palgrave advances in
virginia woolf studies

ᵗim yn l.
ɔ. Sylv
ɹ galw yn
nwyr eraill.

Palgrave Advances

Titles include:

John Bowen and Robert L. Patten (*editors*)
CHARLES DICKENS STUDIES

Phillip Mallett (*editor*)
THOMAS HARDY STUDIES

Lois Oppenheim (*editor*)
SAMUEL BECKETT STUDIES

Jean-Michel Rabaté (*editor*)
JAMES JOYCE STUDIES

Peter Rawlings (*editor*)
HENRY JAMES STUDIES

Frederick S. Roden (*editor*)
OSCAR WILDE STUDIES

Anna Snaith (*editor*)
VIRGINIA WOOLF STUDIES

Jane Stabler (*editor*)
BYRON STUDIES

Nicholas Williams (*editor*)
WILLIAM BLAKE STUDIES

Forthcoming:

Larry Scanlon (*editor*)
CHAUCER STUDIES

Suzanne Trill (*editor*)
EARLY MODERN WOMEN'S WRITING

Palgrave Advances
Series Standing Order ISBN 1–4039–3512–2 (Hardback) 1–4039–3513–0 (Paperback)
(*outside North America only*)

You can receive future titles in this series as they are published by placing a standing order. Please contact your bookseller or, in the case of difficulty, write to us at the address below with your name and address, the title of the series and the ISBN quoted above.

Customer Services Department, Macmillan Distribution Ltd, Houndmills, Basingstoke, Hampshire RG21 6XS, England

palgrave advances in virginia woolf studies

anna snaith
king's college london

palgrave
macmillan

First published 2007 by
PALGRAVE MACMILLAN
Houndmills, Basingstoke, Hampshire RG21 6XS and
175 Fifth Avenue, New York, N.Y. 10010
Companies and representatives throughout the world

PALGRAVE MACMILLAN is the global academic imprint of the Palgrave
Macmillan division of St Martin's Press LLC and of Palgrave Macmillan Ltd.
Macmillan® is a registered trademark in the United States,
United Kingdom and other countries. Palgrave is a registered
trademark in the European Union and other countries.

ISBN-13   978-1-4039-0404-1 hardback
ISBN-10   1-4039-0404-9 hardback
ISBN-13   978-1-4039-0405-8 paperback
ISBN-10   1-4039-0405-7 paperback

This book is printed on paper suitable for recycling and
made from fully managed and sustained forest sources.
Logging, pulping and manufacturing processes are expected to
conform to the environmental regulations of the country of origin.

A catalogue record for this book is available from the British Library.

Library of Congress Cataloging-in-Publication Data
Palgrave advances in Virginia Woolf studies / edited by Anna Snaith.
    p. cm. — (Palgrave advances)
Includes bibliographical references and index.
    Contents: Narratological approaches / Melba Cuddy-Keane — Modernist studies / Jane
Goldman — Psychoanalytic approaches / Makiko Minow-Pinkney — Feminist approaches /
Beth Rigel Daugherty — Bibliographic approaches / Edward Bishop — Postmodernist and post-
structuralist approaches / Pamela L. Caughie — Historical approaches / Linden Peach — Lesbian
approaches / Diana L. Swanson — Postcolonial approaches / Jeanette McVicker — European
reception studies / Nicola Luckhurst and Alice Staveley.
    ISBN-13: 978-1-4039-0404-1
    ISBN-10: 1-4039-0404-9
    ISBN-13: 978-1-4039-0405-8 (pbk.)
    ISBN-10: 1-4039-0405-7 (pbk.)
    1. Woolf, Virginia, 1882–1941—Criticism and interpretation. I. Snaith, Anna. II. Title:
Virginia Woolf studies.

PR6045.O72Z87675 2007
823'.912—dc22

                                                            2006048056

10 9   8   7   6   5   4   3   2   1
16 15 14 13 12 11 10 09 08 07

Printed and bound in Great Britain by
Antony Rowe Ltd, Chippenham and Eastbourne

contents

This, it may be, is one of the first difficulties that faces us in a library. What is 'the very spot?' There may well seem to be nothing but a conglomeration and huddle of confusion [...] Where are we to begin? How are we to bring order into this multitudinous chaos and so get the deepest and widest pleasure from what we read?

(Virginia Woolf, "How Should One Read A Book?" *CR2* 258–9)

acknowledgements

Grateful acknowledgement is due to Palgrave Macmillan for permission to reproduce pages 36–8, 39–42, 44–5, 47, 66–71 and 159 from Jane Goldman's *Modernism 1910–1945: Image to Apocalypse* (Palgrave 2003) in Chapter Two of this volume, and to Continuum for permission to reproduce part of the Introduction to *The Reception of Virginia Woolf in Europe* (eds Mary Ann Caws and Nicola Luckhurst, Continuum Books, 2002) as Chapter 11 of this volume.

Warmest thanks are due to Tory Young and Maggie Humm for their respective advice on reviews of *The Hours* and recent publications on Woolf. I am also greatly appreciative of the support offered by my editor, Paula Kennedy, particularly during the final stages.

notes on the contributors

Edward L. Bishop writes and teaches in the areas of Modernist literature, print-culture history, and creative non-fiction. He has published the Shakespeare Head critical edition of *Jacob's Room* (2004), *Virginia Woolf's Jacob's Room: The Holograph Draft* (Pace 1998), *The Bloomsbury Group* (Dictionary of Literary Biography, 1992), *Virginia Woolf* (Macmillan 1991), and *A Virginia Woolf Chronology* (Macmillan, 1989). His latest book is *Riding With Rilke: Reflections on Motorcycles and Books* (Penguin 2005).

Pamela L. Caughie is Professor of English and Associate Faculty member in the Women's Studies Program at Loyola University Chicago, where she teaches twentieth-century literature and feminist theory. In addition to *Virginia Woolf and Postmodernism* (Illinois 1991), Caughie is the author of *Passing and Pedagogy: The Dynamics of Responsibility* (Illinois 1999) and editor of *Virginia Woolf in the Age of Mechanical Reproduction* (Garland 2000). She is a contributor to two volumes on modernist writing: *Gender in Modernism: New Geographies, Complex Intersections*, ed. Bonnie Kime Scott (University of Illinois Press 2007) and *The Blackwell Companion to Modernist Literature and Culture*, eds David Bradshaw and Kevin Dettmar (2005).

Melba Cuddy-Keane is Professor of English and a Northrop Frye Scholar at the University of Toronto, and a former President of the International Virginia Woolf Society. She has published widely on Virginia Woolf and is the author of *Virginia Woolf, the Intellectual, and the Public Sphere* (Cambridge University Press 2003).

Jane Goldman lectures in English and American Literature at the University of Dundee. She is author of *The Feminist Aesthetics of Virginia Woolf: Modernism, Post-Impressionism and the Politics of the Visual* (1998) and *Modernism, 1910–1945: Image to Apocalypse* (2004), and co-editor of *Modernism: An*

Anthology of Sources and Documents (1998). With Susan Sellers, she is General Editor of the Cambridge University Press edition of Virginia Woolf.

Mark Hussey teaches English and Women's & Gender Studies at Pace University in New York. He is author of *Virginia Woolf A to Z*, has written, edited or co-edited many other books and articles on Woolf, and is founding editor of *Woolf Studies Annual*.

Nicola Luckhurst is Lecturer in Literature at Goldsmiths College, University of London and Distinguished Visiting Fellow at the European Humanities Research Centre, University of Oxford. Her publications include a new translation of Freud's *Studies in Hysteria* (Penguin 2004), *The Reception of Virginia Woolf in Europe* (Continuum 2003), *Science and Structure in Proust's 'A la recherche du temps perdu'* (Oxford University Press 2000) and *Stéphane Mallarmé Correspondance* (Legenda 1998).

Jeanette McVicker teaches at the State University of New York at Fredonia, where she currently chairs the department of English and coordinates the interdisciplinary programme in journalism. She has also directed the women's studies programme. Her work has appeared most recently in *Woolf Studies Annual*; *Converging Media, Diverging Politics: A Political Economy of the News Media in the United States and Canada*, eds David Skinner et al. (Lexington Books 2005) and *Women's Studies On Its Own*, ed. Robyn Wiegman (Duke University Press 2002).

Makiko Minow-Pinkney is a Senior Lecturer in English at the Bolton Institute of Higher Education, where she teaches courses on novels, feminist theory, critical theory and women's writing, and runs the MA in English: Literary Modernism. She is author of *Virginia Woolf and the Problem of the Subject* (1987) and many articles on Woolf, feminist theory and modernism, including, '"The meaning on the far side of language": Walter Benjamin's Translation Theory and Virginia Woolf's Modernism', in *Woolf Across Culture* (2004).

Linden Peach is Dean of the Faculty of Arts and Social Sciences at Northumbria University in Newcastle-upon-Tyne. He was previously Professor of Modern Literature at Loughborough University and at the University of Gloucestershire where he was also Head of the School of Humanities and Faculty Dean. His recent publications on contemporary and twentieth-century literature include *The Contemporary Irish Novel: Critical Readings* (2003), *Virginia Woolf* (2000), *Toni Morrison* (2000) and *Angela Carter* (1998). He is currently editing a definitive edition of Woolf's *Flush* for Cambridge University Press.

Beth Rigel Daugherty teaches English literature, general education Integrative Studies, and interdisciplinary Senior Year Experience courses at Otterbein

College in Westerville, Ohio. She is the co-editor, with Mary Beth Pringle, of the MLA volume on *Teaching* To the Lighthouse, and she has published essays on Teaching Woolf/Woolf Teaching, Woolf's *Common Readers*, her short stories, and individual essays. She is working on a full-length project called *The Education of a Woman Writer: Virginia Woolf's Apprenticeship* and she has plans for two other projects, one tentatively titled *The Teaching of a Woman Writer: Virginia Woolf's Essays* and the other called *The Reception of Virginia Woolf in the United States Before 1975*.

Anna Snaith is a Lecturer in English at King's College London. She is the author of *Virginia Woolf: Public and Private Negotiations* (2000) and has edited 'The *Three Guineas* Letters' (*Woolf Studies Annual* 2000) and *Locating Woolf: The Politics of Space and Place* (with Michael Whitworth, 2007). She is working on a book entitled *Colonial Modernism: Women Writing London 1900–1945* and is editing *The Years* for the Cambridge University Press edition of Virginia Woolf.

Alice Staveley is a Fellow in the Humanities at Stanford University. She received her DPhil from Oxford University in 2001 and taught in the History and Literature programme at Harvard University from 1999–2001. She has published articles identifying the photographs in *Three Guineas*, and on Woolf's *Monday or Tuesday* short fictions, and the feminist narratology of 'Kew Gardens'. Her two current projects include a study of the Hogarth Press' feminist marketing of *Three Guineas*, and a book-length exploration of the relationship between Woolf's role as self-publisher and her emergent modernism.

Diana L. Swanson is Associate Professor of Women's Studies and English at Northern Illinois University. Her articles on Woolf have been published in *Woolf Studies Annual, Twentieth Century Literature*, and *Creating Safe Space: Violence and Women's Writing*.

chronology

For a fuller chronology see Edward Bishop's *A Virginia Woolf Chronology* (Macmillan1989).

1882   Virginia Woolf (née Stephen) born 25 January at 22 Hyde Park Gate, London
1895   VW's mother, Julia Prinsep Stephen, dies
1897   VW's half-sister, Stella Duckworth, dies
1904   VW's father, Leslie Stephen, dies
       VW has nervous breakdown. Recuperates at home of Violet Dickinson
       VW moves with her siblings to 46 Gordon Square, Bloomsbury
       First review appears in the *Guardian*
1905   'Thursday Evenings' commence at Gordon Square
       Begins teaching at Morley College
1906   VW's brother, Thoby, dies
1907   VW's sister, Vanessa, marries Clive Bell
       VW and her brother, Adrian, move to 29 Fitzroy Square
1909   Lytton Strachey proposes to VW
       VW's aunt, Caroline Emelia Stephen, dies, leaving her niece a legacy of £2,500
1910   VW works for Suffrage Movement
       VW participates in *Dreadnought* Hoax
       Roger Fry's first Post-Impressionist exhibition, London
1911   Leonard Woolf returns from Ceylon
       VW and Adrian move to 38 Brunswick Square with John Maynard Keynes, Duncan Grant and Leonard Woolf
1912   VW takes Asheham House
       Marriage to Leonard Woolf and move to Clifford's Inn
1913   VW attempts suicide

1915   *The Voyage Out* published (Duckworth)
       Woolfs move to Hogarth House, Richmond
       VW mentally unwell
1916   VW meets Katherine Mansfield
1917   Woolfs found Hogarth Press and publish *Two Stories* (LW's 'Three Jews'
       and VW's 'The Mark on the Wall')
1919   *Night and Day* published (Duckworth)
       Woolfs buy Monk's House, Sussex
1920   First meeting of the Memoir Club
1921   *Monday or Tuesday* published (Hogarth)
1922   *Jacob's Room* published (Hogarth)
       VW meets Vita Sackville-West
1924   Woolfs move to 52 Tavistock Square
       VW delivers 'Mr Bennett and Mrs Brown' to Heretics Society,
       Cambridge
1925   *The Common Reader* and *Mrs Dalloway* published (Hogarth)
1927   *To the Lighthouse* published (Hogarth)
1928   *Orlando* published (Hogarth)
       VW gives two lectures in Cambridge on which *A Room of One's Own*
       is based
1929   *A Room of One's Own* published (Hogarth)
1930   VW meets Ethel Smyth
1931   *The Waves* published (Hogarth)
       VW delivers lecture to the National Society for Women's Service
1932   *The Common Reader: Second Series* published (Hogarth)
       Lytton Strachey dies
1933   *Flush* published (Hogarth)
1934   Roger Fry dies
1937   *The Years* published (Hogarth)
       Julian Bell, VW's nephew, dies in Spanish Civil War
1938   *Three Guineas* published (Hogarth)
1939   Woolfs move to 37 Mecklenburgh Square
       Woolfs visit Sigmund Freud
1940   *Roger Fry* published (Hogarth)
       Mecklenburgh Square house bombed
       VW delivers lecture, "The Leaning Tower", to the Workers' Educational
       Association in Brighton
1941   VW drowns herself on 28 March in River Ouse, Sussex
       Between the Acts published (Hogarth)
1942   *The Death of the Moth and Other Essays* published (Hogarth)
1943   *A Haunted House and Other Stories* published (Hogarth)
1947   *The Moment and Other Essays* published (Hogarth)
1950   *The Captain's Death Bed and Other Essays* published (Hogarth)

abbreviations

Woolf, Virginia. *Between the Acts*. Ed. Frank Kermode. Oxford: Oxford University Press, 1992. (*BA*)

——. *The Captain's Death Bed and Other Essays*. London: Hogarth Press, 1981. (*CDB*)

——. *Collected Essays*. Vols 1–4. Ed. Leonard Woolf. London: Hogarth Press, 1966–67. (*CE1–4*)

——. *The Common Reader*. Ed. Andrew McNeillie. London: Hogarth Press, 1984. (*CR1*)

——. *The Common Reader, Second Series*. Ed. Andrew McNeillie. London: Vintage, 2003. (*CR2*)

——. *The Complete Shorter Fiction of Virginia Woolf*. Ed. Susan Dick. London: Hogarth Press, 1985. (*SF*)

——. *Contemporary Writers*. London: Hogarth Press, 1965. (*CW*)

——. *The Diary of Virginia Woolf*. Vols 1–5. Ed. Anne Olivier Bell. London: Hogarth Press, 1977–84. (*D1–5*)

——. *The Essays of Virginia Woolf*. Vols 1–4. Ed. Andrew McNeillie. London: Hogarth Press, 1986–94. (*E1–4*)

——. *Jacob's Room*. Ed. Kate Flint. Oxford: Oxford University Press. (*JR*)

——.*The Letters of Virginia Woolf*. Vols 1–6. Eds Nigel Nicolson and Joanne Trautmann. London: Hogarth Press, 1975–80. (*L1–6*)

——. *The Moment and Other Essays*. London: Hogarth Press, 1947. (*M*)

——. *Moments of Being*. Ed. Jeanne Schulkind. London: Hogarth Press, 1985. (*MB*)

——. *Mrs Dalloway*. Ed. David Bradshaw. Oxford: Oxford University Press, 2000. (*MD*)

——. *Orlando*. Ed. Rachel Bowlby. Oxford: Oxford University Press, 1992. (*O*)

——. *The Pargiters: the Novel-Essay Portion of The Years*. Ed. Mitchell A. Leaska. London: Hogarth Press, 1978. (*P*)

——. *Pointz Hall: The Earlier and Later Typescripts of Between the Acts*. Ed. Mitchell A. Leaska. New York: University Publications, 1983. (*PH*)
——. *A Room of One's Own and Three Guineas*. Ed. Morag Shiach. Oxford: Oxford University Press, 1992. (*AROO* & *TG*)
——. *To The Lighthouse*. Ed. Margaret Drabble. Oxford: Oxford University Press, 1992. (*TTL*)
——. *The Waves*. Ed. Gillian Beer. Oxford: Oxford University Press, 1992. (*W*)
——. *A Writer's Diary*. Ed. Leonard Woolf. London: Hogarth Press,1953. (*WD*)
——. *The Years*. Ed. Hermione Lee. Oxford: Oxford University Press, 1992. (*Y*)

introduction

anna snaith

> Virginia Woolf's image generates custody battles over who gets to define her meaning – over whose representation counts as 'truth' – that inscribe clearly demarcated historical moments and ideological positions.
>
> Brenda Silver, *Virginia Woolf Icon*, 1999, 4

Virginia Woolf haunts our culture. Images of Woolf, particularly the famous 1902 Beresford photograph, resurface in unexpected places, redolent with meaning. She has become a ready signifier of highbrow modernism, bohemian London, 1970s feminism, elitism, aestheticism, madness, and the drive to suicide. Her persona has been used to market products ranging from Bass ale to the *New York Review of Books* (Silver 1999, 8) to the new Waitrose supermarket at the Brunswick Centre in London's Bloomsbury.[1] Her cultural influence is eclectic: inspiring Dries Van Noten's 2004 fashion collection and graffiti art in London's Vauxhall (Barkway 2005, 36 and 2002, 29). Fans and detractors alike feel the need to declare their position, often intensely held and heavy with assumptions about art, class and feminism. Few writers, in fact, have triggered such passionate responses. While this is a book about the academic response to Woolf – what we might call Woolf studies – intensity and polarity of response are still to be found. This sense of commitment – Woolf is a writer who matters – makes her reception endlessly fascinating. And her controversial status is a result of her interest in culturally troubling questions, those that still preoccupy us in the twenty-first century. In addition, the plurality of approaches to Woolf speaks to the richness of her writing. That she came at life from so many angles – sexual, political, historical, and psychological – facilitates corresponding critical approaches. Each of these approaches has, in its own way, revolutionized the way one might read Woolf.

Like Sylvia Plath, however, her persona often becomes detached from her writing; her public image seemingly unrelated to the changing ways her texts are taught and read within the academy. Meanwhile, the world of 'Woolf

1

studies' expands exponentially. The vast number of research monographs, biographies, articles, editions, periodicals, societies (in America, Britain, France and Japan), not to mention the gargantuan Annual Conference organized by the International Virginia Woolf Society, indicate her centrality to both research and teaching activity in departments of English Literature and Women's Studies. The task of this volume is to aid readers in their engagement with this plethora of biographical, critical and editorial work by not only grouping and summarizing, but also providing narratives of the genesis of various approaches to Woolf's writing.

The beginning of the twenty-first century has seen Woolf enjoying substantial media attention. The relatively recent release of Stephen Daldry's film *The Hours* (Miramax/Paramount 2002), based on Michael Cunningham's eponymous novel, makes the publication of this volume opportune; it is a pertinent time to reflect upon her reception. Nicole Kidman's Virginia Woolf underlines the often one-dimensional nature of her popular representation. Woolf's suicide is divorced from its Second World War context, she is portrayed as a fragile, victimized woman burdened by her writing, kept going by those around her. Indeed, the film appears indebted to Quentin Bell's 1972 biography of his aunt as an insular aesthete driven by madness and haunted by suicide. None of Woolf's joyousness, her sociability, her wit, or her thoroughgoing concern with both local and global political and cultural environments emerges. Misrepresentations of moments from Woolf's life, such as the scene at Richmond railway station, seem to suggest that she needed the high level of surveillance that Leonard, as her 'keeper', is shown to provide in the film. The key here is, of course, simplification. When Woolf goes to Hollywood she is reduced to 'tormented' Woolf, the experience of writing a tortuous one. She apparently cannot be both a woman with a mental illness *and* a woman who fully appreciated the vibrancy and humour of life.

Reactions to the film underline the gap between Woolf's public and academic reception: in the press she is still 'the brilliant, brittle, snobbish, bitchy, sexually null, mentally unstable Mrs Woolf' (Walsh 2003, 4). As Elizabeth Shih has argued, 'the public Woolf lags behind the academic Woolf' (Shih 2003, 3). Woolf's public persona in the twenty-first century owes much to her early reception in the decades after her death.[2] She supposedly 'deals in prose that aspires to inscrutable poetry; she charts rarified states of mind, subtle shifts of memory and impression' (Walsh 2003, 4). Reviews of the film revivified the polarized character of Woolf's reception. Philip Hensher's subtly titled article 'Virginia Woolf Makes Me Want to Vomit' rails against her 'truly terrible novels: inept, ugly, fatuous, badly written and revoltingly self-indulgent' (Hensher 2003,1) versus Nicola Tyrer's proclamation: 'her message was gothic and doom-laden but still serves as a call to arms to women everywhere; the Woolf howl continues to echo through the generations' (Tyrer 2003, 39). Interesting that even the rallying cries cannot leave the suicide alone.

Support for *The Hours* is often underscored by the assertion that the film has increased the readership of *Mrs Dalloway;* the film's director, Stephen Daldry, has countered criticism with this retort (Young 2003, 75). But the Woolf portrayed in the film bears little relation to the author of the 1925 novel, a woman clearly acutely aware of the discourses and injustices relating to shell shock, the treatment of mental illness, Britain's imperial responsibilities, lack of education for women, eugenics, lesbianism and so on. As Hermione Lee puts it, the film 'evacuates her life of political intelligence or social acumen' (2005, 55). Popular representations of Woolf, then, often insist on reverting to early characterizations, produced prior to crucial work done by scholars working in feminist criticism, cultural materialism and bibliographic studies. This is not to suggest that Woolf critics have discovered the 'real' Woolf, but that they have illuminated the political complexity of her thinking. Woolf's art *was* social criticism; reading and writing were at the centre of Woolf's politics. Furthermore, the minute, fluctuating observations of individual minds found in her novels are synchronic with, rather than divergent from, her overtly feminist or pacifist writing in their illumination of the ways in which cultural discourses are created, perpetuated and resisted. The furore the film produced, however, with its debates about ownership, authenticity and feminism, reminds us again of both the intensity of reactions to Woolf as well as the inevitability of her reinvention.

woolf's early reception

This volume is predominantly concerned with Woolf criticism from the 1960s onwards, when the advent of literary theory radically altered English Studies. We need, however, to address Woolf's early critical reception, in order to understand the legacies of the debates that drove the first three decades of Woolf criticism. Early studies focused largely on Woolf's experimental aesthetics, influenced at this point by the textual rather than contextual emphasis of practical criticism. Given that critics were working without the mass of biographical material now taken for granted (*A Writer's Diary*, edited by Leonard Woolf, appeared in 1953, but the *Letters* and *Diaries* did not start to appear until the 1970s), it makes sense that formalist concerns would take precedence. As Mark Hussey outlines in Chapter 4, apart from Aileen Pippett's oft-forgotten *The Moth and the Star* (1953), the first biography of Woolf did not appear until 1972: Quentin Bell's biography of his aunt. The effect of this explosion of auto/biographical material on the scope of Woolf studies cannot be underestimated.

The 1930s and 1940s saw a series of class-based attacks on Woolf, led by Q. D. and F. R. Leavis, editors of *Scrutiny*. The problem, briefly, was Woolf's perceived insularity. Woolf's novels seem to be written about and for 'the little world of people like herself' 'a class with inherited privileges, private incomes, sheltered lives, protected sensibilities' (Chambers 1947, 1). Her work did not appear to relate to the 'real' world, it lacked relevance. For F. R. Leavis, Woolf's work is without 'public importance' because of its 'lack of moral interest and interest in action' (Leavis, F. R. 1942, 297 and 298). Her writing is characterized by an 'extraordinary vacancy and pointlessness' (295). In her famous 1938 *Scrutiny* article 'Caterpillars of the Commonwealth Unite!', Q. D. Leavis finds *Three Guineas* self-indulgent and ill-informed. She objects specifically to Woolf's focus on the daughters of educated men and deems the equation of 'educated' and 'middle and upper classes' objectionable (203). Leavis' practical, empirical approach to issues like women's education or employment is at odds with what she perceives as Woolf's emotional and prophetic position, another sign of Woolf's distance from the 'real' world.

The first book on Woolf published in Britain was Winifred Holtby's 1932 study, *Virginia Woolf*. As Nicola Luckhurst and Alice Staveley outline in Chapter 11, books also appeared that year in France and Germany, worrying Woolf that her reputation was ossifying. Largely biographical and expository, Holtby nevertheless dedicates sections of the book to Woolf's relationship with politics. She takes a surprisingly progressive line, acknowledging that 'the political world surrounded her' (Holtby 1932, 27), and that she was involved with socialist, co-operative, suffrage and trades union movements. She writes, 'the temptation to be precious, the temptation to be rarefied, and abstract and detached from life, had far less power over her because one side of her mind was continually rubbing up against the minds of people engaged in securing pit-head baths for miners, educational scholarships for women, or a higher standard of administration in the colonies' (33). However, Holtby predicts that 'her range will remain limited, her contact with life delicate' and she will be 'unlikely ever to command the allegiance of a wide contemporary public' (201). Elizabeth Bowen, too, in her review of Bernard Blackstone's *Virginia Woolf* (1949), commends him on his disposal of the 'charge that Virginia Woolf's art was the product of an aerial remoteness from the human norm' (Bowen 1950, 78), but argues that she is consistently a product of her environment, an environment which she knew to be sheltered and privileged (80).

Another version of the 1930s anti-aestheticism came from critics who objected to the plotlessness of her novels. These critics found her characters hard to grasp, such as *Scrutiny* critic M. C. Bradbrook's claim that *The Waves* has 'no solid characters, no clearly defined situations and no structure of feelings' (Bradbrook 1932, 36). For D. S. Savage, whose project was to undermine the prestige associated with Woolf, her novels are 'tenuous, amorphous and vague' (Savage 1950, 70), lacking any 'organic centre' (80), formal coherence or underlying significance. Despite Woolf's search for belief, the novels degenerate into 'meaninglessness' (101) and 'undifferentiated flux' (96).

What was aimless to some was 'technical virtuosity' to others (Beach 1937, 603); Woolf is lauded on exactly the grounds that she is dismissed. The at times hostile studies – and it is easy to single out the polemical reviews – are balanced by those which emphasize Woolf's primary position as 'the reigning goddess of contemporary English letters' (Hawley Roberts 1934, 587). Her acute perception of the minutiae of existence and the revolutionary way in which she recorded sensation captivated critics in their attempt to define, order and understand her technique. As David Daiches wrote: 'she developed a type of fiction in which sensitive personal reactions to experience can be objectified and patterned in a manner that is both intellectually exciting and aesthetically satisfying' (Daiches 1945, 143). The crucial question for these early critics was mimesis: whether Woolf's modernist, formal experimentation suffered from a lack of political or moral relevance or whether it captured the heterogeneity of modern existence and the flux of the human mind in new ways.

The liberal humanist emphasis of early criticism is found in the recurrence of references to 'Beauty', 'Truth' and 'Human nature' (see Bennett 1945, 18), concepts markedly absent from the critical approaches covered in this volume. Furthermore, early critics were often concerned with finding development or continuity in the novels, such as James Hafley's claims that Woolf's purpose was the representation of a unified vision of life, made manifest in the novels as a 'constant and organic development of thought' (Hafley 1954, 2), or John Graham, for whom *Between the Acts* is the culmination of the tension between linear and subjective time in her novels (Graham 1949). Critics felt the need to characterize the *oeuvre* in terms of larger patterns, be they mythic, philosophical or imagistic. Jean Guiguet's influential study *Virginia Woolf et son Oeuvre* (1962 trans. 1965), for example, adopted a philosophical approach in an attempt to capture the unifying, motivating force behind Woolf's aesthetic project: as he saw it, an exploration of 'Being' (462). Guiguet was interested in Woolf's ability to capture the human condition. If 'expression of the inner life was always Virginia Woolf's dominant preoccupation' then the critic's task was to reach 'the very core of her being' (368). The driving questions behind her fiction, 'What am I?', 'What is life?' may remain unanswered, but nevertheless provide a unifying philosophical subtext to her work and link her to various philosophical schools such as Bergsonianism and existentialism (464).

In the 1950s and 1960s Woolf scholarship gained momentum, due in large part, as Melba Cuddy-Keane discusses in Chapter 1, to Erich Auerbach's *Mimesis: The Representation of Reality in Western Literature* (1953). Auerbach's detailed analysis of multiple perspective and temporal fluctuation in a passage from *To the Lighthouse*, lent a gravity and rigour to narratology that inspired a series of studies of Woolf's narrative techniques: Robert Humphrey's *Stream of Consciousness in the Modern Novel* (1954), Melvin J. Friedman's *Stream of Consciousness* (1955), and Ralph Freedman's *The Lyrical Novel* (1963). Auerbach's work also, as Cuddy-Keane elucidates, linked narratological method to post-war cultural crisis, beginning to undermine the perceived autonomy or insularity of her aesthetics. A key development in Woolf studies, as outlined in the second part of Chapter 1 of this volume, has been the fusion of narratology with feminist theory. Similarly, in Chapter 2 on modernist studies, another approach to Woolf which reaches back before the 1960s, Jane Goldman argues that the stark division of avant-garde aesthetics and politics which motivated much early criticism is one which her work actually dismantles.

Nowhere is this more pertinent than in the context of her feminism. Beth Rigel Daugherty argues in Chapter 5 that it was feminist criticism which 'created and now sustains' Woolf studies, indeed it is a category which could encompass all the criticism in this volume. Woolf's feminism is all-pervasive and multifarious, evidenced by the numerous approaches outlined within Daugherty's chapter itself. As usual, most feminist methodologies brought to bear on Woolf's writing are anticipated by Woolf herself: the recovery of lost texts by women, the destabilizing of gender categories, the foregrounding of women's history, the subversion of dominant narrative strategies, the exposure of and resistance to the material and psychological circumstances of women's oppression. These, and others, are the concerns of the vast body of work that Daugherty so expertly describes, nuancing the various strands and shifts in feminist criticism from the 1970s to the present.

Early discussions of Woolf feminism stand in marked contrast to the recent prevalence of this approach. It is either 'aesthetically unacceptable to Virginia Woolf and hardly appears in her writings' (Batchelor 1994, 330) or a 'bleak [...] aggressive streak which can but irritate, disconcert, the adorer of Virginia Woolf the artist' (Bowen 1950, 81). Famously, in his Rede Lecture, E. M. Forster found *Three Guineas* 'cantankerous' and 'old-fashioned' in part because of the feminist 'spots' which mar her work (Forster 1942, 32–3). Naomi Black, who devotes a chapter of her book *Virginia Woolf as Feminist* to responses to *Three Guineas*, argues that the text's polemical pacifism and feminism mean that it has borne the 'most serious brunt of the attacks on Woolf that caricatured her as the ailing maiden queen of the snobbish Bloomsbury Group' (Black 2004, 147). In contrast, Ruth Gruber's recently reprinted, early feminist study of Woolf argues that all aspects of her writing were motivated by feminine self-expression. Gruber reads her as a transitional figure, committed to the intellectual emancipation of women, but searching for a style in which to express the 'psychic consciousness of women' (Gruber 1935, 3). Echoing Woolf's own rallying call, Gruber calls Woolf a 'seeker' paving the way for a woman Shakespeare, 'even a woman Christ' (98).

There is no doubt that during the last decade of her life into the mid-twentieth century, Woolf's reputation was embattled. Despite *The Years'* position at the top of the *New York Times* best-seller list, the post-war years have been called the 'dark ages' of Woolf criticism (Black 2004, 150). Woolf's writing, along with that of many of her modernist contemporaries, seemed decadent in the context of prevailing realism. A key premise behind this book is that the advent of critical theory suited Woolf studies. In this newly theoretical environment her feminism, her politics and her anti-foundationalism came into their own. The dense allusiveness of Woolf's texts combined with her insistence on linguistic instability made critical theory's focus on texts as dynamic signifying systems operating within particular power structures, conducive to the interpretation of her work. As Pamela L. Caughie outlines in Chapter 7, other approaches covered in this volume such as queer theory, new historicism or postcolonial studies are informed and influenced by poststructuralism and postmodernism, which radically altered the way critics thought about language, identity, history and narrative. As Makiko Minow-Pinkney outlines in Chapter 3, after the influx of early psychobiography, came poststructuralist psychoanalytic, particularly Kristevan, readings, focusing on the congruence of sexuality, family relations and identity formation so apparent in her writing. A newly theorized academy kept reading Woolf because she was an important cultural theorist herself whose work anticipated many of the central ideas of feminist theory, new historicism, lesbian studies, and reader response theory.

anglo-american faultlines

While the main focus of this book is Anglo-American, Chapter 11 treats Woolf's reception in continental Europe. As Nicola Luckhurst and Alice Staveley argue, interest in the internationalism of Woolf's publication and reception is burgeoning (see Reinhold 2004). However, thinking about Woolf's reception in the broadest terms means considering the geographical nuances of even Anglo-American responses. As Luckhurst and Staveley contend, there is more divergence in the term Anglo-American than the innocuous hyphen indicates. The evolution of Woolf's reception in the USA is inextricable from the women's movement of the 1970s, whereas in Britain, her persona is more intimately bound up with the Bloomsbury Group and responses invariably circle around class and the relationship between art and politics. Bloomsbury and its creative endeavours have been seen as anathema to politically engaged art, or more moderately, Raymond Williams has argued that the involvement of members of the Group in socialist politics was a 'matter of conscience' rather than 'solidarity' (Williams 1980, 155). As Mark Hussey has discussed, Bloomsbury-bashing comes from the right and the left, Bloomsbury representing 'evils' ranging from the decline of the family and anti-patriarchal sentiment, to dilettantism, exclusivity and aestheticism (Hussey 2004). D. H. Lawrence's homophobic attacks are evidence of the way Bloomsbury was seen to threaten not only the integrity of Britishness, but British masculinity, in particular (Lee 266). Wyndham Lewis' vitriolic blasting of what he saw as the false bohemianism and outmoded Victorianism of the Bloomsbury Group targeted Woolf's formal aesthetics with a fierce misogyny. Stream of consciousness was a myopic 'feminine phenomenon', her writing shrieking, hysterical and 'old-maidish' (Lewis 1987, 138–9). Such contradictory responses belie the complex and various nature of the subject under attack.[3] The problem here again is homogenization. As Regina Marler argues in her engaging study of Bloomsbury as cultural phenomena, 'any name at all for this circle implies fixity where there was flux, and uniformity where there was conflict and innovation' (Marler 1997, 8). Leonard Woolf wrote 'We had no common theory, system or principles which we wanted to convert the world to [....] For there was no more a communal connection between Roger's "Critical and Speculative Essays on Art", Maynard's *The General Theory of Employment, Interest and Money*, and Virginia's *Orlando* than there was between Bentham's Theory of Legislation, Hazlitt's *Principal Picture Galleries in England*, and Byron's *Don Juan*' (L. Woolf 1964, 25–6). And Virginia Woolf was notoriously ambivalent about the idea of a 'set', and her place within it. Leonard Woolf's work for the Labour Party on imperial questions and his anti-imperialist publications, for example, with which Virginia was certainly familiar, are rarely placed in the context of Bloomsbury if they are examined at all (see Brantlinger 1996; Meyerowitz 1982; Wilson 2003). Christine Froula's recent book, *Virginia Woolf and the Bloomsbury Avant Garde: War, Civilization, Modernity*, addresses Woolf as public intellectual within and beyond the context of Bloomsbury, as she engaged with various interwar political debates. Froula refocuses Bloomsbury as a '*modernist movement*' characterized by an internationalist struggle for human rights and freedom from oppression, militarism and totalitarianism (Froula 2005, xi). This work, along with Victoria Glendinning's recent biography of Leonard Woolf, will contribute to a re-evaluation of the political seriousness of Bloomsbury intellectuals. Christopher Reed's *Bloomsbury Rooms: Modernism, Subculture and Domesticity* approaches the artistic endeavours of the Group with the same seriousness by challenging the supposedly oxymoronic relationship between the domestic and the avant-garde, and by arguing that Bloomsbury's political activism was 'animated by the same values' as their aesthetics (Reed 2004, 7). The move towards historicized studies in the 1980s, as Linden Peach discusses in Chapter 8, has meant greater attention to Woolf's own historical, cultural and political environments, be that 1930s politics, suffrage or the First World War, as well as interest in the ways in which Woolf herself thought and wrote about the narrativizing of history. Michael Whitworth's *Virginia Woolf*, part of Oxford University Press's *Authors in Context* series, for example, elucidates the embeddedness of contemporary scientific, political and philosophical discourses (such as evolutionary theory, socialism, Bergsonism, unanimism) in Woolf's writing.[4]

Woolf's British reception continues to be entangled with the question of economic privilege and the ways in which it limited the scope of her writing. Part of her continued interest in culture and power was a need to analyze and dissect the genealogy and manifestations of various kinds of prejudice – her own included. There is no doubt that her privileged class position caused her conflict, an issue central to Alison Light's *Mrs Woolf and the Servants* (2007). She openly admitted concern about inherited views, yet actively sought to counter this by working for the Labour Party, the Workers' Educational Association, Morley College and the Women's Co-operative Guild. She wrote an introduction to Margaret Llewellyn Davies' collection of working-class women's autobiographies, *Life As We Have Known It*, and represented working-class characters and issues in her novels (particularly *To The Lighthouse* and *The Years*). One of the recent trends in Woolf studies has been a more nuanced and contextualized treatment of issues surrounding Woolf, class and gender. Melba Cuddy-Keane's *Virginia Woolf, the Intellectual and the Public Sphere*, with its central concept 'democratic highbrow', is a welcome intervention in this area. Cuddy-Keane highlights reading as central to Woolf's thinking on class and democracy. By uncoupling 'highbrow' from 'upper class', Cuddy-Keane deftly summarizes Woolf's commitment to inclusivity on the one hand and intellectual values on the other. Woolf's insistence that reading and writing which invites independent, critical, dialogic debate is essential to democratic society, and that this not limited to or defined by a particular class, makes her thinking radical rather than elitist.

Cuddy-Keane's work builds on the gradual politicization of Woolf's writing, beginning with the exploration of her feminist politics in the 1970s. Feminist approaches to Woolf have now become commonplace, so it is worth reminding ourselves that this was not always the case. By distancing Woolf from her Bloomsbury Group context, American critics in the 1970s allowed the radicalism of her feminism to emerge. As Jane Marcus put it, 'we have escaped the domination of the Leavises' point of view that still prevents many British readers from seeing Woolf as anything but elitist and mad' (Marcus 1988, 191). As Beth Rigel Daugherty discusses in Chapter 5, the 1970s marked a, perhaps the, revolutionary moment in Woolf studies, resulting in battles across the Atlantic, notably between Jane Marcus and Quentin Bell (Marcus 1988, 191–212). It was as though American critics were laying claim to a Woolf which some British readers could not recognize, resulting in seemingly incompatible versions of Woolf (see Marler 142–53). We have, on the one hand, Quentin Bell's: 'She belonged, inescapably, to the Victorian world of Empire, Class and Privilege' (Bell 1972, II, 186), on the other Jane Marcus' 'She was arguing for total subversion of the world of empire, class, and privilege' (Marcus 1988, 195). While these are not contradictory statements, their implications are certainly divergent. Writing about Coleridge's criticism, Woolf notes that he possesses 'the power of seeming to bring to light what was already there beforehand, instead of imposing anything from the outside' (*E2* 222), but the word 'seeming' belies the universality of imposition. Woolf's reception, with its lack of consensus, is a reminder of the situatedness of critical agendas.

woolf in the age of critical theory

Virginia Woolf's story is reformulated by each generation. She takes on the shape of difficult modernist preoccupied with questions of form, or comedian of manners, or neurotic highbrow aesthete, or inventive fantasist, or pernicious snob, or Marxist feminist, or historian of women's lives, or victim of abuse, or lesbian heroine, or cultural analyst, depending on who is reading her, and when, and in what context. (Lee 1996, 769)

Woolf's words from 'How Should One Read A Book' quoted as the epigraph to this volume could well prefigure responses to her own critical reception. For readers, teachers and researchers of Woolf the feeling of being overwhelmed in a library is a familiar one. Keeping up with the proliferation of new books, articles, approaches, contexts, let alone becoming conversant with close to a century's worth of critical reception is no easy task. The pressure to absorb the 'huddle of confusion' before contributing oneself can be severe. But over the past decades critics have continually found original ways of reading Woolf. For Elizabeth Nielsen, a Danish-American Ph.D. student who visited Woolf on two consecutive days in 1938, it was a lack of criticism that was the problem. Nielsen had been turned down for a Ph.D. on Woolf on the grounds that her subject was too modern. She was given Leslie Stephen instead (D5 145–6). For research students today, the problem is not that Woolf is too modern, but increasingly distant. Now a writer of the last century, Woolf's contexts become ever more alien. As new generations of Woolf critics find their own ways of reading her work, it is important to reread critical texts and to reconsider the trajectories of particular approaches.

The aim of this book is to provide initial routes into Woolf studies, focusing on the explosion of interest in Woolf from the 1970s onwards. Of course, not every piece of criticism is as easily categorized as this volume's chapter divisions suggest, but there are trends in Woolf criticism (as with any other writer) and contextualization is as crucial for secondary as it is for primary material. Each chapter provides an overview of the approach itself and then highlights and summarizes key critical works in the field, and the particular aspects of Woolf's writing they have addressed. The book foregrounds the vicissitudes of scholarship: the gradual accretion of readings and the sudden swerves of direction. New historical contexts, pairings, theoretical approaches, the publication of undiscovered manuscripts – these moments keep happening.[5]

When the first books of criticism appeared on Woolf in the early 1930s, her greatest fear was stasis of reception: 'I must not settle into a figure' (D4 85). Just at this time she was reading Elizabeth Barrett Browning preparatory to writing *Flush* and was concerned with the way in which obsession with Barrett Browning's biography had obscured her writing and dominated her reception. She writes about feeling like a 'mummy in a museum' (L5 37), the books her 'tombstones' (L5 114). One of Woolf's greatest commitments, along with feminism and pacifism, was to dialogue. Her hatred of authoritarianism, and related concepts (egotism, didacticism, summation) informed the way she approached reading, writing, politics, criticism and the ways in which she hoped to be read. Looking at the various approaches to Woolf in a self-reflexive way highlights their historical contingency, their evolution as products of the beliefs and anxieties of particular historical moments. While this volume is by no means comprehensive, it will provide a wider picture, an opportunity to consider the terms and tools of criticism. While reader-response criticism is not an approach covered in a single chapter, this is, in a sense, the overarching remit of the book. It is those 'interpretive communities', to use Stanley Fish's term, which are under scrutiny, their shared reading strategies that are at issue (Fish 1980, 14).

Paying attention to the history of Woolf studies also reveals much about generic hierarchies. Fashion moves with the texts as it does with the readings. For decades focus remained on the 1920s novels: *Jacob's Room*, *Mrs Dalloway* and *To The Lighthouse*. In the last couple of decades more attention has been paid to her later work: *The Years*, *Three Guineas* and *Between the Acts*. Gradually, the dominance of the novel genre is beginning to break. Books on her essays (see Brosnan 1997; Cuddy-Keane 2003; Rosenberg and Dubino 1997; Gualtieri 2000) and short stories (Benzel and Hoberman; Skrbic 2004) have appeared. Rarely the subject of sustained critical attention, the diaries and letters, still tend to be used primarily for biographical evidence. *Flush*, apart from a handful of articles and chapters in books, still evades the critics (see Booth 2000; Caughie 1991; Snaith 2000; Squier 1985).

Other trends emerge, such as the growing interest in the wider bibliographic context of Woolf's work, as Edward Bishop elucidates in Chapter 6. With the gradual publication of Woolf's manuscripts from the 1970s onwards, the question of editions, textual variants and the avant-texte have opened up new ways of talking about Woolf's writing process and have problematized the question of editions. The vast differences between *The Years* (1937) in its published and manuscript versions (*The Pargiters*), for instance, warrants not only further bibliographic but feminist, historical and lesbian approaches in that the essay sections lost in the revision process are more overtly politicized. Julia Briggs' recent *Virginia Woolf: An Inner Life* is unusual yet welcome in its biographical focus on the draft versions of Woolf's novels. At the time of writing, work is underway on *The Cambridge Edition of Virginia Woolf*, which will be an invaluable scholarly edition of Woolf's texts. This edition, fully annotated and including every textual variant in editions produced during Woolf's lifetime, will itself generate further research.

Chapters 9, 10 and 11 represent fairly recent approaches in Woolf studies. The body of criticism on Woolf is growing in each case: lesbian, postcolonial and European reception studies. As Diana L. Swanson outlines, lesbian studies of Woolf are intertwined with feminist criticism, but nevertheless the publication of *Virginia Woolf: Lesbian Readings* in 1997 (eds Barrett and Cramer) marked a crucial moment in Woolf studies. This work began to re-evaluate not only Woolf's own sexuality, but also her portrayal of homosexual relationships in her writing. The silencing and encoding that this required of Woolf leads to cultural and socio-historical work on the signification of female homosexual desire in the late nineteenth and early twentieth centuries. As with postcolonial readings of Woolf, lesbian scholarship has altered the coordinates of Woolf studies, bringing certain texts, characters into focus. In postcolonial studies as Jeanette McVicker elucidates, interest has shifted towards *The Voyage Out, The Waves* and *The London Scene* in particular. Jane Marcus' essay 'Britannia Rules *The Waves*' can be cited as a watershed moment for work on Woolf and empire for its reading of the novel as anti-imperialist. The provocative nature of this article led to an ongoing conversation not only in Patrick McGee's critique of Marcus' argument, but also in Marcus' own reassessment of some of her earlier claims for Woolf. In her recent book, *Hearts of Darkness: White Women Write Race*, for example, Marcus deliberates on whose interests are served in the creation of anti-imperialist readings of Woolf (Marcus 2004, 18–9).

European Reception Studies, too, is an approach crystallized by a single publication: *The Reception of Virginia Woolf in Europe* (eds Caws and Luckhurst, 2002). The politics, logistics and theory of translation come into play here, as well as intercultural exchange within the boundaries of national literatures. The availability of Woolf's texts – the Spanish censorship of *The Waves* a case in point – has elicited discussion on how and to what extent Woolf's writing has served or subverted national ideology. How did Woolf respond to the internationalizing of her reputation during her lifetime, and how has she been read, taught, marketed and translated since her death?

Woolf scholars have not benefited from an abundance of metacritical material. John Mepham's *Virginia Woolf* volume for the *Criticism in Focus* series was published in 1992; a decade and a half of criticism in Woolf studies amounts to a vast amount of material, not to mention the newer approaches that do not feature (postcolonial, lesbian). Jane Goldman's *Icon Critical Guide to To the Lighthouse and The Waves* is more recent, but, of course, only covers the reception of two novels. Eleanor McNees' four-volume *Virginia Woolf: Critical Assessments* is crucial for those working on Woolf, but is an anthology and therefore does not provide commentary on the criticism.

The contributors to this volume have necessarily been limited by space, so we could not even come close to covering all work on Woolf, or even all approaches to her writing. Marxist, ecological, phenomenological, generic, ethical, hypertext approaches, for example, have not been given their own chapter. We have chosen those approaches which, it could be argued, have been most influential in Woolf studies over the last four decades. In an effort to include a wide range of criticism, complex arguments have necessarily been condensed and simplified – this is unavoidable in a book of this kind. This volume is meant to take readers back not only to Woolf, but to criticism on Woolf. And now to Woolf on criticism.

what woolf had to say

[B]ooks pass in review like the procession of animals in a shooting gallery, and the critic has only one second in which to load and aim and shoot and may well be pardoned if he mistakes rabbits for tigers, eagles for barndoor fowls, or misses altogether and wastes his shot upon some peaceful cow grazing in a further field. (*CR2* 270)

Given that this book invites its reader to reflect on the nature of literary criticism in general, it is worth considering Woolf's own substantial body of work on criticism and critics. Not only was Woolf herself a prolific critic, but she thought a great deal about the nature and purpose of criticism. She started her writing life as a critic and essayist, writing her first review for the *Guardian*, an Anglo-Catholic paper, in 1904, and moving to the *Times Literary Supplement* the next year. When applying for a reader's ticket at Dr Williams' library in Gordon Square, she described herself as a 'journalist' (*L1* 190). Her non-fiction writing was never simply a financially motivated or a secondary activity; she maintained a lifelong interest in reviewing, criticism, the essay, and the processes and purposes of reading. As with several of the critical approaches addressed in this volume, not only can Woolf's texts be approached using the methodology but they also make a significant contribution to the approach itself. This self-consciousness certainly applies to her criticism: 'though critics have typically disregarded Woolf's criticism as slight and old-fashioned impressionism, properly seen, Woolf's critical views and attitudes are actually revolutionary. She would hand over criticism to readers themselves and do away with the need for literary journalism, anticipating reader-response criticism by several decades' (Kaufmann 1997, 149). Furthermore, the lack of critical attention paid to the wide range of Woolf's essays has prevented critics from fully recognizing the centrality of the common reader to her politics. Again and again she championed the activities and opinions of the ordinary reader; hers is a democratic and dialogic engagement between text and reader. The reader is an active participant, creating and interpreting the text rather than passively ingesting it, anticipating a Barthesian emancipation of the reader by several decades. 'Perhaps the quickest way to understand the elements of what a novelist is doing is not to read, but to write; to make your own experiment with the dangers and difficulties of words' (*CR2* 259), she writes, 'describing a form of criticism that is grounded in the indissoluble unity of reader and writer rather than in the authority of learning and scholarly pursuits' (Gualtieri 2000, 59). Woolf was always interested in the views of her own ordinary readers, as her responses to the letters from her reading public indicate (see Cuddy-Keane 2003; Daugherty 2006; Snaith 2000).[6] Not only did she keep her fan mail, but replied to as many letters as she could, sometimes developing epistolary friendships with 'unknown' readers. She valued public libraries as places that increased access to books, particularly for working-class readers. In contrast to the moral imperatives behind the Public Libraries movement, Woolf envisaged libraries as spaces free from the constraints of hierarchy: 'to admit authorities, however heavily furred and gowned, into our libraries and let them tell us how to read, what to read, what value to place on what we read, is to destroy the spirit of freedom which is the breath of those sanctuaries' (*CR2* 258).

Her celebration of the common reader is particularly pertinent given her misgivings about the condition of reviewing and literary journalism generally. 'If behind the erratic gunfire of the press the author felt that there was another kind of criticism, the opinion of people reading for the love of reading, slowly and unprofessionally, and judging with great sympathy and yet with great severity, might this not improve the quality of his work' (*CR2* 270). She felt that the sheer volume of books published, the brevity of reviews and the speed required of the reviewer made it impossible for the reviewer to do his or her job. These factors separated the reviewer from the critic, whose judgements were thoughtful, trustworthy, considered, based on extensive reading. Commercialized reviewing had become a careless, dangerous and random sport. In her essay 'Reviewing', therefore, Woolf suggests that the relationship between writer and critic should become a private, professional one, rather than a matter of public entertainment.

While seemingly nostalgic at times for the 'great' critics: Matthew Arnold, Samuel Coleridge, Samuel Johnson, that greatness, it turns out, is down to their vast reading experience rather than any qualities of genius. The authoritarian critic, 'exalted, inspired, infallible', has a weakening effect on the mind of the reader – criticism is best produced through communal effort (*E4* 450). Furthermore, in the modern age – an 'age of fragments' – such constancy of judgement is impossible: 'The most sincere of [our contemporaries] will only tell us what it is that happens to himself' (*E3* 355, 358–9). Critical certainties have vanished in the face of the sheer volume of publications: 'can we go to posterity with a sheaf of loose pages, or ask the readers of those days, with the whole of literature before them, to sift our enormous rubbish heaps for our tiny pearls' (*E3* 355). On the other hand, she does not dismiss cultural waste so easily: 'Every literature, as it grows old, has its rubbish-heap, its record of vanished moments and forgotten lives told in faltering and feeble accents that have perished. But if you give yourself up to the delight of rubbish-reading you will be surprised, indeed you will be overcome, by the relics of human life that have been cast out to moulder. It may be one letter – but what a vision it gives!' (*CR2* 263). Without the canonizing authority of the great critic, the literary field is widened, democratized.

In 'An Essay on Criticism' Woolf 'does' criticism, showing the reader the artificiality of having to 'smooth out all traces of that crab-like and crooked path by which he has reached what he chooses to call "a conclusion"' (*E4* 450). While admitting the necessity of some kind of judgement, the essay reveals the 'prejudices, the instincts and the fallacies out of which criticism is made' (*E4* 455). Hers is a hybrid criticism, one that is relational rather than absolute, tentative rather than dogmatic and eclectic rather than purist. Woolf's criticism, like her fiction, makes demands on its reader. The plethora of responses to Woolf's texts traced in the pages that follow indicate that those demands don't go away.

notes

1. The adverts for the Bloomsbury Waitrose found in Russell Square tube station make frequent reference to the Bloomsbury Group, and one in particular uses a quote from *A Room of One's Own* to celebrate the joys of eating well (September 2006).
2. Elizabeth Shih also notes the parroting of Q. D. Leavis' 1938 review of *Three Guineas* in *Scrutiny* in Theodore Dalrymple's 'The Rage of Virginia Woolf', *City Journal*, 10 August 2002 (Shih 2003, 3).
3. See Jane Garrity's 'Selling Culture to the "Civilised": Bloomsbury, British *Vogue* and the Marketing of National Identity', *Modernism/Modernity* 6.2 (1999): 29–58 for a discussion of the Group's complex relationship to high and popular culture.
4. See also Michael Whitworth's *Einstein's Wake: Relativity, Metaphor and Modernist Literature* for a discussion of Woolf and scientific discourse.
5. Along with *The Hours* (both novel and film), another recent event that brought Woolf extra media and scholarly attention was the discovery of Woolf's 1909 notebook, and its publication in 2003 as *Carlyle's House*. This find provided further opportunity for reflecting on Woolf's image in the twenty-first century, given that any new material subtly alters the Woolf canon.

   As well as *Carlyle's House*, we have recently seen the first publication of all six of Woolf's *London Scene* essays, including the essay 'Portrait of a Londoner', which was not included in the 1975 publication (Woolf 2004). Maggie Humm's *Snapshots of Bloomsbury: The Private Lives of Virginia Woolf and Vanessa Bell*, which includes over two hundred unpublished photographs and the first catalogue of the sisters' domestic photographs, provides a fresh way into the biographical material.
6. Beth Rigel Daugherty's recent edition of the entire collection of fan mail in the University of Sussex's Monk's House archive is an invaluable resource for Woolf scholars (*Woolf Studies Annual* 2006). Virginia Woolf's condolence letters have recently been published as *Afterwords: Letters on the Death of Virginia Woolf*, ed. Sybil Oldfield. These letters, from both friends and members of the general public, make for a fascinating glimpse into Woolf's reception immediately after her death.

1
narratological approaches
melba cuddy-keane

In 1933, one of Virginia Woolf's common readers – a schoolteacher in Omaha, Nebraska – devised an elaborate colour graph diagramming the rhythmic pattern formed by twenty recurrent motifs in *A Room of One's Own*. Although it might seem ironic for Woolf's protest against patriarchal logic to be mirrored in a mathematical chart, its creator, Jessie Towne, was neither a distanced nor an insensitive reader. In a letter to Woolf explaining the graph, Miss Towne described *A Room* as 'a complete and perfect statement for all of us – women who have neither the money nor the rooms of our own', and she praised *The Waves* for its embodiment of 'the inner absolute truth about that strange proceeding, human living'. Furthermore, with narratological acuity, Miss Towne perceived the underlying narrative structure of Woolf's non-fictional essay: the way its *a-logical* power accumulates through an interwoven 'pattern' of repetition and recurrence that seems 'purposed' although perhaps not 'what we commonly call conscious'. The graph was a tool for expressing her intuitive grasp of *the way Woolf's text makes sense*.[1]

Narratology is not a rarefied science, nor is it isolated from literature's fundamental values of affect and meaning. By describing Jessie Towne's approach as narratological, however, I am using the term in its recent, expansive sense. 'Narratology' came into our vocabulary in the late 1960s, when narratological work was structuralist in intent: it sought to identify a universal 'grammar' informing all narrative, analogous to the universal grammar once assumed to underlie all languages and to reflect the structures of the human brain. But narratology has moved beyond such universalist assumptions to diversify and complicate its approach. *Narratology* today encompasses any systematic study of the processes by which narratives make sense, or through which readers make sense of narrative. *Narratological criticism* uses such understanding to analyze specific texts. This broader definition both offers a more flexible future and enables a richer past: early work on the form and style of Woolf's novels becomes part of narratology's history

16

or pre-history, while the possibilities for future analyses are extraordinarily open and diverse.

In this chapter, I will discuss narratological approaches to Woolf in two phases, with the dividing line placed roughly in the late 1970s when the conjunctions of feminism, theory, and narratology were changing the ways in which her work was discussed. Although terminology and theoretical questions become more sophisticated, however, the criticism as a whole is full of insights that deepen our sensitivity to these multifaceted texts. The challenge of Woolf's writing is that it asks readers to think differently, and the distinctiveness of that thinking emerges in the language and form of her expression. Over time, criticism of Woolf has fluctuated between an emphasis on those thinking processes and a focus on the content of her thoughts. Comprehensive reading, however, grasps the two dimensions as inseparable. Narratological criticism testifies to that inseparability, and an overview of its findings thus makes a fitting place to begin any study of Virginia Woolf.

criticism to the 1970s

In the first phase of narratological analysis, studies of Woolf followed the prevailing assumptions of formalist criticism, which aimed to understand a literary work as an aesthetic whole. The era was a time of burgeoning ideas about narrative form; poetry and drama had long possessed their 'poetics' but it was only following Henry James' prefaces to the New York Edition of his collected works (1907–09; [1917]) and Percy Lubbock's *The Craft of Fiction* (1921) that the novel promised to gain a like maturity.[2] But while the excitement, and therefore most often the best work, revolved around questions of technique, it is a mistake to assume – as some theorists have – that aesthetic questions were pursued as relevant only to the aesthetic sphere. Introducing his influential collection, *Forms of Modern Fiction*, William Van O'Connor wrote that form is 'the objectifying of idea' and 'a representation which equips us to understand more fully aspects of existence outside of art' (O'Connor 1948, 3). Later, in *The Turn of the Novel*, Alan Friedman argued that the transition from closed to open endings at the turn of the century was a fundamentally *ethical* move, signifying that the activity of the conscience is never at an end (Friedman 1966, 184–7). As Mark Schorer put it in a widely influential essay, technique was to be regarded as '*achieved* content', not merely a way of organizing material but of exploring and defining value (Schorer 1948, 67).

This implied inseparability of form and meaning informs two of the earliest essays on Woolf to address her style. On the surface, it is true, the essays seem to delineate opposing trends. In 1946, John Hawley Roberts detailed the repetitive motifs in *Mrs Dalloway* and *To the Lighthouse* to argue that these novels offer the verbal equivalent of Roger Fry's 'significant form'.[3] Conversely, two years later, Warren Beck defended *Between the Acts* in political terms, arguing that the novel stands as an indictment of 'totalitarianism's harsh impersonality' (Beck 1948,

253). Whereas Roberts praised Woolf for formal pattern, Beck testified to her social relevance. Nevertheless, although Roberts' analysis of repeated phrases, words, scenes, and images was the more resolutely formalist in approach, he located the significance of Woolf's rhythmic design in a vision of order that counteracts the wilful assertions of the individual ego. In his view, Mr Ramsay is ultimately freed from 'his egocentrism' (Roberts 1946, 846), while the novel's aesthetic design affirms the existence of a deeper 'spiritual design' beyond the attachments of the self (847). In complementary fashion, Beck arrived at his understanding of Woolf's social meanings through a textual analysis of multipersonal consciousness. Extrapolating from the interrelatedness of the minds of Isa, Mrs Swithin, and Miss La Trobe, Beck related Woolf's individual characters to a larger communal consciousness, understanding them as agents for 'the whole population of the mind's immeasurable profundity' (BA 170). Like Roberts, Beck was formalist in conceiving the novel as a 'composite symbol' (Beck 1948, 250), although, unlike Roberts, his emphasis on the ending's rising curtain conveyed a sense of open form and 'a future resolution which human imagination must supply' (253).

The contrast between the two essays is therefore not one of formalist versus thematic approaches. Both critics arrive at thematic meanings through analysis of style, although one analyzes verbal patterns and the other, perceiving consciousnesses. Both critics also agree that Woolf's writing opposes dominance and coercion, although for one critic the domineering threat is individual and for the other, societal. For Roberts, the novels attest to a universal *eternal* order beyond the transience of individual life, whereas, for Beck, the novels oppose a repressive, political, *human* order with the positive fluidity of individual and collective consciousness. But the narratologically significant difference is that one critic celebrates integration, resolution, and closure in Woolf's form, whereas the other finds value in flux, indeterminacy, and open-endedness. This fundamental opposition, as we shall see, continues to haunt studies of Woolf.

The most significant of Woolf's early critics, however, concentrated on the fluidity and multiplicity of her form. In *Mimesis: The Representation of Reality in Western Literature* (1946; trans. 1953) – a monumental study written in Istanbul during the Second World War – Erich Auerbach delineated two basic types of Western realism: the Homeric (externalized, direct, continuous, heroic, and unproblematic) and the Biblical (suggestive, many-layered, nomadic, domestic, and inviting continuous interpretation). And Auerbach's famous last chapter, 'The Brown Stocking', presented Virginia Woolf as a modern representative of the latter type, as demonstrated in three defining characteristics of her style: the 'multipersonal representation of consciousness' (541); the 'polyphonic' and multi-layered handling of time (540); and the discovery of significance in the 'random occurrence' (552), the 'minor happenings' (547) of everyday life. Quoting in its entirety section 5 of Part I of *To the Lighthouse*, Auerbach traced, in more precise detail than Beck, the answers to one of narratology's

most fundamental questions, 'who is speaking?'[4] Marking subtle shifts in tone
and perspective, Auerbach not only identified the differing voices of individual
characters, the collectivized people, and the narrator, but strikingly showed
that the narrator's voice, far from being omniscient and privileged, is woven
into the overall narrative consciousness as one of many multiple perspectives.
Auerbach argued further that, in Woolf's novel, the present moment becomes
an occasion for 'excursuses' (537) that range freely away from 'the framing
occurrence which releases them' (541). Unlike the Homeric flashback, which
prepares for future exterior action, Woolf's fluid movement, through different
time strata and between exterior and interior events, conveys the 'symbolic
omnitemporality of events' (545).

Auerbach's extraordinarily percipient chapter both provided a narratological frame for analyzing the modernist novel and speculated on what, as
cultural meaning, the new trends implied. Modernist form, he posited, betrays
the upheavals of the decades following the First World War: the cataclysmic
eruption of new modes of knowledge and experience, the teeming crowds
of people, the shrinking globe, the clash of the 'most heterogeneous ways of
life', the disintegration of Enlightenment ideologies and even liberalism and
socialism, and the insidious turn to factionalism and extremism in response
(550). The anti-totalitarian implications of decentred modernist narratives
were not lost on Auerbach yet he concluded that, for the most part, modernist
style is 'a symptom of confusion and helplessness' (551). But while recognizing
the note of sadness in *To the Lighthouse*, he found as well a sign of hope.
Woolf's multiplicity, he argued, betokens not confusion but 'something new
and elemental': it seizes upon the isolated random fragments of our experience
and, in surrendering to them, discovers a 'wealth of reality' and 'depth of life'
(552).[5] And, he continued, to draw such richness of existence out of random
everyday occurrences is to look beyond surface conflicts to 'the elementary
things which men in general have in common' (552). Anticipating an eventual
mingling of cultures in which the term 'exotic' would be rendered obsolete,
he found in Woolf's evocation of common life, 'the first forewarnings of the
approaching unification and simplification' (553).

I emphasize – since it is also often missed – that Auerbach did not cast Woolf
as a personal, subjective writer; on the contrary, he identified omniscient or
first-person narrators with subjective views. Woolf's multipersonal perspectives,
he claimed, both undo the authority of the author and testify to the external
existence of the person or object being perceived: the effect is 'a close approach
to objective reality by means of numerous subjective impressions' (536). As to
whether the impressions are finally integrated, Auerbach, although somewhat
ambiguous, leant more towards open than to closed form. He referred to 'the
multipersonal method with synthesis as its aim' (536), yet suggested that
the 'overlapping, complementing, and contradiction yield something that
we might call a synthesized cosmic view or *at least a challenge to the reader's
will to interpretive synthesis*' (emphasis added, 549). Like Beck, he approached •

synthesis not as definitively articulated in the form but as relocated in the
processes stimulated in the reader's mind.

'The Brown Stocking' accorded a new stature to Woolf and what followed
was a groundswell of criticism focused on her form and technique. Such
textual analysis brought a welcome new sophistication to the study of fiction,
but it served another, more specific need in studies of Woolf. At the time,
negative assessments of her writing levelled the charges of insignificance
and aloofness from the 'real' world. A content-based criticism, missing the
traditional signifiers of decisive events, and encountering details from women's
experience and upper middle-class lives, concluded that her works had limited
appeal. But when critics shifted to other ways of reading her texts, more
profound implications began to appear. In 1960, for example, when David
Daiches added a chapter on Woolf to the second edition of his influential
The Novel and the Modern World, it was Woolf's *style* that both provided the
grounds for her inclusion and alerted him to the broader themes of time,
death, and personality in her work. If his label of 'minor fiction at its most
triumphant' (Daiches 1960, 213) now seems rather too subject to his era's
prevailing assumptions, he was nevertheless one of the first to begin reading
Woolf in 'other' ways.

Critical debates of the time revolved around Woolf's multipersonal method,
and the primary feature addressed was her handling of what was, in the
1960s and 1970s, called 'point of view'. To turn back to these early critics
is to see them stumbling over terminology, embroiled in battles over the
way terms were employed, and confronted by a technique that the available
language seemed inadequate to describe. Could Woolf be said to write stream
of consciousness when her language was at the level of articulate thought?
Could she be writing interior monologue when the pronoun designating
the thinker was not 'I', but 'he' or 'she'? Could she be writing soliloquies
given the strong presence of a narrator's voice? But, then, could her narrator
be called omniscient when so much about her characters was left uncertain
and vague, and when the narrator provided no direct guidance about how to
judge the fictional world? The debates over language might seem like quibbles,
but a workable terminology was in the process of being hammered out.
More significantly, underlying and driving these debates were fundamental
questions about the way Woolf perceived the mind and the relation between
the mind and 'truth'. Critics echoed Auerbach in asserting that Woolf, like
other modernists, was confronting the breakdown of a publicly shared system
of values and beliefs. But did the dispersal of the omniscient narrator into
fragmented characters imply the total relativity of all views? Or was there
still, imperceptibly and subtly, behind all this diversity, a coordinating,
unifying force? To some extent the goals were aesthetic – to understand and
articulate the workings of narrative – but the understanding sought was also
psychological (the nature of the mind) and philosophical-epistemological
(the nature of reality and truth).

charge that her novels dealt with mere trivia. Even more significantly, these studies highlight the tension in Woolf's writing between patterns of coherence and the destabilizing effect of fragmented structures and fluid narrator's voice. But perhaps the most important feature of these early critical works is their practice of attentive reading; there is an admirable solidity and detail in a criticism so acutely focused on the language of the texts.

the 1980s to the present

The period from roughly 1980 through to the present sees sufficient change in the study of narrative for us to distinguish a second phase in narratological approaches to Woolf. 'Narratology' (or the French *narratologie*) was coined by Tzvetan Todorov in *Grammaire du Décaméron* (1969), and the rapid adoption of the scientifically inflected 'ology' confirmed a turn to the systematic study of narrative as a descriptive rather than interpretative task.[9] Narratologists, in this more specialized definition, pursue the work of codifying different kinds of narrative discourses or text-types, and of developing an analytic vocabulary for different rhetorical and linguistic forms.[10] The 'high' structuralists – those who sought to uncover a universal narrative 'grammar' – attempted to define the elemental building blocks (actions and 'actants') that form the basis of all stories. For various reasons (the primarily European focus, the objective, positivist approach, Woolf's still peripheral status), her novels do not figure in this work. But as narratology turned from the systematic study of narrated content to examine the *ways* in which stories are narrated ('discourse' rather than 'story'),[11] Woolf's innovative narrative technique became a subject of renewed investigation. At the same time, just as earlier formalist criticism had a strongly thematic component, so most later studies of Woolf approach narratological analysis as inseparable from cultural and ideological critique. Narratology's initial search for universals necessitated the exclusion of context from the analytic field; however, for many critics, the meaning of narrative depends on its function in a communicative system. While feminist critics are not alone in their focus on contextual narratology, their work, by exposing the way in which communicative systems have been pervasively inflected by constructs of gender difference, has played a major role in establishing the ideological implications of narrative technique.

The relation between Woolf's style and gender politics came to the fore with the publication of Toril Moi's *Sexual/Textual Politics* in 1985. Combining the theories of Jacques Derrida and Julia Kristeva with politically oriented critique, Moi argued that the disjunctive pluralism of Woolf's narratives undermines both socially constructed notions of gender identity and the patriarchal political system. Critiquing American feminist critics who, in Moi's terms, continued to essentialize gender identities – by either elevating the female/ maternal identity or constructing androgyny as a union of opposites – Moi claimed that Woolf's writing subverts 'the death-dealing binary oppositions

An excellent summary of the disagreements over point of view can be found in James Naremore's chapter 'Virginia Woolf and the Stream of Consciousness', in *The World Without a Self* (1973). Noting that some critics defined stream of consciousness as the direct rendition of linguistically a-logical and associative processes, while others used the term broadly and conceptually to signify a psychological level which a variety of techniques could represent, Naremore nevertheless concluded that it was not the method that Woolf most frequently employed.[6] *All* definitions concurred that stream of consciousness concerns the private, individual mind, and immersion in the individual was not, Naremore claimed, Woolf's ultimate interest or goal.[7] Indeed, Naremore argued, her objection to Joyce was precisely because he wallowed in the 'individual ego' (Naremore 1973, 63), whereas Woolf urged instead, as evidenced in 'Modern Fiction', a literature that would show a self which 'embraces or creates what is outside itself and beyond' (*CR1* 151). Drawing on Harvena Richter's complex analysis of modes of perception in Woolf's novels, Naremore argued that Woolf modulates between the extremes of 'conscious and unconscious, personal and impersonal, individual and collective' (Richter 1970, 129), until the narrating voice becomes 'the voice of everyone and no one' (Naremore 1973, 75). Seeking a terminology for this narrator, Naremore turned – again following Richter – to Woolf's own language, proposing that a 'nameless spirit' (*PH* 62) brings to life an underlying and inarticulate 'common element' (61), thus conveying 'the world seen without a self' (*W 239*) – the phrase that gave the title to his book.

At approximately the same time, John Graham – with a similar understanding of Woolf's narrative voice – was also searching for a language to describe her technique. He described the narrator in *The Waves* as a 'translator' of the characters' thoughts (Graham 1970, 196), as 'omnipercipient' rather than omniscient (204); he referred to the 'invisible narrating consciousness' (196), 'containing consciousness' (206), and 'narrating Consciousness' (206). These struggles with terminology go to the heart of a significant insight in this early narratological work: however innovative Woolf's approach to character, the greater, more radical innovation was her distinctive narrator. This voice is not so individualized and personalized that it can be regarded as a narrator-character; the narrative mind inhabits an indeterminate position, overlapping but not fully coinciding with the minds of the characters. The overlaps furthermore pose a closely related question, a question pervading Woolf criticism from its beginnings. What connectivity is posited among the various represented consciousnesses in Woolf's novels? Does a unified vision emerge from the blend of voices or not? And, if it does, is this unity one that requires redefinition and reconceptualization, just as much as point of view?

Missing the discrete narrator persona that unifies traditional novels, critics sought organizing patterns in the language of the texts. Naremore emphasized the repeated motifs of fluidity and water, which he identified with feminine eroticism; the dissolution of self in this watery world, he argued, hovers between mystic transcendence into a collective consciousness and the wish for an 'all-embracing union' in death (Naremore 1973, 243). James Hafley (1954) invoked the image of the glass roof from the end of the third narrative section in *The Waves*, finding the moment of coherence in the tumult of noises and sounds that Neville hears surging and crashing together under the vast dome of the London train station. For Hafley – who linked Woolf's representation of interior time to Bergson's *durée réelle* – Woolf's implied synthesis surpasses unity in diversity to become the unity *of* diversity, the one consistency being life's flux itself. Avrom Fleishman employed images of networks and weaving to explain the dense textual fabric of Woolf's novels, detailing the numerous intertextual allusions and tracing a wide variety of recurrent motifs arising out of 'words, names, phrases, quotations, verbal patterns, and mythic figures' (Fleishman 1975, 220). Drawing on such diverse sources as Karin Stephen's work on Bergson, Freud's notion of the uncanny, and Giles Deleuze's theories of *différence* and *répétition*, Fleishman argued that, although Woolf's repetitions suggest a 'temptation to return to a prior state of being that has become known as the "death-instinct"', the continually changing and altering context endows the repeated material with 'new vitality', delineating a process that is ultimately creative and transformative (227).

Like most criticism of the time, these studies seek to understand each novel as a unified whole, although the unity they describe is characterized by fluidity, flux, and multiplicity. And they generally locate the structure of Woolf's novels not in traditional linear progression, but in rhythmic alternations and oscillating binaries, usually related to principles or sensibilities socially gendered as masculine and feminine: land/water; fact/fiction; intellect/intuition; conscious/ unconscious; separation/unity; life/death. But a further accompanying insight was that the *principle* of form in these novels is qualitatively different from that in traditional narratives and that this substantive difference has implications for the reader's activity. Paying increasing attention to the complex way Woolf's narratives *work*, criticism began to foreground the interpretative act itself as part of the narrative's meaning.

The reader's activity becomes the focus, in strikingly different ways, in the work of Mitchell Leaska and Geoffrey Hartman. Leaska was one of the first to pursue a statistical analysis of linguistic elements – the kind of painstaking objective analysis that today can be done more readily with sophisticated software such as TACT.[8] Analyzing the sentence structure, parts of speech, and image clusters attributable to the different characters and the narrator in *To the Lighthouse*, Leaska demonstrated the relations not only among the rhetorical modes of the different voices but also between human time and nature's timelessness. And despite the scientific cast of his lists and tables, Leaska used objective analysis to heighten sensitivity to language and to suggest the affinities of Woolf's style to poetry. Influenced by Louise Rosenblatt's transactional theory of literature, Leaska examined the relation established between text and reader when the author, 'abdicating his [sic] position as

ultimate authority, requires of the reader constant and creative participation' (Leaska 1970, 164). For Leaska, the 'manifold consciousnesses method' – so appropriate for 'an age of such ethical diversity and relativism' (163) – asks us to abandon the practice of reading for 'what-comes-next' (116) and instead to hold accumulated impressions in suspension until 'the whole constellation of emotional and mental processes which make up human experience is revealed' (106).

Somewhat earlier, Geoffrey Hartman advanced a more theoretical understanding of the reader's task in his profound – if somewhat opaque – essay, 'Virginia's Web'. Despite his title's allusion to completed design, Hartman's real interest lay in the gaps, silences, spaces, or what he called 'power failures' (Hartman 1961; 1993, 41) in Woolf's text and the mind's way of supplying connections or 'transitions' (35) between them. In Hartman's scheme, the area of blankness is the phenomenological or existential void, and the fictional world requires, like the leap of faith, an interpolative act of the imagination, filling the gap and affirming continuity, or existence. Hartman further posited a qualitative difference between realist, mimetic plots (which he associated with the male will) and Woolf's expressive prose (which he associated with the female imagination). The realist plot covers or simplifies the gap, relying on the common assumptions of sequence to naturalize continuity; but Woolf's novels, he argued, dwell in the more difficult continuity that must be forged by the mind. But although Hartman read Woolf's *intention* as celebrating the mind's affirmative powers, he proposed that the gaps themselves make visible – or that the reader, in what would be a deconstructive act, makes visible – the contrary and annihilating spectres of 'death, decay, repression, discontinuity' (43). (Why he assumed the *writer* asserts the positive while the *reader* uncovers the negative is not clear.) Hartman then enacted another incipiently deconstructive twist. Although he suggested that the minds of both artist and reader become androgynous in leaping the gap between the two plots (mimetic and expressive), he also hypothesized the danger that feminine desire for the unity of 'mystical marriage' (44) may be a desire for death. Such a possibility would undo the distinction between the gap and the closing of it, since both would signify an annihilating end.

Early discussions of Woolf's form thus focus on point of view, on textual patterns of repetition and oscillating rhythms, on the non-traditional handling of time and structure, and on the reader's role. While there are a few signs of systematic analysis (in addition to Leaska's statistics, Daiches diagrams the structure of *Mrs Dalloway*, and Fleishman provides charts listing the novels' structural units), for the most part narratological analysis is strongly integrated with thematic discussion. There is a marked tendency towards analyzing the novels in terms of a male/female dialectic but little attempt is made to relate such themes to the social and political position of men and women in Woolf's world. Overall, the intense focus on textual analysis produces a somewhat inward-looking Woolf, yet it suggests a philosophical depth adequate to any

of masculinity and femininity' themselves (Moi 1985, 13). Following Kristeva, Moi connected modernist style, with 'its abrupt shifts, ellipses, breaks and apparent lack of logical construction', to 'the rhythms of the body and the unconscious' (15); she then urged a feminist criticism that would add the missing political dimension by showing how such radical deconstruction exposes the arbitrariness of the prevailing rational symbolic order and challenges its exclusionary and oppressive dominance. Implicitly reversing a direction that David Daiches had set when he claimed, 'the material environment [...] was for [Woolf] at most only a background' (Daiches 1960, 188), Moi not only recovered the political Woolf but refuted any separation of aesthetics and politics, 'locating the politics of Woolf's writing *precisely in her textual practice*' (Moi 1985, 16).[12]

Although a work of theory rather than applied narratology, *Sexual/Textual Politics* signalled the direction taken by the first feminist studies to focus on Woolf's 'experimental' style. Analyzing forms of the plot and a variety of elements in story structure, feminists argued that Woolf's apparent lack of logical construction signifies an alternative feminist discourse that subverts the assumptions of authority, progress, unity, and closure implicit in traditional plots. The conventional narrative plot exhibits a forward momentum through conflict towards a point of culmination or denouement – an underlying structure that characterizes the forms known as the *Bildungsroman* (a novel about the formation of identity) and the *Künstlerroman* (a novel about the formation of the identity of the artist), as well as the romance, the courtship plot, and the quest. But are the ideological implications of such plots – heterosexual polarities, discrete unified identities, chronological progress, decisive resolutions – adequate to the experience of women's lives and women's desires? In revisioning the standard plot, do women writers subject the dominant patriarchal institutions to trenchant political critique?

By addressing such questions, feminist narratologists raised the fundamental issue of the way generic expectations affect our interpretations of texts. For, as in the tale of the ugly duckling, what may seem flawed or trivial in the context of traditional conventions may be compelling and meaningful when read as a new genre. Elizabeth Abel (1983), for example, argued that the narrative structure of *Mrs Dalloway* forges an alternative to the epic quest by interweaving, with the heterosexual courtship plot, a submerged narrative of female development. For Abel, subplots of female bonds invoke the pre-Oedipal mother-daughter relationship, subversively resisting the attempt to confine female experience to the male dominated world. In similar fashion, Christine Froula (1993) set Woolf's earlier novel, *The Voyage Out*, against the late Victorian paradigm of female initiation, in which a young woman progresses toward identification with nature, not culture, and finds fulfilment in marriage, maternity, and the private sphere. Showing how the underwater imagery of Woolf's text embodies Rachel's powerful desire to break away from such restrictive plots, Froula concluded that Rachel paves the way for

Woolf's later female *Künstlerromane* in which initiation leads to the birth of
the creative imagination. Rachel Blau DuPlessis's highly influential *Writing
Beyond the Ending* (1985) took inspiration from Woolf's description of a novel
by the fictional Mary Carmichael: 'First she broke the sentence; now she
has broken the sequence' (*AROO* 106). DuPlessis argued that women writers
break from their culture's ideological 'sentencing' by writing beyond the
ending of the traditional forms of closure allotted to them in patriarchal
plots: marriage and death. Woolf's novelistic career, DuPlessis demonstrated,
moves increasingly away from the heterosexual romantic plot, displacing it
in *To the Lighthouse*, for example, by a parent-child tie oscillating between
mother and father and, in Woolf's later novels, by shifting from the individual
quester to the communal protagonist. DuPlessis further theorized that
women's fiction inscribes a 'wavering dialogic structure' (DuPlessis 1985, 38),
vacillating between inclusion (inheritors of culture) and exclusion (outside
and oppositional). Tracing a similar oscillation in women's writing, Susan
Stanford Friedman (1989) defined it in more specifically narratological terms.
Positing a distinction between 'lyric' (a simultaneity or cluster of feelings/
ideas captured in figurative and rhythmic language) and 'narrative' (a story
or structure of events that foregrounds a sequence of dynamic movements in
time and space), Friedman presented Woolf's writing as a complex interplay
between the two modes. Thus, in the *narrative* of *To the Lighthouse*, Lily rejects
the maternal plot of Mrs Ramsay yet, in *lyric* time, mother and daughter are
drawn together in a merging of consciousnesses that becomes the 'wellspring
of the daughter's art' (174).

Like most feminist narratology of the 1980s and early 1990s, these studies
attributed non-conventional aspects of women's writing to a distinctive female
bond with the mother, evidenced in pre-Oedipal as opposed to the Oedipal
plots, or Kristeva's semiotic as opposed to the symbolic. Yet these critics also
resisted the essentialism of proposing a *definitive* female plot, preserving
instead a sensitivity to narrative's *function* within a specific historical and
cultural context. Friedman in particular argued that 'the assumption that all
stories are one story foments an authoritarian plot against narrative itself' and
that 'narrative itself is potentially polyvocal and polymorphous' (180). As a
whole, nonetheless, these studies identify Virginia Woolf's radical ideological
subversions with a corresponding subversion of conventional narrative. In the
words of Margaret Homans (1993), 'Woolf's manifold modernist styles ... are
not incidental but absolutely crucial to her searching critique of patriarchal
institutions' (3).[13]

The studies above approach form as an expression of identity; another closely
related narratological strand understands narrative form as epistemology. As
early as 1961, Samuel Hynes wrote, in a stimulating discussion of Ford Madox
Ford's *The Good Soldier* (1915), 'A novel is a version of the ways in which a
man can know reality, as well as a version of reality itself. The techniques by
which a novelist controls our contact with his fictional world ... combine to

create a theory of knowledge' (Hynes 1972, 54). This vein of enquiry runs throughout Woolf criticism linking, for example, Geoffrey Hartman's earlier work on phenomenological leaps to J. Hillis Miller's later wide-ranging study of fiction and repetition. Miller conceived repetition in two forms: in one, repeated elements echo an originary 'ground', foregrounding the similarity underlying apparent difference; in the other, apparent or fictitious similarities stimulate a perception of gaps and differences. The first generates meaning; the second inhibits the too-easily generated meanings implied by linear sequences. Similarity in repetition informs *Mrs Dalloway*, in which memory functions as resurrection but, in *Between the Acts*, repetition alternates between a powerful rhythmic assertion of wholeness and the possibility that the missing connectives imply a world with 'no centre, no ur-pattern, just echoing differences' (Miller 1982, 219). Then, beyond the oscillation between unity and emptiness, Miller posited a third possibility: that the gaps themselves disclose a positive, a-linguistic, 'ontological principle' – androgynous, but perhaps more readily accessed by women (229). Rejecting Hartman's idea that the mind bridges the textual gaps through acts of interpolation, Miller proposed the opposite dynamic of extrapolation, in which the gaps impel the mind out from known to unknown. But, for Miller, such affirmative silence is no more than glimpsed; by sustaining all three possibilities, the novel 'renders impossible' any resolution of 'truth' (230).

Questions of epistemology and truth then combined with feminist and contextual narratology to engage the political implications, relating to gender and class, embedded in the deployment of narrative authority. In *The Politics of Narration* (1991), Richard Pearce (like Hartman and Miller) focused on Woolf's 'disruptions, discontinuities, silences, absences, holes' (171), seeing (not unlike DuPlessis) a move in Woolf's novels from the 'journey-men's story of adventure and conquest' (140) to, in *The Waves*, an erotic text that 'embodies' relationships in multivalent female forms. Yet Pearce also argued that, in this novel, the male characters appeal to the 'readers' needs for traditional forms of order and unity' (166), producing an *agon* between male and female versions of 'author-ity'. Susan Lanser (1992) more readily accepted Woolf's subversion of traditional masculine consciousness, yet argued that the linguistically homogenizing force of the narrative voice covertly reinstates an authoritative, generalizing voice. Pamela L. Caughie (1992), however, in a postmodernist, deconstructive reading, argued that *To the Lighthouse* displaces its own authorial control. Disputing interpretations of the novel as a three-part progressive narrative (whether recuperating or repudiating the past), Caughie approached the middle section, 'Time Passes', not as transition but as textual disruption. By possessing a 'voice' but not, in *Lily's* terms, a 'vision', the working-class Mrs McNab preserves a space outside and other to the novel's predominantly middle-class norms of agency, signalling the provisionality and limitation of Woolf's own discourse.[14] Locating such disruption not in deconstructive reading but in the text itself, Anna Snaith proposed that the *narrative* of 'Time Passes' subverts the *narrator's* voice-over: whereas the narrator describes Mrs McNab as 'witless' and 'not highly conscious', the narrative, through free indirect discourse (FID), shifts to Mrs McNab's private voice, in which her collected memories and her work of staying corruption constitutes an achievement equal to Lily's painting, though in different terms (Snaith 2000, 76–8).[15]

A general assumption behind much of this criticism is that the classic realist novel, with its authorial distancing and linear sequencing, inscribes a masculinist epistemology, whereas feminist epistemology is more compatible with modernism's perspectivist and associative form. More recently, however, Brian Richardson has argued that *no* form of the plot is inherently ideological, and that its meaning depends on cultural and historical context and also the *content* that it conveys. Claiming that 'some causal connectivity is a necessary precondition of narrativity' (Richardson 1997, 96), and pointing out that chronological progression provides the skeletal frame of most of Woolf's fiction, Richardson observes that the two main story lines in *Mrs Dalloway* come together in an almost motiveless convergence that nevertheless functions as 'deferred causality'.[16] Overall, the studies reveal the complexity of assigning meanings to textual strategies while, at the same time, the importance of understanding 'writing differently' as a way of 'writing back'.

In this light, recent narratological work continues to pursue the study of repeated motifs, but generally without the concomitant universalizing assumption of 'significant form'. Jane Goldman's rich handling of colour in *The Feminist Aesthetics of Virginia Woolf*, for example, is historicized and contextualized in relation to suffragist banner-making and other forms of materialist, feminist intervention; Eileen Barrett's exploration of the networked images of fabric in *To the Lighthouse* turns the motif self-reflexively about to link fabric to fabrication (Barrett 2001). Robert Caserio, in his study of 'tychism', or chance in the form of 'arbitrary and accidental randomness' (Caserio 1999, 6), traces the repeated tropes, in *The Years*, of missed encounters and missed connections, arguing that the novel looks toward a future politics and a future history informed by the positive value of the haphazard and the broken. Caserio's focus on *contradictions*, however, makes his reading alert to the plurality of impulses (toward both coherence and disjunction) that the novel contains. If there is a difference between earlier and recent discussions of motival repetition, it is that the latter are more alert to the multiplicities and contextualizations of patterns, and to the reader's activity in constructing them.

A similar alertness to complexity informs the second wave of criticism to address the problem of defining Woolf's narrating voice, beginning with Dorrit Cohn's *Transparent Minds: Narrative Modes for Presenting Consciousness in Fiction* (1978). Cohn's argument here is that fictional minds are transparent, unlike real minds which are not, and that such transparency depends on a narrative perspective that intersects with, and yet is not identical to, that of the character. Delineating three ways of narrating consciousness – quoted monologue, narrated monologue, and psycho-narration – Cohn made the striking argument that the proportion of unconscious processes in each mode is directly correlated to the proportion of narrator intervention. Stating that there can be no direct transcription of unconscious processes, Cohn posited that we get closest to them in psycho-narration, where the author 'uses his own language rather than his character's' and so 'leads to the sub-verbal depth of the mind'. Cohn described Woolf as employing 'psycho-analogies', or imagist descriptions *analogous* to what a character is thinking (Cohn 1978, 44–5), noting as well, however, Woolf's subtle blurring of the line between character monologue and narrator perception.

Once again, critics of narrative challenged the idea that Woolf's novels immerse us in subjective views. For when narratology subdivided the singular concept 'point of view' to enable a clearer demarcation between 'focalization' (who is seeing) and 'voice' (who is speaking), the latter emerged as the more significant yet more complicated feature of Woolf's texts. The movement from one focalizer to another is admittedly subtle, but *within* one focalization the more difficult question is often whose voice we hear. Whereas one approach – notably that of Ann Banfield (1982) – asserts that, in represented speech and thought (RST), only one point of view can be expressed at any grammatical moment, most narratologists gravitate to the model of free indirect discourse (FID) – a technique in which the focalization can be through the mind of one character but in which voice can shift, almost imperceptibly, back and forth between narrator and character-focalizer, even in a single sentence. Although close to indirect quotation ('she thought that...'), FID displays an indeterminacy that, as Kathy Mezei explains, 'undoes any rigid ... categoric polarization of author, narrator, and character; as a rhetorical figure it mediates between, through, and across voices seeking to be heard' (Mezei 1996, 67).[17] Such discussions of 'discourse' or 'voice' are necessarily technical, but they are also fundamental to any understanding of the values a novel encodes. When a character internalizes a belief or an attitude, can we also distinguish a narrator's voice that is either empathetic or critical? But if there is a distinguishable narratorial voice, does it represent the *narrative's* point of view? Is the narrator ever stable enough throughout a Woolfian text to represent the perspective of an 'implied' author or the 'norms of the text'? Or, if Woolf is writing against the patriarchal voice, is narrator instability part of her anti-authoritarian project? The narratological and hermeneutic questions are inseparable.

In the late 1980s and 1990s, feminist narratological studies of Woolf attempt to give more specificity to the relation between narrative authority and voice. Karen Lawrence (1986), again distinguishing Woolf's use of the *Bildungsroman* from that of male writers like Joyce, argues that *Jacob's Room* presents an alternative to the authority and egotism of patriarchal narration: by eschewing omniscience and even, for the most part, access to her main character's mind, the narrator preserves the enigma of Jacob's personality and refuses to appropriate his voice. For Bette London, Woolf undermines assumptions of authority by exploding the very concept of voice as 'individuated essence' (London 1990, 132). Arguing against readings that claim either Mrs Ramsay or Lily as an authentic female voice, London claims that the disembodied narrator of 'Time Passes' – by disconcerting the surrounding text through 'ruptures, absences and breaks' (146) but also 'echoing conventional forms of authority' (151) – deconstructs the difference between appropriation and de-appropriation and renders unanswerable the questions about narrative authority that the novel repeatedly poses. Kathy Mezei locates the 'textual battle' for narrative authority specifically in FID, where Woolf's narrator both 'orchestrates the movement from one voice into another' (Mezei 1996, 85) yet is also continually effaced by the character-focalizers. Here FID both mimics and mocks conventional narrative authority and, by extension, the patriarchal voice in the social order. Further, the narrator's ability to manoeuvre through the various voices of Septimus Smith, Peter Walsh, Doris Kilman, and Sir William Bradshaw evidences a 'structural indeterminacy' that, Mezei argues, 'shelters and accentuates forms of gender indeterminacy' (67). While early feminist narratological criticism sought distinctively female plots in Woolf's texts, more recent feminist narratology typically foregrounds the refusal of the narrative voice to stabilize into any one position.

The polyvocality of the text – whether manifested within the minds of individual characters or within the larger totality of consciousnesses in the work as a whole – has significant implications for *the way a text means*. Rather than inhering in textual passages, meaning becomes situated in dialectical and dialogic *processes*; the critical subject shifts from ideational content to the relational dynamics of active thought. For Anna Snaith, Woolf's narrative kinetics establish a dialogue between private and public voices, negotiating authority and subjectivity while blurring the distinction between them. Kathy Mezei raises the further complexity that Woolf's narrator is a *constructed* voice to be distinguished from the (implied) author, and that we negotiate not only the differences among the characters and the narrator, but also among the different narrator voices. My own work demonstrates the way these shifts in the narrator's voice constitute the primary rhetorical trope (the 'trope of the twist') in Woolf's essays: the writing voice performatively inhabits different ideological positions, inscribing 'a space for exchange and negotiation' and modelling 'the active and reactive nature of our thinking' (Cuddy-Keane 1996, 144). This strategy of enacting perceptual shifts – a strategy deployed in Woolf's essays and novels alike – encodes multiple voices within the work, leading a number of critics to relate Woolf's technique to Mikhail Bakhtin's notion of the 'dialogic'. One of the most interesting applications of this approach is Patricia Laurence's pedagogical essay on the diverse rhythms in *To The Lighthouse* (2001), in which she demonstrates not only the polyphonic voices of the different characters, but also the added polyphony as those voices are read out loud by a multicultural mix of student voices.[18]

A fundamental question is still how we identify the narrative's different voices. Linguistic narratology seeks to understand just how distinctions between voices are made, to determine, for example, whether grammatical indicators signal the precise moment of a shift. Leaska, as we have seen, attempted to schematize the grammatically characteristic style of each character's speech; today narratologists are more likely to explore greater subtleties and to track dual or multiple voicings. Mezei analyzes the long passage in *Mrs Dalloway* concerning the goddesses Proportion and Conversion to show how 'features of exaggeration such as capitalization, proliferation of phrases, and the heightened language of empire' make us aware of the disparity between the *assumed* patriarchal voice and 'a submerged and ironic voice' that critiques what it mimics (Mezei 1996, 84).[19] Susan Erlich (1994) uses Woolf to argue that, in a crafted written work (unlike ordinary speech), when events representing continuous rather than completed actions are repeated using the same simple past verb tense, the reader interprets the repetition not as redundant information but as the revisiting of an event from a different point of view. Manfred Jahn (1992), however, rejects Erlich's reliance on sentence analysis and the assigning of each utterance to a single point of view, directing attention instead to the way the communicative context inscribes dual voice representation. 'Heard speech,' he asserts, represents the perspectives of both speaker and hearer, so that the reader simultaneously perceives the perspectives of Bradshaw as speaker and Rezia as listener, during Bradshaw's speech. The distinct views are not grammatically marked in Woolf's sentences but emerge out of a context of perspectives that have been accumulating in the novel. David Herman (1995) proposes a model that incorporates both syntactical analysis of meaning and context-dependent functional approaches. *Between the Acts*, he claims, outlines a typology of discourse types (nine in total) that chart the varying relations between discourse and context, distributed on a continuum from most limited, context specific (Bart Oliver) to most unlimited and multiple (Mrs Swithin). In articulating such a spectrum of possibilities, *Between the Acts* helps us 'to develop a polyfunctionalist model for discourse presentation in narrative contexts' (Herman 1995, 181).

If narratology reveals the complexity of Woolf's voices, it also illuminates the challenges they pose for readers. As Mezei states, 'The indeterminacy and instability of FID puts the onus on the reader who has to decide where in all this the author stands' (Mezei 1996, 72). Early critics attempted to define that activity by constructing a hypothetical single reader; now that definitional task includes the way Woolf's texts either invite, or fall victim to, a plurality of readerships or reading experiences. While Sara Blair argues that Woolf's '[t]entativeness, provisionality, skepticism and self-parody' contest the institutionalization of cultural authority, she notes that a 'textual politics of radical hesitation' (Blair 1992, 109) runs the risk of being misread by a straight (non-ironic) reader. My own work shows that Woolf's 'polyvocal rhetoric' (Cuddy-Keane 1996, 156) creates a text that can be entered by readers situated

initially in differing ideological locations; the subsequent twists to new posi-
tionalities inculcate both self-reflexive awareness and flexibility in negotiating
views, adumbrating a conflict strategy with its roots in a female tradition.
Focusing on rhetorical rather than ideological fluctuations in *The Waves*,
James Phelan analyzes the shifts that the reader is asked to make between
attachment and detachment, positing that a 'double vision' emerges from the
juxtaposition of the lyric, mimetic soliloquies, which urge us to feel human
intensity and value, and the distancing, depersonalizing interludes, which lead
us to question the significance of such lived experience in the larger scheme.[20]
Whether seen as a liability or as a *condition* of the texts, multiplicity of reading
practices is another factor now urging a polyfunctional approach.

A proliferation of interpretive contexts also means that narratological
criticism confronts a wealth of new avenues to pursue.[21] Modernism's relation
to technology is generating insights into the impacts of cinema, photography,
broadcasting, and recorded sound – not simply in narrative representations
but very fundamentally in changes in the human body as a medium of
sensory experience. Our understanding of the epistemological dimensions of
Woolf's work is acquiring new sophistication through interdisciplinary work in
literature and cognitive science; at the same time, a release from the limiting
categorization of modernism as the art of subjective impressions is enabling
new perspectives on Woolf's engagement with things, solid objects, and the
ontological status of the non-mental world. Geography's new theorizings of
space and the politics of scale are recasting studies of Woolf's descriptions of
the land and the city, of movement and travel, and of relational shapes. And
there are textual features in her work that urgently need sustained attention
– in particular, the verbal ironies that are so often missed, and the richness
of layered readings that such ironies invoke. Criticism is evidencing a new
interest in questions of aesthetics (the pleasures and functions of beauty)
which a politically conscious age has been inclined to ignore, and, finally
– perhaps the most pressing issue of this time – in textual ethics and the
ethics of reading.

Narratology gives us insight into the power of narrative and the way we use
narratives to shape our lives. It helps us to see the construction of narrative
as a theme in Woolf's novels, and to approach her ideas as always embedded
in a use of language that establishes an attitude, a perspective, a way of
understanding them. As Manfred Jahn asks, 'is it not exactly Woolf's conscious
modulation, her orchestration of all of the techniques, that produces the
remarkable depth-effects and rhythmic quality of her novels?' (Jahn 1992,
361). The reasons *why* we read Woolf will change, but an alertness to the
narratological tradition and the questions it raises will help us, whatever our
interests, to produce better readings. Woolf was first and foremost a worker
in language, and the narratological critic, as Jessie Towne well knew, should
inhabit some part of us all.[22]

notes

1. Miss Jessie Margaret Towne was a teacher of English and later Vice-Principal and Dean of Girls at Central High School in Omaha. I am indebted to the generosity of Lucio Ruotolo (1927–2003) for a copy of the letter and the graph, which he bought at a San Francisco book fair, and to Robert Towne – not, as far as he knows, a relative – for his help in researching Jessie Towne's life. There is no indication Miss Towne's letter was ever sent.

2. John Halperin identifies David Mason's *British Novelists and Their Styles* (1859) as the first work to claim for the novel the kind of high seriousness accorded to poetry, and to advocate a similar critical attention to novelistic style (Halperin 1974, 9). The nineteenth-century followers of Mason's advice, however, were few.

3. Roberts defines significant form as art that embodies 'the uniquely esthetic principle which brings to a complete relationship all the parts within the system' (Roberts 1946, 847).

4. For Auerbach, the question 'whose voice do we hear speaking' is not distinguished from 'through whose consciousness is the event perceived?' I discuss the later narratological distinction between speaking and seeing on p. 29.

5. Contrary to later criticisms that Auerbach was constructing a literary canon (albeit with the inclusion of Woolf), his choice of texts, given the conditions of his exile, was necessarily arbitrary and personal. Woolf's use of the random fragment interestingly parallels Auerbach's historiographic approach.

6. Naremore discusses Lawrence Bowling (1950) as an example of the first approach and Robert Humphrey (1954) as an example of the latter. Today, stream of consciousness is generally distinguished from interior monologue on the grounds that the former presents unconscious impressions as well as conscious thoughts and employs a linguistic style that does not adhere to formal grammatical structures. See Prince (1989, 92).

7. James Hafley (1954) had earlier advanced a similar view, arguing that the characters' views are filtered through the narrator's consciousness.

8. TACT, or Text-Analysis Computing Tools, was developed by faculty and programmers at the University of Toronto and is available, along with a detailed guide, from MLA Publications.

9. See Gerald Prince (1989, 65) and Patrick O'Neill (1994, 13).

10. Indispensable guides for the specialist include Prince's *A Dictionary of Narratology* (1989) and *The Routledge Encyclopedia of Narrative Theory* (2005). *The Cambridge Introduction to Narrative* (2002) offers a shorter and highly useful glossary of crucial terms.

11. See O'Neill (1994, 21) for a useful chart of the various terminologies that critics have employed for these concepts.

12. While Auerbach and Beck considered Woolf's texts posed a counter-vision to both totalitarianism and sectarian factionalism, Moi went further to see Woolf as not merely presenting an alternative, but as radically undercutting the views she opposed.

13. In addition to Woolf's reconfigurations of the *Bildungsroman*, critics have investigated Woolf's generic innovations, for example, in comedy (Little 1983; Cuddy-Keane 1990); short fiction (Head 1992; Benzel and Hoberman, eds. 2004); life-writing (Smith 1993); the epistolary form (Villeneuve 1998); and the elegy (Froula 2002; Wall 2002).

14. Implying a larger point about the way we read plot, Caughie provocatively alerts us to the possibility that *prior* moments may subvert or render equivocal a novel's last words.
15. To extend Snaith's reading, I would also invoke Kathy Mezei's concept of the unreliable, performative narrator. Woolf consistently questions her culture's assumption that not being 'highly conscious' is to be 'robbed of meaning' and, from its opening, *To The Lighthouse* prompts us to ask, 'meaning' in whose terms? Woolf's narrators often perform patriarchal judgements that are undercut by the implied author's alternative view.
16. Richardson still sees Woolf as 'radically challenging the nature of narrative', since the reader must find connectivity through 'analogical correspondences' rather than in direct 'causal ties' (Richardson 1997, 98).
17. The terms and approaches used to define this technique vary, and interested readers will find the debates and differences admirably summarized by Mezei.
18. For a different application of Bakhtin, one that pursues his concept of the chronotope along with Julia Kristeva's invocation of spacialization as a way of charting a text's dialogic processes, see Friedman (1996).
19. Conversely, Edward Bishop (1982) discusses Woolf's use of ambiguous pronoun references in 'Kew Gardens' to show a fusion or merger of consciousnesses.
20. For Phelan, lyric asks us not to judge but to participate in the characters' perceptions, unlike narrative, in which the judging of character is part of the internal structure of the work.
21. Blackwell's *A Companion to Narrative Theory* (2005) offers a broad range of new directions, including Seymour Chatman's work on the narratological relation between *The Hours* and *Mrs Dalloway*, and Melba Cuddy-Keane's discussion of the relation between city consciousness and Woolf's representation of auditory perception.
22. I would like to acknowledge the invaluable research assistance provided by Elizabeth Shih, and to thank James Phelan, Brian Richardson, Anna Snaith, and my former student Cristina Boylan – all of whom commented helpfully on earlier versions of this chapter. I would like also to thank the Social Sciences and Humanities Research Council of Canada for a grant that enabled me to conduct this research.

2
modernist studies
jane goldman

This chapter considers the relationship between Woolf's work and the evolving body of criticism concerned with modernism. Her work as a writer and critic has both shaped and been shaped by modernist criticism. As importantly, her work as a publisher helped to form the cultural economy of the literature we now know as modernism. The Hogarth Press was not only a vehicle for putting Woolf's own work into the public realm, but it was also responsible, for example, for the first major works of Freud in English, and published significant works by key modernist writers such as T. S. Eliot and Gertrude Stein (see Willis 1992). And Woolf herself set the type for the Hogarth edition of Eliot's *The Waste Land* (1923). 'The powerful intellectual developments that made modernism a pan-European phenomenon', as Michael Whitworth observes, 'were sustained at a local level by material institutions like the Hogarth Press' (2000, 150). Just as her press transmitted many important modernist texts, without ever using the term modernism, so Woolf's writing has transmitted modernist theories, oblivious of the term (in its present connotations) that now so thoroughly infuses critical reference to her work. Just as her friend the art critic, Roger Fry bestowed the epithet, 'Post-Impressionist', on the work of the recently deceased 'modern' painters, Van Gogh, Gauguin and others, so Woolf has posthumously received the epithet 'modernist', a term extended to many of her contemporaries, some of whom pronounced themselves Imagists, or Vorticists, Futurists, Cubists, Dadaists, and so on, but not Modernists. In the decades since her death, Woolf studies and modernist studies have grown up together (a claim which is also made about Woolf and feminism), though not always in harmony.

Modernism, it may be understood, was first established as the construct of an historical phase of post-war criticism, deployed to account for the wide and diverse range of experimental and avant-garde literature of the first three or four decades of the twentieth century. And we can now trace the ways this modernism positioned and introduced Woolf, first as the handmaiden to the literary men of modernism (Joyce, Lawrence, Conrad, Ford, Eliot, Pound and Yeats) (see Kenner 1972), and a proponent of Bloomsbury aesthetics (a particularly influential source of formalism for Anglophone modernist criticism), defined with reference to the philosophy of G. E. Moore, and the theories and achievements of Roger Fry, Clive Bell, Lytton Strachey, Duncan Grant, Desmond MacCarthy, Maynard Keynes and Leonard Woolf. General studies of the Bloomsbury Group include those by J. K. Johnstone (1954), Quentin Bell (1968), S. P. Rosenbaum (1975), Leon Edel (1979), Raymond Williams (1980), and David Dowling (1985). Later, as Woolf assisted in the feminist 'unmanning' of modernism (Harrison and Peterson 1997), interest has developed in the influence of women in Woolf's circles, such as Vanessa Bell, Ray Strachey, Jane Harrison, Ethel Smyth, and Dora Carrington (see Marcus 1987; Gillespie 1988; Carpentier 1998; Dunn 1990; Elliott and Wallace 1994). Once feminism took hold of modernism, Woolf became 'Woolfenstein' (see DuPlessis), the mother, for a while, of all modernism and of postmodernism. Subsequent criticism has found Woolf's work, then, the epitome of feminism's modernism, of lesbian modernism, of postmodernism's modernism, of gender studies' modernism, and an important object of postcolonialism's modernism, of new historicism's and cultural materialism's modernism, and of queer modernism. But if modernism's Woolf is now a matter of historical critical record, Woolf's modernism remains the focus of heated critical debate. Woolf's writing was at the heart of influential feminist postmodernist and poststructuralist rereadings of modernism (see Moi 1985; Minow-Pinkney 1987), and of some significance in the recent renewed critical interest in modernism and war (see Tate 1998; Hussey 1991; Wilson 2000). The shifting of modernist critical interest to the 1930s and 1940s, previously considered outside the remit of 'high modernism', has given even more prominence to Woolf's later works such as *Three Guineas*, *The Years*, and *Between the Acts*. Erin G. Carlston's recent book, *Thinking Fascism: Sapphic Modernism and Fascist Modernity* (1998), for example, gives special focus to *Three Guineas* (see also Pawlowski 1995, 2001; Williams and Matthews 1997). Modernism is currently taught and researched with reference to the related term, 'modernity', as indicated in the title of the influential academic journal, *Modernism/Modernity*, which regularly publishes on Woolf (see for example, Brown 1999; Froula 2005; Gordon 2000). Reassessments of modernism go hand in hand with continuing reassessments of Woolf. Although some readers still find that Woolf offers 'lucid, if not systematic, expositions of the essential qualities of Modernist art' (da Silva 1990, iv), and that there is discernible a rigid 'code of modernism' (see Fokkema 1979), others have found it more helpful to talk of multiple and different modernisms (Kermode 1968; Nicholls 1995) and many different Woolfs. If questions of sexual/textual politics, feminism, postcolonialism and cultural context, have informed modernist studies of Woolf in the past couple of decades, the time seems ripe for a return to considerations of formalist modernism. Indeed, one of the most significant contributions to our understanding of Bloomsbury formalism, has been Ann Banfield's recent book, *The Phantom Table: Woolf, Fry, Russell and the Epistemology of Modernism* (2000). Banfield gives fuller consideration to the formalism of G. E. Moore and Bertrand Russell than has been attempted in earlier studies of Woolf and Bloomsbury aesthetics, which have tended to focus mainly on the influence of Roger Fry's formalism and Clive Bell's theory of 'significant form' (see Gloversmith 1984; Koppen 2001; McLaurin 1973; Roberts 1946; Torgovnick 1985). While Banfield has helped to place Bloomsbury and Woolf in the context of Cambridge philosophy, Mary Ann Caws and Sarah Bird Wright, in *Bloomsbury and France: Art and Friends* (2000) have encouraged us to consider Woolf's and her Bloomsbury colleagues' equally important sojourns in France, where they not only enjoyed the physical geography but also had personal contact with many artists and writers of the French avant-garde. Woolf's engagement with visual aesthetics may thus be understood in these wider, international vistas.

Christine Froula places Bloomsbury's and Woolf's modernist aesthetics in broader international and intellectual contexts. Her excellent study of Woolf's *oeuvre* in terms of modernism, modernity, the avant-garde, and Enlightenment thinking, *Virginia Woolf and the Bloomsbury Avant-Garde* (2005), situates Woolf's modernism in the context of Bloomsbury's cultural and political engagements in modernity, giving renewed emphasis to the achievements of Bloomsbury's political and economic wing, such as Maynard Keynes' *Economic Consequences of the Peace* (1919) and Leonard Woolf's *Empire and Commerce in Africa* (1920) and *Imperialism and Civilization* (1928). Froula refreshingly shifts the theoretical framing of Woolf's and Bloomsbury's aesthetics, then, from modernism towards the avant-garde, a term which is currently under renewed scrutiny in modernist studies (see Scheunemann 2000). Froula invokes Peter Bürger's definition of the historical avant-gardes to indicate Bloomsbury's engagement of 'art-for-art's sake in the cause of "forg[ing] a new life praxis from a basis in art"' (Froula 2005, 3; Bürger 1984, 49–50), and shows how it departs from Bürger and connects with Hannah Arendt's conceptions in its integration of 'political and suprapolitical thinking with aesthetics and everyday praxis in addressing a public sphere conceived [...] as "a form of being together where no one rules and no one obeys"' (Froula 2005, 3; Arendt 1982, 8). Froula's shifting of Woolf's modernism on to the previously off-limits terrain of the historical European avant-gardes is very helpful and marks a significant turning point in current critical thinking on modernism.

This chapter explores the various ways Woolf's writing has been understood by critics to embody and to explain 'modernist' aesthetics, however diversely defined. Most notably, Woolf's writing is considered as imitation, a kind of realism, by Erich Auerbach, in his classic book, *Mimesis* (1946), a survey of representation and narrative in Western literature from Homer to the twentieth century. Auerbach dubs her novel, *To the Lighthouse*, the most important modern, twentieth-century work, crowning over two thousand years of literary endeavour. Eric Warner, on the other hand, emphasizing self-reflexive, technical experimentalism in his book devoted to Woolf's 'highest' modernist novel, *The Waves*, observes that this work, like Joyce's *Finnegans Wake*, 'deliberately strives for the palm of innovation so assiduously courted by modernist art', and is considered by critical consensus 'her highest aesthetic endeavour [...] unsettling in the dazzling display of technique, something which [...] renders the book overly enigmatic and elusive' (Warner 1987, 1). More disturbingly, Malcolm Bradbury and James McFarlane, in their still influential introductory collection of essays, *Modernism 1890–1930* (1976), offer the following summation of her art in their 'Brief Biography' of Woolf: 'Mrs Woolf's can seem in some respects a domesticated Modernism, but it contains shrill undertones of disturbance and terror, dark insights undoubtedly related to her suicide in 1941' (639). (Encapsulated here is just about every major patriarchal preconception blocking many students' and readers' first access to Woolf's work.) Bradbury and McFarlane nevertheless lace their introductory essay, 'The Name and Nature of Modernism', with citations from Woolf. Even for them she is a leading, and defining, figure in canonical 'high modernism' (despite her 'strong sense of the female imagination' (639)).

Tim Armstrong's *Modernism* (2005) exemplifies how far received notions of Woolf's modernism and modernism's Woolf have developed since Bradbury's and McFarlane's narrow evaluations. In his wide-ranging and stimulating consideration of cultural modernism, Armstrong offers insightful keyhole readings of Woolf, whom he cites, among numerous other canonical and non-canonical authors, under a range of topics, including modernism and modernity, eugenics, gender, subjectivity, politics, and so on. As well as Woolf's canonical modernist novels, such as *Mrs Dalloway*, *To the Lighthouse*, and *The Waves*, Armstrong refers us to Woolf's essays on Dostoevsky, and 'The Cinema' and 'Street Haunting', her experimental short stories, *Kew Gardens* and 'Solid Objects', and her feminist-pacifist tract, *Three Guineas*. Early orthodox modernist criticism, of Woolf, and through Woolf, foregrounds formalism, transcendent aestheticism, and a mystical sense of organic self-reflexiveness, and focuses primarily on *Jacob's Room*, *Mrs Dalloway*, *To the Lighthouse* and *The Waves* as leading examples of high modernist novels. Close readings of Woolf's fiction, its formalist qualities, its mythic and colour symbolism, for example, and linguistic and structural economies, constitute a rich seam of formalist, modernist studies of Woolf (for example: Alexander 1974; Daiches 1945; Holmesland 1998; Lee 1997; McLaurin 1973; Stewart 1982).

Formalist modernism takes as its yardstick, for Woolf and for the primary male modernists, two influential essays by Woolf: 'Modern Fiction' (1919; 1925) and 'Mr Bennett and Mrs Brown' (1924). These remain Woolf's – and modernism's – most well known and most frequently anthologized and quoted essays. In 'Mr Bennett and Mrs Brown' (first published in 1924 as 'Character in Fiction'), Woolf puts forward her most famous, and most quoted, assertion: 'on or about December 1910 human character changed'. The coincidence of the date with the opening of the formalist art critic, Roger Fry's hugely influential exhibition, *Manet and the Post-Impressionists*, has fuelled modernist critical interest in the influence of the visual arts on Woolf's aesthetic. Paradoxically, such allusions to historical and cultural context have until recently reinforced dehistoricized, formalist and aestheticist readings of her work. In 'Modern Fiction', Woolf outlines an experimental and subjective method of writing characterized by her figure, the 'luminous halo' (CR1 150), an image which has become a founding metaphor of high modernist criticism, frequently put up for comparison with the 'hard' metaphors favoured by other (male) modernist critics such as Ezra Pound, Wyndham Lewis or T. E. Hulme. High modernist critical interest in 'stream of consciousness' technique has also focused on this essay. But Woolf's development of free indirect discourse, allowing for a shifting and collective sense of subjectivity, has sometimes been overlooked by critics anxious to read Joyce's methods, as outlined by Woolf in 'Modern Fiction', as a blueprint for all modernism, including and especially her own.

In short, it seems, Woolf's two most anthologized essays have furnished the theoretical lexis and armature for high modernist criticism, but the cost of this was for many years a limited understanding and definition of modernism and a limited reading of and attention to Woolf's work. The impact of formalist, high modernist criticism is far-reaching and still influential; but both modernism and Woolf have, as mentioned above, been subject to the changing tides in literary criticism and cultural studies. Again, attention to Woolf's writing has *produced* as much as reflected these critical shifts. The common topoi of male modernism, such as myth, the city, time, science and physics, citationality, interiority, gender and sexuality, psychoanalysis, lyric prose, and so on, are sometimes differently inflected in Woolf, sometimes radically revised or challenged. Her 'mythical method' does not follow Eliot's account of Joyce's (in '*Ulysses*, Order, and Myth'), but shows a feminist slant; nor does her writing communicate Eliot's dread of the 'unreal city', and his (related) misogyny, but rather celebrates urban space and the emergence of women in the public sphere. Woolf's famous injunction, in 'Modern Fiction', to 'look within' (CR1 149) was taken literally for a while, and she was presented as a 'naïve', untutored, modernist, obsessed by interior, subjective and mystical experience. Whereas the densely allusive and citational 'difficult' texts of Eliot, Pound, and Joyce, and their learned literary and cultural references, have long since been thoroughly annotated and scrutinized, Woolf's writing is only recently undergoing such treatment. It was not so long ago, for instance, that critics felt able to presume Woolf's lack of classical scholarship, rather than acknowledge her satirical characterization, in her account of Mrs Dalloway's mistaken assignation, in *The Voyage Out*, of Clytemnestra to the *Antigone*. Recent critical interest in Woolf's considerable classical scholarship (for example in her unpublished translation of the *Agamemnon*), and in her vast reading in, and knowledge of, English literature as well as many other literatures and disciplines, has meant a major reassessment of her modernism.

Yet, the rich intertextuality of Woolf's writing was illuminatingly explored in Woolf's lifetime by Ruth Gruber in her 1935 feminist study of Woolf's style, which has recently been republished, and which anticipates more recent feminist engagements with Woolf's modernism (Gruber 2005). Modernist critical focus on Woolf, at the same time, has widened from the canonical modernist essays, and high modernist novels (the sequence from *Jacob's Room* to *The Waves*), to take in such disparate works as her autobiographical writings, for example, the posthumously published, 'Sketch of the Past' (in which she puts forward a philosophical vision, anticipating in some respects Roland Barthes' idea of the 'death of the author', communicating a sense of an ungendered collective aesthetic), and her more popular fiction, for example, *Flush*, her 'low-brow', best-selling biography of a literary lapdog. We can see how feminist modernism might favour *A Room of One's Own* and *Three Guineas* over 'Modern Fiction' and 'Mr Bennett and Mrs Brown'; whereas queer modernism prefers *Orlando*, and so on.

Much of this territory is, of course, covered in other chapters. This chapter, while acknowledging the many different inflections in the rapidly growing body of work where Woolf studies intersects with modernist studies, finds its main concern to be with the rise of formalist, high modernism's Woolf, with attention also to the place of Bloomsbury aesthetics, and of post-Impressionism and the visual arts in such approaches. Given their enduring presence on undergraduate reading lists, it seems sensible to take as the two points of departure for this consideration of Woolf and modernist studies, the essays 'Modern Fiction' (1919; 1925) and 'Mr Bennett and Mr Brown' (1923; 1924). 'Modern Fiction' and 'Mr Bennett and Mrs Brown' have pride of place in several influential modernist readers, introductions, and source books. Bradbury and McFarlane, somewhat elliptically, collapse into a lazy critical shorthand that has proved most enduring some of the key phrases from both essays when they cite Woolf in evidence of modernism's 'great aesthetic revolution':

> Hence Virginia Woolf, holding that the modern stylistic revolution came from the historical opportunity for change in human relationships and human character, and that modern art therefore had a social and epistemological *cause*, nonetheless believed in the aesthetic nature of the opportunity; it set the artist free to be more himself, let him move beyond the kingdom of necessity to the kingdom of light. Now human consciousness and especially *artistic* consciousness could become more intuitive, more poetic; art could fulfil *itself*. It was free to catch at the manifold – the atoms as they fall – and create significant harmony not in the universe but within itself (like the painting which Lily Briscoe completes at the end of *To the Lighthouse*). (1976, 25)

Peter Faulkner, in his *Modernist Reader: Modernism in England 1910–1930* (1986), which for many years was an important source book on university courses, introduces these essays as 'constitut[ing] the clearest statement of the Modernist view of fiction, and link[ing] the advocacy of it to a definite sense of overall social and cultural change' (23). They are cited in the orthodox manner by Peter Childs (80–2) in his New Critical Idiom volume, *Modernism* (2000). But in his introduction to the Longman critical reader *Modernism/ Postmodernism* (1992), Peter Brooker, under the heading, 'Making it old: "Traditionalist Modernism"', gives a negative cast to Faulkner's attention to 'Mr Bennett and Mrs Brown' and to his identification of modernism's inception with Woolf's 1910 statement therein (5). Brooker finds that 'by her own reckoning, however, [Woolf's] method was not the method of modernism, for in the same essay she finds the "modernists" Joyce and Eliot indecent and obscure' (5). More radically, Armstrong omits mention of either of Woolf's seminal modernist essays in his introduction to *Modernism*, although they inform the work of other scholars he has 'synthesized' (Armstrong 2005, x). In his introductory remarks to his *Concise Companion to Modernism* (2003), David Bradshaw also refreshingly opts to deflect attention from Woolf's most cited pronouncements in 'Mr Bennett and Mrs Brown' (2), although one of his contributors, Mary Ann Gillies, passes on received views of 'Modern Fiction' in her very helpful chapter on Bergsonism.

'Modern Fiction' and 'Mr Bennett and Mrs Brown' are reproduced to represent Woolf in Bonnie Kime Scott's groundbreaking anthology, *The Gender of Modernism* where Suzette Henke introduces them, in much the same way, and without reference to gender, as 'constitut[ing] nothing less than a passionate call to aesthetic arms, a rhetorical plea for modernist revolution' (Scott 1990, 627). But they are usefully supplemented in the same volume by the reproduction of Woolf's reading notes on 'Modern Novels (Joyce)', and by other pieces edited by Brenda R. Silver, representing samples of Woolf's work that 'provide glimpses [...] into the historical inscriptions of gender that characterize her revisionary project' (Scott 1990, 647): the story, 'The Journal of Mistress Joan Martyn' (1906), and the essays and notes, 'Byron and Mr Briggs' (1922), 'Notes for Reading at Random', 'Anon' and 'The Reader' (1940–1). Dennis Walder's anthology, *Literature in the Modern World* (1990), avoiding 'Modernism' in his title, represents Woolf with extracts from her major feminist tracts, *A Room of One's Own* (1929) and *Three Guineas* (1938), which are the staple of feminist approaches to modernism, all the same, and a welcome acknowledgement, perhaps, that these works give a better insight into Woolf's modernism. And it is Woolf's language from *A Room of One's Own*, and from other essays ('The Leaning Tower' and 'The New Biography'), but not from 'Modern Fiction', that Maria DiBattista cites, in her introduction to Woolf for the *Modernism and New Criticism* volume of the *Cambridge History of Literary Criticism*, as Woolf's 'critical legacy': 'an image- repertoire rich in symbolic formations: "a room of one's own", "the androgynous mind", the leaning tower, granite and rainbow' (DiBattista 2000, 126). She also points out other familiar images and themes, such as Woolf's advocacy of 'the common reader' in her two published essay collections, and Woolf's vision, in *A Room of One's Own*, of 'Shakespeare's sister', a collectively evolving model for the woman poet, as well as Woolf's memorable accounts of the demons plaguing women writers: 'Milton's bogey' and 'The Angel in the House'. But Woolf's 'luminous halo' imagery, refreshingly, has been elided in DiBattista's list. That said, in selecting material for *Modernism: An Anthology of Sources and Documents* (1998), my colleagues, Vassiliki Kolocotroni, Olga Taxidou, and I, while declaring in our introduction that this anthology 'seeks to unsettle and rethink rather than neatly define the term Modernism' (Kolocotroni et al. 1998, xviii), nevertheless chose to reproduce high modernism's Woolf by extracting the most cited statements from 'Modern Fiction' and 'Mr Bennett and Mrs Brown'. But we also included, in full, 'The Moment: A Summer's Night', another 'much cited document [that] typifies the experimental merging of fact, polemic, and fiction employed in many of [Woolf's] important essays' (392); and Woolf's paper to the Workers' Educational Association, 'The Leaning Tower' (1940), which 'touches [...] on familiar concerns – access to education and to the material spaces for writing and engaging with literature' (610). However we may wish to revise, or even abandon 'modernism', we cannot escape its historical critical formation, embedded in which are Woolf's two 'modernist' essays.

'modern fiction' (1919; 1925)

'Modern Fiction', first published in the *Times Literary Supplement* in April 1919 as 'Modern Novels' and revised for Woolf's first collection of essays, the first *Common Reader* (1925: the revised, 1925, version of the essay is often misdated 1919), is perhaps Woolf's most well known and most frequently quoted essay. Maggie Humm, in her excellent book, *Modernist Women and Visual Cultures: Virginia Woolf, Vanessa Bell, Photography and Cinema* (2002), helpfully explores the centrality of this essay for 'Critical Modernism': 'One of the earliest uses of the term "modern" in relation to literature is by Virginia Woolf herself in "Modern Fiction", where she claims that "the modern practice of the art is somehow an improvement on the old"' (*CR1* 146; Humm 2002, 11), and she points out that this essay 'was chosen by Mark Shorer as a significant introduction to his collection, Modern British Fiction [(1961)]' (Humm 2002, 11). Humm offers a useful discussion of the 'trajectory of the term 'modernism'' (11–14), and she refreshingly, and very helpfully, departs from the orthodoxy by focusing on Woolf's use of the term, 'modern', in 'Modern Fiction', rather than plunging in straight for the famous passage beginning 'Look within [...]'. Humm also points out that 'Woolf's essays in the 1920s specifically about modernism, "Modern Fiction" [...], "The Narrow Bridge of Art" (1927) and "Phases of Fiction" (1929), share [a] concern with perspective. Like snapshots, the essays' momentary reflections often connect by focusing on objects' (Humm 2002, 221).

Woolf distinguishes, in 'Modern Fiction', between the outmoded 'materialism' of the Edwardian novelists, H. G. Wells, John Galsworthy, and Arnold Bennett, and the more 'spiritual' and experimental writing of her Georgian contemporaries. The tyranny of plot and characterization afflicts Bennett's work, she contends, along with the obligation 'to provide comedy, tragedy, love interest, and an air of probability embalming the whole so impeccable that if all his figures were to come to life they would find themselves dressed down to the last button of their coats in the fashion of the hour' (CR1 149). Such writing fails to capture 'life', as Woolf's most famous and most quoted passages of criticism explains:

> Look within and life, it seems, is very far from being 'like this'. Examine for a moment an ordinary mind on an ordinary day. The mind receives a myriad impressions – trivial, fantastic, evanescent, or engraved with the sharpness of steel. From all sides they come, an incessant shower of innumerable atoms; and as they fall, as they shape themselves into the life of Monday or Tuesday, the accent falls differently from of old; the moment of importance came not here but there; so that, if a writer were a free man and not a slave, if he could write what he chose, not what he must, if he could base his work not upon convention, there would be no plot, no comedy, no love interest or catastrophe in the accepted style, and perhaps not a single button sewn on as the Bond Street tailors would have it. Life is not a series of gig lamps symmetrically arranged; life is a luminous halo, a semi-transparent envelope surrounding us from the beginning of consciousness to the end. Is it not the task of the novelist to convey this varying, this unknown and uncircumscribed spirit, whatever aberration or complexity it may display, with as little mixture of the alien and external as possible? (CR1 149–50)

This passage is, according to Randall Stevenson in his introduction to *Modernist Fiction* (1992), 'one of the most comprehensive and celebrated statements of the priorities of modernism' (59). Woolf's story, 'The Moment: A Summer's Night' (c.1929), offers a closer, equally lyrical, account of a luminous 'moment of vision', and is often cited in conjunction with this passage (see Guiguet 1965; Richter 1970):

> Yet what composed the present moment? If you are young, the future lies upon the present, like a piece of glass, making it tremble and quiver. If you are old, the past lies upon the present, like a thick glass, making it waver, distorting it. All the same, everybody believes that the present is something, seeks out different elements in this situation in order to compose the truth of it, the whole of it. (M 9)

Woolf, it seems, sees the novelist's task as to somehow capture the moment – or life – and give the 'truth of it'. As if fiction were a contraption to catch butterflies, or the mind a piece of blotting paper with which to soak in life unadulterated. In 'Modern Fiction', she continues with the injunction:

> Let us record the atoms as they fall upon the mind in the order in which they fall, let us trace the pattern, however disconnected and incoherent in appearance, which each sight scores upon the consciousness. Let us not take for granted that life exists more fully in what is commonly thought big than is commonly thought small. (CR1 150)

Citing 'Modern Fiction', and with particular attention to the 'luminous halo' passage, David Lodge, summarizes in his influential book, *The Modes of Modern Writing* (1977), the dominant, and enduring, formalist modernist critical credo:

> Modernist fiction, then, is experimental or innovatory in form, displaying marked deviations from pre-existing modes of discourse, literary and non-literary. Modernist fiction is concerned with consciousness, and also with the subconscious and unconscious workings of the human mind. Hence the structure of external 'objective' events essential to traditional narrative art is diminished in scope and scale, or presented very selectively and obliquely, or is almost completely dissolved, in order to make room for introspection, analysis, reflection and reverie. A modernist novel has no real 'beginning', since it plunges us into a flowing stream of experience with which we gradually familiarize ourselves by a process of inference and association; and its ending is usually 'open' or ambiguous [...] To compensate for the diminution of narrative structure and unity, alternative methods of aesthetic ordering become more prominent, such as allusion to or imitation of literary models or mythical archetypes, and the repetition-with-variation of motifs, images, symbols – a technique variously described as 'rhythm', 'Leitmotif' and 'spatial form'. Modernist fiction eschews the straight chronological ordering of its material, and the use of a reliable, omniscient and intrusive narrator. It employs, instead, either a single, limited point of view, or a method of multiple points of view, all more or less limited and fallible: and it tends towards a fluid or complex handling of time, involving much cross-reference backwards and forwards across the chronological span of action. (45–46)

Lodge's 'flowing stream' exemplifies standard 'Bergsonian' readings of Woolf's essay in terms of stream of consciousness. Gillies helpfully explains (Bradshaw 2003, 103) how Woolf's recording of atoms is anticipated by the philosopher Henri Bergson, an important source for modernist studies of Proust and Joyce, as well as Woolf (see Kumar 1962). Da Silva finds that in her 'recognition of the significance in the seemingly trivial and insignificant Woolf proves herself to be a true Modernist in line with Joyce as well as Surrealist poets and painters, particularly Marcel Duchamp' (da Silva 1990, 168). Humm advances on the orthodox impressionistic readings of Woolf's famous passage in showing the essay (defined by the imagery of this passage) to be 'a good example of her use of photographic tropes of illumination and reflection [...]. In her seemingly unstructured view of contemporary writing, she applies scopic devices to a commentary on literary features' (Humm 2002, 221). In advocating subjective, fleeting, interior, experience as the proper stuff of fiction along with the abandonment of conventional plot, genre, and narrative structure, Woolf's essay, then, has become one of the standard critical sources in the discussion of modernist literary qualities – particularly 'stream of consciousness' – not least because it includes a (not uncritical) defence of Joyce's work. The most famous example of modernist stream of consciousness technique is Molly Bloom's soliloquy, the 'Penelope' episode, in *Ulysses* (1922), where Joyce represents the myriad, often libidinous, thoughts of a woman as she lies in bed with her husband, in eight extremely long, seamless, sentences. This minimally punctuated episode, according to Joyce himself, 'begins and ends with the female word *yes*' (Joyce 1975, 285). And, interestingly, Woolf's feminist modernist novel, *To the Lighthouse* (1927) begins with the word 'Yes', which is uttered by the submissive, patriarchal wife and mother, Mrs Ramsay, who continuously offers affirmation to her son and husband, and it ends with the rather different self-affirming 'Yes', of the defiantly unmarried artist, Lily Briscoe: 'Yes, she thought, laying down her brush in extreme fatigue, I have had my vision' (*TTL* 281). But the difference between Joyce's technique and Woolf's is more than a matter of who says 'Yes' to whom; it lies in their different deployment and representation of point-of-view, individual and collective (Goldman 2003, 203–4). Woolf's free indirect discourse often renders a most elusive point-of-view. Auerbach's famous question, 'Who is speaking in this paragraph?', remains the most stimulating and helpful one for the reader and critic of modernist Woolf to ask. Auerbach's close reading of a passage from (the fifth section of Part One of) *To the Lighthouse*, offers a most sophisticated analysis of her writing in terms of point-of-view, narrative voice, time, interior and exterior consciousness, epistemology and fragmentation (1953, 525–41; see Chapter 1 in this volume).

Woolf cites, in 'Modern Fiction', Joyce's *Portrait of the Artist as a Young Man* and the extracts from *Ulysses* recently published in the *Little Review* (1918) to exemplify the new 'spiritual' writing. Joyce, she argues, is 'concerned at all costs to reveal the flickerings of that innermost flame which flashes its messages through the brain' (*CR1* 151). Woolf's alchemical imagery here owes much to Walter Pater's aesthetics (see Meisel 1980), and her concern with subjective temporality – the epiphanic 'moment' – to the philosophy of Henri Bergson. And Woolf's 'moments' are compared in modernist criticism with Joyce's 'epiphanies'. Bergson's theory of *la durée* concerns subjective, psychological, non-spatial, time (Bergson 1910, 108). True time is understood to be impenetrable and seamlessly continuous *flux* (a key term), and to exist only within, subjectively: 'Outside ourselves we should find only space, and consequently nothing but simultaneities' (116). Bergson speaks of 'two different selves [...] one of which is [...] the external projection of the other, its spatial and, so to speak, social representation'; but the more 'fundamental' of which is connected to *la durée* and is therefore 'free'. It is reached 'by deep introspection'. Bergson emphasizes that only in 'rare moments' do we have access to *la durée* and to our true selves, and that only in such moments may we 'act freely' (231–2). Bergson's 'rare moments' of introspection seem to resemble Woolf's; and his suggestion of an inner illumination casting its 'colourless shadow' into the external world may also inform Woolf's 'luminous halo' imagery (Stevenson 1992, 104–5). But despite this resemblance, critics were to become wary of fully equating the two. Tony Inglis, for example, in 1977, notes that for some time in Woolf studies 'pondered reading and critical accounts [have] tended to show that Woolf's novels are better read as weapons against flux than as inert surrenders to it'. He continues: 'we swim in the waves of flux instead of drowning in them' (48).

Woolf's 'luminous halo' image also echoes an image from Joseph Conrad's *Heart of Darkness*. Although Woolf identifies, in 'Modern Fiction', a fragment of *Ulysses* ('Hades', extracts of which appeared in the American magazine, *The Little Review* in September 1918, and in the British *The Egoist* in July and September 1919) as a 'masterpiece' for 'its brilliancy, its sordidity, its incoherence, its sudden lightning flashes of significance', she nevertheless finds that it 'fails to compare' with the work of Joseph Conrad or Thomas Hardy 'because of the comparative poverty of the writer's mind' (*CRI* 151). Woolf is less generous to Joyce in private. On reading *Ulysses*, she notoriously captures him in her diary as 'a queasy undergraduate scratching his pimples' (*D2* 188). 'Modern Fiction' nevertheless stands as an early and significant defence of his work, and as a manifesto of modernism (Goldman 2003, 68).

But this complex manifesto-essay is so often reduced in critical discussion to the passages cited above. Woolf's injunction to 'look within' and her description of the mind as *tabula rasa*, passively receptive to 'a myriad impressions', along with her imagery of luminosity, become perfect fodder for interiorized, *reflective*, impressionistic models of modernist aesthetics where literature becomes the subjective site of aesthetic haven, removed from the vicissitudes of life and certainly remote from political life. Woolf's rhetorical questions 'Is life like this? Must novels be like this?' (*CR1* 149), suggest a line of enquiry based on an aesthetics of imitation – that is, art as reflective, imitation of life; and her injunction, 'Let us record the atoms as they fall upon the mind in the order in which they fall', suggests the writer as mere reporter from the interface of subjective consciousness and outer reality. Peter Nicholls, in *Modernisms: A Literary Guide* (1995), puts forward a more considered interpretation of Woolf's luminous imagery in 'Modern Fiction', which he discusses under the chapter heading, 'The Narratives of High Modernism':

> Where Pound had emphasised the need for clarity and 'objectivity', Woolf's sense of interaction with the world is designedly tenuous, a matter of intermittent intensities which seem to befall the perceiver. But the implied passivity is not the only difference, for this 'halo' is also a liminal space in which the self may experience an openness to others, and a temporary relaxing of those psychic defences which had seemed essential to one type of modernist aesthetic. (264)

Nicholls recognizes an implicit collectivity in Woolf's Paterian imagery that is so often (mis)understood in terms of isolated and individuated subjectivity, but he also notes that 'Woolf's desire for some sort of collective "geniality" runs up against her troubled sense of entrenched class divisions'. He finds that the 'resulting tension in her work can be damaging, leading, on the one hand, to brittle and patronizing social judgements, and, on the other, to a certain preciosity in the writing when the everyday is self-consciously elevated to the "poetic"' (265). This seems to be a polite and veiled reference to the crude accusations of effeteness, elitism, and even racism that Woolf's reputation has suffered since Tom Paulin's notorious (British) television programme, *J'Accuse: Virginia Woolf* (Channel Four 1991), and since the politics and prejudices of the right-wing, and sometimes anti-semitic, men of modernism, Lewis, Pound, and Eliot, for example, have been opened up for critical scrutiny (see Tratner 1995). Nicholls subtly acknowledges but also deflects such an approach to Woolf, emphasizing 'the complexity in the best of her work'.

Nicholls' conclusions stem from his discussion of Woolf's aesthetic model in the 'luminous halo' passages in 'Modern Fiction', but it should be noted that these passages arise from Woolf's meditations on *Joyce's* new fictional methods, not her own. Woolf's own 'method' in the essay in which they appear is to describe the attractions of her contemporaries' methods and then show their shortcomings. After questioning whether 'Mr Bennett has come down with his magnificent apparatus for catching life just an inch or two on the wrong side', she finds: 'Life escapes; and perhaps without life nothing else is worthwhile' (*CRI* 149). Having noted the near miss of Bennett's materialist methods, she now turns her attention to Joyce's 'spiritual' methods, before moving on to the 'influence' of the Russians, and of Chekhov in particular. Sympathetic with all of these approaches, she nevertheless exposes their limitations – and this includes the 'luminous halo' approach.

Woolf does not leave 'the comparative poverty of [his] mind' as her explanation of Joyce's failure: 'But is it not possible to press a little further and wonder whether we may not refer our sense of being in a bright yet narrow room, confined and shut in, rather than enlarged and set free, to some limitation imposed by the method as well as by the mind' (151). In referring to the confining space of a 'bright yet narrow room', Woolf seems to be opening up for criticism the 'luminous halo' passage she has used to introduce Joyce's work, or at the very least suggesting his halo is not big or luminous enough! It may well be the 'method' described in that very passage, then, that she seems to be criticizing when she asks:

> Is it the method that inhibits the creative power? Is it due to the method that we feel neither jovial nor magnanimous, but centred in a self which, in spite of its tremor of susceptibility, never embraces or creates what is outside itself and beyond? Does the emphasis laid, perhaps didactically, upon indecency, contribute to the effect of something angular and isolated? Or is it merely that in any effort of such originality it is much easier, for contemporaries especially, to feel what it lacks than to name what it gives? (*CRI* 151–2)

Here we are alerted to the risk of solipsism and isolation inherent in the subjective methodology of the 'luminous halo' approach as practised by Joyce. Joyce's accent – or emphasis – also falls too heavily upon the scatological, Woolf opines. Just as Bennett's materialism misses the mark, so too does the 'spiritual' Joyce, however laudable his experimentalism (Goldman 2003, 69–70).

Critical focus on the 'luminous halo' passage has meant a lack of attention to the oppositional energies at work in 'Modern Fiction', as I have argued elsewhere (70). For example, in pursuing the spiritual aspects of modern literature, Woolf urges us to consider the influence of Russian literature, as a corrective to materialist tendencies in English: 'If we want understanding of the soul and heart where else shall we find it of comparable profundity? If we are sick of our own materialism the least considerable of their novelists has by right of birth a natural reverence for the human spirit' (*CRI* 153). Peter Kaye's chapter on Woolf in his stimulating book, *Dostoevsky and English Modernism 1900–1930*, offers a perceptive reading of Woolf's 'perhaps tongue-in-cheek' admiration of Russian fiction here: 'While recognizing that cultural differences militate against an assimilation of Russian modes of thought or writing, she draws upon their fiction to illustrate the infinite elasticity of the literary imagination' (Kaye 1999, 79). And Kaye recommends that Woolf's essay 'The Russian Point of View' (1925) 'should be read as a companion-piece to "Modern Fiction" (both were first published in *The Common Reader*)' (79). Yet her line of argument does not settle with this point. She also sees something in English letters that is missing in the 'comprehensive and compassionate' Russian mind:

> But perhaps we see something that escapes them, or why should this voice of protest mix itself with our gloom? The voice of protest is the voice of another and an ancient civilisation which seems to have bred in us the instinct to enjoy and fight rather than to suffer and understand. English

fiction from Sterne to Meredith bears witness to our natural delight in humour and comedy, in the beauty of earth, in the activities of the intellect, and in the splendour of the body. (153–4)

In this stimulating passage, which has escaped the sort of critical attention lavished on the 'luminous halo', Woolf points up a distinctly English tradition in a heady mix of dissent, rationalism, humour, materialism, pleasure and sensuousness with which we might temper the spiritual and suffering qualities discerned in Russian literature. It seems ironical, if not somewhat provocative that, in the volatile period after the Russian Revolution, when Woolf was working on this essay, she should choose to characterize Russian culture as long-suffering and stoical, and the English as full of 'protest' and 'fight'. She is, nevertheless, identifying and championing an Enlightenment tradition in English letters overlooked by the many commentators on 'Modern Fiction' whose sights remain so tightly locked on the 'luminous halo'. The passive aesthetic sensibility associated with the 'luminous halo', and then passed as the formula for modernist fiction, should perhaps more properly be read alongside the oppositional credo of 'protest' and 'fight' expressed here in the essay's conclusion.

The essay concludes, not with a recommendation of any one credo for writing fiction ('luminous halo' or otherwise), but with a celebration of 'the infinite possibilities of the art' (154). Woolf's closing line in 'Modern Fiction' figures the art of fiction as a messianic woman seeking transformational violence to her person, as a necessary means for the renewal of her youth and of her beauty ('for so her youth is renewed and her sovereignty assured' (154)). Woolf, at the same time as recommending the renewal of fiction by the violent disruption of tradition, manages both to attack the notion of the feminine as personifying vehicle; and assert a feminine sovereignty by inverting the gender associations of mythic renewal by violence. And it is evident that Woolf's early formulations on what has become known implicitly as 'Modernist Fiction' are bound up with questions of gender, sexuality and feminism, just as the modernist period itself is dominated by them (Goldman 2003).

'mr bennett and mrs brown' (1923; 1924)

'Mr Bennett and Mrs Brown' (the title of an essay published in the *New York Evening Post* and the *Nation & Athenaeum* in 1923; then revised and published in the *Criterion* in 1924 as 'Character in Fiction'; this was reissued with minor revisions as 'Mr Bennett and Mrs Brown' by the Hogarth Press as a pamphlet in 1924), like many of Woolf's essays, evolved from a speech (in this instance to the Cambridge Heretics Society May 1924), and many of its rhetorical features survive into the published text. Here Woolf continues her assault on the Edwardians, Wells, Galsworthy and Bennett, for their materialist conventions, and her uneven defence of the Georgians, Joyce,

Eliot, Forster, Lytton Strachey, and D. H. Lawrence, whose work, she declares, must make us 'reconcile ourselves to a season of failures and fragments' (*E3* 435). The essay's title is derived from its central, virtuoso, conceit whereby Woolf illustrates the inadequacies of the Edwardian novelists as she makes a number of attempts, using their 'tools', to construct a fictional narrative about the character of 'Mrs Brown', a stranger encountered on a train. And Woolf's staging of various paradigms for modern fiction on a train and around the person of 'Mrs Brown' has captured modernist critical imagination (see for example, Bowlby 1997). But these figures, combined with her identifica-tion of December 1910, do not seem to impress Peter Brooker: 'Woolf went on to suggest this had something to do with a perception of changed social relations and attitudes, but did not explore this further, perhaps because her concern was precisely with a new interiorising treatment of character and consciousness in the novel: to present "Mrs Brown" "herself", not as a factoring out of class and environment in the way of an Arnold Bennett or of naturalism' (Brooker 1992, 5). This leads him to conclude that the essay is not a manifesto of modernism (as quoted above). He seems to be reading into this essay, as many critics do, the 'luminous halo' passage and the injunction to 'look within' from 'Modern Fiction'. Brooker seems to be undermining Woolf's status even as a handmaiden to male modernism when he adds: 'We might choose to see her metonymic substitution of the part for the whole, of individual consciousness for "life itself" as equivalent to Joyce's "epiphany" or Eliot's "objective correlative" or the Imagist "doctrine of the image", but Woolf was not consciously contributing to a "modernist aesthetic"' (5). This is helpful in pointing out the retrospective homogenizing of different aesthetic positions under the rubric of modernism, and the role Woolf's essay has played in this process, but Brooker is nevertheless presenting a rather stereotyped view of Woolf's modernism.

Jessica Berman helpfully points out, in *Modernist Fiction, Cosmopolitan-ism, and the Politics of Community*, that Woolf's essay may be bracketed with other Modernist manifestos that 'seek to create, challenge or defend not only particular modes or perspectives but also communities of artists who share those perspectives', but she also instructively asks: 'Yet how many among Forster, Lawrence, Strachey, and Joyce would create Mrs. Brown in the corner of her railway carriage just as Woolf presents her to us, the source not only of modern fiction but also of "life itself"?' (Berman 2001, 25) And Berman argues that: 'Woolf's sense of commonality with these writers [...] is more about how we should read her own work than about how we should read Lawrence. The artistic community she creates for herself provides an imagined context for readership, rather than a real-world bond in the creation of a common project. Thus the manifesto may be thought of as another version of the narrative enactment of community, which ought not be bound by the real-world relationship (or lack thereof) among artists' (25).

'Mr Bennett and Mrs Brown' also contains one of Woolf's most famous, and most quoted, assertions: 'on or about December 1910 human character changed' (*E3* 421). This has come to represent for many cultural commentators the cataclysmic moment of modernity, the inception of the avant-garde, the shock of the new. In the context of the essay, it marks the shift from the Edwardian to Georgian era, when 'all human relations have shifted – those between masters and servants, husbands and wives, parents and children. And when human relations change there is at the same time a change in religion, conduct, politics, and literature' (422). But Woolf is not arguing that literature merely changes in terms of subject matter to reflect new, modern, experience, but that literary form itself undergoes radical, and turbulent, transformation: 'And so the smashing and the crashing began [....] Grammar is violated; syntax disintegrated' (433–4). The work of Joyce, Eliot and Strachey illustrate the point that modern literature has necessarily become caught up in the business of finding new form. Readers must 'tolerate the spasmodic, the obscure, the fragmentary, the failure' (436). The self-reflexive, fragmentary, subjective and momentary qualities of modernist writing are, of course, acknowledged and celebrated by Woolf's avant-garde contemporaries, but her own particular aesthetic was anathema to some. Woolf's 'luminous halo' metaphors, for instance, 'imply an art that rejects precise statement and moral certainty', according to Michael H. Levenson, 'in favour of the suggestiveness and imprecision usually associated with symbolism or Impressionism. [Ezra] Pound on the other hand, opposed all "mushy technique" and "emotional slither", preferring a poetry "as much like granite as it could possibly be"' (1984, 154–5). Levenson alerts us to the critical ruptures of the period. Yet there is common ground between Woolf and Pound. Eliot, who owed much to Pound, for example, was also championed by Woolf.

1910, as her essay suggests, was a significant year for Woolf. It was also a significant one, more broadly, for Bloomsbury. In February, Woolf took part in the notorious *Dreadnought* Hoax. Woolf and her brother Adrian, Duncan Grant, Horace Cole and others, masquerading as the Emperor of Abyssinia and entourage, conned their way past naval high security into a guided tour of the warship, the *HMS Dreadnought*. Bloomsbury notoriety was compounded in November of that year with the opening of Roger Fry's groundbreaking exhibition, *Manet and the Post-Impressionists*, the first major showing in Britain of the work of Van Gogh, Gauguin, Cézanne and other avant-garde continental artists. Fry's neologism, 'Post-Impressionism', is the first of many 'post's in twentieth-century criticism. The exhibition met with huge public and critical outrage. Woolf and Vanessa Bell masqueraded as 'Gauguin girls' at the post-Impressionist Ball. She also joined the suffrage movement in 1910. By 1912 Vanessa Bell and Duncan Grant were among those representing the English artists converted to the new avant-garde aesthetic, in the second post-Impressionist Exhibition. There are many publications on Woolf, Bloomsbury and 1910. Peter Stansky's book, devoted to a detailed exploration of this critical moment for British avant-garde, is probably the most helpful introduction.

But, it was on or about July 1924, it should be noted, that Woolf declared, in her essay, that 'On or about December 1910, human character changed', and it is as well to consider the cultural and literary context in which this declaration was made, as well as the associations and contexts of the designated date of 1910 itself. In a flash of major cultural and political unrest, 1910 ushers in a period which will witness the cataclysm of the Great War, the Russian Bolshevik Revolution, the execution of the Russian Tsar (1918), the establishment of the Irish Free State (1922), the establishment of the Union of Soviet Socialist Republics (1923), and the climate of increasing anger and dissatisfaction at the lot of those who fought and survived the Great War, which led to the General Strike in 1926. In the despondent years after the Great War, 1924 saw the formation of the first Labour government in Britain, headed by Ramsay MacDonald, who in the same year lost the general election to Stanley Baldwin. In the turbulent political context of 1924, then, Woolf looks back over fourteen years of upheaval to 1910, but her statement has only gained in significance in the decades of enormous cultural and political change since it was first published. And 1910 seems to bear the burden of all the upheaval to follow.

Twelve years after Woolf's declaration, in 1936, George Dangerfield memorably sums up 1910's climate of old order decline and exhilarating cultural change: 'People gazed in horror at the paintings of Gauguin, and listened with delighted alarm to the barbaric measures of Stravinsky. The old order, the old bland world, was dying fast' (63–4). In drawing attention to the shocked reception of Gauguin's art, Dangerfield is referring us to the event that has become most powerfully associated with Woolf's designation of 1910 as the moment of change: Fry's notorious exhibition of 'modern' art, *Manet and the Post-Impressionists*, which opened in November 1910. Ian Dunlop reminds us of the political upheavals occurring at the time of Fry's historic exhibition:

> A constitutional crisis over the power of the House of Lords developed, and in the winter of 1910 Asquith dissolved Parliament and called for a general election. In November, a few days after the opening of the Post-Impressionist exhibition, the Home Secretary, Winston Churchill, ordered the troops in to break up the strike of Welsh miners at Tonypandy, an action that was to have lasting effects on labour relations in Britain. Throughout that year the suffragette movement gained momentum. (1972, 132)

Retrospectively, 1910 has been understood as the historical gateway to cultural change, cataclysm and catastrophe. And in the period around 1910 and after, a period of massive social upheaval and major political revolution, the very categories of Art or Literature, as eternal, transcendent values, were under considerable assault, undermined by a wide range of oppositional, avant-garde movements. On the other hand, it must also be acknowledged that the revolutionary date of 1910 has become identified as the moment of inception of a dominant strand of formalist aesthetics, which is considered to entrench Art and Literature even more firmly in separate (from each other, from life), autonomous disciplines, and which by mid-century had become the *modernist* critical filter through which to interpret all avant-garde practices. While, on the one hand, the impact of the exhibition suggests all the hallmarks of a revolutionary avant-garde event, art sending shock waves deep into the praxis of life (see Bürger 1984), the critical apparatus, on the other hand, developed by Fry, and fellow critic Clive Bell, to theorize this retrospectively applied term, post-Impressionism, is recognized as an important foundation for formalist, modernist aesthetics (see Falkenheim 1980). There is a double cultural impetus in post-Impressionism, as both radical, avant-garde and formalist modernist. 'Mr Bennett and Mrs Brown' (and 'Modern Fiction'), in this context, is a prime source for formalist, modernist critical methodologies and reading practices; and Woolf's work is thus considered to perpetuate the ideas put forward by Fry and Bell to define Post-Impressionism. Brooker, for example, concludes: 'if there was any reason for this date [1910] for Virginia Woolf it was presumably less a matter of life itself in the round – which would have something to do, say, with the death of liberal England, with suffrage, Home Rule, trade union militancy, as well as changing domestic relations in the middle-class household – than of the first Post-Impressionist exhibition of that year at the Grafton Gallery' (Brooker 1992, 5–6). On the other hand, the political context, the 'real world' Brooker cites in the streets outside the gallery, may be understood to contribute to the cultural significance of the 1910 exhibition, and Woolf's statement (Stevenson 1992, 61). And there is now a great deal of Woolf criticism concerned with showing the intricate interpenetration of her aesthetics and the public sphere (Snaith 2000; Peach 2000).

Her focus on 1910 in 'Mr Bennett and Mrs Brown' has helped critics, equating 1910 primarily with Post-Impressionism, to forge readings of Woolf's fiction through Fry's aesthetics in particular (Roberts 1946; McLaurin 1973; Torgovnick 1985). And although feminist criticism deflected interest, for a while, to consider other influences, such as the art of Woolf's sister Vanessa Bell (not herself immune, of course, to Fry's theories), there is still important work going on in the exploration of Fry's aesthetics. Banfield, acknowledging that the 'connection between Woolf's thinking about art and Fry's is by now well-established', argues: 'What is not is the extent to which Fry's aesthetic derives from analytic philosophy' (Banfield 2000, 247–8). She shows how Fry mediates Bloomsbury art and Cambridge philosophy, emphasizing that 'Woolf's aesthetic was not [...] articulated in theoretical isolation but in Apostolic Bloomsbury, in which Fry's position was so pivotal that Woolf "wish[ed]" she "dedicated" *To the Lighthouse* to Fry, recognizing "his aesthetic guidance", and came to write his biography after his death' (Banfield 2000, 247, quoting Woolf *L3* 385, and Quentin Bell 1972, II, 129). Banfield has made an important contribution to modernist studies of Woolf in her detailed and informed exploration of Fry's aesthetic hinterland in Cambridge philosophy as shaped by Russell. But the precise nature of Woolf's debt to Fry's aesthetics remains open to question. Here Banfield follows mainstream modernist criticism of Woolf, which reads Woolf's famous letter to Fry on her compositional technique in *To the Lighthouse* as confirmation of her adherence to his theories:

> I meant *nothing* by The Lighthouse. One has to have a central line down the middle of the book to hold the design together. I saw that all sorts of feelings would accrue to this, but I refused to think them out, and trusted that people would make it the deposit for their own emotions – which they have done, one thinking it means one thing another another. I can't manage Symbolism except in this vague, generalised way. Whether its right or wrong I don't know, but directly I'm told what a thing means, it becomes hateful to me. (*L3* 385)

My own view is that in telling Fry she 'meant *nothing* by The Lighthouse' Woolf may be presenting to him a silence that may speak (feminist) volumes. Mrs Ramsay, for example, serves up at her pre-war nuptial banquet '*Boeuf en Daube*', one of Roger Fry's culinary specialities (Spalding 1980, 128), a dish the post-Impressionist painter Lily Briscoe, nevertheless, as we may gather from her opposition to her hostess's promotion of marriage, finds difficult to swallow. If *To the Lighthouse* yields to formalist readings drawn from Fry's theories, it may yet simultaneously disclose a subversive feminist aesthetics at work. It may be that Woolf insubordinately mimes Fry's theories rather than loyally parrots them. This is a point where feminism's impact on modernist studies is felt, opening up questions of gender, politics and form. Modernist experimentation with form may have less to do with art-for-art's-sake or aesthetic autonomy, as high modernist criticism finds, and more with the invention of new avant-garde, political languages, as various other (not only feminist) strands in modernist criticism find. *A Room of One's Own*, for example, is concerned not only with devising the feminine sentence for fiction (*AROO* 99–100) but in speculating on the shape of a fascist poem (134).

But let us turn now to the formalism of post-Impressionism. The 1910 exhibition catalogue preface was anonymous, and not in fact directly written by Fry, but ventriloquized through Desmond MacCarthy (MacCarthy 1945, 124). It declares the post-Impressionist artist's individual expression to be at odds with the naturalistic project of the Impressionists: 'there is no denying that the work of the Post-Impressionists is sufficiently disconcerting. It may even appear ridiculous to those who do not recall the fact that a good rocking-horse often has more of the true horse about it than an instantaneous photograph of a Derby winner' (MacCarthy 1910, 8). Humm, drawing on André Bazin, is instructive on the photographic genealogy of modernism and comments that MacCarthy 'chose to attack spectators' desire for mimeticism by attacking snapshots' (Humm 2002, 23).

The second exhibition, in 1912, gave space to the work of British artists (including Vanessa Bell, Woolf's sister), inspired by the work of the first exhibition, alongside their continental avant-garde masters. Apart from this, the most obvious shift in emphasis from the first exhibition was from romantic to classic, reflected in the new predominance of cubism and an emphasis on the emotional understanding of form for its own sake above everything else. Clive Bell's term, 'significant form', coined for the second exhibition, and further defined in his influential book *Art* (1914), begins to become almost synonymous with post-Impressionism. Fry's theory of 'classic' art arises, like Bell's, from the development of his formalist interpretation of post-Impressionism into a universal formalist aesthetic theory, as the following extract from his *Vision and Design* (1920), illustrates:

> The greatest object of art becomes of no more significance than any casual piece of matter; a man's head is no more and no less important than a pumpkin, or, rather, these things may be so or not according to the rhythm that obsesses the artist and crystallises his vision. [...] It is irrelevant to ask him, while he is looking with this generalised and all-embracing vision, about the nature of the objects which compose it. (52)

Fry's formalism and Bell's 'Significant Form' furnish formalist modernist criticism with the intellectual context in which to explore Woolf's key 'modernist' essays, and provide a formalist resonance to Woolf's choice of 1910 as the date of change – a change understood to occur primarily in the history of art. And, as Fry's and Bell's universalizing development of their formalist theories shows, if this change was perceived as a shocking rupture of artistic tradition in 1910, it was being presented more smoothly as the continuity of universal formalist values by 1912. But to understand, on the other hand, the full avant-gardiste potency of 1910 as a date, we have to consider how the art in question interpenetrates with the period's history and politics, as Dunlop, quoted above, has shown (Dunlop 1972, 132). When Andrew McNeillie glosses Woolf's invocation of 1910 with reference to the post-Impressionist exhibition and the death of Edward VII (*E3* 437), he shows how this art event may be twinned with the end of an era and the start of a new one, eras still designated in terms of the reign of a king. Yet any sense of continuity at this time is severely undermined by the events Dunlop lists. The first post-Impressionist exhibition was understood as not just symptomatic of, but actually stoking contemporary revolutionary tendencies (Wees 1972, 20; Greenslade 1994, 129–33). By 1912 Bell and Fry are putting forward formalist theories that defuse this avant-gardiste frame of reference (see Goldman 1998, 109–37).

'"Mere formalism"', Banfield reminds us, 'has long been a term of contempt for the left which is perhaps not aware that, currently, it is the one aspect of aesthetic theory and practice which right and left are agreed in dismissing' (Banfield 2000, xiv). In opposition to this view, she quotes Michel Foucault's observation that 'formalist culture, thought, and art in the first third of the 20th century were generally associated with critical political movements of the Left – and even with revolutionary movements' (xiv–v). Formalism is the 'aesthetic precursor or accompaniment' of such moments, Banfield contends, 'regardless of the political affiliations of individual practictioners [sic], from Russian revolution to May 68 and even including the neo-classicism of the French Revolution. Only when such revolutionary moments were over – defeated or distorted – did what is more conventionally thought of as political or social literature appear' (xv). This analysis is temptingly neat: avant-garde (revolutionary) formalism yields to more overtly political social(ist) realism, just as romanticism yields to classicism. Transitions between the two poles of formalism and realism, in this period, are more fluid and fluctuating than Banfield's model might suggest, but these terms nevertheless provide useful critical insight. Formalism, however, may refer to several different critical movements, and it is worth briefly considering their basic differences.

Banfield is introducing readers to the philosophical and aesthetic formalism of Bloomsbury, London, that is, to the work of Moore, Russell, Fry and Clive Bell. Formalism is inflected differently by each of these thinkers, and Banfield helpfully opens up the formalism of Bertrand Russell's logical philosophy for special consideration. Moore's influential work *Principia Ethica* (1903) based his proposition that goodness is indefinable and immeasurable on the principle of organic unity: aesthetic and personal pleasures are good in themselves (Roe and Sellers 2000, 166). McNeillie is wary of leaving Woolf's intellectual formation, in particular, 'locked in the wooden embrace of G. E. Moore' (2000, 13), and rightly alerts us to many other important influences on her and on Bloomsbury's thinking, not least the classical anthropology of Jane Ellen Harrison (see Carpentier 1998). But until Banfield's work, Bell's and Fry's formalism has in any case tended to dominate modernist scholarly interest in Bloomsbury's, and Woolf's, aesthetics.

Fry's and Bell's brand of Bloomsbury formalism may be summarized as a concern with form for form's sake, then, and with an emotional and spiritual investment in form, which became known through Bell's influential theory of 'Significant Form'. Their formalism evolved in application primarily to the visual arts, but shows some affiliations with the literary formalism emerging in the early twentieth century which, directly or indirectly influenced by the structural linguistics of Ferdinand de Saussure, 'devoted its attention to concentrating on literature's formalism in an objective manner' (Wolfreys 1999, 847), and which shaped emergent English Studies. Students are still introduced to formalist methodologies based on the 'practical criticism' of the Cambridge scholar I. A. Richards, and of the American New Critics who followed him, all of whom were influenced by Eliot. Indeed Eliot's sense of classicism along with T. E. Hulme's are linked with Fry's and Bell's in modernist criticism (for example, see Brooker 1992, 6). It is the formalism of New Criticism that is most strongly associated with the emergence of Modernism as an aesthetic and critical category, exemplified in the recent volume of *The Cambridge History of Literary Criticism: Modernism and the New Criticism*, in which appears DiBattista's chapter on Woolf (mentioned above).

The central tenet of Russian formalism of the same period, on the other hand, whose connections with the Russian Revolution Banfield emphasizes, stems from Viktor Shklovsky's theory of *ostranenie* or 'defamiliarisation' by which he argues that the 'the function of art is to "defamiliarise" one's habitual perception of the world' (Newton 1990, 6). The politically engaged formal experimentation advanced by Bertolt Brecht's theory of epic theatre (1930) owes something to defamiliarization. The Russian formalists along with The Prague Linguistic Circle 'who continued the work of the Russian formalists after their suppression by the Soviet government during the 1930s', have hugely influenced modern (and modernist) literary and linguistic theory (Womack 2002, 117). The legacy of Soviet socialist realism's antipathy to formalism has been the sometimes crude positioning of formalism almost as the antithesis to politically engaged art. But the spectrum of formalist aesthetics from Bell's significant form to Brecht's alienation technique shows formalism to be highly differentiated and politically nuanced. Woolf's physical and intellectual proximity to Fry and Bell is not surprisingly emphasized in many formalist readings of her work, but this has not precluded, nor should it, Brechtian interpretations (see, for example, Shattuck 1987, 282).

Banfield seeks to elucidate the 'place of formalism in the life and work of a thinker also interested in changing the world' and suggests that the fact of Russell's political activity [...] his existence elsewhere, in a separate political sphere [...] is the counterweight to any charge of "mere" formalism' (2000, xv). This line of argument sits a little oddly with her earlier claim that aesthetic formalism precedes political revolution 'regardless of the political affiliations of individual practitioners'. But, the reception of Fry's and Bell's emergent aesthetic formalism in the public sphere shows it was understood in many quarters as inherently political, rather than political by association. Woolf's position, as central Bloomsburyite and author of the essay that has helped to mythologize Fry's 1910 exhibition, is itself pivotal in the formation of modernist critical discourse. At stake in the interpretation of her statement on 1910 is how we define modernism in general as well as how we interpret post-Impressionism or read Woolf's own work.

In 'Mr Bennett and Mrs Brown', Woolf depicts 1910's shift in human relations, represented in the work of Samuel Butler and Bernard Shaw, in the figure of 'one's cook'. She calls this 'a homely illustration', and Woolf's terms here are, according to Sara Blair for one, 'characteristically domestic (and high bourgeois)' (Blair 1999, 163):

The Victorian cook lived like a leviathan in the lower depths, formidable, silent, obscure, inscrutable; the Georgian cook is a creature of sunshine and fresh air; in and out of the drawing room, now to borrow the *Daily Herald*, now to ask advice about a hat. Do you ask for more solemn instances of the power of the human race to change? (*E3* 422)

The imagery of a woman servant emerging leviathan-like from the dark depths of the kitchen into sunlight may suggest a shift from women's dark, subliminal, creaturely existence to luminous, colourful liberation. For Blair, who discusses Woolf's essay in her chapter on 'Modernism and the politics of culture' for *The Cambridge Companion to Modernism*, Woolf's imagery 'usefully suggests the entanglement of what we call politics and what we call culture as forms of experience; and it evidences the way in which writers committed to socialist, Fabian, feminist, and other left platforms insisted on that connection' (Blair 1999, 164). She offers a perceptive close reading of Woolf's imagery here, showing the cultural significance of each aspect of her 'homely illustration':

> Under the sway of new, mass cultural organs of entertainment and information (like the *Daily Herald*, founded in 1919 as the first mass daily 'worker's paper'), of the forms of fashion and style they promote (like the fetching new hat), and of consumer desire at large (promoted by mass-produced goods that held out promises of material fulfilment to all), traditional and rigidly hierarchical codes of class and national identity, social distinction, and cultural value were being rapidly broken. For all her vaunted aestheticism, Woolf – as well as English and Irish novelists as diverse as H. G. Wells, John Galsworthy, D. H. Lawrence, and James Joyce – would make the newly visible materiality of this everyday, middle- and working-class life-world central to her aesthetic. (164)

I would emphasize that the cook's choice of paper, and possibly even her dress code, suggest a particularly feminist portrait here (see Goldman 1998, 111–112, 123). December 1910 may mean for Woolf, then, material improvement for women workers, and the emergence of women from intellectual darkness into enlightenment, from obscurity into public life. Froula, too, has noticed the suffragist resonances in Woolf's 'watershed year 1910' (Froula 2005, 23). After the creaturely cook, Woolf gives a 'more solemn instance [...] of the power of the human race to change': a revised reading of the *Agamemnon*, in which 'sympathies' (usually reserved for the patriarchal order sanctioned by Athena) may now be 'almost entirely with Clytemnestra' (avenger of her daughter's death). In asking us to 'consider the married life of the Carlyles', she returns to the theme of women's servitude, perhaps mindful of the suffragette scorn for Thomas Carlyle (resulting in a cleaver attack on his portrait in the National Gallery) (Goldman 1998, 112; Atkinson 1996, 163). He personifies 'the horrible domestic tradition which made it seemly for a woman of genius to spend her time chasing beetles, scouring saucepans, instead of writing books'. Woolf spells out this tradition's hierarchized, gendered, relations as she announces its demise: 'All human relations have shifted – those between masters and servants, husbands and wives, parents and children. And when human relations change there is at the same time a change in religion, conduct, politics and literature. Let us agree to place one of these changes about the year 1910' (*E3* 422). Modernism's Woolf, I have been arguing, in its more formalist manifestations, focuses on her stylistic changes, often at the expense of our understanding of the relevance of the cultural and political changes she cites here, and which a new generation of Woolf criticism is now addressing. How precisely aesthetic revolution and change interpenetrate with cultural, social and political revolution and change is where the study of Woolf's modernism begins.

3
psychoanalytic approaches

makiko minow-pinkney

The connection between psychoanalysis and Woolf seems overdetermined. Firstly, the development of psychoanalysis and Woolf's life were contemporaneous and psychoanalysis was profoundly influential on early twentieth-century intellectual life. Woolf's connection with Freud goes further; she was close to the source of dissemination of his theories via the Hogarth Press and her friends and family circle. Bloomsbury played a major role in bringing Freud's theories to England with James Strachey, Lytton's younger brother, and his wife Alix as central figures of this English psychoanalytic movement. Woolf's younger brother, Adrian Stephen, and his wife Karin also became professional psychoanalysts. In 1924 the Hogarth Press became the official publisher of the entire 'International Psycho-Analytical Library', (which means all the writings of Freud and his other followers), and had James Strachey as the official translator as well as the editor of the Standard Edition.[1] While the circumstantial connection between Woolf and psychoanalysis seems so obvious, its actual relationship is far from straightforward and her response seems ambivalent. She maintained a deliberate distance from it until the later years of her life. There is no record until a diary entry late in 1939 that she read Freud, though, according to Leonard Woolf, it seems that she read at least *The Psychopathology of Everyday Life* before she wrote *Mrs. Dalloway*.[2]

Woolf did not receive psychoanalysis for her mental illness. Jan Ellen Goldstein argues in 'Woolf's Response to Freud', that the reason why Woolf stuck with the old-fashioned diagnosis of 'neurasthenia' and treatment of 'rest cure', without resorting to psychoanalysis, which was available in London in 1913, was due to both Virginia and Leonard's belief in the mythic linking of artistic genius and insanity; both feared that scientific analysis and a cure might affect her creativity.[3] Woolf herself certainly seems to encourage us to entertain such a myth when she writes:

... these curious intervals in life – I've had many – are the most fruitful artistically – one becomes fertilised – think of my madness at Hogarth – and

60

all the little illnesses – that before I wrote the *Lighthouse* for instance. Six weeks in bed now would make a masterpiece of *Moths*. (*WD* 146)[4]

Apart from her rejection of psychoanalysis as a treatment for her own illness, Woolf's long-maintained aversion to both writing about and reading Freud is attributed by Elizabeth Abel partly to a discursive rivalry: 'the anxiety provoked by the authoritative discourse on "the dark places of psychology" to which she also staked a claim' (Abel 1989, 14). The 'singularly literary version of psychoanalytic discourse' (15) of the distinctive cast assumed by British psychoanalysis – to which Bloomsbury contributed significantly – may, Abel speculates, have heightened this competitive anxiety in Woolf. There was discursive rivalry because of the recognition of the similarity in the objectives of their pursuits, her modernism and Freud's psychoanalysis.

In her declaration of the modernist aesthetics of her generation in 'Modern Fiction', Woolf directs the reader to 'look within' (*CR1* 149). In fact her writing never stops pointing to this place 'within' our mind, deep beneath the surface. The narrator of 'Street Haunting' comes near to the field of psychoanalytical interest, when she talks of 'instincts and desires' as the natural ingredients of our being and the joy in deviating 'into those footpaths that lead beneath brambles and thick tree trunks into the heart of the forest where live those wild beasts, our fellow men' (*E4* 486, 490–1). The perennial problem of Bernard in *The Waves* is how to write *the* true story without excluding 'a rushing stream of broken dreams, nursery rhymes, street cries, half-finished sentences and sights' (*W* 213), 'any nonsense' (217) which one may be humming under one's breath behind the polite formalities and ready-made phrases of social life. The social and linguistic codes (what Bernard calls 'biographical style') which are 'laid like Roman roads across the tumult of our lives' and compel us 'to walk in step like civilized people with the slow and measured tread of policemen' (216–17) are condemned by Bernard as 'a mistake'; 'this extreme precision, this orderly progress, a convenience, a lie. There is always deep below it ...' (213). So too in the essay 'On Being Ill' health is associated with 'make-believe', punctilious public spirits and even with imperialist endeavours: 'In health the genial pretence must be kept up and the effort renewed – to communicate, to civilize, to share, to cultivate the desert, educate the native [...] In illness this make-believe ceases' (*E4* 321).

If Woolf's interest resides in subterranean life as Freud's does, in the darkness 'when the lights of health go down' where illness discloses 'the undiscovered countries' (*E4* 317), it is not difficult to see why Woolf regards illness ('intervals in life') as artistically most fruitful. In a letter Woolf explains why her mental illness is precious for her art:

As an experience, madness is terrific. I can assure you, and not to be sniffed at; and in its lava I still find most of the things I write about. It shoots out of one everything shaped, final, not in mere driblets, as sanity does. (*L4* 180)

Woolf here reverses the normal hierarchy of values, not by claiming for insanity the power to see a different kind of truth, but the power to see the same truth more intensively and completely than through sanity. While planning *Mrs Dalloway*, Woolf wrote in her diary: 'Suppose it to be connected in this way: sanity and insanity. Mrs D seeing the truth, SS seeing the insane truth.'[5] We know that Septimus was invented later to save the heroine by bearing her destructive impulse so that she lives. Septimus (insanity) and Clarissa (sanity) are one compound character. They see the same truth, but for Septimus the truth manifests itself with completeness and purity. That is the interpretation, anyway, which Clarissa gives when she hears of the young man's suicide. But the point of the novel is that however far apart the two characters are in terms of social status, gender, and age, Clarissa identifies herself with Septimus – 'She felt somehow very like him' (*MD* 158),[6] showing that sanity and insanity are not separate or opposed, but connected.

The continuity between sanity and insanity is also what Freud's genius understood. Psychoanalytic theory's premise is that the psychic problems from which the insane suffer are exactly the problems and conflicts with which the sane struggle. Woolf's proximity to Freud, therefore, is more than circumstantial, suggesting affinity between her literary project and Freud's theory. And yet in spite of, or because of (in Abel's view), this closeness, Woolf maintained a distance from psychoanalysis.[7] She expressed dissatisfaction with the application of psychological/psychoanalytic theory to novel writing, first in L. P. Jack's novel (1918), and then J. D. Beresford's more directly Freudian novel (1920). Woolf attributes the failure of Beresford's *An Imperfect Mother* to the reductionism incurred by his application of scientific theory to the human mind: 'It simplifies rather than complicates, detracts rather than enriches' (*CW* 154).

Probably the first Freudian criticism of Woolf's novels is Erwin P. Steinberg's 'Freudian Symbolism and Communication' published in the periodical *Literature and Psychology* (1953). Assuming that Woolf was conversant with Freud's theory because of her involvement with the publication of his writings, he criticizes what he believes to be Woolf's deliberate use of Freudian symbolism in *Mrs Dalloway* (Peter's 'knife') as 'a good example of [the] failure to subordinate system to aesthetic' (2). On the other hand, he praises Woolf's successful usage of Freud's 'phallic symbols' in *To the Lighthouse*. In it, he argues, 'Freudian symbols: a column of spray, a fountain; a beak of brass, a scimitar' are fused with the more traditional 'imagery of rain, flowering, and fecundity and of aridity and sterility' (4) and the two types of symbolism reinforce each other, resulting in a good communication.[8] It is not difficult to imagine what Woolf would have felt if she had known that she was accused of leaping to use the symbols of the new discovery of 'depth psychology', superimposing a new system on to literature and failing to communicate: the very thing she criticized in her above-mentioned review. In his letter to Steinberg, Leonard Woolf expresses strong doubts that his wife ever used symbols in the way described by Steinberg or she ever read *The Interpretation of Dreams* (see Note 2).

Another contribution in the 1950s is Joseph Blotner's 'Mythic Patterns in *To the Lighthouse*' (1956), in which he refers to the Oedipus myth and Freud's theory of the same myth. His essay features the Demeter-Persephone myth more extensively than the Oedipus myth. Jung is mentioned as the other of 'two old antagonists' (561) who testifies to the Demeter-Persephone myth as a reflection of patterns of human experience (reference to Jung is very rare in Woolf studies). So in the mid 1950s there was some interest in Woolf and psychoanalysis, but, in general, the dominant dualism of art and science operating in Woolf's criticism of Beresford's novel was still an ideological fix in literary criticism, preventing psychoanalytic theory from entering into Woolf studies.[9] Hence Morris Beja's surprise in his introduction to the casebook of *To the Lighthouse* (1970): 'extended attention has not been paid to the possibilities for enlightenment that a psychoanalytic interpretation of this novel might provide' (28). His own very brief demonstration of Freudian interpretation evidences the refinement and subtlety of his understanding of Freudianism.

In the 1970s we saw an explosion of biographical material (see Chapter 4 in this volume): for example, Quentin Bell's biography (1972), *Moments of Being* (1976), the *Letters* (1975–80) and *Diaries* (1977–84). This availability of biographical information, aided by the tide of feminist criticism, roused a surge of interest in Woolf's life, which resulted in vigorous publication of psychobiographical works and the phenomenon of uniquely Woolfian criticism which John Mepham describes as follows: 'Never have literary criticism and psychobiographic investigation been so intimately entwined as in the case of Virginia Woolf' (Mepham 1992, 13). The question of Woolf's mental illness – true insanity, fabrication by conspiracy, psychological disturbance, or psychiatric problems? – started to dominate the critical discourse of Woolf studies as it never had before.[10] Leonard Woolf had remarked in his autobiography that 'the connection between her madness and her writing was close and complicated' (L. Woolf 1964, 103), but it was Quentin Bell's biography which fixed the discourse of madness in Woolf studies. However the psychobiographical works of the 1970s and the early 1980s mostly eschewed 'theory', though issues with which they were preoccupied – Woolf's mental illness, suicide, the problems of sexuality and childhood sexual abuse – have obvious relevance to psychoanalysis. Critical theory was still shunned in literary criticism.[11]

In her review 'Freudian Fiction', though Woolf expresses dissatisfaction with the incompatible combination of science and art which resulted in the simplification of life, she almost immediately qualifies her complaint: 'Partly, no doubt, this is to be attributed to the difficulty of adapting ourselves to any new interpretation of human character' (*CW* 154). Woolf was aware of the historical contingency of thought and this quote indicates her openness to the possibility of radical conceptual change. In the 1970s and 1980s such a change did, indeed, occur together with the change of the relationship between science and art, and theory and literature. This sea change was brought about by the emergence of 'theory' – what Jonathan Culler called 'a new genre' (Culler 1982, 8) – replacing the dominance of new criticism. In this new discursive environment of poststructuralist theory whose antihumanism demystified the concept of the human as ineffable, concerns of reductionism which accompanied the application of scientific theory to the matter of the human mind ceased to be an issue for some (see Chapter 7 in this volume).

In order to examine the significant development in the psychoanalytic approaches of Woolf studies in this new theoretical climate, we need to take into account not only poststructuralism, but also the powerful development of feminist literary criticism during the 1970s. Feminist approaches changed the direction of Woolf studies in a significant way by discovering a new Woolf and redefining her work (see Chapter 5 in this volume). In this surge of assertion of Woolf as a political, feminist thinker, her modernist aesthetics became an awkward irrelevance. It was a poststructuralist approach that rescued Woolf's modernism for use by feminist politics by radicalizing the interpretation of Woolf's narrative strategies, particularly through the issue of feminine writing posited at the theoretical junction of subjectivity, sexuality and language.

Jacques Lacan's poststructuralist psychoanalysis radically changed our understanding of the human subject. The centrality of language in his theory of subject construction, which he claims as a rereading of Freud, made his psychoanalysis particularly pertinent to literary criticsm. But it was Julia Kristeva's modification of Lacan's theory that was especially useful in enabling critics to relate Woolf's modernist aesthetics to her subversive feminism. In Kristeva's theoretical scheme the subject is defined as a dialectic process of two modalities: the symbolic and the semiotic. The semiotic belongs to the pre-Oedipal phase with which the feminine takes its place and is the term whose repression is the conditional foundation of the symbolic order – the sum total of social exchanges including language – which embodies the Law of the Father predicated on castration. She argues that the avant-garde poetics of the late nineteenth and early twentieth century is a literary practice which particularly cultivated the semiotic – the pleasurable and rupturing aspect of language – in order to subvert the symbolic order.

In *Women Writing and Writing About Women* (1979) Gillian Beer and Mary Jacobus make one of the earliest references to poststructuralist psychoanalysis by using Lacan and Kristeva to argue that Woolf's narrative strategies are a narrative politics of feminist subversion rather than escapist aestheticism and that Woolf's writing can be thought of as an exploration of a special language for women. Then Toril Moi, in her influential book *Sexual/Textual Politics* (1985), argued that the true nature of Woolf's radical sexual/textual politics was missed by some Anglo-American feminist critics who could not break the ideological mould of conventional (and therefore patriarchal) humanism and would thus be better understood by a poststructuralist approach. My book *Virginia Woolf and the Problem of the Subject* (1987) addresses the issue fully. It maintains that theoretical readings of Woolf's aesthetics behind her experimental novels reveal Woolf's modernist aesthetics to be a feminist subversion of the deepest formal principles of the very definitions of narrative, writing and the subject, of a patriarchal social order. Recognizing the affinity between Woolf's writing and Kristeva's theory of avant-garde poetics, the book explores Woolf's feminine writing as poised over the chasm between the semiotic and the symbolic, maintaining a difficult and delicate dialectic between submission to the symbolic and refusal of it, for a simple subversion of the symbolic risks expulsion from meaning and sanity.

Though Lacan himself is far from being a feminist, his theory, together with Kristeva's, has given feminism a useful vocabulary and concepts. Terms such as 'the symbolic', 'the imaginary', 'the semiotic', or 'the Law (Name) of the Father' started to have a wide currency in critical discourse both inside and outside of Woolf studies, and arguments presenting (sometimes without theoretical rigour) 'the symbolic order' (and language itself) as inherently masculine or patriarchal, or 'the imaginary' as a utopian feminine realm have been prevalent. As Freudian/Lacanian psychoanalytic theories become an essential conceptual set up through which feminists investigate many of their theoretical concerns like subject construction, sexual difference and its relationship to language, even a criticism of their phallocentricism becomes implicated in the psychoanalytic discourse. This conjunction of psychoanalysis and feminist theory has become a notable tendency in Woolf studies too, and psychoanalytic approaches have become increasingly inseparable from investigation into feminist issues. This also means that such psychoanalytic studies have at last freed themselves from the obsession with Woolf's mental illness, madness or suicide.

Another significant development in this conjunction of psychoanalysis and feminism is a shift in theoretical focus from the Oedipus complex and the father-child relation central to the Freudian/Lacanian paradigm of subject construction to the pre-Oedipal mother-child relation. Kristeva's popularity with feminists could partly be ascribed to her modification of Lacan's theory through her attention to the mother-infant relationship of the pre-Oedipal phase and theorization of the 'affect' side of subjectivity and signification that originates in the imaginary, preceding the symbolic. Before Kristeva, it was Melanie Klein and British object-relations theorists who brought into focus the maternal origin of subjectivity, acknowledged but passed over by Freud. More recently, theorists such as American, feminist, object-relations psychoanalyst, Nancy Chodorow, and French thinker, Luce Irigaray, who condemns Freud's and Lacan's phallogocentrism, also offer alternative theoretical paradigms featuring the mother-daughter relationship. In feminist psychoanalytic studies of Woolf, critics have been turning increasingly to these alternative theoretical schemes for their investigation into the female subjectivity encompassed in Woolf's work.[12]

Elizabeth Abel's universally acclaimed *Virginia Woolf and the Fiction of Psychoanalysis* (1989) constructs the narrative of its argument out of this controversy over the genealogy of subject-hood (particularly female subject-hood) and signification – whether it is maternal or paternal – within psychoanalytic theory since the 1920s. As the title of her book indicates, the premise of her argument is that the project with which both literature and psychoanalysis are engaged is narrativization. Abel's meticulous research historically contextualizes an exchange between Woolf and psychoanalysis and reveals that Woolf's novels echo and rewrite the narrative projects upon which psychoanalysis was embarking concurrently. According to Abel, Woolf's novels of the 1920s interrogate Freud's theory by questioning the paternal genealogies prescribed by nineteenth-century, fictional conventions and reinscribed by Freud; they parallel the narratives which Melanie Klein was formulating simultaneously and anticipate the more radical revisions which were developed by American, feminist, object-relations psychoanalysts like Nancy Chodorow over the next half century. But the story of the 1930s is very different. Abel's own narrativization presents Woolf swerving abruptly from Klein to Freud: Woolf had to abandon her mother-based narrative pitted against Freud's paternal narrative because the ideologies of motherhood were 'appropriated and irretrievably contaminated' by the fascist state (Abel 1989, xvi). Abel's book is unique in that it is not just a psychoanalytic interpretation of Woolf's novels, nor is it just about her responses to psychoanalysis. Abel defends her reading strategies as follows: 'psychoanalysis helps make us the discerning readers she desired. Woolf's fiction, in return, de-authorizes psychoanalysis, clarifying the narrative choices it makes, disclosing its fictionality' (xvi). Through such a dialectic process of reading Woolf's novels and psychoanalysis together and against each other, the book itself becomes an investigation of the developmental narrative of female subjectivity.

Mary Jacobus' essay, 'The Third Stroke': Reading Woolf with Freud' (published originally in 1988) also draws our attention to the narrative choice and fictionality of Freud's psychoanalysis and re-examines its theorization of sexual difference by reading Woolf not only 'with' Freud but also 'beyond' him (Jacobus 1992, 105). Her attempted 'reformulation of the mother's role in representation' is based on Kristeva's revisionary reading of the pre-Oedipal – 'the pre-Oedipal configuration which (re)produces the mother as the origin of all signification' (118). Jacobus argues that *To the Lighthouse*, with its central interlude where not only identity but also sexual difference unravels, inscribes 'the movement of abjection without which there could be no subjectivity, and no signification either'. Jacobus had already referred to Kristeva and Woolf in her introductory chapter 'The Difference of View' in the volume *Women Writing and Writing about Women* (1979). The essay which sets the poststructuralist feminist tone of the book addresses the question of 'the repression of women's desire by representation itself' (12) and women's wish for 'a special language for women', to which, Jacobus suggests, Kristeva's theory of the semiotic has an enlightening relevance. The shift of focus in Jacobus' writing from Kristeva's theory of 'the semiotic' in 1979 to 'abjection' in 1988 seems to reflect a subtle change that took place in feminist critical discourse over the decade. In the beginning feminists discovered the utopian, pleasurable plenitude of the pre-Oedipal and its potential revolutionary power of rupturing and subverting what they regarded as the repressive power of the symbolic order. This euphoric optimism seems to be sobered by an awareness of the risk that such discarding of the symbolic order would incur, the risk for the feminine to be reinscribed as marginal and other. This initiates the search for the possibility of an incompatible desire for subversion and submission (see above, Minow-Pinkney 1987, 8–9). In this context of awareness of the risk posed by the imaginary fusion, a daughter's submerged fear and anxiety, or even anger towards the mother who may exert such a threat of annihilation, started to draw critics' attention rather than the daughter's love and desire to regain the imaginary union with her. The trajectory of this shift is reflected in the tendency for critical attention to move from Kristeva's theory of 'the semiotic' – the pleasurable aspect of language with residue of the maternal and the site of the feminine – to her theory of 'abjection', positing the casting out of the maternal as abject (object) necessary for a subject-to-be to emerge as a subject.

Melanie Klein's increasing popularity is perhaps reflective of this shift of attention from the pleasurable, utopian plenitude of the imaginary to the danger of the imaginary (thus, of the mother herself), for it is Melanie Klein before Kristeva who places the mother-infant relation at the centre of psychoanalytic investigation. Klein's account of the origin of the subject includes a hypothesis of the infant's destructive aggression towards the mother at its developmental stage, and critics started to find that Woolf's works bear out this far less utopian Kleinian relationship between mother and child. As the daughter's feelings are found to be more ambiguous, so is the mother found to be more problematic. In Blotner's 1956 essay (see above, p. 63), Mrs Ramsay is presented as the personification of 'the female force' of ideal motherhood, a universal healer and mitigator of male violence, the unfailing source of 'love, stability and fruitfulness to her family' (Blotner, 562). Woolf's own autobiographical writings about her own mother certainly seem to support such interpretations of the character based upon her. However, more recent studies, re-examining the representations of both the character and the real woman, tend to find Mrs Ramsay and Julia Stephen far less perfect (see below, p. 75).

The notable feature of the feminist psychoanalytic studies of Woolf in the 1980s is that theory is located inside Woolf's texts rather than applied to them from the outside. The feminist psychoanalytic approach takes issues raised by Woolf's literary texts as synonymous with its own theoretical concerns (subjectivity, sexual difference, and its relationship to language). Theory is no longer a mere interpretative expedience, nor is the novel just an explication of theory, adding nothing to what the scientific discipline had already revealed.[13] Mary Jacobus envisages a complex relationship between Woolf's texts, psychoanalysis and feminist theory: 'The pre-Oedipal configuration which reproduces the mother as the origin of all signification in Kristevan theory, not only allows Woolf's novels to read – to be read – beyond Freudian theory but suggests how a reading of Woolf might revise and extend feminist thinking about the pre-Oedipal' (Jacobus 1992, 118). Through such dialectic interweaving of theory and literature, each can give the other insights into new possibilities for reading, theorization and revision; each can assess and specify the other.

Abel brings in history as a third term which 'mediates literature's negotiations with psychoanalysis' (Abel 1989, xviii) in order to make her other triangle of Woolf, Freud and Klein emerge. This also makes irrelevant common charges of the ahistoricism of psychoanalytic approaches. The role of history becomes particularly pivotal in Abel's narrativization of the negotiations between Woolf and psychoanalysis during the 1930s. Historical reality, Abel argues, forced Woolf to change her allegiance from a Kleinian mother-based narrative of the daughter to a Freudian narrative. In *A Room of One's Own* Woolf managed to uphold the matrilineal story by diverting the daughter's hungry disappointment and frustration with her mother who does not feed her amply via, to put in an oxymoron, a female patrilineage, that is a paternal aunt who leaves the narrator £500 a year because of their shared name. The Name of the Father, albeit with a feminine inflection, remains the foundation for cultural and economical heritage. However, Abel argues: 'When biological maternity was glorified by fascism in the 1930s, an oppositional maternal metaphor became untenable' (89). The mother, no longer a nourishing, supportive source of power, is seen as a powerless agent always subjugated by and serving patriarchy. In *Three Guineas* the narrator is the 'daughter of an educated man' rather than a mother's daughter. So at last in 1939 Woolf read Freud's writing in earnest.[14] However, there is a paradoxical twist in Abel's argument here. Woolf may have become a Freudian and embraced the Freudian paradigm of the daughter's story, but Woolf's reading of the political and historical realities which she faced, in Abel's argument, is diametrically opposite to Freud's interpretation of the same realities. Freud read fascism taking over the historical present of the world as 'a catastrophic return of the repressed', 'reviving the sensuous chaos of archaic matriarchy' (14). For Woolf, what she saw both outside and inside Britain was the consecration of patriarchy, extinguishing 'the mother' to whom the daughter can turn. Rejection of fascist ideologies made her repudiate the mother's body appropriated by fascism. Hence, the vanished matrilineage in Woolf's last novel, *Between the Acts*, which encompasses only heterosexuality and disembodiedness.

We find diverse critical responses to the relationship between Freud and Woolf in the 1930s. Diana L. Swanson (1997) criticizes Abel's reliance on the Oedipus complex paradigm, which, she argues, leads Abel to her negative view of Woolf's feminist perspective in the 1930s. Swanson suggests shifting the focus from the Oedipus story of the incestuous sin of patriarchy to the Oedipus-Antigone story of, not father and daughter, but brother and sister, which *The Years*, Swanson believes, is proposing: 'a positive, hopeful new vision of the new world – egalitarian relationship of brothers and sisters instead of father-daughter patriarchy' (Swanson 23).

Nicole Ward Jouve's essay 'Virgina Woolf: Penis Envy and the Man's Sentence' (1998) is closer to Abel's argument in its pessimistic tone, reading Woolf's despair over the relationship between the sexes in her writings in the last decade of her life. She casts grave doubt over the separatist and confrontational attitudes which, in her view, started 'dangerously' surfacing in *A Room of One's Own* when Woolf 'began to see the "man's sentence" as what barred her way to creativity as a woman', and became dominant in *Three Guineas*, finally ending in 'the lack of communication, the submerged violence that pervades *Between the Acts*' (136). Jouve asks: 'Was she being *symptomatic* – responding, giving expression to a worsening relation between the sexes, the rising despair of the 1930s … or was she contributing to it?' (*original emphasis*).

By juxtaposing Freud's 'Anatomical Distinction Between the Sexes' and *A Room of One's Own*, Jouve asks: 'Is Woolf suffering from penis envy, or is the Professor's notion of penis envy a projected dream of superiority?' (131). Vara Neverow offers an unequivocal answer in her essay 'Freudian Seduction and the Fallacies of Dictatorship' (2001). What Neverow sees in the two texts, *A Room of One's Own* and *Three Guineas*, is not the turning point of Woolf's allegiance from a Kleinian genealogy of the female subject to a Freudian story as Abel does, but a mockery and denunciation of Freud's theory and fascist dogma at one stroke by interweaving the two. Woolf regards both as originating from men's 'inferior complex' and 'infantile fixation'. Neverow insists that Woolf's adoption of these two terms in her revisionary interpretations of Freud's castration complex evidences her refutation of his theory of penis envy as a pathological privileging of the phallus. Somewhat equivocally Jouve argues that Woolf makes clear the limited usefulness of such clumsy terms as 'penis envy' or the 'Oedipus complex'. Drawing on Maria Torok, she directs our attention to a complex psychic mechanism involved in 'penis envy'; woman's desire is buried under 'envy', because forbidden, and her desire to have a penis denounces itself as a subterfuge precisely because it is felt as envy; women project all the qualities they want on to an idealized penis. 'What the little girl idealizes, and hates her mother for not giving her is a fantasized object by means of which a girl conceals her own anger at having had her genitality repressed by her mother, at her own anality having had to fall under her mother's control' (Jouve 1998, 133). By 'envying' this fantasized object, the girl expresses the desire to reassure the mother in order to retain her love. Jouve asks if this psychic mechanism of penis envy is working in *A Room of One's Own*, because, she points out, there is a peculiar gap in the logical connection between the narrator's acknowledgement that 'our mothers' gravely mismanaged their affairs, leaving the daughters so little in the way of culture and her insistence that we relate to tradition through our mothers if we are women. 'Is repression talking here? Is it in order to protect the mother from her own aggression?' (133).[15]

Claire Kahane's refined studies (one essay and one chapter of her book)[16] take up the daughter's anger with reference to *The Voyage Out*. Through her detailed textual analysis, Kahane's 'The Woman with a Knife and the Chicken without a Head' illuminates the textual symptoms of the repressed 'rage' of the daughter. Kahane's textual psychoanalysis is concerned with the unconscious dynamics of the text rather than Woolf's or simply the character's. The anxiety of castration is the anxiety of the loss of wholeness, but Freud's theoretical mappings, depending on the phallic economy, figure the subject's primary loss as castration and thus establish the subject as masculine. This cultural fix on the masculine economy causes, Kahane maintains, often unacknowledged female rage. Drawing on Melanie Klein for the infant's destructive aggression towards the mother, and Luce Irigaray and Jessica Benjamin for specifically female rage, Kahane notes that the lack of a specifically female economy of desire is a significant factor in promoting female rage. Women have no symbol of their own for what is lost in order to recuperate the loss except for a borrowed signifier – the phallus. Desire for a signifier of their own, for an 'image' of their own – this desire is what 'penis envy' refers to, according to these theorists. Based on this understanding of the unconscious rage and desire directed at the mother as its primal object, Kahane lets emerge from the textual details of *The Voyage Out* the heroine's ambivalent feelings towards maternal power – rage and desire. However these feelings are culturally not permissible and therefore must be repressed. As the narrative nears the end, Kahane argues, Woolf's increasing suppression of the rage leaves 'a desolate blank space at the centre of female identity', revealing 'the emptiness of the unrepresentable loss' (Kahane 2000, 189).

Kahane's *Passions of the Voice* (1995) – a 'psycho-poetics of hysteria' – locates the emergence of modernism in the 'hysterical narrative voice' effected by the gender subversion witnessed in the unsettling phenomenon of the speaking woman at the end of the nineteenth century. By understanding hysteria 'as a consequence of both repressed rage and repudiated desire', Kahane attempts to define 'links among rage, gender and narrative voice' (xii). The chapter on *The Voyage Out* argues that in the scattered moments of this inchoate modernist novel, the narrative voice breaks up conventional boundaries between subject and object, between masculine and feminine – the uncertainty characteristic of the hysteric – and attempts to excavate 'a beneficent maternal body' which could become a locus of female desire. This connects to the argument that Woolf's feminist/modernist project is to retrieve and inscribe in her writing the repressed, the feminine, or, in Kristevan terms, the semiotic, posited as the imaginary plenitude symbolized by the maternal body (see above, p. 67). However, Kahane contends, in *The Voyage Out* narrative ambivalence to maternal power leads to a hysterical melancholia, due to the lack of cultural signifiers to represent a woman's desire and the cultural inhibition of female rage. Thus the maternal remains a locus of anxiety.

The daughter's rage and melancholia also relate to the central theme of Patricia Moran's *Word of Mouth: Body Language in Katherine Mansfield & Virginia Woolf* (1996). Moran's claim is that fear and hatred of the female body can be traced in both Woolf's and Mansfield's texts, underlying their writings and demonstrated through imagery, despite their self-conscious and mostly successful repudiation of the devaluation and silencing of femininity by patriarchy and narrative conventions. She examines these two writers' revulsion for the female body, prompted by the negative force of society, by drawing on Freud, Klein and Irigaray. Moran understands the psychic configuration of modernist writing in relation to the maternal body differently from some feminist psychoanalytic critics (see Minow-Pinkney (1987) and Jacobus (1992) above). For Moran it is Woolf's and Mansfield's repudiation of and revulsion for the maternal body rather than a desire to retrieve it, as in Kristeva's theory of the avant-garde poetics, which underlie their modernism.

Like Kahane's book, Tony Jackson's *The Subject of Modernism* (1994) also psychoanalytically investigates the emergence of modernism. While Kahane brings in the phenomenon of speaking women as the crossing point between real history and literary history in order to set about her investigation, Jackson's interest is more insulated from historical reality. Based on Lacan's psychoanalytic theory, but also informed by Jacques Derrida and Martin Heidegger, Jackson's book links narrative form to what he claims as the historical shift in the structure of the psychological self, and argues that modernism, articulating a different kind of subjectivity – the 'subject of anxiety' – emerged from a discovery of the unclosable gap in the realist 'subject of certainty'. In the two chapters devoted to *Mrs Dalloway* and *The Waves*, 'the ontological aporia' is at the centre of his mapping of the appearance of modernism. This aporia lies, Jackson explains, 'in the fact that the instruments of violence (language and culture) become the subject's means of overcoming the effects of that violence and attempting a return to a condition of imaginary security, that is, a return to be identical with oneself' (Jackson 1994, 120); but the use of language (symbolic violence) reopens the very wound the subject wants to close. 'The metonymic suturing always tears apart the metaphoric closure it sews up.' In fact, the condition of the human being as a subject is such that this ongoing violence is the means to prevent the split subject from becoming identical with itself, because such 'healing' into metaphoric totality means psychosis.[17]

The ontological aporia is also at the centre of Daniel Ferrer's *Virginia Woolf and the Madness of Language* (1990). Roland Barthes' 'the madness of language' points to the aporia faced by the human subject and her linguistic endeavour. The paradoxical status of enunciation is that '[t]he gulf opened up at every word is simultaneously covered over by every word' (5). In Woolf's case, what gets revealed at every word, Ferrer insists, is her actual madness. It is from death, lack (the place of the 'dead mother') and insanity that her writing originates and to which in the end it returns. Woolf's writing, in trying to fight this ineluctable necessity of language to cover up the 'gulf', 'turns back to its origins and tries to bring them to light through an intense dialectic of revelation and repression' (6).[18]

Ferrer claims our knowledge of Woolf's madness and suicide plays an essential part in the 'author function' (in a Foucauldian sense). So he begins his book by insisting on the continuity between 'the text and what is outside it, the writing and the life' (6), following Woolf's own principle (so he claims) that he will not 'draw a distinction between the [wo]man and [her] work' (quoted in Ferrer 1990, 6). Here Woolf's life, particularly the question of her madness and suicide, which feminist psychoanalytic approaches left behind, resurfaces. However, the relationship of the text and the extra-textual is for Ferrer not 'expression, transposition, or reflection' (6) as it is in conventional psychobiographical studies. His concern 'is not the *theme* of madness, with all its pathos and possible moral and philosophical implication, but rather the relations between the enunciation of the text and madness' (original emphasis) (8). With the opposition between life and work deconstructed, both become a production in psychosocial space and the point is no longer to establish factual truths. In Ferrer's book Woolf's life becomes just a textual phenomenon without any existential density; paradoxically it does not seem to matter whether Woolf was mad or not in the end in spite of his insistence on the centrality of her madness to our understanding of her literature. With madness becoming a synonym of what is excluded from representation,[19] the question is no longer about biographical facts but the limits of discourse and the subject's position in relation to them. So his thesis, Ferrer suggests, may even apply to all fictional texts since their beginning, regardless of their authors' mental status.

Gayatri Spivak's essay 'Unmaking and Making in *To the Lighthouse*' (1980) precedes Ferrer's book in its deconstructive critical approach to the binary opposition of life and work.[20] Her essay is an attempt to insert Woolf's life into the text of her book by undoing the opposition between book and biography, seeing 'the two as each other's "scene of writing"' (Spivak 1985, 244). Spivak suggests that the 'Time Passes' section, mingling life and work inseparably, compresses Woolf's life between 1894–1918, from her mother's death to the end of the First World War, the years marked by madness, and 'narrates the production of a discourse of madness within this autobiographical roman à clef' (Spivak 1980, 316). Spivak proposes a grammatical allegory of the novel that is interpreted as understanding and possessing Mrs Ramsay's essence: 'Subject (Mrs Ramsay) – copula – Predicate (painting)' (311). 'In Part I, Mrs

Ramsay is, in the grammatical sense, the subject. In Part III, the painting predicates her' and the mid section 'couples or hinges I and III'. The quest for the essence of Mrs Ramsay who is under the sway of Mr Ramsay's metaphor of the copula (custodian of copulation of both logics of reason and marriage) in the first part, after the disruption in the middle, is carried out by Lily with a different kind of copula – a copula of art – in the last section. Spivak imagines that an alternative feminine mode of discourse, 'not simply the contemptible text of hysteria' (326), could be produced, not through unhinging the copula as appears in the middle section of the novel, but through this different kind of copula, adumbrated by Lily's art – what Spivak calls 'womb-ing' (325) – which articulates 'a woman's vision of a woman' (326).[21]

The interestingly original approach of the 'thematics of womb-envy' (326), contrasting with 'penis envy' mentioned earlier, has not seen much critical development since, but in other aspects Spivak's essay is a forerunner of many other critical works. Lily's hallucinatory vision of Mrs Ramsay and the completion of her painting have attracted much critical discussion particularly in relation to the issue of an alternative, feminine mode of representation: how to inscribe in representation the repressed and the a-symbolizable (variously termed 'the body', 'the maternal universe', 'the imaginary', 'the real', etc.).[22]

The work of another French critic, Françoise Defromont, also undertakes a poststructuralist psychoanalytical study with a deconstructive approach to the distinction between life and work. Defromont's writing, which is delightfully (sometimes outrageously) imaginative and creative, renders Woolf's half-brother's molestation of her as 'rape' without taking any interest in establishing any factual evidence which could lead her to such a rendition, just as Ferrer cavalierly justifies his labelling Woolf as mad by saying 'her word for it' (Ferrer 1990, 7). Placing the death of her mother and the 'rape' by her half-brother as crucial to both Woolf's life and work, Defromont attempts to unravel how these two traumatic experiences are hidden forces which construct Woolf's texts in a way that addresses issues of the body, identity and sexuality. Her work, published in 1985, contains many points which are to be argued later by other critics: for example, before Louise De Salvo's controversial book, Woolf's sexual abuse is taken up as one of the traumas central to Woolf's person and work.[23] 'The absolute absence of the maternal figure' (Defromont 1992, 65) in *Between the Acts* is also the point made by Elizabeth Abel. Such an absence of the maternal figure, preventing the formation of a narcissistic image, Defromont argues, leads to the uncertainty of sexual identity – 'Am I woman, or am I man?' This ambivalence of the hysteric, which Kahane takes up in her book on the hysterical narrative and modernism, is also the basis of Defromont's thematics. She presents Woolf's problematic split of sexual identity in terms of the conflict between 'the mirror' and 'the book'. The mirror associations, especially linked to the episode of the looking-glass shame, are interpreted as connected to the narcissistic identification with the mother which is crucial for the formation of feminine identity; 'the book' which is associated with the father, who was committed to literature and writing, represents masculine identity. The split of identity is here mapped out as the conflict between femininity and language, which thus leads inevitably to the question of feminine writing.

Charles Bernheimer's 'A Shattered Globe: Narcissism and Masochism in Virginia Woolf's Life-Writing' (1990) psychoanalyses Woolf through a detailed analysis of 'A Sketch of the Past'. This theoretically rigorous and probing Freudian/Lacanian investigation focuses relentlessly on Woolf's psychic structure, reducing questions potentially open to historical, social or aesthetic considerations to issues of her personal psychic structure. So Woolf's 'apparently impersonal' modernist aesthetic project, in his view, is 'the expression of her extremely personal wish' (204), originating from her psychic structure. He contends that Woolf appropriates her masochistic impulses for purposes of artistic production. Hypothesizing Woolf's double-faced narcissism: 'one oriented toward fusion with her ideal ego, the other toward annihilation by her punitive super ego' (203), he explains why her 'shock' experiences, which produced bipolar extremes of despair and rapture as she remembered them, were deemed 'moments of being' essential for her development as a writer. The erotic quality of Woolf's writing emerges from the continual reopening of excitation by shattering the body's integrity and aesthetic wholes, and exposing herself and her art to a proliferation of violent shocks. Woolf 'writes not in opposition to this threat but in collaboration with it' (205). Bernheimer interprets Woolf's mystical vision of a 'fin in the waste of water' which she noted in her diary (*WD* 101, 169) as 'the emblem of the fissure that splits the smooth surfaces of the world as work of art and of the self as patterned whole' (205). His point about her writing being 'simultane-ously a search for re-membered union and a means of perpetuating traumatic disunion', 'at once an attempt at maternal recuperation and an opportunity for masochistic perturbation' (206), features in a number of critical texts in various formulations (see above, pp. 65–6 and p. 72, and below, Berman on p. 75; also see Note 22).

Woolf's shock experiences, extreme bipolar experiences of despair and rapture, and her vision of a 'fin' are taken up also by my essay 'How then does light return … ?' (1997) in order to investigate the issue not only of Woolf's but any human subject's conflict between 'union' and 'disunion' (Bernheimer). That is, the fundamental paradox of the human subject as a linguistic being: only by consenting to lose the mother through language, can we retrieve her through language. With reference to *To the Lighthouse*, the essay attempts to understand the difficult leap involved in Woolf's act of writing from the position of melancholia, identifying with the lost maternal object, to a manic denial of the loss, convinced of reunion with the mother through the act of signification. The key theoretical concept used for the argument is the hypothetical notion of 'the imaginary father' (Kristeva 1987, 40), which

Kristeva elaborated from Freud's 'father in [the individual's] own personal prehistory' (Freud 1991, 370) – the guarantor of primary identification.[24]

Jeffrey Berman, in the introduction of his book, *Narcissism and the Novel* (1990), articulates the validity of treating characters as real people, agreeing with Daniel Schwarz who writes: 'Although modes of characterization differ, the psychology and morality of characters must be understood as if they were real people (quoted in Berman 1990, 47). He defends character analysis and the literary criticism that relates the text back to the novelist's life. A corollary to his belief in character is a belief in 'identity,' 'an essential unity of personality', whether it is the author, fictional character, or reader. He expresses his commitment to this humanist, 'admittedly essentialist position' contrary to poststructuralism which understands a subject as decentred. He asserts this 'revival of character study' as part of the larger resurgence of humanism. The chapter 'Heart Problems in *Mrs Dalloway*' offers with theoretical and literary critical sophistication, a typical, but refined, psychoanalysis of character without simplistically flouting the difference between the fictional world of artistic construction and the real world. Theoretically in line with post-Freudian theorists of Narcissism, he explores 'the link between narcissism and maternal loss' (52) and contends that at the heart of Clarissa's conflicts is the difficulty of reconciling 'distance' and 'desire': distance from the mother necessary for the human subject in order to achieve separation and individuation, and desire for symbiosis with her. (This is a recurrent theme taken up by many critics. See Bernheimer (1990) and Minow-Pinkney (1987), for example.)[25]

The new theoretical climate from the late 1970s onwards, which gave a new legitimacy to psychoanalytic investigation and interpretation, invited contributions from professional psychologists/psychoanalysts too. The main thrust here is to psychoanalyze characters or the author, often treating characters as if they were real people, neglecting the fictionality of character and the textuality of a literary work. Mrs Ramsay becomes Julia Stephen, and Septimus becomes Virginia Woolf. The ultimate interest of these works, whether the object of their analysis is the author or character, seems to lie invariably in Woolf's mental status. Ernest S. Wolf and Ina Wolf's '"We perished, each alone": A Psychoanalytic Commentary on Virginia Woolf's *To the Lighthouse*' (1986) claims to be the only interpretation of the novel in terms of Heinz Kohut's 'self-psychology', which is one branch of post-Freudian theories of Narcissism. They analyze Mrs Ramsay as a narcissistically injured person who needs hyperactivity to keep everyone around her enmeshed with her own personality (what Kohut calls 'selfobjects') in order to protect her defective self from disintegrating. In their analysis, Mrs Ramsay/Julia Stephen, far from being ideal and perfect, emerges as an inadequate mother who, with her own psychic problems, is deficient in her ability to give love and nurture to her daughter.

In *Virginia Woolf: Feminism, Creativity, and the Unconscious* (1997) by a psychologist, John R. Maze, we find another kind of archetypal psychoanalytical criticism – psychoanalysis of the author (strangely, the 'feminism' of the title seems hardly to appear in the book's frame of reference). Following Woolf's novels chronologically one by one, Maze, with tenacious single-mindedness, points out Freudian symbols which, he claims, reveal the author's repressed desires – basically her ambivalent desires of a sexual nature for her mother and her brother, Thoby. Though his approach is simplistic and monotonous, and his interpretation may be regarded by some as exemplifying the vulgarity of crude Freudianism, his close attention to textual details produces some perceptive readings with surprising but sometimes persuasive results. (The difference from E. Steinberg's article mentioned earlier is that here it is Maze, the critic, who applies psychoanalytical tools to Woolf's writing, while Steinberg examines Woolf's use of Freudian symbols in her art.)

The new theoretical environment contributed to the establishment of psychoanalytic approaches as a thriving area of Woolf studies. After a decade of the dominance of feminist psychoanalytical studies, the 1990s started to see more diverse perspectives within psychoanalytic approaches: poststructuralist, anti-poststructuralist, feminist, non-feminist, literary historical, as is evidenced in the works discussed above. What is distinctive about these works is that the relationship of theory to Woolf's texts is external – theory is used as a tool for the interpretation of literary text – rather than intrinsic as in many feminist psychoanalytic studies. Not surprisingly, *Mrs Dalloway* with insanity as its theme, the autobiographical *To the Lighthouse* and 'A Sketch of the Past' are the texts most frequently taken up for the purpose of the application of psychoanalysis. This also means that after having been excluded from feminist psychoanalytic approaches, the theme of 'madness' has resurfaced.

We are 'in the midst of an era pervaded by discourse on madness' according to Shoshana Felman (Felman 1985, 13). This certainly seems true in psychoanalytic studies of Virginia Woolf (except in the field of feminist psychoanalysis), so often obsessed with the question of Woolf's 'madness' and suicide. Frequent references to Michel Foucault, therefore, are not surprising, given his interrogation of the Western discourse of modernity through the history of madness. Stephen Trombley's *All That Summer She Was Mad: Virginia Woolf: Female Victim of Male Medicine* (1982) examines the 'discourse of power' of Woolf's three doctors and questions the presuppositions behind their views on insanity. Foucault's presence is inevitable given Trombley's argument that the concept of Woolf's madness is not so much a medical diagnosis as an attempt to justify certain social, political, sexual moral and aesthetic views. Sei Kosugi's 'Woolf and Psychiatry: In Relation to Mieko Kamiya and M. Foucault' (1998) brings Woolf and Foucault together via this Japanese psychiatrist and clinician in a leprosarium.[26] Reconceptualizing madness as a positive value is the overlapping point in the encounter of this somewhat incongruous pair: the poststructuralist, antihumanist Foucault and the Christian humanist

Kamiya. Kosugi reminds us that well before Foucault, Woolf exposed and condemned the political function of the medical profession in the character of Sir William Bradshaw, a paragon of 'model man', the concept of which, according to Foucault, emerged when the medical profession was nationalized in the eighteenth century.

Michèle Barrett's chapter 'Virginia Woolf Meets Michel Foucault' (1999) is premised on the fruitful interplay of these two thinkers, while aware of the problems involved in such an enterprise – of methodology, anachronism, and Foucault's contentious discoveries. Foucault proposed the historical development and function of the 'caesura' from which the split between sanity and insanity originates. By exposing the distance between reason and nonreason inserted by the 'caesura', Foucault makes a point about, paradoxically, the continuity of the two before the caesura in a different discursive environment. From this Barrett draws the similarity between Woolf and Foucault, for Woolf's literature too is very much about the continuity of sanity and insanity. In fact Woolf's *oeuvre*, her aesthetics of modernism, was a 'search for internal truth where there is no clear dividing line between the sane and the insane truth' (190). Foucault's argument suggests that the exclusion of madness is a historical accident which needs correction, though on the other hand as Derrida argues in his critique of early Foucault, this exclusion is the general condition of language, the constitutive foundation of the very enterprise of speech. If Foucault is right, the emergence of the modernist project to restore the voice of madness in order to expand and revitalize language was an inevitable consequence of Western discourse which constituted itself by this exclusion and lost the force of raw energy.

Freud's enterprise too was to reconnect sanity and insanity. Psychoanalysis is predicated on this insight. Freud's explanation of the 'uncanny' – the return of the repressed – points to the continuity between normal and abnormal. The inherent ambivalence belonging to the uncanny – *unheimlich* is also *heimlich* – could illuminate the compulsive attraction to Woolf's 'madness' witnessed in Woolf studies. The repressed always return, psychoanalysis tells us. So the repressed (madness) haunts our discourse. So, does this fascination derive from our curiosity for the repressed, curiosity for the strange and yet familiar, which involves the simultaneous desire to retrieve the repressed but also exorcise it by marking it off as something incomprehensibly alien, mysteriously 'other'? Following both Freud and Woolf, then, psychoanalytic approaches exist not to separate but to connect sanity and insanity.

It was only after the rigid opposition between theory and literature was dismantled that psychoanalytic approaches really took off in Woolf studies. In the introduction of her *Literature and Psychoanalysis* (1982, originally 1977), a typical volume of this new age of theory, Shoshana Felman suggests the decon-struction of the traditional relationship of literature and psychoanalysis and its replacement by the relationship which has the relation of *interiority* conveyed by the 'inter-implication', instead of 'application' whose notion is based on the relation of *exteriority* and the master (psychoanalysis)-slave (literature) hierarchy of power. In such a new dialogic relationship, literature and psychoanalysis would 'implicate each other, each one finding itself enlightened, informed, but also affected, displaced by the other' (9). Felman points out that '[l]iterature is ... not simply *outside* psychoanalysis, since it motivates and *inhabits* the very names of its concepts'. Psychoanalysis, too, can be located inside literature. Feminist psychoanalytic studies have discovered that psychoanalysis is deeply implicated in Woolf's literary texts, addressing issues such as subjectivity and sexual difference. This recognition of the commonality of concerns between Woolf's writing and psychoanalytic theory has brought forth a true dialogue between the two. Literature is no longer a subservient participant, supplying mere examples for the scientific theory of truth, nor is psychoanalytic theory a mechanical expedience for literary interpretation. I find this development one of the most exciting outcomes of psychoanalytic approaches.

Psychoanalysis, as a science, constitutes a theory of the subject; as practice, it bases itself on a theoretical understanding of the subject. Theory opens up intensely personal problems to issues of universal validity, relevant to any human subject. Salient examples can be found in feminist psychoanalytic studies, which rarely dwell just on Woolf's familial circumstances, mental illness, suicide, and so on, but even works of the most conventional kind, which psychoanalyze Woolf, bring in the principle of the general and thus go beyond the personal and the particular. This distinguishes psychoanalytic approaches from psychobiography whose interests start and end with the particularity of Woolf, with its goal being to find Woolf the person. This ability to go beyond the particular to the universal, I believe, is the fundamental strength and benefit of theoretical psychoanalytic approaches.

notes

1. See Jan Ellen Goldstein, 'The Woolf's Response to Freud: Water-Spiders, Singing Canaries, and the Second Apple', *Psychoanalysis Quarterly* 43 (1974): 441–3. Also Elizabeth Abel, *Virginia Woolf and the Fiction of Psychoanalysis*, Chapter 1.
2. Critics have debated how much and when Woolf actually read and knew Freud's theory. Leonard Woolf writes, in a letter to Erwin R. Steinberg, after receiving his essay on the use of Freud's symbolism in *Mrs Dalloway* and *To the Lighthouse*, 'I don't think my wife had read any of Freud except perhaps the Psycho-pathology of Everyday Life before she wrote Mrs. Dalloway'. Erwin R. Steinberg, 'Note on a Note', *Literature and Psychology* 4.4 (September 1954): 64–5. Though it may be true that she never 'read any of Freud's works', Woolf probably knew them well, since it is hardly surprising if 'he (Woolf) had discussed them with her, having read them as he published them' as Leonard wrote to Blotner (Blotner 1956, 548, n. 2). Woolf, later in her life, in 'A Sketch of the Past', admits that her writing *To the Lighthouse* was a psychoanalytic process (*MB* 81). On this subject, also see Abel (1989, 18).
3. It seems to me that their decision not to seek psychoanalysis for Woolf's mental illness came from a good understanding of Freud's psychoanalysis rather than

'despite' their intimate knowledge of it. Jan Goldstein blames 'the water-spider habits of Bloomsbury' (originally Maynard Keynes' phrase) and Virginia's 'squeamishness' particularly on the sexual aspects of the theory for their decision. If the Woolfs and others around them understood Virginia's problems were of a hereditary nature, it does not seem unreasonable for them to have judged that she would not benefit from Freudian psychoanalysis.

For a discussion of the treatment of Woolf's mental illness by various psychiatric physicians, see Stephen Trombley, *All That Summer She Was Mad* (see above, p. 76); also, Jane Marcus, 'On Dr. George Savage', *Virginia Woolf Miscellany* (Fall 1981): 3–4.

4. In *Beginning Again* (1964) Leonard Woolf expresses his belief that 'Virginia's genius was closely connected with what manifested itself as insanity' (66); ' here surely is an exact description of genius and madness, showing how they occupy the same place in her mind' (67).

5. Quoted by Showalter in 'Introduction' to Woolf, *Mrs Dalloway* (1992), xxvii.

6. Woolf wrote in a letter to a Harvard student: 'the character of Septimus in Mrs Dalloway was invented to *complete* the character of Mrs Dalloway; I could not otherwise convey my whole meaning about her' (emphasis added) (*L4* 36). Septimus is a supplement to Clarissa in a Derridean sense: the 'inferior' term (insanity) is more primary than the 'superior' term (sanity), for Septimus 'preserved' '[a] thing … that mattered' while it was 'defaced, obscured in her own life' (*MD* 156).

7. Goldstein argues that even before Woolf was 'expressively affirming Freud' towards the end of her life, she, in fact, had been 'far from openly accusing Freud' (454). On the other hand Elizabeth Abel maintains that Woolf expresses objections and hostility specifically against the psychoanalysis of Freud but not against the theory of Klein and her followers (Abel 1989, 18).

8. After Steinberg's short article, a series of discussions and responses followed in *Literature and Psychology*. Erwin R. Steinberg, 'Freudian Symbolism and Communication', *Literature and Psychology* 3.2 (1953): 2–5: Frederick Wyatt, 'Some Comments on the Use of Symbols in the Novel', *Literature and Psychology*, 4.2 (1954):15–23; Erwin R. Steinberg, 'Note on a Novelist too Quickly Freudened', *Literature and Psychology*, 23–5; Simon O. Lesser, 'Arbitration and Conciliation', *Literature and Psychology*, 25–7; Erwin R. Steinberg, 'Note on a Note', *Literature and Psychology*, 4.4 (1954): 64–5.

9. L. Woolf relates *To the Lighthouse* to psychoanalysis in his autobiography (L. Woolf 1964, 113).

10. The pioneer of such an investigation is the Japanese psychiatric doctor Miyeko Kamiya's ' Virginia Woolf: An Outline of a Study on her Personality, Illness and Work', *Confinia Psychiatrica* 8 (1965): 189–205. Kamiya was preparing a further, full study on the subject, a creative work of 'autobiography' of Virginia Woolf, written as if it were a memoir narrated by Woolf herself. The psychiatric position in which she believed was the reconstruction of the patient's pathological world as an organic whole through empathy and thus giving it positive value. This work had been eagerly awaited by many internationally but unfortunately was left unfinished because of Kamiya's death while she was waiting for more biographical materials to be published. The outline of this work and fragments of her manuscript which were partly published and partly unpublished in her lifetime are collected in Volume 4 of *A Collection of Kamiya Miyeko's Works* (in Japanese). In her writings Kamiya picks up many issues which were to draw critics' attention well before these become topical subjects in Woolf studies. For example, Woolf's manic-depressive illness

as the central investigation of her study, shock experiences, looking-glass shame, sexual abuse by her half-brother(s), her ambivalent feelings towards her mother and their problematic relationship, which Kamiya suggests, could be related to the staunch feminism of her latter days. See also below Notes 23 and 26.

Another early work of melange of biography, literature and psychology/psychoanalysis, preceding Bell's biography and the series of publication of biographical materials is Nancy Topping Bazin's *Virginia Woolf and the Androgynous Vision*.

Most notable psychobiographical literary studies of Woolf are, for example: Poole, *The Unknown Virginia Woolf* (1978); Rose, *Woman of Letters: A Life of Virginia Woolf* (1978); Spilka, *Virginia Woolf's Quarrel with Grieving* (1980); De Salvo, *Virginia Woolf: The Impact of Childhood Sexual Abuse on Her Life and Work* (1989).

11. Even *Worlds in Consciousness* (1970) written by the psychologist Jean O. Love does not strike the reader very theoretical in its analysis of Woolf's novels; the direct use of theory seems to be deliberately avoided. This shows how much the style of literary criticism changes after the emergence of 'theory' in the late 1970s. B. A. Schlock's 'A Freudian Look at *Mrs. Dalloway*' in *Literature and Psychology* 23 (1973) is exceptional here. Though written before the age of 'theory', it offers a thoroughly psychoanalytic interpretation of the novel (a mixture of character analysis, the author analysis, psychobiography and a perceptive textual analysis), and a cogent comparison of Freud's Schreber and Septimus. As a whole its reading of the novel is interestingly different from the kind of argument which we are now more used to in feminist psychoanalytical approaches. See also Suzette A. Henke, 'Virginia Woolf's Septimus Smith: An Analysis of "Paraphrenia" and the Schizophrenic Use of Language' in *Literature and Psychology* 31 (1981), which examines Septimus' homosexual resonances as well as his schizophrenic language as characteristics of paraphrenia.

12. See for example, Jane Lilienfeld, 'The Deceptiveness of Beauty: Mother Love and Mother Hate in *To the Lighthouse*' (1977); Joan Lidoff, 'Virginia Woolf's Feminine Sentence: The Mother-Daughter World of *To the Lighthouse*' (1986); Ellen Bayuk Rosenman, *The Invisible Presence: Virginia Woolf and the Mother-Daughter Relationship* (1986).

13. This new relationship between theory and literature becomes clear when compared with, for example, the aforementioned Blotner's essay written in the pre-theory age of the mid 1950s; in it he defensively states that his use of the Oedipus myth and of Freud's theory based on the myth is an interpretative method external to the novel and its author's intention and that he applied it in order to illuminate the hidden pattern which would have been otherwise invisible.

14. See Note 1.

15. This is an interesting point that could be compared with Abel's argument of Woolf's manoeuvre of bringing in the paternal aunt in order to complement the mother's deficiency; see above, p. 68.

Though Abel does not use the notion of 'penis envy', Woolf's abandonment of 'the mother' in the 1930s and her identification of the daughter as the daughter of the father in *Three Guineas* as Abel presents, could be explained as directed by 'penis envy'. In fact, rather than Woolf becoming Freudian only in the last decade of her life, what Abel describes as the trajectory of Woolf's position as a whole seems to accord with a Freudian developmental scenario of the female subject: from mother attachment to father attachment via recognition of her castration, ending with penis envy.

16. Kahane 1995, 2000. For another essay of Kahane's, see Note 24.

17. My essay 'Virginia Woolf and the Age of Motor Cars' (2000) also uses psychoanalysis in order to investigate modernism and Woolf through Freud's theory on 'shock' in relation to the new mode of perception which emerged from the new living conditions of the modern city as it entered the technological age.

18. This ontological aporia central to both Jackson and Ferrer's arguments is addressed in Bernheimer's essay differently, in terms of Woolf's specific psychic structure – her need to have her psychic wholeness shattered repeatedly by shock in order to renew her sense of independent wholeness.

19. Also see above, p. 77 on Foucault.

20. Ferrer himself refers to Phyllis Rose's *Woman of Letters* as a work that has affinity with his own except that 'the biographical perspective is the reverse of [his]' (150).

21. For a different argument on hysteria and a new mode of writing, see Claire Kahane's argument mentioned above, p. 70.

22. For example, I describe Lily's aesthetic problems as the impossible paradox that without the symbolic order, the inner picture which Lily locates in the body and which she tries to represent, will be forever muted, yet the former is at the same time the very force that represses the latter (Minow-Pinkney 1987, 113–14). Jacobs, using the notion of fetishism as Spivak does, interprets Lily's 'hallucinatory' moment of restoring Mrs Ramsay as the combination of fetishism and 'abjection', by which Lily manoeuvres between the possibilities of maternal lack and presence. What both Jacobus and I are addressing here is fundamentally the aporia of the linguisitic subject as mentioned above in this chapter (see p. 71.) The thematics of 'hallucination' are central to Ferrer's argument; for him the fictional represen-tation of Lily's hallucination has an effect of, however fleetingly, 'bring[ing] to the surface, within the space of representation, the real' (64). In his argument the a-symbolizable outside the symbolic order is conceived as Lacan's 'the real' rather than 'the imaginary' as in many feminist arguments on feminine writing. So without a feminist slant, Ferrer's point is also about the possibility/impossibility of inscribing the a-symbolizable and the fundamental paradox (aporia) of the human being as a linguistic subject. Spivak also suggests that Woolf questions the orthodox masculinist psychoanalytic position through the Oedipal scene which 'Together Cam-James go through' and which 'involves both father *and* mother as givers of law and language' (original emphases; Spivak 1980, 319–20). On this theme see Abel's '"Cam the Wicked": Woolf's Portrait of the Artist as her Father's Daughter', or *Virginia Woolf and the Fictions of Psychoanalysis* (Chapter 3 and 4); also Margaret Homans, *Bearing the Word* (1986): 16–21, 277–88.

23. Masami Usui points out that it was Miyeko Kamiya, twenty years before DeSalvo's book, who identified Woolf as a victim of sexual abuse in her childhood and recognized the significance of the trauma for the formation of Woolf's personality. Masami Usui, 'Miyeko Kamiya's Encounter with Virginia Woolf: A Japanese Woman Psychiatrist's Waves of Her Own', *Doshisha Literature*, 42 (March 2000) (particularly 4–10). Also Kamiya, *Virginia Woolf Study*, *A Collection of Miyeko Kamiya's works*, Vol. 4, 41, 155–6. On Kamiya also see Notes 10 and 26, and Kosugi (1998).

24. For an antipsychoanalytic study of Woolf's manic-depression, see Caramagno's *The Flight of the Mind: Virginia Woolf's Art and Manic-Depressive Illness* (1992), which evaluates Woolf's life and work in terms of biochemically caused mental illness.

   Claire Kahane's 'The Nuptials of Metaphor: Self and Other in Virginia Woolf' (1980), using D. W. Winnicott and object-relations theory with reference to *To the Lighthouse*, also examines the crucial function of the symbolic field of language in the negotiation of self and other, which enables Woolf to retrieve integrated wholeness out of the fragmentation of self.

25. Post-Freudian theorists of Narcissism maintain that contemporary patients' difficulties originate from the pre-Oedipal stage. Diverting themselves from Freud's drive theory to object-relations theory, they focus on a difficult but key task for the human being to separate oneself from the original state of union, from the first love object. This task is essential for one's mature love relations and mental health, but the wish to merge never completely disappears through one's life. On this, their theoretical interests overlap with feminists'. See Layton and Schapiro (1986, 8–19); also see Berman (1990, 20–35). They acknowledge a great debt to Melanie Klein as the British object-relations school does but they distinguish themselves from both in that they take empirical reality into account.

26. Kamiya translated two of Foucault's works, wrote essays on his works and was also known for her study of Woolf. See Notes 10 and 23.

4
biographical approaches

mark hussey

the female subject and the death of the author

Signing themselves into seeming insignificance in the apron pocket of
history, [turn-of-the-century women autobiographers] anticipated the
present project of women's history to study the signature of the self. What
seems significant is not the female struggle to enter male public discourse
… but the recognition of the inability of that discourse to include their
voices in its history, the necessity of the return to the personal.

Jane Marcus, 'Invincible Mediocrity', 1998

If the inaugural gesture of this feminist criticism is the reduction of the
literary work to its signature and to the tautological assumption that the
feminine 'identity' is one which signs itself with a feminine name, then
it will be able to produce only tautological statements of dubious value:
women's writing is writing signed by women. … If these … are the grounds
of a practice of feminist criticism, then that practice must be prepared to
ally itself with the fundamental assumptions of patriarchy which relies on
the same principles.

Peggy Kamuf, 'Writing Like a Woman', 1980

As modes of discourse explicitly consolidating that bourgeois, white,
heterosexual, masculine 'subject' whose transcendence began to be thoroughly
challenged in the 1960s, biography and autobiography were obvious targets
for a poststructuralist revisioning of literary studies. However, as many critics
have pointed out, the sea change in Anglo-American literary studies effected
primarily by French philosophical theory in the late 1960s and early 1970s
was concurrent with the emergence of a *female* subject that many feminist
academics argued was necessary to redress centuries of neglect. Roland Barthes
may have proclaimed the death of the author in 1968, but workers in 'that
post Woolfian "room of our own" we call Women's Studies' (Stanton 1998,

132) were then busily researching women's lives, designing courses around the work of women writers, and beginning to establish a female literary canon.[1] When Michel Foucault asked 'What difference does it make who is speaking?' (Foucault 1984, 120) some critics answered that it made a very significant difference indeed.[2]

Within the more general transformation in literary and cultural studies, a specific 'transformation in autobiography studies' also took place in the late 1970s (Gilmore 1994, 16 n.6), marked by the publication of several key texts: Elizabeth W. Bruss, *Autobiographical Acts: The Changing Situation of a Literary Genre*; William Spengemann, *The Forms of Autobiography: Episodes in the History of a Literary Genre*; James Olney, ed. *Autobiography: Essays Theoretical and Critical*; and Estelle C. Jelinek, ed. *Women's Autobiography: Essays in Criticism*.[3] Toward the end of that decade, women's auto/biography studies emerged as a significant field of its own.[4] LuAnn McCracken (1990) has reviewed the recent history of autobiography theory, from the traditional view that autobiography is authorized by a stable and unified (implicitly male) self to feminist challenges based on the notion that women's sense of identity tends to be more fragmentary, less stable than men's, resulting in a different kind of life-writing. As this field developed, Woolf became a significant figure in scholarly work on auto/biography precisely because, 'throughout her work, in both fiction and non-fiction, [she] was profoundly concerned with the problems of how to write a life, particularly a woman's life. Her unpublished autobiographical writings have an important connection with her experimentation elsewhere. … Woolf's radicalism and importance as an autobiographer is precisely the extent to which she understood the connection between identity and writing and the need to deconstruct realist forms in order to create space for the yet to be written feminine subject' (Anderson 1987, 13). Furthermore, Woolf studies have been 'a site for debates between post-structuralist and humanist feminisms' (Green 1997, 225 n.49).

As Woolf herself frequently pointed out, 'women's lives deviate from the set stories of traditional biography' (Gordon 1995, 96). Recent critics have argued for the importance of biography for women not only in opposition to that body of thought that would consign women's writing to the personal as a way of denigrating its importance, but also because 'all feminist criticism, however chastely textual, ultimately refers to the specificity of female experience; the "feminine" is never simply a writing effect, but also registers the living effects of female human beings' (Booth 1991, 88). Comparing Woolf and George Eliot, Alison Booth advocates 'the inclusion of the author's biography and of historical context(s) as contributing, unfolding *texts*, not reified entities, in an alert intertextuality' (89). Booth, like several other feminist critics working in the field of auto/biography studies, wishes to challenge 'an aesthetics of impersonality that devalues the feminine' (89). Similarly, Cheryl Walker argues that it is 'important to identify the circumstances that govern relations between authors and texts, as between texts and readers, because without such material we are in danger of seeing gender disappear or become transformed into a feature of textuality that cannot be persuasively connected to real women' (Walker 1991, 110). Walker acknowledges the challenge poststructuralism offers to the turn to biography: 'The difficulty with doing biographical criticism today is that the figure of the author has increasingly come under attack, almost as if the author's portrait, which at one time routinely accompanied critical works, were being anatomized, dissolved in an acid bath of scorn and distrust' (109).

Woolf is often appealed to as prefiguring the destabilized subjects of contemporary auto/biographical writing. For example, Barbara Green finds that Woolf's 'meditations on self-representation have much in common with postmodern concerns with an identity assumed and simultaneously called into question' (Green 1997, 162), and Diane Cousineau refers to Woolf's 'self-consciousness in respect to the very questions raised by theorists of autobiography today' (Cousineau 1993, 51). Modernist women's writing in general, according to Shari Benstock, 'puts into question the most essential component of the autobiographical – the relation between "self" and "consciousness"' (Benstock 1998, 152). Woolf also, of course, has been established as a 'foremother' of women's studies, particularly through her 1929 essay A Room of One's Own. Nancy Miller acknowledges its centrality when she writes, 'By its themes and analysis of the relations between making art and the concrete conditions of its production, A Room in a course on reading and writing women's lives is exemplary' (Miller 1991, 129). That Miller refers to reading *lives* rather than *texts* is perhaps indicative of how theorizing about the relations between life-writing and life itself have made the terms inter-changeable. In another celebrated text about women and auto/biography, A Room of One's Own's themes and questions thread their way through the entire work: Carolyn Heilbrun's *Writing a Woman's Life* draws on Woolf repeatedly in explaining the different shape of women's lives, the importance of female friendships, of appearance, of anonymity and female anger, and of the need to create new forms, to 'break the sequence' as Woolf put it in A Room (Heilbrun 1988, 106).

Additionally, Woolf's characterizing the speaking subject of her essay as 'only a convenient term for somebody who has no real being' (*AROO* 5) goes to the heart of those questions about the ontological status of the written 'I' that have circulated so pervasively in literary and cultural studies for the last half-century.[5] Benstock (1998) writes that 'autobiography reveals the impossibility of its own dream: what begins on the presumption of self-knowledge ends in the creation of a fiction that covers over the premises of its construction' (1998, 146). What has made Woolf so significant a reference in and contributor to contemporary auto/biographical theorizing is not only that, as Hermione Lee writes, 'Everyone who reads has an idea of her and an opinion about her' (Lee 1996, 95), but also her overt concern with 'theories of the subject', which, because many modern theories of autobiography until recently ignored gender, 'have a particular urgency for women' (Raitt 1993, 64). Woolf's 'extremely subtle and provocative thinking about women's auto-biographical writing', as Linda Anderson points out, 'seems to prefigure many of the contemporary debates about writing and sexual difference: she saw the importance of autobiography for women as well as how it was inseparable from the process of its own self-questioning, from a discursive leap into the unknown' (Anderson 1987, 46). In what is in effect the biography of an image, Brenda Silver links Woolf's 'contested appearances' in intellectual and popular culture to 'major shifts in the status of women in society' (Silver 1999, 11).

The proliferation of biographical works taking Woolf as their object themselves form an exemplary recent history of the genre. Given Woolf's centrality in theorizing about women's auto/biography, and her important status in the recuperative work of feminist academics that began in the late 1960s, it is not surprising that a multitude of biographical representations of Woolf, ranging from the traditionally chronological to the iconoclastically forensic, now exist. Aileen Pippett's 1953 *The Moth and the Star* is the first significant, now long-forgotten, biography. An 'official' biography, written by Woolf's nephew Quentin Bell at the invitation of Leonard Woolf and published in two volumes in 1972, quickly attracted controversy for its omission of any consideration of Woolf's writing and for what many critics believed to be its muting of her politics (see, for example, Ozick 1973; Rogat 1974; Cook 1979; Kenney and Kenney 1982). A comprehensive review of biographical work on Woolf would occasion a separate essay, but the following taxonomy might be useful as a guide to the field (open as it will inevitably be to a variety of challenges).

Biographies of Woolf that utilize to varying degrees a chronological narrative of her life as context for the creation of her works include Bell (1972), King (1994), Leaska (1998), Reid (1996) and Lee (1996). Hermione Lee's magisterial biography absorbs into its complex portrait of Woolf over twenty-five years of diverse scholarly work, and takes full advantage of the enormous archive of Woolf's manuscripts now readily accessible in the UK and the USA. It is a self-conscious work, explicitly aware of how the field of women's auto/biography has been profoundly theorized in the past three decades. Closely related to this genre are works that concentrate on telling the story of a writer's life from what might be termed a writerly perspective: Phyllis Rose (1978) and Lyndall Gordon (1984), for example. Most recently, Julia Briggs' *Virginia Woolf: An Inner Life* (2005) traces the biography of Woolf's creative life. Herbert Marder's book-length essay, *The Measure of Life* (2000), is a biography of Woolf's final decade.

The dominance throughout the 1970s and early 1980s of Bell's representation of Woolf was not only contested through reviews and articles. Works by Roger Poole (1982) and by Louise DeSalvo (1989) offered radical challenges to Bell's portrait and to the enterprise of biography itself. Poole's *The Unknown Virginia Woolf*, which has been reissued three times since its initial publication in 1978, each time with a new preface reviewing the state of the argument so far, relies upon a phenomenological investigation of the legitimacy of terming Woolf 'mad'. Seeking to restore Woolf's subjectivity to her own story, Poole concentrates on the tensions in her marriage and other significant relationships, her relation to food and embodiment, and reads her fiction as a source of biographical insight and her diary as an exemplary fiction. DeSalvo's *Virginia Woolf: The Impact of Childhood Sexual Abuse on Her Life and Work* has had a polarizing effect on Woolf studies since its first appearance. Drawing upon the large literature of trauma and abuse which was at that point little known to those working in literary studies, DeSalvo also made controversial interpretations of Woolf's own writings the foundation of the thesis announced in her book's title. These two works are the most significant of a number of challenges to what Susan and Edwin Kenney in 1982 characterized as the 'uncritical acceptance' (162) of the view that Woolf was manic-depressive. The Kenneys wrote that this idea 'derives from all of the "authorized" versions of her life that begin with her husband Leonard Woolf's autobiography ... followed by her nephew Quentin Bell's biography, and most recently Nigel Nicolson's introductions and running commentary to *The Letters of Virginia Woolf*' (161). The causes and character of Woolf's depressions and breakdowns, her suicide, and the extent and effects of incestuous abuse in her childhood have become the most acute emphases of long-running arguments among readers of her many biographies.

Thomas C. Caramagno's *The Flight of the Mind: Virginia Woolf's Art and Manic-Depressive Illness* (1992) criticizes the critics of the 'official' view for what he characterizes as their excessive reliance on Freudian-inspired psychoanalytic readings of Woolf's life to the detriment of a scientific analysis of her condition. Recent works that have also taken illness as their focus include Patricia Moran's *Word of Mouth* (1996) and Allie Glenny's *Ravenous Identity* (1999) (which latter its author describes as complementary to DeSalvo [viii]).

In addition to biographical works on Woolf herself are a number of texts that broaden the view to a biography of, for example, Woolf's relationship with her sister (Dunn 1990; Gillespie 1988) or of her marriage (Spater and Parsons 1977; Rosenfeld 2000), or of her relationship with Vita Sackville-West (Raitt 1993). Stephen Trombley's *All That Summer She Was Mad* (1982), while not strictly speaking biographical, could be seen as ancillary to a work like Poole's in that it provides a rich cultural context for Poole's thesis that late nineteenth- and early twentieth-century medical science itself was to blame for the misunderstanding and mis-labelling of Woolf's condition. Looming behind all these are the ever-multiplying picture books and biographies of Bloomsbury friends, lovers and relations. 'The exact number of Woolf biographies is impossible to ascertain,' Julia Keller wisely states, 'because works on Woolf do not fall neatly into categories' (Keller 1998, 11).

Woolf wrote in 1940 to the composer Ethel Smyth that 'there's never been a womans autobiography. Nothing to compare with Rousseau. Chastity and modesty I suppose have been the reason' (*L6* 453). Nicola Luckhurst comments on Woolf's being 'increasingly preoccupied with the question of writing women's lives' from the 1930s on (Luckhurst 1999, 55), and notes that she 'urged her friends to write their autobiographies' as she began work on her own memoir, 'A Sketch of the Past'.[6] Luckhurst argues that conversations with Smyth created a new context of openness about the body for Woolf, and 'facilitated a new kind of life-writing' (57). 'What I am suggesting,' Luckhurst continues, 'is that from this basic frankness about the body, and by extension through accounts of her illness and its relation to the mind, or, one could say, the novelist's imaginary, Virginia Woolf was able to give the fullest account of her own life' (57). Green also argues that Smyth's auto-biographical collection *Female Pipings in Eden* (1934) provided a model for a practice 'that functioned by inserting the self into the margins of a historical narrative. In Woolf's hands,' Green goes on, 'this practice would develop into the complex "tactic" of carving out a feminist position in the margins of the notebooks that provided the source material for *Three Guineas* as well as in the footnotes and asides of the text itself' (Green 1997, 163).

Woolf had commented on the obstacle to women's autobiography posed by the body in a speech she gave to the London/National Society for Women's Service in January 1931, an occasion on which she shared the stage with Ethel Smyth.[7] The speech is most familiar as the essay 'Professions for Women', in which Woolf writes that although she had killed 'the Angel in the House' of Victorian female convention, she had been unable to find a way to tell 'the truth about my own experiences as a body' (*CE2* 288). Sidonie Smith indicates Woolf's contemporary significance when she describes autobio-graphical practice as 'one of those cultural occasions when the history of the body intersects with the deployment of female subjectivity as the woman writer struggles with multivalent embodiment. And so some kind of history of the body is always inscribed in women's autobiographical texts – muted or loud, mimetically recapitulated or subversive' (Smith 1994, 271).

'who was i then?': woolf's autobiographies

I wonder, parenthetically, whether I too, deal thus openly in autobiography & call it fiction?

Virginia Woolf, *Diary* 14 January, 1920

The most significant event in auto/biographical writing about Woolf was the 1976 publication of *Moments of Being*, a collection of previously unpublished autobiographical pieces from the Monk's House Papers at the University of Sussex, edited by Jeanne Schulkind. '22 Hyde Park Gate', 'Old Bloomsbury', and 'Am I a Snob?' are three papers Woolf read to the Memoir Club. Founded in 1920 by Molly MacCarthy, the Club's members were supposed to present unresearched autobiographical papers of complete honesty (Hussey 1995,

158). Of most interest to Woolf scholars and theorists of auto/biography, however, were two memoirs Schulkind included: 'Reminiscences', a 'life' of Vanessa Bell addressed to Bell's first child, Julian, and begun by Woolf in 1907, and 'A Sketch of the Past', begun by Woolf in 1939, and continued intermittently through the following year. A second edition of *Moments of Being* was published in 1985 after a typescript acquired by the British Library added twenty-seven pages of new material to 'A Sketch', as well as reworked passages of the earlier version.

Several critics have been drawn to comment on Woolf's narration of her memory of the mirror at Talland House, the Stephen family's summer vacation home. The passage incorporates a description of Woolf's sexual abuse at the hands of her half-brother Gerald Duckworth when she was six or seven years old (*MB* 67–9). Shari Benstock examines this passage in terms of the psychoanalyst Jacques Lacan's account of the 'mirror stage'.[8] She sees Woolf's narrative as disrupting 'the linguistic defense networks of male auto-biographers' (Benstock 1998, 149) who see autobiography as what George Gusdorf terms 'the mirror in which the individual reflects his own image' (148). Similarly, Emily Dalgarno reads the mirror scene as figuring 'the process by means of which [Woolf's] fiction both challenges and accommodates the ideology of patriarchy' (Dalgarno 1994, 176). Dalgarno also refers to Gusdorf, noting that the events of the period when Woolf chose to begin her memoir, 1939–40, 'seem to have created the preconditions under which, according to George Gusdorf, autobiography comes into existence' (Dalgarno 1994, 177): Woolf chose 'a moment of imminent historical change to reflect on the constitution of the subject' (177).

Dalgarno's essay extends Benstock's arguments about the function of Woolf's autobiographical narrative: through its 'specular experience' is figured 'the gap through which one glimpses the ideology of gender' (188). Woolf's 'representation of the looking-glass experience closely resembles that of Jacques Lacan' (182), but Woolf's recounting of it makes visible the difference gender makes: 'The site of the confusion of the six- or seven-year old who sees in the mirror features that resemble those of the mother and recoils from them in the name of the father is the body. The discrepancy between herself as subject and object gave rise to a lifelong anxiety' (183).

Cousineau also employs Lacanian theory in her reading of 'A Sketch', which exemplifies for her Woolf's 'ability to engage us simultaneously on the levels of the Imaginary and Symbolic and to direct us toward the Real' (Cousineau 1993, 52). Cousineau does not refer to the incest narrative nor to that mirror outside the dining room recalled by Woolf, but more generally discusses the trope of the mirror in Woolf's memoir, arguing that her 'ambivalence toward the visual marks her awareness that the coherent images of the Mirror Stage always misrepresent the experience of the body at the same time that they are a crucial necessity in the formation of individual identity' (55). Like several other critics, Cousineau highlights the primacy of embodiment in Woolf's memoir: 'for Woolf life begins with the sensations that connect the body to the world' (52–3). Sidonie Smith, comparing Woolf's practice in 'A Sketch of the Past' with that of Cherríe Moraga in *Loving in the War Years*, describes how women 'had to discursively consolidate themselves as subjects through pursuit of an out-of-body experience precisely because their bodies were heavily and inescapably gendered, intensely fabricated ... the universalization of the white male body as the normative source of sexual knowledge, meaning, and identification effectively mobilized the objectification of the female body and its occlusion ... Thus the autobiographical mode solicited the identification of the woman with and against her body' (Smith 1994, 272).

Smith uses that moment in Woolf's memoir when she recalls the incestuous abuse she suffered as a child to argue that Woolf is nostalgic for 'the body before the cultural construction of identity ... intrudes and partitions her off in identity's body' (288). In posing the question of whether the autobiographical body is 'identity's body', Smith suggests that 'More than identity's body ... gender's body or race's body or sexuality's body or ethnicity's body, the body is subjectivity's body' (270). 'A Sketch,' Smith argues, 'sustains the troubled relationship between autobiography and the female body' (288). Smith uses the juxtaposition of Woolf's memoir with Moraga's – wherein Moraga writes explicitly as a lesbian of colour – to point out how 'efficiently the specificities of the body have been erased through Woolf's comfortably middle-class escape from embodiment. After all, Woolf never mentions the color of the skin that needs escaping' (288). Smith's essay marks a concern with race that is relatively new to auto/biographical theory, complicating an earlier exclusive focus on gender and thus recapitulating the trajectory of white American feminist literary criticism in general.

Christopher Dahl compares the earlier and later memoirs published in *Moments of Being*, seeing in them a reflection of Woolf's own 'journey from Victorian to modern and, strangely enough, from self-doubt and insecurity in "Reminiscences" to a kind of acceptance of her own identity in "A Sketch of the Past"' (Dahl 1983, 194). Roger Moss has described 'A Sketch' as 'an act of resistance to the values of Victorian biography' (Moss 1995, 2), joining others who note Woolf's acknowledgment of her place in a specific history of autobiographers. Writing in the same special issue on biography of *Virginia Woolf Miscellany* as Moss, Marylu Hill contrasts Woolf's approach to biography with that of her father, Leslie Stephen, founding editor of the *Dictionary of National Biography*. Woolf's, she writes, is a 'matriarchal paradigm of biography in which the biographer gives birth to a vision of the subject based on regenerative perception rather than dull facts' (Hill 1995, 3). Dahl also places Woolf in her own family's autobiographical tradition, noting 'a divergence between public and private autobiography' (Dahl 1983, 179) in the various memoirs produced by Stephen family members, a tradition also explored recently by Alex Zwerdling (2003). As Julia Briggs has written, Woolf's early childhood coincided with the birth of modern biography (Briggs 1995, 246), as her father worked on his *Dictionary*. Briggs discusses Woolf's recognition of the challenges posed by writing about middle-class Victorian women, and examines her 1907 mock biography of Violet Dickinson, 'Friendships Gallery'.

LuAnn McCracken also compares 'Reminiscences' with 'A Sketch' and finds Woolf absent in the former, present in the latter (McCracken 1990, 72). Both 'Reminiscences' and the novel she was writing concurrently, *The Voyage Out*, according to McCracken, 'suggest Woolf's attempt to form her identity by separation', but 'A Sketch' 'reflects a woman's definition of her identity by relation' (73). The relation in question is with Woolf's mother, Julia Stephen. McCracken believes that in 'A Sketch' Woolf re-established the bond with her mother, thus affirming her 'identity as a woman' (75). She refers approvingly to Ellen Bayuk Rosenman's *The Invisible Presence: Virginia Woolf and the Mother-Daughter Relationship* as endorsing her own reading of Woolf's fictional mother figures as versions of Woolf's relationship with her own mother (McCracken 1990, 76 n.17). Dalgarno also cites Rosenman, but as an example of how critics have taken no note of the mother's consistently unresponsive face in 'A Sketch' when they describe the 'myth of [Woolf's] golden childhood' (Dalgarno 1994, 182, quoting Rosenman 1986, 19).

Hilary Clark reads 'A Sketch' as an example of 'palimpsestic life-writing' (Clark 1990, 6) that can 'enable women writers in particular to open up their life-narratives, drawing forth the ghosts of their mothers in order to both enrich and destabilize their writing and their lives' (7). Merry Pawlowski also focuses on Woolf's attitude to her mother, linking 'A Sketch' to Woolf's analysis of domestic fascism in *Three Guineas* and seeing it as a text of silences and evasions: 'We are invited ... to participate in the stripping away of her polite surface manner and to assist her in saying the unsayable' (Pawlowski 1995, 106).

Drawing on Paul DeMan's 'Autobiography as Defacement', Georgia Johnston sees Woolf reading her life as if it were a text in 'A Sketch', an indication, perhaps, of why this memoir has such currency in feminist auto/biographical theory. Woolf's 'various methods of reading create an unstable subject-object relationship that results in an ironic and fractured narratology of the autobiographical "I"' (Johnston 1996, 140). This fracturing 'affects the theory of autobiography', exemplified in the work of Sidonie Smith, Shoshana Felman, and Shari Benstock. Beth Carole Rosenberg has similarly argued that in 'A Sketch' Woolf does not 'create a narrative of her identity but reproduces the series of beginnings of which that identity is composed' (Rosenberg 1995, 8).

Before the publication of *Moments of Being*, Woolf's life-writing had been available in *A Writer's Diary* (1953) and a selection of her correspondence with Lytton Strachey.[9] As Benstock remarks, 'the bulk of the autobiographical Virginia Woolf exists in her diary and letters, forms whose generic boundaries she extended and reconstructed' (Benstock 1998, 150). Woolf's diary and letters began to be published in 1975; for Lorrie Goldensohn the completion of this project represented 'as material a contribution as we'll ever have to the puzzling relation between fiction and forms of autobiography' (Goldensohn 1987, 2). Susan Sellers has made the case for 'considering the diaries and letters as distinct works of art' (Sellers 2000, 114), seeing them as 'point[ing] to the accomplishment of that new form for writing for which Woolf was searching throughout her career' (122). Several commentators have argued for the 'artistry' of Woolf's diary (Lounsberry 1994, 267), and Roger Poole has even made the provocative suggestion that the diary 'as constituted is very near to being a fictional work' (Poole 1984, 161). Sellers, referring to 'postmodern theory' that 'has taught us to think differently about the nature of the "I"' (Sellers 2000, 116), believes it 'impossible to treat the diaries and letters as the expressions of a coherent self' (116). Poole concurs: 'Who, for instance, is the person referred to as "I" in the *Diary*? What if the *Diary* were Virginia Woolf's longest and most complex novel?' (Poole 1982, xv).[10]

A number of critics have remarked on the interrelations of Woolf's own auto/biographical writing and her fiction. Mepham finds it is 'impossible to keep the literary analysis of Virginia Woolf's fiction separate from the study and interpretation of her life' (Mepham 1992, 3), and Briggs has argued that even in her seemingly conventional second novel, *Night and Day*, her 'exploration of the boundaries between fiction and biography opened the way for further experiments with existing forms' (Briggs 1995, 254).[11]

Even before the publication of 'A Sketch of the Past', the autobiographical nature of *To The Lighthouse* was well established, although critical writing on the novel has ranged from blunt efforts at finding correspondences between biography and fiction to more subtle examinations of how Woolf transmutes life to art. Suzanne Nalbantian argues that Woolf shares with Proust, Joyce, and Nin a 'common aesthetics of transmutation' (Nalbantian 1994, viii) in which 'the referential factor becomes negligible as the artistic analogy has transcended it. The autobiographical ingredients are less than the sum total of the aesthetic product' (156). Galya Diment also focuses on *To the Lighthouse* as an example of how Woolf, similarly to Joyce and the lesser-known Russian writer Ivan Goncharov, developed 'a special way of projecting inner conflicts onto multiple fictional selves' (Diment 1994, 44). Diment notes Woolf's distinction between autobiography and egotism, a quality she felt spoiled the work of Dorothy Richardson and Joyce.[12]

Two early groundbreaking works of biographical criticism are the essays on *To the Lighthouse* by Jane Lilienfeld. In '"The Deceptiveness of Beauty"', she draws on the memoirs in *Moments of Being* to explain why Woolf was 'impelled to write that novel' (Lilienfeld 1977, 345), and discusses the auto-biographical elements of Cam and James Ramsay, and Lily Briscoe. In 'Where the Spear Plants Grew', Lilienfeld argues that most criticism of the novel up to the mid-1970s depended upon 'the ideological persuasion' that the family 'as structured by the patriarchy is the bulwark of morality, the state and stable human character' (Lilienfeld 1981, 149). In her more recent work, Lilienfeld has continued to use biographical investigation, but 'interrogate[s] one-to-one correspondences between art and life' (Lilienfeld 1999, 12). Again taking *Lighthouse* as an exemplary text, Lilienfeld's recent work draws on theories that 'reattach texts and their readers and writers in a more nuanced way to social, economic, and historic life, without losing the gains in analysis of narrative and textual meanings produced by the postmodernist literary revolution' (Lilienfeld 1999, 8–9).

Woolf's two fictional 'biographies', *Orlando* and *Flush*, have also, unsurprisingly, drawn the attention of readers interested in auto/biographical theory. Kathryn Miles (1999) reads *Orlando* in the light of Woolf's 1927 essay 'The New Biography', and Karyn Sproles (1995) links the novel to the 'common genre' of biography as it functioned for members of the Bloomsbury Group. Catherine Peters sees *Flush* as following up 'in a light-hearted way' Woolf's 'earlier essays on biography', and 'suggest[ing] ways of reinventing the genre which are only now being taken seriously' (Peters 1995, 48). A more extensive treatment of *Orlando* is that given by Suzanne Raitt, who places it in the context of biography writing of its time. Raitt's book is one of the most significant recent works of Woolf criticism to draw on auto/biographical theory. Her reading of *The Waves* – which she terms Woolf's 'book of friendship' (Raitt 1993, 147) – is unusual in that it 'examines its formal links with autobiography and biography, and suggests that it was the climax to Woolf's negotiations of images of maternity' (ix).

Distinguishing specific critical works as 'biographical' is probably futile, however; in the case of Woolf criticism, it is almost certainly so. As Stanley Fish points out, 'The choice ... is not between reading biographically and reading in some other way (there is no other way) but rather between different biographical readings that have their source in different specifications of the sources of agency. The only way to read unbiographically would be to refrain from construing meaning – to refrain, that is, from regarding the marks before you as manifestations of intentional behavior; but that would be not to read at all' (Fish 1991, 13–14). Woolf was an artist explicitly concerned with the complex relationship between life and art, between narrative and self-consciousness; it is virtually impossible to find a work of Woolf criticism that is not in some sense 'biographical', whatever its writer may protest. At times, the auto/biographical figures explicitly, as in discussions of Woolf's creation of Septimus Smith in *Mrs Dalloway* (for example Henke 2000); or it may occur in more general considerations of Woolf's narratology (for example Lilienfeld 2000).

woolf and biography

And how could it be possible, in Virginia Woolf's case, to separate the text and what is outside it, the writing and the life? Where could we draw the line in the vast quantity of *intermediate* writings – the diary, the autobiographical fragments, the letters – which occupy such an important place in her *oeuvre* and offer many points of contact with the novels, which they often precede or double? Most critics have been aware of this impossibility of marking a boundary in the continuum which goes from the life to the diary or letters, from the diary to the autobiographical writings; from the autobiographical writings to a novel presented as autobiographical like *To the Lighthouse*; and thence to all the other novels and short stories.

Daniel Ferrer, *Virginia Woolf and the Madness of Language*, 1990

'For Woolf,' writes Linda Anderson, 'the question of a life and its written form – whether in biography, autobiography or fiction – were inseparable and often made her blur the boundaries of genre, disrupting the authority enshrined in masculine convention' (Anderson 1987, 47–8). This inseparability extends also to critical writing about Woolf herself. At the beginning of the 1990s, for example, John Mepham, surveying the state of Woolf studies, noted that 'never have literary criticism and psychobiographic investigation been so intimately entwined as in the case of Virginia Woolf' (Mepham 1992, 13). One of her recent biographers, too, prefaces his work by saying that the 'familiar separation of life and work upon which most literary biography depends does not apply to Virginia Woolf. Her life and work were inseparable, and part of that life was inscribed in every novel she wrote' (Leaska 1998, 16). For Woolf, however, the situation was never so simple: 'Life? Literature? One to be made into the other? But how monstrously difficult!' (*O* 272).[13]

While Alison Booth finds 'the probing of the author's life for the sake of insight into the work ... crucial to a developing interpretation of diverse women's roles in cultural production' (Booth 1991, 87), she acknowledges that Woolf would have dismissed this as irrelevant. In a 1926 essay on *Robinson Crusoe*, Woolf wrote:

Only now and then, as we turn from theory to biography and from biography to theory, a doubt insinuates itself – if we knew the very moment of Defoe's birth and whom he loved and why ... should we suck an ounce of additional pleasure from *Robinson Crusoe* or read it one whit more intelligently? (*CE1* 69–70)

Despite Woolf's suspicion of biography's usefulness for the reader of fiction, she was nevertheless early and long absorbed by the genre. Julia Briggs believes Woolf's earliest writings 'can be read as a series of attempts to reconceive biography, by focusing on the kinds of material and technique that it had traditionally avoided – mundane reality or imaginative flight – while at the same time hankering after its characteristic virtue, its claim to truth' (Briggs 1995, 257). Although Briggs finds that 'biography gradually ceased to provide a model for thinking about the nature of imaginative writing, the issues it raised remained potent for her' (262).

For Barthes, writing is 'the negative where all identity is lost, starting with the very identity of the body writing' (Barthes 1977, 142); for Woolf, writing is the very constituent of identity: 'I make it real by putting it into words' (*MB* 72). In her 1919 essay 'Reading', Woolf wrote 'Somewhere, everywhere, now hidden, now apparent in whatever is written down is the form of a human being' (*E3* 156). Wherever we look in Woolf's essays, we are likely to find her concerned with personality, with the influence of time and custom on a particular writer, or making the effort to reconstruct the outlines of a life. The text for Woolf is always a *social* text – not a sociological deposit, but always fully implicated in those structural determinants of class, epoch, gender and nationality that are the habitual axes of her enquiries. The subject, 'now hidden, now apparent', in anything that is written becomes for Woolf the prime motivator of her own writing, an object at once unattainable and powerfully attractive. If what is written down is biography, it no less partakes of the characteristics of writing: indeterminacy, incompleteness, uncertainty.

Laura Marcus places Woolf alongside her Bloomsbury intimate Lytton Strachey, two radicals who rebelled against the conventions of life-writing represented by such eminent Victorians as Sir Sidney Lee, Lord Morley, and (implicitly at least) Woolf's own father, Sir Leslie Stephen. Both Strachey and Woolf 'open up the question of the historicity of biography and the complexity of the relationship between past and present' (Laura Marcus 1994, 130). In discussing *Orlando: A Biography*, Marcus suggests that Woolf both 'subvert[s] Nietzsche's representations of truth as "becoming a woman"' and 'take[s] up his concept of truth as the veiled gesture of feminine modesty, which creates the illusion of surface/depth' (123). Through its satire of the biographical convention of the truth of self or identity as 'conventionally imaged through the body, especially as clothed/naked' *Orlando* raises two key questions: 'Firstly, what is the place of the body in biography and, secondly, what is the relationship between truth and (in)decency for the moderns?' (123). Marcus sees both *Orlando* and Strachey's *Elizabeth and Essex* as influenced by and contributing to contemporary debates about sexual identity and androgyny in their dual concern with the body (128).

In many essays and reviews, Woolf argues for multiple biographies, works that would tell the story not only of their subjects but also would describe the histories of readers. 'To write down one's impressions of *Hamlet* as one reads it year after year,' she wrote in 'Charlotte Brontë' (1916), 'would be virtually to record one's own autobiography, for as we know more of life, so Shakespeare comments upon what we know' (*E2* 27). Woolf thus can be seen as anticipating the status of her own biography, as it has existed in multiple and proliferating versions over the last thirty years. One of her most recent biographers writes in Woolfian vein, 'Meaning, one inevitably concludes, ultimately does not reside in the text alone: A substantial part of the sense one makes of *any* artifact derives in part from the epistemological history of the particular reader, at a particular time and place, under a particular set of circumstances' (Leaska 1998, 4). Woolf argues in her essays and implies in works such as *Flush* and *Orlando* that the construction of biography is a product of particular ideologies and epistemologies. These influences are felt most sharply when she turns to the occluded history of women's lives, as, indeed, they have been made sharply visible in the contested terrain of writing biographies of Woolf herself. In creating Judith Shakespeare in *A Room of One's Own*, Woolf gave 'a name, a desire, and a history to one of those mute females who lived and died in obscurity' (Modleski 1989, 19). Biographical approaches to Woolf's own writing have made visible much that was obscure before feminist theorizing began to transform literary studies; that theorizing has not only frequently taken Woolf as its example, it has also learned much from her own writing.

notes

1. See Ellen Messer Davidow, *Disciplining Feminism: From Social Activism to Academic Discourse*; Florence Howe, ed. *The Politics of Women's Studies: Testimony from 30 Founding Mothers*.

2. The feminist debate about authorship is wide-ranging; two 'sides' are represented in the epigraphs to this section. A concise statement of the differences can be found in Peggy Kamuf and Nancy K. Miller's 'Parisian Letters: Between Feminism and Deconstruction', in Marianne Hirsch and Evelyn Fox Keller, eds. *Conflicts in Feminism*, 121–33. Also in that volume see Nancy K. Miller, 'The Text's Heroine: A Feminist Critic and Her Fictions', 112–20; and Nancy K. Miller, 'Changing the Subject: Authorship, Writing, and the Reader', in Teresa DeLauretis, ed., *Feminist Studies/Critical Studies*, 102–20.

3. See Gilmore 1994 generally for further bibliographical references.

4. A detailed survey is provided in Smith and Watson 1998, 'Introduction.'

5. 'Today the question of what role the author can claim to perform in writing a poem or a novel is deeply enmeshed in ontological uncertainties that first began to be registered a century ago, when anxieties about authorship also began to surface. Philosophically, this question has become entangled with concerns about the status of the will and intentionality. What do I do when I put my fingers on the computer keys? And who am "I" anyway?' (Walker 1991, 110).

6. In 1927, beginning to contemplate *Orlando*, Woolf even invited Lady Sackville to write her memoirs for the Hogarth Press. See Porter 2001.

7. See Mitchell A. Leaska, ed. *The Pargiters: The Novel-Essay Portion of* The Years, xxvii–xliv.

8. Benstock confuses the identity of the half-brother Woolf mentions at this point in the narrative with her other half-brother, George Duckworth. As Woolf was sexually abused by both, the frequency of this error in commentary on Woolf is understandable.

9. *Virginia Woolf & Lytton Strachey: Letters*. Eds Leonard Woolf and James Strachey. New York: Harcourt, Brace and Company, 1956.

10. Woolf's diary and letters have also been discussed in the broader context of the history of women's autobiography. See Stimpson 1984; Podnieks 2000; and Simons 1990.

11. On biographical sources of *Night and Day*, see McCail 1987.

12. 'I suppose the danger is the damned egotistical self; which ruins Joyce & [Dorothy] Richardson to my mind.' (*D2* 14)
13. Woolf's position in the culture's imaginary is identical in many respects to that of Sylvia Plath, as characterized by Jacqueline Rose: 'As Plath writes herself across her journals, letters, novel, short stories and poetry, her different voices enter into an only ever partial dialogue with each other which it is impossible to bring to a close. To which of these voices are we going to assign an absolute authority...?' (Rose 1992, 104).

5

feminist approaches

beth rigel daugherty

> What more fitting than to destroy an old word, a vicious and corrupt word that has done much harm in its day and is now obsolete? The word 'feminist' is the word indicated.
>
> *Three Guineas*, 302

The word 'feminist' was hardly old when Woolf called for its ceremonial burning in 1938. In its current meaning, it had travelled from France to Great Britain in 1894–95, when she was a girl (Caine 1997, xv; Offen 2000, 19; see also Black 1989, 19). She grew up with feminism, addressing envelopes for the People's Suffrage Federation in 1910 (Black 1983, 183–4), arranging meetings and speakers for the Women's Co-operative Guild for several years, and stating, in 1916, that she was becoming 'steadily more feminist' in response to the war, 'this preposterous masculine fiction' (*L2* 76). She knew and associated with many active feminists in groups such as the Women's International League and the London and National Society for Women's Service and was thus in the web of English and international feminist groups at the time (Black 1983; Harvey 1997; Goldman 1998; Snaith 2000). Even as she worried about the divisiveness caused by the term, she supported the Women's Service Library (later the Fawcett Library and now The Women's Library) with donations of money and books, and used its resources to support her feminist arguments in *Three Guineas* (Pawlowski 2002, 3–8; Snaith 2003). Her call for cremation indicates not only the vexed context for the word in the 1930s (Offen 2000, 373) and Woolf's ambivalence about the organized political campaigns associated with it (Snaith 2000, 34), but also the persistent challenge of identifying oneself and one's work as feminist. Although versions of what is now called feminism have been waxing and waning for centuries, the practitioners of feminist analysis at any time go against the grain of received opinion and risk being attacked. That reality and the anxiety it provokes looms over Woolf's own feminism, over early feminist criticism of her work, and over feminism's current association with Woolf.[1] It has now taken up residence *within* feminism and looms over me.[2]

I am white, heterosexual, middle class, and middle-aged. I am a tenured academic teaching at a private, comprehensive, liberal arts college in the mid-western United States. I live in a house with a room of my own, have a respectable salary, and enjoy my work. My vision is circumscribed by these marks of privilege at the same time it is limited by two marginal positions, female and rural Appalachian. The blinders inherent in my location, to say nothing of the assignment for this chapter, guarantee I will exclude valuable critics, texts, and perspectives. The anxiety I feel about such exclusion stems from my acute awareness of how erasure and partiality have been used against women in the past, my ironic realization that I'm participating in canon building, and my strong commitment to the feminist ideal of inclusiveness. I can only hope that my particular wandering in the trees of feminist approaches to Woolf will open up more paths through the forest. I can also acknowledge the conscious biases guiding (and limiting) my choices for this chapter: a focus on North American and English feminist critics; a preference for feminist critics with a background in Woolf scholarship;[3] an admiration for textual scholarship; a respect for feminist critics who combine theory with close attention to the text and avoid using highly theoretical discourse; and a focus on feminist approaches that have generated excitement, debate, and further study.

introduction

> One wanted fifty pairs of eyes to see with, she reflected. Fifty pairs of eyes were not enough to get round that one woman with, she thought.
>
> *To the Lighthouse*, 266

Virginia Woolf's desire to destroy the word 'feminist' also captures something important and paradoxical about the nature of the feminist project. Its vision is utopian, growing out of a need for political and social change, and it works to transform society. As Sydney Janet Kaplan notes, feminist criticism was brought into existence by 'intense and powerful longings for a better world' (Kaplan 2000, 171), which means it works for its own abolition, for the day when the word and the project are no longer necessary. As a result, the feminist project remains frustratingly and tantalizingly unfinished, but also dynamic.

Lily Briscoe's desire to capture Mrs Ramsay's essence on canvas and her resulting perception that one pair of eyes cannot see the truth of another person, that even fifty pairs of eyes cannot surround and *know* the other, communicates both the initial thrust of feminist analysis and its later awareness that one feminism cannot possibly define all women's experiences. Feminism has become feminisms, and the resulting multiple points of view are exciting, illuminating, and more realistic while still not all-encompassing or conclusive. The various theoretical and practical stances can bewilder, however. Also, as Jodi Dean points out, '[e]fforts to define feminism and to say that gender (or sex or patriarchy) is the key concept within this definition are treated as attempts to replace the hard-won multiplicity of feminisms with yet another exclusive category' (Dean 2003, 733–4), which makes clarifying the nature of feminist approaches seem difficult if not almost impossible.[4]

But just as Lily's awareness does not stop her from painting, feminists' growing self-awareness has not stopped them from writing histories of feminist literary criticism (Benstock, Ferris, and Woods 2002; Thornham 2000), analyzing key components of feminist practice (Tyson 1999; Ahmed et al. 2000; bell hooks 2000), or creating anthologies of feminist thought (Warhol and Herndl 1997; Kemp and Squires 1997; Eagleton 1996; Guy-Sheftall 1995; Humm 1992). Conscious paradox marks contemporary feminist practice, just as it marked Woolf's feminist criticism, so that awareness of multiplicity complicates the need to see, speak, form coalitions, and act, and vice versa (Gunew and Yeatman 1993, xiii).

From my admittedly limited vantage point, feminist literary criticism generally includes, though is not reduced to, the following features. Existing in varying proportions at various times, particular traits often shade into each other, overlap, and move to the foreground or background. During the 1970s, for example, feminism was determined to open the canon to literature by and about women; *recovery and revision* predominated as feminist strategies. In the 1980s, *border crossings* resulted in the growth of hybrid feminisms, interdisciplinary women's studies programmes, and the intersection of Anglo-American feminism and French theory. The 1980s interest in *material circumstances* and a concomitant focus on the body, female sexuality, and gender difference encouraged the focus on *political, historical, and cultural contexts* in the 1990s. Through it all, feminist literary criticism has tried, not always successfully, to remain *self-aware*, critical of its own exclusionary tactics, committed to openness, and vigilant about both pragmatic politics and theoretical questions. As we head further into the twenty-first century, calls for *going beyond* current impasses in feminist criticism can be heard. Although most feminist critics in Woolf studies would identify themselves with several if not all of the above traits, I have, out of organizational necessity, assigned each critic to only one trait in my discussion.

A recent incarnation of feminism in the UK and the USA (often called the 'second wave' to distinguish it from the suffrage-centred 'first wave' of the early twentieth century) developed out of other political struggles in the 1950s and 1960s. In England, a focus on gender issues grew out of a prevalence of class analyses that did not include women, whereas in the USA, a focus on gender issues grew out of a prevalence of race analyses that did not include women. (Ironically, feminists in each country have since been taken to task for not taking into account class or race.) The women's movement of the 1970s coalesced around a political battle for women's rights, an assertion that the personal is political, and numerous journeys of group consciousness-raising and individual assertion. Virginia Woolf, out of favour in the 1950s and 1960s, was rediscovered by the feminists of the 1970s, and *A Room of One's Own* was taken up with excitement and passion. With it, feminist politics entered the academy. Addressed to an audience of young women in a university that had only just made English a primary subject for a degree (Cuddy-Keane 2003, 69), Woolf's text identifies a female literary tradition, analyzes literary history through an economic lens, and asserts that material circumstances matter. Its valuing of obscure lives, obscure work, and obscure literature both for their own sake and for their role as ground for an eventual masterpiece focuses on the real reason for the feminist project: so that when Shakespeare's sister 'is born again she shall find it possible to live and write her poetry' (*AROO* 149). As I write this chapter in the midst of war and terror, I am particularly struck by the enormous and complex political implications of that seemingly simple goal. We should work so that when children are born, they will find it possible to live. And create. That's all. Of course, that's everything.

Basing her knowledge of female literary history on what was in her father's library and weaving fact and fiction in her usual way, Woolf did not set out to create an accurate literary history in *A Room of One's Own*.[5] But she revolution-ized feminist persuasion by creating a layered narration, using exploratory rhetoric, and employing brilliant metaphors; stimulated twentieth-century discussion of androgyny, lesbianism, women's rights, the relationship between creativity and economic circumstances, and the discrepancy between the image of women in literature and women's reality; and identified questions, tensions, and contradictions feminist critics still struggle with. As Michèle Barrett says, 'Many commentators have noted the prescience of Woolf's ideas and her capacity to anticipate the concerns of feminists in the future' (Barrett 1999, 36). An example of feminist criticism at its best – *A Room of One's Own* communicates respect and admiration for women through its content, structure, and rhetoric – its influence has been enormous, for academics in various fields, for feminist literary critics, for students sitting in many sorts of classes, and for writers. Eileen Barrett remembers that when she read *A Room of One's Own* in 1973, it was 'emerging as the blueprint for the women's movement within literary studies and as the guideline for feminist revisions to the literary tradition. "Money and a room of one's own" became the phrase within the academy that succinctly described our demands for women's studies programs, centers, and courses.'[6] What I suspect would most please Woolf, though, is her book's inspirational role in the lives and work of Tillie Olsen, Jeanette Winterson, Rosario Ferré, Toni Morrison, Margaret Drabble, Michelle Cliff, bell hooks, Nancy Mairs, Paule Marshall, and Alice Walker, among others.[7]

Though *A Room of One's Own* was almost a sacred text for feminists both inside and outside the academy in the 1970s, many feminist critics preferred

Three Guineas (1938) (that embarrassment to Leonard Woolf, Quentin Bell, Nigel Nicolson, and E. M. Forster[8]), and its influence has steadily grown. For example, Margo Jefferson used it in a *New York Times Book Review* column to show Woolf's linking of public and private tyrannies and servilities in *Mrs Dalloway* (Jefferson 2003, 31). Jefferson's essay confirms my teaching experience: once students have read *Three Guineas,* they have no difficulty seeing the political thought in all of Woolf's work. Feminist critics have studied Woolf's direct anger in *Three Guineas* (Silver 1991a, 340–70), her strategic use of facts, footnotes, and photographs (Black 2001, lvi–lxiii), her replies to the correspondence of ordinary readers who wrote to her about it (Snaith 2000a), her complex critique of education (Daugherty 1999b), her crucial linking of fascism and the patriarchy (Pawlowski 2001), and her anti-war, anti-fascist, anti-violence rhetoric (Froula 1994, 27–56). Most crucially, however, Woolf clarifies the central paradox for feminists – to gain equality, we must enter the male world, but in doing so, we risk losing the outsider's perspective that might change or transform that world – and articulates the central challenge – to retain the outsider's perspective while inside. For Christine Froula, Woolf identifies 'many of the political, economic, and social challenges that, over half a century later, still confront women and men, races, religions, classes, and nations in our continuing struggles to deal with differences by attempting to speak across, negotiate, transcend, or peacefully erase boundaries rather than by violence' (Froula 1994, 49).

The feminist approach to Virginia Woolf thus began with the recovery of Woolf's feminism, which itself attempted to recover a female writing tradition and to prevent war. Feminists took Woolf's feminist work seriously, brought attention to *Three Guineas* as well as *A Room of One's Own,* and insisted her feminist thought was central to all her work, a stance that changed the way Woolf was perceived. Feminist critics' claim that Virginia Woolf was an important, even canonical, author spawned numerous studies of her work, encouraged the publication of great masses of primary material such as the letters, diaries, holograph manuscripts, and memoirs, inspired numerous biographical visions and revisions, and ultimately led to new editions of her work. Woolf studies – the societies, newsletters, and journals; the conferences, selected papers volumes, chat rooms, and networks; the scholarly debates and passionate advocacy; the dissertations, articles, and books; the influence on contemporary writers and films; the status of cultural icon; the ever-growing bibliography that creates the necessity for volumes such as this; the burgeoning industry, in short – all stem from feminist criticism's insistence that we pay attention to *Woolf's* feminist criticism and revise our opinions of Woolf and her work accordingly. All the contributors to this volume, for example, no matter what other approaches they practice and discuss, could also be called feminist critics: they ground their work in feminist assumptions, rely on feminist strategies, and achieve feminist aims. Feminist criticism created and now sustains what we call Woolf studies.

Woolf did not start it all, of course, but she did restart it, that feminist recursive habit born of necessity: 'think[ing] back through our mothers' (*AROO* 99), going back, picking up stray threads hidden or invisible in the past, pulling them into the present, and re-weaving them into new patterns. Virginia Woolf's own feminist criticism illuminates the main ideas and methodological strategies of feminist critical practice, along with all its questions, paradoxes, and contradictions. Prefiguring current dilemmas and conundrums, Woolf's criticism embodies and anticipates the tension between the essential and the constructed; difference and equality; evolution and patterns; inclusion and exclusion; the desire to resolve and the desire to leave open; politics and art; the communal and the individual; masterpiece and anon; the struggle to speak and the impossibility of speaking; the fear and the courage. Woolf's feminism aims to recover, redefine, and revise. She defies hierarchies, crosses borders, and makes connections. Her work questions, challenges, and changes us. Woolf claimed subjectivity for herself and confronted the difficulty of acknowledging or attempting to imagine the subjectivities of others. She, too, wondered whom she meant when she said 'we'.[9] She, too, tried to walk the fine line between both/and rather than fall into either/or. She, too, wrestled with how to refashion rhetoric so that it did not replicate patriarchal structures and results. She, too, attempted to make judgements, determine value, and yet remain generous and open. She, too, wrestled with whether, and if so, how, writers can have an impact on politics other than through the pen.

Woolf's feminist criticism influenced and continues to influence feminist approaches, which in turn, have radically changed the way she was, and continues to be, read. Virginia Woolf is now read *as* a feminist. She is read *as* political. She is read *as* a body, a physical, sexual being, a private person and a public intellectual, living and acting in the practical, everyday world. Now seen as embedded in her time, place, and culture, she is also read as issuing challenges to those circumstances and demonstrating the difficulties in overcoming them. More than fifty pairs of feminist eyes see various Virginia Woolfs,[10] but none of them bears any resemblance to the mad, frail, apolitical aesthete portrayed by Quentin Bell.

Although the recovery of Virginia Woolf for feminist literary criticism grew apace in reaction to Quentin Bell's publication of *Virginia Woolf: A Biography* in 1972, it had actually begun several years before with Herbert Marder's *Feminism and Art: A Study of Virginia Woolf* (1968). Using only Woolf's work, without the benefit of her letters, complete diaries, or *Collected Essays*, and using the few sources on feminism available to him at the time, [11] Marder insists that Woolf's art and feminism are intertwined. Linking her feminism to a desire for wholeness (4), Marder sees Woolf creating a vision of a better world: 'Her concern began with a sense of personal grievance; it ended with a consciousness of public responsibility' (30). Since the harshest criticism against Woolf then came from those who argued she was detached from the world, his view of her feminism as an engagement with politics that infused

her art was powerful. Although Marder saw *Three Guineas* as an artistic failure
with propaganda getting the upper hand, an opinion he has since revised
(Marder 2000), he argued strongly against the prevailing opinion of Woolf,
calling her feminism her 'moral fervor' (Marder 2000, 175). He gave 1970s
feminist critics a strong foundation, one based on the close reading of texts
and a view of Woolf's feminism as integral, not peripheral or harmful.

Virginia Woolf and the Androgynous Vision (1973) by Nancy Topping Bazin
extended Marder's chapter on the androgynous mind by arguing that Woolf
was on a philosophical and personal quest for balance and that Woolf's
aesthetic theory of androgyny grew organically out of that quest. Bazin,
investigating medical, psychoanalytic, and Jungian literature of the time,
was the first to suggest that Woolf suffered from manic-depression and that
her artistic binaries grew out of that mental state. Appearing at the same time
as Carolyn Heilbrun's *Toward a Recognition of Androgyny*, a general study of
androgyny in myth, history, and literature, Bazin's work makes it clear now
that something was in the air, perhaps the need to look at sexuality (and
women) outside of a rigid Freudian lens. Revolutionary in its more fluid
definition of sexuality, its weaving of autobiographical context and interpretations of the novels, and its portrayal of Woolf as an active agent seeking
health and a balanced world view rather than as a passive receiver of stimuli at
the mercy of madness, Bazin's book was read avidly by Woolf critics. Though
later feminist critics who saw androgyny as reifying essential female and male
qualities and as denying difference criticized Bazin's reading, it has continued
to contribute to debates about the nature and meaning of androgyny within
feminism and within Woolf studies.[12]

recovery and revision

The student was presenting her analysis of feminist literary criticism's effect
on the canon to her senior seminar. She had counted the number of female
authors (4) and pages on those authors (11 out of 3487) included in the
1968 revised edition of *The Norton Anthology of English Literature* and the
number of female authors (52) and the pages on those authors (765 out
of 5819) in the 2000 7th edition. In response, another student said, 'I had
no idea it was that bad. I always thought feminists were just a bunch of
complainers. We owe them a lot, don't we?'

English 400, spring 2002[13]

Feminist literary critics owe a great deal to Virginia Woolf, who devoted her
entire *oeuvre*, novels and stories included, to the recovery of a female writing
tradition, obscure voices, and common readers. Her essays often provide her
audience with reading lists, and the tables of contents in the two *Common
Readers* emphasize the reader's contribution, the often-ignored work by the
famous author, the not-so-famous author, and the 'lesser' genres (see Johnston

1989, 148–58; Daugherty 1995, 61–77). It is no surprise that near the end of her life, she was working to recover 'Anon' (Woolf [Silver] 1979, 356–441). If Woolf's reception history demonstrates how male literary historians can almost write important female writers out of the canon, Woolf's skill at recovery, carried out within the parameters imposed upon her by the male literary establishment, reveals one strategy for counteracting that impulse.

How fitting, then, that a major part of the feminist approach to Woolf has involved not only recovering her feminism, but also, quite literally, her *work* – the photographs in *Three Guineas*, the short stories and essays not collected during her lifetime, the notebooks, the manuscripts. Growing out of feminism's general reclamation project in the 1970s, the feminist recovery of Woolf ignited in the USA just as (or perhaps because) many of her manuscripts became available in the New York Public Library, and the result was numerous transcriptions and textual studies by feminist critics. Poetic justice, surely, that the woman prevented from entering the library at Cambridge to examine the manuscript of *Lycidas* had the huge bulk of her manuscripts end up in a public library where common readers and scholars alike could examine them.[14] In the late 1970s and early 1980s, Woolf's manuscripts were recovered, transcribed, and then published at a rapid rate. Feminist critics were not the only ones working with the holograph manuscripts, but a partial list of transcriptions and manuscript studies published then provides a roster of some of the most important feminist critics of Woolf in North America at the time: Grace Radin, Susan Squier, Ellen Hawkes, Madeline Moore, Brenda Silver, Louise DeSalvo, and Susan Dick. They provided the impetus for a publication process that continues today.[15] The three scrapbooks of clippings Woolf used for *Three Guineas* (housed at the University of Sussex) are now available in an online archive (Pawlowski and Neverow 2002) and have been thoroughly annotated by Black (Woolf *TG* 2001); most of the Sussex Monk's House Papers collection is on microfilm (Woolf 1985); all the Berg Woolf Collection is on microfilm (Woolf 1993); and manuscripts and versions of those manuscripts are available on CD-ROM (Hussey 1997).

In terms of its impact and usefulness, a key text of recovery in Woolf studies is Brenda Silver's *Virginia Woolf's Reading Notebooks* (1983). Not itself a transcription of Woolf's reading notes, but rather a meticulous listing and description of what exists in the major Woolf archives, Silver's text is a feminist classic. Herculean effort, patient categorizing and cross-referencing, and a concern for readers' needs went into producing this generous bibliographic and textual marvel. Since its publication in 1983, Silver's text has given every Woolf scholar easier access to Woolf's reading and her notes on that reading. In addition, her introduction to the volume ('The Uncommon Reader,' 3–31) and her description of each set of reading notes reflect careful detective work based on the information in the letters, diaries, and biographies available to her. Silver gives us a portrait of Woolf working and thinking, revealing the fruitful intersection of feminism and textual scholarship.[16]

Diane Gillespie and Elizabeth Steele, in *Julia Duckworth Stephen: Stories for Children, Essays for Adults* (1987), provide Woolf scholars with some crucial balance in their transcription of the nine stories Woolf's mother wrote for her children and the five essays she wrote for adults. Bringing Julia Stephen into the picture not just as a domestic Mrs Ramsay, but as a thinking, reading, and writing person in her own right, these manuscripts illuminate Woolf's own work and processes and show that Woolf's creativity, humour, and passion for causes stemmed from both sides of the family. In addition, Gillespie's introductory essay, 'The Elusive Julia Stephen' (1–27), thoughtfully investigates Julia Stephen's attitudes about women and feminism within her own historical and cultural context.

Although much exciting, groundbreaking work has been done, twenty-first century feminists in Woolf studies still have important scholarly work to do. Manuscript transcriptions, proof sheets and galleys in archives, substantively differing English and American first editions, and even post-publication variants reveal a revising Woolf for whom 'no text was ever finished' (Briggs 1999, 146) and create a palimpsestic text (Silver 1991b, 193–222). Given the nature of that Woolfian text, 'characterized by change, variation, difference, and [her] refusal to provide a definitive or final version' (Briggs 1999, 144), the questions become, *what* texts then do we read in classrooms and for criticism and *how* do we edit, annotate, and introduce those texts for common readers and students (Gillespie 2002, 91–113)? For Briggs, the feminist approach to Woolf's texts thus far has understandably focused on Woolf's creative processes, but it now needs to shift to the painstaking collation of impressions and editions, the sort of traditional textual criticism that provides the foundation for further bibliographical study (Briggs 1999, 148). Both she and Silver hold out hope for online hypertext editions that would allow all of Woolf's revisions to coexist with various versions of the texts,[17] but such a project must also return to the transcriptions to correct errors and provide more accurate readings of Woolf's notoriously difficult handwriting. Until all such information is readily available, textual scholars and critics will continue to find it difficult to establish reliable and accurate texts for classroom and critical use. Since the scholarly, critical, and theoretical conclusions about Woolf's thought, language, revisions, content, structure, and prose all depend upon having accurate texts, it is crucial that feminists have a hand in establishing those texts (see Chapter 6 in this volume). As the differences between the Oxford and Penguin editions of Woolf's works highlighted in 1992, it matters whether or not feminist scholarship and criticism is part of the scholarly apparatus surrounding Woolf's texts and life. Finally, because of the materials now available, future feminist criticism on Woolf's work can use an intertextuality like that demonstrated in Susan Dick's edition of *The Complete Shorter Fiction of Virginia Woolf* (1989, 1985) or in Naomi Black's edition of *Three Guineas* (2001) where Woolf's drafted, unpublished, and published works rub productive elbows with each other.

Feminist criticism's wholesale recovery of texts, drafts, and notes in the 1970s led to revisions in how women viewed the world and how academics constructed the canon. Woolf's own work could produce such startling revisions, such as the assertion in *Three Guineas* that the traditional English household, with the father at its head, looked suspiciously like a fascist dictatorship, and feminists studying Woolf's texts have produced similar revisions, asserting, for example, that the supposed failed novels, *Night and Day* and *The Years*, rest on strong feminist underpinnings (Marcus 1980, 97–122; Marcus 1977, 276–301) that an essay about aesthetics is also feminist (Daugherty 1983, 269–94), or that colour used in the novels and essays carries suffragette connotations (Goldman 1998).

Michèle Barrett's collection of Woolf's essays in *Women and Writing* (Woolf 1979) revised the negative or lukewarm attitudes about Woolf's feminism derived from Leonard Woolf, E. M. Forster, and Quentin Bell. By grouping together first, several of Woolf's essays about women and literature, and second, essays about individual women writers, Barrett made it apparent that Woolf's feminism consisted of something besides *A Room of One's Own* and *Three Guineas* and that, in fact, it permeated her work. Barrett's compilation revealed the much wider scope of Woolf's feminism and portrayed an essayist dedicated to recovering a female literary tradition. In her introduction (1–39), Barrett, herself trained in sociology, discusses Woolf's insistence that women writers be looked at in their historical context, a strategy the newest generation of feminist literary critics is using to great effect in their studies of Woolf.[18] This essay, together with her 'Towards a Virginia Woolf Criticism' in *The Sociology of Literature* (1978, 145–60), also introduced a much-needed complexity into discussions of Woolf's class attitudes and the intersection of gender and class in her work.

In the early, heady days of Woolf studies, Jane Marcus' essays on Woolf functioned as a tonic, and they continue to inspire or goad others into scholarly action. Her tireless efforts to redefine Woolf as a strong political presence, if not a socialist, were based on exciting contextual research into many of the women (such as Jane Ellen Harrison, Elizabeth Robins, Anne Thackeray Ritchie, Caroline Stephen, Julia Stephen, and Janet Case) and men (such as James Fitzjames Stephen, Oscar Browning, and Leslie Stephen) around and behind Woolf, an insistence on Woolf's radical character, and a provocative reading of texts. Marcus challenged the primarily male and family establishment on their version of Virginia Woolf; she challenged feminist critics to dig, to work, to publish; and she challenged Woolf studies to look where no one else had looked before – at dismissed novels, at obscure references, at textual strategies. Her editing of three collections of essays about Woolf (*New Feminist Essays on Virginia Woolf* [1981]; *Virginia Woolf: A Feminist Slant* [1983]; *Virginia Woolf and Bloomsbury* [1987]) contributed greatly to the explosion of feminist criticism about Woolf in the 1980s and certainly exploded the image of Woolf as apolitical, etiolated, or weak. The research methods underpinning her own essays about Woolf, collected in *Virginia Woolf and the Languages of Patriarchy* (1987) and *Art and Anger: Reading Like a Woman* (1988), led to a great widening of the sphere around Woolf and fed not only the development of new historical and cultural studies within Woolf studies, such as Wayne Chapman and Janet Manson's collection on *Women in the Milieu of Leonard and Virginia Woolf: Peace, Politics, and Education* (1998), but also studies grouping Woolf with other women writers such as Adrienne Rich and Mary Daly (Ratcliffe 1996), Doris Lessing (Saxton and Tobin 1994), Eudora Welty (Harrison 1997), Toni Morrison (Williams 2000), and Lessing, Morrison, Barbara Kingsolver, Julia Alvarez, Anne Tyler, Paule Marshall, and Gloria Naylor (Rubenstein 2001). Marcus' strong and controversial assertions about Woolf's place in the intellectual turmoil of her times pointed the way toward many other ways of seeing Woolf.

In *The Gender of Modernism* (1990), Bonnie Kime Scott brought many strands of feminist criticism together and changed the look of modernism and Woolf simultaneously. Woolf, for example, is no longer the token modernist woman; rather, the volume gives us more nearly the view of modernism *Woolf* must have had: the lively jostling, the diversity of opinions and voices, the sense of living in an exciting time with nothing at all settled, including her own reputation. Widely influential, Scott's introduction (1–18), her 'tangled mesh of modernists' (10), her inclusion of Eliot, Joyce, Lawrence, MacDiarmid, and Pound in the midst of twenty-one female modernists, and her gathering together of some of the finest feminist literary critics between the covers of one book turns the anxious male modernists, the Pound era, and the reign of Eliot on their heads. Not only doing the work of recovery, but the startling work of revision, this brilliant book is filled to the brim with rarely anthologized works by American and English female moderns, statements and reviews and letters by the male moderns about the female moderns, and correspondence, reviews, and journal entries by male and female moderns alike, all of which testify to the rich dialogue about gender, literature, and modernism occurring during the period. As a result, Woolf takes her place alongside not only Dorothy Richardson and Katherine Mansfield, but also Willa Cather, Nancy Cunard, H. D., Jessie Redmon Fauset, Zora Neale Hurston, May Sinclair, Rose Macaulay, Gertrude Stein, and Rebecca West, among others. (Scott's recent book, *Gender in Modernism: New Geographies, Complex Intersections* (2007), continues this important work, with the collected essays focusing on genres and media not covered in the earlier work.) Most usefully for the newest generation of feminist critics, however, the volume serves as a warning, making crystal clear how easily those who write literary history can erase women writers from the accounts: even active women writers, even those writers published, reviewed, and seen as the creators of a new movement in literature.[19] Feminist critics in this century must not only continue to rewrite literary history so that it includes lost voices from the past, but must also ensure that today's cacophony of women's voices is not lost, written off, or left out.

Acutely aware of societal forces that silence women as they aim to revise the prevailing patriarchal paradigm, feminist critics have investigated not only Woolf's revision of women's portrayals and of literary history, but her version of feminism, her negotiation of a male literary culture, and her writing and revising processes. Close work on the manuscripts available, either in archives or transcriptions, led feminist critics to ask general questions about the nature of the feminist text and specific questions about Woolf's narrative practice (Silver 1991b, 193–222). Their work has made it almost a feminist commonplace to say that Woolf's more overt articulation of her political thought, feminist opinion, critique, and/or anger was lost during the revision process (DeSalvo 1980; Radin 1981), although later studies note that Woolf's revision does not always move towards suppression (Friedman 1992, 101–25; Rosenbaum 1992, xiii–xlii; Daugherty 1997, 159–75). A similar dialogue has taken place about the lesbian content of Woolf's work (Barrett and Cramer 1997) (see Chapter 9 in this volume).

border crossings

Have no screens, for screens are made out of our own integument [. . .]. The screen making habit, though, is so universal, that probably it preserves our sanity. If we had not this device for shutting people off from our sympathies, we might, perhaps, dissolve utterly. Separateness would be impossible. But the screens are in the excess; not the sympathy.

Diary 3, 104

Although she understood their necessity, Virginia Woolf continually chafed at boundaries and borders; for her, the lines defining gender, nation, genre, race, and class were in the excess. Dissolving them entirely might be impossible or fatal, but she habitually crossed or blurred them. Feminist criticism, in its fight against patriarchal society's hierarchies, divisions, and polarities, reveals the same impulse, crossing into and using different disciplines, paradigms, and perspectives (Tyson 1999, 92–5).

Gillian Beer's essays on Woolf, published in the late 1970s and throughout the 1980s and collected in *Virginia Woolf: The Common Ground* (1996), situate Woolf 'in the midst of the concerns of her contemporaries at large, rather than sequestered within Bloomsbury' (3). This strategy removes Woolf from a Bloomsbury sometimes viciously portrayed and attacked in England and insists that Woolf was a tough-minded intellectual engaged with the important ideas of her time. Beer's move also frees Woolf from the solely aesthetic realm and shows her crossing over into history, philosophy, and science. Beer argues for Woolf's connections to Darwin, Hume, and Ruskin, suggesting precursors of both genders can function as mothers and contemporaries in the unconscious (100). She also shows the influence of the new physics and Einstein's theories on *The Waves* through Woolf's reading of James Jeans and

Arthur Eddington. In Beer's essays, Woolf is a participant, not an observer, involved in a much wider world than the Leavises and their disciples give her credit for, and she is central to modernism, an assertion that continues to be controversial in the UK.

Beer's work also delineates Woolf's links to the Victorians and her need to resist them, whereas Patricia Waugh and Pamela Caughie cross over into post-structuralism and deconstruction to reveal Woolf's links to the postmoderns. In 'From Modernist Textuality to Feminist Sexuality; Or Why I'm No Longer A-Freud of Virginia Woolf' (1989, 88–125), Waugh explores the historical moment in which postmodernism deconstructed the subject at the same time feminism radicalized it. Waugh claims that feminism 'produced an alternative conception of the subject as constructed through *relationship*, rather than postmodernism/post-structuralism's anti-humanist *rejection* of the subject' (113). Grounding her argument in theories of women's different psychic development, she argues that Woolf, particularly in *Mrs Dalloway* and *To the Lighthouse*, communicates a 'vision of subjectivity which, though opposed to the unified, "imperial" ego, would involve a recognition of both the self's relational connection to others and its separateness and autonomy' (121). Using insights from Lacan and other postmodernists but also arguing with them, Waugh moves away from modernism's emphasis on aesthetics and impersonality, yet refuses to buy postmodernism's antihumanism, either. She portrays Woolf as wending her own way, conceiving of women and of the subject in ways that fit neither the liberal nor the postmodernist definitions of the self.

Pamela Caughie's *Virginia Woolf & Postmodernism: Literature in Quest & Question of Itself* (1991), on the other hand, wants to 'resist the urge' to either polarize or conflate feminism and postmodernism. For her, Woolf's formal experiments are 'material practices' that 'enable her to test out various political positions' (Caughie 1991, 25). Trying to resist binary oppositions herself, Caughie produces numerous provocative readings, 'taking issue' with many prominent feminist Woolf critics and reading Woolf from within postmodern assumptions about art. As a result, the Woolf who emerges from her pages is a fully cognizant artist whose 'contradictions' are themselves radical experiments, a Woolf whose narrative project is 'both more and less radical than we have thought' (207). Caughie challenges both feminists and postmodernists to see their criticism (and views of Woolf) as 'still largely based on modernist assumptions and values' (207), on a need to 'get it right', and Caughie challenges *herself* to avoid predicating her criticism on a demand to get it right, that is, postmodern. Refusing to define postmodernism, Caughie yet performs a postmodern reading, and it *is* a performance; suspended, teetering on a tightrope, she will not tip her balancing pole down on one side or the other of Woolf's contradictions. The result is a combative yet playful feminist discourse, a radically experimental Woolf, a brilliant reading of *Flush*, and an exciting yet exhausting reading experience (see Chapter 7 in this volume).

Patricia Laurence's *The Reading of Silence: Virginia Woolf in the English Tradition* (1991) also mirrors Woolf's refusal to turn oppositions into hierarchies and tries to capture in her own prose the oscillating patterns and wholeness that readers experience when reading Woolf, but the result feels more like a fluid dance than a suspended tension. Laurence defines her view as poststructuralist, emerging from 'structuralism, associated with the disciplines of linguistics and anthropology; deconstruction, springing from a philosophical perspective; feminism, connecting with a historical sense of women; and psychoanalysis, revealing aspects of the mind hitherto ignored' (Laurence 1991, 5), and as she traces Woolf's narrative patterns of language and silence, she models a way through the feminist Scylla and Charybdis of cultural and essentialist criticism. For Laurence, Woolf 'both uses and questions language in creating a narrative space for silence' (7), and she shows that within the tradition of English fiction, Woolf's valuing of women's silence 'undermines not only patriarchal but also Western notions of talk and silence' (8). When Laurence says 'it is now the moment in Woolf criticism for viewing her seeming oppositions as part of a pattern' (218), she agrees with Caughie, but her view of criticism as forming a pattern, a 'dancing rhythm' 'multiplying the forces at work in the field of interpretation' rather than dislodging some views and replacing them with others (10–11), succeeds in creating a participatory space for readers of various critical persuasions and thus a more inclusive kind of feminist discourse.

In *Virginia Woolf Icon* (1999), Brenda Silver crosses over into popular culture and reception studies as she collects and analyzes hundreds of Virginia Woolf 'sightings' in the popular and intellectual media. Focusing on Woolf as a lightning rod for reactions to feminism in the larger culture, Silver traces the uses and abuses to which Woolf, her work, and her feminism have been put. 'Virginia Woolf would become a primary site for the waging of a large number of cultural battles' (Silver 1999, 117), Silver asserts, but she also cannot be contained within those battles, as her epilogue, 'Virginia Woolf Episodes', so cleverly illustrates (272–83). This passionately argued and often funny book illustrates the power and delight that stem from crossing borders. Resisting the disciplinary policing Michèle Barrett exposes (1999, 5–7, 28–32), the intellectual media's definitions, and the barriers erected between popular, intellectual, and academic, Silver (and feminist criticism at its best) follows Woolf's lead, frustrating binaries by writing across them. Barrett captures feminist criticism's admiration for these strategies when she writes, 'May [Woolf] continue to confound, through the complex character of her writing, our attempts at […] classifications' (204).

Feminist critics have also examined Woolf's work for evidence of feminist narrative strategies on the linguistic level (what *is* a female sentence?) or on the more structural level suggested by French theorists Hélène Cixous, Luce Irigaray, and Julia Kristeva (what might an *écriture feminine* be?). As Clare Hanson puts it, 'how is the feminine to be written in our culture?' (Hanson 1994, 14). Makiko Minow-Pinkney, in *Virginia Woolf and the Problem of the*

Subject: Feminine Writing in the Major Novels (1987), illustrates and clarifies this feminist crossing into linguistic, poststructuralist, and psychoanalytic theory, arguing that Woolf writes the feminine in our culture. For her, Woolf's radical androgyny 'has an affinity [...] with Kristeva's theory of poetic language' (Minow-Pinkney 1987, 23), and she argues that Woolf's experimental writing practice links aesthetic innovation and feminist conviction, oscillates between the symbolic and the semiotic, and thus attains the 'impossible dialectic' Kristeva calls for. According to Minow-Pinkney, then, *The Waves* is 'the high point of [Woolf's] achievement in terms of the dialectic of symbolic and semiotic, and of the convergence of modernism and feminism' (187) (see Chapter 3 in this volume).

Determined to portray Woolf as a brilliant, capable, political, real person, feminist critics have used whatever tools come to hand. At the same time, debate has occurred between those who worry that feminism cannot raid patriarchal theories (such as those of Marx, Freud, Lacan) without being co-opted and those who believe feminism can transform those theories – Woolf's *Three Guineas* question once again. R. B. Kershner puts it this way: as 'bridges between European and Anglo-American feminist literary discourse' were built, one could argue that the discourse 'lost its original focus and political impetus' (Kershner 1997, 98). Tension has also existed between identity politics and poststructuralist theories, between difference and free play, between materialist and poststructuralist feminisms, between activism and theory, between the old hegemony of humanism and the new hegemony of antihumanism, all of which exacerbated border disputes between generations and nations. But the crossings have continued nonetheless. Miriam L. Wallace notes that in *The Waves*, Woolf anticipated current border crossings and the concerns about them: 'The tensions between the abstracting power of poststructuralist and antifoundationalist accounts and the still-necessary attention to materialist and cultural approaches to women's differences – economic and experiential – are evoked before their time through Woolf's most stylized novel' (Wallace 2000, 317); Rachel Bowlby wittily summarizes transatlantic crossings in *Still Crazy After All These Years* (1992, 103–16, 131–56); and Susan Stanford Friedman, surveying the larger global movement into cultural geographies and hybridity, calls for negotiation and multidirectional strategies in *Mappings: Feminism and the Cultural Geographies of Encounter* (1998).

material circumstances

But no; with a few exceptions [...] literature does its best to maintain that its concern is with the mind; that the body is a sheet of plain glass through which the soul looks straight and clear, and, save for one or two passions such as desire and greed, is null, and negligible and non-existent. On the contrary, the very opposite is true. All day, all night the body intervenes [...].

On Being Ill, 4

Feminist criticism's focus on the female body has also meant a focus on sexuality, sexual mores and restrictions and conventions, the nature of difference, sexual orientation, violence against women, gender as performance, and so forth. Woolf believed she had managed to kill the Angel in the House, but confessed in 'Professions for Women' that 'telling the truth about my own experiences as body, I do not think I solved' (*CE2* 288);[20] as Black has noted, however, feminists in Woolf's time were not concerned with issues of sexuality the way contemporary feminists are (Black 2001, xlii–xliii). In Woolf studies, feminist approaches have questioned the asexual or frigid labels often pinned on Woolf and illuminated the lesbian attachments in her life and the coded sexual desire in her work (see Chapter 9 in this volume). But Karen Kaivola's 'Virginia Woolf, Vita Sackville-West, and the Question of Sexual Identity' (1998, 18–40) also questions the attempt to pin any sexual label on Woolf, noting that she continues to pose 'a challenge to the way we think about female sexuality today' (Kaivola 1998, 38).

Louise DeSalvo's groundbreaking study, *Virginia Woolf: The Impact of Childhood Sexual Abuse on Her Life and Work* (1989), focuses on the Stephen family and its patriarchal dynamics, examines evidence about all family members, including several on the family tree, and uses contemporary knowledge about abuse to argue that Woolf suffered sexual abuse at the hands of her half-brothers and that this abuse, combined with the pernicious patriarchal atmosphere of the household, had a profound impact on her sexuality, her mental state, and her writing. Criticized for its use of evidence, its emphasis on the psychological, and its methodology, the basic premises of DeSalvo's controversial book remain persuasive because they make sense of Woolf's statements and behaviour.[21] This text also contributed to the feminist portrayal of Woolf as a heroic woman who, far from being detached from struggle, constructed a productive writing life in the face of trauma.

The focus on the body has also led to more attention to the physical in general, the material circumstances of a woman's life, what Woolf called one's room and the need to furnish it – what about food, clothes, money, surroundings?[22] what about the press of the day-to-day, the physical and the local, the products produced and handled, the people met, conversed with, and loved? what about the physical nature of the writing life? Although not overtly feminist, Alex Zwerdling's *Virginia Woolf and the Real World* (1986) supported feminist assertions about Woolf's engagement in the practical and provided feminist critics with a mass of materialist detail, and the more overtly feminist Lee biography (1996) brought such detail out of the academy and into the mainstream.

An excellent example of using feminist criticism to 'read' the physical world and Woolf's place in it, Susan Squier's *Virginia Woolf and London: The Sexual Politics of the City* (1985) describes Woolf's early ambivalent feelings about London and her drive to revise and reshape the city for her own purposes. Using several lesser-studied novels, *Night and Day*, *Flush*, and *The Years* along with *Mrs Dalloway*, and productively weaving in commentary about Woolf's non-fiction, particularly her six essays about London (five of which have been gathered together in *The London Scene*), Squier illustrates how the city allows Woolf to '[link] personal history to culture and [yoke] both to the literary tradition' and thus give both her creative imagination and political analysis a 'place' (Squier 1985, 12). Woolf's London is alive in this study, and Squier carefully traces Woolf's changing attitudes towards it. For Squier, Woolf's maturing vision of the urban landscape contributes to her development of a critique of masculine power and a vision of female energy. The bombing of the city in the Second World War thus destroyed not only the actual city and her home, but also 'the potent image of London that had been central to her writing' (188).

Following Squier's lead but going in a different direction, Rachel Bowlby, in 'Walking, Women and Writing' (1997, 1–33), examines Woolf as a walker, a flâneuse who transgresses, appropriates for herself the male 'place' in the street, and operates out in the open, in public space. Bowlby's 'bit of a ramble' shows how Woolf's use of odd trios disturbs the 'securely dual vision of the difference between the sexes' (3) and thus exposes the masculine norm (30). Bowlby has great fun with language, with Plato's *Symposium* and Freud's 'mis-remembering' of Aristophanes' story, and with Woolf's revision of the *flâneur* and *passante* in Baudelaire and Proust as she asks serious questions about conceptions of women's writing 'as a question of progress' or 'a question of transgressiveness' (30). Using Peter's pursuit of the young woman in *Mrs Dalloway*, the narrator's walks in *A Room of One's Own*, and 'Street Haunting', Bowlby shows how Woolf's placing of herself in the street, as street walker, upsets the representation of woman, challenges the representation of writer, and complicates the representation of woman writer. There may be 'no simple way forward' for the woman writer, Bowlby suggests, but neither is there 'an impasse' (30).[23]

In '"These Emotions of the Body": Intercorporeal Narrative in *To the Lighthouse*' (1994), Laura Doyle argues that Woolf's narrative, 'far from maintaining the prudery or ethereality' she is identified with, actually 'sensualizes metaphysical questions – of death and presence, speech and silence, time and space' (Doyle 1994, 43). Doyle's exciting approach, based on inserting Maurice Merleau-Ponty's work into the postmodern critique of modernism (43–9), illustrates how Woolf intersects with Merleau-Ponty's insights and places them within the larger contexts of race and culture. Taking us through several of Woolf's doublings and narrative turns, such as from Mrs Ramsay's sexualized relationship to the physical world (illustrated in her response to the lighthouse beam's rhythm) to the narrator's irony about the patriarchy's use of such heterosexualized intercorporeality, Doyle shows how Woolf's narrative 'extends the intercorporeality of persons and things beyond the realm and the life of the mother' and thus 'puts at risk the mother-burdening metaphysics of patriarchy' (68). By dematernalizing the ecstatic,

Woolf uses the 'emotions of the body' (*TTL* 241) to 'turn inside out' the 'body-transcending core of traditional Western philosophy and narrative' (42). Doyle's own balance and her portrayal of Woolf's walking a fine line and mingling 'radical critique with recovery of what is submerged' (Doyle 1994b, 155) result in a revolutionary Woolf.[24]

political, historical, and cultural contexts

It suggests that the public and the private worlds are inseparably connected; that the tyrannies and servilities of the one are the tyrannies and servilities of the other. But the human figure even in a photograph suggests other and more complex emotions. It suggests that we cannot dissociate ourselves from that figure but are ourselves that figure. It suggests that we are not passive spectators doomed to unresisting obedience but by our thoughts and actions can ourselves change that figure.

Three Guineas, 364–5

Feminist criticism generally implies or overtly calls for change and transformation; its central impulse, the movement towards autonomy (Black 1989, 9), underlies its analysis and its activism. Woolf saw that in the patriarchy, war is judged important and drawing rooms are judged trivial (*AROO* 116), that the private and the public, the personal and the political are 'inseparably connected' (*TG* 364), that change probably needs to start at the level of the individual and the family and move outward. Though many judged these perceptions apolitical or misguided at the time, Woolf deeply understood how important political, historical, and cultural contexts are to the struggle for transformation.

Berenice A. Carroll's '"To Crush Him in Our Own Country": The Political Thought of Virginia Woolf' (1977, 99–132) was the first systematic gathering of evidence for Woolf as a political thinker, and its insights about Woolf's opinions and methods still have influence (Black 1983, 180; 2001, liv). Noting that Leonard Woolf misunderstands both Woolf *and* Aristotle in his comment about his wife's politics (L. Woolf 1967, 27), Carroll carefully distinguishes between Woolf's boredom with politics as usual (politicians, committees, and organized parties) and her interest in the politics underlying the social order (expressed in her avid reading of newspapers, for example) (Carroll 1977, 101–5). She illuminates Woolf's strategies of derision and concealment, places struggle at the cornerstone of Woolf's political philosophy, tackles Woolf's class bias, and lays out Woolf's political programme, a combination of some standard reform with alternative modes of struggle: truth-telling, living differently, and performing the duties of an outsider. Carroll's article called for and set in motion a still ongoing exploration of the 'actual history and effect of *Three Guineas*' (131), but in the meantime, she showed how Woolf used her weapons, pen and paper, 'to name the enemy, to expose the collaborators, to create new models of resistance to oppression' in all her work (127).[25]

Naomi Black's research into Woolf's feminism includes a careful examination of the early to mid-century feminist organizations in England, the differences among those organizations, and Woolf's connections to and participation in those organizations. Black's 'Virginia Woolf and the Women's Movement' (1983), *Social Feminism* (1989), and the clear introduction to the Shakespeare Head Press edition of *Three Guineas* that summarizes her own and others' research into this now-classic text's composition, context, and reception (2001, xiii–lxxv) serve to ground Woolf in the lived feminism of her time. Her *Virginia Woolf as Feminist* (2003) argues that Woolf's changing representation of feminism in publications from 1920 to 1940 parallels her involvement in the contemporary women's movement, that the illustrations and footnotes of *Three Guineas* subvert male scholarship, and that Woolf's feminism is more relevant than ever. As Black comments in 'Virginia Woolf and the Women's Movement', 'to want to end war is not to be apolitical' (Black 1983, 6).

Given Woolf's pacifist stance, it is not surprising that feminist studies of Woolf as a political thinker committed to change have coalesced around the topic of war in books such as *Virginia Woolf and War: Fiction, Reality, and Myth* (Hussey 1991) and *Virginia Woolf and the Great War* (Levenback 1999). Merry Pawlowski's collection, *Virginia Woolf and Fascism* (2001), puts Woolf's vision of the 'inextricable links between power and gender and her awareness of the roles of fascism and patriarchy in the forging of those links' (Pawlowski 2001, 4) into a wider European framework with essays on Italian fascism and on German women writers.[26]

Feminist approaches put Woolf into other contexts as well – historical, social, imperialist, philosophical, artistic, class, racial/ethnic, educational – and give us a sense of the forces swirling in and around her. In doing so, they function in the ways Woolf's criticism functioned. That is, they generate interest in the writer, the work, and the times, asking the reader to see anew. For example, Kate Flint's 'Virginia Woolf and the Great Strike' (1986, 319–34) puts the writing of 'Time Passes' into the context of the 1926 General Strike and Woolf's conflicted reactions to it. In *Virginia Woolf, the Intellectual, and the Public Sphere* (2003), Melba Cuddy-Keane describes a 'pedagogical Woolf' within a fascinating context of public debates about books, reading, and education, high culture, and democracy (Cuddy-Keane 2003, 1–5).

Jane Goldman's *The Feminist Aesthetics of Virginia Woolf: Modernism, Post-Impressionism and the Politics of the Visual* (1998) uses a deconstructive strategy, not a deconstructive reading, to '[pay] attention to context as much as textuality' (Goldman 1998, 16) and to use feminism to 'enlighten' the Enlightenment (20–1). Working as many other feminist critics have, to suggest the intimate interrelation in Woolf between what's identified as most abstract, aestheticized, and remote and what's most historically aware, materialist, and feminist, she also points feminist criticism in new directions. Goldman's close and creative readings of two years (1927 and 1910), two writings about the solar eclipse, two movements (post-Impressionism and suffrage), and two novels (*To the Lighthouse* and *The Waves*) come together in a claim that Woolf uses colour, particularly the colours of suffrage banners, to produce a feminist aesthetics.

Anna Snaith's *Virginia Woolf: Public and Private Negotiations* (2000a) carefully charts how notions of the public and the private intersected in Woolf's life and work at the same time they were being discussed and debated within the women's movement. Densely argued yet readable, anchored in the textual yet informed by theory, Snaith investigates letters written to Woolf (see also Snaith 'Wide Circles' 2000, 1–82), Woolf's literal Bloomsbury surroundings, and Woolf's use of genres and narrative strategies ('Holes mark the resistance to wholes' [148]) to reveal a Woolf committed to dialogue and heterogeneity. Snaith's claims about Woolf's engagement with working-class women ('speaking to, if not for' them [129]) and Woolf's refusal of unity as a way to resist fascism have a quiet authority because grounded in so much telling contextual and textual detail. Ultimately not wanting to speak *for* Woolf, Snaith produces an exciting work in which Woolf's desire to remain unfixed has public consequences.

In *Virginia Woolf and the Bloomsbury Avant-Garde: War, Civilization, Modernity* (2005), Christine Froula puts Woolf's work, thought and milieu into an even wider context: modernism's Enlightenment project, the shaping of civilization itself. Recalling the Enlightenment's 'self-critical and emancipatory force' and pointing out its inherently 'unfinished and unfinishable struggle for human (including economic) rights, democratic self-governance, world community, and peace' (Froula 2005, xii), Froula brings alive Bloomsbury's attempts to redefine (not save) civilization and Woolf's attempts to '[dismantle] the opposition between women and civilization that Marlow and Freud seek to naturalize' (27). Froula's intellectually rich, deeply feminist, and emotionally bracing readings of Woolf's major works reclaim Bloomsbury for modernism, Woolf for intellectual history, and the Enlightenment for feminism, and her tracking of Woolf's lifelong work 'to forge a public voice' (323) stirs the reader to re-see current battles, re-imagine civilization, and re-act. Meticulously researched, carefully argued, and clearly written, this study of Woolf, ranging from close examinations of single words to wide uses of philosophy and history, is brilliant and moving. Froula has embodied her underlying argument, that Woolf's work continues to inspire 'public thinking and fighting' (324), in a work of literary criticism that attempts no less.

self-awareness

Because the baker calls and we pay our bills with cheques, and our clothes are washed for us and we do not know the liver from the lights we are condemned to remain forever shut up in the confines of the middle classes [...].

Introductory Letter, Life as We Have Known It, xxviii

Virginia Woolf, as Hermione Lee points out, 'was deeply preoccupied with the very categories and demarcations which bias[ed] and inhibit[ed] her' (Lee 1995, 144–5). As Woolf despairingly wondered whether she could ever step outside herself enough to either see herself clearly or to connect with those who were different from her, she tried to do so. Feminist criticism has also tried to gain some distance from itself by examining its own strategies. Thus, for example, Jane Flax suggests that feminist theories should be like postmodernism and 'encourage us to tolerate ambivalence, ambiguity, and multiplicity as well as to expose the roots of our need for imposing order and structure' (quoted in Caughie 1991, 142). Self-conscious, desirous of avoiding the flaws of that which it critiques, and discovering how difficult that is, feminist criticism's most severe critics are often themselves feminist.

Attempting to open up Woolf studies to French feminist theory and French feminist theory to Woolf and asking for readings outside the 'allowable', Bette London's 'Guerilla in Petticoats or Sans-Culotte? Virginia Woolf and the Future of Feminist Criticism' (1991) exposes flaws she sees in the Woolf criticism of Jane Marcus, the feminist genealogies of Sandra Gilbert and Susan Gubar, and ultimately her own commentary. Placing Woolf studies in 1991 at an 'intersection of competing interests' between a 'contested definition of feminism' and a pressure to institutionalize feminisms (London 1991, 13), London interrogates Marcus' 'author-centered criticism', her revolutionary rhetoric, her 'simple reversal within the terms of the dominant discourse, leaving intact its underlying structures of thought, politics, and meaning' (13–15). For London, the danger of Marcus' portrayals of Woolf lies in the ease with which the critical establishment can dismiss them. She wants feminism to be 'more self-conscious about the terms of its participation' in resisting the patriarchy (20) and to open itself up to the radical questions posed by French theorists. Asking feminist critics in Woolf studies to disentangle the project of feminism from 'Woolf's practice and example' (26), London cannot resist using the words about looking-glasses from A Room of One's Own to critique the remaking of Woolf into the mother of feminist literary criticism (20). More self-consciously, she uses a strategic reading of Woolf's 'Time Passes' to demonstrate how Woolf's narrative practices 'dislocate and displace any single system of narrative control' (25) and thus encourage 'the decentering of feminism's established positions' (24). Although this complex essay begins, near its end, to question its own constructions, desires, and flaws, it cannot finally abandon hierarchical discourse or institutional pressures either.[27]

London feared that 'the nature of Woolf's feminine and feminist identity' was in danger of being fixed (21). But feminist critics were already taking up some of the challenges identified in her essay. For example, in 'Virginia Woolf on the Outside Looking Down: Reflections on the Class of Women' (1992, 61–79), Mary M. Childers asks feminist critics in Woolf studies to be willing to 'hear the voice of the relatively privileged woman crack under the pressure of class position' (62), particularly since Woolf's limits are ones 'we have not yet surpassed' (63). In Childers' reading of the introductory letter to *Life As We Have Known It* and *Three Guineas*, whenever Woolf's commitment to aesthetics conflicts with her commitment to politics and reform, beauty wins over truth. For Childers, however, Woolf was often 'more daring in confronting the way her class inflected her feminism' than are contemporary feminist critics, who should do more 'to confront the problem that she poses' (78). In '"Robbed of Meaning": The Work at the Center of *To the Lighthouse*' (1992, 217–34), Mary Lou Emery challenges feminist critics in Woolf studies to acknowledge the ways in which Woolf's novel both 'sets into motion a critique of English colonialist patriarchy that simultaneously repeats colonialist assumptions' *and* represents, through inclusion and suppression, 'the "mumblings" of a counter-discourse' (218). In Emery's reading, Mrs McNab first occupies a central place in the novel but then is robbed of meaning so that Lily can complete her painting (231). Suggesting that Woolf's narrative strategies in her novel should be read dialogically with the discourses of sexology, Emery asks feminist critics to examine 'feminist processes of self-representation and exclusion in historically specific ways' and thus think about the negotiations, self-representations, and exclusions being used now (233).[28]

going beyond

As for her coming without that preparation, without that effort on our part, without that determination that when she is born again she shall find it possible to live and write her poetry, that we cannot expect, for that would be impossible. But I maintain that she would come if we worked for her, and that so to work, even in poverty and obscurity, is worth while.

A Room of One's Own, 149

Addressing her brother Thoby in 1903, Virginia Stephen wrote 'Theres [sic] nothing like talk as an educator I'm sure' (*L1* 77). Conversation, dialogue, and attempts to incorporate conversation and dialogue *within* form Woolf's feminist practice.[29] Current feminist criticism has also begun to return to something more dialogic. Friedman, for example, notes the dangers of 'perpetual problematization' and 'the constant undermining of feminism's discourse' (Friedman 1998, 211–17) and calls for 'creative negotiation' between visions of narrative as political act and narrative as totalizing (227). As problematic and critiqued as they have been, then, Woolf's choices still have value for us. She understood what we are perhaps just beginning to see (or re-see), that criticism as a conversation rather than as a battle invites writers, students, and readers of all kinds to join in. She yearned for 'an inclusive, dialogic mix of voices' able to both 'express their differences without violence' and 'affirm their common bonds' (Cuddy-Keane 2003, 196). As we struggle to include many perspectives in our own criticism, we may discover again that her choices are not, in fact, a retreat, but a conscious attempt to include rather than exclude. Her challenge to us remains – how to refashion academic rhetoric so that it does not replicate patriarchal structures and results.

Jane Lilienfeld's *Reading Alcoholisms: Theorizing Character and Narrative in Selected Novels of Thomas Hardy, James Joyce, and Virginia Woolf* (1999) includes many of the features covered in this chapter – it recovers information from archives and revises our views of famous texts; it crosses borders, working to combine two very different discourses (feminist literary criticism and recovery work); it enriches the historical and cultural knowledge of the authors and their families; it stays on the lookout for ways it might be practicing exclusionary tactics – but it also models the view of feminist work as sharing, passing along, conversing. Not only is Lilienfeld frequently cited by others as having shared an insight, a reading, or an unpublished paper, but a statement from the *To the Lighthouse* chapter in her book is typical: 'These new inter-pretations of *To the Lighthouse* are, like my other readings, meant to reveal hitherto unremarked aspects of the novel, not to displace other arguments' (Lilienfeld 1999, 235). Her deep respect for other critics, other theories, and other systems of thought and her deep appreciation for the work of authors and critics are communicated through her tone and through her attempt to elaborate rather than supplant.

Bonnie Kime Scott uses a similar strategy in *Refiguring Modernism* (1995). In her first volume, Scott continues revising modernism, shifting our gaze from the men of 1914 (Pound, Lewis, Eliot, Joyce, Lawrence, and Forster) to the women of 1928 (Woolf, West, and Barnes). She writes, 'Rather than offering the next in a long series of intergenerational renunciations of feminist precursors, I am pursuing a strategy of strategic attachment' (Scott 1995, xxxii). Similar to Woolf in her uses of metaphor, she employs webs as a way to enlarge and change our sense of Woolf, modernism, and previous feminist criticism. Using as an example Alice Walker's ability to register differences with and yet connect to Woolf, Scott writes, 'The existing scholarship on modernist women writers does convince me that the negotiation of connections, of shared tropes and ontogenies, is a historically and formally varied, fluid, but abiding strategy' (xxxvi).

As the titles of Friedman's first three chapters in *Mappings* (1998) suggest, feminist critics are struggling to move 'beyond' some of the impasses we have created or found ourselves in. Without forgetting lessons learned from an emphasis on gender and then on difference, feminist critics are attempting to move through and across intergenerational conflict (Hogeland 2001), identity politics (Schor and Weed 1994), and national borders (Friedman 1998) and move toward and into fluid and transitory coalitions (Bauer and Wald 2000), frequent shifts 'between the necessarily local and the theoretically general'

(Allen and Howard 2000, 8), broader audiences (Cuddy-Keane 2003, 195), and even a kind of universalism, 'though in such a way as to radically redefine "universalism" itself' (Kavka 2001, xx).

conclusion

Moreover, if you consider any great figure of the past, like Sappho, like the Lady Murasaki, like Emily Brontë, you will find that she is an inheritor as well as an originator.

A Room of One's Own, 143

Amnesia, not lack of history, is feminism's worst enemy today.

Offen 2000, 17

Before Virginia Woolf's death, unable to read or write, fearing her audience was gone, she was trying to work on a third *Common Reader*, her memoirs, and some short stories. To our sorrow, she left those projects unfinished. But such an ending was typical of her: she never wanted to have the last word, so the endings of both *A Room of One's Own* and *Three Guineas* challenge the women and feminist critics of the future to tackle the work left undone by the women and feminist critics of the past. Feminism's project, its very definition, continues to evolve as its locations and commentators change. Both its origins and its recent history resist closure, defer coming to a conclusion, and insist not all the evidence is in. In the previous pages, I have hinted at where I think feminist approaches in Woolf studies may be headed, and I have occasionally suggested projects feminist critics might undertake. But Eleanor Pargiter's question near the conclusion of *The Years* (1937) is the more appropriate 'end': '"And now?" she asked [...]' (413).

notes

1. Both Laura Marcus (2000, 209–44) and Brenda Silver (1999) illuminate the ways in which the fortunes of feminist criticism and Woolf are intertwined.
2. See, for example, Diane Elam and Robyn Wiegman who choose the title of their book, *Feminism Beside Itself* 'to highlight how feminism [has] become increasingly anxious about itself' (1995, 2) and Sneja Gunew and Anna Yeatman who take over ten pages to canvass 'all the dangers inherent in the politics of difference as commonly articulated' and then ask, 'what are the possibilities for producing non-exclusive cultural and gendered representations?' (1993, xxiii).
3. This bias explains, for example, the perhaps conspicuous absence of Elaine Showalter's *A Literature of Their Own* (1977) and Toril Moi's *Sexual/Textual Politics: Feminist Literary Theory* (1985) from my discussion. Neither claims to be a Woolf scholar, yet Showalter, in a book about British women novelists, used Quentin Bell's biography to overdetermine a reading of Woolf's non-fiction *Room* and its supposed retreat (thus, in effect, 'agreeing with earlier critics such as the Leavises on Woolf' [Scott 1995, 260]) and then Moi used Showalter to represent all of Anglo-American

feminist scholarship about Woolf. It should be noted, too, that Showalter did not mean her title to be a reference to Woolf, but to a phrase taken from John Stuart Mill, 'whom I quote on the first page in the third sentence of the book: "If women lived in a different country from men, and had never read any of their writings, they would have a literature of their own"' (1999, xiv).

4. Susan Stanford Friedman provides a useful distinction in *Mappings* (1998) when she defines feminism as 'based on two shared principles: (1) the oppression of women and (2) commitment to social change' but then notes that the 'analysis of the origins and nature of oppression differs widely; so does the theory on the nature of and strategies for change' (243).

5. See my description of Leslie Stephen's library (1999a, 10–17) and Margaret Ezell's criticism of Woolf's 'history' (1990).

6. Eileen Barrett, email message to author, 21 April 2003. To note only one hugely influential spin-off, see Sandra Gilbert and Susan Gubar's *The Madwoman in the Attic* (1979).

7. An interesting study could grow out of tracing the differences, if any, between how writers and how critics respond to and use *A Room of One's Own*.

8. Isota Tucker Epes' recollection of reading it in London after a tour of Germany in 1938 captures a contemporary American reaction not coloured by the masculine Woolf establishment (1994, 19–24). For some sense of that establishment reaction, see Leonard Woolf, who says 'Virginia was the least political animal that has lived since Aristotle', calls *Three Guineas* a political pamphlet, and then does not discuss it in his long 'Downhill to Hitler' chapter (1967, 27, 119–254); Bell, who cites Maynard Keynes' 'angry and contemptuous' reaction (1972, Vol. 2, 205); Nicolson, who calls Woolf's argument 'neither sober nor rational' (1979 [Woolf] L5, xvii); and Forster, who believes feminism hurt Woolf's work and made *Three Guineas* 'cantankerous', but at least realizes that young women should be the ones to judge (1951, 1972, 249–50).

9. Carolyn Allen and Judith A. Howard note that the 1970s made the study of women 'a serious scholarly endeavor', the 1980s 'complicated ideas of what constitutes "women", "race", and "gender"', and the 1990s 'tried to understand more completely those complications in specifying [...] "we"' (2000, 7).

10. For other overviews of the multiple Virginia Woolfs, see Laura Marcus (2000, 209–44), Brenda Silver (1999), Jane Goldman (1997, 86–147), Clare Hanson (1994, 1–27), and John Mepham (1992, 58–86). Rachel Bowlby (1992, 103–16; 131–56), Jane Marcus (1994, 11–14; 1996, 17–23), Julia Briggs (1994, vii–xxxiii), and Susan Stanford Friedman (1998, 107–31) untangle national perspectives and transnational exchanges within feminism in general and within Woolf studies in particular. Mark Hussey's *Virginia Woolf A to Z* (1995) is a readable treasure trove of information about the critical reception of Woolf's work.

11. Marder's bibliography is instructive on what was available in the mid-1960s. On feminism, he lists Simone de Beauvoir, Vera Brittain, Ray Strachey, Caroline Norton's *English Laws for Women in the 19ᵗʰ Century*, Mary Wollstonecraft, John Stuart Mill, Millicent Fawcett, *The Emancipation of English Women*, W. Lyon Blease, and *The Woman Question*, ed. T. R. Smith.

Two much earlier feminist readings of Woolf should also be noted here, Winifred Holtby's *Virginia Woolf: A Critical Memoir* (1932), reissued in 1978, and Ruth Gruber's *Virginia Woolf: A Study* (1935), reissued in 2005 as *Virginia Woolf: The Will to Create as a Woman*.

An interesting history of Woolf studies could grow out of reading bibliographies, noting what was available when, and then researching what was available where. For example, even now, English and American Woolf scholars read a literally different Woolf, with American Woolf scholars unable to easily obtain the Blackwell Shakespeare Head Press Edition or the Oxford and Penguin editions and English Woolf scholars unable to easily obtain American Woolf criticism. An admittedly random survey of online catalogues at a few universities in England revealed that although some libraries had books by Nancy Topping Bazin, Jane Marcus, and Brenda Silver, for example, they did not always have those critics' books on Woolf (see Chapter 6 in this volume).

12. See Makiko Minow-Pinkney (1987), Hussey (1995, 3–6), Kari Weil (1992), and Lisa Rado (2000).

13. I want to thank Shirley Sandridge for her impeccable research and Dr Nancy Woodson for inviting me to her seminar on women writers to hear Shirley's presentation.

14. Now, with the manuscripts beginning to deteriorate, readers in research libraries around the world consult the microfilm copy of the Berg Collection Woolf materials.

15. Early transcriptions included *The Waves* (Woolf [Graham] 1976), *Moments of Being* (Woolf [Schulkind] 1976; 1985), *The Pargiters* (Woolf [Leaska] 1977), and *Pointz Hall* (Woolf [Leaska] 1983). Grace Radin worked on the 'Two enormous chunks' cut from *The Years* (1977). The 25th anniversary number of *Twentieth Century Literature* (1979), ed. Lucio Ruotolo, contained transcriptions of 'The Journal of Mistress Joan Martyn' (Woolf [DeSalvo and Squier]), 'Friendships Gallery' (Woolf [Hawkes]), portions of *Orlando* (Woolf [Moore]), and 'Anon' and 'The Reader' (Woolf [Silver]). *Melymbrosia* (Woolf [DeSalvo]) and the *To the Lighthouse* draft (Woolf [Dick]) appeared in 1982. Since then, critics in Woolf studies have been blessed with *The Passionate Apprentice* (Woolf [Leaska] 1990), *Women and Fiction* (Woolf [Rosenbaum] 1992), *Orlando* (Woolf [Clarke] 1993), *The Hours* (Woolf [Wussow] 1997), and *Jacob's Room* (Woolf [Bishop] 1998) (see Chapter 6 in this volume).

16. *All* Woolf critics should also acknowledge the extraordinary and meticulous bibliographic work B. J. Kirkpatrick has been doing since 1957 and most recently, with the assistance of Stuart N. Clarke, in the 4th edition of *A Bibliography of Virginia Woolf* (1997). On this sturdy foundation, our work rests.

17. Julia Briggs, email message to author, 26 July 2003; Brenda Silver, email message to author, 22 July 2003.

18. To understand, in turn, the context in which Barrett wrote her introduction, see her comment about publishing this essay collection in *Imagination in Theory*: 'One extraordinary sticking point was a subheading that I had put in – Virginia Woolf's Theory of Literature. The director of the Press in charge of this project actually made it a *condition* of granting the rights that this be deleted – since he insisted that she did not have a "theory" of her writing' (1999, 15).

19. Naomi Black notes that in 1941, George Sampson 'included Woolf in his *Concise History of English Literature* only as Leslie Stephen's daughter who wrote "novels of limited renown"' (2001, li).

20. See George Ella Lyon's 'Virginia Woolf and the Problem of the Body' (1983, 111–25). On the other hand, in 'Virginia Woolf's Daily Drama of the Body' (1995, 3–25), Teresa Fulker argues that *Mrs Dalloway* 'involves a deep appreciation of how the corporeal affects all aspects of life, of how the inner life is shaped by that entity which is not precisely inner, nor precisely outer – one's material self' (9).

21. Also persuasive are Thomas C. Caramagno's *The Flight of the Mind: Virginia Woolf's Art and Manic-Depressive Illness* (1992), which uses contemporary knowledge about bipolar disorders and genetics, and Elaine Showalter's 'Virginia Woolf and the Flight Into Androgyny (1977, 263–97), which relates Woolf's breakdowns to key passages in a woman's life. DeSalvo, Caramagno, and Showalter have very different explanations for Woolf's physical and mental states, but they share a strong belief in the impact of the body upon the mind. It seems possible, even probable, that all three forces isolated by these critics were operating in Woolf's life.

22. Anyone studying *A Room of One's Own*, for example, should consult Melba Cuddy-Keane's discussion of the 1928 realities of £500 in 'Opening Historical Doors to the *Room*: An Approach to Teaching' (1995).

23. See also Bowlby's '"We're Getting There": Woolf, Trains and the Destinations of Feminist Criticism', in *Feminist Destinations* (1997, 3–15) and Gillespie's study of Woolf as rural flâneuse in Sussex (2003).

24. 'Voyaging Beyond the Race Mother: *Melymbrosia* and *To the Lighthouse*', in *Bordering on the Body: The Racial Matrix of Modern Fiction and Culture* (1994, 139–73) is a longer version of the argument discussed here.

25. See, too, Michèle Barrett's 'Virginia Woolf: Subjectivity and Politics' in *Imagination in Theory: Culture, Writing, Words, and Things* (1999, 35–67).

26. *The Reception of Virginia Woolf in Europe*, eds Caws and Luckhurst (2002) and Patricia Laurence's *Lily Briscoe's Chinese Eyes: Bloomsbury, Modernism, and China* (2003) refreshingly move Virginia Woolf into global contexts, translation issues, and widening reception studies (see Chapter 11 in this volume).

27. As Bonnie Kime Scott notes, London's essay illustrates a 'new' standard practice: 'the dismissal of a series of former feminist focuses and strategies' (Scott 1995, xxxi).

28. Jane Marcus herself takes up one of London's challenges in *Hearts of Darkness: White Women Write Race* (2004). There, she talks with, questions, and confronts her earlier essay, 'Britannia Rules *The Waves*' in order to further examine Woolf's response to race and imperialism. See also the essays in *Virginia Woolf: Emerging Perspectives* (1994) by Michelle Cliff ('Virginia Woolf and the Imperial Gaze: A Glance Askance') and Barbara Christian ('Layered Rhythms: Virginia Woolf and Toni Morrison') (see Chapter 10 in this volume).

29. Woolf's attempts to create a criticism that used literal conversations can be seen in the clean text and typescript versions of 'Byron & Mr Briggs' prepared by Edward Hungerford (Woolf 1979) and Andrew McNeillie (Woolf 1988) and in 'Mr. Conrad: A Conversation' (*CE1* 309–13). For discussions of Woolf's dialogic form, see Beth Carole Rosenberg (1995, 49–68), Snaith (2000a), and Cuddy-Keane (2003).

6
bibliographic approaches
edward l. bishop

What strikes one first about bibliographic approaches to Virginia Woolf is how few there are. The Roe and Sellers' *Cambridge Companion to Virginia Woolf* (2000) has essays that signal their focus on 'history', 'modernism', 'realism', 'post-Impressionism', 'feminism', and 'psychoanalysis', but nothing dedicated specifically to the bibliographic. Nor does the bibliographic figure as a category in Daugherty and Pringle's *Approaches to Teaching Woolf's To The Lighthouse* (2001), nor in Berman and Goldman's *Virginia Woolf Out of Bounds* (2001), where there are categories such as 'Gender, Sexuality, Feminism', 'Orientalism/ Colonialism', 'Cultural and Material', but nothing on bibliography. Yet there has been a steady stream of bibliographic work. Charles G. Hoffman wrote a series of articles in 1968 and 1969 that initiated study of the drafts, but these short pieces just offered a taste of what was there, and it would be some time before there were more comprehensive studies. The focus in the 1970s and 1980s, and indeed into the 1990s, was in getting the work out. It was as if Woolf was having another publishing career, this time of pre-publication materials. Now, in the early 2000s, Woolf studies seems poised for a new, multifarious phase of bibliographic criticism. But it has been a long time coming.

To look back for a moment, the 1970s was a decade rich in the production of biographical material, and the editing of Woolf's unpublished texts. Quentin Bell's biography came out in 1972, and between 1975 and 1980 Nigel Nicolson and Joanne Trautmann Banks produced the six volumes of the *Letters*. Stella McNichol published her edition of *Mrs Dalloway's Party: A Short Story Sequence* in 1973; in 1977 Mitchell Leaska produced *The Pargiters: the Novel-Essay Portion of The Years*, and the *Bulletin of the New York Public Library* special issue on *The Years*, *The Pargiters*, and *Three Guineas*, which included Grace Radin's '"Two Enormous Chunks": Episodes Excluded During the Final Revisions of *The Years*'. In 1979 the *Bulletin* featured bibliographic work on *The Voyage Out*. That same year Brenda Silver brought out drafts of the essays 'Anon' and 'The Reader' in *Twentieth Century Literature* and Susan Dick discussed the evolution of the 'Time

Passes' section of *To the Lighthouse* in *English Studies in Canada*. However, 1976 must rank as the banner year of the decade, with the publication of both Jeanne Schulkind's *Moments of Being* (revised and enlarged 1985), and John Graham's monumental facsimile transcription of the two holograph drafts of *The Waves*. Schulkind's collection of previously unpublished autobiographical writings from the Monk's House Papers at the University of Sussex – 'Reminiscences', the three Memoir Club contributions '22 Hyde Park Gate', 'Old Bloomsbury', and 'Am I a Snob', and particularly 'A Sketch of the Past' – immediately became indispensable. Graham's transcription, on the other hand, filled scholars with awe but also uncertainty. What could one do with it? And two specifically bibliographic articles, J. A. Lavin's article on the American and British editions of *To the Lighthouse* (1972), and E. F. Shields's on *Mrs Dalloway* (1974), received little attention.

Bibliographic and editorial work in the 1980s included the completion of the five volumes of the *Diary* (1977–84), edited by Anne Olivier Bell and Andrew McNeillie, and in 1986 McNeillie began publishing his multi-volume edition of the *Essays*, a massive project that at this writing has reached volume four. There were book-length studies of the generation of novels at either end of Woolf's career – Louise DeSalvo's *Virginia Woolf's First Voyage* (1980), a study of the drafts of *The Voyage Out*, and Grace Radin's *Virginia Woolf's The Years: The Evolution of a Novel* (1981) – and in quick succession a series of manuscript transcriptions: DeSalvo's edition of *Melymbrosia* (1982), Susan Dick's transcription of the holograph draft of *To the Lighthouse* (1982), and Mitchell Leaska's *Pointz Hall: The Earlier and Later Typescripts of Between the Acts* (1983). Also, in 1985 Susan Dick published her edition of the *Complete Shorter Fiction* (revised and expanded 1989), which included twenty-seven previously unpublished stories. The Hogarth Press itself was becoming an object of scholarly attention, and in the mid-1980s Howard Woolmer and Mary Gaither's *Checklist of the Hogarth Press* and Donna Rhein's *The Handprinted Books of Leonard and Virginia Woolf at the Hogarth Press 1917–1932* appeared. Amidst all this activity Glenn Wright's examination of 'The Raverat Proofs of *Mrs. Dalloway*', a 1986 article in *Studies in Bibliography*, went almost unnoticed by literary critics.

In the 1990s more unpublished material emerged, Leaska's *Passionate Apprentice: The Early Journals, 1897–1909* (1990), and then another round of holograph transcriptions: Rosenbaum's *Women and Fiction* (1992); Clarke's *Orlando* (1993), and Scott's article on the proofs of *Orlando* (1994); Wussow's *The Hours* (1997); my *Jacob's Room* (1998). The decade also saw the publication of the foundational work on the Hogarth Press, J. H. Willis' *Leonard and Virginia Woolf as Publishers: The Hogarth Press 1917–1941* (1992). And Woolf's work began to appear in new forms. Mark Hussey produced the *Major Authors on CD-ROM: Virginia Woolf (1997)*, which includes almost all of her published writings, including the diary and letters, a great deal of unpublished manuscript and typescript material, and a recording of Woolf's broadcast,

'Craftsmanship', as well as Hussey's *Virginia Woolf A–Z* (published in book form in 1995). As we move into the first decade of the twenty-first century we are seeing a proliferation of online resources such as Stuart N. Clarke's *Virginia Woolf and Bloomsbury: A Bibliography*, and critics such as Hussey and Silver are exploring what it means to have Woolf in electronic forms. Inevitably, the notion of what constitutes bibliography and a bibliographic approach has been considerably expanded.

Early bibliographic work appeared either in the introductions of editions, or in specialized articles, and focused primarily on the principles of establishing copy-texts (the text upon which a new edition would be based) or laying out the editorial principles which governed a transcription. Not heady stuff and readers, to judge from the footnotes in critical articles, stayed away in droves. Certainly readers were consulting the drafts (Jane Novak's 1974 *The Razor Edge of Balance* draws on *The Years* material in the Berg Collection at the New York Public Library) and the first Virginia Woolf seminar at the Modern Language Association Convention in 1970 was organized by J. J. Wilson on 'The Uses of Manuscripts in Virginia Woolf Studies', but J. A. Lavin's fine article, 'The First Editions of Virginia Woolf's *To the Lighthouse*', appeared in 1972, and was almost universally ignored.

As Lavin said defensively at the time, 'Detractors of textual criticism sometimes call it "comma hunting", implying that accidentals of punctuation are relatively unimportant in a long literary work such as a novel' (Lavin 1972 189). Yet it can make a difference. Lavin cites the substitution of a comma for a dash in the American edition.

> When she originally wrote 'her daughters – Prue, Nancy, Rose –' (E1, 16.15), the dashes put the names of the girls in apposition with the words 'daughters.' The implication here is of comprehensive inclusion: but in fact Mrs. Ramsay has not included young Cam in her observation about the private thoughts of the older girls. So the revision in the American edition, to 'her daughters, Prue, Nancy, Rose –' (A1, 14.11) is an improvement because it indicates that not all of the daughters are included in the comment.

But there are more substantial changes. In the American edition Woolf softens the character of Charles Tansley by omitting the italicized phrase in the following passage:

> ...what they complained of about Charles Tansley was that until he had turned the whole thing round and made it somehow reflect himself and disparage them, *put them all on edge somehow with his acid way of peeling the flesh and blood off everything*, he was not satisfied. (E1, 18.13)

A small alteration, crucially placed, can have an enormous effect. Consider the ending of Part I of *To the Lighthouse*. The English edition reads,

'It's going to be wet tomorrow.' She had not said it, but he knew it. And she looked at him smiling. For she had triumphed again.

The passage, Lavin argues, is 'melodramatic and unfortunately gives the impression of Mrs. Ramsay gloating over her husband' (Lavin 1972 196). In the American edition Woolf made an addition, but, more significantly, rearranged the phrases:

'It's going to be wet tomorrow. You won't be able to go.' And she looked at him smiling. For she had triumphed again. She had not said it: yet he knew.

The changes 'substitute for the gloating a further link of intimate communication between husband and wife' (197). If Mrs Ramsay's character is softened here, so is that of Mr Ramsay later when Woolf mutes the earwig-in-his-milk episode for the American edition. The ten-page list of variants at the back of the article is still useful today, not only for scholars but for teachers who want to introduce issues of textual stability. Woolf made the changes and saw them through the press, yet when she revised the novel eleven years later for the Everyman edition she ignored the substantive changes made for the American edition. Which text, which relationship between Mr and Mrs Ramsay, which portrait of Tansley, is the 'true' one?

These insights are still valuable, why are they not commonplaces of Woolf criticism? In part, I would suggest, because Lavin's article appeared in *Proof: the Yearbook of American Bibliographical and Textual Studies*, which like *Studies in Bibliography* is filed under a Z call-number, far from the bustling PRs with all of Woolf's works, and periodicals such as *Modern Fiction Studies* or *Twentieth Century Literature* (which featured special issues on Woolf in 1972 and 1979 respectively). The problem is that even if the literary critic does venture into the trackless wastes of the Z sector and takes down a volume of *Studies in Bibliography* she or he is probably not going to read the whole article. E. F. Shields's fine piece, 'The American Edition of *Mrs Dalloway*' (1974) begins opposite the appendix of an article on the Beaumont and Fletcher Folio of 1647, with eight columns of figures that mean nothing to a convention-ally-trained literary critic: the 'bibliographic environment', to use Jerome McGann's phrase, is daunting. After two paragraphs of background Shields tells us 'A collation of the American and English editions of *Mrs Dalloway* reveals numerous changes; many of them are minor...but some are substantive' (Shields 1974, 158). All but hardened textual editors will close the volume at this point. Yet if you persevere, twelve pages in you learn that at a pivotal moment late in *Mrs Dalloway*, at the point separating Clarissa's scene in the small room from the closing scene with Peter and Sally, the British edition has a space break, but the American edition does not. Further, the text is significantly altered at this point. In the passage preceding the break, the proofs read:

The leaden circles dissolved in the air. He made her feel the beauty; the fun. But she must go back.

Harcourt, following Virginia Woolf's directions that accentuate the parallelism, changes the second sentence to 'He made her feel the beauty; made her feel the fun.' Yet in the Hogarth edition the sentence does not appear at all. What British readers get is this:

She felt glad that he had done it; thrown it away while they went on living. The clock was striking. The leaden circles dissolve in the air.

Harvena Richter in 1970 had mentioned the lost sentence in a footnote and argued that it emphasizes Clarissa's sense of catharsis (120 n.16); readers might have built on Shields' observations, but most literary, as opposed to textual, critics would not read this far.

Over a decade later Glenn P. Wright published another important article on *Mrs Dalloway* in *Studies in Bibliography*, this time on the proofs that Woolf sent to Jacques Raverat to read as he was dying (he would be dead before the book was published). Wright establishes that the revisions were made earlier in the proofreading process than those on the proofs Shields was looking at. For most readers, the fascinating part of the essay comes in an appendix in which Wright provides a transcription of Woolf's typed revision of one of the most powerful scenes in the book (and indeed in all of Woolf): Septimus' suicide. It should be consulted by anyone working on the passage, but the format makes it difficult for the ordinary scholar to get a sense of what it looked like:

**Life ['L' *alt. fr.* 'l'] was [*insrtd. for del.* 'As for himself (he had raised himself on the sill now – could see Mrs. Filmer's pots were down below) life was'] *good; the sun^n hot [*insrtd. for del.* 'pleasant, the air cooler after the heat; he had no wish to die']. (Wright, 1986 260)

Critics still are disinclined to work through such texts. George Bornstein, in his *Material Modernism: the Politics of the Page* (2001) demonstrates in a chapter on 'Joyce and the colonial archive' how Hans Walter Gabler's synoptic edition of *Ulysses* can be used. Bornstein links postcolonial theory with genetic criticism to show how the text's construction of alterity, particularly of black, Jewish, and Irish Nationalist identities, is itself constructed at a particular stage in the construction of the text, thus throwing into relief the linkages between these identities. Bornstein's book, published in 2001, is one of the first to actually use (as opposed to contesting, supporting, or analyzing) Gabler's three-volume synoptic edition, which was published in 1984, two years before Wright's essay, an edition that convinced many literary critics that textual critics came from, perhaps belonged on, another planet. Few readers of Wright's essay would have worked backward through the transcription to reconstruct,

> As for himself (he had raised himself on the sill now – could see Mrs. Filmer's pots were down below) life was pleasant, the air cooler after the heat; he had no wish to die,

to compare it with the Hogarth's

> (He sat on the sill.) But he would wait till the very last moment. He did not want to die. Life was good. The sun hot.

and to consider what effects are gained and lost by eliminating Septimus' action of raising himself on the sill, and looking at the pots, of feeling the air cool rather than the sun hot, and feeling he 'had no wish to die' rather than 'did not want to die'. Textual critics and literary critics were not writing for each other.

The editors of the Woolf concordances came to recognize this. When James Haule and Philip Smith Jr. published their *Concordance* to *The Waves* in 1988, they wrote, 'It is our hope that this kind of research tool will not merely expose the technical details of a great novel, but make its mystery and delicate power more accessible to us all' (Haule and Smith 1988, 14). It didn't. The concordance itself seemed more mysterious than the text. Nearly a decade later, in 1997 when Haule took to the pages of *Woolf Studies Annual* to counter this neglect, he opened with Philip Smith Jr.'s recipe for

HOW TO USE A CONCORDANCE
1 large country-type, roundish bread loaf (about 1 pound)
¼ cup virgin olive oil
1 ½ cups basil leaves
2 very ripe tomatoes (about ¾ pound), thinly sliced
1 cucumber (8 to 10 ounces), peeled and thinly sliced
3 cloves garlic, peeled and thinly sliced
½ teaspoon freshly ground black pepper
½ teaspoon salt
2 tablespoons vinegar

Cut the bread loaf in half horizontally and sprinkle the cut surface of each half with the olive oil. Cover with the basil leaves and arrange the tomato slices, the cucumber slices and then the garlic slices on top, distributing them evenly on both bread halves. Sprinkle with the pepper, salt and vinegar. Join both halves together and press the bread under a concordance for at least a few minutes, but longer if possible, to allow the vegetable juices to blend with the oil and seasonings. Cut into 6 large wedges and serve. This is an excellent lunch sandwich.

Note: Traditional cooks have always used the *Oxford English Dictionary* for this purpose, but with the advent of cheaper and faster computers more and more cooks are using concordances. Printed concordances are recommended. The newer microfiche concordances are unsatisfactory and under no circumstances should any attempt be made to use an interactive CD-ROM concordance. (143–4)

This sounds delicious, and it raises the issue of how the materiality, or lack thereof, of the new technologies will have an impact on the text, but it also points to a salient feature of bibliographic articles: from the point of view of the literary critic, the good stuff is buried in the middle. 'A concordance is a textual microscope,' Haule tells us, declaring, 'You do not go searching for meaning, the way a committee might search for a scandal. You must interrogate the text first, and then use the concordance as a scientist might use a microscope, not to see what you are looking for, but to see what was there but you were too blind to notice' (144–5). But then follows nine pages of discussion of how to establish the 'copy-text' and how to determine a 'hard hyphen': key concepts in bibliography and key signals to the common reader that it is time to leave. Yet if you hang on until the middle, Haule demonstrates how the concordance can be used to explore questions of identity and gender. He checks how often each character in *The Waves* uses character names, including his or her own. Haule discovers that Bernard uses his own name twelve times, Louis four, Neville once. 'However, none of the female characters ever uses her own name' (153). (Haule's chart also reveals that Bernard uses 'myself' sixty-two times, where Jinny uses it thirteen times, Rhoda twelve, Louis and Neville eleven, and Susan only seven.) Intriguingly, the vivacious Jinny uses names least of all the characters. Looking at the passages in context, Haule concludes, 'Names for Jinny, Rhoda and Susan are dangerous. They are somehow a reflection of a social caste that obliterates them' (156). Further, 'Rhoda is chiefly concerned with names and the loss of identity [...] but the concordance leads us to understand that the other female characters share her fear of identity and her anger at those who would rob women of that distinction' (157). By this point you may want to argue with Haule, maybe even to get hold of the *Concordance* and check out a few key terms yourself. By the mid-1990s questions of textual scholarship and literary meaning were converging.

Things had already begun to change. In his 1985 Panizzi Lectures, *Bibliography and the Sociology of Texts*, D. F. McKenzie took issue with Sir Walter Greg's view that bibliography is only concerned with 'pieces of paper or parchment covered with certain written or printed signs', and that these signs should be treated 'merely as arbitrary marks' whose 'meaning' is no business of the bibliographer (McKenzie 1986, 27) – the tradition that Shields and

Wright were working in. McKenzie wanted to redefine bibliography as 'the study of the sociology of texts'. He argued that physical bibliography alone was inadequate because we have to account 'for the processes, the technical and social dynamics, of transmission and reception, whether by one reader or a whole market of them', and he maintained that 'the material forms of books, the non-verbal elements of the typographic notions within them, the very disposition of space itself, have an expressive function in conveying meaning' (31). He declared that 'the border between bibliography and textual criticism on the one hand and literary criticism and literary history on the other' in fact does not exist: 'in the pursuit of historical meanings, we move from the most minute feature of the material form of the book to questions of authorial, literary and social context' (34).

McKenzie said, 'I am not bold enough to speak of paradigm shifts' (28), but that is precisely what it was, a shift he was helping to consolidate and perpetuate. His questions about his own reading of an epigraph by Congreve (is the reading a meaning imposed by the printer, John Watts? Or was Watts following the directives of the publisher Jacob Tonson? 'Who, in short, "authored" Congreve?' (36)) echoed the questions of Pierre Bourdieu in 'The Production of Belief' (first translated into English in 1983): 'Who is the true producer of the value of the work – the painter or the dealer, the writer or the publisher, the playwright or the theatre manager' (76). McKenzie is talking about the production of the text while Bourdieu's focus is the reception of it, but both see the need to situate the text in the larger context of its making. The work of other French critics such as Roger Chartier and Michel de Certeau were finding their way into English, changing the way we thought of reading practices, and Gerard Genette's *Paratexts* (1987, trans. 1997) devoted a whole volume to the 'thresholds' we must cross before encountering a text. Bourdieu theorized the 'cultural field' and on the other side of the Atlantic Robert Darnton diagrammed the 'communications circuit' in his now foundational article, 'What is the History of Books?' (1982) which placed the text in a web that included printers and warehousemen, shippers and smugglers, libraries and book clubs, publicity and legal sanctions, and much more. Jerome McGann argued in his 1985 *Historical Studies and Literary Criticism* that, 'The price of a book, its place of publication, even its physical form and the institutional structures by which it is distributed and received, all bear upon the production of literary meaning' (McGann 1985, 4), a theme he came back to in the introduction to *The Textual Condition* (1991), resorting to italics to insist on the link between materiality and meaning:

> the material (and apparently least 'signifying' or significant) levels of the text ... the physical form of books and manuscripts (paper, ink, typefaces, layouts) or their prices, advertising mechanism, and distribution venues. The *meanings* ... are a function of all these matters, *whether we are aware*

of such matters when we make our meanings or whether we are not. (McGann 1991, 12)

Woolf critics are now attending to these elements. Anna Snaith in her 2000 *Virginia Woolf: Public and Private Negotiations*, writing on the readers who responded to *Three Guineas* foregrounds the issues of price and dissemination:

> Jane Walker [a reader] says *Three Guineas* ought to have been published as a Penguin Special, noting 'it ought to have a far wider public than it will get as a seven & six penny book.'... Penguin made books a 'mass medium', which is what the majority of readers argues needed to happen to *Three Guineas*. Constance Cheke, a working-class woman, writes that she would not have bought it if Smiths had not reduced it to 2s. (Snaith 2000, 126)

Price alone is not the issue:

> Yet another respondent, Ernest Huxley, a bus conductor from Merseyside who writes Woolf two extremely long letters, addresses the question of availability in the difficulty he has had obtaining her books (72). ... One correspondent notes that *Three Guineas* should be 'broadcast to millions' (Annie Coles, 44); in other words a change in medium would be a way of increasing accessibility. The letters testify to the urgency of dissemination. (126)

Thus the kind of 'study of the sociology of the text' that McKenzie was calling for in 1985 was now firmly in place; a 'bibliographic approach' in 2000 embraces a whole range of issues that it would not have in the mid-1980s.

And, back at the ranch, as it were, in *Studies in Bibliography* Louis Hay was asking in 1988 'Does "Text" Exist?' Against the notion of a pure formal text, founded on the principle of closure, he opens up the concept of a text to include pre-publication documents, the 'avant-texte'. Manuscripts, he says, 'force us to take into account the unpredictable'; they

> have no respect for the convention of linearity, overflowing the page into multiple spaces. The ways in which the text is laid out on the page, with marginal notations, additions, cross-references, deletions, alterations, in different handwriting styles, and with drawings and symbols, texture the discourse, increase the significations and multiply the possible readings. (Hay 1988, 69)

He concludes, 'Perhaps we should consider the text as *a necessary possibility*, as one manifestation of a process which is always virtually present in the background, a kind of third dimension of the written work' (75).

Woolf critic Susan Stanford Friedman was arguing in 1989 that such a concept of text is essential, for drafts in effect constitute the textual unconscious of the final text:

> The 'draft,' in other words, may contain narrative elements that are repressed and transformed as the author revises the text by the linguistic mechanisms of the dream-work: by condensation, displacement, non-rational modes of representability and secondary revision.... In political terms...the earlier text may erupt into the gaps of the later text just as cultural and political rebellion disrupts the social order. (Friedman 1989, 145)

We need to read 'both ways',

> instead of regarding the 'final' texts as the endpoint and teleological goal of 'drafts,' or instead of reading texts solely as autonomous entities. Repression and resistance can be present at both ends of the process. Rather than searching for the 'authentic' version, this approach regards all versions as part of a larger composite, palimpsestic text. (146)

Christine Froula in 'Modernism, Genetic Texts and Literary Authority in Virginia Woolf's Portraits of the Artist as the Audience' (an important article that deserves wider currency) insisted in 1995 that 'Genetic texts not only document the evolution of literary works through the stages of their compositional history but ... emphasize their interdependence with historical conditions' (Froula 1995, 512). She begins with the reference to Charles Lamb in *A Room of One's Own* and his shock at seeing the manuscript of 'Lycidas' and realizing it could have been different than it was. Froula quotes Lamb's anguished footnote to 'Oxford on Vacation':

> I had thought of the Lycidas as of a full-grown beauty – as springing up with all its parts absolute – till, in evil hour, I was shown the original written copy of it... How it staggered me to see the fine things in their ore! interlined, corrected! as if their words were mortal, alterable, displaceable at pleasure! as if they might have been otherwise, and just as good! as if inspirations were made up of parts, and those fluctuating, successive, indifferent! (514)

Woolf's concept of text, Froula argues, is precisely the opposite. Woolf presents self-portraits and portraits of audience rooted in social conditions, 'with all the risks and chances this involves'

> As notions of literary authority shift from transcendent to social ground, the modernity... entails the death of the Lamblike reader, who shrinks from risking life and limb in the difficulties and dangers of collaboration.... And it entails the birth of the socially organic, historically rooted, indefinitely

branching collaborative authority whose boundaries can never be fully or finally drawn, of which genetic textuality forms an exemplary yet partial and accidental material trace. (526)

Mark Hussey's discussion of hypertext, 'How Should One Read a Screen', draws together concerns with the materiality of the text and protocols of reading, and takes them back to Woolf. He quotes Woolf from 'How Should One Read a Book?' where she explains that there is in reading a process that works against linearity: 'Wait for the dust of reading to settle.... [the book] will float to the top of the mind as a whole. And the book as a whole is different from the book received currently in separate phrases' (*CE2* 8, Hussey 2000, 251). Here we see Woolf anticipating Roland Barthes' notion of 'text' not as something fixed but as a methodological field. Further, Hussey argues that Woolf was 'concerned not only with the sound of her words, but also with their visual display upon the page. Her use of repetition ...and, especially, her use of space breaks all contribute to the effort Woolf made to shape the *reading* of her fiction after about 1917 – the date of her and Leonard's acquisition of the Hogarth Press' (Hussey 2000, 253). This aspect of the text can be lost in digitized texts: 'The electronic format of a novel like *Mrs Dalloway*, complete with blue "hyperlinks" that lead to selected information and opinions...[leads] to an emphasis on the text as *information*, made up of discrete "bits" of text. The spaces on the page that contribute to the rhythmic context of the words on the page are insignificant, "unreadable," in effect by the machine' (254). For Hussey then it is axiomatic that any consideration of the text is inseparable from consideration of its material embodiment. Hussey's article is part of the collection *Virginia Woolf in the Age of Mechanical Reproduction*, evidence that bibliography and cultural studies are beginning to overlap, a fact reflected in the new rubric 'print culture history'. And indeed the fourth edition of the *Bibliography of Virginia Woolf* (1997) by B. J. Kirkpatrick and Stuart N. Clarke reflects the change in bibliography. The new edition includes more items, of course, but if you consult the entry for the first editions of the novels you will find in addition to a description of the edition a narrative of the publishing history, references to the *Concordance*, and a list of articles on the manuscripts.

The first collection devoted specifically to editorial work has recently appeared (2002) and its title announces its dual focus: *Editing Virginia Woolf: Interpreting the Modernist Text*. The editors note that not much has been done with the pre-print documents, and that 'disappointingly few genetic studies have, in fact, appeared' (Haule and Stape 2002, 6). Yet critics of all different persuasions are increasingly likely to include elements of the genetic in their work, and the essays in this book give examples of the ways in which that might be done. The contributors (and I should declare here that I am one) are all involved in the Shakespeare Head edition of Woolf, but the approaches are very different. Anne Olivier Bell's deceptively casual piece, 'Editing Virginia

Woolf's Diary', raises important issues about the physical text and archival preservation. She points out, for instance, that in dealing with the letters often the letter was undated, and the envelope with its postmark lost, but

> post-office workers used to thump the postmark on by hand; and if they were sufficiently enthusiastic, the blind echo of their thumb could be impressed upon the folded sheet within the envelope. So, if one refolds a letter and examines it under strong and raking light, sometimes, eureka! the blind postmark is revealed – as it might be WELLS SOM/4AU 08. I rather fear that in the superior conditions in which manuscripts are now preserved in institutions such evidence, and the possibilities for its detection, will have been ironed out. (Bell 2002, 14)

She reminds readers of the bureaucratic difficulties and actual physical labour of editorial work: 'I began by getting photocopies from the Berg Collection of the 2317 pages of the original diaries (they tried to persuade me to have microfilm but I resisted, and got full-scale sheets – else I would be blind by now)' (18). Bell draws two morals that are salutary cautions for anyone contemplating bibliographic work, which, if it's done right, always looks so easy after it's done: 'One, that it is nearly always necessary to find out about ten times as much about your problem as you will eventually use in elucidating it. Two, that the element of luck, or serendipity, in research is very arbitrary but often immensely valuable' (21).

Joanne Trautmann Banks, in 'The Editor as Ethicist' draws attention to another kind of luck, the luck of manuscript dealers in placing their wares:

> One of the reasons we know so much about the life of Virginia Woolf…is because of …Miss Hamill and Miss Barker of Chicago. They were manuscript dealers, who read English obituaries to see which writers had lately died. They then arrived on the doorsteps of the freshly aggrieved, offering to buy the literary remains for sums so small that they afterwards made a good deal of money selling them to both private and public collections. This was good business, but was it ethical? If the means were suspicious, the ends were certainly good as far as Woolf scholars are concerned. After all, the foundation of the major Woolf manuscript collection at the Berg was achieved through 'the ladies'.…It is sobering to contemplate that had Hamill and Barker been successful in their first plan – to sell the Woolf manuscripts to an eccentric collector called Frances Hooper – there would have been little or no Woolf editing, and not as much biography and criticism, until the late 1980s after Miss Hooper's death. (Banks 2002, 35)

The role of the dealer is a crucial factor in cultural production, but seldom addressed, and about which we need to know more.

Like Olivier Bell, Banks reminds the reader of how the physicality of the text can generate literary meaning, rehearsing her disagreement with biographer Panthea Reid over the dating of the suicide notes, which is based not just on language but on 'stationery, ink, and handwriting' as well as 'levels of soiling'; she wants 'to underscore how readings of manuscripts corrupted by such things as folds, dirt, and subsequent handling may affect the author's identity as it passes down to later generations'. In Banks and Nicolson's version Woolf's suicide 'is a more considered decision…(ten days' meditation as opposed to three). Our Woolf thinks pointedly about her husband at the end; Reid's recycles a letter written several days earlier. Probably most important, the Woolf that our editing creates is someone who wrote at least one letter on the last day that she lived. But which tale is true cannot be known with certainty' (39).

Banks also takes up what has become a contentious issue in Woolf studies: annotation. She notes that she and Nicolson decided to be more 'telegraphic' than Olivier Bell (31). But (and this is where the issue of 'the editor as ethicist' appears) she also talks about how her response to Woolf's gossip and references to the 'bedding behavior' of her acquaintances has changed over the years. She used to be, she says, 'like a pig hunting for truffles: it seemed to me that the public we served had a right to know everything we could uncover'; now, seeing the power of published language to cause suffering, even though there is material that she could supply without fear of libel, she declines to do so: 'for me, legal permission is no longer congruous with ethical choice' (44). It is a good discussion of the kinds of behind-the-scenes attitudes and choices that determine even factual, rather than interpretive, annotation, leading to the question of whether there can ever be purely objective annotation.

Bringing the issue back to Woolf's own practice, Naomi Black in '"Women Must Weep": The Serialization of *Three Guineas*' reminds us that Woolf famously grappled with these issues, and explores the enormous effect the elimination of the footnotes had on *Three Guineas* when it was serialized in *Atlantic Monthly* as 'Women Must Weep'. Black discovers that 'the deletion of the endnotes removes memorable parts of the book. It is in the endnotes, not the text, that Woolf jeers at the academic teaching of English as sipping literature through a straw…'. Further, removing the notes 'removes a whole dimension of satire', constituting as they do 'a feminist undercutting of the masculine scholarship they utilize' (81). In the process the text becomes both 'less feminist' and 'less fun to read' (82). Thus the editorial work highlights the ways in which Woolf achieves her feminist project in *Three Guineas* and establishes more precisely what that project is. Diane Gillespie argues that although Penguin editor Julia Briggs claims that Woolf's 'commitment to textual indeterminacy…should act as an awful warning to those of us who have, with the best of intentions, enchained her flying texts and tied them down to the stone breaking apparatus of notes, commentaries and appendices', in fact editorial apparatus can be enabling to the reader. Gillespie's model is Woolf's notes in *Three Guineas* that challenge the hierarchical model of annotation, which is all about the editor's ego, and 'substitute for this adversarial model mediation, negotiation, and collaboration among editor, author, text, and reader' (102). Gillespie's own examination of the variants for *Roger Fry: A Biography* provides a model for the way such material can be used. Rather than simply pointing them out and stepping back, as bibliographic critics did in the 1970s, she weaves them into a larger argument about censorship and self-censorship. Her inclusion of deleted passages, such as the quotation from Fry's memoirs in which he links his first erection to assisting with a flogging at his school (97), makes a powerful argument for the examination of variants in any approach to Woolf's texts.

James Haule, in 'Version and Intention in the Novels of Virginia Woolf' provides a detailed account of the French translation of the 'Time Passes' section (something he had written about earlier, as had Susan Dick). Haule argues that the section as Woolf first wrote it 'did not fit the novel she was writing' (Haule 2002, 185). For instance, the Mrs McNab of the typescript is ten years older than in the published editions and her 'message to a world' is originally 'more confused but more profound' than those 'solitary watchers' who 'pace the beach at midnight' (186). Haule suggests that 'Woolf saw periodical publication as a way to present a version of the entire section in a form that conveyed her original intention: a separate but important statement of belief and unbelief.' Further, 'by publishing it in translation, she not only saw it into print, but…reduced her risk of unfavorable impact from what she claimed was a "hopeless mess" by publishing it in a language other than English' (186–7). The questions surrounding the 'Time Passes' section lead back to the larger question of a definitive text, and Haule concludes,

> These examples make several things clear. First, there is not one version of a text but several. More than one edition is authoritative, and other versions of the text, while not always an issue in the establishment of a copy-text, certainly reveal that Woolf had several things in mind. Of least importance in many cases was the production of a clean, error-free text that would represent her final 'intentions'. (187)

The most important reader is not the literary scholar but the common reader: 'the person who does not want to put a book together, but to read one', according to Morris Beja, in 'Text and Counter-Text: Trying to Recover *Mrs Dalloway*' (Beja 2002, 128). Having said that, Beja demonstrates how having the apparatus to 'put a book together', or, more properly, to show how a book has been put together, can be vital. He takes up questions such as the famous (to editors at least) 'red dress' in *Mrs Dalloway*:

> In all editions published during Woolf's lifetime, the dress is referred to as 'pink' in a couple of instances up to the party itself, when it becomes

'red.' Wright's [Oxford] edition changes the word 'red' to 'pink,' remarking that 'Woolf simply overlooked the error in the factual details' and citing as supportive corroboration the fact that a similar 'correction' was made in a British edition published in 1947, six years after Woolf's death. (132)

For Beja, the editor's job is not to correct Woolf's 'errors' but to point them out, for 'we cannot be sure that there may not be a point in the apparent inconsistency' (132), and he points to the disastrous example of Danis Rose's edition of *Ulysses* in which he added punctuation to the notoriously unpunctuated monologue of Molly Bloom. Editors of the Hogarth *Mrs Dalloway* corrected Woolf's word 'vagulous' ('that vagulous phosphorescence, old Mrs. Hilbery') to 'vagous' – yet it is a word that now appears in the *OED*, cited as appearing 'only in the writings of Virginia Woolf' (135).

For his edition of *Mrs. Dalloway* Beja chose to present a complete list of variants, not distinguishing as previous editors had between 'accidentals' and 'substantives', because such lists

enable us to become 'genetic' critics and scholars, to see Woolf working on and revising her prose and clarifying it – or, sometimes, making it more enigmatic. Brenda Silver has compared the resulting interpretive process to the 'tunnelling process' that Woolf felt she had discovered while writing *Mrs Dalloway*, and that enabled her to reconstruct 'the past by instalments' (*D2* 272; see Silver 1991, 194).

In a way we have come full circle here: we do want to read a book, rather than put one together, but part of that 'reading', after the initial consumption of the text, may well be an exploration, a 'tunnelling' into the alternate and pre-texts.

But the 'text' of *Mrs Dalloway*, with our more expansive notion of text, now includes so much more. Gerard Genette contends that the text is inseparable from its paratext, a 'threshold' or 'vestibule', 'a zone not only of transition but of *transaction*' that we negotiate before engaging with the text proper (Genette 1997, 2). He further separates paratext into 'peritext' (those materials that are part of the book, such as the cover, title page, name of the author, titles, dedications and inscriptions, epigraphs, prefaces, intertitles, notes) and 'epitext' (materials outside the book, such as letters, diaries, interviews, conversations, pre-texts). He asks, 'How would we read Joyce's *Ulysses* if it were not entitled *Ulysses*?' (2). Woolf readers, even non-scholarly ones, cannot help but ask, 'How would we read *Mrs Dalloway* if it were called *The Hours*?' For the paratext of the novel now includes not only Woolf's diary entries that speak of 'The Hours', and Helen Wussow's transcription of 'The Hours' manuscript, but Michael Cunningham's novel of that name, and Stephen Daldry's film, *The Hours*, in which Virginia Woolf becomes Nicole Kidman with a prosthetic nose.

The most extensive study of the Woolf paratext (specifically the epitext, the material outside the book) is Brenda Silver's *Virginia Woolf Icon*. She insists on putting Woolf's texts in the context of her celebrity – a context often ignored or disavowed in the study of her work, yet which permeates our consciousness, even if only as something to be actively resisted. Edward Albee's 1962 play *Who's Afraid of Virginia Woolf?* and particularly the 1996 film version starring Richard Burton and Elizabeth Taylor, which was nominated for fourteen Academy Awards and won five, 'transformed Virginia Woolf into a household name' (Silver 1999, 9). Thus the difficulties of modernist texts and fear of feminism became forever linked with the phrase, 'Who's afraid of...' and Woolf 'acquired an iconicity that exists independently of her academic standing or literary reputation'. It is sobering to reflect that for a full decade before Quentin Bell's biography appeared in 1972, readers (particularly but not only North American readers) had a Virginia Woolf mediated by the title of Albee's play.

We may seem to be a long way from textual editing, but in fact Silver grounds her study in editorial practices, specifically in the practice of 'versioning', which in literary studies means 'publishing all the different "versions" of an individual work, including prepublication texts (holographs, typescripts, etc.)'. The effect, she says quoting Donald Reiman, is to provide '"enough different *primary* textual documents and states of major texts"' to allow readers to explore their '"distinct ideologies, aesthetic perspectives, or rhetorical strategies"'. But where Haule states that 'more than one edition is authoritative', Silver argues further that the larger effect of versioning

> is to challenge the authority of any one version of the work, and, by implication, both the author's intention and the editor's authoritative final word. Seen in this light, versioning signifies a rebellion among textual scholars against the eclectic edition of a single 'authorized' text and posits the coming-of-age of the unstable, unfixed, postmodern work whose meanings are derived by readings of the differences among the multiple versions. (13)

All of which is part of a larger shift in editorial theory from the intention of the author to affect on the reader. What Silver does is to examine the 'versioning of Virginia Woolf across the cultural terrain' (15).

Once we begin placing the text in its manifold contexts we see that the work of establishing a text, and annotating it, begins to touch on and overlap with the work of cultural critics. Melba Cuddy-Keane in 'Virginia Woolf, Sound Technologies, and the New Aurality' argues that even Woolf's early 'Kew Gardens' is as 'intensely aural' as it is visual, and locates it in the 'new acoustical perception' fostered by new sound technologies (Cuddy-Keane 2000, 82). She further suggests that the form of *The Waves* resembles a radio broadcast, and points to Woolf's discussion with her cousin Virginia Isham for a BBC adaptation (87). We can see how Cuddy-Keane's statement that 'there is a marked resemblance to the listening experience in wireless and electroacoustic reception when the same or similar sounds are auscultated in *The Waves* by different listeners situated in different geographical and narrative positions' (90) could take us back to the *Concordance* to trace the disposition of these sounds, or to Graham's holograph transcription to see how in the process of composition these sounds entered the text, but also outward conceptually to ask with McKenzie and Hay, 'What is a text?' In short, the boundaries between the bibliographic and other approaches to Woolf have become more porous.

And the issues more fraught. Of the editions readily available today, the Harcourt Brace, surprisingly, has no introduction, no annotations, no textual apparatus. Even the inexpensive Signets, printed on pulpy paper, include an introduction along with a list of primary works by Woolf and a 'Selected Biography and Criticism'. The Oxford World's Classics and the Penguin both provide an introduction and annotations, with the Penguin giving their commentary a frankly, but not stridently, feminist slant. The Hogarth Definitive Collected edition unfortunately repeats printers' errors or introduces new ones and offers only brief introductions. The edition that aims to be most thorough is that of the Shakespeare Head Press, which includes a history of composition and reception, factual annotations, and a discussion of the choice of copy text – the text, such as the first British or first American, upon which a current edition is based. Unfortunately cost is a real issue in the textual production and reception of Woolf's work. At £65, ten times that of the Oxford paperback, the Shakespeare Head editions will more likely be consulted than read, and only then if readers have access to a major research library. Students are more likely to encounter Woolf at the other end of the scale, through a Wordsworth Classics edition at £1.50, or perhaps through editions downloaded off the internet, texts which at this writing are notoriously inaccurate.

The Shakespeare Head edition collates those editions known to have been seen through the press by Woolf herself; it does not – and this is an important distinction for bibliographers – collate all the editions produced during Woolf's lifetime, editions on which she could have had, though she cannot be proven to have had, an editorial influence. Although the letters and diaries tend to indicate that once the first British and first American editions were in print Woolf tended to let them go, Julia Briggs argues forcefully in 'Between the Texts: Woolf's Acts of Revision' that while Woolf tended to pay little attention to the variants in her American editions, she continued to make changes to her British editions. Part of the problem is that in the *Bibliography* Kirkpatrick defines an 'edition' as a version in which the text as a whole has been reset; anything else she labels an 'impression'. This has misled scholars, Briggs contends, because Leonard Woolf referred to any version that required even partial resetting as an 'edition'. Thus a given text might be largely identical, and have the same page numbers, but include substantive variants. Here again the conditions of production are significant: Briggs points out that, 'When Woolf made changes in her published texts, she was printer enough to ensure that they corresponded exactly to the space available' (Briggs 1999, 159). A full study of the history of Woolf's texts remains to be written.

In this short discussion I have provided examples merely, not a survey, and thus have left out much excellent bibliographic work. But, and this is not to slight the studies and editions already in place, I believe that with the debates in editorial theory, with the new interests in social contexts and the materiality of Woolf's texts, the most exciting era of bibliographic approaches is about to begin.

7
postmodernist and
poststructuralist approaches

pamela l. caughie

'In or about December 1985, Virginia Woolf criticism changed' (Caughie 1991, 1). Thus begins my book, *Virginia Woolf and Postmodernism*, which demonstrates how postmodernist and poststructuralist theories can change, and have changed, the way we read Woolf – that is, the kinds of questions that motivate our readings, the objectives that guide our analyses, and the contexts in which we place her works. 1985 was the year Toril Moi published *Sexual/Textual Politics* and first articulated the opposition between French feminist *theory* and Anglo-American feminist *criticism*, establishing 'feminist postmodernism' as a new methodology that disrupted the cultural consensus among feminist critics of the 1970s (see Chapter 5 in this volume). In her introduction, 'Who's Afraid of Virginia Woolf?', Moi interrogates the 'theoretical assumptions about the relationship between aesthetics and politics' that made so many American feminist critics resistant to Woolf's modernist style. Relying on a 'realist aesthetic', these critics, Moi argues, assess Woolf's writing and politics in terms of whether 'the right content [is] represented in the correct realist form' (Moi 1985, 3–4, 7). (The relationship between form and content, as we will see, is one of the first casualties of a poststructuralist critical reading.) In contrast, Moi locates Woolf's politics *precisely in her textual practice* (16), focusing on the *politics of language* rather than on the politics *expressed* by Woolf's language (see Chapter 1 in this volume). Although Moi's rigid division between the French and the Anglo-Americans may lead to reductive readings, in which all American feminists are represented by Elaine Showalter, Moi was the first to articulate the difference French theory makes for feminist literary criticism. What this change in thinking means for reading Woolf is the subject of this chapter.

poststructuralism

Imagine giving or receiving the following assignment: choose any work by Woolf and write a critical essay on its stylistic features. Although vague, the

143

assignment would probably be comprehensible to most English students. Now, what if the assignment was worded somewhat differently: choose any text by Woolf and write a critique of its discursive conventions. Are these assignments asking the student to do the same thing but simply using different terminology? Or do the different terms – *text* v. *work*, *critique* v. *criticism*, *discourse* v. *style* – make a difference in what is expected? To grasp the significance of 'the linguistic turn' in literary criticism, the phrase used to designate the emergence of structuralist and poststructuralist theory, one must understand the difference between what these two assignments are asking students to do.

'The linguistic turn' dates from the writings of Ferdinand de Saussure, or more accurately, the transcriptions of his lectures produced from his students' notes. *Course in General Linguistics* (first published in French in 1949 and translated into English in 1960) changed the way linguists and literary critics think about language. Along with Sigmund Freud in psychology, Emile Durkheim in sociology, and Claude Lévi-Strauss in anthropology, Saussure helped to found structuralism, a methodology that attends to how events or objects function within a system rather than to what they mean in themselves. Saussure's *Course* gave us the concept of the *sign* that led to the development of a general science of signs called *semiology* (Roland Barthes' *Mythologies* [1957] is one of the best examples) as well as to the distinction cited above between *work* and *text*.

The sign is composed of a *signifier*, a form that signifies or carries meaning, and a *signified*, an idea or concept. The relation between the signifier and signified, which are inseparable, is arbitrary, by which Saussure meant unmotivated. A sign has significance or value in terms of its place within a system of language – that is, in terms of its relation to other signs within the system – not in relation to some pre-existing thing in the world or concept in one's head. The advantage of *sign* over *word* is that the sign consists of a relationship between two elements so that meaning is understood to be *relational* and *differential* (a sign carries meaning because of its difference from other signs), not *referential* (pointing to something in the world). In language, Saussure says, 'there are only differences *without positive terms*' (Saussure 1976, 120). That is, nothing has value or meaning in itself. A good example of this is our monetary system. An American dollar bill, for example, no longer carries value because it represents a certain amount of gold in the U.S. Treasury; rather, it has value because of its function within a system of exchange.[1] For Saussure, signs, not words, are the basic components of language.

One cannot grasp the significance of Saussure's concept of the sign if one translates *signifier* and *signified* into *word* and *meaning*. Yet it is the very inevitability of that mistake among beginning students of theory that can help us understand why Saussure needed the concept of the sign in the first place: namely, to challenge precisely the notion of language bound up with word-meaning.[2] The initial slip in translating the theoretical concept into familiar terms is a necessary one in order to conceptualize the difference a theory of the sign makes. Saussure's relational, as opposed to referential or expressivist, theory of meaning challenges our common sense thinking about language. The concept of the sign shifts our understanding of meaning from word-world relations (the reference theory of meaning) to signifier-signified relations, where meaning obtains from the relations among elements within a system. For we tend to think of a word's meaning as 'pointing to' something beyond language. The sign, in contrast, conceives meaning as something that is produced by and within the system of language itself. Whenever you have an explanation of meaning in terms of the place, function, or relations of elements within a system – rather than in terms of intrinsic value, characteristic features, or authorial intention – you have a structural analysis. In *The Psychopathology of Everyday Life*, for example, Freud analyzes slips of the tongue not in terms of their content, the secret truth about the subject that the slips reveal, but in terms of unconscious processes, such as displacement and condensation, which describe relations of substitution and combination.

Because structuralism, especially Saussure's linguistics, isolates or 'brackets' everyday social practices in order to focus on the functioning of the system itself, it is a type of formalism. Formalist critics, such as the New Critics of the 1940s and 1950s, analyze genres and individual works apart from their specific historical and cultural contexts. In literary studies, this focus was in part a reaction against nineteenth-century criticism that read literature as expressive of the author's biography and the work's historical moment. Formalists sought to isolate the conventions of writing that were specifically literary, categorizing different types of writing into distinct genres.

Poststructuralism is sometimes understood as a reaction against the rigidity of formalist or structural analysis that sought to identify and codify structures or sign systems conceived as coherent, complete, and relatively stable. However, as Jonathan Culler says, 'when so many of yesterday's structuralists are today's poststructuralists, doubts arise about the distinction' (Culler 1982, 25). Some of those theorists initially identified with structuralism, such as Barthes and Foucault, have become key figures in poststructuralist theory. More important than the distinctions between them (which vary widely in different disciplines) are the ways poststructuralists have acted on the implications of structuralism. Where structuralists explain how sign systems work, poststructuralists analyze how they came about, what exclusions were necessary to their formation, and how their power to organize reality might be resisted and changed. That is, poststructuralists focus on how something comes to be an object of interpretation rather than interpreting the meaning of the object itself or concentrating solely on how meanings are produced within signifying systems. Put differently, whereas structuralists are concerned with systems of meaning, poststructrualists are concerned with relations of power.

Some key texts can serve to illustrate the turn from structuralism to poststructuralism. Barthes' *S/Z* (1970) marks the turning point for some scholars who date poststructuralism from the student revolt in France in May 1968, the year Barthes began the series of lectures that culminated in this book length essay. In *S/Z*, he sets out to do a structuralist analysis of a story by Balzac only to find that the five codes into which he had divided the text didn't hold. That discovery gave rise to a series of digressions (*les divagations*) that interrupt and disrupt the structural analysis. What began as an analysis of the text's structure turned into a long meditation on reading. 'To interpret a text,' Barthes writes, 'is not to give it a ... meaning, but on the contrary to appreciate what *plural* constitutes it' (Barthes 1970, 5). Appreciating the plurality of the text means attending to the play of meanings. In the Preface Richard Howard writes that Barthes's conviction is 'that all telling modifies what is being told, so that ... what is told is always the telling' (xi).

Foucault's *Les Mots et les choses* (literally *Words and Things* but translated into English as *The Order of Things*), published in 1966, is another example of the shift from structuralism to poststructuralism. Foucault argues that Reason is an historical invention – that is, a kind or style of thinking, not the triumph of thinking over superstition or received opinion – and this kind of thinking gave us the notion of language as a means of representing a world apart. Thus, what seems 'natural' (language reflects reality, literature represents life) is understood as historical and cultural. Although *The Order of Things* retains a structuralist concern with the system of rules that determine what a given discourse can do, such as the systems of classification that characterize Enlightenment thinking, Foucault considers as well the way various systems of thought justify a certain economic and social order.[3]

Jacques Lacan's *Écrits*, also published in 1966, rereads Freud through Saussure, moving from a structuralist analysis of unconscious processes to a poststructuralist analysis of the place of the subject in the broader cultural domain. Language speaks us, Lacan declares, in that we become subjects only through entry into the Symbolic order of language and culture.[4] The unconscious is not the seat of instincts or the receptacle of repressed desire; rather, it is a structure that functions like a language. That is, unconscious processes reveal themselves in our linguistic practices. Culture is not what lies outside the subject, in the social institutions and practices of everyday life; on the contrary, culture is what structures the very emergence of the subject.

The writings of Jacques Derrida, however, and the style of reading known as deconstruction, epitomize poststructuralism for scholars and laypersons alike. Derrida's 'Structure, Sign and Play in the Discourse of the Human Sciences' (also 1966) and *Of Grammatology* (1967), among other publications, critique the 'logocentrism' of the Western philosophical tradition (literally, centred on the word, but referring more broadly to notions of grounds or essences) and its 'metaphysics of presence', the notion that a rational individual consciousness is at the centre of all communication. In logocentric thinking, speech is primary and writing derivative because in speech the intending subject is present and thus there is only a single source of authority linking the subject to his words.

To deconstruct a text is to show how the devalued term in binary oppositions, such as speech/writing, always already inhabits the privileged term.

What all these various writings do is to expose the essential difference, division, disorder, or discontinuity that gives rise to the seemingly unified, self-sufficient, coherent identity, whether of the individual or the system. Thus, poststructuralism concerns itself more with 'unravelling' systems of meaning than with explaining them.[5] Where structuralism was concerned with discovering the big structure that explained all others, poststructuralism reveals how every structure leads to yet another structure.

Saussure once said, 'it is often easier to discover a truth than to assign it its rightful place' (Saussure 1976, 68). It is one thing to understand Saussure's concept of the sign; it is quite another to determine precisely what this new concept means, how it changes what we do, not just how we talk. The structuralist revolution produced a shift in the *locus* of explanation, from the nature of meaning to the place of the signifier in a system of differential relations. Thus, structuralism required a new object of study. In literary studies, this object is the *text*, named and conceptualized by poststructuralists.[6] In *The Archaeology of Knowledge* (1969) Foucault argues that one of the first unities or familiar concepts that scholars must question is that of the book (or work): 'The frontiers of a book are never clear-cut: beyond the title, the first lines, and the last full stop, beyond its internal configuration and its autonomous form, it is caught up in a system of references to other books, other texts, other sentences; it is a node within a network' (quoted in Rivkin and Ryan 1998, 423). Julia Kristeva provides a name for this textual network, *intertextuality*, which she defines as 'a field of transpositions of various signifying systems' (Kristeva 1984, 60).

The notion of the *book* or the *work* is bound up with hermeneutics, the practice of exegesis or the finding of meaning in a work, and with the metaphysics of presence, the idea that a rational human mind is at the centre of human communication. Such thinking makes authorial intention a privileged concept in literary criticism. Even the New Criticism, which dismissed authorial intention as a fallacy, retained the notion of the *work* as opposed to the *text*, for its close attention to form and its bracketing of meaning kept the form/content dichotomy intact. Poststructuralism changes the concept of the object itself, which requires a change in the very nature of what readers and critics do. In other words, the shift from *work* to *text* entails a shift in the definition of writing itself, from a mode of communication to a signifying system. 'Writing is read,' writes Derrida, 'it is not the site … of hermeneutic deciphering, the decoding of a meaning or truth' (Derrida 1988, 21). Thus, poststructuralists are concerned not with questions of meaning but with forces of production. Barthes identifies the *work* with consumption and the *text* with production. When critics take Derrida's well-known statement, 'There is nothing outside the text', to mean that there is no social, historical, or material reality outside the pages of the book, they are reappropriating the notion of *text* to the concept of the *book*. There is nothing outside the text because text means a field of relations, not a physical object or self-contained system of meaning. The concept of the text dissolves the boundaries between types or genres of writing (central to New Criticism), and between literary and non-literary cultural productions (central to the institutionalization of literary studies).

This change in the concept of writing and in the object of study explains Barthes' infamous phrase, the 'death of the author'. Often misunderstood as simply dismissing authorial intention, as if what the author thought was irrelevant, the phrase refers to a particular historical conception of the author (as Foucault's essay 'What is an Author?' helps to make clear). To declare the death of the author, to displace the author as the centre or origin of meaning, is to affirm that language as a signifying system precedes and conditions thought. The notion of the author as the conscious, intending subject wholly responsible for the work's creation and meaning makes no sense in terms of the notion of a text conceived as 'a methodological field' (Barthes 1977a, 157), as a 'field of forces' and 'not the book' (Derrida 1986, 167–8). When Barthes writes in 'The Death of the Author', 'it is language which speaks, not the author' (Barthes 1977b, 143), he is following the structuralist notion of language to its logical conclusion (one Lacan also reached). Barthes and, more directly, Foucault treat *author* as a concept, not a person, and one that is related to other concepts (such as *originality*, *genius*, *oeuvre*) that function in a certain discourse of literary interpretation called hermeneutics.

Discourse, for poststructuralists, refers not simply to a way of speaking or a certain genre of writing, but to a systematic mode of enquiry defined by certain kinds of practices, based on certain shared assumptions, and producing a certain kind of knowledge, thereby legitimizing certain kinds of questions and invalidating (or ignoring) others. A minister can pronounce you husband and wife, a medical doctor can pronounce you cured, but if the doctor proclaimed you were married and the minister asserted you were well, one might well challenge the legitimacy of such statements. In 'Teaching Ignorance', Barbara Johnson shows how textbook questions about literary readings focus students' attention on certain kinds of questions ('Is Molière a feminist?') that deflect attention from other kinds of questions ('Who would want to call him that and why?'). Discourses entail power relations, linking power to knowledge, institutions, and disciplinary practices. Those symbolic systems that enable us to conceptualize ourselves as subjects and that establish the possibilities of meaning in a culture at a certain historical moment are discourses. To study discursive conventions, then, is to study the practices that produce, and legitimate, knowledge.

For poststructuralists, the relevant question is not 'what does it mean?' but 'how does it function within a system to produce meanings?' Whereas literary *criticism* concerns itself with exegesis, determining the meaning of a work or else bracketing its meaning to analyze its form (that is, the stylistic features, figures of speech, or rhetorical strategies employed to produce certain effects in the reader), poststructuralist *theory* concerns itself with *critique*, a detailing of the systematic ways in which meanings are produced by certain discourses. A critique recognizes that reading is 'deeply involved in questions of authority and power' (Johnson 1990, 46). As opposed to an interpretive practice oriented toward the revelation of meaning or truth, a critique interrogates the effects of designating something as the origin of meaning or truth, noting how what we think of as an origin or cause is the effect of certain historical, material, and institutionalized practices.

Gayatri Spivak's 1980 essay, 'Unmaking and Making in *To the Lighthouse*', provides an example of a poststructuralist – specifically, deconstructionist – reading, as signalled by its title. Spivak begins by insisting that she is not interpreting the novel: 'This essay is not necessarily an attempt to illuminate *To the Lighthouse* ... It is rather an attempt to use the book by deliberate super-imposition of two allegories – grammatical and sexual – and by reading it, at moments, as autobiography' (Spivak 1988, 30). Her approach 'produces a reading,' Spivak says, not 'the "truth" of the text' (30). Spivak plays with (that is, produces plural readings of) the concept of the 'copula', the fundamental structure of grammar and logic. The copula links two things, as in the statement 'Beauty is truth', and thus forms the basic grammar of the logical proposition: e.g., P is Q. But 'copula' also 'carries a sexual charge', Spivak says, 'copulation', a coupling not of ideas or grammatical elements but of persons. Structurally, Part II of *To the Lighthouse* serves as the copula, linking the first and third parts of the novel, yet the language of Part II, which Spivak calls the language of madness, 'uncouples' the logic of the narration. Any effort to read the novel linearly, as progressing from the pre-war narrative of Part I to the post-war narrative of Part III, must necessarily elide the equivocating language of Part II. 'Time Passes' marks the limit that makes the narration of Parts I and III possible. Spivak writes, 'I should like to propose that, whatever her writing intent, "Time Passes" narrates the production of a discourse of madness within this autobiographical roman à clef. In the place of the copula or the hinge in the book a story of unhinging is told' (35). (Note that the phrase, 'whatever her writing intent', does not deny that Woolf had intentions in writing the novel, but implies that such intentions, even if recoverable, no longer govern the reading of a text.)

Such a reading cannot be summed up by the logic of the proposition: that is, 'Spivak's reading argues that the novel means such-and-such.' Instead, one must pay attention to how the essay proceeds, the kinds of moves it makes. Spivak attends closely to the grammar of the novel. For example, quoting the passage in Part I in which Mrs Ramsay, knitting, looks up to see the third stroke of the lighthouse, and thinks, 'It was odd ... how if one was alone, one leant to inanimate things; ... felt they expressed one; felt they became one ...', Spivak notes that *one* 'can be both an "identity" (the word for the unit) and "difference" (an impersonal agent, not she herself)' (33). This is a characteristic poststructuralist move, noting how grammar functions to disrupt the notion of identity as sameness, revealing its dependence on difference. What Spivak's reading elucidates is how 'knowledge as noncontradiction (identity) is put in question' throughout the novel, 'unmaking' meaning to expose the suppressed elements giving rise to it (43). In another example, citing passages from Part II that carry a 'sexual charge', Spivak notes how 'the disappearance of reason and the confusion of sexuality are consistently linked' (38), again playing on the relation between the copula and copulation as well as noting the way the novel undermines the binary oppositions on which the logic of non-contradiction depends.

Spivak's reading of the copula brings to mind another key text in the emergence of poststructuralism, even though no one would call the text itself poststructuralist. J. L. Austin's *How to Do Things with Words* (1962), based on the William James Lectures Austin delivered at Harvard University in 1955, challenges the tendency of grammarians to think of statements as describing some state of affairs. Such statements Austin terms 'constatives' and distinguishes them from another category of statements he calls 'performatives'. Performatives bring into existence something that did not exist prior to the utterance itself. Austin's most famous example is the marriage ceremony, where the statement 'I now pronounce you husband and wife' brings the couple into being. Another often-used example is the U.S. Declaration of Independence, which begins, 'We the people of the United States ...'. The act of declaring independence from Britain brings into existence the 'we' of this statement, the people of the United States that the pronoun seems to refer to. Performatives are conventional acts, produced by certain persons in certain circumstances following certain practices or procedures. As such, they are evaluated in terms of their effects rather than their accuracy or truthfulness. By the end of the book, however, Austin has muddled the distinction between these types of statements by declaring that all speech acts, even constatives, are conventional.

What Austin's theory of the performative does, far more radically than declaring that certain statements bring something into being through the utterance itself, is to undercut the integrity of the subject, and this move in particular provides the poststructuralist connection. The 'solid moralist,' Austin says, believes that 'accuracy and morality alike are on the side of the plain saying that *our word is our bond*' (Austin 1962, 10, original italics). Austin's performative decouples the copula of that formulation, for a performative statement, as a conventional act, does not belong to the speaker. A performative act, such as promising, is accomplished in the language itself. By introducing a category of statements that are not capable of being evaluated in terms of truth or accuracy (what Austin terms the true/false fetish of the Descriptive Fallacy), and then suggesting that all speech acts, insofar as they are conventional, are performatives, Austin drives a wedge between word and bond, undercutting our tendency to attribute positions to the speaker alone (thereby ignoring the force of language and convention) and thwarting our desire for a guarantee that the speaker means what she or he says. The necessary connection between word and bond can no longer be assumed because assessing the truth or falsity of a statement can never be done 'outside' the performative dimension of language.

This is the kind of reading presented in Derrida's 'Signature, Event, Context,' (1972) which pushes Austin's theory of the performative to the limit. Derrida's reading of Austin has given us the concept of performativity so central to postmodern theory, a concept which has profoundly changed contemporary thinking about identity formation. Performativity conceives identity as the *effect* of the subject's performance of various cultural practices, a *product* of various discursive regimes (e.g., linguistic, psychological, sexual).[7] One reason poststructuralists speak of the *subject* rather than the *individual* is that the individual is an embodied person conceived as an autonomous, inviolable self, whereas the *subject* is a linguistic concept signifying a position within a structure (e.g., the subject of a sentence). *Individual* and *subject* are two very different ways of conceptualizing an object of study. Thus, poststructuralists challenge not just a way of thinking about language but, as Culler puts it, the very 'priority of the subject itself' (1997, 111). No wonder Catherine Belsey refers to the linguistic turn as a '"Copernican" revolution' (Belsey 1980, 130).[8]

postmodernism

In the weeks following September 11, 2001 many commentators and columnists read in the attacks on the World Trade Center in New York City and on the Pentagon in Washington DC the demise of postmodernism. In article after article, bearing such titles as 'Attacks on U.S. Challenge Postmodern True Believers' (*The New York Times*, 22 September, 2001) and 'After the Attack, Postmodernism Loses its Glib Grip' (*Chicago Tribune*, 27 September, 2001), writers proclaimed postmodernism the latest victim of the horror of the terrorist attacks. Why would an assault on symbols of US economic and military hegemony be interpreted as the end of a type of theory?[9] Insofar as postmodernism is identified as challenging objective notions of truth, rejecting foundationalist thinking and universal values, and conceiving reality as a 'fiction' or 'cultural construction', the argument goes, it leaves us with no position from which to respond, morally or militarily, to the terrorist attacks. If there is no reality, if values are relative (which is often misunderstood as 'subjective' rather than as 'contingent' and 'arbitrary', in Saussure's sense of that term), if all distinctions (fact/fiction, good/evil, truth/falsehood) are unstable and untenable, then, the argument continues, we have no way of justifying our condemnation of terrorism.[10] And since we all must condemn these attacks, postmodernism is given the lie.

Although these critics rightly point to some common themes identified with postmodernism, they fail to *read* any of the array of theories subsumed under this term and instead reduce the theories to a handful of propositions. In this way, they recuperate postmodernism through the very kind of thinking it challenges. Rather than argue with specific positions attributed to postmodernism in response to its critics, we can look, as we did with poststructuralism, at its emergence as a discourse and its relation to post-structuralist theory.

Some scholars insist on a distinction between poststructuralism and postmodernism while others conflate the two. What creates confusion is the grammar of the coordinating conjunction (poststructuralist *or* postmodernist theory, poststructuralist *and* postmodernist approaches) that suggests at once that one term is an alternative to the other and that the two terms are equivalent. Julie Rivkin and Michael Ryan assert that in or about 1979 'Post-structuralism changed names' and became 'Post-Modernism' (Rivkin and Ryan 1998, 352). Fredric Jameson argues for keeping the two terms distinct. Unlike 'poststructuralism,' which is tied to certain disciplines and takes as its 'fundamental component' the critique of interpretation, 'postmodernism' is a much more general term that describes an era rather than a theory or practice (Jameson 2001, xiv). Understood as a cultural dominant, postmodernism designates 'macrolevel' changes, such as in information technologies, global economies, biological and digital cloning, and life online. Jeffrey Nealon understands poststructuralism as a new logic, specifically, the logic of the postmodern (Nealon 1993, 20–1). But perhaps the best formulation of the connection between the poststructuralism emerging from the structuralist revolution and the broader implications of this revolution that now go by the name of postmodernism is Lacan's statement in 'The Insistence of the Letter in the Unconscious' (1957): 'The slightest alteration in the relation between man and the signifier, *in this case in the procedures of exegesis*, changes the whole course of history by modifying the lines which anchor his being. ... everything involving not just the human sciences, but the destiny of man, politics, metaphysics, literature, advertising, propaganda, and through these even the economy, everything has been affected' (321–2). That destiny is postmodernism.

As we have already seen with theorists such as Lacan and Foucault, postmod-ernists take language, conceived as a signifying system, as the starting point for thinking about the subject, politics, and justice rather than beginning with material reality, economic production, or social institutions. In general, one could define the project of postmodernism as Moi describes Kristeva's project: an effort 'to articulate a *politics* [and one might add, an ethics] which would constitute the logical consequence of a non-representational understanding of writing' (Moi 1986, 4). Jean Baudrillard provides one example. In a series of books from *The System of Objects* (1968) through *Simulations* (1983), Baudrillard contends that the real is a matter of signification, a 'simulacrum'. Whereas the system of representation presumes the sign bears some relation to the real (often conceived as a reflection of the real), simulation operates in the absence of a referent and thus, as Baudrillard puts it, simulation 'bears no relation to any reality whatever: it is its own simulacrum' (Baudrillard 1983, 11). Andy Warhol's seriograph of Marilyn Monroe (arguably the most famous image of postmodernism and parodied on the cover of *Virginia Woolf and Postmodernism*) points to the primacy of the image, its power to produce the 'real thing' it purportedly represents, even the power to usurp its place, and thereby undermining distinctions between the authentic original and the spurious reproduction. (Simone from the eponymous film by Andrew Niccol is a more contemporary example.) Reality is not so much denied by such theory as redefined: 'The very definition of the real becomes: *that of which it is possible to give an equivalent reproduction*' (Baudrillard 1983, 146).

Such thinking has led to the characterization of postmodernism in terms of apocalyptic statements about ends that recent news reports echo: the end of reality, the end of history, the end of meaning, the dissolution of the social bond, the death of the subject, and so on. In one sense, this characterization has a certain legitimacy insofar as postmodernists critique discourses of knowledge oriented toward a *telos*, or end, where truth or meaning will be revealed (Nealon 1993, 74–5). But in another sense, this characterization of loss assumes that there once was an organic society or an autonomous and rational self that has since suffered in a post-industrial, technologized, and globalized economy.[11] Those postmodernists who produce postmodern theories (as opposed to those who analyze postmodernism) understand such concepts of society and the self as 'fictions', narratives that have gained a certain legitimacy, what Jean-François Lyotard calls 'metanarratives' (Lyotard 1984, 34). In *The Postmodern Condition: A Report on Knowledge* (1984), Lyotard defines postmodernism as an 'incredulity toward metanarratives', those legitimizing discourses or languages based on a belief in universal values, objective knowledge, and rationalist thought that are oriented toward some end: truth, self-knowledge, freedom, progress. For postmodernists, such concepts as *freedom* or *progress* are historical productions, not transcendental values. Metanarratives are always narrated from the perspective of a 'metasubject,' Lyotard says, not a subject 'mired in the particular positivity of its traditional knowledge' (34). Today, metanarratives have given way to micronarratives, Lyotard says, so that 'the problem of legitimation ... has itself been legitimated as a problem' (27). Lyotard adopts the methodology of language games (from Ludwig Wittgenstein's *Philosophical Investigations* (1953)) where legitimation is a matter of a temporary consensus among players on the rules of the game in order to get something done. 'That is what the postmodern world is all about,' writes Lyotard. 'Most people have lost the nostalgia for the lost narrative. It in no way follows that they are reduced to barbarity. What saves them from it is their knowledge that legitimation can only spring from their own linguistic practices and communicational interaction' (Lyotard 1984, 41).

Commentators on September 11th have prematurely declared the death of postmodernism. For they mistook postmodernism for a set of beliefs, a philosophy of life that could be tested against the reality of the terrorist attacks and found wanting. Conceiving postmodernism as a new logic or a mode of analysis, or in terms of the problem of legitimation, provides a different response. Given that postmodernism seeks out the conflicts and instabilities in any system of value, it challenges the 'us-against-them' thinking that resulted in the terrorist attacks and justified the US response to them. Lyotard defines terror as 'the efficiency gained by eliminating, or threatening to eliminate, a player from the language game one shares with him' (63). Postmodernism exposes the potential terror in any practice of justice rooted in universal values or consensus (65).

Wittgenstein's concept of language games that informs Lyotard's theory of the postmodern helps us to understand the problem of defining a concept like 'postmodernism' as a problem of grammar. As Wittgenstein puts it, the difficulty stems from our 'tendency to look for something in common to all the entities which we commonly subsume under a general term' (Wittgenstein 1965, 17). Yet the change in thinking we have been discussing in terms of poststructuralism would shift the question, from 'What is postmodernism?' or 'What is its essential difference from modernism?' to 'What is the point of the distinction between these terms? How are we using this term, in what context, and for what purposes?' (the kinds of questions raised in *Virginia Woolf and Postmodernism* (Caughie 1991)).[12] As we have learned from the poststructuralist revolution, when we ask the meaning of a word, we are, to quote Wittgenstein again, investigating 'its use in the language' (Wittgenstein 1953, 43) or in a particular discourse. Thus, it is important to keep in mind that postmodernism is employed differently in different disciplines. In philosophy, for example, postmodernism designates the end of metaphysics and the projects of the Enlightenment. In architecture, it refers to a specific style, a 'double-coding' that incorporates both new (modernist) techniques and more traditional patterns in an effort to respond to social reality (Jencks 1989, 14). In history and sociology, it functions as a periodizing concept, denoting a particular era that Jameson calls late capitalism. In literary studies, the term is used in both senses, as the literary period that follows modernism, which dates roughly from the 1890s to the 1940s, and as a style of writing that retains some modernist traits (experimentation, irony, self-reflexivity) while rejecting other aspects of modernism (its notion of art's autonomy, its belief in individual subjectivity, its assumed resistance to mass culture).[13]

By virtue of its very name, concepts of postmodernism depend on how a discipline conceives modernism, which means that definitions of postmodernism must necessarily change as concepts of modernism are challenged and revised. Since literary history is made, not simply recorded, we cannot speak of modernism as, to borrow Foucault's language, 'that which was already there' but only as something 'fabricated in a piecemeal fashion' after the fact (Foucault 1984, 72). When we contrast postmodernism with modernism, then, we are not comparing two things but rather different ways of conceiving writing and reading. Revisionary readings of modernism have been underway for over twenty years now, uncovering, as Jonathan Arac puts it, 'an ever-receding history of postmodernism' (Arac 1986, x–xi) by challenging received interpretations of a largely white, Western, and masculine modernist tradition and its New Critical legacy that have shaped the canon of twentieth-century British and American literature.[14] Such revisionary readings make apparent what *Virginia Woolf and Postmodernism* emphasizes: namely, that what we single out as 'features' of modernist or postmodernist texts are not properties of the texts themselves but the values created by a particular approach to literature (Caughie 1991, 16). Which brings us to the question of how to read modernist writers such as Virginia Woolf from the perspective of postmodernism.

As one example, let's return to *To the Lighthouse* and consider what a postmodern approach might entail.[15] Not surprisingly, given the affinities between poststructuralism and postmodernism, such an approach will produce a reading that looks a lot like Spivak's poststructuralist reading discussed above. Given that postmodernists attend to the way any discourse produces its own non-knowledge, that is, the structural exclusions that make the functioning of any discourse possible, and thereby reveal, in Foucault's words, 'the heterogeneity of what was imagined as consistent with itself' (Foucault 1984, 82), we can begin by asking what structural exclusions does Woolf's novel produce? As in Spivak's reading, 'Time Passes' functions in a postmodern reading as a problematizing disruption in the family-romance narrative constructed in Parts I and III of the novel, exposing what that developmental narrative cannot account for. But whereas Spivak focuses on the dissolution of reason in 'Time Passes', with its language of madness and its associative logic, the unhinging of the copula, a postmodern reading might well focus on the inclusion of stories often left out of our metanarratives, or what Foucault calls our 'monumental histories'.[16]

Part II narrates the gaps between the acts of history not only in presenting the minute particulars of the passage of time (such as the fold of a shawl loosening from a boar's skull or a rock dislodging from a cliff) over major historical events (such as war and death, presented in parenthetical asides) but also in testifying to what has not been narrated in fiction or history: specifically, the memories and interior monologues of Mrs McNab, the woman who cleans and tends the Ramsays' summer home. What matters, though, is not simply the inclusion of 'others', but the way in which those others function within the narrative. Instead of recuperating Mrs McNab's story, 'Time Passes' seems to confront its own difficulties in imagining the inner life of this lower-class woman: 'Visions of joy there must have been at the wash-tub, say with her children [....] Some cleavage of the dark there must have been ...' (*TTL* 178). Although Erich Auerbach first pointed out that such narrative uncertainty is characteristic of the novel as a whole, in his famous close reading of a scene from Part I of the novel, the objective of Auerbach's modernist reading is to describe and classify the narrative techniques; the objective of a postmodern reading is to interrogate their function (see Chapter 1 in this volume). The narrative uncertainty does not produce the same effect throughout. The narrative speculations about Mrs Ramsay in Part I ('Was it wisdom? Was it knowledge' [*TTL* 69]) endow her with an aura of secrecy and a depth of meaning denied to Mrs McNab, who 'continued to drink and gossip as before' (*TTL* 179).

Vision, so important for the modernist artist, is denied Mrs McNab. When Mrs McNab remembers Mrs Ramsay, she thinks of concrete things: 'boots and shoes', 'a brush and comb', 'a grey cloak' (*TTL* 185); when Lily remembers Mrs Ramsay, she tries to imagine her thoughts and desires: 'What did the hedge mean to her, what did the garden mean to her, what did it mean to her when a wave broke?' (*TTL* 267). Mrs McNab's memories consist of isolated things; Lily puts things together, 'write[s] them out in some sentence' (*TTL* 199), a process that, in this novel, defines vision, the ability to forge relationships out of disparate experiences. Although given some voice in this novel, Mrs McNab is denied narrative agency, the ability to select and order events into a meaningful sequence, the power to imaginatively reconstruct the past and thus fulfil some present desire, as Lily does in one medium and Woolf in another. Thus far from recuperating Mrs McNab into the narrative, Part II acknowledges the limits of its vision.

Whereas a poststructuralist reading analyzes the language and structure of the text, a postmodernist reading considers as well the motivated, non-innocent nature of reading. It draws attention to the structural exclusions created by any reading that, like Auerbach's, emphasizes continuity in history, unity and closure in narrative, and commonality in culture. A postmodern reading is less concerned with defining a modernist classic like *To the Lighthouse* than with interrogating how and why it has been defined as it has; less concerned with tracing the evolution of modernism than with tracing the conflicts and motives behind its emergence as a literary concept; less concerned with interpreting the novel than with scrutinizing what is at stake in any interpretation. Aesthetic appreciation is occluded by such a reading; notions of beauty and truth become irrelevant – or rather, they are understood to be imposed notions of value, not qualities of the text itself.[17]

(re)reading woolf

It seems appropriate at this point to ask, in the opening words of Part III of *To the Lighthouse*, 'What does it mean then, what can it all mean?' (*TTL* 197). What difference does it make for what we do as Woolf scholars, literary critics, and teachers of literature? What happens to literary criticism when we stop thinking of texts in terms of form and content, and when we acknowledge the 'undecidability' of writing, the inability to reduce a text to its themes? We can begin to answer these questions by contrasting some of the different ways critics have responded to the challenge of rereading Woolf in the aftermath of poststructuralist and postmodernist theories.

As early as Harry Levin's 'What Was Modernism?', published in that decisive year of 1966, critics began comparing modernist writing with the *nouveau roman* of the 1950s and the American postmodernist literature of the 1960s. Initially such readings tended to mine modernist texts for postmodernist features, intimating the ways modernist writers anticipated postmodernism. Such readings might emphasize, for example, the metafictional devices in *Jacob's Room*, where the text calls attention to itself *as* a text as in 'What do we seek through millions of pages? Still hopefully turning the pages – oh, here is Jacob's room' (*JR* 132). Or they might cite the line from 'Time Passes' quoted by Spivak, 'The mirror is broken', and elaborate on the poststructuralist implications of such a line, suggesting the end of representation and mimesis. Yet, as *Virginia Woolf and Postmodernism* shows, to begin with a general definition of postmodernism and then to identify isolated instances of postmodern themes and strategies in modernist writings may change thematic emphases but not necessarily the motives and objectives for reading. The assumptions that the text is an autonomous entity existing prior to and apart from our reading of it; that all texts grouped under the same rubric share certain common features; that these features are properties of the texts themselves; and that the text bears a reflective relation to its historical moment belong to a *modernist* paradigm.

More recently, in the aftermath of the linguistic turn, postmodernist approaches tend to recontextualize modernists, not just to challenge the inherited critical tradition established by modernists like Eliot, but also to bring together otherwise separated cultural discourses through the text itself. That is, postmodernist readings (as opposed to readings that discuss modernists in terms of postmodernism) move through poststructuralism to change the kinds of questions that may be productively raised in a reading and thereby to reconsider what a text might do.[18]

Virginia Woolf and Postmodernism was the first book-length study of Virginia Woolf to bring the various strains of poststructualist and postmodernist theory to bear on Woolf's writings and to change our thinking about what texts do. What is most distinctive about the book is its way of proceeding. Chapters do not move chronologically through Woolf's major novels and essays; instead, each chapter sets up a particular problem in Woolf criticism and reads several works (both primary texts by Woolf and secondary texts on her) against each other to illustrate how poststructuralist theories of language and postmodernist theories of narrative can get us unstuck from certain habitual modes of thinking that give rise to the problem to be resolved. That is, the book does not set out to explain postmodernism, nor to do poststructural-ist readings of individual works (as Spivak does with *To the Lighthouse*), nor to claim Woolf as a postmodernist. Instead, it demonstrates how to read differently in response to poststructuralist insights. 'Through a series of related explorations', *Virginia Woolf and Postmodernism* enacts 'a way of thinking about and responding to narrative discourse that considers different ways of relating things rather than the distinction between two things' (Caughie 1991, xii).

Virginia Woolf and Postmodernism opens by showing that even Woolf's deconstructing feminist critics, who challenge modernist readings of her works, rely on critical assumptions and methods bound up with the modernist aesthetics they claim to reject. What would it mean to act on a different set of assumptions is demonstrated in subsequent chapters. Chapters 1 and 5 can provide examples. Chapter 1 argues that as long as we accept authenticity, autonomy, permanence, and uniqueness as our aesthetic standards, we will interpret a novel that is fragmentary, contradictory, or imitative either as a failed endeavour or as an accurate reflection of the chaos or banality of life itself. Yet in much postmodern fiction, as in Woolf's last novel, what was once narrated – the doubts and difficulties of the artist – in modernist novels (such as Joyce's *Portrait of the Artist as a Young Man*) becomes the *structural* principle of the works themselves. Thus, *Between the Acts*, with its numerous breaks and interruptions, its cacophony and banalities, need not be read as the artist's loss of faith in the efficacy of art or as reflecting the social disruptions caused by the advent of war; rather, these structures are the *logical consequence* of a novel that makes error, uncertainty, frustration, and discontinuity elements of – not obstacles to – the reading and writing of literature, and one that seeks to engage the public in the production and preservation of art (55). What we find in Woolf's writings, then, are not her ideas about art or patriarchy or gender expressed through her particular style, but the theoretical, political, and aesthetic implications of her changing textual practices. In this late novel, Woolf no longer conceives art as unifying a culture because, as she writes in a 1927 diary entry, national divisions are being eroded by new technologies, such as airplanes and airwaves (*D3* 145). In the cacophonies of Woolf's novel one can hear the sounds of a unified and univocal audience dispersing.[19]

Chapter 5 takes up the question of aesthetic value by reading what is perhaps the least valued of Woolf's novels, her mock biography of Elizabeth Barrett Browning's dog, *Flush* (1933). Woolf's best-selling novel in England, and a Book-of-the-Month Club selection in the US, *Flush* is often dismissed as simply a commercial venture not a serious work of art meriting critical attention. Those who do take the novel seriously read through the surface joke to the serious subtext beneath: its critique of London's class and sex oppression. However, insofar as postmodernism bears a different relation to the categorical distinction between the serious and the commercial, or high art and popular culture, rereading *Flush* from the perspective of postmodern art can change our way of valuing so that distinguishing absolutely between the high and the low, the canonical and the marginal, the serious and the spurious is no longer worthwhile, no longer a valuable service rendered by critics and teachers of literature (Caughie 1991, 145). Instead we can read *Flush* as the waste product of a canonical economy, what has been discarded from Woolf's modernist canon, and in doing so expose the functioning of that valuational system. For in terms of its own valuational history (that is, the history of choices Woolf made in producing the novel and that readers and critics have made in consuming it), *Flush* reveals that aesthetic value (defined as intrinsic) and economic value (determined by exchange worth) are mutually dependent (147) and, further, that readings, texts, and canons are never pure but always the product of divergent systems of value. As a waste product (at once necessary to the process of production and a superfluous by-product) *Flush* exposes the illusion of purity, prestige, and consensus that shores up a canonical economy.

Virginia Woolf and Postmodernism sets out to change our critical responses, not to codify a poststructuralist or postmodernist critical approach. As such, the book provides an example of a *performative* approach, one that sets out to enact the difference poststructuralism and postmodernism make to our ways of proceeding, to stage an engagement between Woolf and postmodernism that changes our ways of reading, not just our readings of Woolf.

Another excellent example of a performative reading is Peggy Kamuf's essay, 'Penelope at Work: Interruptions in *A Room of One's Own*' (1982). Kamuf reads Woolf through Foucault, pointing to both the similarities and differences in their writings. Her purpose is less to shed light on either author than to set up a confrontation between the two to see what might emerge from the encounter. As in Spivak's reading of *To the Lighthouse*, Kamuf's reading concerns the way Woolf's essay 'entails as well its own undoing' (Kamuf 1982, 7). Interruptions and digressions structure *A Room of One's Own*, its movement forwarded by 'unruly associations' (8) rather than by logical connections, 'always deferring the promised ends of its labor' (10) – that is, withholding any final signified. 'Through these deflections,' Kamuf writes, '*A Room of One's Own* defines a novel position in relation to the locked room of history' (9). Kamuf emphasizes the 'place' (7) or 'space' (9) of women's writing, its *position* and function rather than its *meaning*. 'Since women's writing,' she continues, 'cannot be studied in the library', because women have been written out of (literary) history, 'it will have to be read into the scene of its own exclusion' (9). That is, the history of women's writing, as Woolf shows, will have to be 'invented' not simply discovered (9).

To illustrate how this might work, Kamuf interrupts her own reading of Woolf's essay with a turn to Foucault's writings, specifically the first volume of his *History of Sexuality*. This engagement between these writers exposes the 'fault lines' (10) or omissions in each. If we read Woolf's essay as a model for a feminist practice that attacks male authors and 'the authority of masculine privilege', the interruption by Foucault gives us pause. For Foucault's writing exposes the masculine subject and its privilege as the effect, not the origin, of 'an historical production' (10). That is, that masculine subject is a product of history, not its determining source. Thus, Foucault's analyses of power and subjectivity provide another context in which to read Woolf's essay, showing us how 'to read *A Room of One's Own* as turning away from [the] historical preoccupation with the subject, closing the book on the "I"' (11). The encounter with Foucault marks an interruption or hiatus in the history of both the Enlightenment subject and the woman writer.

Kamuf's essay does not end with this Foucauldian reading of Woolf, however. Rather, Kamuf offers another digression, this time by reading Foucault through Woolf. Where Woolf's essay proceeds by interruptions and digressions, Foucault's writing brooks no distractions, Kamuf says (12). Thus, the one who theorizes power relations occupies the historical position of power by following 'a train of thought which has been trained ... to think without interruptions' (13). Despite his theorizing, Foucault retains the place of the privileged, undivided subject, the 'I' of Cartesian discourse from which *A Room* has turned, even as he argues that the Cartesian subject of Reason comes into being through 'an exclusion – of unreason, of madness' (13). In contrast, Woolf's essay actually accomplishes a disruption of power by interrupting its narrative with fictionalized scenes of what has been excluded from history, such as the imagined (and historically inaccurate) scene of Jane Austen hiding her manuscripts from visitors, or the scene of the great scholar leaving his study for the nursery to find his mind revitalized by his wife's creation in 'a different medium from his own' (quoted in Kamuf 1982, 14). Such fictionalized interruptions function to throw power off course, so to speak, by inventing moments when power is dislodged from discourse (14).

If Kamuf were to end her essay here, explaining how these two writers differ, she would risk turning her performative reading into a discursive one. Instead, Kamuf plays with the concept of interruption by interrupting her own argument, anticipating objections from the reader that 'all of this is quite fanciful speculation' (16) – or as students sometimes complain, 'you're reading too much into Woolf's essay'. (Of course, that's precisely what post-structuralist theorists do, they read too much into texts in that they read for the excess of meanings and conceive the text as a 'field of forces' not an autonomous object.) Kamuf concedes that this objection to her scenes of encounters (between Woolf and Foucault, between Jane Austen and the male intruder) is valid and professes that she will 'try to conclude on more solid ground' (16). But what does she do but turn her attention to yet another interruption in *A Room* (16), performing the kind of approach that works against an argument that moves logically toward some final signified.

Such readings as Kamuf's, Spivak's and mine treat Woolf's fictional writings in the same way they treat the theoretical texts, rather than taking the theory as offering explanatory paradigms for the fiction. In this sense they are *performative*. Reading Woolf in relation to poststructuralist discourses also entails more *discursive* approaches. Makiko Minow-Pinkney's *Virginia Woolf and the Problem of the Subject* (1987), the first full-length study of Woolf in terms of poststructuralist theory, draws heavily on the writings of Lacan and especially Kristeva and other French feminists, such as Hélène Cixous. Minow-Pinkney explains the significance of the principle of *difference* as opposed to the logic of identity in understanding the intimate relation between Woolf's 'aesthetic innovation and [her] feminist conviction' (Minow-Pinkney 1987, 8) (see Chapter 3 in this volume). Woolf's feminist writings call into question precisely the notion of identity that would conceive the subject as separate from and confronting an external reality, and presenting a more poststructuralist understanding of the subject as 'constituted in and by' a network of sign systems. Androgyny becomes, in Minow-Pinkney's reading, not 'false transcendence of sexual identity' or an 'evasion' of reality, as it is for Elaine Showalter, but a 'play of heterogeneity, a fertile difference' that rethinks unity as multiplicity (12).[20]

Similarly, in *Imagination in Theory: Culture, Writing, Words, and Things* (1999), Michèle Barrett argues that reading Woolf through poststructuralism enables us to see, for example, that for Woolf the problem of femininity takes root at an unconscious level rather than in social convention (Barrett 1999, 41). Barrett identifies poststructuralism with what Foucault calls 'dispensing with things', understood as anterior to discourse, and instead focusing on the formation of objects that emerge only in discourse (18). Barrett points out the many ways in which Woolf's writing lends itself to a poststructuralist reading, as in Woolf's questioning of the assumptions of unitary, uncontradictory identity and her exploration of a multiple, divided consciousness. In her chapter 'Virginia Woolf Meets Michel Foucault', Barrett explains how Foucault's account of the history of the reason/madness division helps to explain critics' obsession with Woolf's madness (186–7). This area offers 'resonances' between the works of these two writers; both are 'pre-eminently interested in words, in language, in what is said and can be said' (187). Yet there is another side, what Barrett terms a 'mystic' side, to Woolf that still believes in those Enlightenment values of freedom, truth, and vision (45). Poststructuralism may illuminate aspects of Woolf's thinking, but Woolf is no poststructuralist.

Such critics as Minow-Pinkney and Barrett advance a poststructuralist understanding of Woolf by explaining how these theories can better account for Woolf's feminist beliefs, her changing narrative strategies, and the political implications of her writings. They are *discursive* insofar as they set out to explain the relation between Woolf and poststructuralism or postmodernism. (*Discursive* is one of those ambiguous words that poststructuralists love, meaning both a rational analysis that moves coherently from topic to topic and an explanation that rambles. Although I mean it here in the first sense, a poststructuralist would remain sensitive to the implications of the alternative meaning, which cannot simply be set aside but which marks the difference within this concept. Thus, the distinction I am drawing here between the discursive and the performative is useful, not ontological. A performative approach is not an alternative to the discursive but rather one that brings out the double meaning of that concept.) Both Barrett and Kamuf caution us about forcing parallels between Woolf's and Foucault's writings, but Barrett emphasizes the values or arguments in Woolf's writing that work against a poststructuralist reading whereas Kamuf notes the insights that emerge as much in the contradictions as in the affinities between Woolf and Foucault. Both readings, the discursive and the performative, run risks. If you perform the difference postmodernism makes, you risk that your readers or students won't get it; if, instead, you explain postmodernism, reducing it to a set of themes or positions, then you would seem not to grasp the difference it makes. Perhaps one final example can make this clear.

Kamuf's essay and my book implicitly raise the issue of how to situate Woolf in a literary history delineated as a movement from modernism to postmodernism. This is the problem Patricia Waugh faces directly in *Feminine Fictions: Revisiting the Postmodern* (1989), which contains a chapter on Woolf. Acknowledging that feminism and postmodernism share the goal of 'deconstructing both the subject and the "master narratives" of history', Waugh cautions that any effort to bring these two discourses together must also contend with 'their historical differences' (Waugh 1989, 16). In the 1960s, when postmodernists were proclaiming the death of the author and undermining the unified subject, women writers were beginning, '*for the first time in history*,' Waugh says, to construct a unified subjectivity that would give them 'a history and agency in the world' (6, original italics). Drawing on object-relations theory, Waugh argues that women writers have developed a relational and collective concept of identity. While this concept may appear to be the same as a poststructuralist concept of identity, as expressed in Lacan's 'The Mirror Stage', for example, Waugh argues that for women writers, this sense of identity must be seen in terms of women's material lives and a history of women's writing. To those marginalized by society and by history, Waugh says, 'a sense of identity as constructed through impersonal and social relations of power' – that is, a 'postmodern' sense of identity – has been part of their self-concept all along (3, 10, 14).

Waugh's book goes a long way towards explaining how and why women writers have largely been written out of the historical narrative of modernism's evolution into postmodernism, and towards creating an alternative literary history that can accommodate women's writing. But Waugh's is not a postmodern reading, as I will explain. Waugh reads retroactively from our postmodern moment to show how women writers anticipated what will have been a postmodern critique of the subject.[21] 'It is the gradual recognition of the value of construing human identity in terms of relationship and dispersal', a recognition that came with the failure of feminism's essentialist stage and feminists' growing awareness of women's heterogeneity, 'which has led feminist writing closer to a "postmodernist" concept of subjectivity' (12–13),

Waugh states. Yet the syntax here – 'it is the gradual recognition' – posits a collective agency. That is, the very sentence in which Waugh acknowledges the heterogeneity of women posits feminists as a single entity coming to share the same awareness. Likewise, when Waugh says that Woolf was 'among the first feminist writers' to recognize the inauthenticity of unitary concepts of identity and to move closer towards a postmodernist concept, she reveals the tension in the revisionary history she has been creating. For Woolf was writing long before feminism's essentialist phase of the 1960s, which Waugh says was a necessary stage in the emergence of a relational concept of identity. In other words, Waugh's revisionary history is narrated in traditional terms. To provide a coherent, continuous history of women's writing, Waugh must eschew historical specificity (for example, by neglecting the historical changes informing postmodernism, reifying it as a set of propositions, as well as the historical conflicts informing feminism, such as the conflict between women's rights and women's desires). In Waugh's history, a belief in a unitary concept of identity is not so much proven inauthentic as it is displaced, from individual, empirical subjects to collective, historical agents – that is, from the 'I' to the 'we'.[22]

What happens to a narrrative of history once the collectivity is called into question, as it is in Lyotard's definition of postmodernism as an incredulity toward 'metanarratives'? For one thing, it means a change in the kinds of narratives we create, both fictional and historical. In narrating a story of the progressive liberation of women's writing, in constructing a plot that reveals women's writing as moving from the inauthentic to the authentic, the limited to the inclusive, Waugh's revisionary history relies on a particular kind of narrative, a story of conflict between the subject and her society, a story of the quest for a new, more equal society that can better accommodate a new sense of self. It is a distinctively *modern* plot, a logical progression of events toward some *telos*. One consequence of this history is that Waugh praises *To the Lighthouse* (that pillar of modernism) for its movement towards an authentic concept of self and slights Woolf's last novel, *Between the Acts* (1941), for its 'partial and extremely tentative' vision of social change (123). But what might make *Between the Acts* resistant to Waugh's reading is that it puts into question the very concept of history and narrative that informs it.[23]

If 'make it new' was the catchphrase of modernism, Woolf's 'dispersed are "we"', a refrain from *Between the Acts*, might serve as a slogan for postmodernism.[24] In her last novel, Woolf confronts her own belief, as expressed in her contemporaneous essay, 'The Leaning Tower', in the ability of outsiders to come together in a shared collective vision. The discontinuous structure of that novel, with its numerous breaks and interruptions and its incompatible interpretations, puts into question the expectation of shared meaning, questioning, as Rachel Bowlby puts it, 'the supposed collectivity of "ourselves"' – 'dispersed are "we"' (Bowlby 1988, 152–3).[25] *Between the Acts* confronts the tension between the historical need to recognize diversity in the polity that was increasingly thrust upon modernist writers in the interwar period, and the equally compelling psychological need to seek identity in the collectivity, especially when facing war or creating a movement such as feminism. In confronting the possibility that outsiders may not come to share a social vision, Woolf was compelled to face what postmodernists recognize as the crisis of the collectivity. Such a realization does not necessarily result in despair but rather can serve to create a willingness to tolerate the incompatibilities and discontinuities that any collective concept engenders. Woolf's artist, Miss La Trobe, is no longer the isolated individual coming to terms with her artwork, or a spokesperson for a culture or a constituency. Like Miss La Trobe's play within the novel, Woolf's narrative raises questions about who can produce art and for what audience, and who can provide narratives of our past.[26]

This is the kind of critique presented in *Virginia Woolf and Postmodernism*, with which I began this section. In seeking to change the way we approach Woolf's writings in the wake of postmodernism, not to argue that Woolf was a postmodernist *avant la lettre*, it does not attempt to narrate a continuous history, explaining how Woolf's writing comes to resemble a postmodern aesthetic or theory of the subject. Rather, each chapter interrogates a different set of texts and a different set of problems that postmodernist theories can help us to unravel. In trying to free us from certain habitual ways of thinking about language, literature, history, and politics, *Virginia Woolf and Postmodernism* attempts to change the structure of debate informing Woolf studies that has trapped us in certain kinds of arguments, to remove the impasses created as much by our own descriptions as by the object of study, and thereby to open up new questions to pursue. Its objective is best described by Wittgenstein's phrase, 'Now I know how to go on' (Wittgenstein 1965, 154).

where do we go from here?

No one today would call her or himself a structuralist critic, and increasingly identifying oneself as a poststructuralist, deconstructive, or postmodernist critic is becoming equally passé. Instead today we hear scholars identified with movements such as cultural studies, gender studies, and queer theory. Still, such approaches have evolved from poststructuralism, however much they may also diverge from it, by taking its notion of the text to the limit. Once we conceive our object of study as the text rather than the work, and turn our attention from a criticism of literature to a critique of discourse, the field of analysis for literary scholars opens up. Once we conceptualize subjectivity in terms of difference rather than identity, traditional distinctions, such as masculine/feminine and heterosexual/homosexual, break down, giving rise to a proliferation of gender and sexual identities.

We can see the effects of questioning traditional boundaries between discourses, such as literary studies and popular culture, in Woolf studies as well.

Scholars such as Brenda Silver, Jennifer Wicke and Jane Garrity, for example, have explored Woolf's place in popular and mass culture.[27] In *Virginia Woolf Icon* (1999), Silver takes as her subject the proliferation of images of Woolf, both in academic scholarship and in popular culture, that the cover of *Virginia Woolf and Postmodernism* flaunts. Her purpose is less to shed light on Woolf as a woman or a writer than to interrogate the significance of her iconicity, reading beer ads and book covers along with Woolf criticism. Wicke's discussion of *Mrs Dalloway* moves beyond a focus on Clarissa's shopping to analyze the 'marketing' of modernism and Bloomsbury as 'an experiment in coterie consumption' (Wicke 1994, 6). Reading Woolf's image in *Vogue* magazine, Garrity analyzes not just the relation between high and popular culture, but also the relation between Bloomsbury as a 'mass-market phenomenon' and the formation of a nationalist identity (Garrity 1999, 29). These writings show that 'there is nothing outside the text', nothing that cannot be read as text, conceived as a 'field of forces' and relations of power and production, and thus nothing that falls outside the purview of the Woolf scholar. While some fear that cultural studies is opening the floodgates, undermining the distinctiveness of literary studies,[28] one can also see this change more positively, as a rethinking of inherited notions of aesthetics, the kind of rethinking that has long sustained humanistic enquiry. This change in the object of study, this shift from literary studies to cultural studies, attests to the continued influence of poststructuralist and postmodernist theories.

notes

I want to thank my research assistant, Brendan Balint, for his help on this chapter.

1. Michel Foucault discusses the functioning of the monetary system in *The Order of Things: An Archaeology of the Human Sciences*, trans. Alan Sheridan.

2. For a fuller discussion of Saussure's significance to the linguistic turn in literary criticism, see Pamela L. Caughie's *Passing and Pedagogy: The Dynamics of Responsibility*, Chapter 2, 'Dead Subjects', 68–80.

3. Expressive realism in literature is another example. 'Still the dominant popular mode in literature, film and television drama', Catherine Belsey writes, and often used as the standard against which modernist and postmodernist literature is measured, expressive realism 'coincides chronologically with the epoch of industrial capitalism' and works with other systems of meaning to shore up the ideology necessary for the functioning of that economic system. Catherine Belsey, *Critical Practice*, 13, 67 ff.

4. 'Language speaks us' is a characteristic expression that captures Lacan's theory of language and subjectivity. For example, in chapter 4 of seminar XVII Lacan states, 'When I say, "the use of language", I do not mean that we use it. It is language that uses us.' I am grateful to Levi R. Bryant of Loyola's Philosophy Department for this reference. The quotation in question can be found on page 75 of Seminar XVII, L'envers de la psychanalyse. Russell Grigg translates it in *The Other Side of Psychoanalysis* (forthcoming).

5. 'Unravel' is used by many critics to describe a deconstructive approach. See, for example, Peggy Kamuf's essay discussed below.

6. See, for example, Roland Barthes, 'From Work to Text', in *Image, Music, Text*, trans. Stephen Heath.

7. Here it is important to distinguish 'performativity' in this poststructuralist sense from the use of 'performativity' meaning maximum efficiency in production, with an emphasis on results.

8. Lacan tells us that Freud himself referred to his discovery of the unconscious as a Copernican revolution. See 'The Insistence of the Letter in the Unconscious' (Lacan 1972, 311).

9. As Stanley Fish writes, 'it seemed bizarre that events so serious would be linked causally with a rarefied form of academic talk'. See 'Condemnation without Absolutes', *The New York Times*, 15 October 2001: A23.

10. Judith Butler says such characterizations of postmodernism are 'articulated in the form of a fearful conditional' that 'warn[s] against an impending nihilism'. See 'Contingent Foundations: Feminism and the Question of "Postmodernism"', in *Feminists Theorize the Political*, eds Judith Butler and Joan W. Scott, 3.

11. This is Jameson's historicist argument in *Postmodernism*, which he contrasts with the 'poststructuralist' argument that such a subject never existed 'but constituted something like an ideological mirage' (Jameson 2001, 15).

12. Another excellent poststructuralist analysis that raises these questions is Eleanor Honig Skoller's *The In-Between of Writing: Experience and Experiment in Drabble, Duras, and Arendt*.

13. Linda Hutcheon defines postmodernism as both period and style along these lines. See *A Poetics of Postmodernism: History, Theory, Fiction*.

14. We might date these revisionary readings from Robert Kiely's edition, *Modernism Reconsidered*, though as far back as the 1960s and 1970s critics were rereading modernist writers through postmodernist discourses. See, for example, Ihab Hassan, *Paracriticisms* and Harry Levin, 'What was Modernism?', in *Refractions: Essays in Comparative Literature*.

15. Here I am drawing on two of my essays: 'Virginia Woolf and Postmodernism: Returning to the Lighthouse', in *Rereading the New: A Backward Glance at Modernism*, ed. Kevin Dettmar, 297–323, and 'Returning to the Lighthouse: A Postmodern Approach', in *Approaches to Teaching Woolf's* To the Lighthouse, eds Beth Rigel Daugherty and Mary Beth Pringle, 47–53. In *Rereading the New* Dettmar points out that what we call postmodern criticism is not a unified movement but a 'loose affiliation' of a variety of theories (11).

16. Foucault defines monumental history as 'a history given to reestablishing the high points of historical development and their maintenance in a perpetual presence, given to the recovery of works, actions, and creations through the monograms of their personal essence' (Foucault 1984, 94).

17. I elaborate on the occlusion of aesthetics in the shift from criticism to critique in 'How Do We Keep Desire from Passing with Beauty?', *Tulsa Studies in Women's Literature*, 19.2 (2000): 269–84.

18. This is Kevin Dettmar's characterization of a postmodern reading in *The Illicit Joyce of Postmodernism*. Other examples of poststructuralist and postmodernist readings of modernists include: *Post-Structuralist Joyce: Essays from the French*, eds Derek Attridge and Daniel Ferrer; Pamela L. Caughie, 'Virginia Woolf and Postmodernism: Returning to the Lighthouse' in *Rereading the New: A Backward Glance at Modernism*, ed. Kevin J.H. Dettmar; Rainer Emig, *W.H. Auden: Towards a Postmodern Poetics*; Ihab Hassan, *Paracriticisms*; *Yeats and Postmodernism*, ed. Leonard Orr; Bonnie Kime Scott, *Refiguring Modernism*, Vol. 2. *Postmodern Feminist Readings of Woolf, West, and Barnes*; and Patricia Waugh, *Practicing Postmodernism, Reading Modernism*.

19. Other critics who read this novel in terms of postmodern theories of language, subjectivity, and aesthetics (respectively) are Marilyn Brownstein, 'Postmodern Language and the Perpetuation of Desire' (1985), Magali Cornier Michael, 'Woolf's *Between the Acts* and Lessing's *The Golden Notebook*: From Modern to Postmodern Subjectivity' (1994), and Beth Rigel Daugherty, 'Face to Face with "Ourselves" in Virginia Woolf's *Between the Acts*' (1993).

20. Other full-length studies that explicitly read Woolf through poststructuralist theories of language and subjectivity, especially Lacanian theory, are Daniel Ferrer's *Virginia Woolf and the Madness of Language* (1990) and Emily Dalgarno's *Virginia Woolf and the Visible World* (2001). Dalgarno's book in particular illustrates the direction poststructuralist criticism has taken since the 1980s by moving beyond a more formalist focus on Woolf's texts themselves and reading her writing in relation to events, technologies, and ideologies of the early twentieth century. Though relying heavily on Lacan and acknowledging its indebtedness to Minow-Pinkney, Dalgarno's book covers a wide range of topics, from photojournalism to astronomy to Woolf's Greek translations, in exploring Woolf's understanding of language and subjectivity. Molly Hite's 'Virginia Woolf's Two Bodies', *Genders* 31 (2000) also presents a reading of Woolf's representation of female sexuality informed by poststructuralist theories.

21. Michael (1994) similarly argues that in focusing on womens' lives and subjectivities, modernist women writers anticipate the more radical critiques of subjectivity that we have come to associate with postmodernism.

22. A critique along the lines of the one I offer here is not meant to prove a writer wrong, but to show what a reading necessarily excludes and what difference those exclusions might make. Any reading, including mine of Waugh, can be deconstructed to reveal the suppressed differences within.

23. It is postmodernism's different understanding of history, rather than Woolf's place in literary history, that informs some critical discussions of Woolf and postmodernism. In 'Virginia Woolf's Postmodern Literary History' (2000), for example, Beth Carole Rosenberg offers an implicit critique of Waugh's approach in demonstrating how Woolf constructs an alternative concept of literary history, one that focuses more on the process of historical production, especially the production of readers, than on history as a continuum. 'By viewing Woolf's historical project as postmodern,' she writes, 'that is, as a method removed from time and the historical moment – we are freed from the burden of trying to establish the "truth" of Woolf's writing of the past' (1115). Instead, we can see how Woolf's history, as presented in *A Room of One's Own*, 'is a constructed fiction'. It is the way Woolf 'makes us read history as a series of unrelated moments, moments whose unity comes through a narrative that tells us more about its own construction than it does about the past' (1128) that makes Woolf postmodern, Rosenberg argues, not her position in literary history as a transitional figure between the modern and the postmodern. This notion of history as a constructed fiction makes Woolf's *Orlando*, along with *Between the Acts*, a popular topic in discussions of Woolf and postmodernism, especially with the release of Sally Potter's campy film version of the novel in 1993. See, for example, Roberta Garrett's discussion of Potter's '"postmodern" interpretation' of the novel in 'Costume Drama and Counter Memory: Sally Potter's *Orlando*' (1995) and Suzanne Ferriss, 'Unclothing Gender: The Postmodern Sensibility in Sally Potter's *Orlando*' (1999).

24. 'Maybe the target nowadays,' says Foucault, 'is not to discover what we are, but to refuse what we are' by resisting those 'techniques of power' that attach the

individual subject to an identity. See 'The Subject and Power', in *Michel Foucault: Beyond Structuralism and Hermeneutics*, eds Hubert L. Dreyfus and Paul Rabinow, 212–16.

25. Bowlby's book is another excellent example of a reading of Woolf informed by post-structuralism and postmodernism. In her first chapter, she connects her controlling metaphor of the train with Saussure's example in *Course*.

26. For a more elaborate postmodernist critique of Waugh, among other modernist and feminist critics, see Caughie, 'Virginia Woolf and Postmodernism: Returning to the Lighthouse', in *Rereading the New: A Backward Glance at Modernism* (1992), ed. Kevin J. H. Dettmar.

27. Brenda R. Silver, *Virginia Woolf Icon*; Jennifer Wicke, '*Mrs Dalloway* Goes to Market: Woolf, Keynes, and Modern Markets', *Novel: A Forum on Fiction* 28.1 (1994): 5–23; Jane Garrity, 'Selling Culture to the "Civilized": Bloomsbury, British *Vogue*, and the Marketing of National Identity', *Modernism/modernity* 6.2 (1999): 29–58; and 'Virginia Woolf, Intellectual History, and 1920s British *Vogue*', in *Virginia Woolf in the Age of Mechanical Reproduction*, ed. Pamela L. Caughie, 185–218.

28. See, for example, Stanley Fish, *Professional Correctness: Literary Studies and Political Change* and Elaine Scarry, *On Beauty and Being Just*.

8

historical approaches

linden peach

The appreciation of Woolf's historical context is inseparable from the renewed interest generally in historical approaches to literary studies, after a period in which critical methodologies from Practical Criticism in the late 1920s and 1930s, to New Criticism in America in the 1940s, to the stress on post-structuralism in the 1970s and 1980s tended to advocate studying texts in isolation. Of course, it would be too much of a simplification to suggest that historicism in literary studies ever really disappeared. But, what is important about this new found interest in historical context is the effect that it has had upon our thinking about history and historiography.

While new historicism, concerned with rethinking the concepts of history and historiography in the 1980s, was in part a reaction against ahistorical criticism, it also developed from philosophical thinking about the nature of language, especially structuralist approaches, broadly speaking concerned with how language organizes our thinking and perception of the world, and what is called deconstruction, which highlights the contradictory and ambivalent nature of language. Inevitably, a greater awareness of how the language available to us determines our thinking and world views and is itself contradictory led to more rigorous questioning of the nature of history and the reliability of historical narrative. This rethinking of history is informed by a general scepticism as to whether we can conceive of history as anything other than a particular narrative, based on selection and occlusion, representing particular viewpoints and interests. Aware of the subjective and relative nature of historical narrative, it became difficult in the 1980s to think of 'history' as other than 'histories'.

New historicism, which was initially identified with a group of Renaissance scholars, principally Stephen Greenblatt (1988) and Jonathan Dollimore (1984), is a difficult concept to define, as it has not emerged as a single, coherent movement. Although Greenblatt (1989) comes closest to a definition, there is considerable debate and conflict among those scholars who might be identified as new historicists. The term 'new historicism' itself is misleading

169

as it implies that it is a radical departure or movement beyond historicism. In actual fact, historicism, which John Brannigan traces back to nineteenth-century practioners and philosophers such as Vico, Schleirmacher and Dilthey, shares with new historicism suspicion 'of the practice of history as the objective description of a knowable past or as the empathetic recreation of that past' (Brannigan 1998, 29). Where they differ is in new historicism's rejection of the model that informed traditional literary history – relating literary texts to singular trends which are taken to characterize a particular period such as the Renaissance – and its emphasis upon 'the past as consisting of very diverse configurations of beliefs, values and trends, often coming into conflict and contradiction with each other' (Brannigan 1998, 31).

The focus on Woolf as a novelist engaged with the socio-historical milieu in which she was living is very recent. In 1986, the American critic Alex Zwerdling lamented: 'Why has Woolf's strong interest in realism, history, and the social matrix been largely ignored? Why has it taken us so long to understand the importance of these elements in her work?' (Zwerdling 1986, 15) Kathy Phillips, eight years later, observed, 'it is only in the past fifteen years or so that Woolf has been recognised as a social thinker, let alone someone with a sophisticated grasp of ideologies' (Phillips 1994, xi). Nevertheless, despite the newness of historicist scholarship on Woolf, it is possible to discern trends, issues and debates. The earlier work, as Zwerdling's comment suggests, begs a number of questions; not least, what is the nature of Woolf's interest in history? This question, in turn, presents us with concerns about distinguishing between the intellectual context in which Woolf thought about history, and the context in which we now read history from critical perspectives developed half a century after her death which have preoccupied more recent historicist criticism.

In the 1970s and 1980s, a historical approach to Woolf's fiction was bound up with the rediscovery of her as a sociopolitically committed writer. This was inevitable given, as Anna Snaith has observed, that it was post 1970s feminist literary criticism that brought 'Woolf firmly back into the "real" world, back to life' (Snaith 2000, 3). In other words, feminist literary critics, such as Jane Marcus (1984 and 1988), argued for the political significance of Woolf that studies of her art and aesthetics earlier in the century had overlooked (see Chapter 5 in this volume). Snaith's reference to the 'real world', implicitly recalls Zwerdling, who, in the first key work to foreground Woolf as a socio-political writer, saw himself redressing the balance between the emphasis in scholarship up to then on Woolf's 'psychological, aesthetic, philosophical, and quasi-religious concerns' and her 'much less familiar ... interest in the life of society and its effect on the individual' (Zwerdling 1986, 4).

Unveiling Woolf's 'interest in the life of society' determined the nature of 1980s historicist criticism, one of the consequences of which was the new found emphasis on her political activities such as her work for women's suffrage, the Richmond branch of the Women's Co-operative Guild and the

Rodmell Labour Party. Indeed, Susan Squier suggested that it was the nature of her previous intellectual pursuits that encouraged her to explore the social dimensions of life in her novels (Squier 1985, 92). Zwerdling argues that it was the Bloomsbury Group that broadened Woolf's political awareness and thinking, and that she had more varied, practical political experience than has commonly been allowed (Zwerdling 1986, 26–8). While this is true, we must be careful, as Hermione Lee has warned, not to exaggerate this dimension of her life as some mid-1980s criticism was prone to do (Lee 1996, 223).

Generally speaking, 1980s historicist scholarship is distinguished from that written in the 1980s by a more theorized concern with how Woolf read her own milieu, and with her own interest in historiography. This work is quite varied. Michael Tratner (1996) employs political, aesthetic and psychological theories to examine how modernists such as Woolf developed new forms to participate in the mass politics that was emerging in the early twentieth century. Karen Levenback (1999), on the other hand, explores how the First World War influenced Woolf's war consciousness, her narrative art and the political content of her essays. Scholarship's interest in theorizing Woolf's political awareness of her milieu will be the focus of this chapter.

When, in the 1990s, the writing of history was subjected to as much scrutiny as history itself, scholars were prepared to argue vigorously that Woolf's novels were themselves the product of a speculative engagement with history and based on a realization that historical narrative was an important cultural phenomenon. Thus, a recurring thesis in late twentieth-century criticism of Woolf is that even in her ostensibly most 'social realist' work of the 1930s, Woolf is not a writer who seeks to present an objective description of the past or one who would have any faith in such a project. Scholars, working on an author that 1980s feminist criticism had invested with a new found social relevance, were disposed to reclaim Woolf as a writer concerned with the way history and historiography impacted upon culture. But the interest in Woolf as a writer concerned with history in the 1990s is inseparable from wider feminist, historical scholarship such as Barbara Green's (1997) linking of autobiography and suffrage and Wayne Chapman and Janet Manson's (1998) exploration of women writers and intellectuals, such as Margaret Llewelyn Davies, Margery Perham and Ray Strachey, within the context of early twentieth-century politics.

In their theorized concern with women's history, historical scholarship on Woolf and more general historical studies converged in the 1990s in recognizing culture as a sign system, an approach indebted to the new historicism which emerged in the previous decade. In order to discover the 'beliefs, values and trends' that in any historical period were in conflict with each other, new historicism was interested in reading the sign systems of the past as anthropologists read the sign systems of another culture (Brannigan 1998, 32). It is not surprising that historical criticism of Woolf should have followed this approach in the 1990s, as her writings lend themselves to this method. The practice of decoding signs and sign systems, that new historicists such as Greenblatt made the linchpin of new historicist criticism in the 1980s, is evident, for example, in *Three Guineas* (1938), where Woolf observes the significance of the way men dress:

> Every button, rosette and stripe seems to have some symbolic meaning. Some have the right to wear plain buttons only; others rosettes; some may wear a single stripe; others three, four, five or six. And each curl or stripe is sewn on at precisely the right distance apart; it may be one inch for one man, one inch and a quarter for another. Rules again regulate the gold wire on the shoulders, the braid on the trousers, the cockades on the hats – but no single pair of eyes can observe all these distinctions, let alone account for them accurately. (*TG* 178)

Thus, the historicism that in the 1980s and 1990s led to a reclamation of the historical context of Woolf's work found an author whose own approach to history was not only as speculative as that of the new historicist critics but was in sympathy with its emphasis upon culture as a sign system. But what makes Woolf, as this passage demonstrates, such an interesting precursor of new historicism is not simply her awareness of the political significance of symbolism, which Fascism in the 1930s brought to the fore, but the way in which that symbolism is embedded in 'rules'. In other words, the focus in this chapter is not upon the individual but the larger regulations and discourses in which individuals are situated.

New historicist approaches to Woolf are inevitably indebted to the French philosopher Michel Foucault in two key respects. First, central to new historicism is the Foucauldian thesis that historical narrative is not simply the product of individual human consciousnesses but of the wider discursive system in which the individual is placed. Foucault's quarrel with structuralism's assertion that discourses are always closed, preventing any deviation from them, is especially important because it allows literary texts the possibility of rupturing or reconfiguring the dominant discourses in which individuals are situated. This does not mean that Foucault argues for a return to Hegelian notions of the capacity of the human imagination to bring about change. But, as Claire Colebrook points out, Foucault maintains that 'discursive formations' 'grant some statements a force, validity and truth effect which is achieved *inter alia* by the exclusion of other statements' (Colebrook 1997, 43). Second, Foucault influenced new historicism's interleaving of historical narrative and the claims of interested groups to power. What is especially relevant to Woolf's works, and the way they have been placed in a historical context, is his concept of power 'as a complex strategical situation in a particular society' (Foucault 1981, 93) rather than the responsibility of any one group, class or sex, even though that 'strategical situation' might serve the interests of particular groups.

Too rigid a distinction between the way 1980s and 1990s scholarship on Woolf has historicized her concern with power would ignore the extent to which the latter evolved from the former and the fact that many Woolf scholars have produced work in both decades. In recommending Woolf as a political writer, Zwerdling was the first major critic to approach Woolf from what was, fundamentally, a new historicist perspective. He takes the term 'real world' to 'mean the whole range of external forces that may be said to influence our behaviour; familial ideals, societal expectations, institutional demands, significant historical events or movements that affect our lives' (Zwerdling 1986, 4). His study indirectly highlights two subjects that subsequently proved essential to historical approaches to Woolf in the 1990s: the extent to which Woolf's *oeuvre* can be considered from a historical perspective, and the extent of the conceptual reach of the historical enquiry in the scholarship and in Woolf's writings themselves.

It is also important not to overlook the differences between scholars who share fundamental convictions about Woolf as a historical writer. Zwerdling establishes a canon of texts in which Woolf is concerned with 'how people are shaped (or deformed) by their social environment, by how historical forces impinge on an individual life and shift its course' (Zwerdling 1986, 13–14): *Night and Day, Jacob's Room, Mrs Dalloway, To the Lighthouse, The Years*, and *Between the Acts*, and her two feminist essays *A Room of One's Own* and *Three Guineas*. The impact of the environment upon the individual is also the backbone of Squier's exploration of Woolf's fascination with the city published the year before Zwerdling's book. Squier argues that the figure of the flâneur in novels such as *Mrs Dalloway* is a vehicle for exploring a society segregated by gender and class (Squier 1985, 94). But Squier's approach is different from Zwerdling's in that she focuses upon the changing way in which London is depicted throughout her novels. The thesis of her study is that while the early writings depict a patriarchal, urban environment that is threatening to women, the later work – including memoirs and essays – recreate an environment that is energized by women's capacity to reconfigure their surroundings.

The absence of two principal texts concerned with empire from Zwerdling's canon – *The Voyage Out* and *The Waves* – betrays the way that a number of scholars in the 1980s, including Squier, privileged a sociopolitical rather than historical approach. Generally speaking, they also failed to theorize the sociopolitical and the historical within wider cultural sign systems. Although Zwerdling attaches more importance to historical context than previous criticism and, occasionally draws attention to the specific events in the text to which Woolf alludes, the focus is primarily on reading the thoughts, feelings and fantasies of key protagonists within specific historical and political contexts. His tendency to read Woolf's fiction thematically within a historical context is also one that has characterized historically-based approaches to Woolf in the 1980s and early 1990s.

It is possible to see 1990s historical scholarship as having been written, at least to some extent, in response to the elisions in 1980s scholarship – a point that can be illustrated through a comparison of Zwerdling's work with that produced in the following decade. Zwerdling's own approach to history is Marxist – Foucauldian in that he stresses Woolf's 'understanding of the inter-relationship of the social forces at work – familial, institutional, ideological, historical' and the fact that her characters are not free agents but must respond to the demands of the world in which they live (Zwerdling 1986, 5). He argues that at the heart of Woolf's social vision are a 'power relationship' and an awareness that 'historical eras differ in the nature and the demands they make upon the individual' (5–6). But what remains underexplored in his study is the relationship between individual agency and the way 'discursive formations' operate, and the extent to which Woolf's texts understand how, as historical eras change and give way to others, they define the individual subject in different ways.

The lack of developed consideration of these two subjects is the principal weakness in Zwerdling's discussion of *Jacob's Room*. The most obvious point to make about the novel is that although it is set in the years that led up to the First World War, it is about the war. Zwerdling rightly stresses the book's concern with the social forces that shape Jacob, and emphasizes Woolf's critique of the institutions that impinge upon Jacob's life. But the discourses that are embedded in these institutions, in the curriculum of the education system for example, are not identified. Zwerdling does not consider how the historical era leading up to the war was defined and how it changed in the way it sought to define itself as the war approached. Zwerdling draws attention to the way Woolf alludes to very specific historical events – the Irish Home Rule Bill and the transformation of the House of Lords, for example. But he sees them only as reminders to the reader of particular dates. Their significance in the larger process by which certain 'discursive formations' achieve dominance over others as well as the way that any era is defined by what is repressed and silenced as much as by what achieves a voice are not considered.

Zwerdling highlights the significance of the elections of 1922 and 1923 that brought the Conservative Liberal coalition in British politics to an end and made the Labour Party the official government opposition for the first time. Within this framework, he discusses how the novel presents a class that is 'decadent rather than crescent', and 'unable to take in or respond to the transformations of the present' (Zwerdling 1986, 121, 123). Again his essay exemplifies the way in which historical approaches to Woolf's novels in the mid-1980s tended to place Woolf's concern with psychological, aesthetic, philosophical, and quasi-religious subjects within a historical context rather than explore Woolf's interest in history and historiography. This is disappointing, with hindsight, because historical change between the years 1918 and 1923 is quite fully realized in *Mrs Dalloway* and Woolf's historical approach is conscientiously, if at times a little cryptically, sustained. Zwerdling's essay on *Mrs Dalloway* exemplifies two subjects that Woolf scholarship in the 1980s did not fully explore – her concerns with how dominant social discourses determined and interpreted key historical events according to prevailing ideologies, and the way that particular historical periods were determined by conflict between different ideologies.

In recognizing more fully the importance of ideology to Woolf's writings, post-1980s scholarship has stressed how *Mrs Dalloway* presents a nation that has been relocated by the war, especially by the return of shell-shocked war veterans and physical invalids, but is uncertain as to how to redefine itself. Within this historical context, allusions to past and present events relating to India, the Armenian crisis, Ireland, and domestic politics in *Mrs Dalloway* have been used by historicist scholars to highlight historiography as a principal sociopolitical discourse. For example, Woolf's allusions to the Armenian crisis are discussed in detail by Trudi Tate. Like many of the works taking a historical approach to Woolf in the 1980s, Tate is indebted to feminist readings of *Mrs Dalloway*. However, she sees the novel as more complex than many of the post-1970s feminist readings allowed. Thus, she argues that the text 'poses some difficult questions about the ways in which women and men are located in relation to political power' (Tate 1994, 469). The shift in Tate's essay from individual agency to historical forces is important as far as historicist approaches to Woolf is concerned, even if it is not sustained – the focus in the last third of the essay returns, in a way reminiscent of Zwerdling, to a reappraisal of Clarissa Dalloway and whether women's participation in politics will transform it or whether they will be transformed by politics. In her discussion of the allusion to the Armenian crisis, Tate goes further than Zwerdling in addressing how power is not simply a matter of individual agency but of the way in which 'strategical situations' are created by the priority that certain discursive forces acquire over others.

Clarissa Dalloway's refusal to think about the Armenians is indicative of the low priority they are given in the larger political world in which her husband participates as an MP. In signing the Lausanne Treaty on 24 July 1923 – shortly after *Mrs Dalloway* is set – Britain, as Tate points out, abandoned the Armenians for whom they had some responsibility (Tate 1994, 474). Readers in the 1920s, as Tate persuasively argues, would have been well aware of the debates about Armenia in the press and political journals. They would also have been aware that the dominant concern was with Britain's wider political interests in the region and the necessity of restoring good relations with Turkey. Tate places Septimus' death within this framework by which history is seen in terms of competing historical forces. Thus, its reception by members of the upper class is not simply the product of their removal from the horrors of war but of the way in which they were now beginning to see the war.

The view of history as involving the privileging of one set of discourses over another, which nevertheless remain in a dialectical relation to each other, has encouraged post-1980s critics taking a historicist approach to Woolf to be attentive to many of the details in the text that had been previously overlooked. For example, Masami Usui sees the privileged position of men over women reflected in *Mrs Dalloway* in the relative status of Westminster Abbey and the forgotten church of St Margaret's that stands close to it, but which is associated with the female in the novel. Westminster was identified with the Great War and had become 'the center of politics, religion and legislation. Westminster is, in other words, men's place and represents men's history' (Usui 1991, 154). Nevertheless, St Margaret's, as Usui points out, has a history comparable to that of the Abbey in whose shadow it stands. Interleaving of these two sites within the novel anchors its concern with the privileging of male-centred over female-centred discourses and histories. This perspective is extended to consider the novel's concern with issues that have a direct bearing on women. For example, Elizabeth Dalloway, whose ambition is to become a doctor, wants to enter one of the most conservative, male-dominated professions of that time. Moreover, her status as an educated woman serves to remind readers that London University only opened its degrees to women in 1878 and Oxford University awarded women degrees for the first time in 1919.

Because of Woolf's own feminist preoccupations, and because of the strong feminist predilection of the initial work on Woolf as a political writer, the first serious historical approaches to Woolf's work, especially her earlier fictions, drew upon new theoretical conceptions of culture as a sign system to stress their critique of the way in which women were positioned by misogynistic discourse. This helped to make 1990s historical criticism of Woolf less thematic than that written in the 1980s. For example, in interleaving war and predatory male desire in her reading of *The Voyage Out*, Helen Wussow retrieves what could have been a somewhat crude thesis in arguing that the novel's principal protagonist Rachel 'takes to heart the misogynist messages she has around her and the cultural aggression towards women she observes' (Wussow 1991, 108). The critical language here not only implies that Woolf analyzed her own milieu as a system of dominant 'messages' which anticipates discourse theory, but also reflects the way in which historically-based literary scholarship in the late 1980s and 1990s was taking a more theorized, Foucauldian approach to history than that to be found in 1980s Marxist-Foucauldian critics such as Zwerdling.

Wussow's point that Rachel 'takes to heart' misogynist discourse eschews the part played by interruption in Woolf's text. One way of theorizing the concept of 'interruption' in this context is to employ Pierre Bourdieu's concept of the 'hiatus', which, as Colebrook says, 'allows for a play of irregular, local or *ad hoc* interests within a system of regularities' (Colebrook 1997, 93). Thus, while Victorian historians tended to write history in terms of its continuities, Woolf, through characters such as Rachel in *The Voyage Out* and Elizabeth in *Mrs Dalloway*, writes history around discontinuity or 'interruption'.

In contrast to Wussow's essay, the notion of Woolf's work disrupting or interrupting prevailing discourses has produced closely focused rereadings of some of the most written about texts. For example, Masami Usui (1991) interprets Lucrezia Smith in *Mrs Dalloway* as a critique of the war bride, brought to Britain as a symbol of male triumph, power and egoism, into a life of loneliness, anxiety and horror. Usui's focus on the war bride as victim rewrites even liberal histories of the war that tended to acknowledge only male victims such as Septimus Smith. Usui's essay also demonstrates that critics in the late 1980s and 1990s were beginning to achieve a more equal balance between the historical forces in Woolf's work and the way in which the emotions and thoughts of characters in Woolf's fiction can be seen as a response to a particular historical milieu. Thus, Lucrezia is not only discussed as a victim of patriarchy or misogyny but as a narrative device to highlight two conflicting forces in British politics: the spirit of the 1844 Naturalization Act by which any foreign woman married to a British subject would become a British citizen herself and the anti-alien attitudes encapsulated in the 1914 and 1919 Aliens Restrictions Acts. Thus Usui goes further than Zwerdling, and even Tate, in stressing power in terms of historical forces.

Usui's essay exemplifies how, initially, the development of historically-based scholarship of Woolf that conflated history with discourse was indebted to the research in the 1980s and early 1990s on Woolf and war. Again what distinguishes 1980s and 1990s criticism is the theorized awareness of the relation between discourse, history and cultural formation. For example, Karen Levenback's exploration (1999) of how the First World War influenced Woolf's 'war consciousness', her narrative art and the political content of her essays, theorizes how the War became reconfigured through individual memory, the popular press, official war histories and popular consciousness. In fact, Woolf's own interest in what we might now label as discourse stemmed from her awareness of the role of propaganda, on which she based her own rejection of what she called 'historians' histories' (*E3* 3).

Again, this brings us back to the notion of power as 'a complex strategical situation in a particular society' which is underdeveloped in Zwerdling's 1980s work but which has proved important in the 1990s to reclaiming Woolf's post-1930s novels as important political works. For example, it was only in the late 1980s and 1990s that *The Years* was recognized for its complexity as a historically situated text. The novel highlights family histories and either marginalizes or approaches obliquely the Boer War, the death of Queen Victoria, the First World War, the rise of the Labour Party, the demise of the Liberals, the suffragettes, the General Strike, the Wall Street Crash, and the British Union of Fascists. Patricia Cramer (1991) argues that in *The Years*, Woolf presents us with history in terms of culturally privileged and culturally marginalized narratives. Her essay is significant in that she pursues the implications of Woolf's own reading of history in terms of signs inscribed with cultural meaning. Such an approach, Cramer recognizes, must involve reading history in terms of myth and myth in terms of psychology. Thus, Cramer's essay opens by recognizing that Woolf in *The Years* 'represents British daily life as a social text – a symbolic network organizing all levels of life in accordance with dominant aims' (Cramer 1991, 207). But in a novel that spans the period from 1880 to 1937 and which marginalizes many of the key events in traditional histories of these years, Woolf is interested in the way in which different historical eras have been defined and redefined. Thus, one way of looking at the novel, Cramer contends, is as 'the story of patriarchy from a woman's point of view'. Within this framework, she shifts the focus of her essay from the way in which 'seemingly innocuous events' have profound political meanings to examining how the discursive dominant formations lose their privilege over time. Thus, the novel moves from the apex of male power, symbolized by the Colonel's control over his family, to his increasing isolation and lack of relevance to the new order, to the end of the heroic ideal signified by the death of Digby and Eugenie, to the sale of the house and the break up of the family with women entering into different kinds of living relations.

Despite its strengths, many of which might be seen as characterizing historicist scholarship on Woolf in the 1990s, the problem with Cramer's study is that the concept of myth is never defined and the relationship between myth and history is never theorized. Moreover, in emphasizing a linear narrative in which patriarchy loses its privileged position, Cramer overlooks the debate that the novel sets up between different models of the family. The model of the nuclear family advocated in post-war Britain is very different from the upper- or upper-middle-class Victorian model of the family (Peach 2000, 174). Woolf's novel might be seen as interleaving several discourses on the family that were circulating in Britain during the period in which it is set: the Victorian, social paternalist view of the family which relied heavily upon social-family metaphor; the domestic integrationist approach that was sceptical about the organization of family life upon which it focused; and the anti-family perspective that stressed personal independence and liberalization from social structures. There is also a tendency in Cramer's essay to essentialize female experience whereas *The Years* presents a range of different women with different life experiences.

One of the criticisms that can be made of new historicism, as Brannigan points out, is that it tends to 'overlook the complexities of subject positions by interpreting all texts as functioning unproblematically within a power system' (Brannigan 1998, 122). The weakness that Brannigan pinpoints in this tendency is that new historicism does not sufficiently take into account that 'subjectivity is fractured, incoherent, rife with contradiction and a sense of difference' (123). Directly or indirectly this view of subjectivity has been important to scholars taking historical approaches to Woolf's work. Unlike Cramer, Gillian Beer (1996) is concerned with the extent to which Woolf is herself the product of Victorian culture – reminding us not to press too rigid a distinction between 1980s and 1990s criticism. Her assessment of Woolf's subjectivity in its historical context is more complicated than that which we find in Zwerdling (1986) and Cramer (1991). Beer maintains that 'the Victorians are not simply represented (or re-presented) in her novels ... the Victorians are also in Virginia Woolf. They are internalised, inseparable, as well as at arm's length' (Beer 1996, 93). But, like much 1990s criticism of Woolf, her approach is decidedly culturally materialist – cultural materialism is concerned with how cultural forms are deployed in everyday life – and different from Zwerdling's and Cramer's work in that she argues that Woolf's writings about culture are 'incoherent' and 'rife with contradiction'. Cultural materialism's emphasis upon the way objects and artefacts are used to carry specific meanings has led, in fact, to *The Years* being seen in the 1990s as a cultural materialist rather than social realist text because of Woolf's own interest in the cultural significance of everyday objects.

Intriguingly, cultural materialist criticism in the late 1990s became as concerned with Woolf as a cultural object as with the cultural significance of the objects in her writings. The key work in this respect traces and analyzes Woolf as an icon in Anglo-American culture. Brenda Silver argues that, as an icon, Woolf is highly subversive, 'crossing the boundaries, dislocating the categories, illustrating how culturally specific and arbitrary they are' (Silver 1999, 74).

Generally speaking, criticism that identifies the subversive nature of Woolf's work tends to be culturally materialist rather than new historicist. The crux of the difference between the two approaches is that the latter demonstrates how the dominant culture is resisted in a text. Cultural materialists such as Alan Sinfield argue that the social order produces 'fault lines', 'through which its own criteria of plausibility fall into contest and disarray' (Sinfield 1992, 45).

In exploring Woolf's 'reading' of the Victorians, especially Ruskin, Beer sees Woolf as appreciating the extent to which the Victorians themselves were 'fractured'. Implicitly, Beer perceives the dominant discourses of the Victorians falling into 'contest' if not 'disarray' in Woolf's work. Broadly speaking, this is seen in the essay as a positive aspect of Woolf's work. Thus, she takes the fact that Orlando's husband, Shelmardine, is a 'woman' as an analogy of Woolf's appreciation of Ruskin's androgyny: 'Fortunately, in the whimsical good sense of the unconscious, fathers can be mothers, and so in looking back through our mothers, as she says women must do, Ruskin may be among them' (Beer 1996, 100).

Of course, *Orlando* is an appropriate text to invoke in a discussion of the fractured nature of Woolf's historically located subjectivity. As I have argued elsewhere, in defamiliarizing over three hundred years of history including the Elizabethan Age, the Courts of King James and Charles II, seventeenth-century Constantinople, eighteenth-century English coffee-house society, and London at the time of the Great Exhibition, *Orlando* encourages its readers to consider the extent to which their own identities are constructed (Peach 2000, 142). Beer argues that Woolf not only defamiliarizes the Victorian past but also casts a new light on the fragments, vestiges and shards that in Victorian literature and culture constitute a synthesis. Thus, in Woolf's fiction, as is evident in *Orlando*, 'the scraps of the communal and personal past are recuperable only *as* gossip and pastiche, a flotsam of significant fragments' (Beer 1996, 110). However, Beer does not pursue the dialectic between history that the imagination recognizes as distinct from itself and the symbolism that mediates between the individual's consciousness and the given world.

1990s criticism of Woolf has tended to see her interest in the way symbolism mediates our perception of 'reality' as an important aspect of her fiction. This has led to the argument that 'reality' in Woolf's writings is 'coded' – exemplifying to the reader how 'reality' outside her texts is also codified and has to be deciphered before it can be reinterpreted (Peach 2000, 31). This is also the perspective of David Bradshaw who takes issue with critics who, in historicizng Woolf, perceive of her as 'both a product and a victim' of 'a civilisation disfigured by patriarchy, imperialism, militarism, homophobia, class prejudice and xenophobia' (Bradshaw 1999, 179-80). At one level, he follows Zwerdling (1986) and Cramer (1991) in emphasizing the critical cultural alignment of *The Years*. But not only is Bradshaw's focus different from theirs – he is concerned with the criticism in the text of the British Union of Fascists and the Pargiters' anti-Semitism – his approach serves to emphasize 'the way in which [Woolf] inscribes her resistance to such bigotry' (Bradshaw 1999, 180).

The extent to which Woolf was a product or a critic of her culture is a strong motif in late 1990s criticism generally. While Sinfield argues for the dissident reader or critic, Bradshaw makes a strong case for Woolf as a dissident reader of culture and history. This is also the conclusion of Merry Pawlowski (2001) who stresses that Woolf's contribution to the wider political consciousness of her day lay in arguing against the menace of Fascism in Europe. But although Pawlowski sees Woolf as the first writer in *Three Guineas* to analyze the psychology of fascism, she does not examine the symbolism of Woolf's writings in as much detail as Bradshaw.

Like the historically-based scholarship of the 1980s and early 1990s, Bradshaw reads *The Years* thematically within a historical framework. That framework – the modern history of the Jews in Britain – is more developed than the historical contexts in Zwerdling (1986) and, in this respect, is closer to Tate (1994). But whereas Zwerdling focuses on the thoughts, feelings and fantasies of the protagonists in the texts he discusses within his historical frameworks, Bradshaw stresses the symbolism that mediates between the individual consciousness and the external world: 'Encoded within the novel is a complementary narrative in which a sequence of references to blue-and-white things emphasises the long history and legitimate place of the Jews in Britain' (Bradshaw 1999, 186). Seeing Woolf, like Beer, but unlike Pawlowski, as internalizing her cultural past while keeping it at arm's length, Bradshaw is concerned to 'record, subtly but unmistakably, her abhorrence of, and resistance to, the harassment of Jews in London and beyond' (187). According to Bradshaw, Woolf's repetition of the blue-and-white of the tallith, the Jewish prayer shawl, may be read as 'symbolic of the rootedness of the Jews' in England. But the encoded nature of the work also represents the encoded nature of reality. She does not simply anatomize her culture but analyzes the way in which an individual's consciousness of the 'real' world is mediated in symbols. Thus, the individual consciousness and the 'real' world exist in a different relationship in Bradshaw's work from Zwerdling's. The former's work is typical of new historicist approaches to Woolf in that the signs in her work are read vertically – in terms of their connotations – as well as horizontally – the way in which they are integrated within the wider sign system of the text. However, Bradshaw does tend to take the cryptic and obscure nature of Woolf's critique of her historical milieu for granted, without considering the contradiction in a political writer who seems to deliberately make the cultural politics of her texts difficult for all but the most attentive readers to grasp.

A potential weakness in new historicist criticism based on the analysis of signs is its tendency to ignore the way in which the sign has changed over time. However, in a discussion of the trope of the aeroplane and the island in Woolf's fiction, Beer considers patriarchy and imperialism 'in shifting relations to air and aeroplane' (Beer 1996, 150). In conceiving of the aeroplane as a 'crucial presence' in *Mrs Dalloway*, *Orlando*, *The Years*, and *Between the Acts*, Beer usefully stresses how Woolf is concerned with the representation of England at 'difficult moments of historical national change' (149–50). These moments of 'historical national change' are linked to moments when a historically-based concept of England changed. Thus, the aeroplane undermines 'the ideas of aptness and sufficiency' which contributed so much to the Victorian's understanding of England. But in bringing about change that causes it to be seen differently, the aeroplane is analogous to the historical perspective bringing about different viewpoints that leads to the concept of history itself being perceived differently.

The fluidity with which Woolf invested history in her later novels does not make history appear ethereal. In fact, *Between the Acts* finds a new sense of energy in the English past. Mr Oliver, for example, observes in the text, as Beer points out, that from an aeroplane the historical landscape becomes clear: 'The aeroplane, in the opening of [*Between the Acts*], allows history to surface in the landscape and be seen anew' (171). However, if the aeroplane then becomes analogous to the historical imagination, one can take the argument further than Beer. Woolf's interest in each of the texts that Beer cites is not only with moments of historical change but moments when the concept of history itself might be said to have changed.

Moreover, Woolf is concerned with the nature of intellectual and cultural space that is created by moments of significant change. The nation, like the villagers in *Between the Acts*, finds its version of England and its past interrupted. Like the villagers, it is metaphorically relocated by the social changes taking place. But the nation, like the village, finds itself occupying a space rife with uncertainty. Thus, while Beer stresses that the disruption of the pageant lies in its interruption of the villagers' view of history, the pageant disrupts the concept of history as a coherent and stable narrative.

One of the dangers that cultural materialist criticism must avoid is that in its focus upon specific subjects such as the war bride in Woolf's fiction, or even its anti-Semitism, it does not eschew Woolf's larger concerns with the totalizing nature of power, history and representation. But an even greater danger lies in the way new historicism has tended to overlook how events are not only constantly changing but are interpreted differently by different cultures and peoples. One of the aspects of Woolf's work, from a historical perspective that has not been fully explored, is the extent to which Woolf was aware of different cultures. While *The Waves* has been reinterpreted as a political novel that critiques the way Englishness for a particular generation was bound up with notions of empire and the imperial project in India (for example Peach 2000, Phillips 1994), it does not consider India and imperial history from the perspective of the colonized (see Chapter 10 in this volume).

Whereas historical-based studies of Woolf in the 1980s stressed her concern with the way in which identity was determined by discourses in which the subject was situated, cultural materialist work in the 1990s (Cramer 1991, Bradshaw 1999) has argued that Woolf is interested in how identity is determined by different subject positions. One of the most innovative of such studies is Lisa Williams's comparative study of Woolf and the contemporary African-American novelist Toni Morrison, who wrote her Master's thesis on Woolf and William Faulkner. Williams reads in tandem texts that have not previously been read in relation to each other, such as Woolf's *The Voyage Out* and Morrison's *The Bluest Eye* and *Mrs Dalloway* and Morrison's *Sula*. Such readings are used to examine how 'from their different subject positions, Morrison and Woolf [dismantle] the madonna/whore, white woman/black woman paradigm'. Williams maintains that 'Woolf, because of the very privilege of her whiteness, does not always succeed in her endeavour' (Williams 2000, 4). Thus, Woolf's strength, and her limitation, as a writer is that she understands the way in which a particular class at certain moments of time was historically situated. But even her writing about women, such as the prostitutes in *The Voyage Out*, *Jacob's Room*, and *Orlando*, outside of this particular class is more schematic even though she retains a coherent focus on how, for example, women are positioned within materialist discourses.

Perhaps, with hindsight, Woolf has been too easily shoehorned into the post-history argument about the end of a linear, coherent history. Even in texts that range over a period of time and consider how particular milieu are defined, Woolf is interested in reading different periods through and against each other. Although *Orlando* would appear to exemplify a cyclic, discontinuous view of history, it is based largely on analogies between fragments of the past and the present. Thus, the Great Thaw can be read as analogous of the Great War in the vast numbers of people killed and the emphasis upon the unburied bodies, the carnival on the ice as analogous of the Roaring Twenties, and the episode set in Constantinople as alluding to Britain coming close to war with Turkey in the 1920s.

Although, as I have demonstrated above, Woolf follows the new historicists in their emphasis upon the analysis of cultural signs, she cannot be entirely equated with the new historicist quarrel with historicism's preoccupation with epoch. Although Woolf keeps the Victorian view of history at arm's length, to appropriate Gillian Beer's metaphor, she internalized its tendency to think in terms of world views and epochs – as is clear from *Between the Acts*. Throughout her work, there is the suggestion that historical change often provides the key to an epoch, but, conversely, that understanding how an epoch has been created and defined at particular moments of time helps us appreciate historical change.

9
lesbian approaches

diana l. swanson

introduction

Lesbian studies of Virginia Woolf have been central to the reframing and reconceptualizing of Woolf's life and work that have occurred over the last thirty years or so. The apolitical, asexual, elitist whose writing was primarily concerned with stylistic experimentation and the nuanced representation of fine shades of feeling has metamorphosed into a politically aware, passionate woman whose writings bear witness to her feminist, pacifist, socialist, and anti-imperialist convictions. It is impossible to separate clearly the development of lesbian approaches to Woolf from the other approaches covered in this volume. In particular, feminist criticism has been central to lesbian criticism of Woolf (see Chapter 5 in this volume). The feminist emphasis on attending to and elucidating women's issues, experiences, and relationships with other women and on tracing women's intellectual and literary traditions and influences made possible lesbian approaches to Woolf; most scholarship on lesbianism in Woolf's life and work is feminist in critical and theoretical orientation. (Feminist criticism and theory, of course, encompass a wide range of approaches: radical feminist, historical, biographical, psychoanalytic, poststructuralist, socialist, and more.) Lesbian studies of Woolf have brought about serious attention to the importance of Woolf's friendships with and erotic feelings for women. This basic insight has led to an understanding of Woolf as a more multifaceted and less isolated person, of her politics as more comprehensive and incisive, of her literary criticism as more revolutionary, and of her fiction as more rich, complex, and subtle than the character and work of the delicate aesthete promulgated by the first four decades of Woolf criticism and biography. The varied scholarship enabled by this basic insight has led to new understandings of Woolf's sexuality, feminism, and politics; of theme, form, style, allusion, and figurative language in her writing; and of Woolf's place in literary history.

biography

As with Woolf's feminism and the Duckworth brothers' sexual abuse of her, the existence of Woolf's lesbian, or 'Sapphist' as Woolf and many in her circle termed it, desire has not been so much the subject of debate; rather, what has been at issue is its strength, physicality, meaning, and importance in Woolf's life and work. Some biographers hold that Woolf was frigid and her passions for women emotional and cerebral. Some present Woolf's homoerotic desires as pathological in some way, often as a type of maternal fixation. Other biographers, in contrast, hold that Woolf was a passionate, vibrant woman who loved women both physically and emotionally. These biographers tend to agree that Woolf's love for women was, to varying degrees, central to her feminist, socialist, and pacifist politics, and her writing. Biographers disagree on whether Woolf self-identified (as Sapphist, lesbian, or woman-loving) on the basis of her homosexual desires and relationships.

Quentin Bell, in his 1972 biography of Woolf, recognized Woolf's homoerotic attachments to several women before her marriage to Leonard Woolf (Violet Dickinson, Madge Vaughan, Kitty Maxse) and her passionate friendship later in life with the writer and gardener, Vita Sackville-West, whom she met in 1922. For example, Bell states that by the age of twenty-five heterosexual desire seems to have played no part in her life: 'All her passions, her jealousies and tenderness are kept for her own sex and above all for Violet [Dickinson]' (Bell 1972, I, 18). But Bell plays down the importance of Sapphism, and sexuality in general, in Woolf's life, repeatedly describing her as 'virginal'. Discussing the sexual failure of Virginia and Leonard's honeymoon, Bell calls her 'sexually frigid'. He 'suggest[s] that she regarded sex, not so much with horror, as with incomprehension; there was, both in her personality and in her art, a disconcertingly ethereal quality' (Bell 1972, II, 6). About her relationship with Vita Sackville-West, Bell writes that she 'felt as a lover feels' (117) and that 'there may have been – on balance I think that there probably was – some caressing, some bedding together. But whatever may have occurred between them of this nature, I doubt very much whether it was of a kind to excite Virginia or to satisfy Vita' (119). Nor does Bell present Woolf's relationships with women as particularly important for her writing or her social analysis. For example, he notes that Woolf used biographical details about Vita and her ancestral estate, Knole, as source material for *Orlando* but does not discuss any thematic or stylistic import their relationship may have for the book.

A year later, Joanne Trautmann's short monograph, *The Jessamy Brides*, treats Woolf's relationship with Sackville-West in greater detail and makes the first argument for its formative impact on Woolf's writing. Trautmann follows Bell's lead in seeing Woolf as largely asexual, focused more on emotional and intellectual than sexual aspects of relationships and life in general. She distinguishes between Woolf's 'physical sexuality' which was tenuous and her 'mental sexuality' which was 'androgynous'. She uses the term 'homo-emotionality' (taken from Charlotte Wolff's *Love Between Women*, which asserts that the core of lesbian love is romance and emotion, not physical sex) to describe all the lesbian relationships in Woolf's fiction. Trautmann also presents Woolf's and Vita's sexualities as 'narcissistic', infused with a desire for coalescence with the beloved and a kind of solitude together that she compares to the experience of cloistered nuns. Thus, like Bell, Trautmann acknowledges Woolf's attraction to women but maintains the notion of Woolf as essentially ethereal and virginal. She also uncritically accepts the Freudian view of lesbianism as narcissistic and maternally fixated.

However, Trautmann does argue that Woolf's relationship with Sackville-West had a significant influence on her writing. *The Jessamy Brides* begins on a strongly affirmative note: 'Virginia at forty found a magnificent companionship which was to be among the most creative in the history of literary friendships' (Trautmann 1973, 2). The influences Trautmann traces are thematic. In the books Woolf wrote during the most intense period of their relationship (*Mrs Dalloway*, *To the Lighthouse*, *Orlando*, and *A Room of One's Own*), friendship between women becomes a more central concern than in her earlier books. Similarly, Trautmann argues that the 'theory of sexuality' in *A Room of One's Own* and the 'conception of friendship' central to *The Waves* 'owe a great deal of their assurance and detail to Vita Sackville-West's prominence in Virginia's life' (49). Finally, like most critics, Trautmann follows the lead of Woolf's own diary and letters (in which Woolf speaks of *Orlando* as a biography of Vita) by treating *Orlando* as the most direct and important literary outcome of Woolf and Sackville-West's relationship. In fact she sees it as the symbolic narrative of that friendship. She makes this argument by referring to Woolf's original conception of 'The Jessamy Brides', a novel which was to be the wild and fantastic story of two women who live together and travel to Constantinople. Trautmannn's theory is that these two figures, suggestive of Vita and Virginia, merge into the figure of Orlando, whose name also alludes to *As You Like It* and suggests that Orlando is also the merging of 'Orlando the nobleman and Rosalind the quick-witted controlling spirit' of Shakespeare's play (Trautmann 1973, 41). This interpretation is consonant with Trautmann's interpretation of Orlando as the embodiment of the androgynous qualities that Woolf was so attracted to in Sackville-West and as the expression of Woolf's theory that women and men should recognize their masculine and feminine qualities respectively in order to know themselves better and to enable the union between the sexes Woolf envisions in *A Room of One's Own*.

Blanche Wiesen Cook's 1979 essay, '"Women Alone Stir My Imagination": Lesbianism and the Cultural Tradition', marks the beginning of the feminist critique of the heterocentric trivializing and (mis)interpretation of Woolf's lesbianism. Cook's essay reviews the treatment of lesbianism in literary history and criticism, charging that the historical record has been distorted by denial and erasure of women's friendships, networks, and lesbian relationships. Woolf figures as an exemplary case in this argument, which also treats Gertrude Stein,

Radclyffe Hall, Djuna Barnes, Natalie Barney, Dorothy Strachey Bussy, Vita Sackville-West, and others. Cook specifically criticizes Quentin Bell for painting a picture of Woolf as frigid, elitist, and apolitical when a contradictory picture arises from Woolf's own words in her diary and letters, such as the letter to Ethel Smyth from which Cook takes her title. Cook's reliance on documentary evidence signals an important development for Woolf scholarship in the second half of the 1970s: the publication of Woolf's letters and diaries. These sources allowed more scholars to evaluate for themselves the sources that Bell had used in his biography and Trautmann in her monograph. Cook also offers the first analysis of Woolf's relationship with Ethel Smyth as Sapphic and as formative of her politics and writing. She criticizes Bell for neglecting to note that 'Woolf's friendship with Smyth, a formidable crusader for women's rights, coincided with a new level of uncompromising militancy in her own work' (Cook 1979, 729). Cook sums up her analysis of Woolf's treatment by scholars thus: 'We were told ... that she was a mad, virginal Victorian spinster-wife, precious and elitist. And so we were denied access to the most eloquent creator of a woman-loving socialist feminist vision of the early twentieth century' (730).

Published in 1982, Louise A. DeSalvo's 'Lighting the Cave: The Relationship Between Vita Sackville-West and Virginia Woolf' shows both the development of feminism and the greater availability of primary documents since Trautmann's work. DeSalvo takes up again the subject of Woolf's relationship with Sackville-West but presents it as more mutually influencing, more clearly erotic, and more important than Trautmann does. DeSalvo suggests that their love gave them each support to re-examine their childhoods and family histories. They both found insight in exploring the similarities in the emotional lives of their families, particularly with demanding, inconsistent, but lovable parents: Woolf's father and Sackville-West's mother. Woolf also spoke to Sackville-West about George Duckworth's molestation of her as a teenager. Addressing this incident with an intimate, sympathetic listener allowed Woolf 'to enter into an erotic relationship for the first time in her maturity' (DeSalvo 1982, 199). In turn, Sackville-West was able to enter into a relationship that engaged and enriched both her emotions and her intellect, unlike her self-destructive love affairs of the past. In the end, it was Woolf's difficulty acting on her sexual desires, Sackville-West's promiscuity, and the divergence of their views on pacifism in the early 1930s that cooled their relationship.

DeSalvo argues that the ten-year period of their closest friendship (ca. 1923 to 1933) was the most productive and creative period of both Woolf's and Sackville-West's writing lives. The love, support, and erotic energy of the relationship enabled both writers to achieve more ambitious and innovative work. Woolf influenced Sackville-West to be more painstaking in the crafting of her works and challenged her intellectually. DeSalvo sees the mark of Woolf's feminist analysis of family structure and economics in Sackville-West's *All Passion Spent* (1931) 'a fictional treatment of the themes in her friend's polemical tract' (DeSalvo 1982, 211) in the sense that it is about a woman without a room of her own whose whole life has been taken up with serving her husband, family, and empire. *Family History* (1932) shows Woolf's intellectual influence in its exploration of the idea that imperialism begins in the patriarchal family. For her part, Sackville-West offered Woolf an understanding of herself as stronger, more productive, more energetic, and healthier than her family's version of her, enabling Woolf to see herself as capable and accomplished. This sense of greater self-worth helped Woolf to accomplish more with less angst. And of course Sackville-West inspired Woolf's *Orlando*. DeSalvo suggests that Woolf drew many of the ideas about time and historical process in *Orlando* from Sackville-West's *Knole and the Sackvilles*. Also, taking up more emphatically a suggestion of Trautmann's, DeSalvo argues that in *Orlando* Woolf gives Knole back to Sackville-West, which the inheritance laws of Kent had denied her as a woman. In turn, in *Family History*, Sackville-West gives Woolf the children she never had, through the character of Viola Anquetil (married to Leonard Anquetil).

Cook and DeSalvo work from a definition of lesbianism consonant with the radical feminism of the 1970s and 1980s in its emphasis on the continuity between women's friendships and lesbian love and on the mutual support such relationships provide in a patriarchal culture. In contrast, Sherron Knopp grounds her analysis of the biographical basis of *Orlando* in the sexological definitions of lesbianism current in the 1920s on which, she asserts, women such as Radclyffe Hall and, to a lesser extent, Sackville-West based their self-images.

In 1988, Sherron Knopp must still criticize what she calls 'petty niggling' over what Vita and Virginia did in bed (Knopp 1988, 24). She, too, calls on the evidence of the letters – including Sackville-West's to Woolf that were published in 1984 – to argue that the relationship was intense, important, and sexual beyond the few months, possibly a year, that Bell and Nigel Nicolson speculate. Scholarly ambivalence over the relationship extends to the novel *Orlando*, which is considered so unlike the rest of Woolf's *oeuvre* that it is usually absent in studies of her novels. Knopp argues that 'to see just how large and attached to life *Orlando* is, one must first get the relationship between Virginia and Vita right and then see it in context' (25). Thus Knopp uses passages from the letters and diary to show that Woolf, not just Sackville-West, actively desired sexual intimacy. Knopp also draws on historical material – the *Well of Loneliness* obscenity trial and theories about gender and sexual identity by sexologists such as Havelock Ellis and Richard von Krafft-Ebing – to illuminate the lesbian subject matter of the novel. She writes that the Sapphic character in Woolf's novel is not androgynous, in which masculine and feminine elements are balanced, but one who displays a female masculinity – a woman who 'acts like a man'. Orlando's body changes in Constantinople but the change 'did nothing whatever to alter [Orlando's] identity' (*O* 133). Orlando is both a man *and* a woman. Thus Woolf uses fantasy to represent Vita's own sense of what she called her dual personality not as freakish (contra the sexologists) but as scintillating and erotic. Thus Knopp offers a quite different view of what Woolf gives to Vita than Trautmann and DeSalvo: 'The remarkable achievement of *Orlando* – and Virginia's *public* gift to Vita – is the book's joyous celebration, in the very teeth of society and psychiatry, of just such a personality as Vita's and its attendant "connections"' (Knopp 1988, 30).

Like Knopp, Ellen Bayuk Rosenman believes the sexual ideology and theory of the 1920s are key to an accurate understanding of Woolf's sexuality. She focuses on how Woolf herself understood her sexuality, a subtle shift from previous debates about whether Woolf was a lesbian. Rosenman's thesis is that Woolf did not identify herself as a lesbian as it was defined in her day and that she resisted equating sexual desires and actions with personal identity. In the 1920s, lesbianism 'entered the cultural consciousness ... in a particularly male-identified form'. That form, influenced by the sexologists Krafft-Ebing and Ellis, relied upon the 'trapped soul' theory in which a lesbian was a man's soul trapped in a female body. 'Lesbian experience, culturally formulated, was actually inappropriate within Woolf's theory of influence, which sought to establish a distinctively feminine consciousness and iden-tification' (Rosenman 1989, 639). According to Rosenman, the figure of the mannish lesbian dominant in the cultural consciousness at the time participated in a devaluation of the feminine and a calcification of identity and sexuality that conflicted directly with Woolf's feminist principles (of valuing women's experiences, traditions, values, and sensibilities) and her understanding of selfhood as shifting, various, multiple. Thus Rosenman challenges the assumption current among many feminists in the 1980s that 'expressing a lesbian identity' is *necessarily* a feminist position (635). Rosenman also disagrees with Knopp's interpretation of Woolf's sense of Sackville-West; she argues for an androgynous Vita, for whom the categories of masculine and feminine are irrelevant.

Thus, by the late 1980s, lesbian feminist criticism had achieved not only the ability to speak of Woolf as a sexual person, but it was also developing a sophisticated debate about sexuality in Woolf's life and work, grounded in an emerging field, the history and theory of sexuality. It asked crucial questions about the cultural construction of sexualities and drew upon Woolf's private and public texts as well as the history of her family. Thus the trajectory of the biographical scholarship on Woolf and lesbianism moves from 'Was Woolf one?' to 'What is one?' to 'How did Woolf identify?' to 'How did she understand lesbianism?' and 'What difference does it make to her writing and her feminism?' This path has been explored most fully and subtly in the literary criticism of the 1980s and 1990s, but before I go on to review those developments, this section must end with attention to the most well-received biography of the 1990s.

Hermione Lee straightforwardly states that Woolf's sexual desires were for women: 'Virginia's preference for her own sex had been a fact of her life since childhood'. However, says Lee, Woolf 'did not define herself as a Sapphist. She could not bear to categorize herself as belonging to a group defined by its sexual behaviour (just as she didn't want to think of herself as an ordinary "wife," or as a writer of "novels"). She wanted to avoid all categories' (Lee 1996, 484). Yet, at the same time, Woolf's writing life was centrally enabled and influenced by her relationships with women, particularly what we would call her lesbian relationships with Violet Dickinson, Vita Sackville-West, and Ethel Smyth. Lee refreshingly calls Woolf's relationships with Dickinson, Janet Case, Madge Vaughan, Kitty Maxse, and Nelly Cecil 'first loves'. In particular, she makes a strong case that Dickinson's role as Woolf's first critic and unconditional supporter was crucial to Woolf's early development as a writer. Vita 'gave her the central relationship of her forties', and the concerns of Woolf's writing – 'the lives and friendships and sexuality of women, ... biography and history and class, and ... freedom and censorship' – were all connected to Vita (Lee 1996, 515). Finally, Lee gives a quite detailed account of Woolf's relations with Ethel Smyth and emphasizes how *Three Guineas* and *The Years* grew out of a speech, 'Professions for Women', that Woolf gave when she appeared with Smyth at a meeting of the London and National Society for Women's Service in 1931. Based on Lee's biography, the centrality of lesbian relationships to Woolf's life and literary work seems largely to be accepted by scholars at the beginning of the twenty-first century. James King's biography, however, demonstrates that this view is not universal. Published in 1994, a year before Lee's, King's biography reverts to the asexuality school (calling her a 'eunuch') and ascribes her lesbian feelings to a psychological inability to get over the loss of her mother.

literary criticism

As the previous section demonstrates, it is impossible to separate biography and literary analysis completely in discussions of Woolf and lesbianism. Literary criticism, however, addresses how Woolf represents lesbian (or Sapphist or homoerotic) desires and relationships in her fictional and non-fictional writing; how her sexuality inflects her writing on the levels of language, theme, and form; and how Woolf's work fits in the larger lesbian literary tradition, in addition to the questions about Woolf's life and work discussed above.

One of the first critics to address lesbian sexuality in Woolf's writing was Sallie Sears in 'Notes on Sexuality: *The Years* and *Three Guineas*' (1977) in the important Woolf issue of *The Bulletin of the New York Public Library*. Sears's central focus is not lesbianism per se, but sexuality in general. Her thesis is that in both the essay and the novel 'the meaning of sexuality ... is "political" rather than "personal."'.... Sexuality is defined in terms of its relationship to power' (Sears 1977, 211). Sears suggests that women in *The Years* are attracted to other women who seem to have escaped the 'tyrannies and servilities' of patriarchal society and who live freer, bolder lives than their own. Sears asserts that the women in *The Years* 'eroticize liberty; the males, tyranny' (220).

Another early study that identifies lesbian passion in Woolf's work is Suzette Henke's '*Mrs Dalloway*: The Communion of Saints', which reads the novel as 'a scathing indictment of the British class system and a strong critique of patriarchy' (Henke 1981, 125). Henke claims that both Clarissa and Septimus are 'repressed homosexual characters who refuse to conform to the stereotypical patterns ascribed to their sex' (134). While the discussion of homosexuality is incompletely tied to the main argument of the essay, the article implies that Clarissa's and Septimus' homosexuality is part of their nonconformity to the patriarchal system and part of the meaning of Septimus' suicide and of Clarissa's communion with him when she hears of his death at her party.

Henke's essay is also an early example of a significant strand in lesbian studies of Woolf: Woolf's spiritual themes, particularly matriarchal ones influenced by the work of classicist Jane Harrison (the 'great J. H. herself' of *A Room of One's Own*). Henke delineates an innovative argument that the symbolic frame of the novel is a 'pagan mass' with scapegoat/Christ (Septimus) and high priestess (Clarissa). At her party, Clarissa offers her guests 'spiritual nourishment'; she is 'a worshipper of life whose spring "fertility rite" is blessed by the scapegoat who "revitalises" the community that destroys him' (126). Henke suggests that through Clarissa the novel valorizes a feminine life force and affirmation of social connection in the face of the absurdity of war and oppression. Readers interested in exploring this strand of criticism further should consult the work of Beverly Ann Shattuck, Patricia Cramer, Evelyn Haller, and Jane Marcus.

Emily Jensen's article, 'Clarissa Dalloway's Respectable Suicide' (1983) also focuses on *Mrs Dalloway* and is an example of the power of close reading. Without reference to biography, Jensen traces the story of both Clarissa's and Septimus' denial and stifling of their homosexual love through what she calls 'the verbal network in the novel – the phrases and images that by repetition take on the nature of a metaphor' – and through how Clarissa responds to other characters (Jensen 1983, 163). Jensen argues that Clarissa's choice to deny her love for Sally and to marry Richard to find a serene and respectable life is presented in the novel as parallel to Septimus' suicide. 'Crippled by heterosexual convention' (162), Clarissa has committed a respectable kind of suicide and has learned, following Peter Walsh's lead, to see her actions as 'civilized' and the memory of her love for Sally as 'sentimental' (166–7). At the end of the novel, Clarissa realizes this truth. Reflecting that the 'treasure' that Septimus holds as he 'plunged' to his death is the 'thing, wreathed about with chatter, defaced, obscured in her own life' (*MD* 156), Clarissa recalls her love for Sally. She has not been true to 'the most exquisite moment of her whole life' (*MD* 30).

Jane Marcus finds a conscious and articulate lesbian in Woolf. Marcus' work on Virginia Woolf has been a galvanizing influence in the study of Woolf as a socialist, a pacifist, and a lesbian feminist. She began publishing her work on Woolf in the late 1970s, and the publication of *Virginia Woolf and the Languages of Patriarchy* in 1987 brought some of her earlier essays together with new ones in an important collection. While not the only essay in the collection that analyzes Woolf's lesbianism, 'Sapphistry: Narration as Lesbian Seduction in *A Room of One's Own*', may be the most influential in lesbian studies. Like all the essays, 'Sapphistry' is full of historical research into the sources of allusions and the material circumstances of Woolf's writing. It presents Woolf's lesbianism as intricately entwined with her feminism. Marcus' main argument is that *A Room of One's Own* responds to the obscenity trial of Radclyffe Hall's lesbian novel, *The Well of Loneliness*, at which Woolf and other Bloomsbury Group figures were ready to testify against censorship. (Their testimony was, however, disallowed by the presiding judge.) Marcus reminds us that *A Room of One's Own* was originally written as talks for the female Girton and Newnham College students at Cambridge, and Woolf maintains that trope in the published essay. Marcus tells us that when Woolf interrupts her description of Mary Carmichael's supposed new novel to ask if Sir Chartres Biron and Sir Archibald Bodkin are hiding somewhere in the room, her audience would have recognized the names from the newspapers as the presiding magistrate of the *Well of Loneliness* trial and the Director of Public Prosecutions. Thus, Woolf brings her female audience into league with her against the censorious patriarchs who want to silence stories of women together. Marcus calls this seduction of the woman reader by the woman writer 'sapphistry': 'An earnest feminist appeal to political solidarity would not be half as effective as shameless flirtation, Woolf seems to feel. Not only narration but even punctuation is enlisted in her seductive plot: "Chloe liked Olivia. They shared a ..." Dot dot dot is a female code for lesbian love' (Marcus 1987, 169). And the 'interrupted text' transforms the material circumstances of the women writer's oppression, her interruption by domestic matters or fear of censorship, into a 'positive female form' (187).

Like Marcus' analysis of *A Room of One's Own*, Patricia Cramer's essay presented at the first annual conference on Virginia Woolf in 1990 explores how Woolf invents a literary language to represent lesbian desire and a lesbian feminist social critique. Cramer also implicitly rebuts Ellen Rosenman's argument that Woolf did not identify herself as Sapphist. Cramer concedes that 'women, like Woolf, writing before the lesbian feminist movement could not adopt the identification "lesbian" in precisely the same ways as contemporary writers' (Cramer 1992, 177), but she then asserts that Woolf participated in a lesbian literary tradition in which 'defining a lesbian or woman-centered identity and eroticism was a central preoccupation' (177). Writers in this tradition include Sappho, Emily Dickinson, Amy Lowell, and Gertrude Stein. For these writers, lesbian identity enables their opposition to patriarchy and provides a lens through which to re-envision self and community. Cramer focuses on *Mrs Dalloway*, which she reads as a coming out story inspired by Woolf's new relationship with Sackville-West. Cramer theorizes the coming out story as a ritual narrative in which a lesbian affirms herself and 'names coming out as a turning point for seeing the world in a new way' (179). In addition, 'the goal of coming out narratives is not only self-affirmation but creation of lesbian community' (181). Cramer sees Woolf's use of this story as part of Woolf's ongoing project of creating new plots in which marriage and motherhood are not the only stories for women. She also links Woolf's use of the coming out story to Woolf's reading of Jane Harrison's work on Greek rituals, especially matriarchal fertility rites that revitalize the community. Cramer sees Clarissa Dalloway coming to a realization of her lesbianism through her memories and through Septimus' experience: 'At the end of the novel when Clarissa identifies with Septimus on the basis of their homosexuality, she changes her life narrative from a tale of heterosexual failure to a story of homosexual resistance and compromise' (180). Cramer's essay is also important for its elucidation of labial and clitoral imagery (through flowers and diamonds) as code for powerful female sexuality, especially lesbian sexuality. Again, Cramer sets this analysis within a lesbian literary tradition, referring to the scholarship of Paula Bennett and Priscilla Pratt on Emily Dickinson's imaging of the female body. She concludes that Woolf repeatedly counters patriarchal images and myths with those based in the female body and lesbian eroticism, transforming our cultural paradigms based in war and violence to ones based in peace and communal vitality.

Toni A. H. McNaron also turns to *Mrs Dalloway* in '"The Albanians, or was it the Armenians?": Virginia Woolf's Lesbianism as Gloss on her Modernism'. Presented at the second annual conference in 1992, McNaron delineates a less optimistic picture than Cramer's of Woolf's living and writing her lesbianism. McNaron's thesis is that Woolf's affinity for modernist aesthetics in which narrative fragmentation and irresolution are central arose from her inability to act fully on her lesbian desires, her 'self-imposed interruption in her pursuit of sexual intimacy with women' (McNaron 1993, 136). McNaron focuses on Clarissa Dalloway as an example of Woolf's women characters who live interrupted and fragmented lives. She reads the moment when Sally kisses Clarissa as Clarissa's experience of wholeness and vitality, which is violently interrupted by Peter Walsh. In her later years, Clarissa's life is marked by 'interrupted surfaces, snatches of memory from her past, and a certain inability to focus' (137). She is a disintegrated character, as is Septimus Smith who has also repressed his homosexual feelings. McNaron suggests that 'like Clarissa, [Woolf] allowed heterosexist culture to interrupt her ecstasy with Vita and her homoerotic impulses toward other women, while her incest experiences cast a cool and restraining shadow over her sexual impulses toward anyone' (138). Clarissa is a portrait of internalized homophobia in her drifting and frittering away of her life. Woolf's own internalized homophobia caused her to find 'the modernist tenet of fragmentation and loss of centeredness ... unusually compatible and useful' (140).

Cramer's and McNaron's essays are just two examples of the flowering of scholarship on lesbianism in Woolf's work beginning in the early 1990s. A brief survey of other essays published in 1993 in *Virginia Woolf: Themes and Variations*, selected papers of the second annual conference, gives a sense of the varieties of lesbian feminist approaches and topics pursued in the decade. Jessica Tvordi and Donna Risolo trace lesbian subtexts in *The Voyage Out* and *To the Lighthouse* respectively. Ruth Vanita analyzes how Woolf uses allusion in *Flush* to represent homosexual love. Pamela J. Olano investigates the question 'How can we readers, within the margins of lesbian narrative space created by the writer, all become intertextual lesbians regardless of our own sexual preferences or orientations?' (Olano 1993, 158) and proposes that self-identified heterosexuals as well as lesbians can read Woolf through a lesbian lens. Annette Oxindine analyzes drafts of *The Waves* to trace Woolf's self-censorship in her revising of the character Rhoda from a recognizable lesbian figure to an ambiguous one. Danell Jones speculates on the influence of the Ladies of Llangollen, famous eighteenth-century romantic friends, on *Orlando*. Other essays published in the early 1990s address class and sexual orientation (Heather Levy) and conflicts over marriage and passion in both Virginia and Leonard Woolf's early fiction (Mark Hussey).

The 1997 publication of Eileen Barrett and Patricia Cramer's anthology, *Virginia Woolf: Lesbian Readings*, marks both a culmination and a beginning. As the first book devoted to lesbian scholarship on Woolf, it is the fruit of two decades of lesbian feminist scholarship. This collection of thirteen original essays gathers together a wide range of lesbian approaches to Woolf: intertextual, textual, biographical, and socio-historical studies; analyses of the encoding of lesbianism in her texts; and personal narratives on experiences of reading Woolf as a lesbian. As such, the volume also forms a foundation for scholars to build upon and a benchmark against which to compare and contrast their work.

Eileen Barrett's introduction to the first section of the anthology is an important contribution to the debate about Woolf's self-identification. Responding to arguments such as Rosenman's that Woolf should not be called a lesbian, Barrett refers to Bonnie Zimmerman's observation that the same rationale is not used in discussing the lives and work of heterosexual writers, for example in discussions of marriage. She quotes Zimmerman: '"Why can we not use the word lesbian," Zimmerman asks, "as we use marriage or wife or mother: to refer to a recognizable structure with content and meaning that may vary according to era or culture?"' (Barrett 1997a, 7; Zimmerman 1983, 174). Barrett's chapter in the collection, 'Unmasking Lesbian Passion: The Inverted World of *Mrs Dalloway*', clarifies this approach by considering the 'competing discourses about lesbianism and male homosexuality' familiar to Woolf. Barrett argues that Woolf first came to understand lesbianism through observing and participating in romantic friendships and through the feminist milieu of the women's movement that provided a supportive environment for lesbian partnerships. This understanding of lesbianism mingled 'the intellectual and the erotic, the personal and the political' (Barrett 1997b, 151), and did not see lesbianism as pathological. The sexologists' theories of lesbianism, with which Woolf was familiar, conflicted with this lesbianism developed among middle-class women themselves. The sexologists saw homosexuality as either congenital (the 'true' lesbian who was 'masculine') or situational (the naturally feminine woman who could be 'normal'); in either case, abnormal. Although the sexologists opposed legal persecution of homosexuals, they did claim that homosexuality was a defect, and some of them linked it with criminality and insanity. The sexologists also linked feminism and lesbianism in ways detrimental to both, describing feminists as arrogant, 'mannish', latent inverts.

Barrett traces the influence of these competing discourses in *Mrs Dalloway*: Sally and Clarissa's relationship exemplifies a turn-of-the-century romantic friendship; Septimus Smith's struggles (internal and external) reveal the destructive effects of the idea that homosexuality is unnatural; Doris Kilman and other minor characters exemplify the negative characteristics the sexologists depicted in lesbian feminists. The conflicts among these discourses of lesbianism converge in Clarissa's ambivalence:

> Clarissa rejects the idea that same-sex love is a crime against nature, yet she projects onto Doris [Kilman] all the negative, distorted stereotypes of lesbians. Clarissa's erotic fantasies reflect the ideal of romantic friendship. But by echoing the imagery of Clarissa's fantasies in her descriptions of Doris's and other characters' lesbian desires, Woolf also illustrates the power of the sexologists to pervert the erotic language of romantic friendship into the language of homophobia and self-hatred. At the same time, the repeated association of Clarissa's lesbian passion with the soul suggests Woolf's efforts to embrace a philosophy of lesbianism, however inadequate, influenced by the trapped soul theory of the sexologists. . . . Through the relationship between Clarissa and Doris, then, Woolf not only challenges the sexologists and their stereotypes but also attempts to reconcile public and private expressions of lesbian passion and identity. (Barrett 1997b, 148)

Thus Barrett models a historically responsible way of discussing the lesbianism of women in the past without assuming their understanding of 'lesbian' is identical to ours today *and* without discarding the reality of women's sexual love for other women in the past and its often central role in their lives and sense of self.

In the confines of this chapter, it is impossible for me to do justice to all the chapters in *Lesbian Readings*. In the rest of my discussion of the anthology, I will focus on those essays that offer intertextual readings of Woolf's work.

Jane Lilienfeld's chapter on Woolf, Violet Dickinson, and Charlotte Brontë explores Dickinson's influence on Woolf, especially on her understanding of

Charlotte Brontë's life and work. Drawing on the work of Sandra Harding, Julia Penelope, Sarah Hoagland, and others, Lilienfeld argues that the love, sexual passion, and woman-centred emotional and intellectual space that Woolf found in her relationship with Dickinson (and later Sackville-West and Smyth) enabled Woolf to develop an empathic mode of knowledge creation and, over the course of her life, to reassess Brontë as a radical model of the woman writer. Woolf's 'life-long writing relationship with the idea of Charlotte Brontë' (Lilienfeld 1997, 39) begins with one of her first published pieces (published through a connection of Dickinson's), an essay on a trip to Haworth Parsonage, and continues through *Three Guineas* and beyond. Noting that Brontë and her biographer Elizabeth Gaskell were contemporaries of Woolf's parents, Lilienfeld draws the connections among Woolf, Dickinson, and Brontë through primary and secondary evidence. Lilienfeld finds that Woolf goes beyond her rejection of Brontë's anger in *A Room of One's Own* and even uses Brontë's imagery of fire to represent feminist anger in *Three Guineas*. She concludes:

> The growth of Woolf's insight into Brontë depended in part on Woolf's developing what Penelope and Hoagland have both cited as a lesbian ethic of resistance to and outspokenness against heteropatriarchy. Woolf's increasing empathy for and identification with Brontë as the flame-throwing figure of the woman oppressed by 'the fathers' depended on strong support from women. Only when joined with other women such as Violet Dickinson, Vita Sackville-West, and Ethel Smyth, among others, could Woolf have moved beyond Elizabeth Gaskell's official view of Charlotte Brontë, a movement that symbolized her leaving her father's library in order to help other women excavate and establish another literary tradition. (55)

Lilienfeld's contribution to understanding Woolf's place in lesbian literary tradition is extended in *Lesbian Readings* by chapters by Janet Winston, Corinne E. Blackmer, and Tuzyline Jita Allan. Winston's 'Reading Influences: Homoeroticism and Mentoring in Katherine Mansfield's "Carnation" and Virginia Woolf's "Moments of Being: 'Slater's Pins Have No Points'"' proposes that Mansfield and Woolf had a relationship of 'mutual mentorship' (Winston 1997, 58). Winston also compares Mansfield's understanding of lesbianism, influenced by Oscar Wilde and the Decadents, with Woolf's, influenced by romantic friendship and feminism. Mansfield tends to portray lesbianism as 'fleshly, exotic, reckless, and menacing' whereas Woolf often 'emphasiz[es] an idealized, sacred communion' between women (59). Winston reads 'Slater's Pins' as Woolf's rewriting of Mansfield's 'Carnation'.

Blackmer's chapter also focuses on Woolf's similarities and differences to another modernist lesbian writer, Gertrude Stein. Blackmer argues that while Woolf engages and revises earlier literary traditions of representing lesbians,

Stein challenges the representability of lesbians and of identity and sexuality in general. According to Blackmer:

> Woolf uses encoding to reveal and *re*conceal her lesbian subject position, fashioning an enclosed, protected site of self-articulation that is constitutive of modern lesbian identity as an ethical domain. In contrast, Stein's experiences impelled her to discard the epistemological distinctions between public and private and literal and encoded knowledge of (homo)sexual identities. For Stein, conscious actors cannot articulate their sexualities as stable identities because sexuality remains occluded by subconscious process. (Blackmer 1997, 93)

In contrast, Allan finds significant similarities between Woolf and Nella Larsen. Invoking the revisionist scholarship on modernism by feminist and African-Americanist critics, Allan asserts the importance of comparative studies of writers such as Woolf and Larsen who are seemingly worlds apart by virtue of race, nationality, and critical success. Allan discusses Woolf's and Larsen's lives as well as analyzes the subtexts and imagery in *Mrs Dalloway* and *Passing*. She argues that

> beneath the surface realities that have sequestered Woolf from Larsen in the universe of feminist criticism – white/black, high modernism/the Harlem Renaissance, family pedigree/half-breed, woman-loving/heterosexual – lies a core of shared experiences, artistic and sexual sensibilities that is revealed to the critical eye through the subtexts of *Mrs. Dalloway* and *Passing*. Both novels inscribe a strong, spiritually-charged critique of the patriarchal institution of marriage and its repression of female same-sex desire in strikingly similar ways. (Allan 1997, 96)

In particular, in both novels the trope of the death of the soul signals the suppression of lesbian sexuality in women's lives and in the authors' own fictions and expresses the immorality of such suppression.

A number of book-length studies published in the last ten years indicate that Woolf is indeed central to the scholarship on lesbian modernism and on lesbian literature in general. These books, however, do not generally investigate the links across race that Allan advocates. The first of these studies is Elizabeth A. Meese's *(Sem)erotics: Theorizing Lesbian: Writing* (1992), a literary/theoretical tour de force that pulls together theory, text, and sex through epistolary form. Contemplating the experience of reading and the experience of sex and riffing on the writing of Woolf, Gertrude Stein, Djuna Barnes, and Olga Broumas, Meese writes letters to these authors and to her own lover and invents letters they might have written as well. Thus Meese pursues a series of dialogues on the lesbian body and lesbian sex, dialogues informed by literary theory and criticism. The chapter, 'When Virginia Looked at Vita, What Did She See;

or, Lesbian: Feminist: Woman – What's the Differ(e/a)nce?' is most directly relevant to Woolf studies.

Julie Abraham's *Are Girls Necessary: Lesbian Writing and Modern Histories* (1996) reads Woolf alongside Willa Cather, Mary Renault, Gertrude Stein, and Djuna Barnes and challenges some of the accepted strategies of literary criticism. She raises a crucial question about defining lesbian literature: 'Does a text have to be "about" desire between women in order to be "lesbian"'? (Abraham 1996, xiii). Abraham answers no and argues that criticism about lesbian literature has been limited by the assumption that it must, in some way, be about two women who fall in love with each other; thus the 'lesbian novel' has been practically equivalent to lesbian literature. The lesbian novel, like all literature, is dependent on the conventions of genre, in this case the decidedly heterosexual conventions of the romance plot. Thus, the 'subject of the lesbian novel is always, in a sense, the problem of not-heterosexuality, which is to say, finally, that the subject of the lesbian novel remains, like the subject of all other novels about women, heterosexuality' (4). Abraham argues for recognizing that sexuality is inscribed in literature in more and more complex ways than representations of sex and romance and explores the uses that the five writers in her study make of history as an alternative way to write 'lesbian'. Regarding Woolf, Abraham analyzes 'the interdependence of her accounts of history, her uses of history as a source of narrative, and her representations of lesbians and gay men. In a pattern that can be traced back to and through the work of Cather and Renault, Woolf's recourse to "history" at once enables and limits possibilities both for the representation of homosexuality and for the lesbian as writer' (xxi). The centrality of Woolf to Abraham's book as a whole is suggested by the title, which quotes from *Orlando*, and by the fact that her reading of *Between the Acts* pulls together the themes and issues of her study.

In contrast to Abraham, *Lesbian Panic: Homoeroticism in Modern British Women's Fiction* (1997), by Patricia Juliana Smith, argues that Woolf uses the conventions of the romance plot to devise new forms for the representation of lesbianism. Smith defines lesbian panic as 'the disruptive action or reaction that occurs when a character – or, conceivably, an author – is either unable or unwilling to confront or reveal her own lesbianism or lesbian desire' (Smith 1997, 2). This idea is based on Eve Kosofsky Sedgwick's concept of homosexual panic. Sedgwick in turn bases her theory of the repressed homosociality/sexuality of canonical English literature on the feminist theories of Gayle Rubin and Luce Irigaray, who both argue that patriarchal social structure is homosocial in that it depends on bonds between men created by the exchange of women. Homosexual panic is a man's fear of becoming the object of exchange and thus becoming feminized and losing his status as a subject. Smith points out that women do not have that status to lose – they are the exchanged object; 'what is at stake for a woman ... is nothing less than economic survival' and a meaningful social identity (6). Smith proposes that moments of lesbian panic are central to the female tradition of the novel because the romance plot, which inscribes compulsory heterosexuality, is itself central to that tradition. Lesbian desire often provides the conflict that drives the plot. In a chapter on *The Voyage Out*, *Mrs Dalloway*, and *To the Lighthouse*, Smith argues that 'in seeking a new novelistic form ... Woolf analyzes in exacting detail the causes and effects of lesbian panic. And it is through this process that Woolf is able to arrive, at the end of her career, at the representation of the lesbian who, despite her marginality, is nonetheless central to the (re)ordering of society' (18). Smith's analysis here contributes to the building consensus among feminist critics that Woolf's feminism and lesbianism are key to her narrative experimentation and restructuring of the novel. Smith also argues for the influence of Woolf's work on the endeavours of later women novelists to write their way out of the structures and strictures of the romance plot – what Rachel Blau DuPlessis calls 'writing beyond the ending'.

Smith is also represented in the collection *Lesbian Readings*, as is the next critic I will discuss. Whereas Smith traces influence forward *from* Woolf to contemporary British writers such as Brigid Brophy, Maureen Duffy, and Jeanette Winterson, Ruth Vanita traces literary influence forward *to* Woolf from the Romantics. *Sappho and the Virgin Mary: Same-Sex Love and the English Literary Imagination* (1996) began, Vanita tells us in the introduction, as a study of Woolf and became a study of same-sex love in English literature from the Romantics to the Moderns. Vanita's innovative argument is that Sapphic love was not always invisible and that lesbian and gay writing is part of the mainstream of the English literary tradition. Tracing allusion, symbolism, and imagery, she focuses on Woolf and her literary indebtedness to Shelley, Keats, Byron, Pater, and Wilde. In the final three chapters of the book, Vanita argues that Woolf countered the sexological and psychoanalytical stigmatizing of same-sex love by using literary language developed by the Romantics and the Aesthetes.

Gay Wachman's *Lesbian Empire: Radical Crosswriting in the Twenties* (2001) places Woolf and other modernist lesbian writers in the context of imperialist politics in the 1920s. Wachman's interest is in 'sexually radical fiction written by British women in the years following World War I' (Wachman 2001, 1), and her book's central focus is the novelist and poet Sylvia Townsend Warner. Wachman juxtaposes Warner's work with that of Radclyffe Hall, Virginia Woolf, Clemence Dane, Rose Allatini, and Evadne Price as she investigates how they 'crosswrite' the rigid cultural boundaries of imperialist society. According to Wachman, lesbian crosswriting 'transposes the otherwise unrepresentable lives of invisible or silenced or simply closeted lesbians into narratives about gay men' (1). While Wachman discusses a number of Woolf's works, *Mrs Dalloway* receives sustained attention.

These comparative studies of Woolf in the larger context of lesbian modernism and postmodernism demonstrate a wide range of approaches within lesbian studies of Woolf and argue for a repertoire of strategies Woolf used to represent lesbianism: allusion, symbolism, imagery, encoding, historiography, genre disruption, and transposition.

the poststructuralist debate

To introduce the debate about the place of poststructualism (and its offshoot, queer theory, developed for the study of homosexuality, bisexuality, and transgenderedness), I turn to Suzanne Raitt's study, *Vita and Virginia: The Work and Friendship of V. Sackville-West and Virginia Woolf* (1993). Raitt focuses on the relationship between Woolf and Sackville-West as 'one between married lesbians' (Raitt 1993, 4). Pointing to evidence of their contentment within their marriages in Woolf's and Sackville-West's letters, Raitt holds that for Woolf and Sackville-West lesbianism 'was not disruptive of marriage. There was no simple way in which, for them, unconventional sexual behaviour was inevitably either socially or politically subversive' (5). She points out that other homosexuals in the late nineteenth and early twentieth centuries, such as Vera Brittain and John Addington Symonds, also held similarly conventional views of marriage and homosexuality. Raitt finds a nostalgic conservatism within both Woolf's and Sackville-West's constructions of lesbianism. This nostalgia is for the experience of 'maternal femininity... . The idea that lesbian energy originated in a past golden age, either pastoral or pre-Oedipal, meant that it could be deployed as often to resist change, as to encourage it' (16). Raitt argues for a view of social institutions as, like texts, full of their own silences and gaps. Thus Woolf's and Sackville-West's lesbianism existed in the gaps in the institution of marriage, and they 'both were and were not lesbian' in the sense that no institution of lesbianism contained their experience of themselves and in that they continually reinvented themselves in relation to each other and to other women (167–8).

Raitt's study attaches, awkwardly, a poststructuralist theory of identity to a largely historical and biographical study. In this way, it is emblematic of the somewhat uneasy place of poststructuralist feminist theory in lesbian Woolf studies. Lesbian feminist criticism of Woolf has largely taken historical, materialist, and radical feminist theoretical approaches. It has been concerned with the oppression of lesbians in a heteropatriarchal society and with the politics of lesbian (in)visibility and silencing in Woolf's day and ours. Such criticism is more directly and intentionally connected to activism than poststructuralist feminist criticism (see Chapter 7 in this volume). Poststructuralist feminist criticism focuses on how discourses operate to create our realities and has been concerned with how lesbianism functions within systems of representation. Poststructuralist studies of Woolf and lesbianism have tended to focus on particular passages or texts by Woolf as exemplary of the problems and possibilities of representing lesbianism/lesbian desire in language and narrative rather than on developing a coherent understanding of Woolf's *oeuvre* or her development as an artist, a lover, or a feminist. Such notions of coherency and teleology, in fact, contradict poststructuralist theories of identity as provisional, ever changing, inconclusive. For that reason, poststructuralist theory is not likely to be the most conducive to a scholar's ongoing involvement in single-author studies. But there is also a basic political difference between the feminist belief (whether socialist or radical or some combination thereof) in the possibility of the individual to develop a liberating sense of self and envision and make social change (in concert with others) and the poststructuralist scepticism about the possibility of achieving any viewpoint or toehold outside the phallocentric, patriarchal world of discourse. Therefore, the debates in lesbian Woolf studies that tend to form around this theoretical divide carry a certain intensity; the debate is also about what it means to live a scholarly life – its ethical and political efficacy – and about what it means to live a lesbian life – the scope of its oppressions and possibilities.

Cramer's elucidation of the two key lesbian passages in *Mrs Dalloway*, 'the match burning in the crocus' and Sally and Clarissa's kiss, and Judith Roof's interpretation and use of them to elaborate her theory of lesbian representation offer a telling example of the contrasts between radical lesbian feminist and poststructuralist feminist approaches to Woolf's work. Cramer reads the crocus, and the flower Sally picks before kissing Clarissa, in the English literary tradition of associating flowers with women's sexual parts, a tradition that writers such as Emily Dickinson, Amy Lowell, and others have drawn on to represent lesbian desire. She reads the petals of the flowers as labial and the match in the crocus, as well as the image of a diamond that Clarissa associates with Sally's kiss, as clitoral images. In contrast, Roof argues that lesbian sexuality is unrepresentable within Western phallocentric language and literature. The three parts of the passage – 'illumination; a match burning in a crocus; an inner meaning almost expressed' (*MD* 27) – are successive attempts by Woolf to express what cannot be expressed.

Roof's position is based in a Lacanian psychoanalytic theory of discourse and identity in which 'sexuality itself is a product of the impact of culture, language, and representations of sexuality on the unconscious' (Roof 1989, 101) (see Chapter 3 in this volume). In this view, the phallus is the primary signifier, the symbol of differentiation that makes language and thought possible. Sexuality is based on a symmetry of the visible/invisible, presence (phallus-penis)/lack (vagina), and 'completing this symmetry, Lacan says "of what cannot be seen, of what is hidden, there is no possible symbolic use"' (101). Because women's genitals are hidden, two women together disrupt the symmetry of both sexuality and meaning. Roof sees the 'match burning in the crocus' as a 'masked and burning phallus' (100) and suggests that the rest of the passage indicates that what is trying to be represented (lesbian sexuality) is 'almost expressed' but ultimately cannot be. 'What is evident in the narrator's description is the difficulty of locating the place of lesbian sexuality in relation to the requisite visibility of a phallocentric system of representation' (100). Speaking of both the match burning in the crocus and the wrapped diamond, Roof says 'while the images appear to strip away obscuring layers in an effort to see the source of the pleasure felt, the end of the stripping is a feeling, a revelation which evades sight but provides insight ... Lesbian sexuality is transparent, invisible, and ubiquitous, figured as light rather than shape' (111). To avoid being reinscripted into the phallic economy of representation, lesbian sexuality must be represented as 'the hidden but radiant other-than-phallus' (114); once the petals of the crocus are peeled back and we see the match it becomes phallic. Roof concludes that women writers trying to represent lesbian sexuality are inevitably reactive to and dependent on the phallic system of representation itself. This belief is at the centre of her criticism of encodement theory which posits that lesbian writers used coded language (figurative language, usually) to convey lesbian subject matter. Roof argues:

> Encodement theories envision the text as a translation of an identity and experience that will be recognized by readers who share that identity and experience. ... This necessarily assumes a very certain and monolithic lesbian identity that correlates with the encoded lesbian meaning of the text. Not only, then, does encodement rely on a notion of an essential lesbian identity, but it also tends to define the text in terms of the 'true' biographical identity of the author, inadvertently limiting textual interplay and contradiction in favor of a correct translation. (Roof 1991, 165)

This critique calls into question many of the studies discussed in this chapter.

Calling on critics/theorists such as Terry Castle and Paula Bennett, Ruth Vanita offers an interesting critique of poststructuralist assumptions that 'writers perforce operate in a phallocentric universe and with heterocentric biases' (Vanita 1996, 1). She argues that this theory of representation is based in a Protestant bias that reads Western culture through the Judaic and classical Greek traditions and the European Renaissance and ignores a thousand years of 'medieval' or 'premodern' culture and its continuing influences, for instance, on the Romantics and Aesthetes. She focuses on the Marian and Sapphic myths with their attendant elaborations of imagery and story as long and varied traditions of representing non-heterosexual and non-reproductive sexual joy, love, companionship, and intellectual contemplation, traditions reclaimed by the Romantics. For example,

> the fascinating 'impossibility' of Mary's virgin motherhood constitutes precisely its attraction for those constructing antimarriage and antire-productive narratives in the nineteenth century and ... they drew on old traditions of reading this figure. Mary, flying in the face of biology and heterosexual normativity, is the exemplary figure for the odd lives of male

and female saints who choose same-sex community over marriage, the 'miracle' of creativity over reproduction. (8)

Vanita criticizes Lacan's, Sedgwick's, de Lauretis', and Foucault's theories for denying women agency and, at times, even presence. Rather than agreeing that lesbian sexuality is unrepresentable, Vanita proposes that a quite elaborate literary tradition does exist to represent lesbian as well as gay male love. Of Woolf, she argues that 'the common language [about homoerotic love, non-reproductive creativity, and the life of the mind] I have traced in texts by late-nineteenth-century men and women writers writing homoeroticism was received by Woolf' (174), who draws on this literary resource to valorize same-sex love.

Leslie Hankins is concerned that queer theory approaches often ignore lesbian feminism or present it as passé. Isolating the gender/sex boundary blurring in Woolf's texts, they miss the feminism entwined with Woolf's play with gender and sexuality. As Hankins points out, 'The 1990s did not invent conflicts between lesbian feminism and other voices in gay and lesbian culture; they were there for Woolf in the 1920s' (Hankins 1997, 182). Abraham (discussed in the previous section), while drawing many insights from post-structuralist theory, also points to the importance of feminist perspectives on gender and oppression. The new work of lesbian and gay studies and queer theory

> often divorces the study of sexuality from the study of gender, while proposing to consider gay male and lesbian subjects in conjunction. I am skeptical about both of these efforts. ... While I share the goals of the gay literary criticism that draws on feminist models and offers an expansive reading of lesbian and gay subjects, what follows is a study of lesbian subjects. It could not be otherwise, given all that feminist criticism has indicated about the particular conditions of the representation of women and of women writing. (Abraham 1996, xxiv)

Other critics have found poststructuralist and queer theory useful for the study of Woolf and lesbianism. Smith, Meese, Wachman, and Blackmer, for example, use poststructuralism, or some aspects of it, in their work. Some critics have developed hybrid modes that combine poststructuralism with the feminist approaches Roof criticizes. For example, Karen Kaivola's 1998 essay, 'Virginia Woolf, Vita Sackville-West and the Question of Identity', blends post-structuralist ideas of identity and sexuality with a lesbian feminist attention to the importance of making lesbian desire and relationships culturally visible. Kaivola's thesis is that Woolf's and Sackville-West's sexualities exceed the sexual identities available to them at the time and that *Orlando* expresses an understanding of sexuality and identity as multiple and always in process. Kaivola draws on Judith Butler's theories to discuss how gender, desire, sex, and sexuality are not necessarily linked in any coherent and stable way. Of Woolf and identity, Kaivola writes that, 'describing her own erotic interests in women as "a turn towards Sapphism," a phrase which suggests lesbian *desire* but stops short of adopting a lesbian *identity*, Woolf resists identifying or reifying herself as a sapphist or a lesbian. She does not see her lesbian desire as an expression of gender or sexual identity; she does not link her gender or sexual identity to her lesbian desires' (Kaivola 1998, 35). Kaivola concludes that 'given the historical tendency to diminish or hide the centrality of their lesbian relationships', critical work emphasizing the significance of Woolf's and Sackville-West's lesbian love provides 'an important corrective both to earlier criticism and to current heterosexist bias ... but efforts to demonstrate that either woman was *really* heterosexual, lesbian, or bisexual remain locked within ideas about identity that obscure the realities of these women's lives' (38). In another example of a hybrid approach, '"Queer Fish": Woolf's Writing of Desire Between Women in *The Voyage Out* and *Mrs Dalloway*', Kathryn Simpson uses encodement theory to show how Woolf uses the related images of fish, fishing, fins, and mermaids to represent lesbian existence and desire. Yet she arrives in the end at a position similar to other poststructuralist and queer critics: that Woolf's writing about women's same-sex desire defies clear-cut definition and categorization. Troy Gordon, in turn, challenges queer theory to attend to feminist analyses of gender so as 'to include a more complex vision of ... historical, social, and economic configurations of gender' (Gordon 2000, 105).

At the 1999 annual Woolf conference, a panel titled 'New Applications of Queer Theory' put Judith Roof, Eileen Barrett, Patricia Cramer, and Troy Gordon in dialogue. In her presentation, Roof again argued that psychobiographical studies, historical-materialist studies, and analyses of encodement are all based in the same theoretical assumptions: 'there is such a creature as a lesbian and we know what that is' (Roof 2000, 94) and lesbianism represents both an alternative to patriarchal relations and a subversion of it. According to Roof, these ideas limit our understanding of the function of literature in culture and society and produce narrow interpretations of texts. She asserts that 'apart from heterosexuality and a system of binary gender, lesbianism has no meaning as such. The question here is not how heterosexuality oppresses lesbians, but rather how lesbian sexuality inflects the heterosexual, what functions it has in the complex problems of representation, power, cultural anxiety, and aesthetics' (97). In response, Barrett (2000) argues for the ongoing importance of biographical criticism in making visible that which is still ignored, glossed over, explained away – that is, lesbianism. Barrett's reading of Doris Kilman suggests that for Woolf as well as for many readers today lesbianism and feminism are intimately connected.

Cramer, in turn, remarks on the differences between poststructuralist and radical feminist theories in politics and intellectual origins. 'For example,' she states, 'structuralist/post-structuralist and queer theories derive primarily from male theorists (Foucault, Derrida, et al.), with queer theorists adding to this the influence of gay male and lesbian activism around AIDS. In contrast, lesbian-feminist theories derive from lesbian life experiences and the interactions between lesbian and feminist movements' (Cramer 2000, 117). Poststructuralist theorists posit theory itself as political action, whereas radical lesbian feminists aim toward concrete social action, propose an idealistic vision of society, and aspire to social action and transformation. Such differences necessitate different theoretical perspectives and produce different kinds of literary criticism. In their own ways, Barrett and Cramer each suggest that these differences are valuable, like Woolf's belief in *Three Guineas* that the value of women's efforts to prevent war lies in the different perspectives and approaches they bring to political and public affairs.

woolf and gay men

A corollary to lesbian approaches to Woolf is investigations of Woolf's relations with and attitudes towards male homosexuals. In 'Sapphistry: Narration as Lesbian Seduction in *A Room of One's Own*', Jane Marcus presents her controversial argument that Woolf asserts a difference in privilege and power between women and homosexual men in her class, including her Bloomsbury friends, through the figure of Oscar Browning. When Woolf read the 1927 biography of Oscar Browning she discovered that her uncle Fitzjames Stephen protected Oscar Browning when he was accused of homosexual affairs with his students, sent his son J. K. Stephen on holiday with Browning to show his support, and Woolf's father covered up the whole affair in his biography of Fitzjames. Writes Marcus,

> for women like Virginia Woolf, the homosexual men of Cambridge and Bloomsbury appeared to be, not the suffering victims of heterosexual social prejudice, but the 'intellectual aristocracy' itself, an elite with virtual hegemony over British culture. E. M. Forster, Lytton Strachey, Goldsworthy Lowes Dickinson, and their friends were misogynist in their lives as well as their writing. Virginia Woolf, already exacerbated by her own sense of sexual difference was, I think, confused and disturbed by the woman-hating of her male homosexual friends, and this is the origin of that difficult passage in *A Room of One's Own* on Oscar Browning, which appears to be uncharacteristically intolerant in a writer who produced so many sympathetic portraits of homosexuals in her fiction. (Marcus 1987, 177)

Woolf had thought of these gay men as allies, but realized they did not see the patriarchal family and social system to be the source of oppression and injustice that she did.

David Eberly's 'Talking It All Out: Homosexual Disclosure in Woolf' (1993) strikes a different note than Marcus' about Woolf and gay men. Eberly focuses on Woolf's sympathy and points of connections with the gay men in her circle. Noting the modernist goal of bringing the censored into public speech, Eberly points out the primary role of Lytton Strachey in Bloomsbury's developing ideal of free speech as well as the vitriolic homophobic attacks made against Strachey because of his stereotypically gay appearance and mannerisms. Eberly also notes that while they spoke freely about homosexuality among themselves, those in Woolf's circle were self-protective in public; most of the homosexual members of Bloomsbury, for example, 'maintained the social fiction of heterosexual partnership: Virginia Woolf with Leonard, Duncan Grant with Vanessa Bell, Keynes with Lydia Lopokova. Even Strachey's relation with Carrington can be viewed as a socially self-protective one' (Eberly 1993, 130). In Woolf's writing in all genres, Eberly argues (reminiscent of McNaron), she uses the strategies of 'reticence, concealment, and disguise' (130). Characters in her fiction, for example, often do not speak their minds; instead, the narrator imparts them to the safer hearer, the reader. In *Jacob's Room* (a novel by the way not often discussed in lesbian readings of Woolf but more often in regard to Woolf's relations with men, heterosexual and homosexual), Woolf hints at Dick Bonamy's homosexuality through a report of gossips who interrupt themselves suggestively. In *Between the Acts*, William Dodge wanders among the guests, his name continually forgotten, despised by Giles, unrecognized as a person except by Lucy Swithin and Isa Oliver. With Isa, he exchanges first names and spontaneous conversation, and thus the two of them experience a moment of freedom of speech as the young Bloomsberries experienced it. Eberly concludes that 'in creating Bloomsbury, its initial members created a haven ... to explore – men and women together – the thoughts and feelings that they could only hint at in their published work ... and so made a place where they could admit what had to be hidden even in the modernist period in which they played so large a part – their remarkable, still barely understandable, love' (133).

Jean Kennard seems to answer both Marcus and Eberly in her article 'From Foe to Friend: Virginia Woolf's Changing View of the Male Homosexual'. Kennard argues that Marcus' view of Woolf's attitude towards male homosexuality only applies through the publication of *The Waves* in 1931. After that, Kennard argues, Woolf's attitude changes significantly. Kennard 'trace[s] the evolution of Woolf's presentation of male homosexuality from an equation with anti-feminist, patriarchal power to a portrayal of male homosexuals in *The Years* (1937) and *Between the Acts* (1941) as fellow outsiders, pacifist and empathic with women' (Kennard 1998, 67–8). She uses evidence from Woolf's letters and diaries as well as her published writing to show that Woolf did equate homosexuality with the masculinist privilege and misogynist attitudes fostered in the public schools and universities of men of her class. However, after Lytton Strachey's death, Woolf comes to realize how much she had counted on hearing his response to *The Waves*, how much she misses his presence and conversation. While writing *The Years*, Woolf reread her diaries from the first World War and thus her many entries on her friendship with Strachey. In *The Years*, Woolf presents for the first time a male homosexual character who espouses pacifism and has empathy for women: Nicholas Pomjalovsky. In *Between the Acts*, Woolf links not only pacifism and empathy for women but also appreciation for art and literature with male homosexuality through the character of William Dodge. Because *Between the Acts* is centrally concerned with the role and value of art in a world facing the destruction of war, Dodge, homosexuality, and its persecution are also central to the novel: 'The battle for civilisation is also fought between the male characters, between Giles Oliver and his father Bart, ... and William Dodge, a gentle, self-deprecating homosexual with aesthetic interests' (81). Kennard ends by pointing out that Woolf did not make Nicholas or Dodge members of the Cambridge elite, unlike Lytton; Woolf 'needed to separate the literary and artistic culture a Cambridge education offered from the militarism and misogyny she also saw it fostering' (83).

Troy Gordon focuses on Woolf's representations of non-sexual relationships between women and men, especially between women and gay men, as important for elucidating Woolf's views of social relations, gender, and the promise of feminist transformation. Gordon sees William Dodge and Lucy Swithin in *Between the Acts* as emblematic of an ideal of the self in relation but not in hierarchical relation nor swallowed up by the other. Gordon delineates the 'heterosocial' as an important category of analysis that opens up new possibilities for transformative plots and social relations. To Gordon, 'Woolf's particular representations of cross-sex associations to my mind make her *more* of a lesbian writer, not less of one, and make lesbian writing itself an expansive category' (Gordon 2000, 107).

future directions

Lesbian approaches to the study of Virginia Woolf's life and work originated in feminist scholarship and activism. This subfield of Woolf studies will continue both to be shaped by and to shape the development of feminist studies and activism. And as feminism has been shaped by intellectual developments such as poststructuralism and critical scientific studies of gender, sex, and sexual orientation (like those by Anne Fausto-Sterling) and by political developments such as the collaboration of lesbians and gay men in the face of the AIDS epidemic and the emergence of transgender rights movements, so lesbian approaches to Woolf will reflect the complexity and diversity of ever-developing understandings of sexuality and gender identity. Scholarship in the history and theory of sexuality will necessarily have an impact on lesbian studies of Woolf. In addition, lesbian, gay, bisexual, and transgender (LGBT) studies is emerging as an interdisciplinary field in its own right; Woolf studies participates in LGBT studies and will be influenced by its new theories and scholarship. However, whether and how all these different constituencies and categories can be encompassed within one field and what the relationship between LGBT studies and feminist studies is and will be is unclear. What seems certain, though, is that ongoing debates about the definitions of sexual orientation and gender identity and about the nature and cultural functions of literary representation will be played out in Woolf studies.

Areas I see as fruitful for the future include continued work on Woolf as part of a lesbian literary tradition that is still in the process of being defined and delineated by scholars. In this regard, the extant intertextual and comparative studies of Woolf's writing of lesbianism have just begun to scratch the surface. Particularly interesting, though I am less hopeful that these will burgeon soon, would be comparative studies across race, ethnicity, class, and nationality such as Tuzyline Jita Allan proposes. The connections between Woolf's strategies for representing lesbianism and her innovation and manipulation of literary form and language also deserve further investigation. Another area ripe for more exploration is Woolf's representations of gay men and of heterosociality (as Troy Gordon terms it). The work of feminist men's studies may be of interest in this regard. Lesbian-feminist epistemology, and lesbian-feminist philosophy in general, are also underused resources for generating illuminating studies of Woolf's work.

I cannot, of course, foretell the future, but what is reasonably sure is that lesbian approaches to Woolf will continue to make innovative and vital contributions to most if not all aspects of Woolf studies as a whole as well as to lesbian studies.

10
postcolonial approaches

jeanette mcvicker

Civilization is not an incurable disease, but it should never be forgotten that the English people are at present afflicted by it.

Mahatma Gandhi, 'Hind Swaraj or Indian Home Rule', 1938

But why is decolonization – defined as the process of unlearning historically determined habits of privilege and privation, of ruling and dependency – such a difficult intellectual matter that we cannot acknowledge our past or present location and simply get on with the business of interpreting the other as honestly and objectively as possible?

Satya P. Mohanty, 'Colonial Legacies, Multicultural Futures: Relativism, Objectivity, and the Challenge of Otherness', 1995

It may be a difficult challenge for white feminists, facing the problem of reading race in that revered classic of the rights of women *A Room of One's Own*. Is the empire written there? Or, rather, how and why is the empire written there?

Jane Marcus, *Hearts of Darkness: White Women Write Race*, 2004a

While being Arachne, unveiling the face of Empire, in matters of capital, the state, war, and women, Woolf may become – or remain – Athena in matters of race, repeating 'received iconography,' using imperial language, unquesting and unquestioning in black matters, to use Toni Morrison's phrase. And black *matters* in Virginia Woolf.

Michelle Cliff, 'Virginia Woolf and the Imperial Gaze: A Glance Askance', 1994

The metaphors that come easily to mind – surveying, navigating, mapping, exploring, investigating – in undertaking literary and cultural analysis reveal the problematic ways in which the English language as well as the nature of literary studies are (still) permeated by the discourses of imperialism and

209

colonialism. One charts (plots, maps) a field (area, domain) of study; one adopts a stance – a centre or grounding point in the familiar – from which to undertake this exploration into the *unknown*, in order to bring it into one's sphere of knowledge and understanding (manipulate, make visible) and *do something* with it (make useful, domesticate). That space between worlds, between the known and the unknown (contact zone, site of encounter), is a highly charged one, shot through with complex power relations. The process of deterritorializing, defamiliarizing, deprivileging one's place within such discursive systems is thus, as Mohanty (1995) ironically points out in the epigraph above, always already a complicated one. Simply naming this particular approach is a fraught process: how to engage with the *post-* prefix given that it comes with its own discursive, temporal and spatial issues; whether to use a hyphen, or not. These contentious questions generated debate among critics and theorists in the 1990s, the decade in which postcolonial studies established itself in the academy.[1] This chapter seeks to open readers to that rich debate as it has emerged over the past twenty years in relation to Woolf studies, reviewing critical work that focuses broadly on the issues generated by the intersection of British colonialism and its imperialist legacies with modernist cultural production. How Woolf articulated this intersection as it marked itself through gender, race, class and nation is the subject of fascinating analysis, lively discussion and intense critical reflection.

Reading Woolf through a postcolonial lens offers readers a deeply historicized approach. It necessitates situating her texts within the discursive and ideological conflicts of the period that witnessed imperialism's wane, fascism's rise, consumer capitalism's growth as the force that would replace the colonial economy, the changing role and power of women, and, not least, the emergence of colonized peoples into a state of independence, however uneven and complicated that emergence. Further, postcolonial studies invites readers to explore the myriad dimensions of the aesthetic in relation to this complex social milieu, providing a critical bridge between the contemporary reader and Woolf's historical moment. Such an interpretive strategy has the potential to unsettle the reader who has grown comfortable with Woolf's relatively recent canonical status within women's studies and English departments generally, for it foregrounds her complex political critique of the social system while revealing her deep inscription within and blindness to some of its most egregious practices. As the epigraphs above illustrate, critics wrestle with the contradictions and complexities that are the legacy of modernism's complicitous role in cultural imperialism, in the establishment of *civilization*, to invoke the quotation from Gandhi that serves as the first epigraph. Woolf critics in particular have struggled to squarely engage with her often problematic response to imperialism and the dehumanizing effects of racism, not only because they admire her articulate, materially grounded critique of fascism and the deep insight (especially in *Three Guineas)* that fascism's patriarchal roots lay in domestic political institutions (the family, the church, the nation), but because Woolf also indicts imperialism directly in work spanning the length of her career. This critical struggle is illustrative of a specific historical moment within the academy: Woolf's establishment as a canonical author (particularly for women's studies scholars) just as postcolonial studies was being hailed as the theory *en vogue*. Indeed, one can read the Jane Marcus/Patrick McGee debate on *The Waves* in 1992 as emblematic of this struggle (of which more will be said below). The academic debates were further complicated by Woolf's *arrival* as a pop culture icon, guaranteeing that Woolf studies would become the site for passionate debate on a whole range of issues focusing on representation (and gender, nationality, race, Englishness). Significantly, Jane Marcus' most recent book, *Hearts of Darkness: White Women Write Race* (2004a), offers an intellectually compelling yet uniquely personal articulation of the effort to decolonize fully her own writing about Woolf, imperialism and race; a passage from her introduction serves as the third epigraph above and illustrates such a dilemma.

Because of the frequently conflicting perspectives generated among those currently working in postcolonial studies, this chapter aims to provide readers with a brief summary of the major theorists, issues and debates within the field and then to situate postcolonial studies in relation to contemporary rereadings of modernism. The last half of the chapter highlights, more overtly, key texts informed by that nexus as they engage specifically with the work of Virginia Woolf, engagements that focalize the profound tensions embedded within Woolf's complex, sometimes contradictory identities. As a white, English, middle-class, feminist, bisexual, socialist, pacifist, anti-fascist, anti-imperialist writer she, sometimes by default and sometimes by choice, was *also* a proud inheritor of the English literary tradition, a beneficiary of the British Empire's imperialist practices, and an enabler of its *civilizing mission*, however unevenly. Laura Doyle characterized this tension insightfully in her introduction to the most recent special issue of *Modern Fiction Studies* devoted to Woolf:

... Woolf is after all an *English* writer. Her *Common Reader* volumes, for instance, were mostly meditations on English writers for English audiences. Of course, as [Mark] Hussey shows, Woolf's critiques of nationalism, especially its sexist and fascist tendencies, earned her a reputation comparable to that of university professors today – as poisoners of citizens' patriotism. Yet Woolf's self-conscious sense of her English identity and her critical attitude toward England's empire, like her awareness of her class, do not undo her imperial Englishness. Her awareness only heightens the volatility of her representations. It only makes her writing all the more indelibly English insofar as English literature has been inflected by the accents of empire since the seventeenth century. (Doyle 2004, 5)

While recent threads of critique in Woolf studies attempt to think Woolf vis-a-vis her historical place within the British Empire by acknowledging her inescapable inscription within its institutional and cultural practices, they diverge sharply in how they theorize the *weight* of her complicity with such practices. Some of the earliest criticism dealing specifically with Woolf's critique of empire, for example, more or less exempted her from *conscious, deliberate* promotion of imperialism by focusing on her textual strategies of anti-imperialist critique and resistance, even while acknowledging her overt complicity (for example, the *use of non-Western discursive structures* for Jane Marcus, 1992; the use of *ironic juxtaposition* for Kathy J. Phillips, 1994). Such a critical feat was frequently performed by way of invoking Woolf's undeniable stance against imperialism's foundations in patriarchal ideology. Woolf's strongly anti-fascist, anti-patriarchal politics, best exemplified in *Three Guineas*, have served as a focal point for extension into an anti-imperialist stance, a controversial linkage, as Urmila Seshagiri notes:

> Woolf always challenges the master narratives of patriarchy and British imperialism, but she does not additionally trouble England's representa-tions of the world outside itself. And because her anti-imperialism does not manifest itself through claims about racial or cultural equality, Woolf's novels often reproduce a wide range of assumptions about nonwhite otherness as well as inscribe tropes of racial differences onto white English identity. (Seshagiri 2004, 60)

As postcolonial studies has gained strength in the academy, then, a distinct shift in assessing the weight of Woolf's complicity with the narratives of *Englishness* has taken place, unsurprisingly. Critics have sharpened the theoretical indictment of Woolf's blindnesses: for example, to the 'material and formalist politics of race' (Seshagiri 2004); to her universalizing of women's situation based on the experience of (privileged) white Western women alone (Kaplan 1994; 1996). Most critics stop short of an all-out indictment, choosing instead to focus on Woolf's frequent gestures, however uneven, toward awareness of her own complicity within imperialism and her efforts to use writing to think through that complicity, analyzing the implications of that struggle for a privileged woman writing from the imperial centre (the final epigraph above, from Michelle Cliff's featured presentation at the third annual Woolf conference, is a wonderfully rich example of this). As Andrea Lewis writes in one of the early critical essays adopting this approach: 'What we seem to be left with is the need to acknowledge the concurrent inside/outside positions that Woolf's work occupies. And I would suggest that we read these not as a contradiction but as a reflection of the powerful social divisions embedded in the British empire and thus an inevitable part of any cultural text produced within the empire at that time' (Lewis 1995, 119). Such work signals the passage of Woolf studies through a critical opening to new reading strategies that can be seen less as competing for institutional dominance, more as metonymic anchoring points for stimulating and exciting cross-critical discussions.

varieties of post(-)colonial studies

The Orient is not only adjacent to Europe; it is also the place of Europe's greatest and richest and oldest colonies, the source of its civilizations and languages, its cultural contestant, and one of its deepest and most recurring images of the Other.

Edward W. Said, *Orientalism*, 1978

... it is a paradox, I suggest, that shapes the term *post-colonialism*. I am doubly interested in the term, since the almost ritualistic ubiquity of *post-* words in current culture ... signals, I believe, a widespread, epochal crisis in the idea of linear, historical *progress*.

Anne McClintock, 'The Angel of Progress: Pitfalls of the Term "Post-colonialism"', 1992

Theory must be flexible and prudent enough to say: the post-colonial is dead; long live postcolonialism.

Vijay Mishra and Bob Hodge, 'What is Post(-)colonialism?', 1991

Defining the terms *colonialism, imperialism, neo-colonialism* and *postcolonialism* is still no easy task, as the epigraphs above suggest. Ania Loomba contributes helpful definitions and contexts for exploring how terminology reflects particular historical processes and, thus, why the debate among postcolonial critics seems, at times, strained. Those entering into this field of enquiry can benefit from her observation that

imperialism, colonialism and the differences between them are defined differently depending on their historical mutations. One useful way of distinguishing between them might be to not separate them in temporal but in spatial terms and to think of imperialism or neo-imperialism as the phenomenon that originates in the metropolis, the process which leads to domination and control. Its result, or what happens in the colonies as a consequence of imperial domination is colonialism or neo-colonialism. Thus the imperial country is the 'metropole' from which power flows, and the colony or neo-colony is the place which it penetrates and controls. Imperialism can function without formal colonies (as in United States imperialism today) but colonialism cannot. (Loomba 1998, 6–7)

We can complicate these distinctions a bit more, in order to better understand Woolf critics' engagement with the complexities of Woolf's position as an imperial subject who sometimes blindly supported the *civilizing mission* even while she articulated strongly anti-imperialist stances in her life and work. Gyan Prakash offers a relevant expansion of these ideas:

> Placed against the background of colonialism's functioning as a form of relocation and renegotiation of oppositions and boundaries, the colonial aftermath does not appear as a narrative framed by the hierarchical knowledges and subjects instituted by Western domination. There is another story in that Western domination that, in fact, surfaces precisely at the point where the encounter with cultural difference is organized into the colonizer/colonized polarity, where the historicist notion of history gathers 'people without history' into its fold, and where the metropolitan culture speaks to the marginalized in the language of its supremacist myths. There emerges in these constitutive processes of colonial power an estrangement and displacement of colonial constructions. ... In these performances, as the myths of the civilizing mission and historical progress find perverse expressions in caricatures of indigenous traditions and racist stereotyping and exploitation of blacks, the colonial reality appears in its estranged representation. ('Introduction' 1995, 4)

Prakash's observations provide a strategic theoretical framework for understanding the increasingly pointed postcolonial readings of Woolf's work initiated in the wake of Jane Marcus' signal essay, 'Britannia Rules *The Waves*' (1992), and Patrick McGee's direct engagement with Marcus in 'The Politics of Modernist Form or, Who Rules *The Waves?*' (1992); Marcus' reconsideration of her own analysis of Woolf's complicity with the ideologies of racism in 'A Very Fine Negress' (2004b) contributes yet another layer to this already dense thread of critique. That rich trajectory of Woolf criticism will be discussed more fully below, but readers might note at this juncture the profound tension inhering between the two symptomatic epigraphs, quoting Cliff and Marcus in texts a decade apart, which introduce this chapter as they contemplate Prakash's important point regarding the displacement of colonial constructions enacted during the scene of encounter. To engage in an in-depth postcolonial reading of Woolf today is also to engage in a multi-voiced postcolonial reading of the *criticism* that forms part of that constellated body of work called 'Woolf studies'.

'Colonialism was not an identical process in different parts of the world but everywhere it locked the original inhabitants and the newcomers into the most complex and traumatic relationships in human history' (Loomba 1998, 2). Postcolonial studies takes as its subject matter an analysis of those traumatic relationships: the writings and cultural practices that established them as well as those contributing to their transformation. As Linda Hutcheon noted in her introduction to a special issue of *PMLA* in 1995, postcolonial studies interfaces – not always smoothly – with multiple critical approaches and theoretical practices, notably cultural studies, race and ethnicity studies, and feminist and gender studies, as well as with theories and practices of the postmodern. Emphatically, however, postcolonial studies does not offer itself as a grand system theory that subsumes these other approaches. Rather, it recognizes, for example, that 'race and gender are mutually constitutive' of subjectivity, and that 'sexual difference' is historically problematized 'within specifically nationalist thought' (Hutcheon 1995, 11). 'A key point informing postcolonial criticism,' Loomba states, is that in spite of 'a variety of techniques and patterns of domination ... all of them produced the economic imbalance that was necessary for the growth of European capitalism and industry' (4). Robert Young complicates this relation between colonialism and the rise of capitalism (as do many other critics). In a passage that establishes a dialogue with Gayatri Chakravorty Spivak (her words are in single quotes in the passage below, as they are in Young's text), he writes:

> Europe has been, as ... Spivak has suggested, constituted and consolidated as 'sovereign subject, indeed, sovereign and subject.' Just as the colonized has been constructed according to the terms of the colonizer's own self-image, as the 'self-consolidating other', so Europe 'consolidated itself as sovereign subject by defining its colonies as *Others*, even as it constituted them, for purposes of administration and the expansion of markets, into programmed near-images of that very sovereign self' (Young 1990, 17; quoting Spivak, 'The Rani of Sirmur', 1985)

Such an insight is critical for understanding the multi-faceted processes by which imperialism constructed subjectivities both in the 'zones of encounter' as well as in the metropolis, and how these subjects were reinscribed as capitalism gradually replaced the economics of empire (a process Woolf critics have analyzed in her texts of the 1930s particularly; see below). Moreover, these imperial subjectivities, in the process of becoming *undone* by capital, unravel according to equally complex processes as those that constructed them, with significant implications for writers and political activists such as Leonard and Virginia Woolf, living in the particular historical moment of this transformation. Retrieving the politics of sexual difference as it entwines with imperialism's marking of London's topography, for example, Jeremy Tambling writes, 'Character, in *Mrs Dalloway*, is not something merely inherent within a person: it is the result of an interrelationship between individuals and the space they inhabit. ... One such place is the formal, public, squared-off London of statues in rigid poses which helps to form those who live within its environment. Here is the Modernist sense of character not as something innate, but produced from without, from the lived practices (which must include the ideology) of a society, rather from a deep personal subjectivity' (Tambling 1989, 144). Scott Cohen retrieves another kind of imperial politics marking London through its monumental art, focusing more closely on the British Empire exhibitions such as the one that Woolf wrote about in

'Thunder at Wembley', composed while she was drafting *Mrs Dalloway*. In his reading, these two texts are interwoven in order to uncover 'the force of empire on the streets of London and the role that the Wembley exhibition had in structuring the imaginary relations between the metropole and periphery between the wars' (Cohen 2004, 87). Analyses of the politics of representation informing statues and monuments, as well as determining the boundaries of literary form, have become important points of departure for contemporary postcolonial approaches within Woolf studies particularly and revisions of modernism more generally.

Postcolonial studies sits in a sometimes uneasy tension with theories of postmodernism as well as poststructuralism, even while many critics have utilized these theoretical intersections in compelling ways. Edward W. Said, whose book *Orientalism* (1978) can be said to have inaugurated contemporary postcolonial studies, drew on the critical and philosophical writings of Michel Foucault, Jacques Derrida and Jacques Lacan, among others, to critique the Western *invention* of *the Orient* as an *idea* or *fantasy* in order to constitute itself as *the West*; his signal contribution for literary and cultural studies in particular – *Culture and Imperialism* (1993) – aims at the imperial project as manifested through canonical cultural texts (such as those by Jane Austen), revealing the permeation of everyday life by imperialist ideology. Such an invention was accomplished through cultural texts as much as government and economic policies with far-reaching implications for colonized and colonizer alike. Yet, the West's *metaphorical* construction of itself brought about the disruption of native and indigenous cultural traditions, physical, psychic and emotional trauma, and dislocation for those who found themselves victims of its very real violence. Many contemporary critics are therefore sceptical of the poststructuralist commitment to the idea that 'human subjects are not fixed essences, but are discursively constituted. Human identities and subjectivities are shifting and fragmentary' (Loomba 1998, 233). Critics who enter into such debates about gendered and racialized subjectivities in relation to Woolf include Tambling (1989); Marcus (1992; 2004); Cliff (1994); Suzette Henke (1994); Elleke Boehmer (2002), and Robin Hackett (2004). Their work has helped to reclaim what had previously been marginal in Woolf's textual practice and to produce what Patrick Williams and Laura Chrisman call 'other knowledge, better knowledge' about the Other: for our purposes, 'better knowledge' within the space of Woolf's *oeuvre*:

> Orientalism's enormous appetite for forms of knowledge – scientific, historical, geographical, linguistic, literary, artistic, anthropological – derives in part from its location within the period of the Enlightenment. The Enlightenment's universalizing will to knowledge (for better or worse) feeds Orientalism's will to power. The latter then stands as an example of the production of knowledge as certainly on balance, if not categorically, negative: stereotyping, Othering, dominatory. Colonial discourse analysis

and post-colonial theory are thus critiques of the process of production of knowledge about the Other. As such, they produce forms of knowledge themselves, but other knowledge, better knowledge it is hoped, responsive to Said's central question: 'How can we know and respect the Other?' (Williams and Chrisman 1994, 8)

Another way of understanding the importance of postcolonial studies' ability to engage with multiple interpretive reading practices, even as this generates *contestatory dialogue* rather than *critical consensus*, can be found in Anne McClintock's important 1994 essay, 'The Angel of Progress', in which she clarifies what's at stake at this moment, for such readings and strategies:

> Asking what *single* term might adequately replace 'post-colonialism', for example, begs the question of rethinking the global situation as a *multiplicity* of powers and histories, which cannot be marshalled obediently under the flag of a single theoretical term, be that feminism, marxism or post-colonialism. Nor does intervening in history mean lifting, again, the mantle of 'progress' or the quill-pen of empiricism. 'For the native,' as Fanon said, 'objectivity is always against him.' Rather, a *proliferation* of historically nuanced theories and strategies is called for, which may enable us to engage more effectively in the politics of affiliation, and the currently calamitous dispensations of power. Without a renewed will to intervene in the unacceptable, we face being becalmed in an historically empty space in which our sole direction is found by gazing back, spellbound, at the epoch behind us, in a perpetual present marked only as 'post'. (McClintock 1994, 302–3)

Such a proliferation has dramatically altered studies of modernism, and fundamentally shifted the terms of debate within Woolf studies. The explosion of rereadings over the past decade alone has upended previously inscribed conceptions of modernism as an international movement led by an elite (white, male) avant-garde centred in Europe and Britain, and foregrounded the exclusionary practices involved in valorizing particular aesthetic forms, critical approaches, geographic locations and political affiliations involved in cultural production.

topographies of modernism and englishness

Modernism and post-colonial studies are both seen in ways that have militated against the consideration of 'modernism and empire'. Accounts of literary modernism that crystallised in the decades after the Second World War did not mention the late colonial context, while post-colonial studies has often only sketched in its relation to modernism.

Howard J. Booth and Nigel Rigby,
'Introduction,' *Modernism and Empire*, 2000

But there was another, more serious reason that [Raymond] Williams's book [*Culture and Society*] could not address the questions generated by Britain's postimperial decline, the very crisis that had motivated his work in the first place: beneath the majestic analysis of the crisis of Englishness from which *Culture and Society* derived much of its authority, there lay a faulty conception of culture not simply as 'an abstraction and an absolute' but also as a general response that did not take account of colonialism as the event that structured the integers – industry and democracy – that Williams considered imperative to understanding Englishness.

Simon Gikandi, *Maps of Englishness:*
Writing Identity in the Culture of Colonialism, 1996

... [T]hough emphases and even theories about the Empire fluctuated greatly, imperialist discourse, like the actual expansion of the Empire, was continuous, informing all aspects of Victorian culture and society.

Patrick Brantlinger, *Rule of Darkness:*
British Literature and Imperialism, 1830–1914, 1988

Postcolonial studies' ascension within the academy initiated a strategic rereading of the ways in which modernism had been defined for generations (to put it very simply: as an international movement of the mostly male, Anglo-European avant-garde masters of innovative, experimental artistic form seeking to reclaim a vanishing historical agency through aesthetics[2]) as well as the classic texts sustaining that particular definition. Its force was even more profound coming on the heels of a significant revision of the modernist literary tradition focusing on the politics of gender that had been underway for several years, launched by feminist and lesbian scholars (Shari Benstock's *Women of the Left Bank*, 1986; Bonnie Kime Scott's edited collection *The Gender of Modernism*, 1990; and Marianne DeKoven's *Rich and Strange: Gender, History, Modernism*, 1991 were significant in that rewriting, among many other texts). The effort to retrieve not only *forgotten* women modernists but to interrogate more deeply the gendered politics of modernist canonization and aesthetic values continues. Patrick Williams' essay in the collection *Modernism and Empire* (2000) provides a succinct overview of the way in which postcolonial studies interrogates constructions of modernism, and both his and Howard Booth's essays feature analysis of Woolf's novels. David Adams offers a compelling reading of the importance of epic (particularly Homer) in modernist *colonial odysseys* (the title of his book), including *The Voyage Out*. What makes his reading so interesting is its invocation of the ontological realm as a fundamental category in the use of epic narrative structures for modernist writers such as Woolf, Conrad, Waugh and Forster:

Despite their settings and structure, the explicit concerns of the narratives are often less political or literary than metaphysical: in each of the novels a central character dies as a result of the journey, inviting reflection on the negation of existence. ... The modernist colonial odysseys, in short, are unable to dispense with questions about the totality of the world and of history, yet they are able to expose the deficiency of available answers. This ambivalence about reoccupation shapes the way they reinforce and critique imperial culture, and it shapes their use and abuse of the odyssey tradition'. (Adams 2003, 4, 6)

Many critics engaged in this revisionary project have adopted postcolonial approaches in order to foreground more overtly the dynamics of race, ethnicity and nation as these combine with gender to form identity; such a multilayered critical approach has caused modernism's contours to shift dramatically over the decade of the 1990s, and Woolf studies has participated overtly in this realignment. In the past decade, these readings have come to reposition our understanding of Woolf's complex relation to *nation*, to the broad concept of *Englishness* and its geopolitical implications.

Several important rereadings of modernism focalizing a postcolonial, gendered politics of the visual as it relates to the aesthetic have contributed significantly to studies of Woolf and imperialism, among them those by Karen Jacobs (2000), Jane Goldman (1998), and Janet Winston (1996). Goldman, in a fascinating 'prismatic' reading of 'the feminist implications of Woolf's aesthetics' concentrating on *The Waves*, suggests that Woolf 'appropriates and adapts' imperial tropes 'for feminism. ... Although effective, this allegorical tactic was unsettling in its contradictory positioning of women in opposition to, yet struggling for better representation within, Empire' (Goldman 1998, 195). Winston also notes the importance of allegory in her brilliant reading of *To the Lighthouse* as an 'imperial allegory, foregrounding the many tropes of imperialism embedded in the text and the conflicting ideologies these tropes suggest. ... If imperialism is the unconscious subject in *To the Lighthouse*, then the question of how to represent imperialism is a meta-textual one, implicating the novel's own allegorical mode. In place of realist portraiture, the novel offers abstraction as a method of interrogating imperialism' (Winston 1996, 43, 65). Utilizing a quite different aesthetic focus, Laura Doyle contributes a unique, insightful reading of *The Waves* (1996) in which she articulates how 'the sublime form[s] the inscape of an emergent imperial self in willed confrontation with a vast world beyond its immediate perception yet over which it claims dominion. This self is a narrated self, a self in extension and transformation, a self born of violent colonization and then converted into colonizer. Without imperial, racial-patriarchal motive, does the sublime have a story to tell? It is exactly this question that Virginia Woolf takes up in *The Waves*' (Doyle 1996, 337).

One of the most significant rearticulations of modernist history and practice over the past ten to fifteen years – crucial also for Woolf studies – foregrounds the geographical/geopolitical/topographical as a methodology that loosens the increasingly dead end claims of identity-centred, *locational* politics. Susan Stanford Friedman's *Mappings: Feminism and the Cultural Geographies of Encounter* (1998) offered readers an approach that honoured the locational politics deriving from Adrienne Rich's signal work in the late 1970s and early 1980s (especially 'Notes Toward a Politics of Location', *Blood, Bread and Poetry: Selected Prose, 1979–1985*) while acknowledging its limitations in the wake of multicultural feminist challenges in the 1980s put forward in work by Gloria Anzaldua (*Borderlands/La Frontera: the New Mestiza*), Audre Lorde (especially *Sister Outsider: Essays and Speeches*) and others, offering a crucial engagement with the postcolonial studies that had restructured the entire range of cultural studies by the 1990s. 'The main project of this book', Friedman writes in the introduction,

> is to propose future lines of development for feminism by examining its encounters with other progressive movements as they are staged in the realms of cultural theory and the practices of scholarship and teaching in the institutions of knowledge. ... The book insists on going 'beyond' both fundamentalist identity politics and absolutist poststructuralist theories as they pose essentialist notions of identity on the one hand and refuse all cultural traffic with identity on the other. It argues for a dialogic position in the borderlands in between notions of pure difference and the decon-structive free play of signifiers. (Friedman 1998, 4)

Her use of the term *geopolitical* to attempt 'a new singularization of feminism that assumes difference without reifying or fetishing it' (4) takes on fascinating dimensions as she reads Woolf, whose work permeates the text and to whom a pivotal chapter is devoted. There, she provides a valuable summary of the critical work focusing on Woolf and imperialism up to that point, enjoins feminist and poststructuralist debates pertinent to Woolf studies, and acknowledges the eventual futility of attempting to determine categorically whether Woolf is or isn't an imperialist. 'As vital as discussions of Woolf's relation to empire are, the geopolitical axis of Woolf's life, work and reception is broader than the politics of imperialism. For an English writer born at the height of the British Empire and dying in its twilight, the story of empire is clearly central. But it is not the whole geopolitical story' (119).

Friedman's work becomes point of departure for many Woolf critics, among them Mark Wollaeger (2001), Scott Cohen (2004), and Sonita Sarker (2000; 2001). Sarker, for example, expands on Friedman's reading: 'The solution is not simply to search for "new" theories in an attempt to expand our territory of knowledge about the author. In that sense, "using" or "applying" postcolonial discourse, a new area in Woolfian studies, still leaves us within the texts, leaving her immediate contexts unquestioned. What is needed is to place Woolf in relation to circumstances that are overlooked but that ... form an extensive background to her art as well as to that of other Modernists' (Sarker 2001, 58).

Gyan Prakash (1995) articulates another dimension of the geopolitical when he talks about the use of postcolonial knowledge in the contemporary world:

> The alternative sources of knowledge and agency released by the return to the cracks of colonial disciplines are heterogeneous: they cannot be classified into some global postcolonial other. This is because postcolonial knowledge takes shape at the specific and local points of disciplinary failures; it arises at certain conjunctures and affiliates with particular traditions of thought. Therefore, while returns to the interpellation of different regions, cultures, and histories undo colonial disciplining, they do not use the heterogeneous colonial sites to fabricate a homogenous account of colonial history. (Prakash 1995, 12)

Gillian Beer and Artemis Leontis contribute fascinating topographical readings of Woolf's work, providing a postcolonial-inflected historical dimension for Woolf's conscious and unconscious articulation of Englishness. In 'The Island and the Aeroplane', Beer offers a reading across Woolf's *oeuvre* to focus on her use of the *island story* to 'dislimn' the construction of the island as self-contained within its own national/imperial narrative, a process achieved with the geo-perspective offered by the 'aeroplane': 'The patchwork continuity of an earth seen in this style [i.e., from the air] undermines the concept of nationhood which relies upon the cultural idea of the island – and undermines, too, the notion of the book as an island. Narrative is no longer held within the determining contours of land-space' (Beer 1990, 266). Beer and Leontis both register the importance of discerning how the concept of *home* is inscribed by the discourse of Englishness, wherever that discourse is *located*, topographically speaking. In her important book, *Topographies of Hellenism: Mapping the Homeland* (1995), Leontis reads the short story 'A Dialogue upon Mount Pentelicus' symptomatically as Woolf's 'ironic, polyphonic rewriting of the familiar travel narrative. Its *logos* is of special interest here because it records a British modernist's revaluation of the *topos* of Hellenism. It generates skepticism about both the sentimental Victorian claim to command the values of Hellenism and the tendency to berate the "barbarian" Neohellenes for their mixed genealogy' (Leontis 1995, 107). For Leontis, the story provides evidence of Woolf's 'self-reflexive skepticism about the value of Englishness and a thoughtful identification of the modern Greeks with real Greeks' (107).

In contrast, Jed Esty's recent study of what he calls 'the end-stage of a London-based modernism' (Esty 2004, 3) assigns to Woolf an important place in the maintenance of a particular version of national culture even while it signals the passing of imperialism:

... [I]t is possible to see that English modernists like T. S. Eliot, Virginia Woolf and E. M. Forster did not (as is often assumed) resist the anthropological turn in a rearguard defense of the literary, but actively participated in the rise of an Anglocentric culture paradigm. ... Taken together, their works of the thirties and forties begin to deemphasize the redemptive agency of *art*, which, because of its social autonomization, operates unmoored from any given national sphere, and to promote instead the redemptive agency of *culture*, which is restricted by national or ethnolinguistic borders. (2–3)

implications: rereading woolf through a postcolonial lens

Nigel Rigby succinctly reviews the turning point in postcolonial approaches to studies of Virginia Woolf's writing:

Other contributors to *Modernism and empire* have noted the critical tendency to detach the works of the 'great' modernist writers from any suspicion of contamination by imperial writing, although even before publication of this volume ... the conceit of a modernism untouched by empire had begun to look increasingly unconvincing. Jane Marcus has pointed out recently in her study of *The Waves* that even Virginia Woolf, one of the highest of the 'high modernists', admitted to being moved to tears after watching the Hollywood imperial epic *Lives of a Bengal Lancer,* in 1935. Whether they were tears of laughter, of course, is more difficult to determine, but her point is that empire was simply a part of life in between-the-wars Britain, whatever one's social class, habits or politics, and that all writers were inevitably exposed to the wide range of imperial narrative being produced at the time. *The Waves* pushes modernist form to its limits – it is in many ways the ultimate expression of an anti-realist text – but Marcus argues that the challenging structure of *The Waves* is, in fact, a sustained and unambiguous attack on empire. The lack of ambiguity about imperialism that Marcus sees in Woolf has in turn been challenged by Patrick McGee, who argues persuasively that her attitudes to empire were far more complex than Marcus allows. The broader implication of Marcus's argument, however, that Woolf is representative of a more general modernist concern with imperialism is, I would agree, far more convincing than the image of the modernist artist living in Olympian detachment from such "mundane" issues'. (Rigby 2000, 225)

Marcus, whose many collected volumes of essays had already established her as a major critic within Woolf studies, altered the critical landscape with 'Britannia Rules *The Waves*' (1992). By recasting the emblematic text of high modernist aesthetics as a sustained critique of imperialist politics, she raised the stakes of Woolf studies for a post-Reagan-Thatcher era that was witnessing the so-called culture wars inside the universities of North America as well as the geopolitical realignment of the postcolonial world by the United States and Great Britain.

To suggest that even Virginia Woolf was criticizing imperialism in a novel such as *The Waves* signalled an important end to the formalist domination of modernism that had managed to exclude discussions of politics generally, women writers particularly, and the politics of imperialism as it manifested itself through literary form specifically. Marcus states unambiguously in her opening paragraph that this novel's 'canonical status has been based on a series of misreadings' that include a misreading of Woolf's sociopolitical self. Her reading 'claims that *The Waves* is the story of "the submerged mind of empire"' (Marcus 1992, 136), invoking J. M. Coetzee's novel *Waiting for the Barbarians* that serves as her first epigraph. Her understanding of the novel as imploding empire from within by framing the Western narrative with Eastern references in the interludes marked a brilliant reading strategy that still generates repercussions within the scholarly community. The broad brush strokes of Marcus' reading opened her to the kinds of critique offered so articulately by Patrick McGee, but the essay continues, nevertheless, to serve as an anchoring point for anyone wishing to read Woolf through a postcolonial critical frame.

McGee's rejoinder and subsequent reading of *The Waves* (1992) both anticipated work on Woolf and Englishness as well as utilizing the post-structuralist critique of discourse and narrative form with precision. The contestatory dialogue that his essay engages in with Marcus' provides one of the most intellectually stimulating debates in Woolf studies, for each essay contributes key insights that continue to reverberate for readers of this and other of Woolf's novels. When McGee argues:

That modernist works have exposed the limits of European culture does not necessarily mean they have articulated the space in which the voice of the other can be heard – the other whose exclusion from the discourse of modernism is one of the grounds of its authority. The lie of imperialism still survives, even in the most radical constructions of Western culture like *The Waves* and *Finnegans Wake*, in the belief that Western culture is able to know itself from the outside, is able to produce its own self-critique without entailing the exclusion of the others who have traditionally suffered from the construction of European subjectivities. (McGee 1992, 648)

readers understand that the work initiated by Marcus in 1992 continues to need strong articulation, for the 'lie of imperialism' still survives.

The first book-length study of Woolf and imperialism appeared soon after, with Kathy J. Phillips' crucial contribution *Virginia Woolf Against Empire* in 1994. Widely reviewed, critics noted that 'the Woolf that Phillips describes is a far cry from the Bloomsbury guardian of civilization' (Gaipa 1996, 120). Phillips' participation in the first annual conference on Woolf held at Pace University in 1991 announced her project with a reading of *The Years* that drew heavily on Leonard's *Empire and Commerce in Africa: A Study in Economic*

Imperialism (1920) which, she suggested, had significant impact on Woolf's conceptualization of empire. 'Virginia and Leonard Woolf essentially agree about the folly of Empire,' Phillips stated. 'As a Socialist, Leonard traces the root of the problem to economic imperialism and eventually to capitalism. Woolf concurs and adds other causes, such as gender relations' (Phillips 1992, 30). By the time her book appeared a couple of years later, Phillips was able to state her thesis quite boldly (not incidentally, of course, the stir over Marcus and then McGee's contributions to the topic had already begun to ripple through the critical Woolf community): 'From her first book to her last, Virginia Woolf consistently satirizes social institutions. She accomplishes this criticism in her novels chiefly by means of incongruous juxtapositions and suggestive, concrete detail, which can be interpreted as metaphor. One of her most interesting juxtapositions associates Empire making, war making, and gender relations in a typical constellation' (Phillips 1994, vii). Phillips' study is exhaustive and historical, though as many reviewers have noted, her methodology leads her to what are frequently traditional conclusions in spite of her highly untraditional subject matter and research. Jennifer T. Kennedy, reviewing the book for *Modernism/Modernity*, registers a widely shared response when she suggests that Phillips uses 'an "Images of Empire" approach, in that her work resembles the "Images of Women" style of feminist literary criticism that catalogues representations of women in literature and judges them in terms of their political progressiveness. ... The narrowness of Phillips's approach necessarily limits the ambitiousness of the claims her findings certainly justify' (Kennedy 1996, 123). In spite of such limitations, Phillips' book represents, along with Marcus' essay, a groundbreaking and inaugural moment in postcolonial readings of Woolf.

   Over the course of the next decade, postcolonial approaches to Woolf increased in their theoretical sophistication and their articulation of postcolonial studies' interweavings with other critical strategies. Jane Garrity's compelling reading of *The Waves* enters into dialogue with Marcus' essay, but like McGee, 'diverges from her claim that the novel sustains a consistent anti-imperialist critique' (Garrity 2003, 244). Reading Marcus alongside Simon Gikandi's conceptualization of and critique of Englishness, Garrity claims that this novel reveals Woolf attempting a critique of 'the master narrative of imperialism' while also providing a means of access for women to 'the very discourse that has, historically, excluded and marginalized them'. In attempting this enormously difficult task, the novel 'reflects Woolf's unstable interpellation by the ideological structures of empire' (245). Breaking new critical ground, Garrity reads *The Waves* as emblematic of an effort by Woolf to re-imagine the function of literary form in relation to these political questions. 'Whereas Marcus reads Woolf's formal strategy as a representation of the effects of cultural hegemony', Garrity discovers 'evidence also of a desire to blur the boundary between self and Other in order to re-imagine the novelistic space in which the nation is produced' (246). '... [B]y unifying and thus equalizing her narrative voices,' Garrity suggests, 'Woolf creates the imaginative possibility of equal access to discourse among characters who occupy incommensurate social positions, even though, in reality, the social inequities that underpin such linguistic fluency never actually disappear' (246).

Sonita Sarker's work on Englishness threads Friedman's geopolitical framework through Marcus' in order to establish a version of postcolonial studies that is historically and materially grounded but also encompasses the rethinking of democracy which she observes in Woolf's writing. Her essay on Woolf's 1931 *Good Housekeeping* articles better known as 'The London Scene' (reissued in 2006 by HarperCollins under its Ecco imprint as *The London Scene: Six Essays on London Life* and containing all six original pieces) suggests that these minor texts reveal 'a particular notion of Englishness' and in fact form 'an exegesis on Woolf's particular Englishness, a voyage in, rather than a voyage out'; that 'while Woolf's feminism informs her ambivalent nationalism, both are inflected by an Englishness which constitutes itself as the unracialized norm against which Others are marked' (Sarker 2000, 6).

A number of critics have used the *Good Housekeeping* essays to situate a reading of the profound transformation taking place within British society in the late 1920s and early 1930s, as it moved from an imperialist to a consumer capitalist social and economic formation, analyzing the implications for Woolf's appropriation of *Englishness*, her use of rhetoric, her participation in the public sphere, and her evolving conceptions of gender construction. Among them are Susan Squier (*Virginia Woolf and London: The Sexual Politics of the City*, 1985); Pamela Caughie (particularly in 'Purpose and Play in Woolf's London Scene Essays', *Women's Studies* 16, 1989: 389–408); Leslie Kathleen Hankins ('Virginia Woolf and Walter Benjamin Selling Out(Siders)', *Virginia Woolf in the Age of Mechanical Reproduction*, ed. Pamela Caughie); Michael Whitworth ('Virginia Woolf and Modernism', *The Cambridge Companion to Virginia Woolf*, eds Sue Roe and Susan Sellers), and Melba Cuddy-Keane (*Virginia Woolf, The Intellectual, and the Public Sphere*). My own essay, which appeared as part of a special topic section on 'Virginia Woolf and Literary History' appearing in double issues of *Woolf Studies Annual* (2003–04), reads the London of these essays as 'a geopolitical space as well as an idea, ceaselessly in transition yet always "the same"' (McVicker 2004, 142). Each essay contributes to a palimpsest of London constructed historically, spatially, temporally, discursively and geopolitically, revealing

the multiple ways by which 'London' extends its space into the arena of the global, an extension in the process of tremendous transformation as political, economic, social and cultural affiliations are being reformulated. Through imperialism, parliamentary democracy, commodity capitalism, the English tradition of literature, language, culture, social manners and customs, London by turns dominates/influences/impacts the nations of the world. The world, in turn, including the subjected nations of empire, naturally reciprocates such influence, however minutely or invisibly. Thus 'London' is always London, yet it is never the same at any particular moment. (143)

I argue that Woolf uses these articles to begin working through both the negative and positive implications that lay ahead for women in this transitional moment of imperialism, issues that will preoccupy her more significant writings of the 1930s.

As this review has attempted to illustrate, those critics working in the broad field of postcolonial studies have re-imagined Woolf's writings yet again, for another historical time and place, for a new audience of readers.[3] The suggestiveness of this interpretive reading strategy has already yielded dazzling new ways of understanding Woolf's political engagement with her world and the depth of her literary imagination. Those who pursue the work only glossed here will certainly be richly rewarded for their efforts.

notes

1. Those early texts and anthologies include, but are not limited to: *The Empire Writes Back: Theory and practice in post-colonial literatures*, eds Bill Ashcroft, Gareth Griffiths, and Helen Tiffin; *Colonial Discourse and Post-Colonial Theory: A Reader*, eds Patrick Williams and Laura Chrisman; *After Colonialism*, ed. Gyan Prakash; *The Post-Colonial Studies Reader*, eds Ashcroft, Griffiths and Tiffin. The book that perhaps single-handedly launched postcolonial studies in the humanities is, of course, Edward W. Said's landmark, *Orientalism*. His *Culture and Imperialism* provides a still-vital model for reading Western cultural and literary texts against the grain of imperialism. Early articulators of postcolonial and nationalist struggle such as Frantz Fanon – especially *The Wretched of the Earth*, trans. Catherine Farrington and *Black Skin, White Masks*, trans. Charles Lam Markmann – C. L. R. James, Leopold Sedar Senghor, Amilcar Cabral and Aime Cesaire remain crucial precursor figures for theorizing postcolonial studies in all its dense layerings.
2. The redefinition of modernism that has taken place in the last twenty-five years has produced too many books to itemize here. See Ellen Carol Jones' introduction to a special issue of *Modern Fiction Studies,* 38.3 (1992) on 'The Politics of Modernist Form', for an early discussion that anticipates the critical fullness coming in on the wave of postcolonial studies: 'To what extent were the artistic practices of modernism aligned with the ideologies and politics of imperialism and capitalism?' (550). She makes extensive references to Neil Larsen's compelling analysis, *Modernism and Hegemony*, another important book for the redefinition of modernism. The journal *Modernism/Modernity* is a key critical source for this ongoing redefinition, as is, for our purposes here, *Woolf Studies Annual* and the volumes of selected papers from the annual conferences on Virginia Woolf.
3. As this essay was going to press, a special issue of *Modernism/Modernity* on the topic of 'Modernism and Transnationalisms' (13.3) was being announced. While the issue had not yet been distributed, the table of contents indicated several essays by Woolf scholars – among them, Susan Stanford Friedman, Jessica Berman, Urmila Seshagiri, Laura Doyle and Sonita Sarker – that will, no doubt, contribute to the lively critical discussion reviewed here. Berman and Doyle's essays specifically address Woolf; Simon Gikandi authors the introduction to the volume.

11
european reception studies
nicola luckhurst and alice staveley

At the 1996 annual Virginia Woolf Conference in Clemson, South Carolina, Jane Marcus wondered aloud, with a nod and a wink at her largely Anglo-American audience, how Virginia Woolf might have viewed her transatlantic appeal at the end of the twentieth-century: 'Is she breathing a sigh of relief, so long critically captive in foreign lands, that we are now shipping that unmistakably English figure, body wrapped in the stars and stripes, with full anti-military honors, back to a country beginning to claim her as their own?' (Marcus 1996, 15). Marcus' parodic repatriation of Woolf-as-corpse invokes the spectre of an Anglo-American Woolf scholarship less critically monolithic than its hyphenation would suggest. It volleys a pointed challenge at the special relationship between the two nations long privileged by that tiny dash. While Marcus takes to task her own countrywomen for adoring Woolf to death, she is even more critical of the English whom she fears will 'reclaim' their cultural possession only to maintain the etiolated woman, gutted of the political complexity that a generation of American feminist criticism has ensured for her.

Marcus' words are, of course, deliberately provocative and knowingly playful in their iconography. However, they also expose the kind of linguistic-cultural anxiety that informs, as well as complicates, her admirable goal of demanding for Woolf 'world-scale interest as a social thinker' (Marcus 1996, 18), a position of enduring importance as an international public intellectual. If England and America speak the same language, it is undoubtedly with 'forked tongue', a phrase that defines for Ann Massa and Alistair Stead 'the commonplace paradox of the two nations divided by the barrier of a common language' (Massa and Stead 1994, vii). Marcus argues implicitly for the affective critical significance of this invisible linguistic barrier while calling explicitly for rigorous literary-historical examinations into the different cultural responses to Woolf's writings subsumed in that 'vigorous hybrid of Anglo-American' (Massa and Stead 1994, vii). Have Americans always read Woolf differently from the English? If, as Julia Briggs asserts, 'the British sense of Woolf as an "insider" [is] counterbalanced by the American recognition of her claims to being an "outsider"' (Briggs 1994, xxiii), to what extent have the evolving claims of a bifurcated tongue influenced the cultural, political, and historical 'versioning' of Woolf, to resituate Brenda Silver's useful terminology (Silver 1999, 13)?[1] Marcus is right that there is currently insufficient attention paid to the contexts and chronological developments in transatlantic readings of Woolf, an oversight this *Palgrave Advances in Virginia Woolf Studies* begins to address.[2] Yet, Marcus' depiction of the transatlantic crossings between Woolf and her American readership is most compelling for its implicit focus on *translation*: we may encounter Woolf under the guise of a common language, but we translate her as much in the spirit of our own linguistic cultural geography as in the *de jure* claims of a common tongue. And if this is true for that hegemonic monolith, Anglo-America (who, in fact, do we mean by 'we'?), how much more true when Woolf's works cross that other waterway, the English Channel, requiring translation, in its most literal sense, at the first port of entry? How might translation, as Mary Louise Pratt recently asks, act 'as a point of departure or metaphor for analyzing intercultural interactions and transactions' (Pratt 2002, 25)?

The European reception of Virginia Woolf has traditionally been an under-explored topic in Woolf studies, even though there has lately been an upsurge of interest in Woolf as an international phenomenon, both critically and popularly. (There are currently separate Woolf societies in Japan, France, Korea, and Britain, and the Virginia Woolf Society based in North America has undergone a notable name change to become an umbrella organization, the International Virginia Woolf Society.[3]) But this critical oversight has recently been challenged with a new book dedicated solely to considering Woolf's place in the diverse, intercultural place that is Continental Europe. Edited by Mary Ann Caws and Nicola Luckhurst, *The Reception of Virginia Woolf in Europe* (2002) stands to change the landscape of reception study on Woolf. Published by Continuum Books as part of the Athlone Critical Traditions series documenting the reception of British authors in Europe, the volume contains essays by scholars and translators on the most resonant and vital areas of Woolf's European reception. Essays address the socio-historical, political, editorial, and critical influences on Woolf's reception in Catalonia, Denmark, France, Galicia, Germany, Greece, Italy, Poland, Spain, and Sweden from the 1920s to the present day.[4]

Within this alphabetized list reside even more interesting geographic contours that reveal their own narratives about the geopolitics of reading and reception. Focusing exclusively on Continental Europe, the volume contains one essay for each of Denmark, Greece, Italy, Poland, and Sweden. Germany, however, merits two very long essays that correspond to its post-Second World War division into East and West Germany, as well as to the extent of its published scholarship that quantitatively rivals Anglo-American criticism. France covers four separate essays, clear testimony to its long-standing artistic and intellectual connections with Bloomsbury, its historically privileged position within Europe as cultural conduit and linguistic arbiter, and its formative role as the first European translator of Woolf's work. Throughout the 1920s and 1930s, France would translate Woolf's works more quickly than any other country. Charles Mauron, the esteemed French writer and close friend of Roger Fry, initiated the European response when he translated the 'Time Passes' section of *To the Lighthouse* for the winter 1926 issue of the Paris journal, *Commerce*, almost six months before the Hogarth Press published the novel in England.[5] More unexpectedly, Spain contributes the lion's share of articles. Its five essays include commentary on Woolf's Argentinean publishing history, as well as her reception in Catalonia and Galicia, districts in the respective north-eastern and north-western corners of Spain. Their distinctive linguistic and cultural heritages complicate the question of a monolithic national reception, revealing how crucial are regional voices to the project of mapping Woolf's larger European reception.

It is perhaps no small irony that in the vast body of Anglo-American scholarship on Woolf, there is no comparable collection of essays, or full book-length study, dedicated to analyzing the historical stages of Woolf's monolingual, if arguably cross-cultural reception which attempts to span, as does this collection, Woolf's entire corpus, beginning with her earliest critical reviews to the present.[6] On the one hand, it might be argued that Europe, sitting at Woolf's back door (or is it her front door?), is the obvious place to begin any study of Woolf's foreign reception. On the other hand, this European reception study's comparatively late intervention in Woolf scholarship might be said to restage larger social and political traditions that have conditioned Britain's historically ambivalent relationship with the Continent. These real or perceived divisions may even have provided a useful foil for the comparable unity perhaps too frequently assumed in any Anglo-American transatlantic dialogue.[7] Yet, as the euro itself slowly infiltrates British shores, the timing of this volume is fortuitous. It proves not only that Woolf has always had important currency in Europe, but also that a comprehensive study of the historical valence of that currency can highlight submerged or unquestioned preconceptions which have shaped the hegemonic formations of an ambiguously cohesive Anglo-American Woolf criticism.

While the following chapter focuses largely on the intersections of culture, criticism, and translation in *The Reception of Virginia Woolf in Europe* itself, we also suggest through glancing comparative references to the Anglo-American tradition how the volume's very existence, bibliographically speaking, effectively prods all Woolf scholars to question the linguistic, geographic, national, institutional, and cultural-historical forces that inform their criticism. Implicit in our argument is that the volume's contributions to the study of Woolf's non-British and non-American reception histories forces current and future Woolf scholars to position themselves and their criticism even *more* acutely along a 'geopolitical axis' (Friedman 1998, 118) of readership and response. If there is a 'European Woolf', of how many nations is she made? If there is an 'Anglo-American Woolf', what are the scholarly, transnational preconditions of her existence? Mapping the divergences as well as the convergences within this kind of diachronic European study helps to initiate deeper thought about the questions of place, publication, and periodization that, inter alia, we need to begin to apply more rigorously to the cultural semantics that symbolically bind – as well as separate – a hyphenated Anglo-American Woolf criticism; if beyond the purview of this chapter, we nonetheless speculate that what might be called the 'meta-cultural criticism' introduced into Woolf studies by *The Reception of Virginia Woolf in Europe* promises to have ramifications far beyond the boundaries of Continental Europe.

reception histories: nation and critical narration

Woolf was first read in translation in Europe in the 1920s. While she was first translated in France, as we have noted, she quickly attracted the attention of publishers and translators throughout Europe. The extent of her appeal reveals unexpected idiosyncrasies. For instance, while France inaugurated her European reception in 1926 with Mauron's translation of 'Time Passes', followed the next summer by a full translation of 'Kew Gardens' in the periodical *Les Nouvelles Littéraires*, it was not until 1929 that a complete novel appeared in French.[8] Instead, Sweden wins historical honours for having introduced Woolf's first novel to Europe. The Swedish translation of *Jacob's Room* appeared in 1927 in a series entitled 'Den Nya Romanen' (The New Novel) devoted to promoting new experimental writing from around the world. According to Catherine Sandbach-Dahlström, Woolf's inclusion in this series signaled the publisher's investment in her as one of the 'elite of the younger authors in Europe' (Sandbach-Dahlström 2002, 151). This distinction soon led to a proliferation of translations, reviews, and the first book-length studies of Woolf's writing, so that by the early 1930s, a definable 'European reception' begins to emerge.

By the end of the decade, however, Europe was at war. With fascism's steady rise, writers such as Woolf, a modernist and a feminist, whose husband was Jewish, were no longer acceptable on the Continent. The legacy of those repressive war and post-war years indelibly shapes Woolf's European reception history. Almost all the nations included in this volume experienced either Nazi occupation during the war years, or struggled with their own home grown fascist or communist regimes. For all the censure, neglect, or misunderstanding Woolf may have experienced during the phases of her British or American receptions (and, of course, from 1917 the Hogarth Press protected against outside editorial intervention), the Anglo-American Woolf never had to confront outright censorship. Whether European publishers directly refused publication, cut passages from her texts, or subtly chose to prioritize her more socially realist texts (*The Years* almost always preferable to *The Waves*), the book histories of Woolf's European translations throw new light on connections between national politics and political aesthetics, connections Anglo-American scholarship frequently critiques, but without recourse to the material conditions of Woolfian censorship within the Continental context.

The Reception of Virginia Woolf in Europe not only reveals the fascinating dynamics of direct and indirect censorship on the highly various conditions of Woolf's textual arrival in Europe, but it also offers discrete case studies for how Woolf's own utopian feminism is put to the test, whether affirmed or contested, once her translated texts cross national borders. '[A]s a woman, I have no country. As a woman I want no country. As a woman my country is the whole world' (*TG* 313), Woolf famously wrote in her 1938 anti-patriarchal tract, *Three Guineas*, celebrating the radical, border-dissolving claims of a pan-global feminism. But what might strike the British or American reader of this volume most forcefully is the extent to which appreciation of Woolf's feminism – almost unanimously deemed to have emerged across Europe in the 1970s and 1980s congruent with, if not allied to Anglo-American feminist movements – intersects discourses of national self-discovery. Feminism and nationalism for the 'European Woolf' are not always mutually contradictory terms. If 'second wave' feminism in Britain and America owes much to their long-established if ever-evolving democratic histories, it is salutary to witness, as we will discuss later, the almost simultaneous emergence of post-dictatorial European nations and a critical rediscovery of Woolf's feminism.[9] Whether this convergence of literary and historical realities supports or subverts Woolf's 'as a woman' mantra, it nonetheless positively informs current debates about the limitations of the term 'post-feminism'. As one feminist critic wryly puts it, to speak of a 'post-feminist' world is as meaningless (and invidious) as a 'post-democratic' one.[10]

In 1940, at a time when national boundaries were shifting, and it was becoming increasingly difficult to envision democracy's survival in Europe, Woolf mounts a brave linguistic resistance to fascism in the final words of 'The Leaning Tower':

...literature is no one's private ground; literature is common ground. It is not cut up into nations; there are no wars there. Let us trespass freely and fearlessly and find our way for ourselves. It is thus that English literature will survive this war and cross the gulf – if commoners and outsiders like ourselves make that country our own country, if we teach ourselves how to read and to write, how to preserve, and how to create. (*CE2* 181)

In the unimpeded movement of people, ideas, and books which here symbolically dissolves national boundaries, Woolf touches on the contradictory, but generative relationships between the particular and the universal – between nationalism and, possibly, a new sense of European union – that uncannily anticipate some of the critical issues raised by *The Reception of Virginia Woolf in Europe*. Several of the contributors even excerpt this quotation in recognition of its visionary, willfully optimistic take on Anglo-European relations at the start of a war whose outcome Woolf would not live to see. Yet, its interpolation within these essays reveals more keenly a meta-textual commentary on the problems and possibilities of mapping Woolf's wider European reception. Its syntactical tension, the contrary way it expresses both progressive and reactionary views, seems to mirror the bibliographic contradictions of a project that seeks a collective European reception history from a disparate series of essays which each demand an unusual amount of self-reflexive national speculation on the part of its contributors. On one level, it is a project that compels precisely the kind of national meta-consciousness that has yet to inform any survey of Anglo-American Woolf criticism. On another level, Woolf herself lets us in on the high stakes of the attendant double bind. For in a passage that celebrates the transgression of national boundaries, which effectively declares that literature has *no* nation, there lurks the defiance of patriotic prophecy: it is *English* literature that 'will survive this war and cross the gulf'. Written during a time when the English Channel would certainly have lived up to its metaphoric figuration as 'the gulf', Woolf prophecies the advancement of English texts on Europe in a manner not dissimilar to how the D-Day planners will have to envision the liberation of Europe, from a defensive, coastal point of departure.

The anxious conservatism of these lines ultimately pivots, however, on Woolf's subversion of the military metaphor by subtly eliding battles with books. Expanding the reach of the feminist-pacifist discourse of her outsiders' society from *Three Guineas*, Woolf pointedly turns *all* English patriots into students of foreign language and culture. From the perspective of *The Reception of Virginia Woolf in Europe*, it is hard not to read her exhortation to 'teach ourselves how to read and to write' as an indication of her canny recognition of the literal and metaphoric translation practices such a prophecy implicitly demands. Even so, the passage does not erase the claims of national specificity. English literature will both liberate and be liberated by this commingling of the domestic and the foreign; while it will only be able to 'preserve' its historical authority by 'creat[ing]' something new by contact with its European neighbours, it is primarily the oscillating tensions *between* preservation and creation, tradition and innovation, the domestic and the foreign, which ensure the generative creativity Woolf craves. Woolf seems to be agitating against the political hegemonies that monolingualism implies, even as she simultaneously declares a bold affection, a deep nostalgia for Englishness, the annihilation of whose linguistic and cultural histories was foremost in her mind at this time.[11] Furthermore, the spirit of Woolf's words – the way their brave ambivalence insists on the sustaining power of distinction within communality, of specificity within universality – anticipates recent educational theories that advocate bilingualism as foundational to democratic society. Bi- and multilingual programmes also insist on the political and mental empowerment that comes from having to negotiate the linguistic and cultural boundaries that Woolf figures here in geographic metaphor. For Doris Summers, for instance, what Woolf describes as the necessity 'to read and to write' in languages other than English creates an 'edge' or an 'edginess' which sounds distinctly Woolfian in its political aesthetics: 'Being on edge sharpens the wits, flexes democratic systems, and generally spurs creativity' (Summers 2002, 8).

While most of the contributors to *The Reception of Virginia Woolf in Europe* are themselves bilingual, there is a cognate, if not always direct or easily definable association between linguistic alterity, cultural aesthetics, and the 'trespass' between them that furthers critical thinking. Forced to review Woolf's reception history through the lens of nationality, many contributors are forced to confront the claims that nationhood has on the production of criticism. If Woolf needed to be literally translated to gain a general readership in Europe, the contributors of this volume make it clear that criticism, as an act of interpretation, is its own form of translation, a unique brand of transliteration from one linguistic register to another. Under this aegis, criticism becomes part of George Steiner's expansive continuum: '...a human being performs an act of translation, in the full sense of the word, when receiving a speech-message from another human being...*[I]nside or between languages, human communication equals translation*' (Steiner 1998, 48–9; original emphasis).[12] While the contributors demonstrate varying degrees of response to this issue, ranging from a brief aside to a more thematized analysis of the critical traditions that govern Woolf's reception, none can avoid the fact that the differentiating claims of nation on narration apply as much to criticism as to literary production itself.

For several contributors, the tensions between 'accurate' and less accurate readings of Woolf – which at times run up against the authenticating imprints of Anglo-American dominance within the field – expose their own double-consciousness as scholars writing in English about national receptions which for the most part (but not always exclusively) speak another language. Sandbach-Dahlström is candid about the difficulties of adjudicating Woolf's reception in Sweden: 'The reader from a different country will, of course, always already be an Outsider displaced from the type of understanding that characterizes a national interpretive community' (Sandbach-Dahlström 2002, 148). She asserts that this displacement has sometimes meant that Woolf's Swedish reception has been too affected by the 'ideological preconceptions of the culture' such that 'some responses appear as reading against the grain or even as misunderstanding' (148). At the same time, however, Sandbach-Dahlström's subsequent analysis supports Woolf's own belief that outsiderness cuts both ways. In her discussion of recent innovative Swedish criticism, she singles out a 1996 article by Maura Tavares whose 'Scandinavian background' (160) gives her special insight into connections between the post-Impressionism of *Jacob's Room* and the art of Eduard Munch. Arguing that Woolf's feminist politics and her modernist aesthetics have not always been as segregated in Swedish criticism as they have been until very recently in Anglo-American scholarship, she cites a 1939 article by Urjan Lindenberger that not only offers a formative reading of Woolf's political aesthetics within the Swedish context, but also appears to have established an important precedent for male feminist scholarship on Woolf that continues as a national 'tradition' to the present day. 'Secular idealism is congenial to the Swedish spirit' (162), Sandbach-Dahlström notably reminds us. It is a spirit that has also shaped institutional policy. In a fascinating exploration of the library lending records in rural Swedish villages, Sandbach-Dahlström discovers that Woolf's translated modernist works enjoyed a fairly wide readership, the result of governmental policy to disseminate high culture to promote the democratic project of mass education. This materialist approach to Woolf's reception history is unprecedented in the collection as a whole and suggests a new avenue that future reception histories on Woolf might pursue. Comparative projects rooted in the specificities of distinct cultural reading traditions may help us to answer, non-rhetorically, the question of whether or not there is, in fact, a commonality amongst nationally disparate 'common readers'.

Other contributors register playfully the serious question of how cultural distinction informs the project of critical reception. Mary Ann Caws, whose article focuses equally on French translation practices and on what might be called the socio-history of the Woolf conference, artfully titles her essay, 'A Virginia Woolf with a French Twist'.[13] Twisting Woolf into a Francophone writer takes many forms, starting with the act of the translator, something we discuss in greater detail later. But it also occurs at the level of the conference venue. Part memoir, part social history, Caws' article analyzes the first major European conference on Woolf, held in 1974 at the Chateau de Cerisy-la-Salle. Titled 'Virginia Woolf et le groupe de Bloomsbury', the conference expended much energy trying to classify Woolf's relationship to the Bloomsbury Group, lamenting that such brilliant intellectuals refused to formalize their group identity in an English equivalent to the *Nouvelle Revue Française*. Caws notes that Jean Guiguet, author of the seminal 1962 book, *Virginia Woolf et son Oeuvre* (translated into English 1965), initiated the 'twist' of the conversation by 'avowing his perplexity, with a typically French question, having to do with classification, terminology and specificity' (Caws 2002, 61). Caws remarks that the tenor of the conference seems to have been informed, for better or worse, by 'the very French desire to pin things down now. That desire, so un-English, is also very un-Virginia Woolf, and thereby hangs much of the tale' (62). For Sergio Perosa, chronicling Woolf's reception history in Italy, a coy remark about the Italian cultural affection for the 'painful burden of the writer' (Perosa 2002, 210) opens up serious political analysis about the influence on criticism of the Italian publication of *A Writer's Diary* in 1959. For Anglo-American critics versed in the shortcomings of this editorialized version of Woolf's life, it is salutary to read that its 'strong appeal for writers and critics of diverse allegiances' (210) contributed to the seriousness with which Woolf was newly appropriated by the Italian Left, after a long post-war eclipse when her writings did not suit the 'neo-realist and engagé tendency of the time' (201).

Cultural inflections that inform the tenor of conferences or emotive-national responses also, of course, have their parallels within the critical dynamics of academic institutions. Particularly in France and Germany, where Woolf's critical response has been the largest, there are clearly defined dominant traditions. Carole Rodier, in her detailed investigation into the *état présent* of French scholarship on Woolf, explores the dominance of non-materialist and non-historical approaches to Woolf that contrast the material-historical scholarship which, as the Norwegian critic Toril Moi has argued, predominate in Anglo-American criticism (it is notable, in fact, that most European critics make *no* distinction between British and American scholarship on Woolf). For Rodier, '[w]hereas Anglo-American criticism emphasizes the historical and social contexts, the French reception of Woolf has historically taken the form of a quest for textual autonomy, whereby her works fly free of any deterministic notion of literature' (Rodier 2002, 39). Liberated from a social (but not perhaps institutional) matrix, Woolf's French critical reception has flourished in areas such as phenomenology, narratology, and genetic criticism, but has made fewer inroads into feminist criticism. Arguing that '[f]eminist interests are always subsumed by aesthetic issues' (52) in the broadest French critical tradition, Rodier speculates that the 'absence of any subject such as "Women's studies" or "Gender studies" in France (apart from the Centre d'Études Féminines at the University of Paris, Vincennes, where Hélène Cixous teaches)' (42) partly explains the dominance of non-feminist criticism in Francophone Woolf scholarship.

In Germany, there exists a similar history of dominant critical response, informed by early pioneers in textual scholarship. Ansgar and Vera Nünning, in an extraordinarily detailed article on the phases of Woolf's West German reception (they register three, the last, beginning in 1982, further subdivided into four areas), conclude their analysis with an informative summary of the ways in which West German scholarship differs from the Anglo-American tradition. Like the French response, German Woolf reception has been short on feminist-historical approaches, but long on narratology and textual criticism. The Nünnings argue that, not only did Erich Auerbach rescue Woolf's work from a post-war Germany that had deemed it not sufficiently 'realist', but his advocacy of her as a major writer helped other European critics concentrate on her technical originality. In Italian Woolf scholarship, for instance, Auerbach is credited with 'invit[ing] a form of acceptance even by socially committed critics' (Perosa 2002, 209). Narratology and formalism became a highly developed focus of German response, particularly under the influence of Franz Stanzel. This strong narratological tradition continues in German scholarship, well worth the attention of Anglo-American critics, particularly in the recent work of Monika Fludernik. Although the Nünnings don't emphasize how her innovative narratological approaches have, in fact, been informed by feminist criticism, Jonathan Culler has made that precise connection in declaring Fludernik's work the most significant development in narratology in recent years.[14] It promises a generational shift, a successful merging, perhaps, of certain 'Anglo-American' and Continental traditions.

points of departure I: facing translation

While several contributors argue that Woolf showed little interest in the ultimate fate of her translated texts, others note that she was neither indifferent to the translation process nor to its implications for her growing reputation. Not only did she meet or correspond with several of her translators, she was also, as Laura Marcus analyzes in her study of the European dimensions of the Hogarth Press, a translator herself, well aware of both the estrangement and creative liberation which results from that 'twofold activity...at once critical and creative' (Felstiner 1980, 2) at the heart of translation.

For Woolf, reaching new readers in Europe was a source of both anxiety and delight. 'Two books on Virginia Woolf have just appeared in France and Germany. This is a danger signal. I must not settle into a figure,' she notes in March 1932. The two books that provoke her alarm are Floris DeLattre's *Le Roman psychologique de Virginia Woolf* (Villeneuve 2002, 21) and Ingeborg Badenhausen's *Die Sprache Virginia Woolfs: Ein Beitrag zur Stilistik des modernen englischen Romans* (A. and V. Nünning 2002, 71). They are not, however, the only inaugural national appraisals to appear that year. Joined by Winifred Holtby's *Virginia Woolf: A Critical Memoir*, these triumvirate texts turn 1932 into something of an *annus gravis* in the history of Woolfian reception. That Woolf did not see it as an *annus mirabilis* is perhaps understandable. Her words betray an ironic anxiety of hardening into the profile of a canonical writer, the kind of 'figure' that might impede her flexibility towards the world and writing. What distinguishes this anxiety, however, is that she does not apply it uniformly to all three texts; the two foreign monographs seem to cause the most initial discomfort. She appears positively sanguine about the imminent appearance of Holtby's book – 'Miss Holtby is writing a book on me' (*D4* 13) – in March 1932, and by October she takes pleasure that '[m]y C[ommon] R[eader] doesnt cause me a single tremor. Nor Holtby's book' (*D4* 125). If she is perhaps protesting too much here, betraying a more inchoate, ineffable fear of domestic criticism by denying that it scares her, she is nevertheless drawing a suggestive (if possibly self-protective) connection between critical consolidation, authorial canonization, and the *literal* act of translation itself. Criticism and translation sit (un)comfortably beside their hermeneutic cousins – appropriation and foreignization – to set her temporarily on guard.

While Woolf certainly expresses a mistrust of foreign criticism, she was not ready to dismiss its reciprocal benefits. Letting her texts loose in another language gave them life, vigour, newness. In correspondence with Victoria Ocampo, the primary advocate of her Spanish translations, Woolf eagerly offers up three of her texts – *Room* first, then *Orlando* and *To the Lighthouse* – in ritualized, almost incantatory language that links the anticipation of translation to developmental rites of passage. The books appear to her now, she tells Ocampo as she symbolically passes them on, 'like faces seen in childhood', 'remote books, about which I felt so passionately, as I wrote them' (*L5* 358). As Laura Lojo Rodríguez argues in her history of Woolf's Spanish reception, it was this very mixture of intimacy and distance that appealed to Woolf's temperament for defamiliarization. Foreign translation could, 'on the one hand, preserve this "remoteness"...but...also make [Woolf's texts] appear brand new to a somehow "remote" readership' (Lojo Rodríguez 2002, 233). Equally, Woolf could be quite mercenary about the prospect of seeing her texts made 'new' in another culture. The Nünnings' article (2002, 68) recounts Woolf's snide response to the imminent appearance of her first German translation, *Mrs Dalloway*; although she discredits German translation practice as 'very effusive and very ineffective', she nonetheless consoles herself with the knowledge that 'any notice is likely to be to my good' (*L3* 460).

As a practising translator, Woolf was well aware of the risks and the creative opportunities that the activity entailed. In her various essays concerning Russian fiction, and most notably in her essay, 'On Not Knowing Greek', she invariably laments the linguistic and cultural losses that attend translation, while turning that consciousness of loss to creative advantage. Her sensitivity to linguistic alterity is so finely tuned that she not infrequently comments on the distinctions between the English and American languages, as if goading her future critics to contextualize the difference for themselves.[15] In fact, recent scholarship on Woolf as a translator (she could read French, Russian, Greek, and Latin) has emphasized her attraction to the discipline precisely because of its intellectual engagement with estrangement and difference. Nicoletta Pireddu, citing Emily Dalgarno's recent study of Woolf's lifelong fascination with Greek, writes that Woolf 'transcend[s] a practice of translation as mere communication of the sense of the original text...by recodifying the semiotic conventions of the target language so as to foreground the instability and the divergence of meaning' (Pireddu 2004, 63). Laura Marcus even intimates that Woolf's practice translating Russian for the Hogarth Press in the early 1920s helped her to theorize a modernist poetics. While it is widely acknowledged that Woolf often used railway metaphors to signal the deficits of the Edwardian writers, as well as the rapid and jarring movement from one outmoded literary period to the current 'spiritualist' movement embodied in large part by the Russians (Bowlby 1997, 4), it is less well known that Woolf actually spent a large amount of time learning her Russian on the commuter train between Richmond and Waterloo (Marcus 2002, 351). For a writer so attuned to the material conditions that influence creativity, this highly (self-) reflective scene of translation is one of the more delightful, hidden gems in the history of Woolf's writing practice. As a *tableau vivant* of the obligations and productive experimentation that accompanied Woolf's duties as co-owner of the Hogarth Press, it also evocatively situates the Press' role, not only as a key player in the production of British modernist writing, but also as 'an important site and conduit for the European and internationalist dimensions of modernist culture' (328).

If translation as both practice and creative metaphor called up competing agendas for Woolf – between a desire for greater 'notice' and a fear of mis-translation; between her older works and their 'new' incarnations; between loss and creative regeneration – these same ambivalences get replicated in her encounters with her contemporary translators. At times, the scene of translation is almost comical in its reciprocity; Woolf infamously mangles the name of the famous French novelist, Marguerite Yourcenar – 'Madame or Mlle Youniac (?) Not her name' (*D5* 60) – when Yourcenar visits her to solicit help in translating *The Waves*, a book that responds by being, as Françoise Pellan wryly argues, 'insidiously unfaithful to the original' (Pellan 2002, 55). But more commonly, Woolf's encounters with her translators mix enthusiasm for the dissemination of her writing with anxiety about the manipulation of her image. Given Brenda Silver's recent extensive critique of how, in an Anglo-American context, Woolf has attained the status of a cultural icon who can signify, visually, independently of her writing, it is clear that a similar cultural dynamic informs her European reception. Yet, in a twist on the Anglo-American context, where Silver argues that what Woolf's proliferating images most frequently signify is fear (Silver 1999, 5), it is Woolf's fear of her *own* image, how it gets generated and regenerated within a multilingual context, that haunts her encounters with her European translators.

When she meets Jacques-Émile Blanche in the summer of 1927, the anticipation of her passage into French culture comes with all the trappings of a celebrity promotion Woolf does her best to deflect. Meeting Blanche at Ethel Sands' house in Auppegard, France, Woolf partakes in a rare interview that gets published on the front page of *Les Nouvelles Littéraires*, beneath the 1902 Beresford portrait, and alongside Blanche's translation of excerpts from *To the Lighthouse* and the complete 'Kew Gardens'.[16] An editorial byline explains the rationale for publishing 'Kew Gardens': 'pour illustrer l'entretien... avec Virginia Woolf'. So Woolf passes into European culture simultaneously as text and image, her art literally following her double figuration – in picture and in print – as artist. Blanche engages his role as portraitist with glee, spending much of the interview commenting on Woolf's greeting, her posture, her famed beauty, all while deliriously questioning how much of *To the Lighthouse* is based on her 'real' family. Frustrating for Blanche, Woolf keeps trying to escape his grasp, insisting they talk about Proust instead.[17] Years later, however, Woolf will have much greater difficulty eluding capture by the foremost advocate of her Spanish translations. Victoria Ocampo is an almost larger-than-life figure in the history of Woolf's Spanish reception, 'one of Virginia Woolf's first feminist readers' according to Laura Lojo Rodríguez (2002, 220), founder of the South American journal *Sur*, and self-appointed cultural intermediary between Europe and Spanish America (Larkosh 2002). Yet her intensely feminist (and colonialist) identification with Woolf as a mirror of her own artistic and cultural longings ends up foundering, ironically, in the glare of the camera lens. It is Ocampo who arranges the infamous sitting for the portrait photographer Gisèle Freund in 1939; the larger-than-life colour portraits that result seem frightful to Woolf, a 'petty vulgar photography advertizing stunt' (*D5* 220), and the overexposed friendship with Ocampo comes to an abrupt end.[18]

When Woolf's works are about to make the passage from one language to another, when her direct involvement comparable to her Anglo-American reception is passive (it was often her habit, for instance, to correct her English and American proofs simultaneously and to choose the same, or closely contemporaneous, publication dates for her transatlantic editions[19]), it is perhaps unsurprising that the tyranny of visual appeal rears its head. The face, after all, has no native 'language'; it at once transcends linguistic particularity and speaks every language, making it a particularly polymorphous object of fascination in a multilingual context. Woolf undoubtedly intuited how this paradox might play itself out given her close contact with key European translators who were also, quite literally, image makers. If she was defiant about not becoming hardened into a canonical 'figure', she was equally wary of being 'figured' or profiled in ways that might compensate for whatever losses she knew from experience inevitably attended the processes of textual translation. She might well have characterized these losses as creative advantages in her own writing, but did she want foreign readers attaching her face to the lacunae of textual translations she herself had no way of authorizing? Certainly, the number of contributors to *The Reception of Virginia Woolf in Europe* who gloss Woolf's image as a constituent feature of her passage into a foreign language and culture suggest that the internationalism of her appeal needs further cultural study. From Pierre-Éric Villeneuve's discussion of how Simone de Beauvoir was haunted by Woolf's face (Villeneuve 2002, 25), to Laura Lojo Rodríguez' analysis of Victoria Ocampo's zealous identification with Woolf's facial and textual persona (Rodríguez 2002, 225), to Urszula Terentowicz-Fotyga's observation that even in Poland publishers use Woolf's 'face ... [as] a kind of lure' (Terentowicz-Fotyga 2002, 147), to the Nünnings' revelation that the Beresford portrait 'did more than anyone or anything...to popularize Woolf in Germany' (A. and V. Nünning 2002, 84), the ways in which Woolf's textual translations intersect her iconic receptions in Europe are suggestively dense. They have already generated articles by European scholars, notably in Denmark (Klitgård 2002, 176) and Germany (A. and V. Nünning 2002, 84).

Yet, whereas the Anglo-American interest in Woolf's image engages a celebratory poststructuralist interrogation for how Woolf's iconicity transgresses fixed borders between high and low culture – fuelled undoubtedly by America's historical fascination with the commercial power of the image – the current European academic response seems more afraid that her image reaffirms an all-too-eager popularizing of Woolf's feminism as it is has been received through her polemical essays. The public absorption with the popular Woolf – both image and feminist essayist – has threatened what the Nünnings describe as the more 'refined critical appreciation' (85) of her texts. This is just one example where European Woolf critics and their Anglo-American counterparts appear at times to be looking at each other on opposite sides of the same mirror. The resulting critical refractions are undoubtedly linked to historical differences of emphasis and cultural 'uptake' for both feminism and popular culture within transnational academies. If the 'culture wars' of 1980s America ultimately validated media studies, popular culture, and women's studies (to name just a few upstart fields) as academic disciplines, those who write about Woolf's European reception suggest greater resistance within the academy to the hybridization of these fields. Commentaries such as the Nünnings' suggest the European academy still has a vested interest in its own high cultural status in ways that inevitably affect interpretations of Woolf's iconicity, no less her feminism. They are issues, as we shall see, that also affect the practices of translation which provided Woolf's texts with European audiences who might read her, as much as gaze at her.

points of departure II: theorizing translation

If translation theory traditionally has occupied, as Edwin Gentzler argues, a 'marginal status...within literary studies' (Gentzler 2001, 2), it is particularly true of Woolf studies that the history, contexts, and methodologies behind her countless European translations have received almost no scholarly attention.[20] Almost all the essays in *The Reception of Virginia Woolf in Europe* narrate some aspect of her 'arrival' in translation. A few of the contributors are themselves translators whose candid explorations, notably Mary Ann Caws', Françoise Pellan's, and Wolfgang Wicht's, of the private deliberations made in the processes of translating or editing Woolf provide the kind of genetic documentation of translation practices that theorists since George Steiner have demanded (Felstiner 1980, 3). Woolf studies could only be enriched by similar investigations: what might the Yourcenar archives tell us, for instance, about the drafts of her apparently disastrous rendition of *The Waves*? Taken en masse, the accounts offered in this collection gloss many theoretically pressing issues about the role of the translator as cultural mediator, the place of gender in translation practice, and the competing claims of 'foreign versus free' translations (Gentzler 2001, 41), or, in Ida Klitgård's analysis of Danish translations, between 'literariness and localness' (Klitgård 2002, 170). Moreover, their commentaries promise new approaches to modernist studies, questioning how translation practices reflect debates about the politics, history, and gender of modernism itself. One of the most intriguing but not always straightforward commonalities, for instance, among several of Woolf's 'mistranslated' European novels is how frequently her feminist politics attract translators in nations struggling to emerge from political, linguistic, or cultural oppressions, an attraction which does not always 'translate' into sensitive renditions of the feminist lyricism of her novels. The oscillating claims of art versus politics that often vexed Woolf herself at times waylay her own translators, narrowing the scope of her European reception. Certainly, further study of her vast array of translations would help to illuminate more clearly the *material* factors that influenced their production and reception; to help us to answer, in the words of contemporary translation theory, how translation is not just a practice, but a 'message' (Larkosh 2002, 101), 'a process of mediation which does not stand above ideology but works through it' (Simon 1996, 8).

For Anglo-American critics, Woolf's publication history is so well known, starting with *The Voyage Out* (1915) and ending with *Between the Acts* (1941), they are likely to be able to recite it on command (perhaps even forwards *and* backwards). In the European context, however, Woolf's book history is so various that no European country shares the same chronology. As shown in Appendix I documenting the list of Woolf's first translated European novels, this variability results in different timelines as well as different reception narratives within individual nations. Decisions to translate Woolf, and the choice of which texts to select for translation are themselves various, based on factors including censorship, the prevailing responses to modernism, the demands of the marketplace, and even the presence of dynamic personalities willing to advocate for her writings. These factors contour Woolf's European reception in ways that are both divergent and convergent. For instance, while Sweden might have shown an avant-garde spirit for inaugurating Woolf's European reception in 1927 with the highly modernist *Jacob's Room*, their follow-up translation of *The Years* in 1942 was a more conservative choice, influenced by the 'epic … [and] proletarian' (Sandbach-Dahlström 2002, 149) concerns of traditional Swedish fiction. These same concerns, under very different historical conditions, influenced both Denmark's (in 1941 during German occupation) and Poland's (in 1958 during communism's entrenchment) selection of *The Years* as first translation. Of course, the more realist use of language in *The Years* would also have made it an attractive option for translators, its ease of translation coinciding with, and certainly congenial to, the prevailing political climates. It might be argued, for instance, that in America, where the novel hit the best-seller lists in 1937 (Silver 1999, 74–5), its comparatively fluid readability smoothed its cross-cultural translation even there.

More recently, in nations newly emerging from communist or fascist regimes, there has been a notable increase in the number of Woolf translations, some coinciding with her emergence from copyright in 1991. For Urszula

Terentowicz-Fotyga, however, the pressures of the new market economies have not always ensured a high quality of translation; Woolf's novels in Poland are still 'waiting for a faithful translator so that [they] will cease to pulse according to different rhythms and styles' (Terentowicz-Fotyga 2002, 127). Not that this post-communist desire for textual uniformity is without some historical irony. Wolfgang Wicht, in his article about the politics of translating Woolf in the former East Germany, highlights the literary costs of a uniform, but implicitly biased, editorial policy, noting that 'close cooperation with the publishing house' (answerable to the Ministry of Culture) led to a 'consistent policy' of editing Woolf's texts that nonetheless 'precluded...a louder pro-modernist voice' (Wicht 2002, 108). Although Wicht is referring to editorial policy and Terentowicz-Fotyga to translation policy, both wrestle with how culture and politics inevitably mediate Woolf's European reception, raising questions about what agendas get hidden in aspirations for and claims to textual fidelity. Terentowicz-Fotyga's anxiety about translation quality is certainly apropos of a broader fear about the authoritative value of editions read by European university students whose widespread access to cheap, editorially corrupt copies of Woolf's novels is a credible pedagogical problem (Abranches 2002, 325). It reverses the problem of teaching Woolf in America where copyright restrictions on English publishing imports have meant that students have only had access, until recently, to the endlessly reprinted, unannotated Harcourt Brace editions. If not corrupt in themselves, since they are based on Woolf's original proofs, their intransigent lack of any editorial apparatus, whether explanatory footnotes or scholarly introductions (not to mention commentary on how Woolf herself inserted distinctions between her American and English editions), does a disservice to readers for whom England is, after all, a foreign country. Good news is, however, on the horizon for American readers at least; Harcourt Brace has agreed to publish moderately priced editions, annotated and introduced by contemporary Woolf scholars.[21]

While proliferating, competing translations bring problems of authority and selection, they also elaborate the postmodernity of Woolf's politic aesthetics, contributing to debates within textual and editorial studies where a text's manifold publication history, its many 'bibliographical environments' (McGann 1985, 85), trump any claim to textual autonomy. Terentowicz-Fotyga writes about two competing 1994 Polish translations of *Orlando*: one, a plodding, word-by-word transcription that is technically 'closer to the original' (Terentowicz-Fotyga 2002, 141); the other, a richly stylized, playful reinvention whose translator, Tomasz Bieron, adds explanatory notes about the translation process, making claims that Orlando's poem finds its most faithful interpreter in a renowned *Polish* poet. Certainly, the textual transgressions (and canny nationalist appropriations) enacted by Bieron in his role as translator are consistent with the text's own self-questioning; they also, however, draw back the curtain on the too-often invisible role of translator and/as critic in mediating the cultural power of any given text.[22] It is even tempting to make a political allegory of Bieron's playfulness, his transgressions sanctioned and celebrated in the atmosphere of post-martial law Poland. As several other contributors attest, *Orlando* has been a particularly popular translation choice in newly democratic European nations where screenings of Sally Potter's 1992 film also contributed to the text's appeal.

Yet, Bieron's paratexts, however postmodern, are not without precedent. Graça Abranches argues that Manuela Porto, Woolf's most vigorous and feminist defender during the years of Salazar's dictatorship in Portugal (1924–74), made 'conscious use of translation and preface writing ...to say by proxy that which was forbidden in [her] social context, that which [she was] not allowed to say in an autonomous text' (Abranches 2002, 317). Translation attempted a kind of protective political cover, codifying 'a poetics of marginalization' (317) that Abranches argues needs further study as a defining trope for Portuguese writers of the period. In addition, she highlights a connection between translation and modernist reading practices that we suggest merits further theorization within the broader European context.[23] Arguing that Woolf's two most talented Portuguese translators, Manuela Porto and Cecilia Meireles, frequently used preface writing to 'comment on the risks of translating Woolf into another language' (2002, 317), Abranches notes that they also admonished their readers to think *like* translators, that the protocols for a modernist reading practice were not dissimilar to the interventions and recreations enacted by the activity of translation itself. Certainly, under the pall of fascism, the commonplace risks of translation must have been placed in sharp relief for these particular translators.

If the politics of Woolf's style has been the predominant focus of recent Anglo-American scholarship, these examples prove its different interpretations in the context of translation study.[24] But it also resides, of course, at the level of language. From the earliest days of her passage into European culture, Woolf's translators complained about her difficult prose. Laura Marcus cites a previously unpublished letter from Maurice Lanoire who wrote to Woolf when he was preparing his translation of *To the Lighthouse*, commending her on the 'flow, the admirable flow of your sentences or periods', but lamenting that the 'French language does not possess the plasticity of the English and its roll cannot always have the same length' (Marcus 2002, 331). Mary Ann Caws concurs with Françoise Pellan that the tendency towards abstraction in the French language – both as a lexical reality and an *expectation* on the part of the French reader – poses legitimate barriers. Yet, in her effusive praise of Charles Mauron's translations, Caws credits part of his success to a 'Provençal joy in words' (Caws 2002, 65), directly implicating language politics in the aesthetic valuation of translation practice. Caws implies that modernism's own linguistic challenges to dominant narrative codes may find a natural affinity with dialects or idioms that are themselves marginal to the dominant national tongue. Woolf herself certainly preferred Mauron's prose, harbouring a secret desire that he would translate *Orlando* (Marcus 2002, 332).

While it might be argued that Woolf's modernism was already enforcing a foreignizing reading practice on English readers, making them approach difficult prose as new territory, her writing was also being domesticated by foreign markets for reasons of politics and prevailing cultural mores.[25] Sergio Perosa explores how Woolf's Italian translations of the 1930s and 1940s were consistently regularized to conform to the *bello scrivere* (fine writing) tradition in Italian fiction, obscuring the 'revolutionary nature of her writing' (Perosa 2002, 201) and providing anodyne templates that would suit the socially committed politics of the 1950s. Even when the prestigious publishing house Mondadori commissioned a canonizing reprint in the 1970s of Woolf's works (under Perosa's editorship), it would not correct the mistranscriptions that made Woolf more realist than modernist.[26] Gender also plays a significant, if not yet fully theorized role in the hierarchical politics of language and genre translation. Perosa opens his article by noting that '[e]arly Italian translations of Virginia Woolf were mostly by women' (200), but much further work needs to be done on *how* these women reconciled the tensions between Woolf's feminist modernism and national literary traditions that had problems swallowing modernism at all. If someone like Manuela Porto made incursions using paratexts, Anna Banti appears to have split the difference between criticism and translation. Nicoletta Pireddu's recent work on Banti's Italian translations (independent of the *European Reception* volume) offers incisive analysis, for instance, of the conflict between Banti's overt advocacy of Woolf's feminist essays and her normalizing translations of Woolf's novels. In other contexts, the inflected grammar of many European languages forces gendered choices Woolf could afford to leave polemically ambiguous, thanks to her native syntax: should Orlando become (a Polish or Italian) Orlanda?

Within *The Reception of Virginia Woolf in Europe*, Jacqueline Hurtley's article on the importation of Woolf into Catalonian culture – an already politicized act since Catalan was a minority Spanish language whose 'vernacular [was] struggling to come into its own' (Hurtley 2002, 296) – plays a variant theme on these conflicted allegiances. While the Catalonian *Mrs Dalloway* held distinction as the first mainland Spanish translation of Woolf in 1930, its translator a strong proponent of the modernizing Noucentista movement, Hurtley excoriates his heavy-handed translation of Woolf's free indirect discourse which consistently foregrounds a masculine perspective (notably culminating in a last line that celebrates, not Clarissa's autonomy, but Peter Walsh's gaze). As an act of political subversion, a modernist challenge to hegemonic language laws, the translation nonetheless replays, in a different key, debates about the gender of modernism that have received considerable critical attention in the last decade.[27] When Hurtley notes the paucity of feminist criticism on Woolf within Catalonia today (Hurtley 2002, 310–11), it is hard not to speculate on the connections between cultural-historical trends in translation practices and prevailing orthodoxies in local academic scholarship. Without doubt, Woolf's translations sit at the cross-hairs of any number of debates about language politics, cultural and gendered identities, and competing histories of modernism that we expect will shape the next generation of scholarship on Woolf's foreign reception history.

embargoed goods: censorship

The national and ideological contexts of translation practice that exert a regularizing – or grossly distorting – effect on Woolf's novels arguably constitute forms of censorship. Yet, the publication of Woolf's writings within Europe had many other mediators, aside from translators, whose interventions ranged from direct censorship to general censoriousness. Censorship was, of course, an uneven and irregular process, but reading its imprints on Woolf's European book history brings home, quite literally, how important was the Hogarth Press to Woolf's creative autonomy. It provides the palpable backdrop against which Woolf's expressions of liberation achieve emotional depth: '[I]t makes all the difference writing anything one likes, and not for an Editor' (L2 169).

In France, where Woolf entered a literary culture already appreciative of modernism – she was, in Nathalie Sarraute's ambiguous label, 'une seconde Proust' (Caws and Luckhurst 2002, 3) – her high modernist novels were easily assimilated. Éditions Stock eagerly published both To the Lighthouse and Mrs Dalloway, but swiftly rejected Orlando, A Room of One's Own and Three Guineas. In Laura Marcus' assessment, 'Woolf's most overtly feminist texts were received by Stock as untranslatable in cultural terms' (Marcus 2002, 331). Hidden in the Hogarth Press archives at Reading University is the outcry of one French woman declaiming the sexism of the publisher's 'stock' response, hoping in turn to land translation rights to Room for herself: 'I have repeatedly stressed to [Éditions Stock] the interest of this volume, but the interest of women is the last concern of men over here...' (331). These rallying words certainly highlight the feminist value of the Hogarth Press, etching in stark outline what might have been the book's fate in England (not to mention whether it would ever have been written) in its absence. Indeed, when Manuela Porto presented an adapted version of A Room of One's Own as part of a lecture on Woolf for the January 1947 Exposiuao de Livros das Mulheres (Exhibition of Books Written by Women), the censors were waiting to pounce. The impact of the exhibition led to its cancellation by the Portuguese authorities in June 1947, and a ban on all independent women's groups during the next three decades of Salazar's regime (Abranches 2002, 315–16).

In other contexts, Woolf's books find safe haven as offshore translations published in South America, bearing unconventional witness to that commonplace postcolonial trope, 'the empire writes back'. Victoria Ocampo's fervently feminist response to Woolf's work meant, for instance, that Argentina become 'the centre of pioneering translations of her texts in Spanish' (Lázaro 2002, 249); similarly, the culture of translation in Brazil which had flourished from the early 1940s supplied Portugal with 'some exemplary Portuguese versions of modern ... world literature' (Abranches 2002, 317), including two of its three pre-revolution translations of Woolf. But, as Alberto Lázaro points out, the official censorship processes on the continent could be quixotic. In Spain, the censors allowed the translation (of *Flush*, *The Years*, *Night and Day*, *The Voyage Out* and, more unexpectedly, *Jacob's Room*) and Argentinean importation (of *Mrs Dalloway* and *To the Lighthouse*) and critical commentary of English modernism in prominent journals like *Ansula* and *Escurial* was generally favourable (Lázaro 2002, 252); yet, the 1953 censor's report on *The Waves* sanctioned its publication only with major suppressions, including all 'references to the body, God, crucifixes or the Spanish language' (251). Again, in 1957, the censors recommended cuts to twenty-nine pages, concluding that *The Waves* was of 'undoubted literary quality; but...a monstrosity that cannot be authorized' (251–2). It was not until 1972, six years before Franco's death, that the ban on *The Waves* was lifted.

The Waves, in fact, becomes something of a flashpoint in debates about Woolf, censorship, and political criticism. In Poland where, in Urszula Terentowicz-Fotyga's description, the fragile post-war national identity privileged writing that was socially 'committed', and 'Virginia Woolf was seen as too ethereal and uncommitted to fit into the "burdened" Polish context' (Terentowicz-Fotyga 2002, 128), *The Waves* finally emerges, phoenix-like, in 1983. As the crowning achievement of Woolf's canon, it also signals the triumph of modernism '[a]fter the silent years of martial law' (140). Extrapolating political parables from publication histories does not, however, always guarantee a uniformly political *textual* critique. Ida Klitgård also notes that the 1994 Danish translation of *The Waves* holds a privileged place in Woolf's Danish reception, a 'classic' of the genre that similarly has thrown off a prior burden. For Klitgård, however, that albatross is not social realism (or martial law), but 'the feminist burden of the 1970s whereby [Woolf] was solely linked with *A Room of One's Own*' (Klitgård 2002, 183). In part, Klitgård's words are on a continuum with our previous analysis of the ambivalent relationship within the European critical reception between the popular and the academic, the 'feminist' and the 'high modernist' Woolf, but they also speak to the chameleon politic impulses of *The Waves* itself.

For Wolfgang Wicht, for instance, sole editor and official critic of Woolf in the former GDR, the struggle to write the official 'Nachwort' (Afterword) to his 1988 translation of *Die Wellen* offers a deeply revealing portrait of a critic's complicity with prevailing national politics. From the vantage point of reunification, Wicht deconstructs his Nachwort word-by-word, showing how the valence of each term resonates with both socialist and (subversively) modernist readings; it is the kind of destabilizing tension, he suggests, that not only animates *The Waves*, but also haunts a regime that needs the communitarian narrative to predominate. Wicht surprises himself that, for all his subversive pro-modernist leanings, he could still not bring himself to include the word 'modernism' in his appraisal. His microscopic self-analysis makes his account the most comprehensive reading yet of Woolf in the context of censorship. Arguing that Woolf's East German reception was part of the 'installation of modernism' in the former GDR – both a sign of and a contribution to the political changes that effectively brought down the Wall – Wicht's canny introspection nonetheless refuses any easy triumphalism. Asserting the political hybridity of Woolf's novels, he offers a revealing exposé of the corresponding partiality of *all* critical arguments. '[D]e- and reconstruction of cultural discourses is primarily a task for insiders,' he writes (Wicht 2002, 105). Partly a defensive statement, it also glosses an ethic we have been arguing is bibliographically constituent of *The Reception of Virginia Woolf in Europe*. History might have forced Wicht to reassess the conditions that shaped (and censored) his criticism on Woolf, but his disarming candour primarily demonstrates how any deep consideration of the historical, geographical, institutional, political, linguistic and bibliographical factors that influence Woolf's reception take us all 'inside' our readings of Woolf, making us (in Woolf's political aesthetics) always already canny outsiders to the multiple canonizations of her work.

feminist arrivals: multiplying *the hours*

We began this survey of Woolf's European reception recapitulating Jane Marcus' concern for the loss of the feminist politically engaged Woolf in her transatlantic 'voyage back'. The metaphors associated with any discussion of translation and travel are inevitably bound up in narratives of ownership, change, losses, and gains that all attend a mobile, and thereby ultimately international canonical writer. If we have suggested that some of Marcus' fears might gain a certain momentum east of the cliffs of Dover, we have also argued that the history of feminist reception narratives themselves, and the national and institutional cultures upon which they are predicated need much finer interpellation within Woolf studies itself. Reading the roots of Woolf's European reception reminds us that we have not yet done the necessarily arduous, even tedious work of excavating the fullest material cultural history of Woolf's textual receptions in her hyphenated Anglo-American contexts from the beginning of the twentieth century to the present. We have also argued that criticism itself is a kind of translation, one that involves encountering Woolf under different banners – feminist, narratological, phenomenological, to name just a few – that necessarily condition and situate the type of engagement we have with her. Translation and criticism are both forms of rewriting; they are transformations that alter and renew our meetings with Woolf, even as their mobility and mutability ensure there is no final, definitive critique, no static or transparent 'European' or 'Anglo-American' Woolf.

On a popular level, the reclamation of Woolf within Europe, her ever shape-shifting identity, has perhaps no clearer proof than her transformation in fiction. Michael Cunningham seems not to have a global hold on Woolf's fictional persona, even though *The Hours* arguably charts a uniquely American Woolfian liberation story where generation and geography are key players. In European countries that have experienced political dictatorships, Woolf's popular feminist emergence can often be gauged by the speed with which *A Room of One's Own* and *Three Guineas* sold out upon publication in the 1970s or 1980s, or by her stealthy reassertion in a country like Poland where women began to suspect that Solidarity had left them behind (Terentowicz-Fotyga 2002, 142). Yet, European writers have been working equally hard at creating a cultural space for Woolf, particularly in countries whose relatively new democracies are searching for their own national literary traditions. Thus, we can find Woolf discussing art, gender, politics and history with the contemporary Italian left-wing politician and writer, Rossana Rossanda (Klitgård 2002, 182); visiting Santiago de Compostela in the guise of 'Lady Woolf' and returning to England to write the Galician Ur-narrative of national liberation (Palacios 2002, 289–91); meeting Greek novelist Argiro Mantoglou in London's Virginia Woolf Café to save Emma (Aima is Greek for blood), a doomed heroine of Thomas Hardy's (Kitsi-Mitakou 2002, 198); revisiting her own past in 'Regreso a Monks House', accompanied, contextually, by two regionally prominent Spanish women artists, the nineteenth-century Aragonese writer Maria del Pilar Sinués and the twentieth-century Aragonese painter, Julieta Aguilar (Gámez Fuentes 2002, 263); taking part, with Shakespeare and the overlooked Portuguese modernist writer, Irene Lisboa, in an Orlandoesque journey through contemporary postcolonial Lisbon (Abranches 2002, 318).

We can only meet Woolf in these guises, of course, if we read and speak these national and regional languages. Here, at the end – or the end of what we hope will provoke new beginnings – of our survey, we come up against the claims of language and place. If not insurmountable, they certainly suggest that future Woolf scholarship will need more translators, as well as a keener sense of comparative critical scholarship. We might well have to 'teach ourselves to read and to write' in languages other than English, as Woolf reminded us in 1940, if we want to cross the gulf between her Anglo-American criticism and its European counterparts. Otherwise, we risk losing out (or worse, becoming culturally complacent) on fields that are making new inroads: Werner Wolf and Franzila Mosthof's writings on 'intermediality' that offer new interpretations of Woolf's musical and artistic cross-currents as they intersect her narratological innovations (A. and V. Nünnings 2002, 95); Sabine Hotho-Jackson's search for a more conservative Woolf, always skirting the borders of tradition and modernity (88); Catherine Lanone's 'rhizomatic' mapping of *Jacob's Room* as it reveals new perspectives on Woolf's postmodernism (Rodier 2002, 46); Nadia Fusini's work on Woolf's 'scrittura al femminile' (Perosa 2002, 215) which might, in turn, help us to better interrogate Fusini's new 1998 Italian translations of Woolf, letting us answer if and how her feminist criticism has updated the older Mondarori imprints. As Woolf arrives gradually in other European countries, as the European Union itself expands, and as Woolf takes on the colourations and perspectives of differently situated critical traditions that are themselves in flux, one thing seems clear: Woolf will never entirely be lost in translation.

notes

1. While Silver grounds her conception of 'versioning' in the reproducibility of the image, it might be applied to Woolf's many textual receptions as well, especially in light of the renewed interest in bibliographical and editorial approaches to her work (see Chapter 6 in this volume).
2. There are, however, promising signs of development in this field. Recent articles by Mark Hussey ('Woolf in the U.S.A.'), and Andrew McNeillie ('Virginia Woolf's America') begin to close the large publication gap since Elaine K. Ginsberg's mid-1980s essay, 'Virginia Woolf and the Americans'. Additionally, Melba Cuddy-Keane's paper at the 2001 Virginia Woolf Conference ('Flexible Englishness: Virginia Woolf Reading Americans'), Beth Rigel Daugherty's 2003 MLA paper ('The Transatlantic Woolf: Essaying an American Audience'), and the papers given by Cheryl Mares ('The Making of Woolf's America(s)'), Eleanor McNees ('The English Tourist in/on America: Leslie Stephen vs. Virginia Woolf'), and Thaine Stearns ('Others wanted to travel': Woolf and 'America herself') on the panel 'Woolf and the United States' at the 2005 Virginia Woolf Conference all indicate increased attention to transatlantic figurations of Woolf.
3. The Sixth Annual Virginia Woolf Conference (1996) devoted a special session to an International Symposium on Woolf. The plenary papers were subsequently published in the Fall 1996 *South Carolina Review*. While the majority of Woolf conferences continue to be hosted by American academic institutions (see Note 13), there has been an increase in European (and international) attendance and scholarship in recent years.
4. 'European Reception Studies' is a substantially revised version of the original introduction to *The Reception of Virginia Woolf in Europe* published after the completion of this article. Natalya Reinhold's edited *Woolf Across Cultures* (2004) also provides a helpful complementary perspective for some of the issues and arguments we present here. Derived from papers delivered at a summer 2003 conference at the Russian State University for the Humanities in Moscow, the volume offers informative commentaries on Woolf in translation, not only in parts of Europe, but also in Asia, including Japan and Korea. While less of a sustained diachronic survey of Woolf scholarship across continental Europe than *The Reception of Virginia Woolf in Europe* (2002), *Woolf Across Cultures* (2004) draws important attention to Woolf's international appeal and, appropriate to its origins, devotes a large section to Woolf and Russia.
5. That a fragment of her still unpublished novel, *To the Lighthouse*, could appear independently and in advance of its narrative context shows not only that it entered a well established, pre-existing modernist literary culture in France, but also that it acted as early promotion for Woolf's actual novel. In 1928, the English language version of *To the Lighthouse* would win the prestigious *Femina Vie Heureuse* prize for the best foreign book of the year (Lee 1996, 514).
6. While there are certainly good anthologies within Woolf studies that provide chronological surveys of key critical works, beginning with Woolf's easiest reviews (see Majumdar and McLaurin (1997), and more recently Eleanor McNees' massive

four-volume anthology (1994)), these works have not yet generated scholarly criticism on the comparative history of Woolf's English and American receptions.

7. For a highly engaging debate between American and British academics over the state of the transatlantic feminist dialogue, see the special issue, 'Is There an Anglo-American Feminist Criticism', *Tulsa Studies in Women's Literature*, 12.2 (1993). Laura Marcus draws attention to some distinctions when, in a moment rare in discussions of Woolf and Anglo-American criticism, she draws explicit attention to the hyphen: 'For...a number of North American Woolf critics, "anger" runs throughout Woolf's texts, even where it is most displaced or denied' (Marcus 2000, 233).

8. Both *Mrs Dalloway* and *To the Lighthouse* appeared in France that year.

9. See Sheila Rowbotham, *A Century of Women: The History of Women in Britain and the United States in the Twentieth Century*, for an informative comparative history of transatlantic feminism.

10. A perceptive, if off-the-cuff remark made by Naomi Wolf in the question-and-answer session following her talk at the 1996 Amnesty International Lectures, Oxford University. The text of her lecture appears in *Women's Voices, Women's Rights, Oxford Amnesty Lectures 1996*, ed. Alison Jeffries.

11. A preoccupation noted by recent critics of *Between the Acts*, the novel Woolf was concurrently writing. See Beer (1996).

12. Steiner's distinction between 'interlingual' and 'intralingual' translation practices provides him formidable scholarly reach to include almost all acts of reading, writing, and speaking as acts of translation. Shifting the conventional thinking about translation as a decryption and re-encryption of one language into another, he recognizes the potential for the metaphoric and practicable import of the act to expose the non-transparent aspects of monolingual communications as well: 'On the inter-lingual level, translation will pose concentrated, visibly intractable problems; but these same problems abound, at a more covert or conventionally neglected level, intra-lingually' (Steiner 1998, 49). Since these theories first appeared in *After Babel* in 1973, they have aroused both controversy and acclaim. While we have deliberately extrapolated Steiner's ideas to incorporate acts of criticism as acts of translation, we do so in the spirit of his work, as much to emphasize how a consideration of Woolf's European reception helps us to rethink the 'covert or conventionally neglected' differences within American and British Woolf scholarship as to explore what it means for European critics to investigate their national reception histories in light of the dominance of Anglo-American criticism on Woolf.

13. Since 1991, an Annual Virginia Woolf Conference, originated by Mark Hussey, Vara Neverow and Patricia Cramer, has been held at various universities across the USA. In 2001, the conference crossed the Atlantic for the first time, arriving in Wales. The 2004 conference, 'Back to Bloomsbury', was held in London, and the Sixteenth Annual Conference (2006) was held again in the UK in Birmingham. As noted, in 2003, a major Woolf conference was held in Russia, proof that Woolf's European reception continues to expand.

14. Jonathan Culler, 'Narratology Today', Ian Watt Memorial Lecture, Stanford University, 1 April 2003.

15. In her role as a reviewer, Woolf sometimes reviewed American books, linking the distinction of American English with colonial rebellion, as when she wrote of Sherwood Anderson: '...the first step in the process of being American [is] to be not English....to dismiss the whole army of English words which have marched so long under the command of dead English generals' (*E4* 271). Her anti-imperialist approbation of American English did not, however, always fall on appreciative ears.

When her essay 'On Not Knowing French' was published in the *New Republic* in 1929, it raised accusations of snobbery and condescension which Woolf rebutted with even more forthright praise (cloyingly certain to offend her accuser): '...how magnificent a language America is, how materially it differs from English....I envy it the power to create new words and new phrases of utmost vividness. I ha[ve] even gone so far as to shape a theory that the American genius is an original genius and that it has borne and is bearing fruit unlike any that grows over here.' See Wilson (1952) for the larger context of this debate.

16. While Blanche conducts the interview, and translates excerpts from *To the Lighthouse* that are printed in italics alongside his own non-italicized explanatory notes linking the excerpts, 'Kew Gardens' is actually translated by a woman, Georgette Camille.

17. Woolf's letters to Vita Sackville-West on 7 and 22 August 1927 (*L3* 409, 412) show a canny awareness for Blanche's need to back up his glamour magazine discourse with photographic proof. Complaining that Blanche needs to 'substantiate his statements by a large untouched portrait', Woolf asks Sackville-West to take some snapshots of her as a possible replacement for what would ultimately become the Beresford portrait ('an old photograph of me at 19 – which is just as well').

18. For further study of the phenomenon of literary photojournalism in the 1930s and Freund's ambivalent responses to the movement, see Luckhurst and Ravache (2001). Luckhurst characterizes Ocampo as 'the silent third party to the photo-conversation between Freund and the Woolfs' (7) and notes that Woolf's fears about the photos were compounded by historical events which prevented her from ever seeing them.

19. See Gabler (2004) for a thorough investigation of the various stages from proof to transatlantic publication that resulted in what he characterizes as the 'simultaneous versions' of *To the Lighthouse*. Gabler also argues that, for this text at least, Woolf appears to have spent more time on her English proofs than her American.

20. For an excellent survey of the history and contemporary state of translation study, see Gentzler (2001). For an insightful model of what future scholarship on Woolf and translation theory might look like, see Pireddu (2004) and Reinhold, ed. (2004). The entire Fall 1999 issue of the *Virginia Woolf Miscellany*, ed. Patricia Laurence, was devoted to the theme 'Virginia Woolf in/on Translation'. Several of the contributors subsequently published longer essays in *The Reception of Virginia Woolf in Europe*, but the issue also contains interesting articles on Woolf's translations in non-European contexts, specifically Brazil, Israel, Japan, China, and the Arab world.

21. Annotator's and introducer's name in parentheses: *A Room of One's Own* (Susan Gubar); *Mrs Dalloway* (Bonnie Kime Scott); *To the Lighthouse* (Mark Hussey); *Orlando* (Maria DiBattista); *The Waves* (Molly Hite); *Three Guineas* (Jane Marcus).

22. For an extended analysis of the trope of invisibility within translation study, see Venuti (1995). Jorge Luis Borges turned the trope into an insider's joke; for years he teased interviewers with the suggestion that his 1930s Spanish translations of *A Room of One's Own* and *Orlando* were undeclared (and unverifiable) collaborations with his mother (Lojo Rodríguez 2002, 234). If the joke hides Freudian aggression, it might relate to Borges' anxiety for what Sherry Simon describes as a possibly more pervasive disciplinary trope: 'Whether affirmed or denounced, the femininity of translation is a persistent historical trope. "Woman" and "translator" have been relegated to the same position of discursive inferiority' (Simon 1996, 1).

23. For a fascinating recent study of the relationship between translation as a 'literary mode' and the modernism of Pound, Yeats, H. D., and Joyce, see Yao (2003).

24. Since Alex Zwerdling's 1986 study, *Virginia Woolf and the Real World*, there has been an ever-increasing focus on what David Bradshaw calls the 'ethical and political "sympathies"' (Bradshaw 2000, 191) of Woolf's writing. So much contemporary work on Woolf positions itself against the backdrop of earlier formalist and ahistorical criticism that, in certain contexts, it has almost become a cliché to assert that Woolf is not the 'ethereal and apolitical' doyenne of earlier imaginings. Her feminist and pacifist politics have been widely acknowledged, and continue to inform new readings of both her life and narrative poetics. See particularly Lee (1996), Snaith (2000), and Mezei (1996). It seems high time we apply these wider developments in Woolf criticism to a critical history of Woolf's translations, helping us to understand more fully what the translation process itself reveals about the reception of Woolf's political and materialist sympathies in foreign countries.

25. For the most thorough study to date of modernism as a self-consciously difficult art form, see Diepeveen (2003).

26. Should one ever forget that modernism relies on specifically technical innovations of language, these mistranscriptions serve as useful reminders: free indirect discourse becomes direct discourse; third person pronouns are inserted for 'clarification'; English proper nouns become Italianate.

27. For an excellent summary of the contradictory debates that define modernism as a reaction against the feminine or its quintessence, see Pykett (1994). See also Felski (1995) and Scott (1990).

appendix I

Chronological list of Woolf's first European novel translations:
  Swedish – (*JR* 1927)
  German – (*MD* 1928)
  French – (*MD* and *TL* 1929)
  Czech – (*O* 1929)
  Catalan – (*MD* 1930)
  Italian – (*O* 1933)
  Spanish – (*ROO* 1936)
  Hungarian – (*Y* 1940)
  Danish – (*Y* 1941)
  Croatian – (*Y* 1946)
  Portuguese – (*MD* and *W* 1946)
  Dutch – (*MD* 1948)
  Norwegian – (*TTL* 1948)
  Serbian – (*MD* and *TTL* 1955)
  Polish – (*Y* 1958)
  Macedonian – (*TTL* 1965)
  Greek – (*MD* 1967)
  Romanian – (*MD* and *O* 1968)
  Icelandic – (*ROO* 1973)
  Slovak – (*MD* 1976)
  Bulgarian – (*MD* 1983)
  Basque – (*TTL* 1993)
  Galician – (*TTL* 1993)
  Lithuanian – (*MD* 1994)
  Estonian – (*O* 1997)

selected primary bibliography
(in chronological order of publication)

major works

The Voyage Out. London: Duckworth, 1915; New York: Doran, 1920.
Night and Day. London: Duckworth, 1919; New York: Doran, 1920.
Jacob's Room. London: Hogarth, 1922; New York: Harcourt, 1923.
Mrs Dalloway. London: Hogarth, 1925; New York: Harcourt, 1925.
To the Lighthouse. London: Hogarth, 1927; New York: Harcourt, 1927.
Orlando: A Biography. London: Hogarth, 1928; New York: Harcourt, 1928.
A Room of One's Own. London: Hogarth, 1929; New York: Harcourt, 1929.
The Waves. London: Hogarth, 1931; New York: Harcourt, 1931.
Flush: A Biography. London: Hogarth, 1933; New York: Harcourt, 1933.
The Years. London: Hogarth, 1937; New York: Harcourt, 1937.
Three Guineas. London: Hogarth, 1938; New York: Harcourt, 1938.
Roger Fry: A Biography. London: Hogarth, 1940; New York: Harcourt, 1941.
Between the Acts. London: Hogarth, 1941; New York: Harcourt, 1941.

essays and shorter fiction

The Mark on the Wall. London: Hogarth, 1917.
Kew Gardens. London: Hogarth, 1919.
Monday or Tuesday. London: Hogarth, 1921; New York: Harcourt, 1921.
Mr Bennett and Mrs Brown. London: Hogarth, 1924.
The Common Reader. London: Hogarth, 1925; New York; Harcourt, 1925.
The Common Reader, Second Series. London: Hogarth, 1932; *The Second Common Reader.*
   New York: Harcourt, 1932.
The Death of the Moth and Other Essays. Ed. Leonard Woolf. London: Hogarth, 1942;
   New York: Harcourt, 1942.
A Haunted House and other Short Stories. London: Hogarth, 1944; New York: Harcourt,
   1944.
The Moment and Other Essays. Ed. Leonard Woolf. London: Hogarth, 1947; New York,
   Harcourt, 1948.

The Captain's Death Bed and Other Essays. Ed. Leonard Woolf. London: Hogarth, 1950;
    New York: Harcourt, 1950.
Granite and Rainbow: Essays. Ed. Leonard Woolf. London: Hogarth, 1958; New York:
    Harcourt, 1958.
Contemporary Writers. London: Hogarth, 1965; New York: Harcourt, 1966.
Nurse Lugton's Golden Thimble. London: Hogarth, 1966.
Collected Essays by Virginia Woolf. Ed. Leonard Woolf. 4 vols. London: Hogarth, 1966–
    7; New York: Harcourt, 1967.
A Cockney's Farming Experiences. Ed. Suzanne Henig. San Diego: San Diego State
    University Press, 1972.
Mrs Dalloway's Party: A Short Story Sequence. Ed. Stella McNichol. London: Hogarth,
    1973; New York: Harcourt, 1975.
Freshwater: A Comedy. Ed. Lucio P. Ruotolo. London: Hogarth, 1976; New York:
    Harcourt, 1976.
*Books and Portraits: Some Further Selections from the Literary and Biographical Writings of
    Virginia Woolf*. Ed. Mary Lyon. London: Hogarth, 1977; New York: Harcourt, 1978.
Women and Writing. Ed. Michèle Barrett. New York: Harcourt, 1979.
The Complete Shorter Fiction of Virginia Woolf. Ed. Susan Dick. London: Hogarth, 1985;
    New York: Harcourt, 1985.
The Essays of Virginia Woolf. Ed. Andrew McNeillie. 4 vols. London: Hogarth, 1986–94;
    New York: Harcourt, 1986–94.
Carlyle's House and other sketches. Ed. David Bradshaw. London: Hesperus Press, 2003.
The London Scene. London: Snowflake, 2004.

autobiographical writings

A Writer's Diary. Ed. Leonard Woolf. London: Hogarth, 1953; New York: Harcourt, 1954.
The Letters of Virginia Woolf. Eds Nigel Nicolson and Joanne Trautmann. 6 vols. London:
    Hogarth, 1975–80; New York: Harcourt, 1975–80.
Moments of Being: Unpublished Autobiographical Writings. Ed. Jeanne Schulkind. London:
    Chatto & Windus, 1976; New York: Harcourt, 1977.
The Diary of Virginia Woolf. Ed. Anne Olivier Bell. 5 vols. London: Hogarth, 1977–84;
    New York: Harcourt, 1977–84.
Congenial Spirits: The Selected Letters of Virginia Woolf. Ed. Joanne Trautmann Banks.
    San Diego: Harcourt, 1989.
A Passionate Apprentice: The Early Journals 1897–1909. Ed. Mitchell A. Leaska. London:
    Hogarth, 1990; New York: Harcourt, 1990.

published manuscripts

The Waves: The Two Holograph Drafts. Ed. John W. Graham. Toronto: Toronto University
    Press, 1976.
The Pargiters: The Novel-Essay Portion of The Years. Ed. Mitchell A. Leaska. New York:
    New York Public Library, 1977.
To The Lighthouse: The Original Holograph Draft. Ed. Susan Dick. Toronto: University of
    Toronto Press, 1982.
Pointz Hall: The Earlier and Later Typescripts of Between the Acts. Ed. Mitchell A. Leaska.
    New York: John Jay Press, 1982.
Melymbrosia: An Early Version of The Voyage Out. Ed. Louise A. DeSalvo. New York: New
    York Public Library, 1982.

Women and Fiction: The Manuscript Version of A Room of One's Own. Ed. S. P. Rosenbaum. Oxford: Blackwell, 1992.
Orlando: The Original Holograph Draft. Ed. Stuart Nelson Clarke. London: S. N. Clarke, 1993.
The Hours: The British Museum Manuscript of Mrs Dalloway. Ed. Helen M. Wussow. New York: Pace University Press, 1996.
Jacob's Room: The Holograph Draft. Ed. Edward Bishop. New York: Pace University Press, 1998.

reference works

Bishop, Edward. *A Virginia Woolf Chronology*. Basingstoke: Macmillan, 1989.
Clarke, Stuart N. *Virginia Woolf and Bloomsbury: A Bibliography* (online) <http://www.uk.geocities.com/stuart.n.clarke@btinternet.co.uk>, 2006.
Goldman, Jane, ed. *Icon Critical Guide on To the Lighthouse and The Waves*. Cambridge: Icon Books, 1997.
Haule, James M. *A Concordance to the Novels of Virginia Woolf*. New York: Garland, 1991.
Hussey, Mark. *Virginia Woolf A to Z*. Oxford: Oxford University Press, 1996.
Hussey, Mark, ed. *Major Authors on CD:ROM: Virginia Woolf*. Reading: Primary Source Media, 1997.
Kirkpatrick, B. J. and Stuart N. Clarke. *A Bibliography of Virginia Woolf*. 4th edn. Oxford: Clarendon Press, 1997.
Majumdar, Robin and Allen McLaurin, eds. *Virginia Woolf: The Critical Heritage*. London: Routledge, 1997.
McNees, Eleanor, ed. *Virginia Woolf: Critical Assessments*. 4 vols. Sussex: Helm Information, 1994.
Mepham, John. *Virginia Woolf*. Bristol: Bristol Classical Press, 1992.
Pawlowski, Merry M. and Vara Neverow, eds. *Reading Notes for Three Guineas: An Edition and Archive*. California State University-Bakersfield. <http://www.csub.edu/woolf/tgs-home.html> (by subscription), 2002.
Rice, Thomas Jackson. *Virginia Woolf: A Guide to Research*. New York: Garland, 1984.
Silver, Brenda R. *Virginia Woolf's Reading Notebooks*. Princeton, NJ: Princeton University Press, 1983.
Woolmer, J. Howard. *A Checklist of the Hogarth Press 1917–1938*. London: Hogarth Press, 1976.

websites

The International Virginia Woolf Society <http://www.utoronto.ca/IVWS/>
Virginia Woolf Society of Great Britain <http://www.virginiawoolfsociety.co.uk>
Virginia Woolf Society of Japan <http://wwwsoc.nii.ac.jp/vwsj/>

major manuscript collections and archives
(See *woolf studies annual*, vol. 11, 2005 for further details of holdings)

The Beinecke Rare Book and Manuscript Library, Yale University
Henry W. and Albert A. Berg Collection, New York Public Library
British Library Manuscripts Collection, London

Harry Ransom Humanities Research Centre, The University of Texas at Austin
Hogarth Press Archive, University of Reading
King's College Archive Centre, King's College, Cambridge
Library of Leonard and Virginia Woolf, Washington State University
The Lilly Library, Indiana University
Monk's House Papers and Leonard Woolf Papers, University of Sussex Library

virginia woolf journals

Woolf Studies Annual. New York: Pace University Press
Virginia Woolf Miscellany. New Haven: Southern Connecticut State University
Virginia Woolf Bulletin. London: Virginia Woolf Society of Great Britain

special woolf issues

Modern Fiction Studies 2 (1956); 18 (1972); 38 (1992); 50 (2004)
Twentieth Century Literature 25 (1979)
Women's Studies 4 (1977)
Conference Proceedings from the Annual Virginia Woolf Conference are available
from Pace University Press (1991–2000).

works cited and suggestions for further reading arranged by chapter

introduction

Auerbach, Erich. *Mimesis: The Representation of Reality in Western Literature*. Trans. Willard R. Trask. Princeton, NJ: Princeton University Press, 2003.

Barkway, Stephen. 'Virginia Woolf Today'. *Virginia Woolf Bulletin* 18 (2005) and 10 (2002): 36–9 and 27–9.

Barrett, Eileen and Patricia Cramer, eds. *Virginia Woolf: Lesbian Readings*. New York: New York University Press, 1997.

Batchelor, John. 'Feminism in Virginia Woolf'. In *Virginia Woolf: Critical Assessments*. Vol. 1. Ed. Eleanor McNees, 322–31. East Sussex: Helm Information, 1994.

Beach, Joseph Warren. 'Virginia Woolf'. *The English Journal* (October 1937): 603–12.

Bell, Quentin. *Virginia Woolf: A Biography*. Vols 1 and 2. London: Hogarth Press, 1972.

Bennett, Joan. *Virginia Woolf: Her Art as a Novelist*. Cambridge: Cambridge University Press, 1945.

Benzel, Katherine and Ruth Hoberman, eds. *Trespassing Boundaries: Virginia Woolf's Short Fiction*. Basingstoke: Palgrave, 2004.

Black, Naomi. *Virginia Woolf as Feminist*. Ithaca, NY: Cornell University Press, 2004.

Blackstone, Bernard. *Virginia Woolf: A Commentary*. New York: Harcourt Brace, 1949.

Booth, Alison. 'The Scent of a Narrative: Rank Discourse in *Flush* and *Written on the Body*'. *Narrative* 8.1 (2000): 3–22.

Bowen, Elizabeth. 'The Achievement of Virginia Woolf'. In *Collected Impressions*, 78–82. London: Longman, 1950.

Bradbrook, M. C. 'Notes on the Style of Mrs Woolf'. *Scrutiny* 1.1 (1932): 33–8.

Brantlinger, Patrick. '"The Bloomsbury Fraction" Versus War and Empire'. In *Seeing Double: Revisioning Edwardian and Modernist Literature*. Eds Carola M. Kaplan and Anne B. Simpson, 149–67. Basingstoke: Macmillan, 1996.

Briggs, Julia. *Virginia Woolf: An Inner Life*. London: Allen Lane, 2005.

Brosnan, Leila. *Reading Virginia Woolf's Essays and Journalism*. Edinburgh: Edinburgh University Press, 1997.

Caughie, Pamela L. *Virginia Woolf and Postmodernism: Literature in Quest and Question of Itself*. Urbana, IL: University of Illinois Press, 1991.

Caws, Mary Ann and Nicola Luckhurst, eds. *The Reception of Virginia Woolf in Europe*. London: Continuum, 2002.

Chambers, R. L. *The Novels of Virginia Woolf*. London: Oliver and Boyd, 1947.

Cuddy-Keane, Melba. *Virginia Woolf, the Intellectual and the Public Sphere*. Cambridge: Cambridge University Press, 2003.

Daiches, David. *Virginia Woolf*. London: Nicholson and Watson, 1945.

Daldry, Stephen. *The Hours*. Miramax/Paramount, 2002.

Daugherty, Beth Rigel, ed. 'Virginia Woolf's "How Should One Read A Book?"' *Woolf Studies Annual* 4 (1998): 123–85.

——, ed. 'Letters from Readers to Virginia Woolf'. *Woolf Studies Annual* 12 (2006): 1–212.

Fish, Stanley. *Is There A Text In This Class? The Authority of Interpretive Communities*. Cambridge, Mass.: Harvard University Press, 1980.

Forster, E. M. *Virginia Woolf*. New York: Harcourt Brace & Co., 1942.

Freedman, Ralph. *The Lyrical Novel: Studies in Hermann Hesse, André Gide and Virginia Woolf*. Princeton, NJ: Princeton University Press, 1963.

Freidman, Melvin J. *Stream of Consciousness: A Study in Literary Method*. New Haven: Yale University Press, 1955.

Froula, Christine. *Virginia Woolf and the Bloomsbury Avant Garde: War, Civilization, Modernity*. New York: Columbia University Press, 2005.

Garrity, Jane. 'Selling Culture to the "Civilised": Bloomsbury, British *Vogue* and the Marketing of National Identity'. *Modernism/Modernity* 6.2 (1999): 29–58.

Glendinning, Victoria. *Leonard Woolf*. London: Simon and Schuster, 2006.

Goldman, Jane, ed. *Icon Critical Guide on To the Lighthouse and The Waves*. Cambridge: Icon Books, 1997.

Graham, John. 'Time in the Novels of Virginia Woolf'. *University of Toronto Quarterly* (January 1949): 186–201.

Gruber, Ruth. *Virginia Woolf: A Study*. Leipzig: Verlag von Bernhard Tauchnitz, 1935.

Gualtieri, Elena. *Virginia Woolf's Essays: Sketching the Past*. Basingstoke: Macmillan, 2000.

Guiguet, Jean. *Virginia Woolf and Her Works*. Trans Jean Stewart. London: Hogarth Press, 1965.

Hafley, James. *The Glass Roof: Virginia Woolf as Novelist*. Berkeley, CA: University of California Press, 1954.

Hawley Roberts, John. 'Toward Virginia Woolf'. *Virginia Quarterly Review* (July 1934): 587–602.

Hensher, Philip. 'Virginia Woolf Makes Me Want to Vomit'. *Telegraph*, 24 January 2003.

Holtby, Winifred. *Virginia Woolf*. London: Wishart & Co., 1932.

Humm, Maggie. *Snapshots of Bloomsbury: The Private Lives of Virginia Woolf and Vanessa Bell*. New Brunswick, NJ: Rutgers University Press, 2005.

Humphrey, Robert. *Stream of Consciousness in the Modern Novel*. Berkeley, CA: University of California Press, 1954.

Hussey, Mark. 'Mrs Thatcher and Mrs Woolf'. *Modern Fiction Studies* 50.1 (2004): 8–30.

Kaufmann, Michael. 'VW's *TLS* Reviews and Eliotic Modernism'. In *Virginia Woolf and the Essay*. Eds Beth Carole Rosenberg and Jeanne Dubino, 137–55. Basingstoke: Macmillan, 1997.

Leavis, F. R. 'After *To The Lighthouse*'. *Scrutiny* 10.3 (1942): 295–8.

Leavis, Q. D. 'Caterpillars of the Commonwealth Unite!' *Scrutiny* 7.2 (1938): 203–14.

Lee, Hermione. *Virginia Woolf*. London: Chatto and Windus, 1996.

———. *Virginia Woolf's Nose: Essays on Biography*. Princeton, NJ: Princeton University Press, 2005.

Lewis, Wyndham. *Men Without Art*. Santa Rosa: Black Sparrow Press, 1987.

Light, Alison. *Mrs Woolf and the Servants*. London: Viking, 2007.

Llewellyn Davies, Margaret. *Life As We Have Known It*. London: Hogarth Press, 1931.

Marcus, Jane. *Art and Anger: Reading Like a Woman*. Columbus: Ohio State University Press, 1988.

———. 'Britannia Rules *The Waves*'. In *Decolonizing Tradition: New Views of Twentieth Century 'British' Literary Canons*. Ed. Karen R. Lawrence, 136–62. Urbana: University of Illinois Press, 1992.

———. *Hearts of Darkness: White Women Write Race*. New Brunswick, NJ: Rutgers University Press, 2004.

Marler, Regina. *Bloomsbury Pie*. New York: Henry Holt, 1997.

McGee, Patrick. 'The politics of modernist form; or, who rules *The Waves*'. *Modern Fiction Studies* 38 (1992): 631–50.

McNees, Eleanor, ed. *Virginia Woolf: Critical Assessments*. Vols 1–4. Sussex: Helm Information, 1994.

Mepham, John. *Virginia Woolf*. Bristol: Bristol Classical Press, 1992.

Meyerowitz, Selma. *Leonard Woolf*. Boston: Twayne, 1982.

Oldfield, Sybil. *Afterwords: Letters on the Death of Virginia Woolf*. New Brunswick, NJ: Rutgers University Press, 2005.

Pippett, Aileen. *The Moth and the Star: A Biography of Virginia Woolf*. New York: Viking, 1957.

Reed, Christopher. *Bloomsbury Rooms: Modernism, Subculture, and Domesticity*. New Haven: Yale University Press, 2004.

Reinhold, Natalya, ed. *Woolf Across Cultures*. New York: Pace University Press, 2004.

Rosenberg, Beth Carole and Jeanne Dubino, eds. *Virginia Woolf and the Essay*. Basingstoke: Macmillan, 1997.

Savage, D. S. *The Withered Branch: Six Studies in the Modern Novel*. London: Eyre and Spottiswoode, 1950.

Shih, Elizabeth. 'When Woolf Goes Missing (From Herself)'. *Virginia Woolf Miscellany* 62 (Spring 2003): 2–3.

Silver, Brenda. *Virginia Woolf Icon*. Chicago, IL: University of Chicago Press, 1999.

Skrbic, Nena. *Wild Outbursts of Freedom: Reading Virginia Woolf's Short Fiction*. London: Praeger, 2004.

Snaith, Anna, ed. 'The *Three Guineas* Letters'. *Woolf Studies Annual Vol. 6* (2000): 1–168.

———. 'Of Fanciers, Footnotes, and Fascism: Virginia Woolf's *Flush*'. *Modern Fiction Studies* 48.3 (2002): 614–36.

Squier, Susan. *Virginia Woolf and London: The Sexual Politics of the City*. Chapel Hill: University of North Carolina Press, 1985.

Tyrer, Nicola. 'Why Hollywood Moguls Are Still Afraid of Virginia Woolf'. *Mail on Sunday*, 5 January 2003: 38–9.

Walsh, John. 'Bloomsbury to Beverly Hills'. *The Independent Review*, 21 January 2003: 4–5.

Whitworth, Michael. *Einstein's Wake: Relativity, Metaphor and Modernist Literature*. Oxford: Oxford University Press, 2002.

———. *Virginia Woolf*. Oxford: Oxford University Press, 2005.

Williams, Raymond. *Problems in Materialism and Culture*. London: Verso, 1980.

Wilson, Peter. *The International Theory of Leonard Woolf*. Basingstoke: Palgrave, 2003.
Woolf, Leonard. *Beginning Again: An Autobiography of the Years 1911–1918*. London: Hogarth Press, 1964.
Woolf, Virginia. *Carlyle's House*. Ed. David Bradshaw. Hesperus Press, 2003.
———. *The London Scene*. London: Snowflake, 2004.
Young, Tory. *Michael Cunningham's The Hours*. London: Continuum, 2003.

narratological approaches

Abel, Elizabeth. 'Narrative Structures and Female Development: The Case of *Mrs Dalloway*'. In *The Voyage In: Fictions of Female Development*. Eds Elizabeth Abel, Marianne Hirsch, and Elizabeth Langland, 161–85. Hanover: University Press of New England, 1983.
Abbott, H. Porter. *The Cambridge Introduction to Narrative*. Cambridge and New York: Cambridge University Press, 2002.
Auerbach, Erich. *Mimesis: The Representation of Reality in Western Literature*. Trans. Willard R. Trask. Princeton, NJ: Princeton University Press, 1953.
Banfield, Ann. *Unspeakable Sentences: Narration and Representation in the Language of Fiction*. Boston: Routledge & Kegan Paul, 1982.
Barrett, Eileen. 'The Language of Fabric in *To the Lighthouse*'. In *Approaches to Teaching Woolf's* To the Lighthouse. Eds Beth Rigel Daugherty and Mary Beth Pringle, 54–9. New York: Modern Language Association of America, 2001.
Beck, Warren. 'For Virginia Woolf'. In *Forms of Modern Fiction*. Ed. William Van O'Connor, 243–53. Minneapolis: University of Minnesota Press, 1948.
Benzel, Katherine N. and Ruth Hoberman, eds. *Trespassing Boundaries: Virginia Woolf's Shorter Fiction*. New York: Palgrave Macmillan, 2004.
Bishop, Edward. 'Pursuing "It" through "Kew Gardens"'. *Studies in Short Fiction* 19.3 (1982): 269–75.
Blair, Sara B. 'Good Housekeeping: Virginia Woolf and the Politics of Irony'. In *The Politics of Irony: Essays in Self-Betrayal*. Eds Daniel W. Conway and John E. Seery, 99–118. New York: St Martin's Press, 1992.
Bowling, Lawrence E. 'What is the Stream of Consciousness Technique?' *PMLA* 55 (1950): 333–45.
Caserio, Robert L. *The Novel in England, 1900–1950: History and Theory*. New York: Twayne, 1999.
Caughie, Pamela. 'Virginia Woolf and Postmodernism: Returning to the Lighthouse'. In *Rereading the New: A Backward Glance at Modernism*. Ed. Kevin J. H. Dettmar, 297–323. Ann Arbor: University of Michigan Press, 1992.
Chatman, Seymour. '*Mrs. Dalloway's* Progeny: *The Hours* as Second-degree Narrative'. *A Companion to Narrative Theory*. Eds James Phelan and Peter J. Rabinowitz, 269–81. Oxford: Blackwell, 2005.
Cohn, Dorrit. *Transparent Minds: Narrative Modes for Presenting Consciousness in Fiction*. Princeton, NJ: Princeton University Press, 1978.
Cuddy-Keane, Melba. 'The Politics of Comic Modes in Virginia Woolf's *Between the Acts*'. *PMLA* 105 (1990): 273–85.
———. 'The Rhetoric of Feminist Conversation: Virginia Woolf and the Trope of the Twist'. In *Ambiguous Discourse: Feminist Narratology and British Women Writers*. Ed. Kathy Mezei, 137–61. Chapel Hill: University of North Carolina Press, 1996.

——. 'Modernist Soundscapes and the Intelligent Ear: An Approach to Narrative through Auditory Perception'. *A Companion to Narrative Theory*. Eds James Phelan and Peter J. Rabinowitz, 382–98. Oxford: Blackwell, 2005.

Daiches, David. 'Virginia Woolf'. In *The Novel and the Modern World*. Chicago, IL: University of Chicago Press, 1960.

DuPlessis, Rachel Blau. *Writing Beyond the Ending: Narrative Strategies of Twentieth-Century Women Writers*. Bloomington, IN: University of Indiana Press, 1985.

Ehrlich, Susan. 'Repetition and Point of View in Represented Speech and Thought'. In *Repetition in Discourse: Interdisciplinary Perspectives, 1 and 2*. Eds Barbara Johnstone and Roy O. Freedle, 86–97. Norwood, NJ: Ablex, 1994.

Fleishman, Avrom. *Virginia Woolf: A Critical Reading*. Baltimore and London: Johns Hopkins University Press, 1975.

Friedman, Alan. *The Turn of the Novel: The Transition to Modern Fiction*. London, Oxford, New York: Oxford University Press, 1966.

Friedman, Susan Stanford. 'Lyric Subversion of Form in Women's Writing: Virginia Woolf and the Tyranny of Plot'. In *Reading Narrative: Form, Ethics, Ideology*. Ed. James Phelan, 162–85. Columbus: Ohio State University Press, 1989.

——. 'Spatialization, Narrative Theory, and Virginia Woolf's *The Voyage Out*'. In *Ambiguous Discourse: Feminist Narratology and British Women Writers*. Ed. Kathy Mezei, 109–36. Chapel Hill: University of North Carolina Press, 1996.

Froula, Christine. 'Out of the Chrysalis: Female Initiation and Female Authority in Virginia Woolf's *The Voyage Out*'. In *Virginia Woolf: A Collection of Critical Essays*. Ed. Margaret Homans, 136–61. Englewood Cliffs, NJ: Prentice-Hall, 1993.

——. 'Mrs Dalloway's Postwar Elegy: Women, War, and the Art of Mourning'. *Modernism/Modernity* 9.1 (2002): 125–63.

Goldman, Jane. *The Feminist Aesthetics of Virginia Woolf: Modernism, Post-Impressionism and the Politics of the Visual*. New York and Cambridge: Cambridge University Press, 1998.

Graham, J. W. 'Point of View in *The Waves:* Some Services of the Style'. *University of Toronto Quarterly* 39 (1970): 193–211. Repr. in *Virginia Woolf: A Collection of Criticism*. Ed. Thomas S. W. Lewis. New York: McGraw-Hill, 1975.

Hafley, James. *The Glass Roof: Virginia Woolf as Novelist*. Berkeley, CA: University of California Press, 1954.

Halperin, John, ed. *The Theory of the Novel: New Essays*. New York, London, Toronto: Oxford University Press, 1974.

Hartman, Geoffrey. 'Virginia's Web'. *Chicago Review* 14 (Spring 1961): 20–32. Repr. in *Virginia Woolf: A Collection of Critical Essays*. Ed. Margaret Homans, 35–45. Englewood Cliffs, NJ: Prentice-Hall, 1993.

Head, Dominic. 'Virginia Woolf: Experiments in Genre'. In *The Modernist Short Story: A Study in Theory and Practice*, 79–108. Cambridge: Cambridge University Press, 1992.

Herman, David. *Universal Grammar and Narrative Form*. Durham and London: Duke University Press, 1995.

Herman, David, Manfred Jahn and Marie-Laure Ryan, eds. *The Routledge Encyclopedia of Narrative Theory*. London: Routledge, 2005.

Homans, Margaret, ed. *Virginia Woolf: A Collection of Critical Essays*. Englewood Cliffs, NJ: Prentice Hall, 1993.

Humphrey, Robert. *Stream of Consciousness in the Modern Novel*. Berkeley and Los Angeles: University of California Press, 1954.

Hynes, Samuel. 'The Epistemology of *The Good Soldier*'. In *Edwardian Occasions: Essays on English Writing in the Early Twentieth Century*, 54–62. London: Routledge & Kegan Paul, 1972.

Jahn, Manfred. 'Contextualizing Represented Speech and Thought'. *Journal of Pragmatics* 17 (1992): 347–67.

Lanser, Susan Sniader. *Fictions of Authority: Women Writers and Narrative Voice*. Ithaca and London: Cornell University Press, 1992.

Laurence, Patricia Ondek. '"Some Rope to Throw to the Reader": Teaching the Diverse Rhythms of *To the Lighthouse*'. In *Approaches to Teaching Woolf's* To the Lighthouse. Eds Beth Rigel Daugherty and Mary Beth Pringle, 66–71. New York: Modern Language Association of America, 2001.

Lawrence, Karen. 'Gender and Narrative Voice in *Jacob's Room* and *a Portrait of the Artist as a Young Man*'. In *James Joyce: The Centennial Symposium*. Eds Phillip Herring, Morris Beja, Maurice Harmon, and David Norris, 31–8. Urbana: University of Illinois Press, 1986.

Leaska, Mitchell A. *Virginia Woolf's Lighthouse: A Study in Critical Method*. London: Hogarth Press, 1970.

Little, Judy. *Comedy and the Woman Writer: Woolf, Spark, and Feminism*. Lincoln: University of Nebraska Press, 1983.

London, Bette. *The Appropriated Voice: Narrative Authority in Conrad, Forster, and Woolf*. Ann Arbor: University of Michigan Press, 1990.

Mezei, Kathy. 'Who Is Speaking Here? Free Indirect Discourse, Gender, and Authority in *Emma*, *Howards End*, and *Mrs. Dalloway*'. In *Ambiguous Discourse: Feminist Narratology and British Women Writers*. Ed. Kathy Mezei, 66–92. Chapel Hill and London: University of North Carolina Press, 1996.

Miller, J. Hillis. *Fiction and Repetition*. Cambridge, Mass.: Harvard University Press, 1982.

Moi, Toril. *Sexual/Textual Politics: Feminist Literary Theory*. London and New York: Methuen, 1985.

Naremore, James. 'Virginia Woolf and the Stream of Consciousness'. In *The World without a Self: Virginia Woolf and the Novel*, 60–76. New Haven: Yale University Press, 1973.

O'Connor, William Van, ed. *Forms of Modern Fiction*. Minneapolis: University of Minnesota Press, 1948.

O'Neill, Patrick. *Fictions of Discourse: Reading Narrative Theory*. Toronto, Buffalo, and London: University of Toronto Press, 1994.

Pearce, Richard. *The Politics of Narration; James Joyce, William Faulkner, and Virginia Woolf*. New Brunswick, NJ: Rutgers University Press, 1991.

Phelan, James. 'Character and Judgment in Narrative and in Lyric: Toward an Understanding of Audience Engagement in *The Waves*'. In *Narrative as Rhetoric: Technique, Audiences, Ethics, Ideology*, 27–42. Columbus: Ohio State University Press, 1996.

Prince, Gerald. *Dictionary of Narratology*. Lincoln and London: University of Nebraska Press, 1989.

Richardson, Brian. *Unlikely Stories: Causality and the Nature of Modern Narrative*. Newark, Delaware: University of Delaware Press, 1997.

Richter, Harvena. *Virginia Woolf: The Inward Voyage*. Princeton, NJ: Princeton University Press, 1970.

Roberts, John Hawley. '"Vision and Design" in Virginia Woolf'. *PMLA* 61 (1946): 835–47.

Schorer, Mark. 'Technique as Discovery'. *Hudson Review* 1 (1948): 67–87.
Smith, Sidonie. 'The Autobiographical Eye/I in Virginia Woolf's "Sketch"'. In *Subjectivity, Identity, and the Body: Women's Autobiographical Practices in the Twentieth Century*, 83–102, 206–8. Bloomington and Indianapolis: Indiana University Press, 1993.
Snaith, Anna. *Virginia Woolf: Public and Private Negotiations*. Basingstoke: Macmillan, 2000.
Towne, Jessie Margaret. Letter to Virginia Woolf. 2 October, 1933. Unpublished.
Villeneuve, Pierre-Eric. 'Epistolary Narrative and the Addressee as Influence: "Christmas Day 1922"'. In *Virginia Woolf and Her Influences: Selected Papers from the Seventh Annual Conference on Virginia Woolf*. Eds Laura Davis and Jeanette McVicker, 269–74. New York: Pace University Press, 1998.
Wall, K. 'Significant Form in *Jacob's Room*: Ekphrasis and the Elegy (Virginia Woolf)'. *Texas Studies in Literature and Language* 44.3 (2002): 302–23.

modernist studies

Alexander, Jean. *The Venture of Form in the Novels of Virginia Woolf*. Port Washington: Kennikat Press, 1974.
Arendt, Hannah. *Lectures on Kant's Political Philosophy*. Ed. Ronald Beiner. Chicago, IL: University of Chicago Press, 1982.
Armstrong, Tim. *Modernism*. Cambridge: Polity Press, 2005.
Atkinson, Diane. *The Suffragettes in Pictures*. London: Sutton Publishing, 1996.
Auerbach, Erich. *Mimesis: The Representation of Reality in Western Literature*. Trans. Willard R. Trask. Princeton, NJ: Princeton University Press, 1953.
Banfield, Ann. *The Phantom Table: Woolf, Fry, Russell and the Epistemology of Modernism*. Cambridge: Cambridge University Press, 2000.
Bell, Clive. 'The English Group'. In *Second Post-Impressionist Exhibition*. London: Grafton Galleries, Exhibition Catalogue, 1912.
——. *Art*. London: Chatto & Windus, 1914.
Bell, Quentin. *Bloomsbury*. London: Weidenfeld and Nicolson, 1968.
——. *Virginia Woolf: A Biography*. 2 vols. London: Hogarth Press, 1972.
Bergson, Henri. *Time and Free Will: An Essay on the Immediate Data of Consciousness*. Trans. F.L. Pogson. London: Macmillan, 1910.
Berman, Jessica. *Modernist Fiction, Cosmopolitanism and the Politics of Community*. Cambridge: Cambridge University Press, 2001.
Blair, Sara. 'Modernism and the politics of culture'. In *The Cambridge Companion to Modernism*. Ed. Michael Levenson, 157–73. Cambridge: Cambridge University Press, 1999.
Bowlby, Rachel. *Feminist Destinations and Further Essays on Virginia Woolf*. Edinburgh: Edinburgh University Press, 1997.
Bradbury, Malcolm and James McFarlane, eds. *Modernism 1890–1930*. Harmondsworth: Penguin, 1976.
Bradshaw, David, ed. *A Concise Companion to Modernism*. Oxford: Blackwell, 2003.
Brooker, Peter, ed. *Modernism/Postmodernism*. London: Longman, 1992.
Brown, Bill. 'The Secret Life of Things: Virginia Woolf and the Matter of Modernism'. *Modernism/Modernity* 6.2 (1999): 1–28.
Bürger, Peter. *Theory of the Avant-Garde* (1974). Trans. Michael Shaw. Minneapolis: University of Minnesota Press, 1984.
Carlston, Erin G. *Thinking Fascism: Sapphic Modernism and Fascist Modernity*. Stanford, CA: Stanford University Press, 1998.

Carpentier, Marta C. *Ritual, Myth, and the Modernist Text: The Influence of Jane Ellen Harrison on Joyce, Eliot, and Woolf.* Amsterdam: Gordon and Breach, 1998.

Caws, Mary Ann and Sarah Bird Wright. *Bloomsbury and France: Art and Friends.* Oxford: Oxford University Press, 2000.

Childs, Peter. *Modernism.* London: Routledge, 2000.

Daiches, David. *Virginia Woolf.* Bournemouth: Poetry London, 1945.

Dangerfield, George. *The Strange Death of Liberal England.* London: Constable & Co., 1936.

da Silva, N. Takei. *Modernism and Virginia Woolf.* Windsor: Windsor Publications, 1990.

DiBattista, Maria. 'Virginia Woolf'. In *The Cambridge History of Literary Criticism* Vol. 7: *Modernism and the New Criticism.* Eds A. Walton Litz, Louis Menand and Lawrence Rainey, 122–37. Cambridge: Cambridge University Press, 2000.

Dowling, David. *Bloomsbury Aesthetics and the Novels of Forster and Woolf.* Basingstoke: Macmillan, 1985.

Dunlop, Ian. *The Shock of the New: Seven Historic Exhibitions of Modern Art.* London: Weidenfeld and Nicolson, 1972.

Dunn, Jane. *A Very Close Conspiracy: Vanessa Bell and Virginia Woolf.* London: Bloomsbury, 1990.

DuPlessis, Rachel Blau. *Writing Beyond the Ending: Narrative Strategies of Twentieth-Century Women Writers.* Bloomington, IN: University of Indiana Press, 1985.

Edel, Leon. *Bloomsbury: A House of Lions.* London: Hogarth Press, 1979.

Eliot, T. S. '*Ulysses*, Order and Myth' (1923). *A Modernist Reader.* Ed. Faulkner, 100–4.

Elliott, Bridget and Jo-Ann Wallace. *Women Artists and Writers: Modernist (Im)positionings.* London: Routledge, 1994.

Falkenheim, Jacqueline V. *Roger Fry and the Beginnings of Formalist Art Criticism.* Ann Arbor: UMI Research Press, 1980.

Faulkner, Peter, ed. *A Modernist Reader: Modernism in England 1910–1930.* London: Batsford, 1986.

Fokkema, Douwe W. 'An Interpretation of *To the Lighthouse*: With Reference to the Code of Modernism'. *PTL: A Journal for Descriptive Poetics and Theory* 4 (1979): 475–500.

Froula, Christine. *Virginia Woolf and the Bloomsbury Avant-Garde: War, Civilization, Modernity.* New York: Columbia University Press, 2005.

Fry, Roger. 'Introduction'. In *Second Post-Impressionist Exhibition.* London: Grafton Galleries, Exhibition Catalogue, 1912.

——. *Vision and Design.* London: Chatto & Windus, 1920.

Gillespie, Diane Filby. *The Sisters' Arts. The Writing and Painting of Virginia Woolf and Vanessa Bell.* Syracuse: Syracuse University Press, 1988.

Gloversmith, Frank. 'Autonomy Theory: Ortega, Roger Fry, Virginia Woolf'. In *The Theory of Reading.* Ed. Frank Gloversmith, 147–98. Brighton: Harvester, 1984.

Goldman, Jane. *The Feminist Aesthetics of Virginia Woolf: Modernism, Post-Impressionism and the Politics of the Visual.* Cambridge: Cambridge University Press, 1998.

——. *Modernism, 1910–1945: Image to Apocalypse.* Basingstoke: Palgrave, 2003.

Gordon, Craig. 'Breaking Habits, Building Communities: Virginia Woolf and the Neuroscientific Body'. *Modernism/Modernity* 7.1 (2000): 25–41.

Greenslade, William. *Degeneration, Culture and the Novel 1880–1940.* Cambridge: Cambridge University Press, 1994.

Gruber, Ruth. *Virginia Woolf: The Will to Create as a Woman.* New York: Carroll & Graf, 2005.

Guiguet, Jean. *Virginia Woolf and Her Works*. Trans. Jean Stewart. London: Hogarth Press, 1965.

Harrison, Elizabeth Jane and Shirley Peterson, eds. *Unmanning Modernism: Gendered Re-Readings*. Knoxville, TN: University of Tennessee Press, 1997.

Holmesland, Oddvar. *Form as compensation for Life: Fictive Patterns in Virginia Woolf's Novels*. Columbia: Camden House, 1998.

Humm, Maggie. *Modernist Women and Visual Cultures: Virginia Woolf, Vanessa Bell, Photography and Cinema*. Edinburgh: Edinburgh University Press, 2002.

Hussey, Mark. *Virginia Woolf and War: Fiction, Reality and Myth*. Syracuse: Syracuse University Press, 1991.

Inglis, Tony. 'Virginia Woolf and English Culture'. First published in French in *Virginia Woolf et le groupe de Bloomsbury*. Ed. Jean Guiguet, Paris, 1977. First English version in *Virginia Woolf*. Ed. Rachel Bowlby, 46–61. London: Longman, 1992.

Johnstone, J. K. *The Bloomsbury Group: A Study of E. M. Forster, Lytton Strachey, Virginia Woolf and Their Circle*. London: Secker & Warburg, 1954.

Joyce, James. *Selected Letters of James Joyce*. Ed. Richard Ellmann. New York: Viking, 1975.

Kaye, Peter. *Dostoevsky and English Modernism 1900–1930*. Cambridge: Cambridge University Press, 1999.

Kenner, Hugh. *The Pound Era: The Age of Ezra Pound, T. S. Eliot, James Joyce and Wyndham Lewis*. London: Faber and Faber, 1972.

Kermode, Frank. 'Modernisms'. In *Continuities* 1–32. London: Routledge & Kegan Paul, 1968.

Keynes, Maynard. *Economic Consequences of the Peace*. London: Macmillan, 1919.

Kolocotroni, Vassiliki, Jane Goldman and Olga Taxidou, eds. *Modernism: An Anthology of Sources and Documents*. Edinburgh and Chicago: Edinburgh University Press and University of Chicago Press, 1998.

Koppen, Randi. 'Embodied Form: Art and Life in Virginia Woolf's *To the Lighthouse*'. *New Literary History: A Journal of Theory and Interpretation* 32.2 (2001): 375–89.

Kumar, Shiv K. *Bergson and the Stream of Consciousness Novel*. London and Glasgow: Blackie, 1962.

Lodge, David. *The Modes of Modern Writing*. London: Edward Arnold, 1977.

Lee, Hermione. *The Novels of Virginia Woolf*. London: Methuen, 1977.

Levenson, Michael H. *A Genealogy of Modernism: A Study of English Literary Doctrine, 1908–1922*. Cambridge: Cambridge University Press, 1984.

——, ed. *Cambridge Companion to Modernism*. Cambridge: Cambridge University Press, 1999.

MacCarthy, Desmond. 'The Post-Impressionists'. In *Manet and the Post-Impressionists*. London: Grafton Galleries, Exhibition Catalogue, 1910.

——. 'The Art Quake of 1910'. *The Listener*, 1 February 1945.

Marcus, Jane, ed. *Virginia Woolf and Bloomsbury: A Centenary Celebration*. London: Macmillan, 1987.

McLaurin, Allen. *Virginia Woolf: The Echoes Enslaved*. Cambridge: Cambridge University Press, 1973.

McNeillie, Andrew. 'Bloomsbury'. In *The Cambridge Companion to Virginia Woolf*. Eds Roe and Sellers, 1–28.

Meisel, Perry. *The Absent Father: Virginia Woolf and Walter Pater*. New Haven: Yale University Press, 1980.

Minow-Pinkney, Makiko. *Virginia Woolf and the Problem of the Subject*. Brighton: Harvester, 1987.

Moi, Toril. *Sexual/Textual Politics: Feminist Theory*. London and New York: Methuen, 1985.

Moore, G. E. *Principia Ethica*. Cambridge: Cambridge University Press, 1903.

Newton, K. M. *Interpreting the Text: A Critical Introduction to the Theory and Practice of Literary Interpretation*. New York: St Martin's Press, 1990.

Nicholls, Peter. *Modernisms: A Literary Guide*. Basingstoke: Macmillan, 1995.

Paulin, Tom. *J'Accuse: Virginia Woolf*. Directed and produced by Jeff Morgan, Fulmar Productions for Channel Four, London, 29 January 1991.

Pawlowski, Merry M. 'Reassessing Modernism: Virginia Woolf, *Three Guineas*, and Fascist Ideology'. *Woolf Studies Annual* 1 (1995): 47–67.

——, ed. *Virginia Woolf and Fascism: Resisting the Dictators' Seduction*. Basingstoke: Palgrave, 2001.

Peach, Linden. *Virginia Woolf*. Basingstoke: Palgrave Macmillan, 2000.

Richter, Harvena. *Virginia Woolf: The Inward Voyage*. Princeton, NJ: Princeton University Press, 1970.

Roberts, John Hawley. 'Vision and Design in Virginia Woolf'. *PMLA* 61 (1946): 835–47.

Roe, Sue and Susan Sellers, eds. *The Cambridge Companion to Virginia Woolf*. Cambridge: Cambridge University Press, 2000.

Rosenbaum, S. P., ed. *The Bloomsbury Group*. London: Croom Helm, 1975.

Scheunemann, Dietrich, ed. *European Avant-Garde: New Perspectives*. Amersterdam: Rodopi, 2000.

Scott, Bonnie Kime, ed. *The Gender of Modernism*. Bloomington, IN: Indiana University Press, 1990.

——. *Refiguring Modernism*. 2 vols. Bloomington, IN: Indiana University Press, 1995.

Shattuck, Sandra D. 'The Stage of Scholarship: Crossing the Bridge from Harrison to Woolf'. In *Virginia Woolf and Bloomsbury: A Centenary Celebration*. Ed. Jane Marcus, 278–98. London: Macmillan, 1987.

Snaith, Anna. *Virginia Woolf: Public and Private Negotiations*. Basingstoke: Macmillan, 2000.

Spalding, Frances. *Roger Fry: Art and Life*. London: Granada, 1980.

Stansky, Peter. *On or About December 1910: Early Bloomsbury and Its Intimate World*. Cambridge, Mass. and London: Harvard University Press, 1996.

Stevenson, Randall. *Modernist Fiction: An Introduction*. Hemel Hempstead: Harvester, 1992.

Stewart, Jack. 'Spatial Form and Color in *The Waves*'. *Twentieth Century Literature* 28 (1982): 86–107.

Tate, Trudi. *Modernism, History and the First World War*. Manchester: Manchester University Press, 1998.

Torgovnick, Marianna. *The Visual Arts, Pictorialism, and the Novel: James, Lawrence, and Woolf*. Princeton, NJ: Princeton University Press, 1985.

Tratner, Michael. *Modernism and Mass Politics: Joyce, Woolf, Eliot, Yeats*. Stanford, CA: Stanford University Press, 1995.

Walder, Dennis, ed. *Literature in the Modern World*. Oxford: Oxford University Press, 1990.

Warner, Eric. *The Waves*. Cambridge: Cambridge University Press, 1987.

Wees, William C. *Vorticism and the English Avant-Garde*. Manchester: Manchester University Press, 1972.

Whitworth, Michael. 'Virginia Woolf and Modernism'. In *The Cambridge Companion to Virginia Woolf*, eds Roe and Sellers, 146–63.

Williams, Keith and Steven Matthews, eds. *Rewriting the Thirties: After Modernism*. Essex: Longman, 1997.

Williams, Raymond. 'The Bloomsbury Fraction'. In *Problems in Materialism and Culture*, 148–69. London: Verso, 1980.

Willis, Jr., J. H. *Leonard and Virginia Woolf as Publishers: The Hogarth Press 1917–1941*. Charlottesville: University of Virginia Press, 1992.

Wilson, Travis D. 'The Ghosts of War: Modernism, Conflict, and Memory in the Twentieth Century'. In *The Image of the Twentieth Century, Media, and Society*, eds Will Wright and Steven Kaplan, 434–38. Society for the Interdisciplinary Study of Social Imagery. Pueblo: University of Southern Colorado, 2000.

Wolfreys, Julian, ed. *Literary Theories: A Reader and Guide*. Edinburgh: Edinburgh University Press, 1999.

Womack, Kenneth. 'Russian Formalism, the Moscow Linguistics Circle, and Prague Structuralism'. In *The Edinburgh Encyclopaedia of Modern Criticism and Theory*, ed. Julian Wolfreys, 114–19. Edinburgh: Edinburgh University Press, 2002.

Woolf, Leonard. *Empire and Commerce in Africa*. London: George Allen and Unwin, 1920.

——. *Imperialism and Civilization*. London: Hogarth Press, 1928.

psychoanalytic approaches

Abel, Elizabeth. '"Cam the Wicked": Woolf's Portrait of the Artist as her Father's Daughter'. In *Virginia Woolf and Bloomsbury: A Centenary Celebration*. Ed. Jane Marcus, 170–88. London: Macmillan, 1987.

——. *Virginia Woolf and the Fictions of Psychoanalysis*. Chicago and London: University of Chicago Press, 1989.

Barrett, Michèle. 'Virginia Woolf Meets Michel Foucault'. In *Imagination in Theory: Essays on Writing and Culture*, 186–204. Cambridge: Polity Press, 1999.

Bazin, Nancy Topping. *Virginia Woolf and the Androgynous Vision*. New Brunswick, NJ: Rutgers University Press, 1973.

Beja, Morris, ed. *Virginia Woolf: 'To the Lighthouse' (A Casebook)*. London: Macmillan, 1970.

Bell, Quentin. *Virginia Woolf: A Biography*. Vols 1 and 2. London: Hogarth Press, 1972.

Berman, Jeffrey. *Narcissism and the Novel*. New York and London: New York University Press, 1990.

Bernheimer, Charles. 'A Shattered Globe: Narcissism and Masochism in Virginia Woolf's Life-Writing'. In *Psychoanalysis and ....* Eds Richard Feldstein and Henry Sussman, 187–206. New York and London: Routledge, 1990.

Blotner, Joseph. 'Mythic Patterns in *To the Lighthouse*'. *PMLA* 4.1 (1956): 547–62.

Caramagno, Thomas C. *The Flight of the Mind: Virginia Woolf's Art and Manic-Depressive Illness*. Berkeley, Los Angeles and London: University of California Press, 1992.

Culler, Jonathan. *On Deconstruction*. Ithaca, NY: Cornell University Press, 1982.

Defromont, Françoise. 'Mirrors and Fragments'. In *Virginia Woolf*. Ed. Rachel Bowlby, 62–76. London and New York: 1992.

DeSalvo, Lousie. *Virginia Woolf: The Impact of Childhood Sexual Abuse on her Life and Work*. London: The Women's Press, 1989.

Felman, Shoshana, ed. *Literature and Psychoanalysis: The Question of Reading Otherwise*. Baltimore and London: Johns Hopkins University Press, 1982. (Originally *Yale French Studies* 55/56, 1977.)

——. *Writing and Madness*. Trans. Martha Noel Evans and the author with the assistance of Brian Massumi. Ithaca, NY: Cornell University Press, 1985.

Ferrer, Daniel. *Virginia Woolf and the Madness of Language*. Trans. Geoffrey Bennington and Rachel Bowlby. London and New York: Routledge, 1990.

Freud, Sigmund. *The Penguin Freud Library Vol. 11*, On *Metapsychology*. Trans. James Strachey. Ed. Angela Richards. Harmondsworth: Penguin, 1991.

Goldstein, Jan Ellen. 'Woolf's Response to Freud: Water-Spiders, Singing Canaries, the Second Apple'. *Psychoanalysis Quarterly* 43 (1974): 436–76.

Henke, Suzette A. 'Virginia Woolf's Septimus Smith: An Analysis of "Paraphrenia" and the Schizophrenic Use of Language'. *Literature and Psychology* 31 (1981): 13–23.

Homans, Margaret. *Bearing the Word: Language and Female Experience in Nineteenth-Century Women's Writing*. Chicago and London: University of Chicago Press, 1986.

Jackson, E. Tony. *The Subject of Modernism: Narrative Alterations in the Fiction of Eliot, Conrad, Woolf, and Joyce*. Ann Arbor: University of Michigan Press, 1994.

Jacobus, Mary, ed. *Women Writing and Writing about Women*. London: Croom Helm, 1979.

——. '"The Third Stroke": Reading Woolf with Freud'. In *Virginia Woolf*. Ed. Rachel Bowlby, 102–20. London and New York: Longman, 1992.

Jouve, Nicole Ward. 'Virginia Woolf: Penis Envy and the Man's Sentence'. In *Female Genesis: Creativity, Self and Gender*, 119–37. Cambridge: Polity Press, 1998.

Kahane, Claire. 'The Nuptials of Metaphor: Self and Other in Virginia Woolf'. *Literature and Psychology* 30.2 (1980): 72–82.

——. *Passions of the Voice: Hysteria, Narrative, and the Figure of the Speaking Woman, 1850–1915*. Baltimore and London: Johns Hopkins University Press, 1995.

——. 'The Woman with a Knife and the Chicken without a Head: Fantasms of Rage and Emptiness'. In *Psychoanalysis/Feminism*. Eds Peter L. Rudnytsky and Andrew M. Gordon, 179–91. Albany: State University of New York, 2000.

Kamiya, Miyeko. 'Virginia Woolf: an Outline of a Study on her Personality, Illness and Work'. *Confinia Psychiatrica* 8 (1965): 189–205.

——. *A Collection of Miyeko Kamiya's Works*. (In Japanese).Tokyo: Misuzu, 1996.

Kosugi, Sei. 'Woolf and Psychiatry: In Relation to Miyeko Kamiya and M. Foucault'. (In Japanese with an English resume.) *Virginia Woolf Review* 15 (1998):1–15.

Kristeva, Julia. *Tales of Love*. Trans. Leon S. Roudiez. New York: Columbia University Press, 1987.

Layton, Lynne and Barbara Ann Schapiro, eds. *Narcissism and the Text: Studies in Literature and the Psychology of Self*. New York and London: New York University Press, 1986.

Lesser, Simon O. 'Arbitration and Conciliation'. *Literature and Psychology* 4.2 (1954): 25–7.

Lidoff, Joan. 'Virginia Woolf's Feminine Sentence: The Mother-Daughter World of *To the Lighthouse*'. *Literature and Psychology* 32.3 (1986): 43–59.

Lilienfeld, Jane. 'The Deceptiveness of Beauty: Mother Love and Mother Hate in *To The Lighthouse*'. *Twentieth Century Literature* 23.3 (1977): 345–76.

Love, Jean O. *Worlds in Consciousness: Mythopoetic Thought in the Novels of Virginia Woolf*. Berkeley, Los Angeles and London: University of California Press, 1970.

Marcus, Jane. 'On Dr. George Savage'. *Virginia Woolf Miscellany* (Fall 1981): 3–4.

Maze, John R. *Virginia Woolf: Feminism, Creativity, and the Unconscious*. Westport, Connecticut and London: Greenwood Press, 1997.

Mepham, John. *Virginia Woolf: Criticism in Focus*. London: Bristol Classical Press, 1992.

Minow-Pinkney, Makiko. *Virginia Woolf and the Problem of the Subject*. Brighton: Harvester, 1987.

——. 'How then does light return … ?' In *Virginia Woolf and the Arts: Selected Papers from the sixth Annual conference on Virginia Woolf*, eds Diane F. Gillespie and Leslie K. Hankins, 90–8. New York: Pace University Press, 1997.

——. 'Virginia Woolf and the Age of Motor Cars'. In *Virginia Woolf in the Age of Mechanical Reproduction*. Ed. Pamela L. Caughie, 159–82. New York and London: Garland, 2000.

Moi, Toril. *Sexual/Textual Politics: Feminist Theory*. London and New York: Methuen, 1985.

Moran, Patricia. *Word of Mouth: Body Language in Katherine Mansfield & Virginia Woolf*. Charlottesville: University Press of Virginia, 1996.

Neverow, Vara S. 'Freudian Seduction and the Fallacies of Dictatorship'. In *Virginia Woolf and Fascism*, 56–72. Basingstoke and New York: Palgrave, 2001.

Poole, Roger. *The Unknown Virginia Woolf*. Cambridge: Cambridge University Press, 1978.

Rose, Phyllis. *Woman of Letters: A Life of Virginia Woolf*. London and Henley: Routledge & Kegan Paul, 1978.

Rosenman, Ellen Bayuk. *The Invisible Presence: Virginia Woolf and the Mother-Daughter Relationship*. Baton Rouge: Louisiana State University Press, 1986.

Schlock, Beverly Ann. 'A Freudian Look at *Mrs. Dalloway*'. *Literature and Psychology* 23 (1973): 49–58.

Spilka, Mark. *Virginia Woolf's Quarrel with Grieving*. Lincoln: University of Nebraska Press, 1980.

Spivak, Gayatri C. 'Unmaking and Making in *To the Lighthouse*'. In *Women and Language in Literature and Society*. Eds Sally McConnell-Ginet, Ruth Borker, and Nelly Furman, 310–27. New York: Praeger Publishers, 1980.

——. 'Three Women's Texts and a Critique of Imperialism'. *Critical Inquiry* 12 (1985): 243–61.

Steinberg, Erwin R. 'Freudian Symbolism and Communication'. *Literature and Psychology*, 3.2 (1953): 2–5.

——. 'Note on a Novelist too Quickly Freudened'. *Literature and Psychology* 4.2 (1954): 23–5.

——. 'Note on a Note'. *Literature and Psychology* 4.4 (1954): 64–5.

Swanson, Diana L. 'An Antigone Complex? The Political Psychology of *The Years* and *Three Guineas*'. *Woolf Studies Annual* 3 (1997): 28–44.

Trombley, Stephen. *All That Summer She Was Mad: Virginia Woolf, Female Victim of Male Medicine*. New York: Continuum, 1982.

Usui, Masami. 'Miyeko Kamiya's Encounter with Virginia Woolf: A Japanese Woman Psychiatrist's Waves of Her Own'. *Doshisha Literature: A Journal of English Literature and Philology* 42 (2000): 1–26.

Wolf, Ernest S. and Ina Wolf. '"We Perished, Each Alone": A Psychoanalytic Commentary on Virginia Woolf's *To the Lighthouse*'. In *Narcissism and the Text: Studies in Literature and the Psychology of Self*. Eds Lynne Layton and Barbara Ann Schapiro, 255–72. New York and London: New York University Press, 1986.

Woolf, Leonard. *Beginning Again: An Autobiography of the Years 1911–1918*. London: Hogarth Press, 1964.

Woolf, Virginia. *Contemporary Writers*. London: Hogarth Press, 1965.

——. *Mrs Dalloway*. Ed. Stella McNichol and intro. Elaine Showalter. Harmondsworth: Penguin, 1992.

Wyatt, Frederick. 'Some Comments on the Use of Symbols in the Novel'. *Literature and Psychology* 4.2 (1954): 15–23.

biographical approaches

Anderson, Linda. *Women and Autobiography in the Twentieth Century: Remembered Futures*. London: Prentice Hall and Harvester Wheatsheaf, 1987.

Ashley, Kathleen, Leigh Gilmore, and Gerald Peters, eds. *Autobiography & Postmodernism*. Amherst: University of Massachusetts Press, 1994.

Barthes, Roland. 'The Death of the Author'. In *Image-Music-Text*. Essays selected and trans. Stephen Heath, 142–8. New York: Noonday, 1977.

Bell, Quentin. *Virginia Woolf: A Biography*. Vol. 1. *Virginia Stephen 1882–1912*. Vol. 2. *Mrs Woolf 1912–1941*. London: Hogarth Press, 1972.

Benstock, Shari, ed. *The Private Self: Theory and Practice of Women's Autobiographical Writing*. Chapel Hill: University of North Carolina Press, 1988.

——. 'Authorizing the Autobiographical'. In *Women, Autobiography, Theory: A Reader*. Eds Sidonie Smith and Julia Watson, 145–55. Madison: University of Wisconsin Press, 1998.

Booth, Alison. 'Biographical Criticism and the "Great" Woman of Letters: The Example of George Eliot and Virginia Woolf'. In *Contesting the Subject: Essays in the Postmodern Theory and Practice of Biography and Biographical Criticism*. Ed. William H. Epstein, 85–107. West Lafayette: Purdue University Press, 1991.

Briggs, Julia. 'Virginia Woolf and "The Proper Writing of Lives"'. In *The Art of Literary Biography*. Ed. John Batchelor, 245–65. Oxford: Clarendon Press, 1995.

——. *Virginia Woolf: An Inner Life*. London: Allen Lane, 2005.

Bruss, Elizabeth W. *Autobiographical Acts: The Changing Situation of a Literary Genre*. Baltimore: MD, Johns Hopkins University Press, 1976.

Caramagno, Thomas. *The Flight of the Mind: Virginia Woolf's Art and Manic-Depressive Illness*. Berkeley, CA: University of California Press, 1992.

Clark, Hilary. 'Living with the Dead: Narrative and Memory in Virginia Woolf's "A Sketch of the Past" and Marlatt's *How to Hug a Stone*'. *Signature* 4 (1990): 1–12.

Cook, Blanche Wiesen. '"Women Alone Stir My Imagination": Lesbianism and the Cultural Tradition'. *Signs* 4.4 (1979): 718–39.

Cousineau, Diane. 'Virginia Woolf's "A Sketch of the Past": Life-writing, the Body, and the Mirror Gaze'. *a/b: Autobiography Studies* 8.1 (1993): 51–71.

Dahl, Christopher C. 'Virginia Woolf's *Moments of Being* and Autobiographical Tradition in the Stephen Family'. *Journal of Modern Literature* 10.2 (1983): 175–96.

Dalgarno, Emily. 'Ideology into Fiction: Virginia Woolf's "A Sketch of the Past"'. *Novel* 27.2 (1994): 175–94.

Davidow, Ellen Messer. *Disciplining Feminism: From Social Activism to Academic Discourse*. Durham, NC: Duke University Press, 2002.

DeMan, Paul. 'Autobiography as Defacement'. *Modern Language Notes* 94 (1979): 919–30.

DeSalvo, Louise A. *Virginia Woolf: The Impact of Childhood Sexual Abuse on Her Life and Work*. Boston: Beacon, 1989.

Diment, Galya. *The Autobiographical Novel of Co-Consciousness: Goncharov, Woolf, and Joyce*. Gainesville: University Press of Florida, 1994.

Dunn, Jane. *A Very Close Conspiracy: Vanessa Bell and Virginia Woolf*. London: Pimlico, 1990.

Ferrer, Daniel. *Virginia Woolf and the Madness of Language*. Trans. Geoffrey Bennington and Rachel Bowlby. New York: Routledge, 1990.

Fish, Stanley. 'Biography and Intention'. In *Contesting the Subject: Essays in the Postmodern Theory and Practice of Biography and Biographical Criticism*. Ed. William H. Epstein, 9–16. West Lafayette: Purdue University Press, 1991.

Foucault, Michel. 'What Is an Author?' In *The Foucault Reader*. Ed. Paul Rabinow, 101–20. New York: Pantheon, 1984.

Gillespie, Diane Filby. *The Sisters' Arts: The Writing and Painting of Virginia Woolf and Vanessa Bell*. Syracuse: Syracuse University Press, 1988.

Gilmore, Leigh. 'The Mark of Autobiography: Postmodernism, Autobiography, and Genre'. In *Autobiography & Postmodernism*. Eds Kathleen Ashley, Leigh Gilmore, and Gerald Peters, 3–18. Amherst: University of Massachusetts Press, 1994.

Glenny, Allie. *Ravenous Identity: Eating and Eating Distress in the Life and Work of Virginia Woolf*. New York: St Martin's Press, 1999.

Goldensohn, Lorrie. 'Unburying the Statue: The Lives of Virginia Woolf'. *Salmagundi* 74–5 (1987): 1–41.

Gordon, Lyndall. *Virginia Woolf: A Writer's Life*. Oxford: Oxford University Press, 1984.

——. 'Women's Lives: The Unmapped Country'. In *The Art of Literary Biography*. Ed. John Batchelor, 87–98. Oxford: Clarendon Press, 1995.

Green, Barbara. *Spectacular Confessions: Autobiography, Performative Activism, and the Sites of Suffrage 1905–1938*. New York: St Martin's Press, 1997.

Heilbrun, Carolyn G. *Writing a Woman's Life*. New York: W. W. Norton, 1988.

Henke, Suzette A. 'Virginia Woolf and Post-Traumatic Subjectivity'. In *Virginia Woolf: Turning the Centuries. Selected Papers from the Ninth Annual Conference on Virginia Woolf*. Eds Ann Ardis and Bonnie Kime Scott, 147–52. New York: Pace University Press, 2000.

Hill, Marylu. 'Mothering Her Text: Woolf and the Maternal Paradigm of Biography'. *Virginia Woolf Miscellany* 46 (1995): 3.

Howe, Florence, ed. *The Politics of Women's Studies: Testimony from 30 Founding Mothers*. New York: The Feminist Press, University of New York City, 2000.

Hussey, Mark. *Virginia Woolf A–Z: The Essential Reference to Her Life and Writings*. New York: Oxford University Press, 1995.

Jelenik, Estelle C., ed. *Women's Autobiography: Essays in Criticism*. Bloomington, IN: Indiana University Press, 1980.

Johnston, Georgia. 'Virginia Woolf's Autobiographers: Sidonie Smith, Shoshana Felman, and Shari Benstock'. In *Virginia Woolf: Texts and Contexts: Selected Papers from the Fifth Annual Conference on Virginia Woolf*. Eds Beth Rigel Daugherty and Eileen Barrett, 140–4. New York: Pace University Press, 1996.

Kamuf, Peggy. 'Writing Like a Woman'. In *Women and Language in Literature and Society*. Eds Sally McConnell-Ginet, Ruth Borker, and Nelly Furman, 284–99. New York: Praeger, 1980.

Kamuf, Peggy and Nancy K. Miller. 'Parisian Letters; Between Feminism and Deconstruction'. In *Conflicts in Feminism*. Eds Marianne Hirsch and Evelyn Fox Keller, 121–33. New York and London: Routledge, 1990.

Keller, Julia. 'Inventing Virginia Woolf: Literary Biography as Art Form'. In *Virginia Woolf and Her Influences: Selected Papers from the Seventh Annual Conference on Virginia Woolf*. Eds Laura Davis and Jeanette McVicker, 11–12. New York: Pace University Press, 1998.

Kenney, Susan M. and Edwin J. Kenney, Jr. 'Virginia Woolf and the Art of Madness'. *Massachusetts Review* 23.1 (1982): 161–85.

King, James. *Virginia Woolf*. London: Hamish Hamilton, 1994.

Leaska, Mitchell. *Granite and Rainbow: The Hidden Life of Virginia Woolf*. New York: Farrar Straus Giroux, 1998.

Lee, Hermione. 'Biomythographers: Rewriting the Lives of Virginia Woolf'. *Essays in Criticism* 46.2 (1996): 95–114.

——. *Virginia Woolf*. New York: Alfred A. Knopf, 1997.

Lilienfeld, Jane. '"The Deceptiveness of Beauty": Mother Love and Mother Hate in *To the Lighthouse*'. *Twentieth Century Literature* 23 (1977): 345–76.

——. 'Where the Spear Plants Grew: the Ramsays' Marriage in *To the Lighthouse*'. In *New Feminist Essays on Virginia Woolf*. Ed. Jane Marcus, 148–69. Lincoln: University of Nebraska Press, 1981.

——. *Reading Alcoholisms: Theorizing Character and Narrative in Selected Novels of Thomas Hardy, James Joyce, and Virginia Woolf*. New York: St Martin's Press, 1999.

——. 'Accident, Incident and Meaning: Traces of Trauma in Virginia Woolf's Narrativity'. In *Virginia Woolf: Turning the Centuries: Selected Papers from the Ninth Annual Conference on Virginia Woolf*. Eds Ann Ardis and Bonnie Kime Scott, 153–8. New York: Pace University Press, 2000.

Lounsberry, Barbara. 'The Art of Virginia Woolf's Diaries'. In *Virginia Woof: Emerging Perspectives: Selected Papers from the Third Annual Conference on Virginia Woolf*. Eds Mark Hussey and Vara Neverow, 266–71. New York: Pace University Press, 1994.

Luckhurst, Nicola. '"To quote my quotation from Montaigne"'. In *Virginia Woolf – Reading the Renaissance*. Ed. Sally Greene, 41–64. Athens: Ohio University Press, 1999.

Marcus, Laura. *Auto/biographical Discourses: Theory, Criticism, Practice*. Manchester: Manchester University Press, 1994.

Marder, Herbert. *The Measure of Life: Virginia Woolf's Last Years*. Ithaca, NY: Cornell University Press, 2000.

McCail, Ronald. 'A Family Matter: *Night and Day* and *Old Kensington*'. *Review of English Studies* 38.149 (1987): 23–39.

McCracken, LuAnn. '"The synthesis of my being": Autobiography and the Reproduction of Identity in Virginia Woolf'. *Tulsa Studies in Women's Literature* 9.1 (1990): 59–78.

Mepham, John. *Criticism in Focus: Virginia Woolf*. New York: St Martin's Press, 1992.

Miles, Kathryn. '"That perpetual marriage of granite and rainbow": Searching for "The New Biography" in Virginia Woolf's *Orlando*'. In *Virginia Woolf and Communities. Selected Papers from the Eighth Annual Conference on Virginia Woolf*, eds Jeanette McVicker and Laura Davis, 212–18. New York: Pace University Press, 1999.

Miller, Nancy K. 'Changing the Subject: Authorship, Writing, and the Reader'. In *Feminist Studies/Critical Studies*. Ed. Teresa DeLauretis, 102–20. Bloomington, IN: Indiana University Press, 1986.

——. 'The Text's Heroine: A Feminist Critic and Her Fictions'. *Conflicts in Feminism*. Eds. Marianne Hirsch and Evelyn Fox Keller, 112–20. New York and London: Routledge, 1990.

——. 'Teaching Autobiography'. In *Getting Personal: Feminist Occasions and Other Autobiographical Acts,* 121–42. New York: Routledge, 1991.

Modleski, Tania. 'Some Functions of Feminist Criticism, or The Scandal of the Mute Body'. *October* 49 (1989): 3–24.

Moran, Patricia. *Word of Mouth: Body Language in Katherine Mansfield & Virginia Woolf*. Charlottesville: University Press of Virginia, 1996.

Moss, Roger. 'The "Sketch of the Past" as Biographical Criticism'. *Virginia Woolf Miscellany* 46 (1995): 1–2.

Nalbantian, Suzanne. *Aesthetic Autobiography: From Life to Art in Marcel Proust, James Joyce, Virginia Woolf and Anais Nin.* New York: St Martin's Press, 1994.

Olney, James, ed. *Autobiography: Essays Theoretical and Critical.* Princeton, NJ: Princeton University Press, 1980.

Ozick, Cynthia. 'Mrs. Virginia Woolf'. *Commentary* 56 (1973): 33–44.

Pawlowski, Merry M. 'From the Country of the Colonized: Virginia Woolf on Growing Up Female in Victorian England'. In *Violence, Silence, and Anger: Women's Writing as Transgression.* Ed. Deirdre Lashgari, 95–110. Charlottesville: University Press of Virginia, 1995.

Peters, Catherine. 'Secondary Lives: Biography in Context'. In *The Art of Literary Biography.* Ed. John Batchelor, 43–56. Oxford: Clarendon Press, 1995.

Pippett, Aileen. *The Moth and the Star: A Biography of Virginia Woolf.* New York: Viking, 1957.

Podnieks, Elizabeth. *Daily Modernism: The Literary Diaries of Virginia Woolf, Antonia White, Elizabeth Smart, and Anais Nin.* Montreal: McGill-Queen's University Press, 2000.

Poole, Roger. *The Unknown Virginia Woolf.* 2nd edn. Atlantic Highlands, NJ: Humanities Press, 1982.

——. 'Panel Discussion 2'. In *Virginia Woolf: A Centenary Perspective.* Ed. Eric Warner. New York: St Martin's Press, 1984.

Porter, David. '*Orlando* on Her Mind? An Unpublished Letter from Virginia Woolf to Lady Sackville'. *Woolf Studies Annual* 7 (2001): 103–14.

Raitt, Suzanne. *Vita and Virginia: The Work and Friendship of V. Sackville-West and Virginia Woolf.* Oxford: Clarendon Press, 1993.

Reid, Panthea. *Art and Affection: A Life of Virginia Woolf.* New York: Oxford University Press, 1996.

Rogat, Ellen Hawkes. 'The Virgin in the Bell Biography'. *Twentieth Century Literature* 20.2 (1974): 96–113.

Rose, Jacqueline. *The Haunting of Sylvia Plath.* Cambridge Mass.: Harvard University Press, 1992.

Rose, Phyllis. *Woman of Letters: A Life of Virginia Woolf.* New York: Oxford University Press, 1978.

Rosenberg, Beth Carole. 'How Should One Write a Memoir? Virginia Woolf's "A Sketch of the Past"'. In *Re: Reading, Re: Writing, Re: Teaching Virginia Woolf: Selected Papers from the Fourth Annual Conference on Virginia Woolf.* Eds Eileen Barrett and Patricia Cramer, 7–12. New York: Pace University Press, 1995.

Rosenfeld, Natalia. *Outsiders Together: Virginia and Leonard Woolf.* Princeton, NJ: Princeton University Press, 2000.

Rosenman, Ellen Baynk. *The Invisible Presence: Virginia Woolf and the Mother-Daughter Relationship.* Baton Rouge: Lousiana State University Press, 1986.

Sellers, Susan. 'Virginia Woolf's Diaries and Letters'. In *The Cambridge Companion to Virginia Woolf.* Eds Sue Roe and Susan Sellers, 109–26. Cambridge: Cambridge University Press, 2000.

Silver, Brenda R. *Virginia Woolf Icon.* Chicago, IL: University of Chicago Press, 1999.

Simons, Judy. 'The Safety Curtain: The Diary of Virginia Woolf'. *Diaries and Journals of Literary Women from Fanny Burney to Virginia Woolf.* Iowa City: University of Iowa Press, 1990.

Smith, Sidonie. 'Identity's Body'. In *Autobiography & Postmodernism.* Eds Kathleen Ashley, Leigh Gilmore and Gerald Peters, 266–92. Amherst: University of Massachusetts Press, 1994.

Smith, Sidonie and Julia Watson, eds. *Women, Autobiography, Theory: A Reader*. Madison, WI: University of Wisconsin Press, 1998.
Spater, George and Ian Parsons. *A Marriage of True Minds: An Intimate Portrait of Leonard and Virginia Woolf*. New York: Harcourt Brace Jovanovich, 1977.
Spengemann, William. *The Forms of Autobiography: Episodes in the History of a Literary Genre*. New Haven: Yale University Press, 1980.
Sproles, Karyn. 'Orlando's Self-Conscious Biographer and Challenges to the Patriarchy'. *Virginia Woolf Miscellany* 46 (1995): 2.
Stanton, Domna C. 'Autogynography: Is the Subject Different?' In *Women, Autobiography, Theory: A Reader*. Eds Sidonie Smith and Julia Watson, 131–44. Madison, WI: University of Wisconsin Press, 1998.
Stimpson, Catharine R. 'The Female Sociograph: The Theater of Virginia Woolf's Letters'. In *The Female Autograph*. Ed. Domna C. Stanton. Chicago, IL: University of Chicago Press, 1984.
Strachey, Lytton. *Eminent Victorians*. Harmondsworth: Penguin, 1975.
Trombley, Stephen. *All That Summer She Was Mad: Virginia Woolf, Female Victim of Male Medicine*. New York: Continuum, 1982.
Walker, Cheryl. 'Personal Criticism and the Death of the Author'. In *Contesting the Subject: Essays in the Postmodern Theory and Practice of Biography and Biographical Criticism*. Ed. William H. Epstein, 109–21. West Lafayette: Purdue University Press, 1991.
Zwerdling, Alex. 'Mastering the Memoir: Woolf and the Family Legacy'. *Modernism/Modernity* 10.1 (2003): 165–88.

feminist approaches

Ahmed, Sara, Jane Kilby, Celia Lury, Maureen McNeil, and Beverley Skeggs, eds. *Transformations: Thinking Through Feminism*. London and New York: Routledge, 2000.
Allen, Carolyn and Judith A. Howard. 'Feminisms as Provocation'. In *Provoking Feminisms*. Eds Carolyn Allen and Judith A. Howard, 1–8. Chicago, IL: University of Chicago Press, 2000.
Barrett, Eileen and Patricia Cramer, eds. *Virginia Woolf: Lesbian Readings*. New York: New York University Press, 1997.
Barrett, Michèle. 'Towards a Virginia Woolf Criticism'. In *The Sociology of Literature: Applied Studies*. Ed. Diana Laurenson, 145–60. Sociological Review Monograph 26. Keele: University of Keele, 1978.
——. *Imagination in Theory: Culture, Writing, Words, and Things*. Washington Square, NY: New York University Press, 1999.
Bauer, Dale and Priscilla Wald. 'Complaining, Conversing, and Coalescing'. In *Feminisms at a Millennium*. Ed. Judith A. Howard and Carolyn Allen, 287–91. Chicago, IL: University of Chicago Press, 2000.
Bazin, Nancy Topping. *Virginia Woolf and the Androgynous Vision*. New Brunswick, NJ: Rutgers University Press, 1973.
Beer, Gillian. *Virginia Woolf: The Common Ground*. Edinburgh: Edinburgh University Press, 1996.
Bell, Quentin. *Virginia Woolf: A Biography*. 2 vols. New York: Harcourt and Harvest, 1972.
Benstock, Shari, Suzanne Ferriss, and Susanne Woods. *A Handbook of Literary Feminisms*. New York and Oxford: Oxford University Press, 2002.

Black, Naomi. 'Virginia Woolf and the Women's Movement'. In *Virginia Woolf: A Feminist Slant*, ed. Jane Marcus, 180–97. Lincoln: University of Nebraska Press, 1983.

——. *Social Feminism*. Ithaca, NY: Cornell University Press, 1989.

——. 'Introduction'. *Three Guineas* by Virginia Woolf. Ed. Naomi Black, xiii–lxxv. Oxford: Blackwell, 2001.

——. *Virginia Woolf as Feminist*. Ithaca, NY: Cornell University Press, 2003.

Bowlby, Rachel. *Still Crazy After All These Years*. London and New York: Routledge, 1992.

——. *Virginia Woolf: Feminist Destinations and Further Essays on Virginia Woolf*. Edinburgh: Edinburgh University Press, 1997.

Briggs, Julia. 'The Story So Far ...' In *Virginia Woolf: Introductions to the Major Works*. Ed. Julia Briggs, vii–xxxiii. London: Virago, 1994.

——. 'Between the Texts: Virginia Woolf's Acts of Revision'. *Text: An Interdisciplinary Journal of Textual Studies* 12 (1999): 143–65.

Caine, Barbara. *English Feminism: 1780–1980*. Oxford: Oxford University Press, 1997.

Caramagno, Thomas C. *The Flight of the Mind: Virginia Woolf's Art and Manic-Depressive Illness*. Berkeley, CA: University of California Press, 1992.

Carroll, Berenice A. '"To Crush Him in Our Own Country": The Political Thought of Virginia Woolf'. *Feminist Studies* 4 (1977): 99–132.

Caughie, Pamela. *Virginia Woolf & Postmodernism: Literature in Quest & Question of Itself*. Urbana, IL: University of Illinois Press, 1991.

Caws, Mary Ann and Nicola Luckhurst, eds. *The Reception of Virginia Woolf in Europe*. London: Continuum, 2002.

Chapman, Wayne K. and Janet M. Manson, eds. *Women in the Milieu of Leonard and Virginia Woolf: Peace, Politics, and Education*. New York: Pace University Press, 1998.

Childers, Mary M. 'Virginia Woolf on the Outside Looking Down: Reflections on the Class of Women'. *Modern Fiction Studies*. Special Virginia Woolf issue. Ed. Ellen Carol Jones. 38.1 (Spring 1992): 61–79.

Christian, Barbara. 'Layered Rhythms: Virginia Woolf and Toni Morrison'. In *Virginia Woolf: Emerging Perspectives: Selected Papers from the Third Annual Conference on Virginia Woolf*. Eds Mark Hussey and Vara Neverow, 164–77. New York: Pace University Press, 1994.

Cliff, Michelle. 'Virginia Woolf and the Imperial Gaze: A Glance Askance'. In *Virginia Woolf: Emerging Perspectives: Selected Papers from the Third Annual Conference on Virginia Woolf*. Eds Mark Hussey and Vara Neverow, 91–102. New York: Pace University Press, 1994.

Cuddy-Keane, Melba. 'Opening Historical Doors to the *Room*: An Approach to Teaching'. In *Re:Reading, Re:Writing, Re:Teaching Virginia Woolf: Selected Papers from the Fourth Annual Conference on Virginia Woolf*. Eds Eileen Barrett and Patricia Cramer, 207–15. New York: Pace University Press, 1995.

——. *Virginia Woolf, the Intellectual, and the Public Sphere*. Cambridge: Cambridge University Press, 2003.

Daugherty, Beth Rigel. 'The Whole Contention Between Mr. Bennett and Mrs. Woolf, Revisited'. In *Virginia Woolf: Centennial Essays*. Eds Elaine K. Ginsberg and Laura Moss Gottlieb, 269–94. Troy, NY: Whitston, 1983.

——. 'Virginia Woolf Teaching/Virginia Woolf Learning: Morley College and the Common Reader'. In *New Essays on Virginia Woolf*. Ed. Helen Wussow, 61–77. Dallas: Contemporary Research Press, 1995.

——. 'Readin', Writin', and Revisin': Virginia Woolf's "How Should One Read a Book?"' In *Virginia Woolf and the Essay*. Eds Beth Carole Rosenberg and Jeanne Dubino, 159–75. New York: St Martin's Press, 1997.

—— 'Learning Virginia Woolf: Of Leslie, Libraries, and Letters'. In *Virginia Woolf and Communities: Selected Papers from the Eighth Annual Conference on Virginia Woolf*. Eds Jeanette McVicker and Laura Davis, 10–17. New York: Pace University Press, 1999a.

——. 'Virginia Woolf's Educational Inheritance: The Stephen Household and 19th Century Debates about Education for Girls'. Paper presented at the Ninth Annual Conference on Virginia Woolf, University of Delaware, 10–13 June 1999b.

Dean, Jodi. Rev. of *Why Feminism? Gender, Psychology, Politics*, Lynne Segal and *Feminist Debates: Issues of Theory and Political Practice*, Valerie Bryson. *Signs: Journal of Women in Culture and Society* 28.2 (2003): 733–6.

DeSalvo, Louise. *Virginia Woolf's First Voyage: A Novel in the Making*. Totwa, NJ: Rowman and Littlefield, 1980.

——. *Virginia Woolf: The Impact of Childhood Sexual Abuse on Her Life and Work*. Boston: Beacon, 1989.

Doyle, Laura. '"These Emotions of the Body": Intercorporeal Narrative in *To the Lighthouse*'. *Twentieth Century Literature* 40 (1994a): 42–71.

——. 'Voyaging Beyond the Race Mother: *Melymbrosia* and *To the Lighthouse*'. In *Bordering on the Body: The Racial Matrix of Modern Fiction and Culture*, 139–73. Oxford: Oxford University Press, 1994b.

Eagleton, Mary, ed. *Feminist Literary Theory: A Reader*. 2nd edn. Oxford: Blackwell, 1996.

Elam, Diane and Robyn Wiegman. 'Contingencies'. In *Feminism Beside Itself*. Eds Diane Elam and Robyn Wiegman, 1–8. New York: Routledge, 1995.

Emery, Mary Lou. '"Robbed of Meaning": The Work at the Center of *To the Lighthouse*'. *Modern Fiction Studies* 38.1 (1992): 217–34.

Epes, Isota Tucker. 'How Virginia Woolf Brought Me Up'. In *Virginia Woolf: Emerging Perspectives: Selected Papers from the Third Annual Conference on Virginia Woolf*. Eds Mark Hussey and Vara Neverow, 19–24. New York: Pace University Press, 1994.

Ezell, Margaret J. M. 'The Myth of Judith Shakespeare: Creating the Canon of Women's Literature'. *New Literary History* 21 (1990): 579–92.

Flint, Kate. 'Virginia Woolf and the Great Strike'. *Essays in Criticism* 36 (1986): 319–34.

Forster, E. M. 'Virginia Woolf'. In *Two Cheers for Democracy*, 242–58 [1951]. London: Edward Arnold, 1972.

Friedman, Susan Stanford. 'Virginia Woolf's Pedagogical Scenes of Reading: *The Voyage Out, The Common Reader*, and Her "Common Readers"'. *Modern Fiction Studies* 38.1 (1992): 101–25.

——. *Mappings: Feminism and the Cultural Geographies of Encounter*. Princeton, NJ: Princeton University Press, 1998.

Froula, Christine. 'St. Virginia's Epistle to an English Gentleman: or, Sex, Violence, and The Public Sphere in Woolf's *Three Guineas*'. *Tulsa Studies in Women's Literature* 13.1 (1994): 27–56.

——. *Virginia Woolf and the Bloomsbury Avant-Garde: War, Civilization, Modernity*. New York: Columbia University Press, 2005.

Fulker, Teresa. 'Virginia Woolf's Daily Drama of the Body'. *Woolf Studies Annual* 1 (1995): 3–25.

Gilbert, Sandra and Susan Gubar. *The Madwoman in the Attic: The Woman Writer and the Nineteenth-Century Literary Imagination*. New Haven: Yale University Press, 1979.

Gillespie, Diane F. 'The Texture of the Text: Editing *Roger Fry: A Biography*'. In *Editing Virginia Woolf: Interpreting the Modernist Text*. Eds James M. Haule and J. H. Stape, 92–113. Basingstoke: Palgrave, 2002.

——. 'Woolf and Walking: Mapping a Rural Flâneuse'. Paper presented at the Thirteenth Annual Conference on Virginia Woolf, Smith College, Northampton, MA, 5–8 June, 2003.

Gillespie, Diane F. and Elizabeth Steele, eds. *Julia Duckworth Stephen: Stories for Children, Essays for Adults*. Syracuse, NY: Syracuse University Press, 1987.

Goldman, Jane. ed. *Icon Critical Guide on* To the Lighthouse *and* The Waves. Cambridge: Icon Books, 1997.

——. *The Feminist Aesthetics of Virginia Woolf: Modernism, Post-Impressionism and the Politics of the Visual*. Cambridge: Cambridge University Press, 1998.

Gruber, Ruth. *Virginia Woolf: The Will to Create as a Woman*. New York: Carroll & Graf Publishers, 2005. Reprint of *Virginia Woolf: A Study*, 1935.

Gunew, Sneja, and Anna Yeatman. 'Introduction'. In *Feminism and the Politics of Difference*. Eds Sneja Gunew and Anna Yeatman, xiii–xxv. Boulder: Westview Press, 1993.

Guy-Sheftall, Beverly, ed. *Words of Fire: An Anthology of African-American Feminist Thought*. New York: The New Press, 1995.

Hanson, Clare. *Virginia Woolf*. London: Macmillan, 1994.

Harrison, Suzan. *Eudora Welty and Virginia Woolf: Gender, Genre, and Influence*. Baton Rouge: Louisiana State University Press, 1997.

Harvey, Kathryn. 'Historical Notes on Woolf and the Women's International League'. In *Virginia Woolf and the Arts: Selected Papers from the Sixth Annual Conference on Virginia Woolf*. Eds Diane F. Gillespie and Leslie K. Hankins, 142–9. New York: Pace University Press, 1997.

Heilbrun, Carolyn. *Toward a Recognition of Androgyny*. New York: Harper & Row, 1973.

Hogeland, Lisa Maria. 'Against Generational Thinking, or, Some Things that "Third Wave" Feminism Isn't'. *Women's Studies in Communication* 24.1 (2001): 107–21.

Holtby, Winifred. *Virginia Woolf: A Critical Memoir* [1932]. Chicago: Academy Press, 1978.

hooks, bell. *Feminist Theory: From Margin to Center*. 2nd edn Cambridge, Mass.: South End Press, 2000.

Humm, Maggie, ed. *Moderns Feminisms: Political, Literary, Cultural*. New York: Columbia University Press, 1992. [In UK, *Feminism: A Reader*]

Hussey, Mark, ed. *Virginia Woolf and War: Fiction, Reality, and Myth*. Syracuse, NY: Syracuse University Press, 1991.

——. *Virginia Woolf A to Z*. New York: Oxford University Press, 1995.

——. *Major Authors on CD-ROM: Virginia Woolf*. Woodbridge, CT: Primary Source Media, 1997.

Jefferson, Margo. 'Unreal Loyalties'. *The New York Times Book Review* 13 April 2003: 31.

Johnston, Georgia. 'The Whole Achievement in Virginia Woolf's *The Common Reader*'. In *Essays on the Essay: Redefining the Genre*. Ed. Alexander J. Butrym, 148–58. Athens, GA: University of Georgia Press, 1989.

Kaivola, Karen. 'Virginia Woolf, Vita Sackville-West, and the Question of Sexual Identity'. *Woolf Studies Annual* 4 (1998): 18–40.

Kaplan, Sydney Janet. 'On Reaching the Year 2000'. In *Feminisms at a Millennium*. Eds Judith A. Howard and Carolyn Allen, 168–71. Chicago, IL: University of Chicago Press, 2000.

Kavka, Misha. 'Introduction'. In *Feminist Consequences: Theory for the New Century*. Eds Elisabeth Bronfen and Misha Kavka, ix–xxvi. New York: Columbia University Press, 2001.

Kemp, Sandra and Judith Squires, eds. *Feminisms*. Oxford Readers Series. Oxford and New York: Oxford University Press, 1997.

Kershner, R. B. 'Gender Criticism'. In *The Twentieth-Century Novel: An Introduction*, 93–103. Boston: Bedford Books, 1997.

Kirkpatrick, B. J. and Stuart N. Clarke. *A Bibliography of Virginia Woolf*. 4th edn. Oxford: Clarendon Press, 1997.

Laurence, Patricia Ondek. *The Reading of Silence: Virginia Woolf in the English Tradition*. Stanford, CA: Stanford University Press, 1991.

——. *Lily Briscoe's Chinese Eyes: Bloomsbury, Modernism, and China*. Columbia: University of South Carolina Press, 2003.

Lee, Hermione. 'Virginia Woolf and Offence'. In *The Art of Literary Biography*. Ed. John Batchelor, 129–50. Oxford: Clarendon Press, 1995.

——. *Virginia Woolf*. New York: Knopf, 1997.

Levenback, Karen. *Virginia Woolf and the Great War*. Syracuse, NY: Syracuse University Press, 1999.

Lilienfeld, Jane. *Reading Alcoholisms: Theorizing Character and Narrative in Selected Novels of Thomas Hardy, James Joyce, and Virginia Woolf*. New York: St Martin's Press, 1999.

London, Bette. 'Guerilla in Petticoats or Sans-Culotte? Virginia Woolf and the Future of Feminist Criticism'. *Diacritics* (Summer/Fall 1991): 11–29.

Lyon, George Ella. 'Virginia Woolf and the Problem of the Body'. In *Virginia Woolf: Centennial Essays*. Eds Elaine K. Ginsberg and Laura Moss Gottlieb, 111–25. Troy, NY: Whitston, 1983.

Marcus, Jane. '*The Years* as Greek Drama, Domestic Novel, and Götterdämmerung'. *Bulletin of the New York Public Library* 80.2 (1977): 276–301.

——. 'Enchanted Organs, Magic Bells: *Night and Day* as Comic Opera'. In *Virginia Woolf: Revaluation and Continuity*. Ed. Ralph Freedman, 97–122. Berkeley, CA: University of California Press, 1980.

——. *Virginia Woolf and the Languages of Patriarchy*. Bloomington, IN: Indiana University Press, 1987.

——. *Art and Anger: Reading Like a Woman*. Columbus: Ohio State University Press, 1988.

——. 'A Tale of Two Cultures'. *The Women's Review of Books*. January 1994: 11–14.

——. 'Wrapped in the Stars and Stripes: Virginia Woolf in the U.S.A'. *The South Carolina Review* 29.1 (1996): 17–23.

——. *Hearts of Darkness: White Women Write Race*. Brunswick, NJ: Rutgers University Press, 2004.

Marcus, Jane, ed. *New Feminist Essays on Virginia Woolf*. Lincoln: University of Nebraska Press, 1981.

——. *Virginia Woolf: A Feminist Slant*. Lincoln: University of Nebraska Press, 1983.

——. *Virginia Woolf and Bloomsbury: A Centenary Celebration*. Bloomington, IN: Indiana University Press, 1987.

Marcus, Laura. 'Woolf's Feminism and Feminism's Woolf'. In *The Cambridge Companion to Virginia Woolf*. Eds Sue Roe and Susan Sellers, 209–44. Cambridge: Cambridge University Press, 2000.

Marder, Herbert. *Feminism and Art: A Study of Virginia Woolf*. Chicago, IL: University of Chicago Press, 1968.

——. *The Measure of Life: Virginia Woolf's Last Years*. Ithaca, NY: Cornell University Press, 2000.

Mepham, John. *Criticism in Focus: Virginia Woolf*. London: Bristol Classical Press, 1992.

Minow-Pinkney, Makiko. *Virginia Woolf and the Problem of the Subject. Feminine Writing in the Major Novels*. Brighton: Harvester, 1987.

Moi, Toril. *Sexual/Textual Politics: Feminist Literary Theory*. London: Methuen, 1985.

Offen, Karen. *European Feminisms, 1700–1950: A Political History*. Stanford, CA: Stanford University Press, 2000.

Pawlowski, Merry M. 'The Virginia Woolf and Vera Douie Letters: Woolf's Connections to the Women's Service Library'. *Woolf Studies Annual* 8 (2002): 3–62.

——, ed. *Virginia Woolf and Fascism: Resisting the Dictators' Seduction*. New York: Palgrave, 2001.

Pawlowski, Merry M. and Vara Neverow, eds. *Reading Notes for* Three Guineas: *An Edition and Archive*. California State University-Bakersfield <http://www.csub.edu/woolf/tgs-home.html (by subscription)>, 2002.

Radin, Grace. '"Two enormous chunks": Episodes Excluded during the Final Revisions of *The Years*'. *Bulletin of the New York Public Library* 80.2 (1977): 221–51.

——. *Virginia Woolf's* The Years: *The Evolution of a Novel*. Knoxville, TN: University of Tennessee Press, 1981.

Rado, Lisa. *The Modern Androgyne Imagination: A Failed Sublime*. Charlottesville and London: University Press of Virginia, 2000.

Ratcliffe, Krista. *Anglo-American Feminist Challenges to the Rhetorical Traditions: Virginia Woolf, Mary Daly, Adrienne Rich*. Carbondale: Southern Illinois University Press, 1996.

Rosenbaum, S. P. 'Introduction'. In *Women & Fiction: The Manuscript Versions of* A Room of One's Own. By Virginia Woolf. Ed. S. P. Rosenbaum, xiii–xlii. Oxford: Blackwell, 1992.

Rosenberg, Beth Carole. 'Virginia Woolf and Samuel Johnson: Conversation and the Common Reader'. In *Virginia Woolf and Samuel Johnson: Common Readers*, 49–68. New York: St Martin's, 1995.

Rubenstein, Roberta. *Home Matters: Longing and Belonging, Nostalgia and Mourning in Women's Fiction*. New York: Palgrave, 2001.

Saxton, Ruth and Jean Tobin, eds. *Woolf and Lessing: Breaking the Mold*. New York: St Martin's Press, 1994.

Schor, Naomi and Elizabeth Weed. 'Introduction'. In *The Essential Difference*. Eds Naomi Schor and Elizabeth Weed, vii–xix. Bloomington, IN: Indiana University Press, 1994.

Scott, Bonnie Kime. *Refiguring Modernism. Volume 1: The Women of 1928*. Bloomington, IN: Indiana University Press, 1995.

——, ed. *The Gender of Modernism: A Critical Anthology*. Bloomington, IN: Indiana University Press, 1990.

——, ed. *Gender In Modernism: New Geographies, Complex Intersections*. Urbana, IL: University of Illinois Press, 2007.

Showalter, Elaine. 'Virginia Woolf and the Flight Into Androgyny'. *A Literature of Their Own: British Women Novelists from Brontë to Lessing*, 263–97. Princeton, NJ: Princeton University Press, 1977.

——. 'Introduction. Twenty Years On: *A Literature of Their Own* Revisited'. In *A Literature of Their Own: British Women Novelists from Brontë to Lessing.* Expanded edn, xi–xxxiii. Princeton, NJ: Princeton University Press, 1999.

Silver, Brenda R. *Virginia Woolf's Reading Notebooks.* Princeton, NJ: Princeton University Press, 1983.

——. 'The Authority of Anger: *Three Guineas* as Case Study'. *Signs* 6.2 (1991a): 340–70.

——. 'Textual Criticism as Feminist Practice: Or, Who's Afraid of Virginia Woolf Part II'. In *Representing Modernist Texts: Editing as Interpretation.* Ed. George Bornstein, 193–222. Ann Arbor: University of Michigan Press, 1991b.

——. *Virginia Woolf Icon.* Chicago, IL: University of Chicago Press, 1999.

Snaith, Anna. *Virginia Woolf: Public and Private Negotiations.* Basingstoke: Macmillan, 2000a.

——. '"Stray Guineas": Virginia Woolf and the Fawcett Library'. *Literature and History* 12.2 (2003): 16–35.

——, ed. 'Wide Circles: The *Three Guineas* Letters'. *Woolf Studies Annual* 6 (2000b): 1–82.

Squier, Susan Merrill. *Virginia Woolf and London: The Sexual Politics of the City.* Chapel Hill: University of North Carolina Press, 1985.

Thornham, Sue. *Feminist Theory and Cultural Studies: Stories of Unsettled Relations.* London: Arnold, 2000.

Tyson, Lois. 'Feminist Criticism'. In *Critical Theory Today: A User-Friendly Guide*, 81–116. New York: Garland, 1999.

Wallace, Miriam L. 'Theorizing Relational Subjects: Metonymic Narrative in *The Waves*'. *Narrative* 8.3 (2000): 294–323.

Warhol, Robyn R. and Diane Price Herndl, eds. *Feminisms: An Anthology of Literary Theory and Criticism.* Rev. edn. Basingstoke: Macmillan, 1997.

Waugh, Patricia. 'From Modernist Textuality to Feminist Sexuality; Or Why I'm No Longer A-Freud of Virginia Woolf'. In *Feminine Fictions: Revisiting the Postmodern*, 88–125. London: Routledge, 1989.

Weil, Kari. *Androgyny and the Denial of Difference.* Charlottesville and London: University Press of Virginia, 1992.

Williams, Lisa. *The Artist as Outsider in the Novels of Toni Morrison and Virginia Woolf.* Westport, CT: Greenwood Press, 2000.

Woolf, Leonard. *Downhill All the Way: An Autobiography of the Years 1919 to 1939.* New York: Harcourt, 1967.

Woolf, Virginia. '"Anon" and "the Reader": Virginia Woolf's Last Essays'. Ed. Brenda Silver. General ed. Lucio Ruotolo. *Twentieth Century Literature* 25 (Fall/Winter 1979): 356–441.

——. 'Bryon & Mr Briggs'. Ed. Edward A. Hungerford. *Yale Review* 68 (1979): 321–49.

——. 'Friendships Gallery'. Ed. Ellen Hawkes. General ed. Lucio Ruotolo. *Twentieth Century Literature* 25 (Fall/Winter 1979): 279–302.

——. *The Hours: The British Museum Manuscript of* Mrs Dalloway. Ed. Helen M. Wussow. New York: Pace University Press, 1996.

——. 'Introductory Letter to Margaret Llewelyn Davies'. In *Life as We Have Known It.* By Co-operative Working Women. Ed. Margaret Llewelyn Davies, xv–xxxix. New York: Norton, 1931.

——. *Jacob's Room: The Holograph Draft.* Ed. Edward L. Bishop. New York: Pace University Press, 1998.

——. 'The Journal of Mistress Joan Martyn'. Ed. Susan M. Squier and Louise A. DeSalvo. General ed. Lucio Ruotolo. *Twentieth Century Literature* 25 (Fall/Winter 1979): 237–69.

——. *The London Scene.* 1975. London: Hogarth, 1982.

——. *Melymbrosia: An Early Version of* The Voyage Out. Ed. Louise A. DeSalvo. Scholar's Edition. New York: The New York Public Library, 1982.

——. *On Being Ill.* 1930. Intro. Hermione Lee. Ashfield, MA: Paris Press, 2002.

——. '*Orlando*: An Edition of the Manuscript'. Ed. Madeline Moore. General ed. Lucio Ruotolo. *Twentieth Century Literature* 25 (Fall/Winter 1979): 303–55.

——. *Orlando: The Original Holograph Draft.* Ed. Stuart Nelson Clarke. London: S. N. Clarke, 1993.

——. *The Passionate Apprentice: The Early Journals, 1897–1909.* Ed. Mitchell A. Leaska. San Diego: Harcourt, 1990.

——. *Three Guineas.* Ed. Naomi Black. Shakespeare Head Press Edition. Oxford: Blackwell, 2001.

——. *To the Lighthouse: The Original Holograph Draft.* Ed. Susan Dick. Toronto: University of Toronto Press, 1982.

——. *The Virginia Woolf Manuscripts: From the Henry W. and Albert A. Berg Collection at The New York Public Library.* Microfilm. 21 reels. Woodbridge, CT: Research Publications, 1993.

——. *The Virginia Woolf Manuscripts: From the Monks House Papers at the University of Sussex and Additional Manuscripts at the British Library, London.* Microfilm. 6 reels. Brighton: Harvester Press Microform, 1985.

——. *The Waves: The Two Holograph Drafts.* Ed. J. W. Graham. Toronto: University of Toronto Press, 1976.

——. *Women and Fiction: The Manuscript Versions of* A Room of One's Own. Ed. S. P. Rosenbaum. Oxford: Blackwell, 1992.

——. *Women and Writing.* Ed. Michèle Barrett. New York: Harcourt and Harvest, 1979.

Zwerdling, Alex. *Virginia Woolf and the Real World.* Berkeley, CA: University of California Press, 1986.

bibliographic approaches

Banks, Joanne Trautmann. 'The Editor as Ethicist'. In *Editing Virginia Woolf: Interpreting the Modernist Text.* Eds James M. Haule and J. H. Stape. Basingstoke: Palgrave, 2002.

Beja, Morris. 'Text and Counter-Text: Trying to Recover *Mrs Dalloway*'. In *Editing Virginia Woolf: Interpreting the Modernist Text*, eds James M. Haule and J. H. Stape, 127–38. Basingstoke: Palgrave, 2002.

Bell, Anne Olivier. 'Editing Virginia Woolf's Diary'. In *Editing Virginia Woolf: Interpreting the Modernist Text*, eds James M. Haule and J. H. Stape, 11–24. Basingstoke: Palgrave, 2002.

Bell, Quentin. *Virginia Woolf: A Biography.* 2 vols. London: Hogarth Press, 1972.

Black, Naomi. '"Women Must Weep": The Serialization of *Three Guineas*'. In *Editing Virginia Woolf: Interpreting the Modernist Text*, eds James M. Haule and J. H. Stape, 74–90. Basingstoke: Palgrave, 2002.

Bornstein, George. *Material Modernism: the Politics of the Page.* Cambridge: Cambridge University Press, 2001.

Bourdieu, Pierre. 'The Production of Belief: Contribution to an Economy of Symbolic Goods'. In *The Field of Cultural Production*. Ed. Randal Johnson, 74–111. London: Polity Press, 1993.

Briggs, Julia. 'The Story So Far...: An Introduction to the Introductions'. In *Virginia Woolf: Introductions to the Major Works*. Ed. Julia Briggs, vii–xxxiii. London: Virago Press, 1994.

——. 'Editing Woolf for the Nineties'. *South Carolina Review* 29 (1996): 67–77.

——. 'Between the Texts: Virginia Woolf's Acts of Revision'. *TEXT: Transactions of the Society of Textual Scholarship* 12 (1999): 143–65.

Caughie, Pamela L., ed. *Virginia Woolf in the Age of Mechanical Reproduction*. New York: Garland, 2000.

Cuddy-Keane, Melba. 'Virginia Woolf, Sound Technologies, and the New Aurality'. In *Virginia Woolf in the Age of Mechanical Reproduction*, ed. Pamela L. Caughie, 69–96. New York: Garland, 2000.

Darnton, Robert. 'What is the History of Books?' In *The Kiss of Lamourette: Reflections in Cultural History*, 107–36. New York: Norton, 1990.

Daugherty, Beth Rigel and Mary Beth Pringle, eds. *Approaches to Teaching Woolf's To the Lighthouse*. New York: The Modern Language Association of America, 2001.

DeSalvo, Louise. *Virginia Woolf's First Voyage: A Novel in the Making*. Totowa: Rowman & Littlefield, 1980.

Friedman, Susan Stanford. 'The Return of the Repressed in Women's Narrative'. *The Journal of Narrative Technique* 19.1 (Winter 1989): 141–56.

Froula, Christine. 'Modernism, Genetic Texts and Literary Authority in Virginia Woolf's Portraits of the Artist as the Audience'. *The Romanic Review* 86.3 (May 1995): 513–526.

Genette, Gerard. *Paratexts: Thresholds of Interpretation*. Trans. Jane E. Lewin. Cambridge: Cambridge University Press, 1997.

Gillespie, Diane. 'The Texture of the Text: Editing *Roger Fry a Biography*'. In *Editing Virginia Woolf: Interpreting the Modernist Text*, eds James M. Haule and J. H. Stape, 91–113. Basingstoke: Palgrave, 2002.

Haule, James M. 'Virginia Woolf Under a Microscope'. *Woolf Studies Annual* 3 (1997): 143–59.

——. 'Version and Intention in the Novels of Virginia Woolf'. In *Editing Virginia Woolf: Interpreting the Modernist Text*, eds James M. Haule and J. H. Stape, 172–89. Basingstoke: Palgrave, 2002.

Haule, James M. and Philip H. Smith Jr. *A Concordance to The Waves by Virginia Woolf*. Ann Arbor, Michigan University Microfilms International, 1988.

Haule, James M. and J. H. Stape, eds. *Editing Virginia Woolf: Interpreting the Modernist Text*. Basingstoke: Palgrave, 2002.

Hay, Louis. 'Does "Text" Exist?' *Studies in Bibliography* 41 (1988): 64–76.

Hoffman, Charles G. 'From Short Story to Novel: the Manuscript Revisions of Virginia Woolf's *Mrs. Dalloway*'. *Modern Fiction Studies* 14 (Summer 1968): 171–86.

——. 'From Lunch to Dinner: Virginia Woolf's Apprenticeship'. *Texas Studies in Literature and Language* 10 (Fall 1968): 609–27.

——. 'Fact and Fantasy in *Orlando*: Virginia Woolf's Manuscript Revisions'. *Texas Studies in Literature and Language* 10 (Winter 1968): 435–44.

——. 'Virginia Woolf's Manuscript Revisions of *The Years*'. *PMLA* 84 (1969): 79–89.

Hussey, Mark. 'How Should One Read A Screen?' In *Virginia Woolf in the Age of Mechanical Reproduction*, ed. Pamela L. Caughie, 245–65. New York: Garland, 2000.

Kirkpatrick, B. J. and Stuart N. Clarke. *A Bibliography of Virginia Woolf.* 4th edn. Oxford: Clarendon Press, 1997.

Lavin, J. A. 'The First Editions of Virginia Woolf's *To the Lighthouse'. Proof* 2 (1972): 185–211.

McGann, Jerome. *Historical Studies and Literary Criticism.* Madison, WI: University of Wisconsin Press, 1985.

——. *The Textual Condition.* Princeton, NJ: Princeton University Press, 1991.

McKenzie, D. F. *Bibliography and the Sociology of Texts: The Panizzi Lectures, 1985.* London: British Library, 1986.

Moore, Madeline. 'Virginia Woolf's *Orlando*: an Edition of the Manuscript'. *Twentieth Century Literature* 25.3/4 (1979): 303–55.

Novak, Jane. *The Razor Edge of Balance.* Coral Gables: University of Miami Press, 1974.

Radin, Grace. '"Two Enormous Chunks": Episodes Excluded During the Final Revisions of *The Years'. Bulletin of the New York Public Library* 80.2 (1977): 221–51.

——. *Virginia Woolf's The Years: The Evolution of a Novel.* Knoxville, TN: University of Tennessee Press, 1981.

Rhein, Donna E. *The Handprinted Books of Leonard and Virginia Woolf at the Hogarth Press 1917–1932.* Ann Arbor: UMI Research Press, 1985.

Richter, Harvena. *Virginia Woolf: The Inward Voyage.* Princeton, NJ: Princeton University Press, 1970.

Roe, Sue and Susan Sellers, eds. *Cambridge Companion to Virginia Woolf.* Cambridge: Cambridge University Press, 2000.

Scott, Alison M. '"Tantalising Fragments": The Proofs of Virginia Woolf's *Orlando'. Papers of the bibliographical Society of America* 88.3 (1994): 279–351.

Shields, E. F. 'The American Edition of *Mrs. Dalloway'. Studies in Bibliography* 27 (1974): 157–75.

Silver, Brenda R. '"Anon" and "The Reader": Virginia Woolf's Last Essays'. *Twentieth Century Literature* 25.3/4 (1979): 356–441.

——. 'Textual Criticism as Feminist Practice: Or, Who's Afraid of Virginia Woolf Part II'. In *Representing Modernist Texts: Editing as Interpretation.* Ed. George Bornstein, 193–222. Ann Arbor: University of Michigan Press, 1991.

——. *Virginia Woolf Icon.* Chicago, IL: University of Chicago Press, 1999.

——. 'Virginia Woolf: //Hypertext'. In *Virginia Woolf Out of Bounds: Selected Papers from the Tenth Annual Conference on Virginia Woolf.* Eds Jessica Berman and Jane Goldman, 157–64. New York: Pace University Press, 2001.

Snaith, Anna. *Virginia Woolf: Public and Private Negotiations.* Basingstoke: Macmillan, 2000.

Willis, J. H. *Leonard and Virginia Woolf as Publishers: The Hogarth Press 1917–1941.* Charlottesville: University Press of Virginia, 1992.

Woolf, Virginia. *'The Hours': The British Museum Manuscript of Mrs. Dalloway.* Transcribed and ed. Helen M. Wussow. New York: Pace University Press, 1997.

——. *Jacob's Room: The Holograph Draft.* Transcribed and ed. Edward L. Bishop. New York: Pace University Press, 1998.

——. *Melymbrosia by Virginia Woolf: An Early Version of The Voyage Out.* Ed. with intro. Louise A. DeSalvo. Scholar's edition. New York: The New York Public Library, Astor, Lennox and Tilden Foundations, 1982.

——. *Mrs. Dalloway's Party: A Short Story Sequence.* Ed. Stella McNichol. New York: Harcourt Brace Jovanovich, 1973.

——. *Orlando: The Original Holograph Draft*. Transcribed and ed. Stuart Nelson Clarke. London: S. N. Clarke, 1993.

——. *A Passionate Apprentice: The Early Journals, 1897–1909*. Ed. Mitchell A. Leaska. San Diego: Harcourt Brace Jovanovich, 1990.

——. *To The lighthouse: The Original Holograph Draft*. Transcribed and ed. Susan Dick. Toronto and Buffalo: University of Toronto Press, 1982.

——. *The Waves: The Two Holograph Drafts*. Transcribed and ed. J. W. Graham. London: Hogarth Press, 1976.

——. *Women & Fiction: The Manuscript versions of A Room Of One's Own*. Transcribed and ed. S. P. Rosenbaum. Oxford: Shakespeare Head Press, 1992.

Woolmer, Howard. *A Checklist of the Hogarth Press 1917–1946*. With a short history of the press by Mary E. Gaither. Revere, Penn.: Woolmer and Brotherson, 1986.

Wright, Glenn P. 'The Raverat Proofs of *Mrs Dalloway*'. *Studies in Bibliography* 39 (1986): 241–61.

postmodernist and poststructuralist approaches

Arac, Jonathan, ed. *Postmodernism and Politics*. Minneapolis: University of Minnesota Press, 1986.

Attridge, Derek and Daniel Ferrer, eds. *Post-Structuralist Joyce: Essays from the French*. Cambridge: Cambridge University Press, 1984.

Auerbach, Erich. 'The Brown Stocking'. In *Mimesis: The Representation of Reality in Western Literature*. Trans. Willard R. Trask. Princeton, NJ: Princeton University Press, 1953.

Austin, J. L. *How to Do Things with Words*. Eds J. O. Urmson and Marina Sbisà. Cambridge, Mass.: Harvard University Press, 1962.

Barrett, Michèle. *Imagination in Theory: Culture, Writing, Words, and Things*. New York Square, NY: New York University Press, 1999.

Barthes, Roland. *Mythologies*. Trans. Annette Lavers. London: Cape, 1972.

——. *S/Z: An Essay*. Trans. Richard Miller. New York: Hill and Wang, 1974.

——. 'From Work to Text'. In *Image, Music, Text*. Trans. Stephen Heath, 155–64. New York: Hill and Wang, 1977a.

——. 'The Death of the Author'. In *Image, Music, Text*. Trans. Stephen Heath, 142–8. New York: Hill and Wang, 1977b.

Baudrillard, Jean. *Simulations*. Trans. Paul Foss, Paul Patton and Philip Beitchman. New York: Semiotext(e) Inc., 1983.

Belsey, Catherine. *Critical Practice*. London and New York: Methuen, 1980.

Bowlby, Rachel. *Virginia Woolf: Feminist Destinations*. New York: Blackwell, 1988.

Brownstein, Marilyn. 'Postmodern Language and the Perpetuation of Desire'. *Twentieth Century Literature* 31 (1985): 73–88.

Butler, Judith. 'Contingent Foundations: Feminism and the Question of "Postmodernism"'. In *Feminists Theorize the Political*. Eds Judith Butler and Joan W. Scott, 3–21. London: Methuen, 1992.

Caughie, Pamela L. *Virginia Woolf and Postmodernism: Literature in Quest and Question of Itself*. Urbana, IL: University of Illinois Press, 1991.

——. 'Virginia Woolf and Postmodernism: Returning to the Lighthouse'. In *Rereading the New: A Backward Glance at Modernism*. Ed. Kevin J. H. Dettmar. Ann Arbor, MI: University of Michigan Press, 1992.

——. *Passing and Pedagogy: The Dynamics of Responsibility*. Urbana, IL: University of Illinois Press, 1999.

——. 'How Do We Keep Desire from Passing with Beauty?' *Tulsa Studies in Women's Literature* 19.2 (2000): 269–84.

——, ed. 'Virginia Woolf, Intellectual History, and 1920s British *Vogue*'. In *Virginia Woolf in the Age of Mechanical Reproduction*. New York and London: Garland 2000.

——. 'Returning to the Lighthouse: A Postmodern Approach'. In *Approaches to Teaching Woolf's* To the Lighthouse. Eds Beth Rigel Daugherty and Mary Beth Pringle, 47–53. New York: Modern Language Association, 2001.

Culler, Jonathan. *On Deconstruction: Theory and Criticism after Structuralism*. Ithaca, NY: Cornell University Press, 1982.

——. *Literary Theory: A Very Short Introduction*. Oxford: Oxford University Press, 1997.

Dalgarno, Emily. *Virginia Woolf and the Visible World*. Cambridge: Cambridge University Press, 2001.

Daugherty, Beth Rigel. 'Face to Face with "Ourselves" in Virginia Woolf's *Between the Acts*'. In *Virginia Woolf: Themes and Variations*. Eds Vara Neverow-Turk and Mark Hussey, 76–82. New York: Pace University Press, 1993.

Derrida, Jacques. *Of Grammatology*. Trans. Gayatri Chakravorty Spivak. Baltimore, MD: Johns Hopkins University Press, 1976.

——. 'Structure, Sign and Play in the Discourse of the Human Sciences'. *Writing and Difference*. Trans. Alan Bass, 278–82. London: Routledge, 1978.

——. *The Illicit Joy of Postmodernism*. Madison, WI: University of Wisconsin Press, 1996.

——. 'But, beyond...(Open Letter to Anne McClintock and Rob Nixon)'. Trans. Peggy Kamuf. *Critical Inquiry* 13 (Autumn 1986): 155–70.

——. 'Signature, Event, Context'. In *Limited, INC*. Evanston, Il: Northwestern University Press, 1988.

Dettmar, Kevin J. H., ed. *Rereading the New: A Backward Glance at Modernism*. Ann Arbor, MI: University of Michigan Press, 1992.

Dreyfus, Hubert L. and Paul Rabinow, eds. *Michel Foucault: Beyond Structuralism and Hermeneutics*. Chicago: IL, University of Chicago Press, 1979.

Emig, Rainer. *W.H. Auden: Towards a Postmodern Poetics*. New York: Macmillan, 2000.

Ferrer, Daniel. *Virginia Woolf and the Madness of Language*. Trans. Geoffrey Bennington and Rachel Bowlby. London: Routledge, 1990.

Ferriss, Suzanne. 'Unclothing Gender: The Postmodern Sensibility in Sally Potter's *Orlando*'. *Literature/Film Quarterly* 27.2 (1999): 110–15.

Fish, Stanley. *Professional Correctness: Literary Studies and Political Change*. Cambridge, Mass. and London: Harvard University Press, 1995.

——. 'Condemnation without Absolutes', *The New York Times*. 15 October, 2001: A23.

Foucault, Michel. *The Order of Things: An Archeology of the Human Sciences*. Trans. Alan Sheridan. New York: Random House, 1970.

——. 'Nietzsche, Genealogy, History'. In *The Foucault Reader*. Ed. Paul Rabinow, 76–100. New York: Pantheon Books, 1984.

——. 'The Subject and Power'. In *Michel Foucault: Beyond Structuralism and Hermeneutics*. Eds Hubert L. Dreyfus and Paul Rabinow, 212–16. Chicago, IL: University of Chicago Press, 1979.

——. 'What is an Author?' In *The Foucault Reader*, 101–20.

Garrett, Roberta. 'Costume Drama and Counter Memory: Sally Potter's *Orlando*'. In *Postmodern Subjects/Postmodern Texts*. Eds Jane Dowson and Steven Earnshaw, 89–99. Amsterdam and Atlanta: Rodopi, 1995.

Garrity, Jane. 'Selling Culture to the "Civilized": Bloomsbury, British *Vogue*, and the Marketing of National Identity'. *Modernism/modernity* 6 (1999): 29–58.

Hassan, Ihab. *Paracriticisms*. Urbana, IL: University of Illinois Press, 1975.

Hite, Molly. 'Virginia Woolf's Two Bodies'. *Genders* 31 (2000).

Hutcheon, Linda. *A Poetics of Postmodernism: History, Theory, Fiction*. New York: Routledge, 1988.

Jameson, Fredric. *Postmodernism, or the Cultural Logic of Late Capitalism*. Durham, NC: Duke University Press, 2001.

Jencks, Charles. *What is Post-Modernism?* 3rd. edn. New York: St Martin's Press, 1989.

Johnson, Barbara. 'Teaching Ignorance: *L'Ecole des femmes*'. In *A World of Difference*, 68–85. Baltimore, MD: Johns Hopkins University Press, 1987.

——. 'Writing'. In *Critical Terms for Literary Study*. Eds Frank Lentricchia and Thomas McLaughlin, 39–49. Chicago, IL: University of Chicago Press, 1990.

Kamuf, Peggy. 'Penelope at Work: Interruptions in *A Room of One's Own*'. *Novel: A Forum on Fiction* 16 (1982): 5–18.

Kiely, Robert. *Modernism Reconsidered*. Cambridge, Mass. and London: Harvard University Press, 1983.

Kime Scott, Bonnie. *Refiguring Modernism*. Vol. 2. *Postmodern Feminist Readings of Woolf, West, and Barnes*. Bloomington, IN: Indiana University Press, 1995.

Kristeva, Julia. *Revolution in Poetic Language*. Trans. Margaret Waller. New York: Columbia University Press, 1984.

Lacan, Jacques. 'The Insistence of the Letter in the Unconscious'. In *The Structuralists: From Marx to Lévi-Strauss*. Eds Richard T. and Fernande M. De George. Garden City, NY: Anchor Books, 1972.

Levin, Harry. 'What was Modernism'. In *Refractions: Essays in Comparative Literature*. New York: Oxford University Press, 1966.

Lyotard, Jean-François. *The Postmodern Condition: A Report on Knowledge*. Trans. Geoff Bennington and Brian Massumi. Minneapolis: University of Minnesota Press, 1984.

Michael, Magali Cornier. 'Woolf's *Between the Acts* and Lessing's *The Golden Notebook*: From Modern to Postmodern Subjectivity'. In *Woolf and Lessing: Breaking the Mold*. Eds Ruth Saxton and Jean Tobin, 39–56. Basingstoke: Macmillan, 1994.

Minow-Pinkney, Makiko. *Virginia Woolf and the Problem of the Subject*. Brighton: Harvester, 1987.

Moi, Toril, ed. *Sexual/Textual Politics: Feminist Literary Theory*. New York: Methuen, 1985.

——. *The Kristeva Reader*. New York: Columbia University Press, 1986.

Nealon, Jeffrey. *Double Reading: Postmodernism after Deconstruction*. Ithaca, NY: Cornell University Press, 1993.

Orr, Leonard, ed. *Yeats and Postmodernism*. Syracuse, NY: Syracuse University Press, 1991.

Rivkin, Julie and Michael Ryan, eds. *Literary Theory: An Anthology*. Malden, MA: Blackwell, 1998.

Rosenberg, Beth Carole. 'Virginia Woolf's Postmodern Literary History'. *MLN* 115 (2000): 1112–30.

Saussure, Ferdinand de. *Course in General Linguistics*, 3rd edn. Trans. Wade Baskin. Eds Charles Bally and Albert Sechehaye. New York: McGraw Hill, 1976.

Scarry, Elaine. *On Beauty and Being Just*. Princeton, NJ: Princeton University Press, 1999.

Silver, Brenda R. *Virginia Woolf Icon*. Chicago, IL: University of Chicago Press, 1999.

Skoller, Eleanor Honig. *The In-Between of Writing: Experience and Experiment in Drabble, Duras and Arendt*. Ann Arbor, MI: University of Michigan Press, 1993.

Spivak, Gayatri Chakravorty. 'Unmaking and Making in *To the Lighthouse*'. In *In Other Worlds: Essays in Cultural Politics*, 30–45. New York: Routledge, 1988.

Waugh, Patricia. *Feminine Fictions: Revisiting the Postmodern*. London: Routledge, 1989.

——. *Practicing Postmodernism: Reading Modernism*. London: Edward Arnold, 1992.

Wicke, Jennifer. '*Mrs. Dalloway* Goes to Market: Woolf, Keynes, and Modern Markets'. *Novel: A Forum on Fiction* 28 (1994): 5–23.

Wittgenstein, Ludwig. *Philosophical Investigations*. Trans. G. E. M. Anscombe. New York: Macmillan, 1953.

——. *The Blue and Brown Books*. New York: Harper & Row, 1965.

historical approaches

Beer, Gillian. *Virginia Woolf: The Common Ground*. Edinburgh: Edinburgh University Press, 1996.

Bradshaw, David. 'Hyams Place: *The Years*, the Jews and the British Union of Fascists'. In *Women Writers of the 1930s: Gender, Politics and History*. Ed. Maroula Joannou, 179–91. Edinburgh: Edinburgh University Press, 1999.

Brannigan, John. *New Historicism and Cultural Materialism*. Basingstoke: Macmillan, 1998.

Chapman, Wayne K. and Janet M. Manson, eds. *Women in the Milieu of Leonard and Virginia Woolf: Peace, Politics and Education*. Lanham: University Press of America, 1998.

Colebrook, Claire. *New Literary Histories: New Historicism and Contemporary Criticism*. Manchester: Manchester University Press, 1997.

Cramer, Patricia. '"Loving in the War Years": The War of Images in *The Years*'. In *Virginia Woolf and War: Fiction, Reality and Myth*. Ed. Mark Hussey, 203–24. Syracuse, NY: Syracuse University Press, 1991.

Dollimore, Jonathan. *Radical Tragedy: Religion, Ideology and Power in the Drama of Shakespeare and his Contemporaries*. Chicago, IL: Chicago University Press, 1984.

Foucault, Michel. *The History of Sexuality, Volume 1: An Introduction*. Trans. R. Hurley. London: Penguin, 1981.

Green, Barbara. *Spectacular Confessions: Autobiography, Performative Activism and the Sites of Suffrage 1905–1938*. New York: St Martin's University Press, 1997.

Greenblatt, Stephen. *Shakespearian Negotiations: The Circulation of Social Energy in Renaissance England*. Oxford: Oxford University Press, 1988.

——. 'Towards a Poetics of Culture'. In *The New Historicism*. Ed. H. Aram Veeser. London and New York: Routledge, 1989.

Lee, Hermione. *Virginia Woolf*. London: Chatto and Windus, 1996.

Levenback, Karen L. *Virginia Woolf and the Great War*. Syracuse, NY: Syracuse University Press, 1999.

Marcus, Jane, ed. *Virginia Woolf: A Feminist Slant*. Lincoln: University of Nebraska Press, 1984.

——. *Art and Anger*. Columbus: Ohio State University Press, 1988.

Pawlowski, Merry. *Resisting the Dictator's Seduction: Virginia Woolf and Fascism*. Basingstoke: Macmillan, 2001.

Peach, Linden. *Virginia Woolf*. Basingstoke: Macmillan, 2000.

Phillips, Kathy. *Woolf Against Empire*. Knoxville, TN: University of Tennessee Press, 1994.

Silver, Brenda. *Virginia Woolf Icon*. Chicago, IL: Chicago University Press, 1999.

Sinfield, Alan. *Faultlines: Cultural Materialism and the Politics of Dissident Reading*. Oxford: Oxford University Press, 1992.

Snaith, Anna. *Virginia Woolf: Public and Private Negotiations*. Basingstoke: Macmillan, 2000.

Squier, Susan M. *Virginia Woolf and London: The Sexual Politics of the City*. Chapel Hill: University of North Carolina Press, 1985.

Tate, Trudi. '*Mrs Dalloway* and the Armenian Question'. *Textual Practice* 8.3 (1994): 467–86.

Tratner, Michael. *Modernism and Mass Politics: Joyce, Woolf, Eliot and Yeats*. Stanford, CA: Stanford University Press, 1996.

Usui, Masami. 'The Female Victims of the War in *Mrs Dalloway*'. In *Virginia Woolf and War: Fiction, Reality and Myth*. Ed. Mark Hussey, 151–63. Syracuse, NY: Syracuse University Press, 1991.

Williams, Lisa. *The Artist as Outsider in the Novels of Toni Morrison and Virginia Woolf*. Westport, Connecticut and London: Greenwood Press, 2000.

Wussow, Helen. 'War and Conflict in *The Voyage Out*'. In *Virginia Woolf and War: Fiction, Reality and Myth*. Ed. Mark Hussey, 101–9. Syracuse, NY: Syracuse University Press, 1991.

Zwerdling, Alex. *Virginia Woolf and the Real World*. London and Los Angeles: University of California Press, 1986.

lesbian approaches

Abraham, Julie. *Are Girls Necessary? Lesbian Writing and Modern Histories*. New York: Routledge, 1996.

Allan, Tuzyline Jita. 'The Death of Sex and the Soul in *Mrs. Dalloway* and Nella Larsen's *Passing*'. In *Virginia Woolf: Lesbian Readings*. Eds Eileen Barrett and Patricia Cramer, 95–113. New York: New York University Press, 1997.

Barrett, Eileen. Introduction to Part One, *Virginia Woolf: Lesbian Readings*. Eds Eileen Barrett and Patricia Cramer, 3–9. New York: New York University Press, 1997a.

——. 'Unmasking Lesbian Passion: The Inverted World of *Mrs. Dalloway*'. In *Virginia Woolf: Lesbian Readings*. Eds Eileen Barrett and Patricia Cramer, 146–64. New York: New York University Press, 1997b.

——. 'Response to Papers by Judith Roof and Troy Gordon'. In *Virginia Woolf: Turning the Centuries: Selected Papers from the Ninth Annual Conference on Virginia Woolf*. Eds Ann Ardis and Bonnie Kime Scott, 111–16. New York: Pace University Press, 2000.

Barrett, Eileen and Patricia Cramer, eds. *Virginia Woolf: Lesbian Readings*. New York: New York University Press, 1997.

Bell, Quentin. *Virginia Woolf: A Biography*. 2 vols. New York: Harcourt Brace Jovanovich, 1972.

Blackmer, Corinne E. 'Lesbian Modernism in the Shorter Fiction of Virginia Woolf and Gertrude Stein'. In *Virginia Woolf: Lesbian Readings*. Eds Eileen Barrett and Patricia Cramer, 78–94. New York: New York University Press, 1997.

Cook, Blanche Wiesen. '"Women Alone Stir My Imagination": Lesbianism and the Cultural Tradition'. *Signs* 4.4 (1979): 718–39.

Cramer, Patricia. 'Notes from Underground: Lesbian Ritual in the Writings of Virginia Woolf'. In *Virginia Woolf Miscellanies: Proceedings of the First Annual Conference on*

Virginia Woolf. Eds Mark Hussey and Vara Neverow-Turk, 177–88. New York: Pace University Press, 1992.

——. 'Response'. In *Virginia Woolf: Turning the Centuries: Selected Papers from the Ninth Annual Conference on Virginia Woolf.* Eds Ann Ardis and Bonnie Kime Scott, 116–26. New York: Pace University Press, 2000.

DeSalvo, Louise A. 'Lighting the Cave: The Relationship between Vita Sackville-West and Virginia Woolf'. *Signs* 8.2 (1982): 195–214.

Eberly, David. 'Talking It All Out: Homosexual Disclosure in Woolf'. In *Virginia Woolf: Themes and Variations.* Eds Vara Neverow-Turk and Mark Hussey, 128–34. New York: Pace University Press, 1993.

Fausto-Sterling, Anne. *Myths of Gender: Biological Theories About Women and Men.* New York: Basic Books, 1992.

——. *Sexing the Body: Gender Politics and the Construction of Sexuality.* New York: Basic Books, 2000.

Gordon, Troy. 'The Place of Cross-Sex Friendship in Woolf Studies'. In *Virginia Woolf: Turning the Centuries: Selected Papers from the Ninth Annual Conference on Virginia Woolf.* Eds Ann Ardis and Bonnie Kime Scott, 102–11. New York: Pace University Press, 2000.

Hall, Radclyffe. *The Well of Loneliness.* Paris: Pegasus, 1928.

Hankins, Leslie Kathleen. '"A Precipice Marked V": Between "A Miracle of Discretion" and "Lovemaking Unbelievable: Indiscretions Incredible"'. In *Virginia Woolf: Lesbian Readings.* Eds Eileen Barrett and Patricia Cramer, 180–202. New York: New York University Press, 1997.

Henke, Suzette. '*Mrs. Dalloway*: The Communion of Saints'. In *New Feminist Essays on Virginia Woolf.* Ed. Jane Marcus, 125–47. Lincoln: University of Nebraska Press, 1981.

Hussey, Mark. 'Refractions of Desire: The Early Fiction of Virginia and Leonard Woolf'. *Modern Fiction Studies* 38.1 (1992): 127–46.

Jensen, Emily. 'Clarissa Dalloway's Respectable Suicide'. In *Virginia Woolf: A Feminist Slant.* Ed. Jane Marcus, 162–79, 1983.

Jones, Danell. 'The Chase of the Wild Goose: The Ladies of Llangollen and *Orlando*'. In *Virginia Woolf: Themes and Variations. Selected Papers from the Second Annual Conference on Virginia Woolf.* Eds Vara Neverow-Turk and Mark Hussey, 181–9. New York: Pace University Press, 1993.

Kaivola, Karen. 'Virginia Woolf, Vita Sackville-West, and the Questions of Sexual Identity'. *Woolf Studies Annual* 4 (1998): 17–40.

Kennard, Jean. 'From Foe to Friend: Woolf's Changing View of the Male Homosexual'. *Woolf Studies Annual* 4 (1998): 67–85.

King, James. *Virginia Woolf.* London: Hamish Hamilton, 1994.

Knopp, Sherron E. '"If I saw you would you kiss me?": Sapphism and the subversiveness of Virginia Woolf's *Orlando*'. *PMLA* 103 (1988): 24–34.

Lee, Hermione. *Virginia Woolf.* New York: Random House and Vintage Books, 1996.

Levy, Heather. '"Julia Kissed Her, Julia Possessed Her": Considering Class and Lesbian Desire in Virginia Woolf's Shorter Fiction'. In *Virginia Woolf: Emerging Perspectives.* Eds Mark Hussey and Vara Neverow, 83–90. New York: Pace University Press, 1994.

Lilienfeld, Jane. '"The Gift of a China Inkpot": Violet Dickinson, Virginia Woolf, Elizabeth Gaskell, Charlotte Brontë, and the Love of Women in Writing'. In *Virginia Woolf: Lesbian Readings.* Eds Eileen Barrett and Patricia Cramer, 37–56. New York: New York University Press, 1997.

Marcus, Jane. 'Sapphistry: Narration as Lesbian Seduction in *A Room of One's Own*'. In *Virginia Woolf and the Languages of Patriarchy*, 163–87. Bloomington, IN: Indiana University Press, 1987.

McNaron, Toni A. H. '"The Albanians, or Was it the Armenians?": Virginia Woolf's Lesbianism as Gloss on her Modernism'. In *Virginia Woolf: Themes and Variations*. Eds Vara Neverow-Turk and Mark Hussey, 134–41. New York: Pace University Press, 1993.

Meese, Elizabeth. *(Sem)erotics: Theorizing Lesbian: Writing*. New York: New York University Press, 1992.

Olano, Pamela J. '"Women Alone Stir My Imagination": Reading Virginia Woolf as a Lesbian'. In *Virginia Woolf: Themes and Variations*. Eds Vara Neverow-Turk and Mark Hussey, 158–71. New York: Pace University Press, 1993.

Oxindine, Annette. 'Sapphist Semiotics in Woolf's *The Waves*: Untelling and Retelling What Cannot Be Told'. In *Virginia Woolf: Themes and Variations*. Eds Vara Neverow-Turk and Mark Hussey, 171–81. New York: Pace University Press, 1993.

Raitt, Suzanne. *Vita and Virginia: The Work and Friendship of V. Sackville-West and Virginia Woolf*. Oxford: Oxford University Press, 1993.

Risolo, Donna. 'Outing Mrs. Ramsay: Reading the Lesbian Subtext in Virginia Woolf's *To The Lighthouse*'. In *Virginia Woolf: Themes and Variations*. Eds Vara Neverow-Turk and Mark Hussey, 238–48. New York: Pace University Press, 1993.

Roof, Judith. 'The Match in the Crocus: Representations of Lesbian Sexuality'. In *Discontented Discourses: Feminism/Textual Intervention/Psychoanalysis*. Eds Marleen Barr and Richard Feldstein, 100–16. Urbana, Illinois: University of Illinois Press, 1989.

——. *A Lure of Knowledge: Lesbian Sexuality and Theory*. New York: Columbia University Press, 1991.

——. 'Hocus Crocus'. In *Virginia Woolf: Turning the Centuries*. Eds Ann Ardis and Bonnie Kime Scott, 93–102. New York: Pace University Press, 2000.

Rosenman, Ellen Bayuk. 'Sexual Identity and *A Room of One's Own*: "Secret Economies" in Virginia Woolf's Feminist Discourse'. *Signs* 14.3 (1989): 634–50.

Sackville-West, Vita. *Knole and the Sackvilles*. London: Heinemann, 1922.

Sears, Sally. 'Notes on Sexuality: *The Years* and *Three Guineas*'. *Bulletin of the New York Public Library* 80.2 (1977): 211–20.

Smith, Patricia Juliana. *Lesbian Panic: Homoeroticism in Modern British Women's Fiction*. New York: Columbia University Press, 1997.

Trautmann, Joanne. *The Jessamy Brides: The Friendship of Virginia Woolf and V. Sackville-West*. University Park: Pennsylvania State University Press, 1973.

Tvordi, Jessica. '*The Voyage Out*: Virginia Woolf's First Lesbian Novel'. In *Virginia Woolf: Themes and Variations*. Eds Vara Neverow-Turk and Mark Hussey, 226–37. New York: Pace University Press, 1993.

Vanita, Ruth. 'Love Unspeakable: The Uses of Allusion in *Flush*'. In *Virginia Woolf: Themes and Variations*. Eds Vara Neverow-Turk and Mark Hussey, 248–57. New York: Pace University Press, 1993.

——. *Sappho and the Virgin Mary: Same-Sex Love and the English Literary Imagination*. New York: Columbia University Press, 1996.

Wachman, Gay. *Lesbian Empire: Radical Crosswriting in the Twenties*. New Brunswick, NJ: Rutgers University Press, 2001.

Winston, Janet. 'Reading Influences: Homoeroticism and Mentoring in Katherine Mansfield's "Carnation" and Virginia Woolf's "Moments of Being: Slater's Pins

Have No Points"'. In *Virginia Woolf: Lesbian Readings*. Eds Eileen Barrett and Patricia Cramer, 57–77. New York: New York University Press, 1997.

Wolff, Charlotte. *Love Between Women*. London: Duckworth, 1971.

Zimmerman, Bonnie. 'Is "Chloe Likes Olivia" a Lesbian Plot?'. *Women's Studies International Forum* 6.2 (1983): 169–75.

postcolonial approaches

Adams, David. *Colonial Odysseys: Empire and Epic in the Modernist Novel*. Ithaca and London: Cornell University Press, 2003.

Anzaldua, Gloria. *Borderlands/La Frontera: the New Mestiza*. San Francisco: Aunt Lute, 1987.

Ashcroft, Bill, Gareth Griffiths and Helen Tiffin, eds. *The Empire Writes Back: Theory and practice in post-colonial literatures*. London and New York: Routledge, 1989.

——, eds. *The Post-Colonial Studies Reader*. London and New York: Routledge, 1995.

Beer, Gillian. 'The island and the Aeroplane: the case of Virginia Woolf'. In *Nation and Narration*. Ed. Homi K. Bhabha, 265–90. London and New York: Routledge, 1990.

Benstock, Shari. *Women of the Left Bank*. Austin: University of Texas Press, 1986.

Bhabha, Homi K., ed. *Nation and Narration*. London and New York: Routledge, 1994.

——. *The Location of Culture*. London and New York: Routledge, 1994.

Boehmer, Elleke. *Empire, the National, and the Postcolonial, 1890–1920: Resistance in Interaction*. Oxford: Oxford University Press, 2002.

Booth, Howard J. and Nigel Rigby, eds. *Modernism and Empire*. Manchester and New York: Manchester University Press, 2000.

Brantlinger, Patrick. *Rule of Darkness: British Literature and Imperialism, 1830–1914*. Ithaca and London: Cornell University Press, 1988.

Caughie, Pamela. 'Purpose and Play in Woolf's *London Scene* Essays'. *Women's Studies* 16 (1989): 389–408.

Cliff, Michelle. 'Virginia Woolf and the Imperial Gaze: A Glance Askance'. In *Virginia Woolf: Emerging Perspectives: Selected Papers from the Third Annual Conference on Virginia Woolf*. Eds Mark Hussey and Vara Neverow, 91–102. New York: Pace University Press, 1994.

Cohen, Scott. 'The Empire from the Street: Virginia Woolf, Wembley, and Imperial Monuments'. *Modern Fiction Studies* 50.1 (2004): 85–109.

Cuddy-Keane, Melba. *Virginia Woolf, The Intellectual, and the Public Sphere*. Cambridge: Cambridge University Press, 2003.

DeKoven, Marianne. *Rich and Strange: Gender, History, Modernism*. Princeton, NJ: Princeton University Press, 1991.

Doyle, Laura. *Bordering on the Body: The Racial Matrix of Modern Fiction and Culture*. New York: Oxford University Press, 1994.

——. 'Sublime Barbarians in the Narrative of Empire; Or, Longinus at Sea in *The Waves*'. *Modern Fiction Studies* 42.2 (1996): 323–47.

——. 'Introduction: What's Between Us?' *Modern Fiction Studies* 50.1 (2004): 1–7.

Esty, Jed. *A Shrinking Island: Modernism and National Culture in England*. Princeton, NJ: Princeton University Press, 2004.

Fanon, Frantz. *Black Skin, White Masks*. Trans. Charles Lam Markmann. New York: Grove Press, 1967 (Orig. pub. 1952 in French).

——. *The Wretched of the Earth*. Trans. Catherine Farrington. New York: Grove Press, 1968 (Orig. pub. 1951 in French).

Friedman, Susan Stanford. *Mappings: Feminism and the Cultural Geographies of Encounter*. Princeton, NJ: Princeton University Press, 1998.

Gaipa, Mark. 'When All Roads Lead to Empire'. Review of Kathy J. Phillips' *Virginia Woolf Against Empire*. *English Literature in Transition* 39.1 (1996): 199–223.

Gandhi, Mahatma. 'Hind Swaraj or Indian Home Rule'. Ahmedabad: Navjivan, 1938. Quoted in Prakash, 'Introduction: After Colonialism'. In *After Colonialism*. Ed. Gyan Prakash. Princeton, NJ: Princeton University Press, 1995.

Garrity, Jane. *Step-Daughters of England: British Women Modernists and the National Imaginary*. Manchester: Manchester University Press and New York: Palgrave, 2003.

Gikandi, Simon. *Maps of Englishness: Writing Identity in the Culture of Colonialism*. New York: Columbia University Press, 1996.

Goldman, Jane. *The Feminist Aesthetics of Virginia Woolf: Modernism, Post-Impressionism, and the Politics of the Visual*. Cambridge: Cambridge University Press, 1998.

Hackett, Robin. *Sapphic Primitivism: Productions of Race, Class, and Sexuality in Key Works of Modern Fiction*. New Brunswick, NJ: Rutgers University Press, 2004.

Hankins, Leslie Kathleen. 'Virginia Woolf and Walter Benjamin Selling Out(siders)'. In *Virginia Woolf in the Age of Mechanical Reproduction*. Ed. Pamela Caughie. New York: Garland, 2000, 3–35.

Henke, Suzette. 'De/Colonizing the Subject in Virginia Woolf's *The Voyage Out*: Rachel Vinrace as *La Mysterique*'. In *Virginia Woolf: Emerging Perspectives: Selected Papers from the Third Annual Conference on Virginia Woolf*. Eds Mark Hussey and Vara Neverow, 103–8. New York: Pace University Press, 1994.

Hutcheon, Linda. 'Introduction: Colonialism and the Postcolonial Condition: Complexities Abounding'. *PMLA* 110.1 (1995): 7–16.

Jacobs, Karen. *The Eye's Mind: Literary Modernism and Visual Culture*. Ithaca, NY: Cornell University Press, 2000.

Jones, Ellen Carol. 'Writing the Modern: The Politics of Modernism'. *Modern Fiction Studies* 38.3 (Autumn 1992). Special issue on 'The Politics of Modernist Form'. Ed. E. C. Jones, 549–63.

Kaplan, Caren. 'The Politics of Location as Transnational Feminist Practice'. In *Scattered Hegemonies: Postmodernity and Transnational Feminist Practices*. Eds Inderpal Grewel and Caren Kaplan, 117–52. Minneapolis: University of Minnesota Press, 1994.

——. *Questions of Travel: Postmodern Discourses of Displacement*. Durham, NC: Duke University Press, 1996.

Kennedy, Jennifer. Review of *Virginia Woolf Against Empire* by Kathy J. Phillips. *Modernism/Modernity* 3.2 (1996): 123–4.

Larsen, Neil. *Modernism and Hegemony*. Minneapolis: University of Minnesota Press, 1990.

Laurence, Patricia. *Lily Briscoe's Chinese Eyes: Bloomsbury, Modernism, and China*. Columbia: University of South Carolina Press, 2003.

Lawrence, Karen R., ed. *Decolonizing Tradition: New Views of Twentieth-Century 'British' Literary Canons*. Urbana and Chicago: University of Illinois Press, 1992.

——. 'Woolf's Voyages Out: *The Voyage Out* and *Orlando*'. In *Penelope Voyages: Women and Travel in the British Literary Tradition*, 151–206. Ithaca and London: Cornell University Press, 1994.

Leontis, Artemis. *Topographies of Hellenism: Mapping the Homeland*. Ithaca and London: Cornell University Press, 1995.

Lewis, Andrea. 'The Visual Politics of Empire and Gender in Virginia Woolf's *The Voyage Out*'. *Woolf Studies Annual* 1 (1995): 106–19.

Loomba, Ania. *Colonialism/Postcolonialism*. London and New York: Routledge, 1998.
Lorde, Audre. *Sister Outsider: Essays and Speeches*. Trumansburg: Crossing Press, 1984.
Marcus, Jane. 'Britannia Rules *The Waves*'. In *Decolonizing Tradition: New Views of Twentieth-Century 'British' Literary Canons*. Ed. Karen R. Lawrence, 136–62. Urbana and Chicago: University of Illinois Press, 1992.
——. *Hearts of Darkness: White Women Write Race*. New Brunswick, NJ: Rutgers University Press, 2004a.
——. 'A Very Fine Negress'. In *Hearts of Darkness: White Women Write Race*, 24–58. New Brunswick, NJ: Rutgers University Press, 2004b.
——. 'The Empire is Written'. In *Hearts of Darkness: White Women Write Race*, 1–23. New Brunswick, NJ: Rutgers University Press, 2004c.
McClintock, Anne. 'The Angel of Progress: Pitfalls of the Term "Post-colonialism"', *Social Text* (1992): 1–15. Excerpted in *Colonial Discourse and Post-Colonial Theory: A Reader*. Eds Patrick Williams and Laura Chrisman, 291–304. New York: Columbia University Press, 1994.
McGee, Patrick. *Telling the Other: The Question of Value in Modern and Postcolonial Writing*. Ithaca, NY: Cornell University Press, 1992.
——. 'The Politics of Modernist Form: or, Who Rules *The Waves*?' *Modern Fiction Studies* 38.3 (1992): 631–50.
McVicker, Jeanette. 'Vast Nests of Chinese Boxes, or Getting from Q to R: Critiquing Empire in "Kew Gardens" and *To the Lighthouse*'. In *Virginia Woolf Miscellanies: Proceedings of the First Annual Conference on Virginia Woolf*. Eds Mark Hussey and Vara Neverow-Turk, 40–2. New York: Pace University Press, 1992.
——. 'Reading *To the Lighthouse* as a Critique of the Imperial'. In *Approaches to Teaching Woolf's To the Lighthouse*. Eds Beth Rigel Daugherty and Mary Beth Pringle, 97–104. New York: The Modern Language Association of America, 2001.
——. '"Six Essays on London Life": A History of Dispersal'. Part One in *Woolf Studies Annual* 9 (2003): 143–65; Part Two in *Woolf Studies Annual* 10 (2004): 141–72.
Midgley, Clare, ed. *Gender and Imperialism*. Manchester and New York: Manchester University Press, 1998.
Minh-ha, Trinh T. *Woman, Native, Other*. Bloomington, IN: Indiana University Press, 1989.
Mishra, Vijay and Bob Hodge. 'What is Post(-)colonialism?' *Textual Practice* 5. 3 (1991): 399–414. Excerpted in *Colonial Discourse and Post-Colonial Theory: A Reader*. Eds Patrick Williams and Laura Chrisman, 276–90. New York: Columbia University Press, 1994.
Mohanty, Satya P. 'Colonial Legacies, Multicultural Futures: Relativism, Objectivity, and the Challenge of Otherness'. *PMLA* 110.1 (1995): 108–18.
Phillips, Kathy J. 'Woolf's Criticism of the British Empire in *The Years*'. In *Virginia Woolf Miscellanies: Proceedings of the First Annual Conference on Virginia Woolf*. Eds Mark Hussey and Vara Neverow-Turk, 30–1. New York: Pace University Press, 1992.
——. *Virginia Woolf Against Empire*. Knoxville, TN: University of Tennessee Press, 1994.
Prakash, Gyan. 'Introduction: After Colonialism'. In *After Colonialism*. Ed. Gyan Prakash, 3–17. Princeton, NJ: Princeton University Press, 1995.
——, ed. *After Colonialism*. Princeton, NJ: Princeton University Press, 1995.
Rich, Adrienne. 'Notes Toward a Politics of Location'. In *Blood, Bread and Poetry: Selected Prose, 1979–1985*. New York: Norton, 1986.
Rigby, Nigel. '"Not a good place for deacons": the South Seas, sexuality and modernism in Sylvia Townsend Warner's *Mr. Fortune's Maggot*'. In *Modernism and empire*. Eds

Howard J. Booth and Nigel Rigby, 224–48. Manchester and New York: Manchester University Press, 2000.

Said, Edward W. *Orientalism*. New York: Vintage, 1978.

——. *Culture and Imperialism*. New York: Alfred A. Knopf, 1993.

Sarker, Sonita. 'Three Guineas, the In-Corporated Intellectual and Nostalgia for the Human'. In *Virginia Woolf in the Age of Mechanical Reproduction*. Ed. Pamela Caughie, 37–66. New York: Garland, 2000.

——. 'Locating a Native Englishness in Virginia Woolf's *The London Scene*'. *NWSA Journal* 13.2 (2001): 1–30.

Scott, Bonnie Kime, ed. *The Gender of Modernism*. Bloomington, IN: Indiana University Press, 1990.

Seshagiri, Urmila. 'Orienting Virginia Woolf: Race, Aesthetics, and Politics in *To the Lighthouse*'. *Modern Fiction Studies* 50.1 (2004): 58–83.

Sharpe, Jenny. *Allegories of Empire: The Figure of the Woman in the Colonial Text*. Minneapolis: University of Minnesota Press, 1993.

Spivak, Gayatri Chakravorty. *The Post-Colonial Critic: Interviews, Strategies, Dialogues*. Ed. Sarah Harasym. New York and London: Routledge, 1990.

——. 'The Rani of Sirmur'. In *Europe and Its Others*. Eds Francis Barker et. al. 2 vols. Vol. 1: 128–51. Colchester: University of Essex Press, 1985. (Quoted in Young, 1990.)

Squier, Susan Merrill. *Virginia Woolf and London: The Sexual Politics of the City*. Durham, NC: University of North Carolina Press, 1985.

Tambling, Jeremy. 'Repression in Mrs Dalloway's London'. *Essays in Criticism* 39.2 (1989): 137–55.

Whitworth, Michael. 'Virginia Woolf and Modernism'. In *The Cambridge Companion to Virginia Woolf*. Eds Sue Roe and Susan Sellers, 146–63. Cambridge: Cambridge University Press, 2000.

Williams, Patrick. '"Simultaneous uncontemporaneities": theorising modernism and empire'. In *Modernism and Empire*. Eds Howard J. Booth and Nigel Rigby, 13–38. Manchester and New York: Manchester University Press, 2000.

Williams, Patrick and Laura Chrisman, eds. *Colonial Discourse and Post-Colonial Theory: A Reader*. New York: Columbia University Press, 1994.

Winston, Janet. '"Something Out of Harmony": To the Lighthouse and the Subject(s) of Empire'. *Woolf Studies Annual* 2 (1996): 39–70.

Wollaeger, Mark. 'Woolf, Postcards, and the Elision of Race: Colonizing Women in *The Voyage Out*'. *Modernism/Modernity* 8.1 (2001): 43–75.

Young, Robert. *White Mythologies: Writing History and the West*. New York and London: Routledge, 1990.

european reception studies

Abranches, Graça. 'The Portuguese Reception of Virginia Woolf'. In *The European Reception of Virginia Woolf*. Eds Mary Ann Caws and Nicola Luckhurst, 312–27. London: Continuum, 2002.

Beer, Gillian. '*Between the Acts*: Resisting the End'. *Virginia Woolf: The Common Ground*. Ann Arbor, MI: University of Michigan Press, 1996.

Bowlby, Rachel. *Feminist Destinations and Other Essays on Virginia Woolf*. Edinburgh: Edinburgh University Press, 1997.

Bradshaw, David. 'The socio-political vision of the novels'. In *The Cambridge Companion to Virginia Woolf*. Eds Sue Roe and Susan Sellers, 191–208. Cambridge: Cambridge University Press, 2000.

Briggs, Julia, ed. *Virginia Woolf: Introduction to the Major Works*. London: Virago, 1994.

Caws, Mary Ann. 'A Virginia Woolf, with a French Twist'. In *The European Reception of Virginia Woolf*. Eds Mary Ann Caws and Nicola Luckhurst, 60–7. London: Continuum, 2002.

Caws, Mary Ann and Nicola Luckhurst, eds. *The Reception of Virginia Woolf in Europe*. London: Continuum, 2002.

Cunningham, Michael. *The Hours*. New York: Picador, 1998.

Dalgarno, Emily. *Virginia Woolf and the Visible World*, Cambridge: Cambridge University Press, 2001.

Diepeveen, Leonard. *The Difficulties of Modernism*. New York: Routledge, 2003.

Felski, Rita. *The Gender of Modernity*. Cambridge, Mass.: Harvard University Press, 1995.

Felstiner, John. *Translating Neruda: The Way to Macchu Picchu*. Stanford, CA: Stanford University Press, 1980.

Friedman, Susan Stanford. *Mappings: Feminism and the Cultural Geographies of Encounter*. Princeton, NJ: Princeton University Press, 1998.

Gabler, Hans Walter. 'A Tale of Two Texts: Or, How One Might Edit Virginia Woolf's *To the Lighthouse*'. *Woolf Studies Annual* 10 (2004): 1–29.

Gámez Fuentes, María José. 'Virginia Woolf and the Search for Symbolic Mothers in Modern Spanish Fiction: The Case of *Tres mujeres*'. In *The European Reception of Virginia Woolf*. Eds Mary Ann Caws and Nicola Luckhurst, 263–80. London: Continuum, 2002.

Gentzler, Edwin. *Contemporary Translation Theories*, 2nd edn. Clevedon: Multilingual Matters Ltd, 2001.

Ginsberg, Elaine K. 'Virginia Woolf and the Americans'. *Bulletin of Research in the Humanities* 86.3 (1983–85): 347–59.

Guiguet, Jean. *Virginia Woolf et son Oeuvre*. London: Hogarth Press, 1965.

Holtby, Winifred. *Virginia Woolf: A Critical Memoir*. London: Wishart & Co., 1932.

Hurtley, Jacqueline A. 'Modernism, Nationalism and Feminism: Representations of Virginia Woolf in Catalonia'. In *The Reception of Virginia Woolf in Europe*. Eds Mary Ann Caws and Nicola Luckhurst, 296–311. London: Continuum, 2002.

Hussey, Mark. 'Woolf in the U.S.A.'. In *Woolf Across Cultures*. Ed. Natalya Reinhold, 47–61. New York: Pace University Press, 2004.

Kitsi-Mitakou, Katerina K. '"The Country or the Moon" and the Woman of "Interior Monologue": Virginia Woolf in Greece'. In *The European Reception of Virginia Woolf*. Eds Mary Ann Caws and Nicola Luckhurst, 186–99. London: Continuum, 2002.

Klitgård, Ida. 'Waves of Influence: The Danish Reception of Virginia Woolf'. In *The European Reception of Virginia Woolf*. Eds Mary Ann Caws and Nicola Luckhurst, 165–85. London: Continuum, 2002.

Larkosh, Christopher. 'Translating Woman: Victoria Ocampo and the Empires of Foreign Fascination'. In *Translation and Power*. Eds Maria Tymoczko and Edwin Gentzler, 99–121. Amherst: University of Massachusetts Press, 2002.

Laurence, Patricia, ed. 'Virginia Woolf in/on Translation'. *Virginia Woolf Miscellany* 54 (1999): 1–9.

Lázaro, Alberto. 'The Emerging Voice: A Review of Spanish Scholarship on Virginia Woolf'. In *The European Reception of Virginia Woolf*. Eds Mary Ann Caws and Nicola Luckhurst, 247–62. London: Continuum, 2002.

Lee, Hermione. *Virginia Woolf*. London: Chatto & Windus, 1996.

Lojo Rodríguez, Laura Maria. '"A gaping mouth, but no words": Virginia Woolf Enters the Land of Butterflies'. In *The European Reception of Virginia Woolf*. Eds Mary Ann Caws and Nicola Luckhurst, 218–46. London: Continuum, 2002.

Luckhurst, Nicola and Martine Ravache. *Virginia Woolf in Camera*. London: Cecil Woolf, 2001.

Majumdar, Robin and Allen McLaurin, eds. *Virginia Woolf: The Critical Heritage*. London: Routledge, 1997.

Marcus, Jane. 'Wrapped in the Stars and Stripes: Virginia Woolf in the U.S.A.'. *The South Carolina Review* 29.1 (1996): 17–23.

Marcus, Laura. 'Woolf's feminism and feminism's Woolf'. In *The Cambridge Companion to Virginia Woolf*. Eds Sue Roe and Susan Sellers, 209–44. Cambridge: Cambridge University Press, 2000.

——. 'The European Dimensions of the Hogarth Press'. In *The European Reception of Virginia Woolf*. Eds Mary Ann Caws and Nicola Luckhurst, 328–56. London: Continuum, 2002.

Massa, Ann and Alistair Stead, eds. *Forked Tongues: Comparing Twentieth-Century British and American Literature*. New York: Longman, 1994.

McGann, Jerome. *The Beauty of Inflections: Literary Investigations in Historical Method and Theory*. Oxford: Oxford University Press, 1985.

McNees, Eleanor, ed. *Virginia Woolf: Critical Assessments I–IV*. Sussex: Helm Information, 1994.

McNeillie, Andrew. 'Virginia Woolf's America'. *Dublin Review* 5 (2000–01): 41–55.

Mezei, Kathy, ed. *Ambiguous Discourse: Feminist Narratology and British Women Writers*. Chapel Hill: University of North Carolina Press, 1996.

Nünning, Ansgar and Vera. 'The German Reception and Criticism of Virginia Woolf: A Survey of Phases and Trends in the Twentieth Century'. In *The European Reception of Virginia Woolf*. Eds Mary Ann Caws and Nicola Luckhurst, 68–101. London: Continuum, 2002.

Palacios, Manuela. '"A Fastness of their own": The Galacian Reception of Virginia Woolf'. In *The European Reception of Virginia Woolf*. Eds Mary Ann Caws and Nicola Luckhurst, 281–95. London: Continuum, 2002.

Pellan, Françoise. 'Translating Virginia Woolf into French'. In *The European Reception of Virginia Woolf*. Eds Mary Ann Caws and Nicola Luckhurst, 54–9. London: Continuum, 2002.

Perosa, Sergio. 'The Reception of Virginia Woolf in Italy'. In *The European Reception of Virginia Woolf*. Eds Mary Ann Caws and Nicola Luckhurst, 200–17. London: Continuum, 2002.

Pireddu, Nicoletta. 'Modernism Misunderstood: Anna Banti Translates Virginia Woolf'. *Comparative Literature* 56.1 (2004): 54–76.

Pratt, Mary Louise. 'The Traffic in Meaning: Translation, Contagion, Infiltration'. *Profession* 2002: 25–43.

Pykett, Lyn. *Engendering Fictions: The English Novel in the Early Twentieth Century*. London: Edward Arnold, 1994.

Reinhold, Natalya, ed. *Woolf Across Cultures*. New York: Pace University Press, 2004.

Rodier, Carole. 'The French Reception of Woolf: An *État Présent* of *Études Woolfiennes*'. In *The European Reception of Virginia Woolf*. Eds Mary Ann Caws and Nicola Luckhurst, 39–53. London: Continuum, 2002.

Rowbotham, Sheila. *A Century of Women: The History of Women in Britain and the United States in the Twentieth Century*. Harmondsworth: Penguin, 1997.

Sandbach-Dahlström, Catherine. '"Literature is no one's private ground": The Critical and Political Reception of Virginia Woolf in Sweden'. In *The European Reception of Virginia Woolf*. Eds Mary Ann Caws and Nicola Luckhurst, 148–64. London: Continuum, 2002.

Scott, Bonnie Kime, ed. *The Gender of Modernism: A Critical Anthology*. Bloomington, IN: Indiana University Press, 1990.

Silver, Brenda. *Virginia Woolf Icon*. Chicago, IL: Chicago University Press, 1999.

Simon, Sherry. *Gender in Translation: Cultural Identity and the Politics of Transmission*. London: Routledge, 1996.

Snaith, Anna. *Virginia Woolf: Public and Private Negotiations*. Basingstoke: Macmillan, 2000.

Steiner, George. *After Babel: Aspects of Language and Translation*. Oxford: Oxford University Press, 1998.

Summers, Doris. 'Bilingual Aesthetics: An Invitation'. *Profession* 2002: 7–14.

Terentowicz-Fotyga, Urszula. 'From Silence to a Polyphony of Voices: Virginia Woolf's Reception in Poland'. In *The European Reception of Virginia Woolf*. Eds Mary Ann Caws and Nicola Luckhurst, 127–47. London: Continuum, 2002.

Venuti, Lawrence. *The Translator's Invisibility: A History of Translation*. London: Routledge, 1995.

Villeneuve, Pierre-Éric. 'Woolf among Writers and Critics: The French Intellectual Scene'. In *The European Reception of Virginia Woolf*. Eds Mary Ann Caws and Nicola Luckhurst, 19–38. London: Continuum, 2002.

Wicht, Wolfgang. 'Installing Modernism: The Reception of Virginia Woolf in the German Democratic Republic'. In *The European Reception of Virginia Woolf*. Eds Mary Ann Caws and Nicola Luckhurst, 102–26. London: Continuum, 2002.

Wilson, Edmund. 'Virginia Woolf and the American Language'. In *The Shores of Light*, 421–8. London: W.H. Allen & Co., 1952.

Wolf, Naomi. '"Women Are Like Cold Mutton": Power, Humiliation, and a New Definition of Human Rights'. In *Women's Voices, Women's Rights: Oxford Amnesty Lectures 1996*. Ed. Alison Jeffries, 93–100. Oxford: Westview Press, 1999.

Yao, Steven G. *Translation and the Languages of Modernism: Gender, Politics, Language*. Basingstoke: Palgrave Macmillan, 2003.

index

Abel, Elizabeth, 25, 61, 66, 68, 69, 78
  n.1, 78 n.2, 79 n.7, 80 n.15
Abraham, Julie, 198, 203
Abranches, Graça, 243, 245–6, 248
Adams, David, 218–19
Albee, Edward, 140
Allan, Tuzyline Jita, 197
Anderson, Linda, 86, 94
Anglo-American reception, 7–9, 227–8,
  229, 230, 231, 235, 236, 238, 239,
  240, 247, 248
annotation, 137–8; *see also* bibliographic
  issues
anti-imperialism, 8, 211, 212, 214,
  222–4; *see also* colonialism; *see also*
  empire; *see also* Englishness; *see also*
  postcolonialism
anti-semitism, 180–1, 230
Anzaldua, Gloria, 220
Arac, Jonathan, 155
archives, 15 n.5, 105, 106, 126, 136, 245;
  see also manuscripts
Arendt, Hannah, 37
Armstrong, Tim, 38, 41
Arnold, Matthew, 14
Auerbach, Erich, 5, 18–9, 33 n.4, 33 n.5,
  33 n.12, 37, 45, 156, 235
Austin, J. L., 150–1
autobiography, 3, 84, 85–6, 87–92; *see*
  also biography
avant garde, the, 37, 51–2, 53, 54, 55, 56

Badenhausen, Ingeborg, 236
Banfield, Ann, 29, 36–7, 53–4, 55–6, 57
Banks, Joanne Trautmann, 136–7, 185–6
Banti, Anna, 244
Barkway, Stephen, 1
Barrett, Eileen, 11, 28, 101, 194–5, 204

Barrett, Michèle, 77, 101, 107, 111,
  161–2
Barthes, Roland, 71–2, 95, 145–6, 148
Batchelor, John, 6
Baudrillard, Jean, 152–3
Bazin, Nancy Topping, 104
Beach, Joseph Warren, 4
Beck, Warren, 17–8, 19, 33 n.12
Beer, Gillian, 64, 109–10, 178–9, 181–2,
  221
Beja, Morris, 63, 138–9
Bell, Anne Olivier, 135–6
Bell, Clive, 53, 55, 56, 57
Bell, Quentin, 2, 9, 63, 86, 103, 122 n.8,
  187
Bell, Vanessa, 89
Belsey, Catherine, 151, 165 n.3
Bennett, Arnold, 43, 47
Bennett, Joan, 5
Benstock, Shari, 85, 89, 91, 96 n.8
Benzel, Kathryn, 11
Bergson, Henri, 5, 22, 41, 44, 45–6
Berman, Jeffrey, 75
Berman, Jessica, 50
Bernheimer, Charles, 74, 81 n.18
bibliographic issues, 11, 106, 125–42; *see*
  also archives; *see also* manuscripts
Bieron, Tomasz, 242–3
Bildungsroman, 25, 29
biography, 2, 3, 63, 83–97, 103, 185–90
  psychobiography, 63, 72, 80 n.10
  see also autobiography
Bird, Sarah, 37
Bishop, Edward L., 11, 34 n.19, 125–42
Blackmer, Corinne E., 196–7
Black, Naomi, 6, 113, 116, 137
Blackstone, Bernard, 4
Blair, Sara, 31, 57, 58
Blanche, Jacques-Émile, 238

298

302 palgrave advances in virginia woolf studies

Marcus, Jane, 9, 12, 83, 107–8, 118,
191–2, 205, 209, 211, 212, 214,
222–3, 224, 227, 228, 247
Marcus, Laura, 95, 236, 237, 243, 245,
250 n.7
Marder, Herbert, 103–4
Marler, Regina, 7–8, 9
marriage, 200
Massa, Ann, 227
materialism, 43, 48, 49, 112, 113, 132–3,
179, 234, 240
maternal relations, 65, 67, 70, 73, 74, 91,
106
Mauron, Charles, 229, 243
Maze, John R., 76
McClintock, Anne, 213, 217
McCracken, LuAnn, 84, 91
McFarlane, James, 38, 40
McGann, Jerome, 132–3, 242
McGee, Patrick, 12, 211, 214, 223, 224
McKenzie, D. F., 131–2
McNaron, Toni A. H., 193
McNees, Eleanor, 12
McNeillie, Andrew, 55
McVicker, Jeanette, 12, 209–26, 225–6
Meese, Elizabeth A., 197–8
The Memoir Club, 88
mental illness, 60–1, 61–2, 63, 72, 76–7,
79 n.3, 81 n.24, 87; see also
psychoanalysis
Mepham, John, 12, 63, 92, 94
Merleau-Ponty, Maurice, 114
Meyerowitz, Selma, 8
Mezei, Kathy, 29, 30, 31, 34 n.15
Miles, Kathryn, 93
Miller, J. Hillis, 27
Miller, Nancy, 85
mimesis, 5
Minow-Pinkney, Makiko, 7, 60–82, 65,
80 n.17, 80 n.22, 111–12, 161
Mishra, Vijay, 213
modernism, 19, 35–59, 61, 65, 71, 108,
120, 154–5, 156, 157, 193, 215–16,
217–22, 223, 234, 240
Mohanty, Satya P., 209
Moi, Toril, 24–5, 33 n.12, 64, 143, 152
Moore, G. E., 56
Moran, Patricia, 71
Morrison, Toni, 182
Moss, Roger, 90

Nalbantian, Suzanne, 92
narcissism, 73, 74, 75, 82 n.25, 186
Naremore, James, 21–2, 33 n.6
narrative voice, 19–21, 27–31
narratology, 5, 16–34
nation, 181–2, 219, 221–2, 232, 233–6;
see also Englishness
Nealon, Jeffry, 152, 153
Neverow, Vara, 69
New Criticism, 56–7
new historicism, 169–70, 172, 173, 178,
179, 181, 182, 183; see also cultural
materialism
Nicholls, Peter, 46–7
Nielsen, Elizabeth, 10
Nünning, Ansgar, 235, 237, 239, 240,
248
Nünning, Vera, 235, 237, 239, 240, 248

Ocampo, Victoria, 237, 239, 245, 251
n.18
O'Connor, William Van, 17
Oedipus complex, the, 26, 63, 65, 66, 67,
68, 69, 80 n.13; see also Freud,
Sigmund; see also psychoanalysis
Olano, Pamela J., 194
Oldfield, Sybil, 15 n.6
orientalism, 216–17; see also
postcolonialism
Oxindine, Annette, 194

Palacios, Manuela, 248
paratext, 139, 140, 243
patriarchy, 64, 65, 68, 69, 70, 178, 201–2
Paulin, Tom, 47
Pawlowski, Merry, 91, 116, 180
Peach, Linden, 8, 169–83
Pearce, Richard, 27
Pellan, Françoise, 238
penis envy, 69, 70, 80 n.15; see also
Freud, Sigmund
performative, 151, 159, 160, 162
Perosa, Sergio, 234–5, 244, 248
Peters, Catherine, 93
Phelan, James, 32, 34 n.20
Phillips, Kathy J., 170, 212, 223–4
philosophy, 5, 20, 53–4, 56, 146, 154
photography, 45, 54–5
Pippett, Aileen, 3, 86
Pirredu, Nicoletta, 237, 244